Out of the Sighs

LEWIS COLEMAN

Copyright © 2021 Lewis Coleman
All rights reserved.

ISBN: 9798778889507

*"Out of the sighs a little comes, but not of grief,
for we have knocked down that"*
– Dylan Thomas

2031

I'd managed to lose them all. Right or wrong, I'd needed to. They wouldn't be far, but far enough that I felt uneasy. I glanced over at the churchyard, the gloomy shadow of yew trees. It was too dark and I didn't have my headtorch.

Behind me, the noisy rabble at Picks, the rumble of the generator, "Don't Look Back in Anger" on the jukebox. They might've still been in there but going back to that place was like going back to the noughties, stale booze and sticky floorboards, the risk of violence, a desire to fuck the wrong women.

I passed the old post office, red bricks mossed, car tyres piled up inside blocking the huge smashed windows. Memories of getting my giro, a world ago, the big pale green cheque with a nice texture which felt like new money. At £44 a week it rarely covered the bills, but New'ky Brown Ale was only 99p a bottle in 'Spoons in the late 90s. We used to stick a straw in it and neck it – four of those and we were well on our way.

I walked along the Queensway. The newsagents, an old café, Barclays Bank: ransacked, blacked-out and smashed up. Pizza No.1, the big windows long gone, a gaping mouth into nothingness. And then…

Click.

A strange sensation, a glooping heartbeat which left me hollow and dizzy. It was as if the lights had come on and it wasn't dark. I was younger, the town wasn't deranged and people were walking the streets, cars parked across the road, old ladies, prams and mums, people on their lunch break and the odd drunk, an addict or two. In a blink. Was this a flashback? A split synapse snaking with electricity and only briefly projecting an image on my retina? Was this the beginning of some kind of madness? One night on acid, I stared at a light for so long that I tricked my brain into thinking it was daytime – I even started getting ready for college, much to the amusement of the boys.

In a millisecond it was dark again, the synapse reattached. I was old again, my bones stiff with cold, all on my own. At least I thought I was. I looked across the road by the side entrance to the graveyard.

There was a bright light and it seemed to vibrate with sound. I found myself curiously drawn to it. God, was I finally going home?

'Ello, bud,' a voice said.

'Shit!' I blurted. 'Made me fucking jump.'

Hacking laughter broke the vision. I couldn't fully see him, but I realised who it was, sitting on a bench.

'Erm… what you bloody doing here, Mick?' like he'd flipped his lid.

'Found this old box, portable DVD thingy, ay it.'

'I can see that.'

'Ar know the rules!' he insisted. 'Doh care. There's no aerial.'

'What you watching?'

'They don't make 'em like this anymore, son.'

I recognised the music. It was The Stripper. 'They probably don't make them at all, Mick,' I laughed.

'That's about right, bud. Yow know it.'

He chuckled watching it. It was good to see, his old face toothless, lit up like an artist's sketch of a prune. When it ended, I asked him to repeat it.

I vaguely remembered it. It was like the Two Ronnies, but it wasn't them, it was the other ones. I sat down next to him, transfixed on the screen. One of the performers was tossing slices of bread to the other in time with the music and something moved in me. Then the other one opened cupboards, again in time with the music. It seemed so daft but it tickled me, then Mick laughed, nudging me in agreement, the sickly sweet colours of the screen brightening the night. There was a kitchen, pyjamas, sausages and pancakes, a fridge with a light. Saft men dancing. There was an audience, laughter. Lots of people laughing.

'Morecambe and Wise!' I remembered.

'That's them,' he said.

The sketch ended when one of the comedians slammed a meat cleaver into the kitchen radio. Perhaps it was a reality check, or perhaps he was just saving the batteries, but Mick immediately shut it down with a click and the light went out. The DVD whirred to a standstill and suddenly I felt colder, my eyes blinded by the light, slowly readjusting to the absence of it. I could see very little, but it wasn't hard to imagine the familiar shapes of the derelict shops across the road, the iron railing around the graveyard, the grasses wildly growing out of a once neatly trimmed green.

Mick patted the DVD player, his little memory box, 'I'm keeping it.'

I nodded but he probably didn't see.

I tried to look at him, blacked out, smashed up. In my mind's eye a tear trickled down his face. It was unlikely, he wasn't the type. But he should've cried, because he clearly missed it. There was laughter and an audience, most of whom, if not all, would be dead.

'Yow'm alright,' he said out of nowhere, like we were in a film.

'Er, thanks.'

He laughed, gravelly, a wheeze which turned into a grating cough.

'Have you seen my lot?' I asked.

He took a deep breath and went quiet.

'Mick?'

Nothing.

'Mick?'

I waited. I found myself listening for his breathing.

'Mick?' I shook his shoulder.

'Shush!' he said – for a second I thought he'd gone, he had to be in his 80s.

I held my breath, then I heard the prattle and witter of a knob head talking to himself.

'He's one, en't he?'

'Ta Mick.'

'No worries, me mon.'

I got up and walked into the graveyard.

'Eh, Tom,' he called.

'Yeah?'

'Your dad, he was one of the good uns,' he said, reverting to the film script.

'Oh, yeah, Mick. He was alright,' I said, conforming.

'An old sod,' he laughed.

Will was at the Greek Grave. Every now and again, when he moved his head, I could see his torchlight. He was rambling to himself, mumbling a tune. Using the light of the half moon, I made my way across and through the damp tall grasses, tentative steps, kicking in all directions to find a safe route through the headstones.

I might've guessed he'd be there. The graveyard had always meant something to us. When we were young, after closing time, we'd sit on

William Shenstone's red sandstone grave, a bottle of take-out wine, smoking joints into the morning. Shenstone was an 18th Century poet, an appendix in the romantic movement. We weren't particularly big fans, but he'd been a landscape gardener and a writer and that was cool. He was an artist and we considered ourselves on that side of life. That's what we wanted to do with our lives – that's what I'd tried to do. I often reminisced on those nights we'd spent on the poet's grave, most of Halesowen asleep – it was now buried under grasses and far too close to St John's for our liking.

The Greek Grave was more hidden. The only one in the whole of Halesowen, smack bang in the middle of the dark, sprawling graveyard. It was the resting place of Leyton who, in 2008, killed his friend Warren outside Picks one night for fifty quid of fruit machine winnings. Leyton never got done for it, but everybody knew. He died of a heroin overdose a year later and was buried at St John's. One of the boys at Picks suggested Leyton's grave, when the slew of Greekings took place in the mad spring of 2027. Mob-drunk, they fetched a bunch of fireworks and paraffin, dug the hole, buried the explosives deep and then blew it, a shudder of mud all around. There was still part of his skull, or somebody else's skull amongst the rotting splinters of wood. People regularly stopped to piss on it, like they had with the old Greek himself.

Will sat with his legs dangling in it, swaying slightly and mumbling he told us so, as per. He'd long known the dirty truth of the Greek – if it even was the truth – and this "evidence" meant all his theories were true, moon landings, Marilyn, global warming, the Rothschilds and the Jewish conspiracy, and whatever else it was he'd stumbled across in his in-depth armchair research – it was hard to keep up.

'Come on, man, you'll reek of it,' I said.

'Who cares?' He swigged the berries, winced slightly as the sourness hit.

'Me. I've gotta sleep with you!'

'Pahahaha!'

'Has Loz gone back already?' I asked.

'Yeah, lightweight. Where's the other one?'

'Dead,' I answered, deadpan.

He laughed.

'No… He is. Died in Picks,' I said with sincerity. 'Someone kicked his stick as he was dancing to "Sweet Caroline". He fell. Cracked his head on the tiles.'

'Pahahahaha! You're a twisted fuck.'
'Yes,' I smiled. 'Now, come on.'
'He could be dead,' Will said.
'Don't say that.'
'Where were you anyway?' he asked.
'Me? Nowhere.'

I heard something behind us, yanked the torch off his head. 'Ow, ya fuck! Where's yours?'

I didn't answer.

'You better not have lost it!'

I glanced back in the direction of the Queensway and saw the "other one" hobbling in the beam. He came to the bench by the entrance. Mick directed him.

Giggling to himself, Marcus looked older than his 50 years. With each heavy step his headtorch came on and then immediately went off again, a loose wire.

'He's a bloody liability,' I mumbled to myself.

Will tried to get up but fell back drunk. 'Help me, then,' he moaned.

I grabbed the collar of his army jacket and pulled on it. He barely moved.

'Hang on!' he nagged.

I pulled harder, mischievous, but determined.

'Bloody stop it!'

I let go, tutted irritably, 'you want my help-'

'Don't want you to fucking throttle me.'

He gave up and lay back, rested his head on the knot of a root. I looked up, lit the skies. The yews were the same, solid and immovable. The grey squirrels still came. It was as if I'd never left. But it wasn't the nineties or the noughties. If it had been, I'd have been in the Greek with him.

Marcus stumbled towards us, one hand on his stick, the other using the gravestones.

'You'll do yourself a right mischief,' I said, mock-camp, as he neared.

He tittered.

'I thought he was dead,' Will said.

'He is.'

'Fuck off,' Marcus squeaked, getting his breath. 'I soon will be. Ooh, this place is like a fucking assault course.'

'Stay away from the Greek,' Will said, like a concerned parent.

'Fucking too right, fucking piss-pot, smell like…' he stopped to think and then looked to me, half-proud, 'smell like a basecamp bog.'

'You what?' I snapped.

'Alright, alright, Ralph Fiennes.'

Will laughed.

'Ranulph!' But he knew, he was just trying to wind me up. 'What would you know about it?'

'I know. Oh, I know… I remember the endless pictures on fuckbook.'

Will turned onto his knees and stood up. 'Everything's fuck with you.'

'Ironically,' I smiled.

'More recent than you,' he bitched.

'*Really*?' I bitched back, smiling.

'That's not hard,' Will said to me, retrieving his torch and putting it back on his head.

Marcus noted Will's choice of words, but before he could feed on the euphemism, '*Leroy*?' I asked.

Will cast a surprised glance. It was a bit dark. I really shouldn't have gone there.

'Ok, ok,' Marcus backtracked, wounded. 'The one we don't talk about,' a melodramatic flick of the hand to joke it off.

But it was a terrible tragedy and I felt guilty for bringing it up.

I started brushing the mud off Will's jacket and pulled a leaf out of his long, matted hair. 'He still cares,' he laughed.

I snorted in realisation. 'I didn't even think. Just started grooming you like a child.'

'That sounds bad,' Marcus laughed. 'You'll have the Sons on you.'

I shook my head, tutted, but then it hit me, like it does – *a child*. 'Boom,' I muttered.

And they knew. They both went quiet. Sick of it, I guess.

We awkwardly made our way through the graveyard in silence, through overgrown grasses and biscuit-broken graves, three men well past their prime.

At the wall, I looked up at the Andrew Road flats. Four maisonettes and one high-rise now gone. One high-rise remained, Bredon, sticking its finger up amongst the remaining knuckles of maisonettes. A few floors had electric lighting, most just the flicker of candle-light or weak solar powered garden lights. There was a headtorch in the distance. Marcus stopped to fumble with his, which had now fully ceased to work.

'Don't you dare,' Will said.

'Calm down!'

'We don't need more than one – *luckily*,' he nagged, half-blinding me with a glance.

'It'll turn up,' I said.

'Mine's buggered anyway,' Marcus said, smacking it. 'But just in case.'

'In case of what?' Will said. 'A pack of bloody wolves!'

'You never know.'

A dog barked in the distance just as Will swigged a mouth of berries. 'Bloody hell,' he dribbled, grabbing my arm like an elderly relative.

We sped up. Just in case.

'Where were you anyway?' Marcus asked me.

'Nowhere.'

'Nowhere?'

'I can't be arsed with Picks. I went wandering.'

'Oooh,' he chimed, enlivened, 'ark at the wandering minstrel.'

───────────────

Ankerdine Court, Block 5, Flat 1. Brown-bricked ground floor flat sinking, or was the ground growing, taking it, taking us with it? My old home. When we first went back there, in the stormy wake of the last bus, we'd had to dig out the bottom to open the back door and reclaim the place – a mud slide had buried three feet of it.

The previous tenants had made a better job of the flat than me. I'd lived there nearly 20 years before in council magnolia, offcuts of linoleum tacked and glued to the concrete floor. We inherited thick warm grey carpets, lime green wallpaper, two brown settees, and a super king in the bedroom. Will and I took the bed, the more comfortable option, we were the alphas. At least that was how Will saw it – I just went along with it.

I opened the back door and Loz was sat on the floor, against the settee, rolling a cigarette.

He looked up, 'want one?' a knowing smile.

'No, you're alright,' I said, tired of it.

'Sooner or later,' a dumb smile, handful of teeth left.

Will barged past me and handed Loz the berries, 'drink!'

'I don't want any.'

'Go on, Loz,' I smiled. 'Don't be a weck. Drink it.'

'Have you had any?' he accused.

'I don't drink,' obviously.

'*Exactly.*'

'Exactly?' I looked to Will and then back to Loz, 'but *you* do.'

He was stumped.

'You're an idiot, Loz,' Will laughed. 'Just drink.'

Loz eyed up the clear bottle. I could see bits floating in the purple juice. Was it the blackberries or bits of sick from when Will threw up earlier? He looked at Will, then down at the bottle. He knew he was going to have to, Will was the alpha. He drank.

'Alright, very funny, wench,' Marcus was yelling from the door.

'What you screaming about?' Will shouted irritably, now on the settee rolling a joint.

'Oh, calm down, misery guts. It's just Ally calling me a cripple.'

'Well, close the door and fuck her.'

'No, thank you.'

'And switch your torch off.'

'It's working!' he squeaked.

He closed the door and sat on the other settee with a groan, rubbing his knee.

I stood in the middle of the room unsure what to do. Loz lit his cigarette, coughed smoke in my direction. Behind him, Marcus reached for the berries, sighed, geed himself up and then took a long swig. Will licked the Rizla and speedily sealed the joint, before tamping it down on his tobacco tin. It could've been 2011, it could've been 1998, or any of the years in between, but it was 2031 and we were in our fifties. It would've been easy to forget the life I'd had after, and perhaps that would've been the best thing to do, but I just didn't want to – especially with everything that had happened. I went and lay down on the bed.

'You having some of this?' Will yelled through, laughing – the other two joined in. I ignored them.

Years before, I would lie in this room, curtains closed, in the dark, trembling. I'd hear a knock at the bedroom window. It'd usually be Will, occasionally Leroy.

"Come on, I know you're in," they'd shout. And I'd freeze, try not to breathe too loudly, just wanting to be left alone. No carpets, just cheap lino, the flat was always cold and echoey. Sometimes I'd be sitting writing at my old computer, right in front of the curtains, and they'd bang at the window. I'd move my feet under the chair and as far back as possible.

"Come on Tom, I'm not stupid, open up," they might shout, three feet away, shielded by a single pane of glass and thin black curtains.

I felt bad ignoring them, dared myself to answer, but I just couldn't. If I had I would've drank and who knew when it would end. One day would turn into two, into a week, or more. One drink would become many, then weed, wraps of speed, anything, coke if Loz and Marcus came down, the only two of us who worked. And then, when we ran out of money, almost against my will, I'd steal bottles of wine, beer, roll the security tag off the French brandy from Asda. French brandy was a big win – it was their own brand but, be it Courvoisier or Asda, the result was the same.

There was a time when there was an Asda. 24 hours too. *I'd love a doughnut. Wouldn't need to be fresh, those late-night discounted ones when the outer bread had gone slightly hard, the inner soft with sticky jam, apple or custard. Cheap Asda doughnuts – no doubt full of chemical poisons, but who cares?*

I drifted away thinking about those yellow labelled bakery products. When I awoke, Will was above my face, 'Tommy,' he smiled.

'Fuck!'

He burst out laughing.

'What you doing man?'

He had that look about him. Childish smile, lost in some reverie. 'I know you don't want any shit but come and join us.'

'I want sleep.'

'Come on,' tempting a baby.

'Piss off!'

'Alright, alright,' he said, backing away through the hall and into the living room.

'He wants to sleep,' I heard him say.

They laughed like teenagers, the low cackle of Loz and Will punctuated by Marcus's high-pitched chortle. A piercing cacophony, paranoia-inducing at times.

I lay in bed trying and failing to fall asleep, half-annoyed that even now they weren't in the least bit sympathetic to my need to stay sober. I tried to drift off imagining I was in a tent, the soft patter of snow on a winter mountain. But it was no good, I could hear them yabbering away about the times we used to go to the underground car park and drink a knock-off bottle of Martini, snorting poppers and rubbing grainy base in our gums. It was nearly 30 years ago, but oddly it felt like yesterday. It was like the Sons weren't a thing. It was like the Chinese, Russians or the Americans – depending on who you believed – had never bombed the south. It was like Burnham-on-Sea had never happened. It was like I'd never met Lucy and got married and lived like a normal human being for a few fucking blissful years. And the kid. *Not again, Tom. Don't go there.*

And they were muttering and giggling, clinking the berries and smoking shit. *God grant me the serenity to accept the things… – don't go there either.*

I got up quietly and snuck through the hall to the front door. I opened it. Clunk. *Damn.*

'Tom?' Will asked.

I quickly slammed the door behind me, ran up a flight of stairs and out the main entrance to the block. There was no door, just a hole which had been smashed through. In front of me was Ground Zero, the remnants from a high-rise which had been demolished and was now used for tipping, the sulphurous whiff less apparent in the damp of night. I climbed over some bricks and rubble onto a path, jumped a short wall and clambered up the grass bank to the park. It was pitch black without my headtorch. The half slice of moon allowed me to see a little, but not enough to avoid the tree. I went down. It didn't knock me out, but I was down and dizzied, lying on the cold grass, dewy and cooling. I was crying, and it wasn't the tree. I closed my eyes.

I awoke on my back in thick grass, shivering. It was early morning blue. The ether fizzed with little atoms as my eyes adjusted to the low light. Exhausted, I curled up on my side for warmth, but it didn't help. I was too wet, my linen trousers stuck to my legs. I summoned the strength to stand up and then gently jogged on the spot for a few seconds to wake myself up and shake my clothes free.

I thought about the boys. Had they followed me? I doubted it. I guessed they'd still be bang at it. I didn't want to go back to that. But where could I go? I found myself feeling nostalgic for the days when I could go grab a newspaper and a coffee. Looking over the unkempt

Highfield park, I decided to go for a run. *Why not?* Like a Sunday afternoon in suburbia in 2026.

Taking a few long breaths to get myself ready, I began jogging through the park. The grasses were neck high in parts and seemed nightmarishly never-ending, like an old Atari game glitch, forced to repeat the same blocky section. When I finally came out the other end, I was even more drenched than when I started, longing for home and bed.

The road was lined with the same empty houses, most of them long since looted. Who knew what you might find amongst the wreckage, dead bodies or people who may as well be. I continued trotting along the pavement, hoping to dry, to warm up, to not think about it, about anything.

On a bench by a bus stop, Mel, an old prune loon, was sat drinking something unrecognisable and muttering to herself.

'Yow!' she yelled, pointing at me.

'Me?' I asked, turning, jogging backwards.

'Ar knows your mother,' she said and cackled.

'I know, Mel, I know. Can't stop.' I turned and ran on.

They'd gone to school together. Mum had always said she was a bully. God only knows how or why she was still going and my mum, who'd lived a largely sober life, was gone. Mel was "gone" though, her days spent on benches, drinking her insides dry, face wrinkled and sunken like she was permanently sucking a lemon sour.

I ran past Halesview, the building where I used to have counselling as an angst-ridden teenager, where I once did a recovery share when I was celebrating two years sober, now half eaten by vandals and thieves, an upturned VW van painted like the Scooby Doo Mystery Machine – I wondered where the Banksy Collective were these days; did they go with the bomb? I carried on past the Button Factory, the pub where I used to pop pills, swallow booze, and sing songs on the karaoke.

I ran about half a mile to the Huntingtree park, my knees hurting, lungs burning, face hot and dripping. The sun was coming up and I was feeling prickly with the effort of it of all, spiky, itching, angry. I pushed myself hard, but it was too much, lactic acid filling my mouth, heart thudding in my tight chest. *You're not having a heart attack, Tom.* I stopped anyway, fearful, and walked alongside the overgrown park where I used to play football pretending to be a normal boy, where I learned to drink pretending to be just one of the lads, a park now free and wild with tall grasses and little pink and blue flowers.

I started to run again. I passed the old Co-op, the metal board cut open, a jagged aperture into the fetid rat-hole – I dreaded to think what was in there now. I continued along the road, the units of shop innards rusting in the street but, before I could get to the park at the bottom of the Squirrels Estate, I suddenly threw up, terrified, my chest aching, panting for breath. *You're not having a heart attack, Tom*!

I looked to Portsdown Road in the distance, the hill of empty homes, caged houses, snaking up towards the tree tufts of Clent Hills. A big part of me wanted to continue, but that part of my life was done. I didn't want to think about the house where I grew up. I didn't want to remember those early years when mum and dad were together. And I didn't want to think about the community centre, those old, lost but hopeful faces. *Where did that get us*?

I started to cry.

'Stop it!'

I told myself it was just my pathetic lack of fitness. But so much of my life happened on that estate and now it was desolate. Dad always used to say, "I remember when it was all fields." I wished I could tell my son, "I remember when it was all homes."

I turned around and started walking back.

Either side of Bassnage Road were more of the pink and grey shells of creatures long since snailed north. Empty houses, some with metal-boarded windows warping my reflection, some caged, preserved like time capsules, mini museums for future generations; their lawns still littered with the rotting remnants of the black bags.

There was rarely anybody this side of town, perhaps the odd prune loon sucking on some intoxicant, or a scag rat lurking about, a living zombie. Most lived in the town centre.

I turned down a side road and started to make my way back. I noticed the old Scout Hut up a little path, overgrown with shrubs and grass. I remembered those late-night walks back from Cubs to dad's, an arm of red badges, twirling my neckerchief like a gymnast's ribbon. The divorce all seemed so minor now, but it was so big for much of my early life. At least until dad died.

I'd spent my morning running away from my current life, only to find myself running towards a life I'd spent years running away from. And now I was running away from it again. And running back to what? 'This is what happens when you don't drink,' I declared out loud, almost independent of myself. 'You find yourself running around, bumping into walls, a pinball of emotion.'

As I made my way back down Andrew Road, aching and tired from the run, the stink of the town became more prominent. The sulphurous whiff of Ground Zero, which the Sons dismantled from the roof down, in 2029, all because Robert Parsons, its most infamous resident, shagged a goat in the 1980s. Would people believe this happened in generations to come? Or had it become the norm everywhere? Was that the world we'd come to live in? It was hardly the Clintons' paedophile ring. No Trump the Poisonous Pump, or Philip the Greek, or the Eton boys' fetish for fucking pigs' faces. Robert Parsons just shagged a goat. I'd never condone the sick act, but all things considered the town response was madness, and people died doing it, two old men and a young girl. But even we'd joined in on the third floor, because that's where dad had lived and, besides, they fed us.

Don't get me wrong, we enjoyed dismantling the thing with sledgehammers. Perhaps it was therapy. But I felt sad too, recalled being a kid lying on the floor, leg reddening by the electric fire, watching the Two Ronnies and Minder with dad. He used to make me grilled cheese on toast, onions and Worcestershire sauce.

I also recalled nicking his prescription drugs, being welded to the floor after swigging diamorphine. But it was all just memories, memories which now resided in the dumping ground at the back of our block, smoky methane in the back of your throat on warm days.

I sat on the kerb, head in my hands, picking the scabs of a lifetime of memories. I didn't hear the scraping of gravel behind me: 'yow alright, mate-'

'You shit!' I punched him in the calf.

It was Jason. Yellowed, thin, an old scag rat. In his mid 50s, he was only a couple of years older than me, but he'd been at it for much longer. I'd had the Burnham-on-Sea years to make me a bit more vital. His legs were heavily swollen, face smooth and liver-tanned.

'Still alive,' I said.

'You too.'

I laughed, but we both knew it wasn't the same thing. His liver was gone and he'd never make it to Derby to get help – if there really was help in Derby.

'I doh suppose yow've got anything?' he asked, wiping sweat from his cheek.

'I don't do anything, do I,' I said, flicking a stone into the road.

'Why yow ere?' Irritated. 'Yow should be up there.'

'Up there? Doing what?'

'Fighting.'

'Fighting what?'

'The… the bastards who did this.'

'And who exactly is that?'

'Ah, forget it,' he said, angry, walking off. 'Yow'm a… yow'm a… fuck it.'

I went to call him back, to appease him, but there was only one thing that would do that and I didn't have it.

I opened the back door. Marcus was asleep on his settee, Loz was sitting cross-legged on his, like a guru, smoking.

'Where were you?' he asked.

'I needed to get out.'

There was an awkward silence.

'I'm sorry.'

'What for?' I sat next to him.

'I was just joking… the roll up… taking the piss. We were just a bit messed up. We spoke about it after.'

I smiled. 'I don't know why you bother.'

'*We* don't know why *you* bother,' he said.

'Other people,' I said.

'*Other people?*' He looked confused.

'I don't know.' I did. I was trying to set an example.

'No one's gonna change in Halesowen,' he laughed. 'It's kinda the point of the place.'

And it was. It certainly always had been to me, but now that's literally all it was. A place to get fucked up, now the country was, well, fucked up. There was a time when I swore I'd never return to Halesowen town, but when the south went I had nowhere else to go. A mate of ours, Eeyore, punned it "Hell's-Own Town" back in the noughties. I was inclined to agree. He was hooked into Six-Kids-Stacey at the time – that was his hell. For me, I just couldn't put down the drink and drugs. Hell was a perfect description, the land of temptation. Yet here I was, I'd been tempted back, back to the boys who were still the boys, even though we were middle aged men.

'Don't you want more from life?' I asked Loz. 'You could actually help. You were a *teacher*.'

He looked a bit hurt.

'I don't mean… I mean, I do mean what I say,' I asserted.

'What do you mean?'

'Hope. A future.'

'I've still… got… hope,' fell out of his mouth unconvincingly. 'It's just Jenny and the kids-'

'Don't you want to find them? It'd probably be very easy.'

'If they're alive,' he stopped. 'I'm sorry.'

I looked around the room. Marcus was half naked, flab splayed, the long scar from his knee injury, a cushion on his crotch. I could hear Will's guttural snore from the bedroom. Behind, the kitchen door was open, and the rancid smell of yeast emanated from the brew.

'It's ok,' I said. 'Shit happens. You know this as much as me.'

'Not quite.'

'You do.'

'Not really.'

'Are we having a pissing contest about who's got it worse?' I laughed.

He smiled.

'The kids are probably at that thing Eeyore was on about, if it even is a thing,' I said.

'The academy?'

'Yeah.'

'25 and 27?' He looked at me like I was stupid.

'Shit,' I laughed. 'Time flies.'

I heard Will stir in the bedroom, sit up and roar into a stretch. He groaned, pulled himself up and came into the living room in his pants, all six foot six of him.

'Better?' he asked me, like I'd come out the other end of another tantrum.

'Not really.'

He went into the kitchen, 'nearly there,' he called through. 'Soon be ready to trade.'

I heard him uncork a bottle, take a swig and then put it down. He came in and put his hand on my head – I could feel a slight tremor. 'I couldn't do it,' he said.

'What?'

'I couldn't live like this and not drink, smoke. I just couldn't.'

'I probably could,' Loz said.

'Piss off,' Will laughed. 'Why don't you then?'

'Don't want to.'

'You don't have to say this shit to me,' I said.

'I know.' Will was adamant.

There was a brief silence and then we heard a high-pitched 'ooooh.' We looked at each other, briefly shocked and confused, then we realised it was Marcus snoring and burst out laughing.

Will went into the kitchen and came back with a bottle of berries. He chucked it at Marcus, who woke up with a start. 'Ow! Fuck off, you cunt.'

'Pahahaha,' Will creased.

'You'd go fucking mental if I did that to you.'

'I know. Then I'd drink.'

Marcus looked at the bottle, held it up, went to pop the cork. 'I can't. Too early.' He looked over at me. 'I see madam's back.'

It would be so much easier to drink, to join in, to be the boy I used to be. 'I need to get away.'

Will knew I was serious. 'Let's go to the woods for a bit.'

'What about the brew?' I asked.

'Let's go home,' he smiled. 'Those two will have to stay here.'

'Oh, right,' Loz grumped, 'so we finish it off, while you go and chill up Leasowes?'

'Basically.'

'We could just wait,' I said.

'No.' He turned to Loz, 'he's our mate, he needs a break.'

'Why don't *you* stay?' Marcus glanced at Loz for back up.

'Yeah,' Loz rebelled.

'It's not just a jolly. There's work to do. Marcus, you up for digging a hole? Loz, you fancy cutting the base and building the shed?'

'I could do that,' Loz said.

'And Marcus?' Will waited. 'Exactly. Shall we leave Marcus on his own, Loz? Or do you think you can look after him?'

'I don't need looking after! I'm not a fucking child.'

'No, you're a fucking queer.'

'No, I'm not.'

'Come on, Marcus,' I tempered.

'I'm not.' He was defiant, but wouldn't look me in the eye.

'Well, whether you are or you aren't is irrelevant anyway, isn't it,' I said.

There was a silence. We all knew it. He was lucky to have lasted this long, despite my friendship with Jake and Christian.

'How many days?' Loz conceded.

'I reckon the brew has three days. We'll build the toilet, be at one with the trees for a bit, and then come back and bottle. Then we can all head up together and chill for a week or so.'

Will went back into the bedroom. Marcus was shooting eyes at Loz, who shrugged.

'I owe you one,' I said.

The hole was a couple of feet over my head and about four feet wide. It had taken me most of the day to dig it. My arms were shaking with fatigue, and now I had to figure out how to get myself out. I could reach the top of it, but I didn't have the strength to pull myself up.

'Will!'

He didn't come.

'Will!'

Nothing.

The sun was going down and now I was in a cold hole in the shade. I thought about my mum, bless her, her communion with the earth. '"Oh, for a draught of vintage that hath been cooled a long age in the deep delved earth."' *Bloody Keats*. I hadn't thought of Keats in a long time. Eight feet down in a hole and dredging up buried memories and Keats.

'Will!'

I had the idea to make little footholds. It seemed so stupid that I couldn't get out of this frigging hole. But even picking up the spade and pick, my arms were seizing. What would happen when we were too old to do things? *The town isn't equipped to deal with that, and the other three are likely to die before me, unless I'm lucky. What if I live to a ripe old age? Gramps had dementia. Perhaps I wouldn't care, wandering around Halesowen in another world. I'd look like just another prune loon with Wernicke-Korsakoff's.*

Perhaps they'd do me in? I'd sooner conk out like dad, hit the tiles and just not come around again.

I sat on the cold earth thinking about him, his memory fast fading in me, wasting away like an old VHS tape I'd watched too many times. The old scientist had once seemed so wise, but he'd got more daft as I'd got older and seen more of the world, which made me feel sad. The recall of drunken violence in my childhood had faded too. I'd forgiven him. Now, mostly I remembered his stupid laugh, moronic, mischievous. It was the warmest memory, but even this was a distortion, a scratched record skipping back and forth. I'd see his smile in reverse, unsmiling, sad, alien and frozen, a waxwork. I'd written so much about him over the years, snapshots of my childhood, but it just didn't feel like an accurate portrait of him. It was all written in moments, sad, happy, angry, and these moments made it unreal – like, was it an actual memory or just the memory of a photograph? *I must try not to write about Lucy. Or the boy. I can still feel her head on my neck. I can still carry him on my shoulders.*

'What you doing?' Will said, hands on hips, like he was talking to a child.

I looked up at him. 'I can't get out.'

'Pahahaha! Climb, mister mountaineer.'

'My arms, I've been digging this hole for 10 hours.'

'10 hours!'

'Yeah, it's hard! Where've you been?'

'I made the base and finished the shed and then had a nap.'

'Bastard! There's been all sorts of things I've had to overcome, rocks, bits of wood, clay-'

'This en't clay.'

'Whatever. It's been hard. 10 hours and all so you can have a shit in your fucking manor.'

'Alright, alright, grumpy arse.'

'Well...'

'I'll get the ladder.'

Of the people left in Halesowen, very few were likely to venture to the sprawling grounds of Leasowes Park. It just didn't serve any purpose. So, this was to be our true home. Not the flat, that was just a bed in town – we had the "office" too, for storing metals. This overgrown park, a temple to childhood, originally landscaped by our very own William Shenstone, the poet whose grave we'd sat upon many a night.

We found a small clearing in the woods and got to work. Will always spoke of finding a girl, falling in love and repopulating the town, but that dream faded after his last blighted romance. At least we'd have someplace of our own to die. Acres of healthy land, rabbits, we'd even seen deer, and there were pools and streams from which to fish and get water.

Will lay the ladder down and I climbed out of the hole. 'I've never claimed to be a mountain climber. I just liked hiking in the hills.'

'Alright,' he smiled.

'What?'

'I'm only playing with you.'

'I know. I just want to say it as it is.'

'Crib Goch was hardly a hike in the hills,' he said.

'Well, no, that was a terrifying scramble.'

He laughed.

'We should go back,' I said. 'Let's walk to Wales like we always talked about.'

'We will die,' he emphasised, laughing.

'We will wherever we are. Not too many years left, and what a place to die.'

'This isn't too bad either,' he said, proud, looking around.

Leasowes Park was definitely Will's manor. When we were young, we'd come here to get stoned in hidden corners. Will always fantasised about the apocalypse and how we'd survive, and how Marcus and Loz would probably fall by the wayside and need us to protect them. He wasn't quite on the money, but here we were, building a house in something which was as good as the apocalypse. But then, this was just the black hole of Halesowen. The sensible part of town had left. There was still a whole world out there. There was a fight somewhere, probably, some said, who really knew? But the closing of the south wasn't the end of this island, I was sure of it.

'I'm getting itchy feet,' I said.

'Talc,' he smiled, thinking he was ever-so funny.

'The world's a big place.'

'Look, Tom, you travelled far and wide when you left Halesowen. The Himalayas for fuck's sake. Haven't you seen enough?'

'You've barely left Halesowen. Don't you want to see more?'

'No.'

'I don't understand.'

'I know you don't. You have trouble understanding anything outside of your periphery. You always did.'

He had a point. I knew this much about myself. This was obviously enough for him, but not for me. Not this shanty town for drunks. Not forever. How could I get him to leave? All sorts of sabotaging ideas had entered my brain. Tell the Sons about the metal store, burn the brew, burn Ankerdine Block 5! Hell, burn this idyllic set up in Leasowes Park. But then I watched him as he dragged the huge sheet of ply over my bog hole, sinewy arms and determined grimace – he didn't even think to ask me to help, could see I was spent. The middle of the wood had been already scored and he popped it out with his foot so that it now lay at the bottom of the hole. Then he carried a dining chair over, flipped the cushioned middle out, and placed the legs in little indents he'd made in the wood.

'Ta daaa!' he smiled.

I stuck my thumb up.

'I know it's not ideal, but we don't have to crouch to shit anymore. Not getting any younger.' He looked up to the skies and authoritatively added, 'it's not gonna rain today. I'll fit the shed later.'

He'd worked so hard to build this place. We'd all worked hard. Loz too. Marcus just sort of pranced about and occasionally cooked beans on a campfire which Will had usually built. None of us were particularly handy, spent our lives doing other things. Will had spent most of his adult life on benefits, searching for truth online, whilst getting stoned. Loz taught in a college, after teaching English in South Korea for a few years. Marcus worked in care homes for the elderly. After my misspent youth, I'd done something similar with people with learning difficulties, but had been trying to eke a career as a writer. Will was more handy than me. I was just good for digging holes and over-thinking things.

We walked over to our little house, about 50 metres from the bog hole. It wasn't big, but it wasn't small. It had two bedrooms at the back and a living space which was about the same size as both rooms. It had taken months to build, made from shed and summer-house beams of wood from many abandoned gardens. Plywood lined the whole cabin, and mixed panelling of various types and shades of wood covered the outer, sanded and painted with a collection of outdoor wood varnishes. In between the panels we'd haphazardly stapled and stuck all manner of insulating materials we'd found. But when it was cold, it was cold – blankets and clothes were aplenty. The roof gradually climbed higher, the highest point at the front door, so any rainwater would trickle off the back of the cabin – in theory. We talked about drainage leading water into vats, which we could purify and use – we talked about it. The roof panels had been felted – in a way. We'd also stapled an army camouflage tarpaulin to it too. It looked like a ramshackle little hut, but it was fairly sturdy. It did the job. We were proud of it. I couldn't just destroy this to make them come with me. Besides, Will would probably just make us build it all again.

―――――――――

'Shit,' he cursed, looking out the window. 'I should've fitted the shed.'

The rain was coming down hard and heavy on our little Leasowes cabin – Will wasn't always right.

'It'll dry out, don't worry about it.'

'But it would've been done and out of the way. This fucking weather. You can never know what they're gonna do with it.'

'Quit with the chemtrails.'

'You'll never learn will you,' he said, irritated.

'I'm with you. It didn't look like it was going to rain. We just guessed wrong.'

'Alright, Tom, you know everything.'

'No, I don't. And I'm good with that.'

'Why do you bother?'

I could feel his annoyance at my cynicism, so I kept schtum to avoid the rising rage.

I was sat on an old sofa which we'd dragged a mile or so from one of the empty houses on Manor Way. It was brown leather, which I'd figured would at least be a little waterproof if we had a leak. Will didn't like it, but I'd never particularly liked the idea of building the cabin when we had a hundred detached houses we could choose from on the surrounding estates. There were even a couple of houses just off the park, yet Will was insistent we played out his dream.

But as I sat listening to the rain pelting the tarpaulin, I was happy we'd built it too. The damp in the air smelt earthy, releasing a fresh fragrance from the bluebells which currently surrounded much of the cabin. Little streams raced each other down the single pane glass window. Confounding gravity, there was a single drip in the corner which fell into a tiny spreading puddle to the front door mat, but otherwise we'd done an alright job with the place. The previous winter, it'd survived the worst snow storms I'd ever seen in the UK – never mind Halesowen. We'd survived it too, locked in for three days, the reek of piss, shit and sick buckets, stale booze and weed. We'd passed the time by painting the inside walls pink – the only paints we had were salmon pink, and ivory cream and pepper red which we used to make a variation on salmon pink.

'I'm sorry about… you know, chemtrails,' I said.

'I don't care,' he smiled. And he meant it.

We'd gotten pretty good at getting past these old couple spats. As long as we stopped it before it went too far. The alpha goats had been known to lock horns. We'd been friends for 35 years.

We met going to a house party when we were at college. He offered to carry my crate of beer, insisted in fact, wooed me with a selfless act. Perhaps it was a way to show his strength, but it didn't feel like that at the time. Then we got talking about music and all sorts of other shit, mostly girls. We hit it off instantly and, in between my dad's flat and his family home, we practically lived with each other during college. We'd had good times and bad times, like brothers. We met Loz and Marcus at college too. Fell together in the middle of a bender and stuck.

'We've got a good thing here,' I added to further appease him.

'We have.'

'I might even find a way to relax, if it wasn't for the bastard Sons and federalis-'

'It's just a couple of days. He'll be alright – Loz probably won't leave the flat and he'll make Marcus stay with him.'

'It depends, doesn't it,' I said.

'Ok, but even if they go to Ally's they'll be alright. She'll look after them,' he laughed.

Ally's house was the lure of sex for most men. Loz, however, was mostly desperate to be the family man again. Ally had two young children by two different men who'd long since left her. Loz had offered himself, but it was never going to happen. Ally also had other children, older, but they'd disappeared. North, presumably.

'I've just,' I said, 'got a bad feeling.'

'You've always got a bad feeling,' he interrupted. 'Quit with the novel.'

Marcus was the runt of the pack. He wasn't a fighter. He was gay, bi, something other than straight, he'd never confirmed it – and in these times he couldn't. He did come out once, many years ago, after his first fling with Leroy, a long since scattered friend of ours – scattered being the operative and somewhat visceral word. He made a right song and dance of it all, took us all to one side, and we all solemnly accepted it as if we'd never expected it. But then after a couple of months he denied it again and it was like the thing didn't even happen – maybe we took the piss a little too much. But however Marcus defined himself, there was no denying he was camp – 1970s Frankie Howerd/Kenneth Williams camp. This made him pretty funny to most people when they didn't think about what that campness suggested, but when some people thought about it, like half of Halesowen, it made him a target. And we'd told him over and over again, but he'd get drunk, flirt around and put us all at risk.

There was a knock at the door. I immediately jumped up. Will motioned me to keep still.

'I knew it!' I whisper-shouted.

'Shush!'

Knock, knock, knock.

'They've had Marcus!' I mouthed.

'Shut up!' he mouthed back.

'Hello… er, um… hello. You there, guys?'

'Bloody Eeyore.' I fell back to settee and sighed, before getting up to answer it.

'What's he doing here?' Will whispered.

'Who cares?' I lifted and opened the front door – it had sunk on the hinges a little.

'Alright, er, mate… how are ya?' he asked, dripping wet.

Will pulled his army jacket on and pushed past us to go outside.

'Come in, Damien. Why are you here?'

'I just em… I er… popped to the flat and er… Marcus said you wuz here.'

'Marcus?' *Bloody blabber mouth.*

He nodded.

I took his sopping green parka and gestured for him to sit down, grateful for the brown leather.

'I thought you were on the canals?' I asked, standing looking out the front door.

'I was for a…' he stopped, 'is he alright?'

'Just checking you're on your own.'

'O…k. I was on the barge for um… a bit. Didn't get too far. Er, you sure he's ok… has he been on the waccy baccy?'

'Always.'

'Wouldn't mind some… er… my… um… self.'

'In the pot,' I said, aimlessly pointing to the porcelain on the coffee table.

I watched Will nervously look around, before heading towards the bog hole. He then picked up the cushioned middle of the chair and placed it back on top, protecting my hole from the rain.

'Nice er… that. What… er…?' he lingered.

'Grecian urn, that's what I call it,' I said, watching Will.

'Oh yeah, how come?'

'Naked wrestlers on it. Probably some tat someone bought on holiday.' I had a sudden recollection of a Spanish bodega, eating olives and anchovies, the smell of sherry casks. Lucy fell off her chair after drinking one glass of rioja.

I snorted a laugh but it hurt. 'Remember holidays?'

Will started dragging his shed to the hole. It looked like four fence panels cobbled together, with a separate piece for the roof. He clearly needed help, but he wasn't going to ask. He looked to the skies, then down to his shed. He decided to give up.

'I um… have holidays all the time,' Damien laughed.

'The barge? I guess it's a kind of holiday.'

'You should come.'

'I should.' My mind drifted to nothingness, 'boom.'

A sad silence filled the air and I tried not to think about it.

'Have you seen her?' he asked.

'Who? Oh,' I realised what he was on about, 'yes, a couple of days ago. She's doing alright.'

I turned to watch Damien clumsily breaking up a bud of weed with damp hands.

'Does he… um know?' he gestured outside.

'Of course not. We were in Picks. I wandered off and met up with her.'

'Did anyone see you?'

'It was pitch black. I left my torch there.'

'She should come north,' he said.

'She won't, but yeah.'

Will pushed past me and shut the door. 'Sky might change.'

'If they let it,' I said, pointing upwards.

He glared at me, irritated.

'*A joke.*'

'Be good for the base to dry out before I fit it.' He looked down at Damien rolling a joint. 'Help your fucking self.'

'I er… Tom… um… I didn't mean, shall I put it back?'

'I said he could have one.'

'Twos,' Will said, sitting next to him.

He watched Damien trying to roll, and Damien knew it. He flopped over the Rizla awkwardly, little movement in his cold fingers, and the weed fell out.

'Fuck sake,' Will said.

Damien looked at him. 'What? Oh… um… you wanna do it?'

'Give it here,' he nagged. 'How'd you get to nearly 60 without learning to roll?'

'I did. I do… um… roll. I do all the time.' He pulled out his packet of tobacco.

'Drum?' Will asked, anxious to get some off him.

'Yeah, from Stafford.' He started to roll a cigarette.

'Black market?' I asked.

'Nah, shop. I keep… um… telling ya, you should come. This town is dead, like a low budget er… Mad Max.'

'I'd sooner a low budget. Safer,' Will said.

Damien looked at me, rolled his eyes.

'We should go see for ourselves,' I said.

'Do we have to keep going on about this stuff?' Will said.

'I'm gonna go-' I tested.

'Go then,' he snapped, like an angry lover.

'One day, I will.'

Will lit up his joint and Damien lit his cigarette. They swapped after a couple of drags. It made me feel hungry for some reason. I looked down at my gut. I used to be podgy. Now it was just skin.

'You really should come, Tom,' Damien said.

'I may well do.'

'There's space for two of you,' he gave me a knowing glance and I stared him down, nervous.

Will looked at me suspiciously.

'*He* isn't gonna come is he?' I said, pointing to Will.

'I'm not going,' Will confirmed, indignant. 'I'm happy here.'

Damien took a big drag on the joint and fell back to the settee, smiling. God knows what was going to come out of his mouth next.

It was too close for comfort. I stood up, 'I'm going to have a lie down.'

I woke up sweating, hot, disturbed, thinking about the bombs. A drinking dream. We were in The George, Six-Kids-Stacey lined up the shots – Wood's Navy rum, nail varnish burn. I knew I wasn't supposed to be drinking, a disappointed Lucy in the back of my mind.

'Oh, forget her,' Stacey said, young and curvy, in a tight leopard print dress, a sexy curl in the corner of her mouth.

I knew we were going to kiss, I wanted it, felt it deep inside. When our lips touched, Stacey picked up the bottle of rum, threw it behind the bar and an explosion ended the dream.

It had been four years since the bombs, another lifetime which had done its best to erase my previous lifetime, the one where I was happy. It was like I'd never left Halesowen. Whilst on the surface the town had changed – whole estates had left en masse, buildings destroyed and ransacked – the core of the Halesowen I used to know and inhabit was pretty much still intact. Only older. Aching faces melted or pickled, stretched and distorted. Decay. A rank odour in the air, the fish and piss of this lifestyle, flesh rotting from within, and the sickly sweet market-rot of rubbish which lined the streets, the smoky whiff emanating from Ground Zero.

For a time, in Halesowen, there had been hope. But it went with the preacher. Now I was longing for a catalyst, praying. *God get me out of Halesowen! No, God give me direction, purpose, let me serve You (preferably not here).* That was a better way of phrasing it, but I was trying to forget the whole God/Higher Power thing.

I tuned into Will in the living room.

'The US just couldn't let us begin to see,' he said, sounding animated.

'Um, I suppose, but-' Damien tried to interject.

'They needed to put a nation to sleep and the only way was to cut off its legs.'

That was quite a nice way of putting it.

'But they're saying it's the Russians,' Damien said.

'Russia?' Will patronised. 'China I get, but-'

'No, not um… I mean they don't… blame… when you go north-'

'North of Stafford, yes, yes,' he replied, tired of Damien's line.

'Look, Will,' Damien was suddenly surprisingly assertive, 'you're living in the butt end of the UK-'

'I'm living in the middle of the UK,' he was adamant.

'Listen, er… um-'

'Yes?'

'I um…'

'Ummmm? Come on.'

'It… I… um…'

'You can't even speak!' Will was proud – he was a bastard at times.

'I can. You. I. That's not what I mean. Um… Halesowen… Oh, forget it.'

The bomb hit London October 4th 2027 at 8.05am. I was back visiting mum in Halesowen. We heard it a hundred miles away, saw the bright flash, the house x-rayed from afar. Outside we saw the cloud turn orange and then purple and black, bruise, like the blood of a million people rising to the surface of the "legs" of the nation. About half an hour later, the sky was still and grey. TV stopped completely for a few hours, all channels out. And then came the crazy emotional reports. The bomb hit the east, over Bethnal Green, a reporter said. They spoke of an 80 mile radius, which soon dwindled to a 55 mile radius, wiped out in one blast. Seven million estimated to be killed. To begin with it was all China's fault, a Chinese bomb, potentially approved by Russia.

I remember trying to call Lucy, but all the networks were down. I went to use the house phone. That was no good either. I knew I had to get back to my family in Somerset, but mum was terrified, said I should wait until we'd heard more news. When the internet came back on, I sent a Facebook message to Lucy. She said she was alright, was with her family. I wanted to talk to her, to hear her voice. The phone networks still down, we tried to messenger call, but the internet was ropey, her tone unreal, a robotic interpretation, like we were living in alternate dimensions. Eventually the Alexa pod showed me their faces and she looked tired.

'Come up here,' I said.

'Mum and dad,' she replied.

'Bring them.'

'Please come back, Tom.' She looked frightened and she was not easily scared.

I swore I'd be home the next day.

The TV was intermittent that first day, they told us London was definitely gone and that the US were blaming China and planning to bomb them.

People were out on their streets crying. They'd left their houses as if to get away from the reality of it, but really it was people needing people. Besides, the ash-filled skies told us it all. In mum's cul de sac they gathered in the road, huddled, a herd of sheep defending against an invisible wolf. Autumn cold, people drank tea from mugs and flasks, as they hopelessly tried to rationalise, to make sense of it and come up with solutions. A few left for Wales almost immediately. One or two for Scotland. Quite literally heading for the hills.

Every now and again someone would come out with a snippet of news from the TV, "the Chinese have bombed the UK for supporting the US embargo on the Chinese internet market". Some even chanced to take information from the net, one read from her phone, "the Russians are the only country who manufacture bombs which explode in this particular shade of orange, best described as bile-yellow", an image of various shades like a Dulux palette. People wondered what the US would do, what Europe would do. The EU remained impartial, other than to offer shocked sympathy and support to rebuild the UK if we wanted it. We heard nothing from China or Russia, no denial or admission.

Radio fizzed crackled waves from various points in the street, and we waited for World War III to be declared. But who would declare it? Parliament had been in session and was undoubtedly wiped out in the blast. On the radio they told us different things, often with opposing information from stations owned by the same people. We heard somebody say the US were not planning on any *more* bombing in China or Russia, which suggested the bomb had been sent from the US out east, implying we'd inexplicably been caught in the crossfire. This seemed ridiculous for many reasons. The fact that London was specifically hit made no sense. Surely this was no accident. But, a target?

There was no newspaper the following day. The Sun, gone, The Times finished, in physical form at least. After the bomb they joined the Mail and Express in ending all ties to print, focusing their attention to the dopes online. So smooth was the transition, conspiracy theories started popping up about their involvement, a meme of Rupert Murdoch's pickled corpse on a *Rosebud* sled to Hades pulling the globe down with him.

TV and radio were more reliable sources, since Labour had imposed the new regulations, but it was still information packaged with an agenda, at least that's what I heard on the radio, which seemed to be slightly left of the TV if you listened to the right stations.

Early next morning, in the confusion of it all, I found myself driving to Will's little bedsit in Old Hill. The roads were surprisingly empty of cars and the streets surprisingly lined with people, gabbing away, drinking and jeering, even cheering as I went past. I'd expected the panic-buying and looting of the viruses and the Greek Riots. Perhaps people had finally given up, after a tough decade of social unrest. Outside Will's block, people were smoking weed, disgruntled but aloof. In a cloud of green smoke himself, Will's tin hat was well and truly planted on his head, but right now his ideas were at least as good as anybody else's.

'It's the Yanks, of course it is,' he told me.

'But why?'

'To get to the Russians.'

'Eh?'

'Bomb the British, blame the Chinese. The EU will also blame the Chinese, who will know they didn't do it. The Chinese will naturally assume it's the Russians-'

'Naturally?'

'And start a war. This destabilises China and an already weakening Russia, after the war with the EU for Georgia's acceptance, and the recent Ukraine talks…' blah, blah, blah… 'It goes way back to the noughties…' blah, blah, blah… 'Putin's bear….' blah, blah, blah… 'Blair's global dream…' blah, blah, blah… 'Finland didn't help things when they cut the train lines in the north, but really that was just a distraction, it was not the Franz Ferdinand.'

'What?'

'That's what this is, a big Franz Ferdinand. Once the Russians get involved, the war begins, then the population will shrink after a few years of it.'

'A few years of it! Christ, Will, it's just happened. This isn't some Austrian king-'

'Prince.'

'Prince, whatever! Seven million dead they reckon!'

'We're the lucky ones.'

'What?!'

'We'll be alright from here on in.'

'What the fuck!'

'It is what it is.'

'Listen to yourself, man. Do you know what's just happened?'

'I know perfectly well. Do you?' He was smug.

I wanted to hit him. None of what he said sounded reasonable. But then I didn't really know – or care. I'd avoided politics for years, just living a normal life with my wife and kid. What was the point in caring about it? What could I do about it?

Looking back, I think the reason I was there, the reason I went to see Will of all people, was to have a drink. But he didn't have any, just weed, and that was the last thing I needed. It was a lucky escape.

'I've gotta see Lucy,' I said.

'You can't.'

'What?'

'Radiation. Have you not seen the direction of the winds?'

'What are you on about? Fucking chemtrails?'

'Nothing to do with it. It's the storms.'

'That's my wife and kid!'

There was a silence. I could see him slowly catching on with what I was saying.

'Do you want me to come?' he asked.

'No.'

I left immediately.

———————

Bang, bang, bang!

'Get up you lazy fuck!' Will shouted.

'Why?' I asked from under the covers.

'You've been asleep for the best part of a day. The sun's going down.'

'So?'

'Damien's off.'

I sat up. 'What?'

This might be my chance. I reached for my jumper on the floor. 'Hold on a sec.' Pulled it on, arms aching, chest aching, back aching from digging the frigging hole. 'Too old for this shit.'

I opened the door to the living room and Will was lying on the settee, smoking a cigarette, smiling.

'Where's Eeyore?'

'He left,' swigged beer from a bottle.

'Left?' I moved to the door. 'When?'

'Hours ago. See a man about the north.'

'What does that even mean?' I was irritated. I opened the front door.

'He'll be at the Netherton canals by now.'

'What?' *Cunt.* 'Why didn't you wake me?' I knew why. 'You're a shit.'

'Pahaha,' he swigged again and burped.

'Where did you get that beer from?'

'Eeyore. Some brewery in Stoke.'

'You see?' I pleaded. 'A world!' Like he was dumb. 'It moves outside of Halesowen. A brewery! Not some shit blackberry brew made in the kitchen of a sinking flat. What's wrong with you?'

'Fuck off,' he smirked.

I stormed out of the cabin, slammed the door.

'Fuck! FUCK! I can't do this anymore! I can't. I can't. I can't.'

I ran over to the toilet. He'd fitted his shed. I kicked its flimsy walls, punched it, kicked it again with an almighty boot and it came off the base, toppled over and the roof fell off. Will ran out.

'Tom! Stop it, you fuck!'

'Why won't you let me leave?' I screamed.

I jumped on his shed, a wobbly box, surfing it. He tried to get to me. I jumped again. It cracked and snapped at the corners. As it crumpled, I fell with it. Will caught me and then threw me to the ground. He jumped over me, trapping me, astride me.

'Boom!' I yelled. 'Fucking boom!'

He pinned my weakened arms back using one hand, then slapped me with the other. 'Four years, Tom!'

I tried to wrestle out of it but he was too strong. 'Boom, boom, boom!' I spat in his face.

He flinched, but just stared me down. 'What. Are. You. Gonna do on a fucking barge?'

'Get away.'

'Run away,' he said.

'Whatever. Let me go!'

He rolled off. I got up awkwardly, brushed myself down. 'Running away?' I said. 'What do you think you're doing?'

'Building a life.'

'You're in hiding.' I mimed smoking a joint. 'This whole town is just running away. Loz is running away. Marcus… Marcus has gone!'

He laughed.

'It's not funny, Will! There's a world out there.'

'Not my world.'

'Where's your fight? The big man. Where's your ambition? The world could be yours, ours – a woman, you could finally settle down!'

'Don't go there!' he warned.

'A home, a life,' I pleaded, changing tack.

'No, this is my home.'

'A pile of rotting planks nailed together, a leaky roof, for Christ's sake! It won't survive too many more snowy winters, that's for sure.'

He looked sad. I felt a pang of regret.

He turned away from me and walked back to the cabin and then, calmly, 'go then, Tom, run to the canals.'

'Come with me.'

He ignored me.

'Where you going, Will?'

'I've gotta fix the shed.'

I turned to look at his broken toilet shed. I'd done it again. I knew I had. I'd had a moment, one of my moments. But he was such a bastard. But he was right too. Four years was a long time.

But I wasn't running away. Was I? In a way, I was the only one in this town who wasn't. I couldn't. I'd tried that. For years. I didn't drink, smoke, get out of my goddam head. I was just ready to move on, wasn't I?

'I'm not running away,' I said to myself more than him.

Fucking boom.

The moon lit the skies. Torch off, we made our way back to town in the purply haze of the night. The drag of our old feet on broken, forgotten roads, the occasional hollow bump and grating twang of Will's guitar, strapped to his back. Icy breath, my hands not quite warming up in the holey pockets of an old leather jacket.

'We know he landed on the moon,' Will said. 'It's a categoric fact that man landed on the moon.'

'What?' I was distracted. 'Oh, I know.'

'The post-Trump files showed us the more important truth.'

'I know. Let's talk about something else. I know all about it,' I looked to the skies. 'Let's sing.'

'What?'

'"Life on Mars?"' I smiled to myself.

'I'm trying to talk to you, Tom.'

'Well don't. Sing to me. Like you used to,' I joked.

'I'm trying to say something important.'

'Again.'

'You what?' he was irritated.

'Oh, ok! The files showed us the government stirred a falsehood that the moon landings were faked to muddy the waters,' I reeled off. 'They did this to ultimately define conspiracy theorists as nutcases as opposed to people who theorise logical reasons for something happening other than the official story.'

I saluted, but he didn't see me.

There was a silence.

'Good lad,' he said.

'You're a patronising fuck. Play the guitar. You know I don't give a shit.'

'It's too cold. My hands won't work.'

'Playing will warm them up.'

He tussled with it and pulled the strap round, muttering and moaning to himself in the process. He took a deep breath and whilst walking started to play the chords to "Space Oddity".

'That's not it,' I said.

'Yes, it bloody is.'

'"Ground control to Major"…' I sang, to illustrate my point.

'Oh, alright. It's one of his fucking space ones.'

Years ago, we played in a band together. Will on guitar, I sang, Loz played bass. Leroy played the drums for a while. Marcus couldn't do anything musical. Because of this, one drug-fuelled night we decided he should sit on the stage on a stool and remain frozen for the entire gig. It was supposed to be some witty arty idea, like a kind of anti-Bez. He did it for about three gigs. It looked terrible, cluttered up the stage and irritated Leroy because nobody could see him. Leroy was a vain bastard – in a room full of egos he shined the brightest.

We sang "Life on Mars" as we made our way down Mucklow Hill. Then we sang something we wrote ourselves years ago. "Bastard Little Jellyfish".

'What the fuck was that about?' he asked.

'A jellyfish.'

'Yeah, but what were we trying to say?'

'I don't remember us ever really trying to say anything,' I laughed. 'But, I guess, we were saying it was just our luck that in something as big as the sea we'd end up getting stung by a relatively tiny man o' war.'

'Big tentacles, though,' he said.

'I guess.'

We walked the rest of the way in silence. I wondered whether the radiation from the bombs could still touch us here from the south. I was too cowardly to want to die a painful death, but I sort of hoped I'd already been stung.

We got back home in the early hours, Will clicked his headtorch on. Loz and Marcus were asleep on the settees. Will shook Loz.

'What's happened?' Loz said, sheltering his eyes from the light.

'We're going to Ally's.'

'What? Why? What time is it?'

Marcus started to stir. I turned to light him, his half-naked pink flesh whitened in the light to a sickly pale.

'We going to Ally's?' he asked me.

'Not us,' I said.

Will hadn't spoken to me about any of this. I knew what he needed to do. He needed to let it all out. He needed to get away from me. He needed to get wrecked.

'Well, I don't want to go,' Marcus defended, typically rejected.

'Good. Cos you're not,' Will said.

'Ooh, ark at you with your anger issues.'

'Don't,' I said.

Will went into the kitchen. I heard the popping of corks, the clinking of bottles, as he tested the brew.

Loz sat up and rolled a cigarette. 'Didn't go well?'

'We got the toilet done,' I said. 'On the second attempt.'

'Second?'

Will walked into the living room, a bottle of berries in each hand. 'Thanks to that fuck. Come on.' He gave him a gentle kick. 'You might find yourself a wife.'

'What? Oh, one mistake! I was drunk,' Loz said, putting his trainers on.

'Yeah, go marry Ally,' Marcus pathetically ribbed. No one reacted.

'It'd be better than sleeping on a beat-up settee.'

'How you gonna marry her?' Marcus asked, giving me a wink.

We'd been taking it out on him for months about this. Loz had finally admitted in all sincerity he wanted to marry Ally, to bring up her kids. Taking the piss, and in all "sincerity", we coaxed him into asking her, knowing full well it would end in comical disaster. Ally laughed in his face. Seeing how wounded he was by this, she tried to assuage his embarrassment by asking him where he could possibly find a vicar.

"I'll go er… north," he told her, for the first time realising his predicament.

But the real predicament was Ally would never be attracted to somebody like Loz. Aside from the fact he was a bit of a div, he was also too nice. Ally only ever went with people who were bound to leave her. She'd be stuck with Loz for life.

"I didn't think," he'd said to her, getting up off his knees.

"You're me mate, Loz," she replied, patting him on the shoulder.

He was so gutted about it we couldn't laugh at him – for a little while.

'You just *didn't think*, did you?' Marcus said, as Loz got up from the settee.

Will laughed and handed Loz a bottle, 'come on mate, ignore the fucker.'

'*She's just your mate*,' I added, laughing.

'Oh, fuck off, Tom!' Will shot back, half-blinding me with his headtorch.

They left with a slam of the back door.

I sat on Loz's settee in the dark, silence, the colourful beads of the ether darting about whilst my brain caught up with the absence of light. I knew Marcus was awake, but he was being very still, as if he was thinking about something. Maybe he just felt left out.

Eventually he spoke. 'The bombs?'

'Yeah.'

I'd left Will's bedsit in Old Hill that morning, back then, thinking about the desolated town of Chernobyl, the people who died of cancer in the wake of the nuclear explosion. It made me think about a trip I'd taken with Lucy to Japan when she was pregnant with the boy. She was determined to go to Hiroshima to see the atomic bomb dome, the famous building left standing when the atom bomb exploded in 1945. I was determined we wouldn't, because I didn't want to put our unborn child at risk of exposure to radiation. I admit it was over-cautious, but I managed to persuade her against it by suggesting a trip to see the snow monkeys in Hakodate.

I drove back to my mum's and explained why I had to go back to Somerset. She begged me to stay, but there was no way I was leaving my wife and child exposed to radiation.

'I'll be back with them,' I promised.

'It's a hundred miles away,' she said.

'The winds!'

'What are you on about? Have you been listening to Will? He smokes that stuff all day. What does he know?'

But he was right. The radio seemed to be talking about nothing but radiation and how anywhere south of the Midlands was a risk, and anywhere south of the M4 was a no-go area in this weather. What could I do? Leave them there? Leave them to get sick?

I called the Alexa pod. She was by the beach with the boy, but had the portable with her. The first thing I noticed was the wind, her hair blowing wild. 'You shouldn't be out.' She gave me a stern look, there was never any telling her what to do. It made me laugh. 'Please go home. I'll be there in a couple of hours.'

When I left mum's, I don't know why, I had the strange feeling that I would never return to Halesowen again. I drove to Ankerdine high-rise, where I used to live with dad. I parked on Andrew Road, lured by nostalgia perhaps, or maybe it was something to do with the crisis, whatever it was I wanted my dad. As I got out of the car and walked over towards it, Mick was coming out of the block.

'Bloody hell, kid, long time no see.'

I nodded. There was an awkward silence. I felt embarrassed to be there, weak. Dad had died 16 years ago, *get over it, Tom.*

'What a mad un, eh?' I said.

'World gone to pot. Let 'em all in and this is what happens.'

'Eh? They're saying it's the Chinese. Or the Russians. My mate reckons it's the Americans, but–'

'What? Nah, fucking Muzzies.'

I didn't have it in me to argue and found myself shrugging my shoulders.

'Yow know it, me mon,' he said. 'Ow come yow'm here?'

'Oh, I just, um-'

He could see I was struggling. 'You remember the Nelson, son?'

I nodded.

'Me and your dad had some bostin' times in the Nelson, Bri was a top bloke. Do you remember… What was his name?'

He expected me to know.

'Yow know,' he said.

'Nigel?'

'Nah!' like I was being daft. 'He was the gaffer down the George.'

'Colin?'

'Nah. Colin died. Din't ya hear?'

'Cancer.'

'Ar,' he nodded. 'The landlord, yow know-'

'Tony Dale?'

'Tony Dale,' he said, reminiscing, satisfied we'd got there. 'He's just moved back and taken on Picks. Didn't even know about your old man. Them wuz the days. Yuh dad, I miss the old bugger.'

'Me too.'

'I know,' he said, and then paused looking at me. 'We got lucky.'

'What?'

'Them southerners.'

I'd almost forgotten, lost in a warm world past. I looked through the flats, down Andrew Road to town. It hadn't changed. These same old maisonettes, the high-rises, the bus station at the bottom. London was gone. Big Ben, Buckingham Palace, Piccadilly Circus, Wembley, Wimbledon, the West End, the museums, universities, churches, the City, the tube, the parks all gone. It was home to some of the most famous people past and present the world had seen, but it was now no more, wiped out, a nuclear waste ground. But my old town in the Black Country was still standing.

Halesowen and its flats, the houses, the pubs, an old church, a swimming baths, two high schools, a handful of primary schools, the trees, fields and a tiny football ground, all still standing.

'All them people,' he said. 'The politicians – good bloody riddance. The fellas off the box – load of rubbish, but I do like that Bradley Walsh chap, shame.'

'Is he dead?'

'He's a Londoner.'

'Had to be close to it, anyway.'

'Ar, too bloody true,' he laughed.

'It's horrible, Mick. I've got mates there.'

'Now, it's no good thinking 'bout them, me mon. Yow gotta think about yourself.'

'And my wife and kid.'

'That's all that matters,' he prodded my chest.

I looked up at the block, to the third-floor window I used to look out of as a kid.

'And he's gone,' he said.

'I know,' I stopped. 'I know he's gone.'

Mick looked at me, his face tanned with age and heavy drinking, and he smiled. Smiled like he was stronger than me, like he pitied me. That's how it felt.

'You want a pint, son?'

'No, ta.' I couldn't tell him I'd long quit, another nail in my wet-cardboard coffin. 'I better be off, Mick. Gotta see to the missus.'

'Ar know that feeling,' he laughed. 'Don't have that no more, thank God.'

I watched him walk down town, short and stocky. Mick had to be in his 70s, but he was pretty solid. He'd been a builder and it showed. Dad was taller and more frail. He was a chemist, not the pharmaceutical kind, but a plastics chemist – before his life fell apart. I always knew him as an old man. When I was at school, people thought he was my grandfather. By the time I was 20, he was well into his 60s. In his last years, he used to make himself walk down town to buy a Daily Mail. He'd stop and sit on a wall every so often, struggling to catch his breath – always swore it was working with chemicals and not the twenty fags a day. Then he'd pop into the Nelson for a couple of pints of mild, followed by a whiskey or three. Often he needed help walking home.

I sat in the car outside and found myself talking to him, saying goodbye to him. Again. When I looked at my watch, a couple of hours had passed. I cursed myself, but I didn't know what was going to happen. How could I? I didn't think an hour or so would make a big difference.

The motorway was empty heading south, ghostly devoid of movement. I saw just one car heading in the same direction as me in the short time I was on the motorway. One car who would witness the same thing as me, from the same perspective and possibly with the same intention of saving a loved one. This was in stark contrast to the other side of the motorway, where a considerable number of cars were heading north, running away from the invisible fallout.

The second bomb hit before I'd even made it to junction six.

'Boom,' I said to nobody, reliving it in the darkness of our flat, Marcus still and silent, perhaps feeling awkward.

'You've gotta let it go, man,' he eventually said, with rare sincerity.

I got up and felt my way to the bedroom. I kicked my shoes off and got into bed. Marcus was very still, no sound of movements, again like he was thinking. I was expecting to hear him say something, to repeat his line like he was in a goddam film. *You've gotta let it go, man.* But he didn't. I heard him move about and settle back down on his settee.

I closed my eyes.

I felt like I'd slept for just a few minutes, but it was lighter outside, so it must've been a couple of hours. Somebody was sitting on the bed. I could see the outline of her old, bony frame.

'Tom,' her voice cracking, hand shaking my thigh.

'What do you want, Stace?'

'Ally sent me over.'

'Ok.'

She squeezed my leg, 'to see if yow'm alright.'

'Ok.' I knew what was going on. It wasn't the first time.

'*Ok?*'

Over the covers, she slowly moved her hand up my thigh. I let it happen. When she neared my balls, I started to morph, to change shape. My legs outstretched, she took hold of my cock and shook it side to side like she was playing with a joystick.

'Yeah?' she asked.

I didn't say anything.

She moved her hand off and under the quilt. She tugged at my pants and I helped her pull them down. I wasn't sure about it, but it felt good – *it's not like I do drugs or drink*. I started to think about fucking her and I reached for her knee and pulled her up the bed. I rubbed hard through the denim of her trousers and she undid her top button. In this light, I could imagine how she looked back then.

Those dresses, a thin skin, that Picasso woman shape bending in the aloofness of her movements, no more or no less than two handfuls of breast, forward facing nipples in the nylon, lycra, whatever the material was. 30 years ago, when I was just a shy kid, before necking a few drinks, then the flirting would start. Then I'd drink until anything else was nigh on impossible. I laughed out loud thinking about it.

'Wha?'

'Nothing.'

I slowly unzipped her jeans, felt the brush of her bush – she wasn't wearing knickers. It was exciting.

BANG, BANG, BANG! The back door.

I jumped up and out of bed too quickly, guilty, caught in the act, 'ow, shit, my bastard back!' – *the bloody hole.*

The back door opened, I pulled my pants up. I heard Marcus jumping off his settee.

'What the fuck?' Marcus.

'Where is she?' Tony Dale.

'Who? Where's who?' Marcus.

He'd obviously not heard Stacey come in. He wouldn't have lied to Tony Dale, he wasn't that daft.

'She's in here, Tony,' me.

I sat down on the bed, Stacey used my shoulders to help her stand up on the mattress, behind me. 'Yow *bastard*.'

She was right, of course, but I didn't have a choice. Honesty in this situation was survival.

Tony came into the bedroom. Ten years older than me but by no means weaker, a brute of a man when he wanted to be, brandishing a brass dipstick like some sort of landlord's whip, which frankly looked nothing short of kinky. Stacey awkwardly stood on the bed, using me as a shield, one hand gripping a tuft of hair on my balding head. I blindly reached for the battery lamp on the bedside table, but couldn't find it. Hazy shapes in the low light.

'What's she doing here?' he asked me.

Be brave, be strong. 'What the hell do you think she's doing?'

He looked up at her, then down at me. '*Stacey?*' confused, surprised even.

'I was nearly fucking there!' I said.

'*Stacey?*' again confused.

'What ya saying?' she spat, still clinging to my tuft.

'Where is it?' he yelled.

'Where's wha?' she clearly lied.

'You know what.'

'Ar doh.'

'Yes, you fucking do.'

'Ar doh.'

'You do.'

'*Ar doh!*'

'Oh, for fuck's sake.' I pulled free from Stacey, losing a couple more hairs in the process. I got up off the bed and quickly went to the window. 'Bloody pantomime.' I opened the curtains to let a little more light in to reveal the farce.

'I'm not playing, Stace,' he said.

She edged back on the bed carefully, my illusion broken, her age apparent in the twilight blue.

'Just give it to him, whatever it fucking is.'

Tony Dale dropped his dipstick and walked towards her, looking like Bill Sykes about to snap her neck. I briefly looked out of the window and could still see candle-light across the way in the window of Ally's flat. I turned back and saw a flicker of light from behind Stacey's back. My brain knew instantly what it was, long before words could formulate. Adrenaline burst into my gut, but before I could even spit out "fuck", the flicker moved across the room like a shooting star in an animation flipbook and into Tony Dale's neck. He immediately stepped back, grabbing hold of the knife, garbling incomprehensibly. Stacey fell back off the bed and I caught her for a split second, before dropping her, instinctively aware I might be complicit. Her old bones crumpled awkwardly to my feet. I stood frozen and watched the dark shape of Tony Dale slide down the wall, gargle, and then stop gargling.

'Marcus!' I shouted.

There was no movement.

Stacey climbed up my legs and torso, her fingers jabbing, crawling. She quickly closed the curtains.

'Marcus!' I yelled.

There was a pause. '… Yeah?' I could hear the wariness in his voice.

'Stacey just killed Tony Dale.'

There was another pause. '…Stacey's here?'

'I was about to fuck her,' I said. I don't know why I said it. It just came out.

Silence.

'About… time?'

I sat on the bed and looked up at Stacey's bony silhouette in front of the curtains. She was staring at me. No emotion. I put my head in my hands to hide from it, pressed my eyes, atoms darting in a fuzzy light show.

BOOM. It was much bigger than a boom. There was the sound of a big crack and then an enormous echo from it. But to me it's a boom. Sometimes I find myself just saying it when I don't even realise I'm thinking about it. Boom. Maybe I'm missing her. Or something reminds me of them. Cereal bowls. For some reason cereal bowls remind me of his hair. His level blond fringe cupping his bronze head, a couple of centimetres above his green eyes.

The indent above and behind my collarbone reminds me of Lucy, because it's like a jigsaw, it's where her head fits.

Boom. It didn't occur to me for what felt like a good minute but what may well have been less than a second. Ahead of me on the motorway, the blinding white cloud, like the earth was running away from the sky. The central reservation clattered like a banged radiator, the road signs breathed and then coughed. I instinctively stopped the car, transfixed. Then the road stopped.

The cars on the other side of the motorway seemed to be doing about 200 mph, they swerved and crossed, missing each other and then started to pull over. First on the hard shoulder, then the first lane slowed to a stop, then second lane. Those who ploughed on trickled along in the third lane. Horns. People got out shouting, screaming. I watched dazed.

Only then did the meaning of it truly hit me, dig under my rib cage, and I saw her face, her wild hair, I heard him laugh. The cloud quickly turned orange, beautiful, and I instantly forgot. Then I woke up again and heaved, opened the door and fell out, half sure a car would take me with her, with him. I lay there looking at the monster, it turned brown, then purple and black. The skies went thick with grey and I stayed under it, a few feet below a thick blanket of history.

They said it was likely aimed at Cardiff, but it hit Burnham-on-Sea. Cardiff or Burnham, they would have died. A tsunami took out Newport and Cardiff, drowned them, and the blast reached as far north as Bristol.

If I'd have gone straight there, I would've died with them.

I lay on the motorway for a while, until a car pulled up behind mine. Somebody got out.

'You need to turn back,' the voice said.

It was a policeman. I stared at him, blank.

'You need to go back.'

'Yes.'

2028

I'm not impervious to conspiracy theories. I'd spent a year back with Will, living between his little bedsit and my mum's house, and no longer did I have my fancy Samsung, fearing cell damage from 6G frequency disruptions. Now I had my third wave revival Nokia 3310, which was even less fancy than the one they brought out a decade ago. But Loz wasn't answering, and he was the only one who had a phone. Will had renounced the use of one, due to the gene altering waves, and Marcus had lost his and given up on it – one less lecture from Will.

I called Picks.

'Ello,' gruff.

'Hiya, Tony, are they still there?'

'Who?'

'It's Tom.'

'Oh, yeah, them here.'

'Tell them to hang on, I'm heading into town.'

'Ar.'

It felt like a Sunday morning in the 90s, before the pubs opened, but it was Tuesday. I walked along the Hagley Road and, when I came to traffic lights, I pressed the button. I continued and a few seconds later the piercing bleeping echoed through the still street. I turned, walking backwards, to see the red orb. I hadn't seen a car on the whole walk, nor a person.

As I came onto the Queensway in town, I saw people heading towards me. An old couple with a dog. I knew who they were, but it was too late to avoid them. I'd drank with them many times in a previous life. I knew her more than him. Barb used to work with my mum down the Co-op. When they were young, they'd go up Brum to the Rom together, get drunk and dance to Barry White. But whereas mum grew away from that life, Barb was still drinking heavily, decades later, her face heavily wrinkled from booze and tanning beds. She looked a bit like a sultana. She was hunched and small, and so was Rex. They spent their days drinking and their nights bickering. God knows how they'd kept it up all these years.

I smiled at Barb. 'Rex,' I nodded.

'How you doing, boy?' His warm Welsh accent, a waft of whiskey.

I looked down to the old black lab, who flopped to the tarmac, clearly glad of a rest. 'I'm ok. What can you do?'

'*This*? Pah! It'll blow over soon enough. Life will go back as it were.'

'Ever the cock-eyed optimist, eh,' Barb said, grabbing his arm.

'We've had it lucky all these years, boy.'

I thought about the Greek Riots not three years ago, which brought the royal family to its knees. We'd only just started to see light at the end of that murky tunnel and then the bombs hit. 'Lucky?' I scoffed. 'That's an interesting way of looking at things.'

'Ah, come on, boy, you…' he belched, losing the end of his sentence. 'You know what you need, you need a good woman.'

He turned to Barb, smiling. I could see her eyes darting about with what he'd just said. He was oblivious.

'Have we really been lucky, Rex? The protests and riots? Two decades of austerity? What about the pandemics?'

'Pandemics now, is it? That was nature's way.'

'Nature?' I asked, suspicious of it.

Barb looked to the dog – it could barely lift his head – and started scratching behind his ears.

'Yes, boy, nature,' he insisted.

Perhaps he was right. Perhaps it was just a bat, a rat, a monkey or an armadillo. Will was adamant it wasn't. But how could he know? How could anyone know? In a way, that was one of the things I loved about Will. He had a belief that there was truth out there and that it was accessible.

'You've got to wipe your glasses, boy!' Rex suddenly impressed upon me, prodding the air with his walking stick.

'Here we go,' Barb rolled her eyes.

'"If the doors of perception were cleansed,"' he said, '"everything would-"'

'"-appear to man as it is,"' I continued the quote.

'Yes, that's right, boy, you know it is so,' he said, musically Welsh. 'But what do you think war is?'

'What I was trying to-'

'Do you not think I know what you were trying to say? Bats, armadillos, laboratories or the military, it's all the same thing. Are we not animals-?'

'This is his latest thing,' Barb chipped in, smiling.

'My latest-?'

'Yes, Rex,' I interrupted, to halt the bickering. 'We're all animals.'

'Are we not nature?'

'Yes, I guess, but–'

'No buts, boy, listen to me. Mother nature has a funny way and we can't explain it. Some of us call it God.'

Oh God. 'God?' I asked, judgementally.

'Yes, God almighty, mother nature, Lord of the lamb and the wolves!' he blarted, the Welsh calm suddenly thick with passionate poetry, the reverence of an old Dylan Thomas recording, walking stick flailing, much deeper and bigger than his thin frame ought to have allowed.

'Come on, Rex,' Barb said, 'he doesn't need–'

'No, it's fine,' I lied.

'He has places to be,' she added.

'Oh, sorry,' his voice dropped back down. 'Do you have places to be?'

Was that sarcasm? 'Well,' I looked at Barb who was eyeballing me, coaxing me, 'I mean, yes, I have to see–'

'A man about a dog, do you?'

Passive-aggression? 'Will, Loz,' I stuttered. 'The boys.'

'Boys?' he asked.

I nodded, then looked beyond them into town. There was no one, it was empty, deserted.

'You call yourself *boys*, but you are *men*,' he said.

A bit bloody ironic coming from you! 'I mean, the guys–'

'Never mind a man about a dog,' he interrupted. 'You'd do well to see a man about God, boy.'

Barb looked away embarrassed, gently tugging on his arm.

'Yes, Rex, you're right,' I said, beaten. 'I must get on.'

He nodded but they didn't move, just stood there. I nodded back, but there was no sign of the end of the interaction, just awkwardness.

Somebody finally spoke. 'Your mother?' Barb asked.

'Good. Yes, I'll remember you to her.'

She smiled and nodded her head like she was expecting me to say more.

'Yeah… good then,' I smirked. 'Better get on… Bye Rex, Barb, bye… doggy.'

'Ben,' Rex corrected.

'Ben, bye Ben.'

The animal opened his eyes briefly at the sound of his name, but couldn't be bothered to move.

I walked around them and on. *How did I do it for so many years? Live here?* I passed the old post office, which had been converted into a now abandoned café, windows surprisingly still intact. Then the William Shenstone, the Wetherspoons, boarded up. Halesowen was dead, the old church opposite, a sandstone sculpture, the solidified eye of an ancient God who'd stopped watching over us.

I casually glanced behind me and they were gone, disappeared around the corner. *Thank God.* Rex never used to be religious. He'd studied physics at Oxford, if he was to be believed, and he was always espousing atheism in the old days. I had no issue with God. Not really. I'd gone enough rounds with Him myself. I'd been sober for nearly two decades. I didn't know too many people who'd stayed sober for that long without having a relationship – or at least a conversation or two – with God, a higher power, something, telling yourself "it is what it is" and "everything happens for a reason". But as the words stumbled drunk out of Rex's mouth, I had the sudden feeling God might be more likely to drive me to drink than away from it.

———

Billy Picks – or Picks as it'd long been known – was one of the oldest pubs in Halesowen, serving Halesonians, and anyone willing to enter, since the mid-1800s. L-shaped and small, I entered through the side door. Straight ahead of me, the regulars. A row of middle-aged men sitting at a mahogany bar, supping cloudy cider, the sweet reek of rancid manure. Behind them, a bench against the wall and three little round tables, older men, and some young who may as well have been old. Most were drinking the same strong juice, except for Ray James, an ex-councillor, who was drinking something from a brandy glass, brandy perhaps. Councillor Ray was small and nattered like a check-out girl, his fast Black Country delivery just a few tones higher than the rest.

It was cramped and busy, low moans and jarring laughter, "I know arr's!" and "ow am ya's?", punctuated by the nasal patter of councillor Ray. It was how I'd always known it, except there used to be more women.

I tight-lip grinned and nodded but mostly avoided eye-contact. I made my way into the right side of the bar, the family side, lilac walls and wooden floorboards. There were always fewer people this side.

A couple were sat at a table, their young boy sitting on a big toy ambulance wearing a Western Flu visor and playing with his paramedic action figures. I winked at the kid and he blushed behind the mask, shy.

At the far end, Will, Loz and Marcus were sat around a small table supping that same pickled juice. It made me think of Somerset, of Burnham-on-Sea, the sour whiff which spilled from high-street beer gardens on warm summer evenings – it made me want to turn around and walk straight back out.

'Boys,' I greeted.

'How is she?' Will asked.

I glanced over my shoulder to see if anyone was serving. Tony Dale was in the back. 'There's just one doctor left at the surgery.'

'But less people to see,' Loz chirped.

'It's manic. There's a shortage of meds, and she's refusing to take the last bus.'

'Too fucking right,' Will banged the table. 'We'll look after her. Don't worry.'

Marcus swigged from his glass, struggling to make eye-contact. Loz was grinning at me like an eight-year-old.

'It's serious, mate.' I sat on a stool. 'She's really not well, coughing up all sorts of shit.'

Loz looked at Will. 'You gonna tell him, or shall I?' he asked.

'Go for it,' uninterested.

'We've got a present!' Loz excitedly handed over an old Asda bag.

'What's this?' I looked inside. Boxes of prescription medications. I quickly closed it, casually looking around. The young kid was edging closer on his ambulance. I shot a bullet from my finger and he giggled, then ran back to his mum.

'*How?*'

'Blackberry Lane,' Will said. 'Inbetween the old police station and the Conservative club, where we used to play snooker.'

'Before some silly twat put a hole in the baize,' I laughed.

'I told you I couldn't fucking play,' Marcus said.

'There's at least eight empty houses on the bend,' Will continued, 'eleven across the road. People are fleeing, the middle class anyway,' he scoffed.

I glanced over my shoulder, Tony Dale nodded. I returned the nod, trying to be cool. 'Usual?' he yelled.

'Ta, Tone.' I turned back to Will, whispered, 'you mean, you nicked them?'

'No, ya daft prat… Jay Bird did.'

'Oh, well, that's alright then,' sarcastic.

'No one's gonna miss it. They're gone. North, west, wherever,' he said, before taking a big swig.

I looked through the bag. 'Phyllocontin, Ventolin, Beconase. Amazing!' Three medications my mum used for her COPD. Then there was Citalopram, simvastatin, propranolol, ramipril, warfarin, Gaviscon and lansoprazole. There was even a week's worth of amoxycillin made up of three unfinished blister packs. Aspirin, paracetamol and ibuprofen – nothing stronger. 'This will definitely help.'

'More will turn up,' Loz said. 'People are leaving all the time.'

'It still feels a bit wrong,' I said.

'Oh, sod off,' Will dismissed. 'You used to rob booze from Asda all the time.'

Tony Dale brought my black coffee over, big brown arms, the blue smudge of tattoo ink. 'What ya got there?' he asked.

'Oh,' I blushed, 'just some… stuff… things.'

'Stuff-things, eh?' he tested, smiling. 'I ay the bloody feds, am I?'

'We in America, now?' Loz was laughing.

Tony wasn't, his face changed, he glanced behind. Smile gone, he homed in on Loz. 'What you fucking say?' voice gaining half an octave and twice the volume, cutting, splitting the sour atoms of rotting apples.

Loz's face dropped.

'Tony-' I tried.

'No, Tom,' he cut me off. 'What ya say?'

Marcus caught my eye, nervous. Will was trying not to smile, which made me want to laugh in hysteria. Behind, the kid had been wheeling closer, curious, trying to get my attention. I looked to the woman, she nervously called him back to the table.

'He doesn't mean-' I stuttered.

'No, come on, Stephen Fry. You picking me up on me grammar?'

Loz looked at me for support. I shrugged, helpless. The whole reaction seemed bizarre and over the top. Will picked up his cider, took a swig, watching the play unfold.

'I don't mean… no… I mean feds is American, isn't it? The FBI.'

'Ok, smart arse, what about the,' he glanced behind again, then turned back and, voice-lowered, 'the federali?'

Loz's eyes darted about, searching for help, 'the Italian… police?'

'Spanish,' Marcus said with authority.

We all turned to him, confused, but Tony Dale didn't seem confused. He looked to Marcus, then back to Loz. He now had both in his sights. Behind me, I saw the kid was now tight in his mum's arms. I smiled, winked again, then gave Tony Dale a nudge in his big hip. He noticed the kid, looked back to Loz, then Marcus, all the time shaking his head. 'You two got a lot to learn about the federali.' He grabbed the bag out of my hand and opened it. '*Meds?*'

'For my mum, the shortage.'

'You need meds, you come to me.'

'You can get 'em?'

'Tony three,' he said, handing the bag back.

'Tony three?'

'Tony Bonham,' he confirmed, walking back to the bar.

I was none the wiser. 'Ok, yeah, thanks Tone, thanks a lot.'

As soon as he was out of earshot, Will muttered under his breath, 'it's always them pair.' He punched Loz in the arm. 'You're always getting us into fucking trouble.'

'Not my fault,' he sulked. 'What's he even on about?'

Marcus looked pale and clammy, side-glancing towards the back of the bar. The room was heavy with quiet. Some of the old men in the back were glaring at us. Councillor Ray looked over his little square glasses, pitying us.

I turned back to the three boys sitting with me, all nearing 50, yet 18 all over again, forever trying to be adults in a bar full of grown men.

Will started rolling a cigarette.

'Roll me one,' Loz said.

'Fuck off.'

'I need one after that.'

'Roll your fucking own, goddam toddler.'

I looked behind to see the family getting ready to go – a good sign for us to leave.

'Don't be a bastard,' Loz said, a look of injustice.

'Oh, for fuck's sake!' Will started to roll another. 'You need to do it for yourself in future. I'm not fucking coddling you anymore. The world has changed. You need to learn to look after yourself.'

It felt like the whole bar was watching us. Not only had we shrunk in Tony's irritation, but now we looked like bickering children. I was embarrassed. 'Come on.' I swigged the coffee, half-scalding my gullet in the process.

Marcus was nodding in agreement, swallowing his cider fast.

'Where?' Will asked.

'I've gotta get back to Jen,' Loz said.

'Jay Bird's!' Will decided. 'He's bound to have found something better than paracetamol.'

As we made our way to the door, I nodded at Tony. He nodded back, unsmiling. I heard the old boys laughing as we left, perforated by councillor Ray's woodpecker laugh. I didn't look back.

'Fat fuck,' Marcus said, outside.

'Is he?' I asked. 'More like bloody muscle to me.'

'Fat, fucking, bug-eyed bitch!'

'Bug-eyed bitch?'

'Bug-eyed, pahahaha,' Will laughed.

The pub door opened and Marcus immediately grabbed my arm. Councillor Ray walked out. 'Yow boys need to be careful,' he warned.

'Piss off,' Will spat.

'Yow lot'll never learn, until one of yow gets clobbered,' he sniffed, walking off in the opposite direction.

'Who the hell are you?' Will argued.

'Come on,' I said, tugging his t-shirt. 'Let him go.'

On the high street, the lime trees were overgrown, big green heads bobbing in the summer wind. Wild roots like unwieldy tentacles were already cracking the concrete, but soon there would be nobody to prevent it getting worse. *There's some things you just can't stop.* I thought about Rex. *That's nature.*

Most of the shops of my youth were already long gone, the hardware store, electric goods, butcher's and the indoor market. The old carpet shop, which had been there for decades, no longer had the big windows, a trolley tossed through them, and no one had done anything about it. The banks had been boarded up. We now just had the government cashpoint, a shuttered cubicle which was only open Wednesdays and Fridays from 9am to 1pm. Amazon gave everyone a run for their money in the teens, then even more went after the big viruses hit a few years later. The Greek Riots saw even more off. And now the mass exodus north. Even the hairdressers had all gone mobile or worked from home. All that now remained in Halesowen was the Supra shop, which was once the pound shop, selling everything the powers-that-be provided.

'I'm not going to Jay's,' I said.

'Come on, Tom,' Marcus pleaded.

'I don't want to.' It was a solid no and they knew it.

Our habitat had changed. But it didn't just happen overnight with the bombs. It started long before and we just let it. Either we didn't mind things changing, we wanted it to change, or we had no choice. Perhaps it *was* just the natural order of things.

'What's the fucking federalis then?' Marcus asked. 'A bit random.'

'God knows,' I smiled – *if He even exists.*

Clutching the bag of meds, I walked up the wide neck of Portsdown Road, passing the many side roads as I climbed higher. Ainsdale Gardens, Quantock Close, Cumbrian Croft, the quaint streets of my youth. Doran Close, where my old best friend Steve Harris used to live, where Leroy made us both listen to the devilish yells of Iron Maiden and we played with Transformers and Thunder Cats.

Every day, since moving back, I walked up this road, and every day I relived my past. The good and the bad.

I turned onto Mendip Road where I used to play tig and tracker with Steve Harris, Leroy and Pete Smith, who we used to bully because he always smelt of shit, and the Turner twins and tiny Ninny Jackson, who my mum said had little man syndrome. He was always threatening us with his older brothers – I smacked him once for punching a girl and spent weeks worrying, when wandering alone on the estate.

The whole area was virtually deserted now, just the spectres of memory. Outside, there'd be children playing kerbie with a football, the gravelly sound of skateboards. Indoors, a kid in front of an 11 inch TV, Streetfighter on the Sega Master System. There was an old upturned bike on the pavement as if somebody had just run in the house to get a pump, before getting sucked out of this world and spat into another.

The images of neatly trimmed lawns and uniform semi-detacheds were still clear in my mind. Ghost shells which fitted over the houses now caged, boarded or just left, the jagged teeth of glass where someone had already broken in; scruffy gardens dandruffed with cans, sweet wrappers and junk mail mulch.

Some people refused to leave. The old or the stubborn, the addicts and the unwell. Ninny Jackson was an addict and could be seen wandering around, shirtless and gaunt, his brothers both long since lost to the needle. You might see the odd car parked on a drive, but most had taken their owners further away from the fallout. My car was dead, somewhere in Old Hill near Will's, probably something to do with the fuel injection, but it was beyond me. All of the town's petrol stations were closed, the nearest was on the motorway.

In some parts, the streets had started to smell sweet with rot, diarrhoetic cabbage, despite the binmen who still came monthly but seemed to remove very little, certainly nothing beyond the pavement. It'd been a hot summer which didn't help things. I remembered the smell from poorer countries with warmer climates. The marketplaces of India, Nepal and Tanzania.

This had been a clean suburb which used to bustle with working mums and dads, kids playing, and cats – where had all the cats gone? A suburb which suggested the promise of a future, where good children made good friends, had a good education and then got a good career. They'd meet a nice partner, get married, and have nice children. At least, this was what I believed growing up.

It'd only been 11 months since the bombs and the estate was now transformed. There were still plenty of people in Halesowen, but the leafy suburbs had emptied fast. The majority now lived where dad had ended up, down town amongst the flats and maisonettes.

I passed Long Mynd where, when we'd grown into yobbos, we'd play knock door run. That's what mum called us, "yobbos", and she was right. I remembered chasing each other down the road with fireworks, little rockets called vampires. Feral and crazy, throwing mini explosives at each other.

I started to steal. I'd sneak into mum's bedroom to nick money out of her purse, the electric fear of being caught. I painfully remember the time I stole her last tenner. I called Leroy to see if he was up for getting two bottles of Thunderbird and a pick n mix. I was tethered to the coiling wire of the house phone, when she came downstairs in a panic, clutching her purse, holding it open for me to see. My guilty heart beat fast and I casually mouthed, "just give me a sec," as if the call was important. She waited in the kitchen, I could hear her pacing up and down. I carefully tore a sheet from the Yellow Pages and wrote, "I'm really sorry, mum, I can't help it." I put the tenner on top of the note on the phone table, opened the front door as quietly as possible and then legged it down the road. She never broached the subject with me and I never stole off her again, but I'd lost her trust. Even now, she wouldn't let me have a key to the front door, 20 years of living right and half the country obliterated.

'But what does any of this matter now?' I asked Purbeck Close, 'the town transformed, the estate desolated.' *Will we ever find a way back?*

Perhaps the few of us left would remain and Halesowen would eventually repopulate. Like Hiroshima. Even London could become a tourist spot. Like Chernobyl. Trees emerging from the flattened capital, the gritty remains of the City, Camden, Soho, the West End – theatres scalped and overgrown with nuclear moss, the Reduced Lloyd-Webber Company playing twice daily. Perhaps they'd hold ghost tours on the tube, a runaway train ride. A laser monument to Buckingham Palace, emanating from robots, statues of the Queen and Prince William – if people still accepted they knew nothing about the whole business.

Or what about a monument to David Icke. The Statue of Lizardy, poised like a hunter, his foot upon the slimy Greek?

'Will would like that idea,' I said to a Curly Wurly wrapper, faded and twisted around the iron grate of a drain. 'I bet people'd pay loads to see Nuclear London, especially the Americans.'

I realised I was stopped still in the middle of mum's road, looking down the drain for answers to an inspired business idea. I heard the scuff of gravel and looked up. An old woman was facing me.

'Tom?' she asked. 'Tom Hanson?'

I was shocked and embarrassed. 'No, I mean, yes.'

'Maureen,' she prompted.

'Maureen?' I shrugged, confused, before it suddenly came back to me. '*Nooo*. Mrs Hayward?'

'Sorry, of course,' she smiled. 'Mrs Hayward. Maureen Hayward, yes. Are you alright, Tom?' She sounded concerned.

Was I dreaming? Facing me was my old primary school teacher, hunched and grey, but still wearing what seemed to be the big brown, plastic specs she used to wear.

'Tom, are you alright?' she repeated.

'Sorry? What? Yes, I mean,' I laughed nervously.

She nodded, slow and inquisitive.

I glanced around us. There was no one in sight. Only two people still lived on mum's road, most houses now had the same caged fronts, as if they'd been put in a giant safe, filed for future use. There was one car, an old Austin Rover, its wheels on bricks – it'd been this way for years before the bombs.

'Ok, Tom,' she said, nervously edging around me.

'I'm fine, miss… Maureen,' I said, turning with her. 'I'm not mad,' I scoffed. *Mad? Why did I say that?*

'No, I wasn't thinking…'

She looked scared. 'What you doing here, miss?' I asked, trying to be casual.

'Maureen.'

'Yes, Maureen, damn it!'

'It's ok, Tom,' she said, calming me with her hands – which made me feel worse. 'I've just been visiting a friend on… Hambleton Road,' she said, wary.

'You're… er… still here then?' I asked, because that's what people say.

'I couldn't leave, not now.'

'But the fallout?'

She smiled, 'and you're still here?'

'Well, no, not really. I mean, I am here, but I'm back. I came back.'

'Back? Why?'

'My home went with the bomb.'

'You lived in London?'

'Somerset.'

'Oh. And your family? A partner? Children?'

'I don't have any.'

I don't know why I lied. I guess I just couldn't face the conversation.

'Oh. It's just you?'

I felt my face burning up with the deceit, hot then cold in the breeze, sick and swimmy. 'And mum!' I asserted, desperately papering over the lie. 'She still lives here. She'll never leave, mum won't. No. There,' I pointed to number 6a. 'She lives… er… there.' But it felt like another lie.

'Ok,' suspicious.

'She does,' I protested.

'I believe you, Tom.'

She was lying, I was sure of it. I started walking to the door. I knocked it. 'Here,' I said. '6a.'

She just looked at me, a blank expression. I felt like I'd just smoked a joint and it was turning on me. 'Mum,' I called.

'It's ok, Tom,' she said, anxious. 'I better be going.'

'You could have a tea. A cup, I mean. Mum has electricity the… er…' I pointed to the roof. 'The panel things, sun panels, solar panels, she's got a good battery. It works. Nearly all of the time. Especially now. The sun. Summer.' I knocked again. 'Mum!'

Mrs Hayward kept on walking.

'Mum!' I knocked harder.

I watched my old primary school teacher quickly turn onto Mendip Road. 'Oh, for God's sake. Mum!'

But I had to break in.

―――――――

I sat on a fallen tree on Lutley park grass bank and emptied the bag of medications. I made my way through them quickly, putting the boxes I didn't want back in the bag. It wasn't some rash panic, I was focused on the task at hand. Most of the meds were unlikely to do anything of note. The only one I was unsure of was Phyllocontin. I'd come across it many years before and dismissed it, but I was desperate. Amongst the side effects were "confusion and change of behaviour". Admittedly, rare side effects, but perhaps the only glimmer of hope in a bag of pointless drugs.

'Fuck!'

What am I gonna do?

I pushed a Phyllocontin out with the hope I might at least escape the shock of seeing mum. It fell on the grass. I picked it up and put it in the middle of my hand. It was round and chalky like a generic paracetamol, but it was off-white, yellow almost. It smelt of nothing. I knew I'd need to take a lot of them to cause any "change of behaviour".

'Maybe life's easier this way,' I said, gesturing to the skies.

I smacked the back of my head. *What the fuck are you saying?*

I thought about finding Will and the boys, but then I didn't want any of them to see her dead. She was in her nightie. And they were with Jay Bird. I saw him yapping over me like a Pomeranian pooch, eager to help and proud of his haul, a litany of proper meds, not the pathetic bag of pills I had. Drugs to bring on bestial nights, a quick spiral out of control and, let's face it, my eventual death. I didn't want to die. I didn't know why I didn't want to die, but I didn't. I just wanted to forget. Like I used to.

I pushed out eight Phyllocontin and rattled them in my fist like I was rattling diazis, temazis, or zoppis. I didn't even have a drink. I'd have to fill my mouth with spit and take them one at a time. *And for what? They might do nothing. They might just make me feel worse.*

The lessons of my recovery flashed through my mind. Taking things a day at a time, sometimes a moment at a time. Playing the tape forward, imagining how I'd feel later and what it'd lead to. And I had such a long stint, nearly 20 years sober.

But mum.

'Fuck it,' I muttered, generating spit – *it's Phyllocontin not fucking psilocybin.*

I placed one on my tongue, and then I heard a scream.

'Get off me!' came from the brook.

I stood up and spat it out, dropped the pills. I looked around. I couldn't tell exactly where it had come from.

I grabbed the bag of meds and started to make my way quickly down the bank, falling in the thick grass and getting back up again. I made a short run and then tripped up on the chain of an old swing. I got up, and then went down on a stifled root of bracken, up again, then down again. 'Fucking life!'

'Let me go!' she yelled.

A surge of adrenalin, I quickly got up and made my way to the far side of the park where a small bridge crossed the brook. When we were kids, there was a muddy route alongside the brook and into a small woods, but now it was thick with brambles.

'I don't want to,' she shouted.

She sounded like a teenager.

The only way to find her was to walk through the brook and risk all sorts of infections in the milky-grey water. I tucked my light linen trousers into my socks. Ankle deep, holding the bag above my head – *must protect the meds* – I started making my way, slowly to begin with, my shoes immediately taking on water. I could hear rustling up ahead, like there was some sort of creature in the bushes.

'Never again,' she shouted. 'I told you. Get off!'

I moved faster and fell in a small trench, thigh-high in the soup, 'Let her go!' I yelled, angry at the fuckers for making me traipse through the brook.

The rustling stopped. I stopped. 'Who's there?' a male voice.

'Who's that?' I asked, suddenly aware of what I was doing, what I was risking.

There was silence.

'I can't breathe,' the girl shouted, struggling.

'Shut up,' he said.

'You better leave her alone!' *Be brave.* 'You don't want to know who this is.'

'Piss off, I've got a gun,' he said.

It made me stop in my tracks, water sucking on my feet in my trainers. 'Put it this way, kid, I'm not the feds.' I don't know why I said it. It worked on Loz, I guess.

'The feds? What does that mean?' he asked.

I could hear her struggling, like he was sitting on her and covering her mouth.

I laughed like a villain – *a fucking villain?* 'You've got a lot to learn, my friend.' I grimaced, annoyed at my stupidity, shrugging at a judgemental weeping willow.

'I've got a gun!' he warned.

'He hasn't,' the girl shouted.

I heard an almighty wallop and she screamed. I snapped a dead branch from a tree and moved quickly through the brook. I could hear a lot of noise from the bushes and half expected to be pounced on – how many were there? I climbed over a branch, and then I caught my first glimpse of her. Her back towards me, smooth skin, half-naked, she was pulling her pants and trousers up.

She looked over her shoulder, 'stop looking, ya deeve. He went that way,' pointing away from me, up through the trees and onto Rosemary Road.

'What was he doing to you?' I tossed the meds bag on the bank and pulled myself up, carefully picking brambles out of my linen shirt and arm.

'What do *you* think?' she snapped.

I grinned, awkward, not really knowing how to respond.

'Is that what you're here to do?' she asked.

'*Me*? No. My mum just died.'

'What's that got to do with it?'

I didn't know. I guess I just needed to say it out loud. 'What are you doing here? In the bushes? Did he drag you here? How did you get here? Did he drug you?'

'20 fucking questions,' she moaned.

She lifted herself up onto the branch of an old oak tree which climbed high above the dense shrubs surrounding the brook. Behind her there was a clearing. In the middle of it, the black ash of a small fire long gone out, a sheet on the floor, which had been used to sit on – amongst other things, I imagined. I noticed a two-litre green plastic bottle, which I assumed was cider, a quarter full.

'Were you having a party?' I asked.

'Were you?' she asked, pointing to my bag.

'Asthma meds and beta blockers.'

'A regular action hero.'

'My mum's.'

She looked away. 'You want some?' She pointed to the bottle.

'No.'

'It's Snakebite,' she tempted, only a tinge of Black Country, probably lower middle class, like most of us on the Squirrels Estate.

I found myself staring at her. She was probably about 20, pretty, but bitter, an arrogant sulking scowl. I'd met many like her.

'I've got some smack,' she said, proud, 'but you don't look like the sort.'

I laughed.

'What?'

'What do you know about me?'

'You're old,' she laughed.

'Thanks.'

'You've just ran through a brook to "save me" and you look like you need a fuck.'

'You almost sound like you know what you're talking about.'

'Thank you,' she said, clearly trying to wind me up.

I walked past her over to the clearing, ducking branches. I looked out through the trees to the road.

'Is that him? Running up Bassnage Road?' She didn't respond. 'What did he do to you?'

He looked small and was quite fast.

'Same thing you want to do.'

'I'm married.'

'So what?'

'Not everyone wants to sleep with you.'

'I didn't say they did,' petulant, defensive.

'I thought he was trying to rape you.' I watched him scuttle over the brow of the hill.

There was silence.

The strike of a lighter.

I turned to see her lighting a metal piece of an Old Jamaica ginger beer can and the dirty powder turned to a dark brown liquid. She inhaled through a plastic straw. She repeated it, and then leant back, her shoulders resting on a higher branch, so she dipped in the middle. There was no denying she was attractive, but I wasn't totally sure if I was more attracted to the effect of the heroin.

'Nah,' she said. 'Not rape. He's my fella.' She dropped the metal.

'It didn't sound like that.'

'Nah,' she cooed. 'Yeah. A bit rough.'

I sat down on the sheet, watching. Her white eyes half-closed, she went to a place I longed to return to, narcotic oblivion, but I just couldn't.

Why was I sober?

Perhaps it's for her.

She tore a small strip off a leaflet to make a roach for a cigarette and then tossed what was left of it on the sheet. She'd been in an irritable mood since she'd woken up. We'd chatted a little. She told me about her dad – "prick died in Afghanistan." She agreed we had to bury mum. I don't know why she felt the need to help me – perhaps secretly she did feel I'd saved her.

She took a hard drag on the cigarette which seemed to soothe her and made me long to smoke again. I had to look away.

I picked up the familiar looking leaflet, an image of the UK sent out by the acting government with an overlay of two misshapen boobs, Bethnal Green and Burnham-on-Sea the nipples – this was how Marcus had described it and it stuck. Inside the boobs, the nipples were red and there were three smaller circles in shades of pink. Halesowen was in the lightest shade, but it was most definitely in the boobs. This was why almost everybody had left. Anywhere north of Shrewsbury or Leicester was deemed safe. The nearest official hospital was Derby.

The fallout map was seen an exaggeration by many. It was a regular debate in the media and continued on the street. A whole section of Halesowen had told themselves the science was nonsense. Will agreed, Loz was on the fence. I didn't care and neither did Marcus.

I waved the leaflet at her, 'what you reckon?'

'Don't care.'

It didn't really matter. We were all expected to evacuate the boobs by September 8th. Nuke-drivers had been coming once a fortnight to take those who had no other means to the halfway houses. The last bus would be leaving next week. We'd never considered taking the bus ourselves, because we knew we could always make our own way. Also, Will didn't want to become ensnared in the system, even though he was the only one of us receiving Supra rations. Regardless, the Supra shop and the cashpoint would be closing September 8th and staying meant finding a new way to survive, independent of the UK and all that entailed – no electricity, communication, food, water and fuel.

She offered me the last few drags of her pathetic looking roll-up, a soggy wick.

'I'm good.'

It looked a little less pathetic when she dragged on it, restorative, despite the phlegmy cough which filled her mouth. She took aim, then fired a bullet of spit into the brook.

'Lovely,' sarcastic.

'Perhaps now you won't want to fuck me.'

'Perhaps,' I flirted, instinctively, then inwardly cursed myself for it.

She tossed her nub end in the brook. 'Purbeck Close?'

I nodded.

She grabbed her tobacco and gear tin, sprung up and immediately started to lead the way out. 'Let's go sort your mum.'

I got up less easily, 'wait up.'

I pushed my way through shrubs and bush, carefully trying to move brambles out of the way, whilst avoiding being whipped by the branches she was letting go of without a thought.

We left the woods in the dark and made our way across and then up the neck of Portsdown Road.

There was an urgency in her movement, I thought perhaps she might need the loo. I was practically running to keep up, the bag of meds intermittently bashing my leg.

'If you left the door wide open, who knows who's been in,' she shouted back.

I hadn't even considered that. I moved faster.

When I'd broken in, mum was just sitting on her chair. I knew straight away she was dead. She seemed much smaller. The TV was blaring out Only Fools and Horses on BBC Gold. It was like she'd just dropped off in front of it. She was 80 and had been ill for a while with COPD. She hadn't smoked for 20 years, but heavily before that. I was in shock, struggling to think straight, so I switched the TV off. This made the room feel incredibly empty, which freaked me out. I started to panic and ran back out of the house looking for Mrs Hayward, another human. I thought she'd know what to do. But I didn't find her, so I just kept making my way down Portsdown Road thinking I'd eventually have to call the boys. When I got to the park, I realised I'd been carrying mum's meds the whole time, my hand tense and hot, welded to the bag. Then it seemed sensible – logical even – to take something, to change the way I felt. To deal with it.

When we got to Mendip Road, I stopped to catch my breath. She turned to see me, hands-on-knees panting, and furiously gestured for to me to hurry up. When we got to mum's road, I could see the lights were already on.

'Is that it?' she asked.

'Yeah.' I walked on fast but she held me back.

'Someone's in there,' she said.

'Who?'

'How the fuck should I know?'

'My mum,' I said. 'I've got to go in.'

'They're animals around here!'

'We're all animals,' I half-smiled, oddly proud of it.

'Don't be saft,' she said.

I pushed her off me and marched to the house.

'Who's in my house?' I yelled, emboldened – in part, proving myself to the young woman.

She waited outside. I went through the hall and into the living room. Mum was still on her seat, looking small and empty, not there anymore. I sensed someone behind me, turned to the settee and jolted back.

'Tom,' she said, jumping up.

She looked more scared than me.

'What did you do?' she asked.

I knew how it looked, which immediately put me on the back foot, feeling inexplicably guilty. 'I didn't do anything.'

'I knew something wasn't right.'

I looked down at my mum, my heart beating fast. 'It's my mum. I told you.'

Mrs Hayward held her phone up. 'Why was the house broken into?'

'I haven't got a key.'

'To *your* home?'

'It's my mum's.'

She shook her head in disbelief. '*You don't live here.*'

I took a step closer and she gasped. I stopped, open-palmed, 'I do. I do live here, but I haven't got a key. She won't give me…' I looked back at mum. 'She wouldn't give me a key. It's a long story.'

Mrs Hayward was breathing deeply, trying to control it, but it was getting faster. I thought she might hyperventilate.

I stepped back again to give her space. 'What do you think I did, miss-?'

'Don't "miss" me,' she sniped.

'Do you seriously think I killed her? Why? And why would I come back?'

'There's a lot of nastiness around here,' she said.

'Believe me, *I know*. I've just stopped somebody being raped.'

'*Raped?*'

She looked down at mum.

'Yes!'

'What? How?' she stumbled. 'I don't know what's going on, but I don't trust you, Tom Hanson.'

I looked around the house, helpless. There wasn't even a single picture of me on the walls, just a large painting of dogs playing snooker – which dad always said was worth something and mum kept up to stop him selling it. We weren't the sort of family to put pictures of ourselves up. They were all kept in a box in the attic. 'Her purse!' I shouted.

'Ooh,' she yelped.

'Sorry. Let me get her purse. I can prove it's Pat Hanson. My mum. You must remember-'

'I remember Mrs Hanson, but that doesn't prove you didn't… You were being very odd earlier, talking to yourself. Are you on drugs?'

'No! This is all very odd. Seeing you was odd, this situation is insane. The Squirrels, the estate where I grew up, went to school, is beginning to feel like something in a horror film, or a war report – I don't even know.'

I reached over my mum to the side of her seat where she kept her handbag.

'Wait!' She held her phone, poised to call.

I stood up straight, sighed, 'who can you even call? The police?'

'My son.'

'What's he gonna do?'

She looked confused, beaten. 'He's… he's in the army.'

'Please,' my hands pleading, talking slowly, 'I'm not trying to scare you. I don't mean any harm. I just want to prove to you this is my mum and then we can take it from there, yeah?' She didn't respond. 'At the far side of her chair is a green leather handbag. She's got some sort of fabric purse in there and somewhere in there will be her bank cards and an old driving licence.'

She looked at me, then my mum, then back to me, gesturing for me to get the purse with her phone like she was holding a gun.

As I reached over mum my hand brushed hers, resting on the arm. It felt cold. Colder than the house and colder than the night. I lifted the bag up over her like I was holding a bomb. I took a deep breath before I defused it – it'd been a long time since I'd been in her handbag. I pulled out the purse, thudding palpitations as if she might wake up and catch me. I dropped the bag and then clicked open the purse. I grabbed a bunch of cards. 'Can I hand them to you?'

'Throw them,' she said, her finger on the button.

I tossed them over and they fell around her. She knelt down, still staring at me, blindly reaching for them. I looked down into mum's purse, saw a scrappy piece of paper which intrigued me. I went to take it out.

'Leave it,' she demanded.

'It's just a piece of paper. It's not money. Just scrap.'

'Leave it!'

'Ok, ok.'

Mrs Hayward had a couple of cards in her hand and stood up.

'P Hanson,' she dropped a bank card. 'Patricia Hanson,' she dropped mum's driving licence. 'Ok, so it's your mother, but it doesn't clear up why you broke in.'

'She wouldn't answer. I was worried.'

'And why's she dead?'

'I don't know. She just died. She wasn't well. I'm as shocked as you.'

'You don't seem shocked.'

'I… don't… What am I,' I stuttered. 'I don't know… I've just found out. How am I supposed to be? When I found her I went looking for you.'

'*For me?*' She sounded frightened.

'No. I thought you might be able to help. I'd just seen you, but I couldn't find you. Then I ran down to the park-'

'The park?' confused.

'The park, yes.'

'Why would I believe-'

'And then there was this girl.'

'Girl?' bewildered.

Of course, the girl. 'The rape! The girl,' I pointed outside.

'What?'

'I don't know. Can I… Girl,' I called out into the hall. 'Woman?' I could hear her on the drive, pacing, the gravel. 'Woman, come in here.'

I heard her enter the hallway. 'I'm not coming in there,' she whisper-shouted.

'It's ok. It's just my old primary school teacher.'

'Teacher,' she said, immediately walking in and standing beside me.

'Sarah,' Mrs Hayward said.

'Nan,' Sarah nodded.

'Nan?'

'Now I know there's something funny about this,' Mrs Hayward said.

'Nan?' I asked again.

'Nothing funny, actually. His mum died and I was coming to help him.'

'Nan?' Again.

'Yes, that's my nan.'

'More's the pity,' Mrs Hayward said.

'But she's my old primary school teacher.'
'And. She's. My nan,' talking to a dolt.
'What have you done to this poor woman?' Mrs Hayward asked her.
'I've never even met her in my life,' she snapped. 'He helped me.'
'Poppycock!'
'He did.'
'She was being raped,' I defended.
'Don't you believe it, Tom Hanson.'
'Honest, nan! I was in the park and he came running through the brook.'
I looked into mum's purse and pulled out the piece of paper.
'What were you doing in the brook?'
I unfolded it.
'I wasn't in the brook,' Sarah said. 'He came out of the brook because he heard me scream.'
It was from the Yellow Pages.
'What was he doing in the brook?'
'I dunno. Grieving.'
I read in my own handwriting, "I'm really sorry, mum, I can't help it."
I fell down on my knees, my head on mum's cold hand.
'What are you doing?' Mrs Hayward asked.
'Grieving! He's allowed to!'
'I'm so sorry, mum.'
I closed my eyes and heard someone move towards me. They could've clobbered me on the head for all I cared. I thought about the way dad hurt mum, the way I hurt mum, the way I've hurt so many people close to me. I found myself crying like a child. I felt a hand on my head.

———————

I finished digging the hole and climbed out.
Sarah put her hand on my arm, it sent tingles through me. It felt like a long time since anybody had touched me like this. My mum, for all her good points, wasn't the touchy-feely sort. She was a tough old bird made in a different time. The boys had their moments, but it was easier to take the piss.
'Thank you,' I said.

She looked uncomfortable. 'You helped me,' a warm waft of stale coffee.

I looked over Sarah's shoulder and saw Mrs Hayward looking at us from the lighted kitchen window. She immediately glanced down, like mum doing the washing up.

'I think your nan's a bit concerned.'

'Oh, she's a bloody…' she stopped herself and turned away from me. 'I'm not always the best,' she mumbled. It felt sincere.

'What do you mean?'

She looked up to the skies and sighed. 'I'm just not… you know.'

'Whatever it is, you can say it. Maybe I can help.'

'I'm not gonna fuck you,' she warned.

'What?' I shook my head. 'I told you, I'm married.'

'Where is she then?'

It was a good question. 'Who said it was a woman?'

'You're not gay!'

I tried my best to look offended, playing. 'No,' I smiled. 'Dunno why I said that.'

She gave me a funny look, like she was trying to suss me out, then half-giggled. It was a kind reaction, feminine and present, her face cracked, split by small laughter lines at the corner of her mouth. The mask fell away and for a moment I forgot what we were doing.

I rubbed my face, as if to wipe away a blush. 'Anyway, we were talking about you. Why?'

'Why what?'

'Why are you not – what did you say? "Always the best?"'

'I'm just a wrong un, en't I,' she smiled mischievously.

'Is it the drugs?'

'No!' It was a hard no. I'd crossed a line. The wall went up and her smile disappeared, the moment of intimacy gone.

I felt the immediate need to retreat. I picked up the spade from beside the hole and started patting the edges as if I was shaping it to fit a pond. 'I'm not who you think I am, you know,' I said, smoothing a corner. 'I've lived a long life.'

'I don't care who you are,' she sulked.

I'd done it now. She was back to her defence stance. Sod it. I decided I may as well be honest about it. 'Drugs, drink, it's a shitty life,' I lectured. 'Crime, violence, people die.' The heavy bags under her eyes were evident even in a garden lit only by the kitchen light. 'Most people wouldn't believe it, but I-'

'Why does everyone blame drugs?' She turned to look at her nan in the window, 'and don't listen to anything she says, she doesn't know anything about what I do or where I go. I'm not an addict.'

'I didn't say you were.'

'Tell me you didn't think I was.'

I looked her in the eye, then down into the hole, thought about jumping in and digging some more. She was right. Had I made a massive assumption? It wouldn't be the first time. Some people take drugs recreationally. Some people can.

'I do what I do. I live my life,' she stated. 'I take drugs, so what? Who doesn't? Who wouldn't these days?'

'Me.'

'That's because you're a geek.'

'A geek? What is it, the fucking noughties?' I said, a little offended.

'That's not an old word! What you on?'

'Nothing,' I said. 'That's my point. I used to use, and probably far more than you've ever taken.' I was bragging, I could feel it. I didn't want her to think I was a "geek".

'I doubt it.'

'Ok, whatever,' I stopped myself. 'I'm just saying you can talk to me, if you want. And I don't wanna… you know… not everybody wants to…'

'Whatever.'

I put the spade down, suddenly remembering why I was digging this hole. 'Is there any chance you could help me get my, you know, mum?'

There was silence. She'd solidified in the coldness of my simple questioning. I felt the harshness of the wall, the sad wall I've hit so many times when trying to help people.

'Yeah,' she said, dead.

I looked into the hole and then back at Sarah, pathetically apologetic, not really knowing what to say and lacking the energy needed to try and work it out.

'Course, yeah,' she melted.

There was hope.

Sarah followed me inside. In the kitchen, I awkwardly grinned at my old teacher. What was she thinking? Me, her granddaughter, my mum dead in the armchair?

As I passed her she tapped my arm.

'Yeah, miss?' a child.

'Maureen-'

'Maureen,' a grown up.

'Tom, I have to ask this. Is it wide?'

'Is what wide?'

'The hole. Your mum. It's been, she's probably… set-'

'Nan!' Sarah cursed.

'Oh, I see,' I said. 'We can fit her in sideways, yeah.'

'Sorry, Tom-'

'No, please,' I said, walking into the living room, mentally trying to detach myself from the situation.

Mum seemed so tiny in the armchair. She had a natural tan and looked at peace. It made me think of that monk who supposedly self-mummified in meditation. We put a sheet over her and then, standing either side, lifted her so she was sitting in our arms. We carefully carried her through the kitchen and then out the back door. Her body felt heavier than she looked and the cold seemed to transfer into my veins and tendons, stiffening me, making me shiver. Sarah looked like she was holding her breath. I couldn't smell anything.

Mrs Hayward just watched, didn't say anything, and remained in the kitchen. We lay mum on the grass at the side of the hole and I climbed in. I pulled her towards me. There was still some movement in her limbs, but she'd been shaped by the chair into almost the foetal position. I lifted her down.

The hole was mud cold, mum was cold in it and I was cold off it. It was like some strange communion with the earth. She would be swallowed by the roots of trees, the grass, the weeds and live on. I arranged the sheet over her like she was going to bed, took one last look at her sunken face and then covered it. After a few moments silence, I climbed out.

Sarah picked up the spade. 'Want me to?'

'No, you go inside. I'll do it.'

'I can help.'

'No, thanks.'

Outside of the hole, the night was mild but chilly, light jacket weather. There were more stars in the sky than ever before, like those purple nights in the Moroccan mountains, the cardiograph wave of Scorpio one side, the kite of Orion the other. I started filling in the hole, just mum and me.

What had happened to us? I'd never dreamt this could happen – not mum dying, I'd been imagining that for years, punishing myself with it – but a situation in our country where it was ok to bury your mum in the garden because there was nobody to check up on it. Where there was nobody to even perform an autopsy; no back-up plan and effectively no rules. *How did it come to this?* Who had been running the country? At the previous election, I'd blocked half of my Facebook feed because of the incessant political opinion. I couldn't be bothered with it all, the fear-mongering about voting one way or another. The usual stuff: the left is like Hitler, the right is like Hitler, centrism is socialism, socialism is communism, conservatism is fascism, the Left is now right and the Right is ever wrong. I couldn't make head nor tail of it. It seemed the prevailing theory from most sides had been we were all pawns in a business war. Labour said it, Conservative said it, the Greens had been whispering it for years, the Lib Dems had said whatever the Labour government said – and that we should legalise cannabis for recreational use.

I held a spadeful of earth over mum's face, took a deep breath and froze – the sound of crickets, the hum of summer flies. 'I'm sorry it didn't end well, mum.'

But then I thought about it. It ended how she'd lived. Little had changed. If anything, her life was better after the bombs, because she'd had me around to help. Otherwise life was pretty much the same. She'd lived a moderate existence, nothing like the life of excess dad and I had lived. She had times of sadness and loneliness, but mostly she just went about her life zen-like, following routines and keeping order.

I carefully shovelled the dirt over her face and, as she disappeared under it, Sarah popped into my head. The loss of her dad – was that why she took drugs? Was that the void she was trying to fill? Family troubles were nearly always at the root of addiction, yet so many parents or siblings, sons or daughters, Maureens and the likes had a harsh stance on it: addicts, the scourge of the earth. I was lucky to get the help whilst it was still there. It took three times in a psych ward and a spell in rehab until I was grateful enough and it stuck. 'And this is why I'm still sober,' I said out loud. 'I'd be a bastard if I pissed on that help now. And they're dead! The ones that helped me. In the mud of Somerset.'

I turned to the window and saw Mrs Hayward staring at me. She didn't look away this time. I patted down the soil and went inside.

'I'm not mad,' I said to her. 'I just think out loud sometimes.'

She didn't say anything, handed me a cup of lemon and ginger tea – it was that or coffee in mum's house, she'd taken a dislike to normal tea, and all things she rightly or wrongly associated with India, after we'd taken her to Goa and she spent a week with Delhi-belly.

'Where's Sarah?'

'In the bathroom, doing you know what.'

'I don't-'

'The heroin.'

'No, I was going to say I don't do drugs, Maureen. I've done them. I've done a lot of things. The note, mum's note. And she kept it after all these years. I guess she felt there was hope in my apology, hope there was a good person somewhere in me, even if everything I did suggested otherwise.'

I sat down with her and told her why I'd written it, I told her about the drink and drugs. I told her I was going to help Sarah and that Sarah didn't realise it, but she was helping me.

'So, you started a new life in Somerset? What about your friends?'

We were both sitting forward on the settee, almost knee to knee in a heart to heart.

'They're all dead. They must be.'

'Did you have family? A girlfriend or-'

I paused. I wanted to say it. 'No.'

'I guess that's lucky. I mean, not lucky, but-'

'I guess so.'

'But why would you stay here, now your mum's gone? There's a whole life up north, a new life.'

I put my cup down on the floor and sat back on the settee. 'I have friends here, and people I can help. Sarah.'

She looked a little wary.

'With the drugs,' I justified.

Expressionless, she nodded.

'I've helped people before. I think that I can mend... help her... Sarah, I mean-'

'What about me?' She walked into the living room, face pale and dirty.

I looked at Maureen and then back to Sarah. 'I was just saying how you helped me and how I hoped I could help you.'

'I don't even know you.'

'Come on, Sarah,' Maureen reasoned.

'You're a bit weird, you know.' She sounded much younger than she looked.

'No doubt,' I joked.

'Can I sleep upstairs? *On my own?*'

'Of course,' I said, certain I was blushing.

She left the room, an angst-ridden teenager.

We sat in silence in the home of my childhood. It was empty without mum, mementoes, the brown Berber carpet worn with age, the green curtains holding onto a funny smell: soapy boiled clothes and chicken nuggets. It felt darker, sharper, the lights flickering on and off from time to time, as if at some point they were going to go out and then all of this would disappear forever, die, like her. It was nothing like my home in Somerset which was a home, a real home. Homely. Light and rounded, the bulbous sofa and bulbous chairs. Lemon and magnolia and blue. Messy and lived in.

'What was she like?' Maureen asked.

'She-' I stopped. 'Mum?'

'Yeah.'

'Oh. She was funny. She had a sadistic sense of humour. Would've made a good host on one of those TV talent shows,' I laughed.

'I noticed she liked music.'

'Yeah, musicals, ABBA.'

'Classical too.'

'The records? No, that was dad. Mum just kept one or two to make her look cultured,' I laughed.

'That's what I miss most,' she said. 'I used to go to the Symphony Hall in Birmingham all the time. You can hear it recorded, but it's not the same.'

'I like music too, but it's books for me.'

'You read a lot?'

'I used to. I rarely ever read new books. Just things which were written years ago, in other worlds. I always figured I was playing catch up. What was it about the Symphony Hall, the acoustics?'

'It was the mistakes.'

I gave her a curious look and she smiled. 'Now, that sounds like mum.'

'You're watching people who've devoted their lives to rehearsing for musical performance. I play the piano-'

'I know. Assembly,' I smiled. *'Jesus gives us the water of life,'* I sang.

'Of course. I devoted a large part of my life to the piano, but very little in comparison to real musicians. At the Symphony, you watch people who spend their lives trying so hard to be perfect actually play imperfectly. There's something so beautifully human about it.'

'That sounds less like mum,' I laughed.

'No?'

'I did love her.'

I awoke on the settee. Maureen was sitting at the far end and I had my feet on her. She was awake. I quickly removed myself from her, embarrassed. Still half-asleep, the surreal events of yesterday passed through my mind. Mum, the brook, Sarah and this little old woman who taught me 40 odd years ago.

Mum. Gone. I'd nearly relapsed on Phyllocontin on the back of it for Christ's sake, if that was even possible. I snorted a laugh thinking about it. Maureen looked at me, then looked away, ahead, staring at the wall. I looked over at mum's empty seat, imagined her face, her thin skin starting to mottle, sitting in her chair watching re-runs on Dave+1*,* a quiet cackle. Then I saw her dead, still, her matte face "set" – as Maureen said. I remembered awkwardly lifting her with Sarah, the coldness.

'Sarah up?' I asked.

'Gone,' Maureen said, shaking her head.

'Gone!' I sat up, electric, the synapses. 'What do you mean?'

'You should probably check for valuables.'

'What?' I stood up, sick.

'I heard the door go,' she said. 'I tried to wake you but you were fast asleep.'

'Is that why…? That's why she helped me with mum.' *It wasn't out of the goodness of her fucking heart.*

Maureen shrugged, cold, *I told you so.*

The rush up Portsdown Road to get to the house, the performance by mum's grave about how she "wasn't always the best". How many times had I witnessed such a performance? Hopeless cases, but you keep trying to change the way you think about it, because sometimes it gets through, sometimes a kind of psychic change takes place and the world changes for a person and the people in their life. *You bloody idiot.*

'I'm sorry, Tom.'

I went upstairs into mum's room, just to confirm what I already knew. It had been turned upside down.

I sat on the bed, head in hands. 'Oh, what does it matter, Tom? What does it matter?' I asked the universe. 'It doesn't matter. It doesn't matter. It's just stuff, just stuff, just stuff,' I told myself.

We had a moment outside, didn't we? There was intimacy.

'Just stuff, damn it!'

I took my phone out of my pocket, switched it on and rang Loz.

'Where you at?'

'Home,' he said.

'And Will?'

'They're here. Asleep. Jenny and the kids have gone out. I dunno what happened. Some shit last night. Jenny was drinking too. I've got stuff to sort out.'

'I need your help.'

'I've gotta sort this first.'

'Mum's dead.' The phone went silent, he didn't say anything. 'Loz?'

'You up there now?'

'Yeah.'

'I'll wake them up. See you in a bit.'

Jewellery gone. Probably money gone. It even looked like ornaments were gone. What was she going to do with them in Halesowen? Perhaps she was planning to head north. For a second, this thought made me feel better, but it seemed unlikely. She was bang at it. Smack, likely crack too. She was probably heading straight for that little bastard I'd watched scuttle up Bassnage Road. I wanted to find him, to hurt him, to stamp on the little rat.

I heard Maureen coming up the stairs. She stood in the doorway, as if not to intrude too much.

'You should take the bus and head out of here, Tom.' She was holding mum's green bag and the note from the Yellow Pages. 'You don't belong here.'

'I told you last night, I used to beg, borrow and steal to get what I needed.'

'But you don't now. You were just a kid.' She handed me the bag and note.

'So's Sarah.'

'No, she's not. She's a woman. A quite attractive one too, when she wants to be.'

'What? What do you mean?' I knew what she was implying, standing over me, pitying me.

'She has a way with men.'

'I'm not some kind of deeve-'

'Deeve?'

'Yeah,' I said, confident, but unsure exactly what it meant. 'In fact, I'm-' I had to stop myself telling her I was married because I'd told her I wasn't and I didn't want her to think I was a liar. 'I'm just trying to stay sober. You don't understand. This is what I have to do.'

'There's plenty of people in the world to help. When the bomb hit your town it didn't eradicate addiction.'

Hit my town. It was strange hearing that sitting in my childhood home in Halesowen, but true. The bomb hit my home town, the town where I'd made a life for myself. The other bomb hit London, but I think we all adapted to that pretty quickly, because we had to. That was the bomb that changed everything. It took out the control centre, the government, what was left of the royals. It struck the epicentre of our green and pleasant land and cracked the country into splinters.

From reports on the radio, the regions in the North East – from Hull to the borders – had now formed an alliance. Liverpool and Manchester joined forces, but split very quickly into individual regions.

The lowlands were controlled by Derby. This was largely because of the central hospital, which had become a symbol of recovery for the South, their NHS staff held up as an example to the rest of the country. The private hospitals were looted for the NHS and quite literally run out of town.

The UK government was now in Edinburgh and representatives from all over the country went up to the Scottish parliament. We had a woman from Birmingham supposedly representing the West Midlands, but she now based herself in Derby. The EU had tried to help, which Scotland initiated. This had resulted in the North East Alliance, which opposed their help, opting instead for US investment in North Sea oil. Will suggested this was evidence of guilt on the Americans' part, because there really wasn't much North Sea oil. But who really knew? What everybody seemed sure of was that the United Kingdom was no longer united. This was what I heard on the radio and in the pub, and this was largely the result of the bomb hitting London.

'Don't let your kindness get the better of you,' Maureen said.

'It's not kindness. It's just recovery.'

The second bomb had a much bigger emotional impact. Burnham-on-Sea was just a small seaside town in the South West. It never hurt anybody. And here in Halesowen and the rest of the Midlands, it had a special place in our hearts as a family holiday spot because it was one of the nearest seaside towns, just slightly further south than Weston-Super-Mare, which was less quaint, the Blackpool of the South West. Of course, both of these were taken out, alongside a good chunk of Bristol, the Mendips, the Quantocks, Newport, Cardiff, Glastonbury and Wells. It sounds bad, but when the bomb hit London, *they* died. When the bomb hit Burnham, *we* died. This was the feeling on the streets and in the pubs of Halesowen and, whether it was rational or not, that was the feeling in my heart.

The bottom half of the country was sunk and the North was still afloat but, here in Halesowen and the Black Country, we were in a nuclear wind, bobbing in and out of a toxic sea. Mum had just fallen in. Why would anybody not claw their way up and out of it to breathe freely and start again? You'd have to be mad or depressed to want to stay. Anyone who wanted to stay was depressed or mad.

'I can't tell you what to do,' Maureen said, 'but you seem like a nice man.'

'I'm better than I was, that's all.' I looked to the note I'd written mum.

'Ok, Tom.'

'I have a lot more in common with Sarah than you realise.'

It dawned on me Sarah had no one. Maureen was a nice lady but she didn't get addiction, she didn't understand it was an illness that made you do horrible things, and that underneath it there's another person. Occasionally a person is rotten to the core, but this is true of all people, drugs or no drugs; occasionally someone is so far gone they will never find a way back. Sarah wasn't a terrible person, I knew it.

'I just hope she doesn't hurt you.'

'Maureen, don't worry about me.' I reached for her hand and, as she squeezed mine, I became suddenly aware I was a 50 year old man, not the 10 year old she once accused of stealing a lollipop from Zoe Hackett. 'Thanks for caring. I appreciate it. Sarah can't hurt me.'

But she already had, *damn it*.

———————

'There's nothing here for you now, mate,' Will said.

Most of Halesowen gone, Will had plans of finding an abandoned house, a longed-for bachelor pad. He'd even suggested building one, ignoring the fact that between us the only thing we could successfully build was a joint. He puffed away on one, whilst we stood around mum's grave.

'We have solar power here,' I said. 'Food to keep us going for a little while, a cooker, water, beds. Mum's even got a room full of candles, just in case.'

'It's too far away from everyone.'

'I can't just leave,' I said, gesturing towards mum's grave. I looked to Loz and Marcus for backup. 'Loz?' I asked.

'What?' oblivious. 'So who's this bird?'

'Bird?'

'The girl,' Marcus said.

'Woman,' I corrected, and then caught Will's knowing grin. 'Like I said, she just appeared out of nowhere.'

'The brook,' Loz said.

'Yes.'

'Fit?' Marcus asked.

'I'm not answering that.'

'So, yes,' he laughed.

'Why's it always have to be about that?'

'What's wrong with you?' Will asked.

'What?' all innocent.

'You know what! I'm gonna smack her if I see her,' he added.

'You don't get it. She's sick, man.'

'We're all fucking sick!' he shouted.

Marcus mimed a *Carry On* "oooh".

I knew they wouldn't understand. We stood in silence whilst they passed around the joint, the cough of old lungs and sore throats – the *grark* of a crow, ominous and irritating, in the rowan tree.

Many years had passed since the four of us would sit in this garden smoking weed and swigging Buds and Stellas. We'd graduated Mad Dog 20/20 in the park, and would drink beer like men at my house. Men giggling like kids every time mum walked back inside, thinking we'd got away with it when we told her it was just fruit tobacco. It wasn't so bad at that point. I was messed up, but the drug and drink consumption was manageable. I still found my way to college, did my exams and worked a part-time job in a cinema. We were young and full of energy. My body could take it.

Looking at us now, I wondered how on earth they could still take it. Marcus was all but bald, red-faced, profusely sweating under his flab, a paisley short-sleeved shirt like some aging hippy, betrayed by his Marks and Sparks chino shorts and leather sandals, toenails yellowing and cracked. Will was tall, he seemed like a foot taller than any of us, but in fact he was about half a foot taller than the next one, me. Strong and stick thin but for his gut, like a rugby ball under his camouflage T-shirt; he wore a fisherman's hat over his long, mousey locks, which hid the beginnings of a bald patch – not that Will was vain, no, of course not, he was above such things. Loz looked about the most normal one amongst us. He tucked his checked shirts into his denims, wore Fila trainers – after the big revival in the mid-20s – and if it hadn't been for the overly wide, not long, grey beard which shaped his face like a spade, he'd probably pass for a new age hipster, denim-striped frames on his glasses. Instead he looked a little like a preacher trying too hard to be cool.

As for me, donned in hippy linen – I'd spent too much time in Morocco and Nepal – and my was hair fast disappearing, greying beard fairly long.

'Blueberry tobacco,' Will laughed, 'remember, Tom?'

'I was literally just thinking about it.'

'She was a cracking bird. Milf,' Marcus said. We all turned in disbelief. 'Too soon?'

Will smacked him on the back of his head. Loz was staring at me to see how I was reacting, but it didn't really bother me.

'She's probably got some booze around the house,' I said. 'Be good if you had a drink to her and got rid of the stuff.'

Will was already making his way back inside. 'Milf?' he tutted.

Marcus laughed, following close behind.

'Lilf more like,' Will mocked.

'Eh?'

'Leroy-I'd-like-to-fuck.'

'Very clever,' Marcus's droll response.

'And he's probably dead,' Will added, 'but that wouldn't stop ya.'

'Every hole's a goal.'

Loz grabbed my arm. 'You ok?'

'What can you do?'

'She was great, your mum.'

'She wasn't perfect, but she was my mum and I wish I'd been a better person sooner.'

'You've been looking after her for the last 10 months-'

'Alright, alright,' I interrupted, unwilling to take anything which even remotely resembled a compliment. 'Now go save me from a relapse.'

———————

Marcus was periodically throwing up in the bathroom, a piquant stench of bile filling the house, the occasional retch punctuating our already stilted conversation. Will was sitting forward on mum's chair, the crème de menthe from a Christmas in the nineties apparently matured to absinthe strength. He occasionally made a circular motion with his body before falling back into his seat, only having to sit up again a moment later to deal with the twirl of the room.

Loz was vocally the more drunk, slurring. 'And I doh see why she's making us leave home cos of the boob,' he said.

'The kids,' I suggested.

A retch echoed in the bathroom.

'Peoples still… live, um, in Chernobyl,' he said.

'Do they?' I asked.

'And Tokyo!'

'Tokyo?'

'Yeah, the Pokémon fucking ninja nuclear 1945er.'

'Cunt!' Will shouted.

'Oh, fuck off Will!'

It was starting.

'Nagasaki! Hiroshima! What do you know about the Little Boy and the Fatman? What do you know about nuclear war?' he ranted, leaning forward too far and falling on his knees, before crawling back onto the seat.

'You can't even stand up straight… sit, sit-straight,' Loz said. 'And who's a fat boy?'

'Ha! You can't even spit straight… speak. The bombs. The Fatman had less effect than the Little Boy because of the mountains.'

'The mountains?' I asked, intrigued.

'Always has to be about the mountains,' Will laughed.

'You brought it up!' Loz accused, laughing.

'Fuck you fat boy!'

'Come on you two,' I said, half-laughing at them. 'Surely the burning question here is, who knows more about Pokebombs?'

'Don't take the piss out of us,' Will said. 'Where's your *girlfriend*?'

There was a brief, painful silence, before Loz spoke up, 'Will! That's evil.'

'What you on?' He was unaware.

I could see what had happened and I knew where they both were coming from. Against reason, I was smarting from the way Loz had misinterpreted Will's piss-take.

'No, Loz!' Will realised. 'I meant the fucking brook pussy… Tom, the brook-'

'I know what you meant,' I said.

'Mean ass,' Loz said, winding him up.

'Don't you fucking dare,' he warned.

'Or what? You'll throw a music stand off my head!'

'Let's not rehash the past,' I reasoned. 'We all know who means what.'

One eye closed, Will tried to look at Loz, went to shout, then waved him away. He looked at me, pointed to his closed eye, then his heart, then in my general direction.

'I know brother,' I said.

At times like this I didn't miss drinking. Marcus was ill with it in the bathroom, the other two were incapacitated. God knows what we'd have done if Sarah and a merry gang of addicts came to steal the rest of mum's things.

Will had a point about moving back to town. We had allies there. I'd spent 15 years of my life living there, grew into an adult there, surrounded by fuck-ups, but all the fuck-ups were my friends and most of the fuck-ups had so far stayed, the ones who were still alive. With mum gone, the only people I'd spoken to on the whole estate were Maureen and Sarah – and she'd robbed me. I was sure there were reasonable people about, but there were also the shady figures of middle-class addiction who made going out at night a risk. Adult-children with some sort of unfulfilled birthright - *it'd be great to think I could help them in some way, but now's not the time.*

'So, what are you gonna do about Jenny and the kids?' I asked.

He groaned at me for bringing it up. 'I guess, I'm gonna go.'

Will looked up and was about to have a go at him for being under the thumb, but I put my hand up to stop him.

'It's shit,' I said, 'but it makes sense.'

'You should too,' he said.

'Yeah, probably, but I'm not gonna. Especially now.'

Loz looked confused, 'the pussy?'

'No – stop calling her that! But because I might be able to help people in Halesowen, yes. They might need it more here than up north.'

They didn't say anything. I knew Will was thinking something along the lines of me being holier than thou, but he also wanted me to stay. Loz just thought I was lying, went to pat me on the shoulder and missed. I caught his hand and he awkwardly tried to shake mine, sincere, man-like.

There was the sound of a God-awful retch from the bathroom. Moments later, Marcus came down, his face dotted with red spots where he'd burst small blood vessels.

Nursing mid-morning hangovers, I made them coffee in the kitchen, slightly smug that ship had sailed.

'It's just not safe up here,' Will said. 'The place is crawling with hunchbacked scag rats-'

'Same everywhere,' I said. 'But you have a point.'

'We need to take whatever we can, like the candles – smart wench, your mum. Obviously, valuables, if there's any left – brook bitch.'

'And personal stuff,' Loz said.

I had the Yellow Pages note in my pocket. There was the box of photos in the attic. A hard drive of my writing, photos and videos – although who knew how long that would be usable – and a few notebooks. The rest was in my head as long as it was in my head.

'We just need to find somewhere in town,' Will said. 'Somewhere big, where we can all live in relative comfort. The three of us, anyway.'

Loz scoffed and looked out into the garden.

'The stuff that junkie took is gone,' Will added, squeezing my bicep. 'I thought maybe we could track her down and get it back, but it's not worth the effort. The town is full of useful things. We've got our own personal shopper in Jay Bird.'

'Until they find him dead,' I said.

'Could be dead now,' Loz laughed.

'You're not in this,' Will said, giving him a shove.

Loz tutted, walked into the living room for a few seconds, then came straight back into the kitchen. I thought he was about to say something, but he just sighed, looking to me for support. I smiled and shrugged. I should've fully supported him. I knew what he was planning to do was absolutely the right thing but, against my better self, there was a little bit of me that sensed the betrayal Will felt so strongly. Or maybe I was just jealous.

'When you think about it, it's all a bit exciting,' Will said, ignoring Loz's frustration.

'Like the frigging Goonies,' Marcus sneered.

Loz laughed, bitter.

But it was. All this talk had even made me a little excited. I liked the idea of the last bus leaving us in the nuclear zone, in this lawless land, leaving us to do whatever we liked, to live how we wanted. It was more like the old graphic novel, The Walking Dead, than the Goonies, except without the dead, unless you counted the heroin addicts and they could be turned back. The walkers could become talkers again. It was like The Walking Dead with a bit more hope. *What a great idea for a drama series, or maybe even a sitcom? One of those metaphysical ones. Or maybe it's even more conventional than that and every week the main guy saves a different addict, like the 80s drama, Highway to Heaven. If we ever decide to head up north, about season eight, perhaps I'd write it, and then, for season eight I could write an arc about the protagonist moving up north to write a TV drama about his soul-saving mission.*

'I'm sold,' I said. 'We need to get a place in town. Somewhere with solar power. But let's at least wait until the last bus leaves.'

'Sounds good,' Will said. 'I'm gonna head home and bring my shit here. Marcus-'

'What?'

'Drink up.'

'It's fucking miles away.'

'We can bike it. I saw one on the road.'

'Tyre's out. Probably chain too,' I said.

'Just a tyre, I checked. We can fix it and I'll take yours. Also, your hiking rucksack-'

'Hold the fuck on a sec!' Marcus said. 'I'm not riding a fucking bike.'

Will looked at me. 'He can take yours. Loz,' he added – we waited for the insult – 'good luck.'

'Cheers,' he smiled.

'You're gonna need it.'

On my own in the house again, mum gone and feeling very alone, I went up to my room. It was now just a bed surrounded by boxes of clothes, candles, Star Wars and He-Man toys, even some of dad's old stuff, records, beer glasses, things she never got rid of, or he never fetched. She didn't usually hang on to things. Her place was minimalist because she got frustrated by clutter. Dad was the opposite. Mum didn't think twice of throwing things out, old knick-knacks, picture frames, DVDs. It was just another thing she didn't need, something else to clean. Even the attic had nothing but a cardboard box of photos and a plastic box of old sheets and towels. My room was an anomaly. Perhaps it was the old world, perhaps she didn't want to get rid of that part of her life, maybe she still loved dad – she certainly respected him despite his misgivings. Whatever it was, she accepted it.

I lay on my bed and thought about masturbating. I didn't. The habit was still there, ingrained, but the hormones weren't. I had to work at it these days.

I wondered what Sarah was doing, 'or perhaps who?' I said out loud.

Fuck sake, Tom. 'What's wrong with you?'

I thought about home again. The homely home. But not too much. Just abstractly, like I knew it was there, toyed with it in my head, closed my eyes and started to dream a bit, the hypnagogic stuff before sleep. I picked the house up in Burnham, like I was a giant digger. I trundled down Love Lane with it, crossed the roundabout and headed towards the motorway, but the house was just a toy and I started to shake it with the digger like a kid shaking pennies out of a piggy bank. People fell out and I came-to with a start.

I didn't manage to sleep.

I had to find Sarah.

The front door broken open, I secured it with a mattress, wedging it between the door and the stairs. I locked the back door and went out through the garage, empty except for a mini-gym I'd rarely used. I locked the garage behind me.

I knew Maureen had a point. I wasn't ignoring the fact that I might be somewhat attracted to her but, if it was that alone which spurred me on, I was lying to myself without knowing any better. I wanted to help. I could sense the good in her. I'd seen it. I'd felt it through me when she touched my arm, an electric force for good. And now I was on a spiritual quest to help. My sobriety had been a series of these quests. Not because I was some kind of saint. Far from it! Because it kept me sober.

I walked slowly through the thick grass alongside the park, on Rosemary Road, linen trousers damp around the ankles. Adjacent to their little hideaway, I stood listening but didn't hear anything.

I made my way through the overgrown shrubs and trees. I climbed awkwardly over a branch, and then under another. Feeling buoyed by the mission, and rather than finding a way around, I climbed up over two branches on a willow tree but then, as I went to swing under a third higher branch, it broke and I came tumbling down, slashing my forearm on a pointy knot. Sitting on the ground, I grabbed my arm, already wet with blood. The cut was deep, just seeing it made me feel queasy. Like a regular Bear Grylls, I tugged at the other arm of my linen shirt, thinking I'd wrap it around the wound, but it was a good shirt from Morocco and it didn't come. I had to take the shirt off and stand on the cuff, pulling at it, all the time blood spilling down my arm, making me feel like I was going to faint.

The sleeve eventually tore away from the shirt and I wrapped it around the wound. Then it occurred to me I could've used a sock. 'If ever there's a bloody sign to walk away from this quest, Tom…'

I crawled awkwardly on my hands and knees to the clearing where I'd first found her. No one was there, but the cider bottle was gone, so someone had definitely been there since we had. I sat waiting on the dirty sheet, cursing her, cursing myself, cursing this cursed world. Eventually, I fell asleep.

I awoke in semi-darkness to the sound of people rustling in the shrubs. My arm throbbed. I listened.

I heard a girl laugh and I knew it was her. I got up quickly, making too much noise in the process.

'There's someone there,' a man said.

'Tom?' she asked.

'Why would he be there?' he nagged.
'He won't,' she said.
'So, why did you call him? Oi! Stalker!' he shouted.
I stayed quiet.
'There's no one there, see,' she said.
'But you called his name,' he said. 'Let's fuck it off.'
'Fine! if you don't want it,' she snapped.
'I don't mean it like that, babe.'
'You're a coward, do you even want to fuck me?'
'Course I bloody do! I ay a weck,' he sulked.
I couldn't listen to this, I took a deep breath, 'Sarah?'
'Shit,' she said.
'Is it him?' he asked.
'I'm not bothered about mum's things,' I said. 'It's just stuff.'
'Go, go, quick, turn around,' she panicked.

I heard them backtracking through the shrubs. I clambered up, nauseously aware of my arm which felt about a foot wider, the shirt sleeve bandage covered in blood. Collecting little cuts from branches and brambles, I pushed my way back through and out. It was nearly dark, the orange blink of a street lamp near the end of its life, and I could just about make out the two figures turning onto Portsdown Road.

Limping with injuries, I moved as quickly as I could, trying to follow them up the hill. But they were too fast and far away, and I was feeling ever more weak with a more pressing concern. I slowed down, telling myself: 'I don't have septicaemia, gangrene hasn't set in, I'm not going to lose my arm – or my life!'

Across the road, I spotted two young guys and a girl, stick thin Lowry characters under the orange light, shifty and slouched-morose. They turned onto Hambleton Road, where Maureen's friend lived. I imagined a little old widow and wondered whether I should follow them in case they were up to no good, but I caught a rotten whiff of marketplace, thought of my arm and continued up Portsdown in a bid to prevent amputation.

As I turned onto Mendip Road, it suddenly occurred me to I'd left the house unguarded and they were heading in that direction. I tried to pick up the pace, but I felt physically sick. I didn't know whether it was my injury or my neuroses, but I was betting on my festering arm.

Where would all this figure in my TV drama? A desperate man on a pathetic chase. Perhaps Sarah would be the protagonist's love interest. A recurring character who kept just out of reach of help, but who would inevitably succumb to him by the end. Or would she? Sometimes characters died, and as long as it was done right, it was acceptable.

'What are you fucking on, Tom?'

There was no sign of anyone when I got back. Inside, the garage closed behind me, I rushed to check the back door was locked and the mattress still secure against the front door.

I sat in mum's chair and unravelled my wound. It was bubbling away and already looked infected – I was certain of it.

I suddenly remembered mum's meds. *Antibiotics*!

I clambered up like a dying man, but I couldn't find them anywhere. *Sarah must've taken them.* 'Perhaps she'll get high on Phyllocontin.'

My arm stinging, I noticed there was a small amount of crème de menthe left in the bottle. I tipped it on the wound, a cold burn which felt nice as it wore off, a refreshing waft of mint. I dabbed my finger on the sticky residue and went to lick it.

Fuck! *Is this a relapse*?

I went to the kitchen and washed it off to stop the alcohol getting into my bloodstream. The water hurt, but revealed just how deep the cut was. I clearly needed stitches and all I had were plasters. In my TV show, maybe the protagonist would have the balls to use a needle and thread. *I'm certainly not there yet.*

I rang Loz, trying my best to remain calm. 'She stole the antibiotics!' I screamed.

There was a pause. 'What?'

'Sarah! Ok… breathe,' I told myself. 'Calm down.'

'I'm calm-' he said.

'I'm talking to myself. I need you to go to Picks to get some amoxycillin off that Tony Bonham fella.'

'Who?'

'Ask Tony Dale.'

There was another pause. 'What?'

'Tony Dale!'

'I don't think that would be wise, do you?'

'Why?'

'…The feds-'

'The feds?'

'The *feds*.'

'Feds,' it dawned on me. 'I need you to get Will to-'

'I'm not with him.'

'Shit! Why haven't they got fucking phones?'

'What's going on, Tom?' He sounded worried. 'Is it life or death?'

'Is it life or death?' I looked down at the wound, three finger plasters, like fat stitches. 'I don't know.'

'Is it life or death?' he asked again.

I thought about it. 'Probably… not. I just… cut my arm. It's deep!'

'You could always call Picks yourself,' he said.

'I didn't think of that.'

He half-laughed. 'Are you alright?'

I felt better just speaking to him. 'I'm probably just being me. Are you alright?'

'You know,' he scoffed.

There was a silence, my arm throbbing, the Nokia hard against my ear. In the background, I heard somebody yell "stop it". It sounded like his lad.

'You there, Tom?' he asked.

'Yeah… I'm sorry about earlier.'

'What for?'

'For not being supportive.'

'It's ok. Will's a wanker.'

I laughed. 'You're doing the right thing. I'd leave… if I… you know.'

'I know.'

There was a silence. I wanted to say more. I wanted to tell him that I'd miss him, that he was about the most normal one amongst us and perhaps we were all destined to descend into madness without him. 'You're lucky, mate.'

'Shame she doesn't feel the same. You sure you're alright?'

'I'm sure she does.'

'Getting evils. Can we chat later?'

He hung up as I said, 'yeah.'

I looked at my phone, the battery was low. I put it on charge.

How long until all that went away? Mobile phones? The ability to charge them? What would happen when we were officially boob-bound, living off the grid in no-go territory? Would we use generators? How did solar power even work? *I know nothing about this shit.* It was exciting, but people were bound to suffer and die because of the lack of infrastructure and the lack of knowledge. I drifted off worrying about it.

I awoke on the settee to a knock at the door. I could barely move my hand. Had I slept on it funny, or was it gangrene? I looked down at my arm and heaved. I felt weak. Hungover almost. My arm was obviously infected.

Knock, knock, knock.

Thank fuck they're here.

Knock, knock, knock.

'Coming,' I tried to say, pushing myself up.

I yanked the mattress back, but fell forward with the weight of it. I got back up and managed to get in front of it to open the door, the mattress weighing heavy against me.

'I'm sorry,' Sarah said.

'You came back?' I sounded pathetic.

'I didn't steal for drugs.'

'That's ok.'

'No, it's not. I stole for a good cause.'

'It doesn't matter.' I felt drained.

'What's happened?'

Woozy, segments of the ether seemed to erase themselves. My arms felt light, my hands cold. Was I breathing? I looked up at Sarah, a plastic taste, anaesthetic. And that was that.

―――――――――

I felt somebody prod my bad arm.

'He's fine,' he said.

It sounded like Marcus but I couldn't open my eyes.

'I didn't mean any harm,' she said. 'He's a nice guy – a bit weird.'

'It's just a big cut.' That was Will and it annoyed me.

My arm felt heavy, like a club, slugged over the arm of the chair.

'It looks bad,' Sarah said.

I knew she'd come back. I knew there was good in her. It's just stuff, just things. Life's more important than objects.

'This is what Tom does. He has-'

'Emotional-' Marcus interrupted, laughing.

'Emotional outbursts, and sometimes he lashes out, breaks things, other times it's just hypochondria,' Will continued.

Fucking smart arse.

Marcus laughed again and I heard a slap. 'Ow! Cunt!'

'Don't laugh at him, you cold bastard. Pat just died.'

'His mum's things,' Sarah said awkwardly. 'It was just-'

'Survival. I get it,' Will said.

He'd soon changed his tune – all it took was a pretty woman. But he was right, I knew I was a hypochondriac. I kept forgetting. Why was I so forgetful? A brain tumour. *Don't be silly*! Perhaps it was early onset dementia. *For God's sake!*

'Sort of,' she said.

Just remembering, my arm felt lighter already. Sore but lighter. I was never great at expressing myself. I was better than I used to be, but mostly it took place in my head or on the page, often coming out sideways.

'It was for the church.'

I coughed, opened my eyes, '*church*?'

'You're alive then?' Will said.

'How did I? What did I?' I pretended. I wasn't going to let him know I'd heard his diagnosis.

'You cut your arm,' Sarah said.

'I know I did,' I lifted it. 'Bloody hurts.'

'You woolly woofter,' Marcus said, lips pursed, talking to a child.

'Woolly what?' Sarah asked, confused.

Will winked at him. 'He's allowed to say it.'

'Fuck off!'

'What's a woolly-?'

'Woofter? Him,' Will laughed.

'Ignore them,' I said.

We were old. I was sitting in mum's chair and I felt old. The cut on my arm had a much more profound effect on my system than it would've even a couple of years ago, and that wasn't the hypochondria, it was just the aging process.

The three of them were standing inspecting me from the middle of the living room. In front of them was my hiking rucksack and three or four Lidl bags of things they'd obviously brought back from Will's. I felt like an elderly relative on my last legs, whilst they sat around divvying up my belongings.

'So what happened?' I asked.

'You passed out, you daft bastard,' Will said.

'We found you wedged in the front door,' Marcus added. 'We had to carry you in.'

'*We?*' Will punched him in the arm.

'Alright, stop fucking hitting me. *They* did. Lank and the brook-'

'Girl-woman,' Will interrupted. 'She helped.'

Sarah glanced down at the bags and Will caught her. She noticed, 'I'm not gonna nick anything!' she bit, before catching herself. 'I'm sorry, Tom. It was for the church, I promise.'

'Really?' It seemed bizarre, but I definitely recognised an inner struggle in her.

'Yes, Lutley Community Church.'

'Never heard of it,' I said.

Will looked suspicious, eyes widening to let me know. But then he was also side-glancing her breasts. Marcus was oblivious – of the church and Sarah's body.

'It's a new church,' she added.

'Christian?'

'Yeah, but not like C of E or Catholic, not "organised" religion, but we follow Jesus-'

Marcus coughed a laugh. We all looked at him. 'Sorry.'

'I don't care,' she said.

'But, don't get me wrong,' Will said, more polite than usual but still smug, 'you robbed Tom. His dead mum's – sorry, Pat's – stuff.'

'The church needed it. We have to help the weaklings to keep the chain strong-'

'Weaklings?' I asked.

'Weak… links. To keep the chain strong. There's, you know, old folk. Some are pretty ill,' she said to Marcus, who looked offended. 'There's addicts,' she said to me.

'Thou shalt not steal,' Marcus chirped.

'It's a pretty big commandment,' I reasoned.

'Oh, fuck it,' she snapped. 'I didn't come here to be judged. Thou shall not judge-'

'That's not a-' Will.

'Don't think it's a-' me.

'I just wanted to apologise, alright! You were nice to me. I told them at church and they said I should apologise. I wasn't going to. Then you were down the brook again-'

Will cast a confused glance. I waved him off.

'And I felt bad… A little bad. Ok, I didn't feel really bad,' she fought with herself. 'I figured it was bad karma.'

'You thought I was going to keep coming after you,' I smiled.

'Oh, whatever. I'm not scared of you. You should come and see for yourself.'

'Go to church?' Marcus asked, incredulous.

'You should,' she pleaded. 'It's alright. A bunch of mess-heads, but we're trying. I'm… trying,' she looked up to the ceiling, to God maybe.

'I mean,' I looked at Will, who looked weirded out but not against the idea, if for no other reason than to stare at her tits. 'I'm up for it.'

'You too,' she said to Will. 'Maybe not the fat one.'

'Pahahaha! Fatty.'

'I've been to church lots of times actually,' Marcus defended.

She looked awkward. An unwilling missionary. It was endearing. It reminded me of making amends to the people in my life. The letters, the messages, the meeting up with people. *I'm sorry I stole off you, I'm sorry I broke up with you, I'm sorry I made you break up with me. I'm sorry I left you lying naked on the floor when you needed me to pick you up but you fucking beat me*! Ok, so some of them were still a work in progress, and maybe they always would be.

'I'd actually quite like to go,' I said. 'Out of curiosity,' I defended, but it was more than that.

'It's not like normal church. It might seem a bit wonk,' she justified, 'but he… they really helped me.'

'That's what I used to say, when I was trying to get people to AA.'

'Lee went to AA,' she said. 'The preacher.'

'So what does your nan think about them?' I asked.

'She thinks it's a cult.'

'People say that about AA too.'

'So, you actually were an addict?' She sounded a bit surprised.

'Don't get him fucking started,' Marcus sneered.

'Pahahaha.'

What on earth had we come to?

Twelve of us in a semi-circle sitting on tiny chairs. Opposite me, Rex and Barb, clearly tipsy. Rex was grinning at me, a self-satisfied look on his face, like he'd shown me the way. But as much as this irritated me, because of the way I'd ended up here, something was telling me this was meant to be. *Everything happens for a reason.*

Sarah was wearing makeup. A faint orange line ran down the blonde soft fur by her ear, like the seams of a tangerine geisha. It masked the gauntness of her addiction but highlighted the wildness of her inexperience. I was trying not to stare at her, but she looked anxious and it made me want to protect her.

We were in the back room of Lutley Community Centre. Built in 1970s, red-bricked and functional. The outside was decorated with white slats of wood and red wording in the kind of font you'd see up and down the country on the walls of old swimming baths or evangelical churches. I had my 8th birthday here, over 40 years ago, playing musical chairs on what appeared to be the same seats. The room used to feel huge, now it was much smaller, even the ceilings seemed lower – Will could touch it without stretching his arm out fully.

A man nodded in my direction, he looked about 35. He was gaunt with black eyes. I would've guessed a heroin addict, which meant he could just as easily have been 50. He wore a white vest and black leather trousers. I felt hot just looking at them. His arms as thin around his biceps as they were around his wrists, a tattoo of a crucifix on his forearm which looked homemade. He nervously nodded at me.

'Tom,' I said.

'Jake,' he replied. 'Squirrels.'

'Squirrels?'

'Squ-squirrels,' he nodded.

O…k…

Marcus kept looking at me, but I refused to acknowledge him. I knew he just wanted to laugh, like it was another one of those drunken situations we used to find ourselves in. Will was trying to be sensible. I was sure he had a thing for Sarah, but I was trying not to think about it.

Sarah was up and down at the door, impatient, like she was waiting for her dealer – it was all a fix one way or another. 'Lee will be here in a bit,' she told us.

Was she his little helper? Who was this Lee fella? Was it the boyfriend? I hoped not. I really didn't want to come face to face with the little rat I saw scuttling over the brow of Bassnage road. But this Lee had been to AA, so addiction figured in there somewhere.

'He's not normally late,' she said to me. 'Probably caught up helping someone.'

Can't be the same guy.

I felt like a gatecrasher. It reminded me of those evenings we'd snuck into events at the Cornbow Hall in town. Weddings usually. We walked into a bar mitzvah once and walked straight back out. At least that's what we assumed it was, the men and boys in yamukkahs. Will had already picked up ideas about Jewish conspiracies and left without hesitation. I just figured it was impossible to blend in without a head covering.

I looked to Will. He mouthed: "what have we got ourselves into this time?" I smiled, then caught Rex looking at me disapprovingly. I just couldn't shake the gatecrasher feeling.

I remembered sneaking into a boxing match with Loz once. We were wrecked on "plant food", the "not for human consumption" legal highs we used to buy in a shop off Broad Street. We strolled into the Cornbow wearing jeans and T-shirts, Loz had a hoodie on when hoodies were synonymous with asbos. Everyone else was in tuxedos and ballgowns. It must've been some sort of posh fundraiser. We wandered around pointing at the lights, pretending to be technicians. When the lights went down, we sat at an available table and they brought starters over to us. We felt so uncomfortable, so out of place. We left before the mains.

'Fuck off!' Will shouted.

'What you doing?' I said, embarrassed.

He turned to me and said loud enough so everyone could hear, 'that little prick keeps staring at me.'

The man was old, glazed eyes, staring in our direction.

Sarah came running over, 'what the hell, man?'

'Him,' Will shouted.

'He's blind.'

'I don't care if he's fucking deaf – oh,' he realised. 'Shit.' He turned to Marcus who was trying not to laugh. 'Pahahaha!'

'For God's sake, Will!... I mean, shitting hell... damn... fuck,' I mumbled awkwardly, noticing the Jake fella in his leather slacks staring at me.

The old man started to laugh. It was deep and jutting, like he was getting it on. This made Marcus laugh, high-pitched and camp. Sarah laughed. Then, 'pahahaha.' Soon everybody started to laugh, except me. I don't know why. I just couldn't. The whole circle vibrated with varying degrees and tones of laughter.

I looked over at a young woman, we made eye-contact, then she laughed and turned away all coy. She glanced back at me again, flicked her hair back, manic with laughter. *What the fuck?*

Had I missed something? It suddenly felt like they were laughing at me. I tried to laugh with them, *that's what I need to do*, but it was fake. They all laughed louder from their little chairs, in the little room where I'd had my 8th birthday party, Thunder Cat toys, He-Man, my mum and dad both alive and young and together; the R2-D2 cake with candles that relit after I tried to blow them out, much to the amusement of everybody else. I felt like I was in a fucking Kafka novel. Will spotted my paranoia and laughed harder. I wanted a drink, I wanted to relax, I wanted to escape. I considered getting up and running out, but that would've made me even more paranoid. Have they spiked me? Is my arm infected? It felt bigger, wider, a machine gun arm resting on a child's stool.

I couldn't take it. I was about to stand up and then the door opened and a man walked in.

'Fucking hell!' came out of my mouth.

I turned to Marcus, the blood fell from his face, he looked ill. I elbowed Will, he saw the man at the door and stopped laughing.

Sarah turned to see him, excited, 'you're here. This is Lee.'

'Leroy,' Marcus said, awkward. 'Alright er… mate.'

Leroy looked like he didn't recognise him. 'Lee,' he said. 'I'm Lee.'

2031

Lucy was sitting on the bar at the George. I knew she was watching me.

'Line them up, Tina,' I said.

Breasts bursting out of her goth basque – a tingle from groin to gut – she leant forward and poured six shots of red syrupy Aftershock.

One sticky shot after the other, I necked the aniseed drink.

Lucy was disappointed, I could feel it. I glanced at Tina's breasts, and then at Tina who was smiling at me. I didn't look over at Lucy, who by now was sitting on the TV stand in the corner, ghostly, the light of the Champions League Final, Man U versus Bayern Munich shining through her. I didn't see it. I just knew it.

It wasn't the drinking, it was the lie that killed me. I hated that I'd lied to people for so many years about my sobriety.

In the back of the pub, Marcus and Will were dancing like they were at a Madness tribute gig to "Come on Eileen", which Loz was singing on the karaoke. Six-Kids-Stacey was dancing too, but her womanly Picasso figure had morphed into his famous blue skeletal guitarist, jeans hanging baggy over her anorexic frame. Ally was on a stool, staring at me, laughing. I couldn't tell any of them how I felt, they didn't care or understand, and Lucy was watching me the whole time. I just had to deal with it alone.

'Tony, line them up,' I said.

'*Tony?*' Tina said, confused.

'Sorry, Lucy–'

'*Lucy?*' like I'd called her the wrong name during sex.

Guilty, I immediately turned to Lucy's ghost on the TV stand, but before catching a glimpse, I fell out of the dream.

For a few moments the dream was my reality. I felt sketchy and embarrassed. I'd had variations on this dream so many times, and it always felt real and disturbing. It was never the drinking, it was always the deception which bothered me. The lie. The thought that I'd been lying to people about being sober for years. Lucy was often in it, like an angel. Even when she was alive she'd been an angel in my dreams, an overseer, she never participated, just watched me let her down. These dreams usually happened when something was bothering me and I saw them as an unconscious trick my mind used to protect me from relapse. In my heart I knew I didn't want to drink, but sometimes I'd stray from the path and needed a metaphysical kick to get me back on track.

Then I remembered what had happened and the dream paled.

Lying on my side, I opened my eyes and Tony Dale was staring at me. He was dead, of course. Empty. He looked green in the dark, his body casting a hazy film noir shadow on the wall and carpet. A tiny beam from a crack in the curtains lit the blade, still in his neck, reflecting a small section of grey stubble. The blood on his face and jowls looked like oil.

At the side of him, on a kitchen stool, was Marcus, St Vitus' dance knee.

'Stop it,' I said.

He put his hands on his knee as if it were independent of him. 'We've got to move him, Tom.'

'Has she gone to get them?'

'I ay going out there,' came from behind.

I sat up. Stacey was standing by the window, curtains closed.

'They could be days if the powder's on the table!' I said.

'Yow get 'em!'

'Fuck you! You did this. You killed him!'

'But it's Tony Dale, ay it. For me. *Please*,' an old wench pleading with long-lost womanly wiles.

'I can't tell Ally,' I said.

'Marcus then.'

'He can't do it!'

'*What?*' a look of typical injustice on his face. 'No,' he conceded, 'I'll fuck it up.'

'Come on Tom,' she begged. 'She doh care about him anymore. Not like that.' Her hands, thick with arthritic knots, shaking, her face twitching. 'I can't, can I? Look at me.'

'How *long* was I out?'

'About 20 minutes,' Marcus said.

'At least an hour,' she countered.

'No,' a child's retort. 'I looked at my watch, actually.'

'Can't you tell the fucking time?'

'Bitch!'

'Queer!'

'Murderer!

'For fuck's sake,' I shouted, 'quit with the bastard tennis!'

'Tennis?' Marcus asked, a dumb smile.

'Don't be a bastard. Have you got any on you?' I asked her, the sweat beading on her pasty forehead.

'All my gear's over at Ally's. Ar just came here to do yow a favour.'

'And now there's a dead Tony Dale in my bedroom.'

'Stop calling him Tony Dale!'

'There's three of the fuckers!'

'Two,' Marcus smiled. 'That'll be easier.'

'Tony Two,' she said, 'that's what he's called. Tony Bonham's three and the other Tony-'

'Moran-'

'He is that,' Marcus quipped.

'Wha?' she asked.

'A moron.'

'Wha?'

'Tony,' he smiled.

'Which one?'

'Tony One-'

'He is what?' she asked. 'You said, "he is that", he is what?'

'A moron!' I shouted, making fists. 'Tony Moran is a moron.'

'I wouldn't tell him that,' she smirked.

'This is ridiculous. Let me think.'

'Last time we did that you fell asleep,' pencil-lined eye-brows raised.

It was nearly light, the veins of linen in blue curtains. I wasn't sure how I'd drifted off. One minute I'd been thinking about Lucy and the bomb, the next I was trying to figure out how we were going to survive this latest bomb. *Maybe the answer's in my dream* – I knew that was the alcoholic talking, angling, looking for a way in.

'Back door?' I asked.

'I've locked it,' Marcus said. 'The front too.'

'We need to take him up to Dan's old flat.'

'What if someone's up there?' he asked.

'Have you heard anything?'

'…No,' he conceded. 'Goddamit,' he stuck his middle finger up at Stacey, 'whore!'

Stacey was now kneeling on the bed over me, trying to look innocent and apologetic. She went to hold my hand. I refused it and got up out of bed.

I prodded the air. 'You need to clean this up. All that blood needs to disappear.'

She nodded, then twitched, rubbing her cheek like a child scrubbing off muck.

The sun was coming up outside and with it a smoky whiff of methane from Ground Zero. Daylight came in through the smashed-in main entrance, but we were nearly two floors up and, with no electricity, it was dark.

'I can't, I can't... he's too heavy,' Marcus panted.

'Hold him, hold onto him,' I pleaded, carrying him backwards up the cold concrete stairs.

He let go and Tony Dale's head hit the step with a smack which echoed like a cough.

'Marcus!'

The weight forced me to drop his feet and his body slid down a flight to the landing between the first and second floor.

'Fuck, sorry,' he said, stretching his fingers, stepping down to the landing. 'I have got the fucking heavy side.'

'I'm going bloody backwards!' I looked beyond him, 'is there any blood?'

We'd wrapped him in two bed sheets, but blood was still coming through to the outer sheet. Marcus looked down, clicked the button on his headtorch. It didn't come on.

'You need a new one.'

'It's fine.' He smacked it and the light came on. He looked to the stairs. 'Yeah, a trail.' He looked behind him. 'All the way down to the first floor too.'

'Shit.' I sat on the step. 'What are we gonna do, Marcus?'

'Wipe it.'

'I don't mean the blood.'

'Oh,' he shrugged, then his torch went out. 'Fucking thing.' He smacked it a few times. 'I need a new one.'

He plonked himself on Tony Dale's stomach.

'*Marcus!*'

'I need a rest!' He put his head in his hands and sighed.

What difference did it make, I guess? Tony Dale was dead, gone, the gaffer of the only working pub left in Halesowen, club house to the Sons, to "dutiful rep and conscientious worker" alike. Someone would pay for this. Tony might not have been a Son, but he was well respected. When they found out what had happened, and I couldn't see how they wouldn't, we'd be in serious trouble. If it wasn't Marcus's loosened lips after a drink or two, it would be Stacey looking for a fix. If it wasn't them, it would be one of the others after we'd inevitably told them about it. It wouldn't be Ally. I was scared to tell her because he was the father of one of her children, but she wouldn't say anything.

But perhaps this was what we needed, a catalyst. Perhaps this was our way out of here and back into civilisation.

'Come on,' I said, geeing myself up. 'Just this flight, then we can hide him in Dan's.'

'Swap?' he asked, getting up.

I nodded. The moment I hulked him up, I realised Marcus had definitely had the raw end of the deal. He grabbed his feet and one step at a time, I forced the bulk of Tony Dale up the stairs. We then dragged the body into Dan's.

I'd been to this flat many times in my previous life. A quick text to Dan, then I'd be up the stairs to buy a ten bag of weed. It was usually only in times of desperation. He took a bit of a shine to me and I couldn't get away from the fucker once he'd started. He had an iguana and a couple of corn snakes. Loved to show them off. He also liked reading about serial killers. Jeffery Dahmer was his favourite. The cold-blooded animals, the murderers, I never felt comfortable. He had a smile that was disarming, and frightening for the very same reason. I wanted to like him, but something told me it wasn't a good idea, that some day he'd make the news for some shocking crime – "kept himself to himself, nice smile, seemed like such a lovely guy". And he did, in a way.

We put Tony Dale's corpse against the back wall of the living room and looked for someway of hiding him.

Dan's old flat had long since been looted. Dan's flat had long since ceased to be Dan's. The upturned, ripped-up furniture and pulled-up carpets belonged to the tenants who came after him, or maybe even a tenant who followed them. But it would always be Dan's flat to me, frozen in time, even though the flat now looked like nearly every other empty flat on the estate.

When the looting began, we never knew what we'd find hidden in these rooms. Most of the estate had just been normal everyday folk, of course, but there were still more dealers and petty criminals than on the Squirrels estate or in Hasbury, or anywhere else in Halesowen. You might find drugs, weapons or a stash of expensive equipment. You'd also find money, which technically we couldn't use, but you could trade it outside of St John's with those who wanted to head north. Most didn't want to leave or were scared to, but when they did want to leave, they really wanted it. If you found the right person, this made money very valuable. But it was also dangerous with the federali around. People had disappeared for it. In Halesowen *spend a penny* was no longer a euphemism for going to the loo. When someone had gone to spend a penny they weren't coming back.

'Pass me the cushions,' I said.

He reached for a sofa cushion and let out a sudden yelp, 'mother fucker!'

The cushion flew towards me and I caught it, 'what now?'

'Woodlice!'

'Oh, you silly shit! I thought it was something serious.'

'It's fucking woodlice!' he shuddered.

I couldn't be bothered to point out we'd just lugged a bleeding corpse up the stairs. I carefully placed the cushion over Tony Dale's head and shoulders, before standing back, taking it off and then placing it back slightly differently like I was making a collage – the Banksy Collective Tracey Emin parody: My Death Bed.

'Do you remember Dan?' I asked him.

'Lover boy?' he laughed.

'You wish,' I countered.

'It was your arse he was after.'

'He wasn't one of your lot,' I said.

'My lot?' the usual look of confusion, like he was hearing it for the first time.

'Forget it,' I conceded. 'Did you ever hear how he went?'

He laughed hard, 'of course! Out the fucking window.'

'You're a sick fuck. Pass them over.'

He started passing the cushions like he was handing over dirty socks. I carefully placed them over Tony Dale's body, making my art, so it looked haphazard as if they'd been tossed mid-ransack. I then pushed the TV table up against his top half and the plastic back of a 50 incher on his lower half. We'd previously mined the TV for metals. We'd also found and broken down a laptop, an Alexa pod, smart pots and nano pans and various phones, of which we'd found quite a few. These were the valuables we now concerned ourselves with, because inside all of these useless items were precious metals in varying quantities. Smart devices, remote controls, glasses, buttons, pen sets, occasionally we'd find jewellery, gold teeth – I vividly recalled Jay Bird's brother's leathery mouth, which was where the whole idea started, after they'd "left" the George. Gold, silver, palladium, copper and platinum. We just had to break it down. We had an office for this – that's what we called it. It was a room at the back of the derelict Zion church.

'One day you're gonna come out with it,' I said. '*Again.*'

'What do you mean?' he pretended. 'Oh, that was a one time thing.'

'I saw you, Marcus. The green frock?'

'Robe.'

'Whatever. Why do you bother? They know. I know – of course, I know.'

'The second time was just the madness of all this. I know you think-'

'In the end it doesn't matter what I think. You need to come clean. For your own sanity.'

We left Tony Dale in suburban quietude and made our way back down to Stacey in silence. When we got to the front door, Marcus mumbled, 'and end up like Dan?'

I turned and smiled and he gently shoved me through the front door. It was as honest as he'd been about it in a long time.

But that wasn't why Dan was killed. He hadn't paid his supplier, the "dutiful rep" Tony Moran, who even back then, before the Sons, before the bombs, might be described as a kind of rep, but his duty was only to himself and his family. Dan was leaving the block, but Tony and his son, Aaron, were waiting for him. He ran back inside and they chased him up the stairs. He locked his front door and they started to kick it in. Dan knew his only option was to climb out of the window, but he fell two storeys down, hit the concrete, headfirst. And that was that.

―――――――――

Will looked haggard, his face crumpled and creased like a Lucian Freud painting. He was beginning to show signs of coming around after drinking half a bottle of berries. Next to him, Marcus sat, twitching, eager to let it all out.

'Ally needs 24 bottles,' Will said.

'Piss off! Two crates for one night's sesh?' I complained.

'No, I got a decent bag for it.' He pulled out the weed and his papers and started to roll. 'I got you a bar of Galaxy… and fucking Six-Kids!'

Marcus prompted me with his eyes, *tell him*.

'I didn't ask for Stacey.'

Loz was lying down facing the back of his settee, depressed, the usual powder comedown, his legs on my lap. Marcus was desperate for me to speak, but I needed Will to have a drink first and come round properly.

'I was only trying to help you,' Will insisted. 'Is she still out of it?'

'Out cold, yep,' Marcus said.

We'd come back to find Stacey passed out, a bottle of berries necked, the blood still staining the carpet.

'Why didn't you just do it?' he asked, disappointed.

'I actually nearly did this time,' I said, shaking my head in disbelief.

'You've gotta move on, Tom. I know she's a bit manky, but you did used to have a proper crush on her.'

'I tried, alright! Tried imagining her back in the day.'

'Best thing to do,' he said, like an authority.

'And what about you? Did *you* find *love*?' I pressed.

He just looked at me, trying not to rise to it.

This was really not the time to go down that road, but he'd irritated me. 'It's ok for you to try to help me, but-'

'Don't take the-'

'I'm not taking the piss.'

'I shagged Ally,' he said, defiant.

'You'll build her hopes up,' Marcus laughed.

'Oh, fuck off, you twat! Anita came down too, but she didn't want it.'

'I'm not on about sex!' I said.

'You don't say!' *Full stop*.

I looked at Marcus who was still prompting me with his eyes to say something about what had happened. He wiped sweat from his bald, wrinkled forehead.

'Have a drink,' I told him.

Will looked at him, then at me. He gave the bottle to Marcus with a thump to the chest. 'Drink! So what's going on?' he asked me.

'Nothing's going on,' I lied, not really knowing how to say it.

'For fuck's sake, Tom,' Marcus snapped with a squeak.

'Calm down,' I whisper-shouted. 'That's not going to help anyone.' Loz's legs felt heavy and hot in my lap, my thighs melting, neck sweaty. I looked to Will. 'We have a bit of a problem.'

Will immediately jumped up, panicking, 'have we been robbed? Has the brew spoiled?'

'The brew? What? No! Tony Dale's… dead.' My lips quivered upwards in a smile. I couldn't control the hysteria.

Will was stood in the middle of the room looking to me, then to Marcus, who was swigging the berries fast, intermittently heaving.

I pushed Loz's legs off. He moved them back. I pushed them off again. 'Stop it,' he moaned, half-asleep, trying to put them back on me.

I stood up. Marcus swigged off the dregs, sick-burped, holding his throat, and then joined me. The three of us were now in a circle in the middle of the living room looking at each other.

'How?' he asked.

'That's the problem.'

'When?'

'A couple of hours ago.'

'Who?'

'It wasn't me,' Marcus said.

'Tom?'

'No, you daft prick.'

'Well, what the fuck are you on about, what does it have to do with us?'

I grabbed his hand and pulled him towards the bedroom. The curtains were closed and Stacey was still out for the count. I used my headtorch to show him the carpet and then the wall. We'd got most of it out, but there was still an obvious brown stain.

'Shit?' he asked.

'Blood.'

'Tony Dale's,' Marcus said.

It dawned on him, '*Stacey.*'

'She nicked something off him,' I said.

'What?'

'I don't know.'

'And *she* killed *him?*'

'It came out of nowhere. A dagger to the neck.'

'Alright, Macbeth,' Marcus quipped.

We both spun round to look at him.

'Shakespeare?' he said. '"Is this a dag-"'

I waved the subject away. 'Stacey killed him, which has put us in a bit of a situation.'

Will was absent, thinking, he took a deep breath and said, 'she's gone right off, hasn't she? You can't fuck her, Tom. We'll find you someone better. You shoulda fucked Sarah.'

'Yeah right,' I scoffed.

'This is more important,' he lied, trying to prove it didn't matter.

'Come off it.'

'Much more. It would've helped to break this grief.'

'Calm down Hamlet.' Marcus was smiling, proud.

'What you on?' I whispered.

'…I could really use something.' He wiped his brow.

'Drink,' Will ordered.

Marcus looked down at Stacey, agreed to it, and left the room.

'We're in a right pickle,' I said.

Stacey was beginning to stir. I hoped she wasn't listening.

'Why didn't you?' he asked.

I knew what he was asking and the answer he wanted from me. This was my life amongst fuck-heads – my fuck-heads, but fuck-heads nonetheless. A person had died. Tony Dale was dead. He'd been killed by the woman who'd been inexplicably sent over to fuck me out of my grief – not for the first time – and who I'd almost let fuck me – for the first time. Then, having a dead Tony Dale in our flat, we'd been forced into action and dragged his bleeding corpse up the stairs and hid it in my ex-dealer's ex-flat, under woodlice ridden cushions and a smashed up TV. The Sons would need to find out what had happened to him. There weren't so many people in Halesowen anymore. It wouldn't be hard to find out, especially as all but one of the people who knew about it were regularly out of their heads. And in the face of all this, Will just wanted me to tell him why I'd never tried it on with Sarah.

'It wasn't about that with us,' I said.

Whether it was or it wasn't he gave me a look which made it hard to deny it.

'Because of Lucy,' I defended.

'But Tammy?' he asked, like I was mad.

'That was years ago!'

'But you still loved her-'

'Tammy?'

He nodded.

'We were kids.'

'Why didn't you go for it with Sarah? Really? Come on, tell me. You were so close.'

The conversation only existed between Will and me. Only the two of us truly understood it all. He puppy-dog eyed me, oblivious to the severity of our plight because his synapses were burning embers after the cocaine binge. I knew what I needed to say.

'I didn't go there because of you.'

He offered his hand. I grabbed it and he pulled me in and hugged me. 'Brother,' he said.

If only he knew. If only he could understand. But I couldn't tell him because he didn't want sobriety. He wouldn't understand what the desire to stay clean motivated a person to do.

'She was never meant for me, was she, Will?'

'I know I'm old,' he said, 'but it was close, wasn't it?'

I looked into his tired eyes, yellowing and vein cracked. I didn't know what to say, I didn't want to lie. I smiled, and a tear trickled down his face.

'Come on, man,' I said. 'We need to do something about this.'

I loved him, there was no doubt about it. Sometimes it felt like he wasn't there anymore but then the hard, crusty shell of bravado cracked and a little light shone back at me. I loved all of them. And all of us were gone one way or another, anyone who stayed in this town was mad or depressed, but we were still there, somewhere, underneath it all.

Will was still there underneath the flickering flame of his desire for love, underneath the anger and madness of his self-abuse. I was still there, underneath my balding head, my never-ending recovery battle and the loss. Even Stacey was still there, underneath the addiction and emaciation. These were all just things which had happened to us along the way. It was life.

Will shook Stacey's foot, she moved it away. 'Oi, Six-Kids.'

She didn't move.

'Oi, wench!'

She rolled on her back, her greasy hair greying and stuck to her face. Her eyes were closed, breathing laboured, breasts reaching for her armpits. I still remembered her introducing me to Fairground Attraction, young, lively and beautiful: *find my love, find my love*. When I was young, naïve and in awe of her, when she had just a couple of kids and was still trying to look after them.

Will knelt on the bed and shook her shoulder, 'oi!'

I looked at her face and all the evidence of a bitter life seemed absent, botoxed away by gravity and heroin.

She opened her eyes and caught me looking. 'What?' angry.

'Nothing, sorry,' looking away, shy again.

'Oi, you!' Will said. 'You've fucked us right up, haven't you.'

Ally lay on the settee, a purple and black tie-dye dress, a bush of ginger hair, tangled and dry. She looked enormous, confident and younger than her 55 years, her wrinkles stretched out. She had a mug in her hand with cider wine in it, orange swill. Red curtains closed, no carpet, Moroccan rugs, one of which Lucy and I had brought back for mum from Essaouira. Candles everywhere, incense smoke choking the air. She wasn't a hippie by any means, just liked the style.

'Stairs?' she asked.

'All wiped. Even shook a load of dust and dirt over it after.'

There was a loud bang upstairs, making me jump.

'Someone about to fuck,' she said. 'Don't worry. They can't hear anything in here.'

'If it's one of them-'

'They can't hear, I promise. So… the world is no more for old Tone.' Wistful, she raised her mug and then drank to him.

'What do we do about Stacey?' I asked.

'I'd say I'll sober her up, but I can't see that happening. She's too far gone. Anita's quit by the way.'

'*Has she*?' I was stunned.

'Yes, 10 days.'

'Why?'

'Just because she wants to. We all want to at times.'

'I thought she might be trying to win Christian back,' I laughed.

'Not at all!'

'Well, that makes two of us in my little club.'

'Not quite,' she said, knowingly. 'How is she?'

'Sober, I think.'
'Where is she?'
'I couldn't say.' She knew I was lying. 'But I'm sure she's sober.'
'Good. Maybe she could help Stace?'
'It's a massive risk.'
'Probably right.'
'Ohhhh,' it suddenly dawned on me, 'that's why Anita didn't shag-'

'Will?' she laughed, then went quiet, looked to her glass and drank.

'So, you-?' I asked.

'He's a bastard, but I do love that man.'

'Love? Will?' I asked, pretending I didn't know.

'Yes, Will.' She looked disappointed in me – I wasn't being loyal. 'He's a good man, and he's really good-'

'Alright, alright, you'll give me a complex.'

'*You?*'

'No need to say it like that.'

'You were just a boy.'

'And I was very drunk.'

'Now you're giving me a complex,' she lied, laughing. She didn't care one way or another about our little drunken fumble all those years ago.

Back then, like now, Ally lived opposite me in this same maisonette, only now she had full run of the block. The main front entrance was boarded up. Many of the ground floor windows too. The only way in was through the back door. The flats were each ornately decorated and themed. Most of the town had contributed to it, dragging furniture from flats and houses all over town. It was before the lines went down and we volunteered our phones in the media cull. We would send photos from each house we looted, then she'd text or call her request.

Before the bombs, Ally was a little fish in a big pond. No one really knew her. She'd survived on benefits, her children running amok in a cramped and messy two bed flat. She was a drinker, like most of us. She held parties, birthdays and what-not, which is how I came to know her – I was the drunk across the way, invited over for a beer. She was intelligent, but struggled. We became close over the years, before I shipped off to rehab.

'You know, Tom, someone has to pay for this.'

'I know.'

'Tony's right up there. This is much worse than when they left the George and look what happened there.' She rolled forward, heaved herself off the settee and then went over to the back window. 'They'll search everywhere, definitely your place,' she said. 'Even if you didn't do it.'

'I didn't.'

'You know what I mean. You'd be high up on the list. You don't involve yourselves. Be more useful. Like me,' she laughed, hiking her knickers up under her dress.

Ally had set up a centre of depravity in the flats. She regularly held parties where she and her friends offered a service. It wasn't officially a whorehouse, that would go against the moral code of the Sons. The women didn't get paid exactly, but they scratched an itch and people thanked them for it. It wasn't a "business", more a "contribution to the community". Essentially, it was tit for tat.

Business was a taboo word in Halesowen, because of its connotations. It was now trade, which was mandated in one solitary all-encompassing law. Most of the workers were looters and they specialised in a trade, such as metals, or clothes and fabrics, furniture, or batteries (that was a good one – councillor Ray controlled it), crockery, gas (another good one), and just about anything you could think up, as long as it was deemed a need. A good trade was one which required less materials, less work, to give you more of what you need. It was an offence to have more than you needed. Likewise, it was an offence to stray from your looter-trade. It was an *offence*. It wasn't a crime, crime was another taboo word – there were no police in Halesowen. This was all part of Jay's Law. It wasn't always this way. In the beginning it had been a free-for-all.

'If you were more of a presence,' she added, 'no one would be suspicious. To begin with, just trade a little more often.'

'We don't really need anything, and surely that's the point,' I smiled.

'Compromise. Decorate the flat. What about paper? Ink? Surely you should be writing all this down,' she smiled. 'Or a new guitar? Jordan would be a good guy to get in with?'

Jordan was a crafter. Crafters would often get their materials from the looters to make necessary items, from tools and utensils to musical instruments. There was even talk of commissioning a huge town sculpture made of nails and buttons, the historic trades of the town, but this was highly controversial – was it a need?

Brewers were also crafters, and lots of people did this, including us. Alcohol was deemed an essential need as an ancient "relaxant-stimulant" – whatever that means – used in the "birthplace of democracy and referenced in the bible". People grew weed too but this was technically against Jay's Law. This was a risk we weren't willing to take, although Will was experimenting with some low grade bush weed outdoors up Leasowes. It wasn't an offence to consume any intoxicant, but almost every drug was illegal to possess, grow or make because they were non-essentials. This was Jay's Law. Of course, no one would search or accuse you… unless they searched or accused you. If you were searched, you'd already committed an offence, or someone who mattered had been offended.

'Jordan's practically a non,' she added.

'*Is he?*'

Tony Dale was a non because he ran an official building, Picks. Other non-bureaucrats included Tony Bonham, the chemist, and the various traders at St John's, including butcher, baker and undertaker. The only doctor in town was a non-bureaucrat too, but technically he wasn't a doctor.

'How can he "practically" be a non?' I asked, cynical. 'This is what's wrong with the whole damn place.'

'Tom,' she said, and I knew not to go there.

After the nons, crafters and looters, were the indies. Painters and builders (the non non-bureaucrat kind), hairdressers, and Doreen the cake-maker. These were acceptable non-essentials. I guess Ally and the girls were indies, unofficially, but then perhaps she was also a non. Unofficially. In the same way Jordan was now, apparently, "practically" a non.

But Ally was different. She was a friend to all. I could spout my opinions to her most of the time and get away with it. The dutiful reps, conscientious workers, prune loons and scag rats alike would mix happily in Ally's Place, which is what everybody now called Wychbury Court Block 6. It was a home away from home, and everyone had contributed to it. All of us had a little stake in it. The Sons liked it that way. Mostly because it meant it was open.

'Jordan chairs the meetings of the federalis,' she said. 'Get a new bloody guitar. Just get a little closer.'

She was probably right. We were four men living in a small flat in a broken down block. Our home wasn't open, we hadn't gone to any effort to extend it or make it welcoming. It was somewhere for us to sleep and a place we were familiar with. We were known looters and crafters, and they knew where we lived, but we weren't always there. We'd spend weeks in the cabin up Leasowes. The Sons didn't know about our Leasowes home. They knew we went away and they didn't like or trust that. But then we'd turn up with a bunch of metal at St John's, as if we'd been looting, but it was mostly metal we'd collected whilst living in town long before.

'What are we gonna do, Ally? Stacey's fucked us.'

'She was trying to help you,' she said, looking out the window.

'The only way she's helped us is by giving us a reason to leave.'

She spun around, 'you're not?'

'What-?'

'Thinking about it?'

'Always.'

'But you wouldn't.'

Of course I would. I was desperate to leave, but I couldn't tell her that when I needed her help. 'Of course not, but we need to sort this mess.'

'What do you *need*?' she impressed.

'What do you mean?'

'How's your back?'

'Fine. Ok, for someone in his fifties.'

'Really?'

'I'm still aching a bit from digging a hole.'

'The bog hole?' she laughed. 'You're mean.'

'I didn't mean to smash it up. I had one of-'

'Your moments, yes,' she smiled. 'You need to get over it.' She moved back to the settee, sat down, and pointed at me. 'You need painkillers.'

'Don't touch them.'

'You need them.'

'I'll be fine.'

'Nothing strong. Just ibuprofen.'

'Honestly, I don't.'

'Honestly, you do.'

'Just say what you mean, Ally, you're doing me bloody nut in.'

'Who would you get pills from?'

'Tony Bonham.'

'Have you ever met him?'

I thought about it. I had a vague idea he was one of the old guys who sat in the back at Picks, but I'd never actually met him. 'Probably at one time or another. I've never really needed to.'

'I doubt it.'

'I've chatted to most of the Sons.'

'He's not a Son.'

'You know what I mean.'

'You haven't met him.'

'I can't picture him.'

'That's because he doesn't exist.'

I was about to argue… '*What?*'

'Who's Tone's favourite band?'

'I dunno.'

'Yes, you do.'

'Yes, I do. Led Zeppelin.'

'His favourite musician?'

'Easy. Robert Plant. He's from Halesowen.'

'Nope, John Bonham.' She was eyes-wide smiling.

'Are you trying to say,' I stopped to gather myself. '*Tony Bonham doesn't exist?*'

'Not anymore. You killed him.'

'Tony?… Fuck.'

'Tone sold the meds. I've still got a roomful here.'

'Who do we get meds off now?' *Like that matters.* 'Can I have a coffee?' I was stunned.

She nodded.

On a sideboard she had a jug of cold black coffee. It'd probably been there for a day or two, but I needed something. I poured it into a dirty mug, wiped a smudge of lipstick off the rim. I took a sip, it tasted weak and nice for it. I necked it and poured another. It felt like a week since I'd had a drink of anything. I was always so busy not drinking alcohol, I'd forget to drink at all.

'So, what do I need to do? I don't understand,' I said.

'You barely go into town anymore, Tom.'

'We were in Picks the other night,' I insisted.

'You disappeared after ten minutes,' she accused.

'I don't drink. I went home,' I lied.

'My point is, you go into town once in a blue moon. You don't go to town meetings, have nothing to do with the federalis-'

'I'm friends with Christian,' I defended.

'You can't walk in without arousing suspicion-'

'And Jake!'

'Especially during the day. You need a reason to go in. You obviously can't just turn up asking for Tony Two, but you can turn up asking for Tony Three-'

'Is that Bonham?'

'You should know!'

'It's Bonham,' I affirmed, not one hundred percent certain.

She nodded, half-smiling. 'You can ask for Tony Three, because you don't know he's Tony Two. The reason: you're in town for meds.'

'I'm confused.'

'Just go into town to ask for Tony Three to get some ibuprofen. Hopefully it will act as some sort of alibi for your ignorance.'

'Ok... That kinda makes sense. What about the body?'

'It's gotta go.'

'How can I do that?'

'You're not gonna do that. The boys are gonna take him out the back of Ankerdine, up over the bank and the back way to the graveyard. Then they're gonna put him in the Greek Grave.'

'Are you mad?'

'It has to send a message, Tom. The last thing you lot would do is send a message. You're cowards.'

She was right. We also weren't stupid hicks with dubious morals who'd blow up the grave in the first place, or go on a killing spree to whittle out all those deemed perverts in the town, or demolish a tower block because some chap shagged a goat.

'I don't know if this is absolute madness or sheer Machiavellian genius,' I said.

'Me neither,' she laughed, before swallowing a mouthful of the orange swill. 'Pour me another.'

I went over for the jug.

'The only problem we might have,' she added, 'is Honest John, but I'll have to deal with that myself.'

It was a war zone outside. That's how it looked anyway. Maisonettes which had crumbled, like half-pulled broken teeth pillaged for gold. Smashed windows, the main doors removed, leaving an expression of shock on their brown-bricked faces. Some of the blocks had been demolished, because there was a need for everything if it was wanted by the right people and aligned with their dubious moral code. Drugs and money were found hidden in the walls, the secret agenda of some – by default, we got lucky in copper. Clumsy sledge-hammering caused incidents, skeleton buildings and collapsed floors. This all happened after they left the George in a bid for order. I couldn't help but wonder what might happen now Tony Dale had "left" Picks.

Six of the blocks, about a third, still looked habitable. Some of these had been converted into single establishments, like Ally's Place and the Fed-House, others were split-up by floor. In Bredon, the remaining high-rise, each floor had become one apartment. The lift had long ceased to work and the shaft had been fitted with ladders, which people scuttled up like rats. There was still the stairwell, but somebody brought up health and safety at a town meeting, claiming it was a fire risk to have only one exit – far safer to have a ladder up a lift shaft! I confess, in the absence of mountains, I found it exciting to use the shaft myself when visiting Christian, a Son, but a friend.

The roads and pathways amongst the flats were barely visible under the dirt and debris, largely blown across from Ground Zero. This wasn't a priority to the Sons. There'd been a meeting about this too, but it was deemed an unnecessary expenditure of time, because the only roads now used were the main ones, and even these looked like the chewed up roads I'd once driven on in Kathmandu.

Some of the grassy areas, however, had become a top priority. This was thanks to Ally. They sent Honest John out to keep the grass trimmed. By chance, this meant the grass leading to our back door was neat, but the bank at the side of the block was left to grow wild which wholly covered our kitchen window, thankfully protecting the brew. Honest had even planted rows of vegetables, like a thick moat around Ally's castle. I saw him banging fence posts in with his mallet as I made my way into town. I nodded, nervously. He looked over at me, before turning away. He was one of those I'd always known on a surface level, but never really knew, fat, strong, tall, a recognisable face of Halesowen. A photograph of him planting tomatoes as a boy popped into my thoughts. I shuddered thinking about it.

I left the flats, crossed the pot-holed Andrew Road and headed down through the old bus station, which sat at the mouth of the indoor shopping mall. The huge glass windows had been smashed, grown adults taking aim with bottles on raucous nights, before the federali cleaned the streets. Now it had boards with the words, "Renovation Pending", as if some wealthy landowner was redeveloping the much sought-after land. But the whole town could've had that sign over it, those perpetual words, awaiting the Sons' promise in the *Declaration of Freedom* to "re-skin the skeleton of our beloved town." They had a real sick poet making this shit up. His name was Ross North.

I passed the derelict shops, the old post office and its windows with the piled-high tyres. Just beyond it, the *William Shenstone*, the Wetherspoons smashed up when all things corporate were deemed evil that carnival night, the night we all agreed that this was our home, *fuck the government*, wherever it lay. We thought we were inventing democracy. We all accepted Tony Moran as a Son. Me too. We didn't care about his criminal past. In a non-judgemental environment, it showed initiative and enterprise. Besides, in the history of the world, what happens when a criminal turns "good"? They become politicians – or "dutiful reps", whatever you want to call it. It made sense, even though it really didn't.

But we were high on the festival, and most were high on much more besides. I wasn't. Sarah wasn't, either. We could've stood up and been counted that night. I could've stood as a dutiful rep. Sarah would've voted for me, Will would've disagreed with the idea but gone along with it. The other two would've followed suit. Ally and some of the girls from the flats, Christian and Anita, too. Leroy may or may not have voted for me, but if he had, many would've gone along with him and he might have survived.

Across the road, in the graveyard, I saw Barb. She was dwarfed by her pink dressing gown, pulling up grass around the graves and throwing it onto the path. She stood up and looked in my direction. I immediately looked away. I'm sure she wouldn't have recognised me anyway. A regular prune loon. That's what happened to the old survivors. I think it probably always did in Halesowen – at least in the Halesowen I moved in.

Two nons were lugging a long box into St John's. I felt my heart beating faster, colder, but they were clueless. Of course I assumed it was a body, which was irrational. It was more likely to be a box of meat or veg, business as usual. I looked straight ahead, trying to walk casually but suddenly losing the ability, my legs lifting in strange intervals like I'd just done a line of ketamine. *No faster, no slower, just get around the goddam corner, Tom.*

I turned onto the old high street and walked down towards Picks. Here the town changed to an old city. A cobbled hill down to the pub, cobbled by the Sons with grey slate cubes, loose teeth, paved with as much pretentious artistry as the words in our declaration by the sick scribe, waving his big red flag, like he cared.

It was the only place in the whole town where there'd been any work done, the big bushy lime trees had been mercilessly chopped down after a heated debate, and we'd been renovated back to the 1800s. It made me think of Blake's poem, "London". Ok, it wasn't abortions and smog, rather liver disease and methane, but I couldn't help but think a soldier's blood may yet run down the ramparts they were planning on building, "Renovation Pending".

We should've fought against this. Will, of all people, should've wanted to fight this regime. But he'd got lost in a dream where his only hope was hiding in the woods.

I was welling up with anger. Mostly it was thinking about what happened to Leroy, but he was the first of many who died for the crime of being themselves. I needed a fight. Not their fight up north, if it even existed, not even a physical fight necessarily, but something. Maybe I just needed to write. Or maybe I needed to escape.

'There's a whole world out there, Tom,' I told myself.

I could feel it calling me. Bittersweet olives in sunny Sicilian towns, the tart meat and pickle of a smorrebrod in Odense, a bowl of steaming snails in Jemaa el-Fnaa. *God, I need to eat.* I needed to eat something other than the Halesowen national dish of faggots and peas, or the bland tins of fruit, vegetables, soup and stew. I needed hot and sour momo in Lukla, a seafood pizza in Boulogne-Sur-Mer, hot provoleta with a cold spoonful of chimichurri on the sweaty streets of Mendoza. No matter what Will thought, it was not my desire to run away, it was my thirst for life. I thought about Lucy, but suppressed the guilt, because I knew I needed to get out of Halesowen.

'Maybe they need to die,' I said.

'Who?' a voice said.

I looked up, embarrassed, but it was only Jason the scag rat, scurrying for something to feed his habit.

'Everyone,' I said.

'You got anything, Tom?' he pleaded. 'Come on man.'

'I'm sorry, I just don't do anything.'

'Why are you here?' he sulked. 'Don't fucking belong here.'

'I'm beginning to think the same thing.'

'Come on, man. A blue, yellow even, a zoppi or codeine?' The blue vein on his sweaty temple pulsating, lip twitching, eyes already pin-headed on something, the whites long beiged.

'Nope, not even a paracetamol.' I suddenly remembered my mission. 'I'm after an ibuprofen myself,' playing the game. 'Bad back.'

'I got some,' he said.

Shit!

'You keep them, Jase. You need them more than me.'

'How about you buy some blues, and I'll trade for ibus?'

SHIT. Why did I say anything? 'Nah, thanks. Er… why don't you ask Tony Bonham?'

'They ain't gonna let me in there, are they?'

He'd broken Jay's Law. He was addict, but then most of us were addicts one way or another. He was one worse. An addict without a use. He wasn't capable of crafting, he wasn't on a looter-team – councillor Ray cut him adrift for holding back a pack of doubles As. Now he was just left begging until the day he stopped begging, and maybe we'd never find the bloated corpse, purpled lips and paled.

'Come on, do us a favour?' he begged.

'Nah, I really can't. Sorry mate.'

'Come on.'

'No, I can't.' I felt bad.

'Help a geezer out, man.'

'There's nothing I can do.'

'Don't be a cunt.'

'Oh, piss off!' It came out wrong, but I was digging a hole for myself, for us all. A Greek sized one. 'I'm sorry. I didn't mean-'

'You're a prick man,' he started walking up the hill. 'Shouldn't even be here,' he yelled down.

'I'm sorry.'

Hunched, he scuttled up the cobbled path and disappeared around the corner.

I would've liked to help him out, but it wouldn't have been convincing if this out and proud sober man suddenly asked for Valium.

Over the din of the generator, I could hear "Daydream Believer" emanating from Picks, the low, gruff voices full of beer singing along. Football supporters, testosterone, the potential for violence. It could've been 2018 when England got to the semis in the world cup, or 2026 when we got knocked out in the group stage, or 1999 when Man U beat Bayern Munich in the Champions League, or any derby day when Wolves played West Brom. A room full of people daring themselves to drink more. This had never been my scene, not really. It was bad enough walking in on a normal day, never mind after dragging the landlord's lifeless body up to the top of my block. The excitement, the revelry was already palpable. And what did they know, I wondered? What would they think? Did they already suspect anything? *Ally better know what she's doing.*

Sunny and light outside, it dimmed considerably as I entered the bar.

'Tom!' Ricky cheered. 'How you doing fella, ay sin yow in a bit?'

I went to school with Ricky, we were never friends, but we knew each other. 'Hiya Rick, not so great. Bit of a bad back.' I grimaced for effect.

'Yow wanna drink sum of the gold,' he said, the waves of cider splashing, sea of dreams in a glass.

'You'm alright, mate,' I replied, appropriating a broader accent.

The place was heaving. Fat, beery men spilling over bar stools. A line of older men seated on the bench running along the wall, waiting to fall off and be replaced by the next generation, who were mostly standing or sitting at the bar. In amongst the parliament of drinkers, were the Sons. All seven of them. They didn't look sinister for the most, but they looked cocksure. Jake, strange in a shirt and tie, saluted, like we'd been through a war – I guess we had. Christian, my old school friend, pretended to putt a golf ball with an imaginary club, then he gyrated his hips like he was shagging, pointing to me and laughing. I fake laughed in response.

They didn't look like a committee of politicians, but ordinary Joes and Johns deciding the fate of a nation with their one vote, which was what it was always meant to be. It often proved to be the same vote, cobble the high street, cut the grass, Jay's Law, knock down Ankerdine high-rise because a goat shagger lived there, kill the preacher, blow up the grave of a murderer – that last one didn't count, because it happened before the Sons even existed, but the signs of what were to come were all there.

Seven Sons. Hasbury, the Squirrels, the Flats, Manor Way, Huntingtree, the College and the Outsider. Seven was enough. By 2029 there weren't so many of us left. It was a loose and informal vote, a show of hands in St John's. At the time it wasn't such a difficult decision. Most people were happy not to be a representative. We just had to agree to let the people who volunteered do the job. It was all councillor Ray's idea, Son of Hasbury. He clearly had no idea what it would become, or what it couldn't.

I avoided the suffocation of the Sons – always avoided it. I went into the quieter side of the bar, the family side, a gaggle of wenches on our usual table, Anita amongst, looking like something from Abigail's Party, skimpy dress, a nouveau perm and a fag hanging out of her mouth. I waved, noticed she had a glass of wine – *that didn't last long*. I wasn't going to say anything. Besides, 10 days sobriety was good going in this town. They were bopping in their seats to some old Cher song which came on.

'"Do you believe in life after love?"' one of them stood up and sang, before cackling and falling back onto her seat.

The men were in one side of the bar, the women in another. It was like I imagined the 1950s might've been, just a little wilder. Apartheid of the sexes. And I was happy to nestle in this side, somewhere in between with old Percy and Jack, a couple of queers in their nineties, fully pruned-but-somehow-not-looned, who'd managed to sneak under the radar for their deviance. Others weren't so lucky.

'Tina,' I said.

'Yes, love,' she leant over the bar, breasts mottled and wrinkled.

'Get us the usual.'

'Kettle's gone, Tom. Sorry. You were the only one who used it and we barely see you these days.'

'Whose idea was that?' I asked. I looked behind her to the other side of the bar and one of the nons was giving me a funny look, his face pale and tired, big and round like a panda. I thought it was the butcher, but I wasn't certain – Marcus and Loz did most of the shopping.

'Tone's,' she said.

'Oh, ok.' I could feel the nerve leaving me, vividly picturing a dead Tony Dale staring at me. I told myself Ally knew what she was on about. 'What can you do me, then?'

'Not a lot really. Water.'

'That it? How much is that then?' What was that fella staring at me for? Everyone else was ranting away. Christian and councillor Ray were firing laughter back at each other; Aaron Moran was choosing music on the jukebox, some were mumbling to the music, but this round-faced non was just still, elbows-on-the-bar focused on me, like a cut out in a moving scene. I felt like he knew what had happened and that he was gonna be the one who killed me in this strange film we were in.

'Same as coffee. Four shillings. I'll stick it on the St-John's.'

'Thanks.'

Actually water didn't seem like such a bad idea. I could feel my hand trembling by the side of me like I was weak, a lack of sustenance.

'And nuts. Can I have nuts?' A child in a world of men. 'Please.'

'All we got is Honest's cob nuts,' she said.

I nodded. When she turned to get them, I closed my eyes, clenched my fists by the side of me, and finally said what I was there to say, 'is Tone in?'

She gave me a funny look.

'What?'

'Which one?'

'Which one?' *Shit*. I went absent, disappeared, my brain left me. *Which one?* 'One.'

'One?'

But before I could say, 'No, Bon, I mean, Bonham,' she'd moved up the bar.

'Tone!'

'I mean, Bon… Tony Bon…' My heart glooped a missed beat. *Shit*!

'Round here, love,' she was saying

'No, I mean–' *One, why did I say one?* I could've said Bonham, Dale, two or three, any or all of those, the same as they are, would've been better than Tony fucking one.

But it was too late. Tony Moran, the impish Irish ogre came round from the back, Son of the Flats. 'What's up?' he asked, looking up at me.

'Tom wants a word.'

'I can see that,' he said. 'What ya want?'

'Sorry Tone, I meant the other Tone.' I laughed, or I tried to. 'I mean, Dale. No, two. No! Three-'

Shit!

'Tony Two's not in.'

'I mean, the other one-'

'What other one?' He was irritated.

'The Two... Three... the chemist... I mean, the,' I nearly said drummer, thinking of Tony Dale's inspiration, 'Bonham.'

I was shaking. I felt the blood fall to my feet. My upper body wobbled like one of those standing punch bags, but if he'd hit me I was sure I'd stay down. In the back of the bar, that same figure, the butcher – he looked like a butcher, I imagined him wiping his meat cleaver on a bloodied tight-fitting apron – was glaring at me like he knew.

'What's the matter with you?' he prodded.

The dead Tony.

'Eh? Come on! What ya need?'

'I...I...buprofen.' I said it.

'That won't help you. What's wrong with you? You need a drink.' And with that he burst out laughing.

I didn't really know Tony Moran. I knew a lot of them, but not him, not the fella who unofficially resided at the top. I remember him being an old face from the George, our karaoke Sundays. He'd been in Halesowen all of my life and I'd always known of him. He was always someone to stay away from. Likewise his son, Aaron, who was in year seven when I was in year eleven and even then we were all afraid of him.

I laughed, nervously, joined in with him.

'What ya laughing for? Eh?' he said, shoving me.

'Leave him alone, Tone,' Tina shouted. 'He's clearly not well.'

I glanced to the back bar and the eerie figure was gone. Jake was watching with a worried look on his face, 'squirrels,' he blurted out, and then put his hand on his mouth. Nobody laughed. Even Christian wasn't laughing. The butcher walked around and stood next to Tony Moran. He was shorter than he looked and fat but somehow he looked fast.

'I'm Tony Bonham,' he said.

The whole bar shook with laughter, even old prune Percy laughed, a nasal machine gun. Christian looked nervous and apologetic but laughed along with them. I knew him for his laughter, his most enduring memory of me is of a stupid schoolboy sketch, playing the laughing game. This was no laughing matter, and he was laughing, but he knew it.

'That's not Tony Three,' a woman shouted from behind me.

'Ah, shut your face,' Tony Bonham said.

I knew he wasn't. Everybody knew he wasn't, but I had to pretend it might be him.

'Nice to meet ya,' I put my hand out. 'Tom. Tom Hanson.'

Everybody in the whole place laughed.

'Like the mild?' he said, laughing at his own joke, ignoring my hand.

'Yeah, like Hanson's mild ale,' I said. 'That's it.'

'What's the frigging matter with you?' Tony Moran asked again.

By now a few of them had come around to see what was actually going on. Councillor Ray bobbed his head around the corner, then disappeared again. A wall of them faced me, Tony Moran, his lad Aaron, Tony Bonham, smirking. There were four of them in the midfield. Three nons and the College Son, Ed, who wore a trilby and cardigan and looked like a choonboy about to burst into Z-Star's hostel cover, "(Daddy) Mack the Knife". Ricky was behind them in goal. He was less of a threat, just being a nosy bastard.

'Nothing. Just my back. Nothing,' I stuttered.

To the side of me, supping some dark spirit at the bar, Percy and Jack were in their summer jackets, turning their noses up at me. Behind, were the gaggle of perpetually single women, spares, most of whom I'd seen at Ally's but didn't really know because it wasn't my thing. People died in situations like this. I'd witnessed it, and then it was forgotten about like it was a collective drunken mistake. Where was Lucy? Where was my boy? Where was my life? I knew they all wanted me to move on and forget them, but I'd had a life, a proper life. Why was I back here in this, sober? Why would anybody sound of mind return to this madness? *I must be depressed, I must be insane.* I wanted to cry, but that wasn't going to help me.

'Why you in here without your bum boys? Eh?' Tony Moran asked.

I was tempted to look at Percy and Jack, to draw attention from myself. I was tempted to point out their hypocrisy to save myself.

'I… I…,' I tried to speak.

'I, I, I,' he mocked.

He then gave me a hard shove and I lost my footing and fell back, tripping over a bar stool. I found myself falling and twisted to try to save myself, but I couldn't. I heard a loud click and let out a squeal. Everybody laughed. I was lying face first on the wooden floor. I turned, caught a glance of Anita, who guiltily looked away.

'My bastard back,' I said.

'You what?' Tony Moran asked like I'd called him something.

'That's why I was here.'

'Want me to medicate him?' Tony Bonham menaced, making jazz hands. In one strange move all his bulldog-toughness left him - a dancing panda. If my heart wasn't beating so hard and fast I might've laughed.

I looked around for councillor Ray, for Jake, Christian, for Tina, for Ricky even, for somebody to make a stand, to help a fella out. This wasn't what we signed up for. It wasn't the dream.

'Leave him to his water,' Tony Moran said, ushering the Sons back. 'Tina, toss him some codeine.'

'I don't do-'

He turned swiftly and looked like he was about to stick the boot in, 'don't what?'

'Thanks Tone,' I said.

'It's Tony to you, bud.'

He went in the back. I took a deep breath, threw my head back and sighed. I saw Anita again, upside down. She mouthed 'are you ok?'

I laughed to myself to mask my fear and embarrassment, got up in pain. I'd done my back in – at least I didn't have to lie. I dusted my clothes off.

How was I ever ok with this town? I'm not saying they were all arseholes. They weren't. I'd had plenty of friends. But I just didn't really fit in. I used to drink to fit in. I wasn't into football and bikes. I wasn't into pool, snooker or darts. I wasn't into casual violence. It was a cattle market really, only I rarely had enough to buy a cow and they rarely looked to this poor bull. And the four of us were the same in our own way. That's why we got on. The pub scene wasn't really who we were but we were born into it, born into the Black Country and now we were gonna fit in, damn it! We were gonna drink real ale, play pub games, ogle wenches and be men. We were gonna moan about immigrants, support the wars, drink to the queen and all that. But it didn't last. I just couldn't do it to myself. No matter how much I thought I wanted it, I was never going to become a son of Halesowen.

I hobbled over to the bar and Tina handed me a blister pack of co-codamols. Ten capsules. Familiar. The idea of taking them seemed very appealing.

'I'll stick that on the tab too,' she said. 'Here's some water.'

'Thanks.'

I could still feel everybody looking at me, but Percy and Jack were nattering about Dancers, the old clothes shop opposite the pub, boarded up, "Renovation Pending". I heard the door and glanced over to see councillor Ray leave. The gaggle of wenches were singing "Dancing Queen" with the jukebox. The panda across the bar was back on his seat, patient, staring at my clearly appealing chops, but the rest of the Sons had returned to their menial talk about whatever it was they wanted to share an opinion on.

'Go on,' she said.

'What?'

'Take them. You can't keep on fighting that pain without taking anything.'

'I will.'

I looked at the foil. Solpadol. An hour or so of some kind of high and then probably a nap. It seemed like bliss.

'Go on.'

I could see the round-faced figure in the background waiting for me to slip up. If I didn't take them, maybe they'd figure out it was all a ruse. Yes, that made sense. I had to take them. I popped the pills out of the packet and looked at them, rattled them. Red and white capsules. Smooth and appealing. Synthetic pain relief, derived from a natural plant. Tina was looking at me, egging me on. She wanted me to relapse. The panda was watching me. I put them in my mouth, but the moment I did it, my dream came back to me, the gloopy Aftershock. I knew it was wrong. I knew why I was taking them, and it wasn't to save myself, to save us, on this crazy nonsensical mission Ally had sent me on. I was taking them to get high. I popped them between my teeth and gums and immediately the plastic, gelatine, whatever it was, sticky, started dissolving in my mouth. I swigged the water back.

'Thanks.'

I made to leave.

'Wait,' Tina called. 'You forgot your nuts.'

I smiled and nodded, the pills making my face feel wider, took the paper bag and shoved it into my pocket and left.

I knew where I needed to go. I needed a friend. I spat the pills into my hand, already powder had started to seep out, but not enough to make me panic.

I'll be fine. I'll be fine. I'm fine.

I casually put them in my pocket, aware they might've been watching, and walked towards the baths. The cobblestones ended and "new" Halesowen, which had been dressed old, turned back into old Halesowen, which looked dated but younger, the same streets I'd traversed for the first 30 years of my life. I was back on the uneven broken slabs of my youth, an ugly mosaic of beige tablets. But it was prettier, it was more real, it spoke of councils and government and people trying to help. A world away from-

'The dumb arsehole who just had me on the floor. Thick prick!' I felt a heavy pang in my chest.

That can't be good. I tried not to think about it.

The steps to the baths were overgrown with tall weeds which had seeped through the cracks to reclaim the earth. I stopped to think on it, taking deep breaths. There was something beautiful about it. It reminded me of my mum, not gone, just deep in the earth, reclaimed by nature. It'll happen to us all.

Pang! There it was again, like I was being jabbed in the chest from within with a porcelain pestle.

Don't think about.

I climbed the steps slowly, breathing heavy. The glass doors were boarded up "Renovation Pending".

The pain started to spread and I knew what was happening.

I slipped in behind one of the boards, which caused the chain of tin cans to come crashing down.

'It's just me,' I panted.

The room started to spin.

'Help! It's me!'

'You… um,' Damien mumbled, dashing over from the changing rooms, his green parka dragged behind him, 'alright, er… um… Tom?'

'What are you doing here?' I asked, breathless, my hands feeling cold and weak. 'Where's Sarah?'

2028

What is he wearing? It was clearly Leroy. Medium build, blond, almost white, hair. He wore a red robe, like a bishop. There was a silver trim around the bottom, and the wrists were frilled. My memory of Leroy was hoodies and band shirts, Iron Maiden when we were kids, before mellowing to Foo Fighters and eventually Snow Patrol in our mid 20s. The most outlandish he'd ever dressed was in his lime green Ben Sherman and black and red bowling shoes phase, when he was all Paul Weller and The Who. Admittedly, it'd been a number of years since I'd seen him, but back then he was in skinny jeans and a black tight shirt, listening to Ed Sheeran and Sam Smith, in what seemed like an early mid-life crisis.

His face was red, white and shiny. He looked younger than us, he could still have been in his late 30s. His voice had a slightly higher pitch than I remembered and was hollow, like he was missing the middle note in his vocal chord. Leroy was always a passionate talker, usually he got like this when he was talking about a sexual conquest. He was always with the "yeahs" and "come ons" and "you knows". When he really got going, he sounded like a scrambler being revved up.

'And that… is when… I found… the Lord Jesus! Yeah!' he said, pacing in the middle of our semi-circle.

'Hallelujah,' Rex declared. One or two others had their hands in the air, surrendering to an invisible gunman.

Leroy closed his eyes. 'Let us pray. Lord,' he said, 'we want to thank you for the food you've put on our tables in the end times. We want to thank you for giving us the strength to keep going while we wait for your…'

It is Leroy, isn't it? He'd told us his name was Lee and there'd been no advance on that, no handshake, no hello. Leroy was one of my oldest friends, I'd known him since primary school, but there'd been no acknowledgment. He'd looked at us and just apologised for being late, before getting on with the gig.

I looked over at Marcus. Mostly he looked down, his balding head red ugly with sun, a Benidorm tan. Occasionally somebody would mumble an "hallelujah" or a "thank you Lord", to which he'd lift his head to see where it was coming from and then briefly glance at

Leroy. Whatever had really gone on between them, it was definitely unfinished business.

Will sat there with a smug look on his face, suggesting he was listening but had formulated an argument more on the money. His sight drifted to Sarah a number of times, and she was nodding along to everything Leroy was saying.

'… and Lord, thank you for giving Sarah the resourcefulness to find items which are sure to help keep the chain strong in the congregation of our little church…'

I knew he was referring to the things Sarah had stolen from mum. I saw her gaze crack when he said it, and she half turned to look in my direction but stopped herself. But I really wasn't bothered. If I'd grown at all in the years of my sobriety, it was in caring less about material things. This was just something I'd had to accept. And my acceptance had brought me to this place. *Perhaps there IS salvation. Maybe I've found a light in this long dark night.*

I'd been seeking the light my whole life, one way or another, but often chose ambition over serenity.

'…Lord, thank you for bringing new members to Lutley Community Church, new people with whom we can share and spread your word…'

He looked over at us. Marcus immediately looked away. Will scoffed. Leroy looked directly at me and smiled, but it was alien and patronising. *Is it Leroy? What am I thinking? Of course it's fucking Leroy.*

"Amens" abounded the room.

'Please stay and have refreshments,' Leroy said. 'There's currently no electricity here, but we have water and some lovely biscuits Barbara made for us.'

Barb was blushing, proud. That was odd, too. My memory of Barbara was not one of domestication, but of alcoholism and flirting, kisses which tried to break the barrier of tepid association, hands breaking promises to Rex. I never went there, of course, she was the same age as mum, but there were dark times in my addiction when she'd nearly broke down my wall. Looking at her now, she seemed older and sweeter. Similarly, Sarah had lost her wild edge, tamed by her service. What was going on?

'I'm out of here,' Marcus said, getting up.

'Wait, let's speak to him,' I said.

'Who? Leroy or "Lee" the fucking cunt vicar?'

'Calm down, batty-boy,' Will smirked. 'It was one shag.'

Now standing, Marcus looked more serious and furious than I think I'd ever seen him. Too angry and upset for quips, he stormed out of the room.

'What did you say that for?' I said.

'Oh, it was one drunken fuck. A mistake, clearly.'

'Obviously it was more than that to him. He came out.'

'You can pussy-foot around it if you want, Tom, but I'm not playing that game. Either he says it how it is, or he has to take the consequences.'

Most of the congregation were standing in small circles talking amongst themselves. Rex called over, 'want a biscuit, boy?'

It occurred to me I hadn't really eaten properly all week. Maureen heated a tin of soup after I buried mum on Tuesday, then Sarah gave me a lump of old cheese and a stale cracker on Friday after I'd fainted. No wonder I'd passed out. I hadn't been looking after myself.

'Yes, please, Rex,' I thumbed, patting my gut – that was still there, but my arms were much thinner.

I stood up.

'Where you going?' Will asked.

'To speak to the "vicar",' I grinned.

'Don't leave me here.' He got up, 'I'll come.'

'No, stay here.'

'Why?'

'Because you'll say something stupid or start a fucking argument.' I could see he was pissed off at me for saying this. 'Go grab a biscuit, better still go ogle Sarah.'

'Ogle?' he smirked. 'I'll go and stare at her tits. There'll be no ogling like a dirty old man.'

'What age do you cross over into dirty old man territory?' I laughed.

'Not yet!'

Rex was wandering towards me, I took a couple of biscuits from an old Celebrations tub. 'So, you listened to me, boy. You came to see a man about a God.'

'Something like that.'

'Surrender, boy,' he said.

'I've been down this road many times, Rex.'

I took a bite of a biscuit. Round and hard with a salty taste.

"'Come to me, all you who are weary and burdened, and I will give you rest,'" Rex preached.

Leroy was standing by the door, lips pursed in a smile which surely subdued some strange truth, listening to the old blind man Will had accused of staring at him.

'*So?*' Rex asked.

'What?' I snapped.

'The biscuits, boy.'

'Sorry, Rex. Thanks. Nice and salty.'

'Salty? Oh, bloody *Barb*!'

I took that as my cue and made for Leroy. He saw me coming and smiled that same alien grin, a pious head-tilt. *What's he playing at?* As I neared, he saw the man out of the room and then turned to face me. He held his hand out.

'You made it,' he said.

'Yep,' I half-smiled, assuming he was referring to the bombs.

'I hope it won't be the last time.'

We shook hands, cold and formal.

'Oh. Sarah asked me to come.'

He started shaking his head and then pointed upwards to remind me it wasn't Sarah, but it was in fact God.

'God?' I asked.

He nodded.

It irritated me, mostly because I was thinking along the same lines. I couldn't help feeling it was meant to be. Mum dying, bumping in Maureen, nearly relapsing, meeting Sarah and now Leroy and the church. 'Could be,' I said, playing along.

He gave a deep sigh: *when will you learn?* The performance was convincing.

'So what's the deal, Leroy?'

'I'm Lee,' he said, a little too quickly.

'You haven't been Lee since we were at primary school.'

He shook his head in confusion.

'Come off it,' I said. 'Stop mucking about.'

He reached for my hand and I flinched. He gave it a little squeeze and I can't pretend it wasn't slightly comforting. Now I was the confused one. I looked across the room to see Will spitting a biscuit out on the floor. There was a bit of a commotion, which Sarah was trying to deal with.

I pulled my hand away. 'What's going on?' I asked him.

'It tells us all about it in revelations.'

'I mean, *you*.'

'Me?'

'You. Lee. Leroy. Lee, if you like.'

'I'm perplexed,' he said – not a Leroy word. 'You keep calling me Leroy. That's not my name.' He looked embarrassed. 'I can see you don't believe me, but it's really not who I am.'

He seemed genuine, but I knew I was standing talking to Leroy. That dry curl in his lip, like he was playing a joke but you were in on it the whole time. That was his charm. That was how he slept with just about every woman we knew – and Marcus.

'Come off it!' I insisted.

'What? Please, you're troubling me now.'

'*Troubling me*? What's wrong with your words?'

He genuinely seemed confused. Maybe it wasn't Leroy. It'd been well over a decade since I'd seen him. But then we couldn't all be mistaken. Marcus, Will and me. *Perhaps he's had some kind of breakdown.*

'You look just like him,' I said, smiling.

He raised his finger in the air like he had an idea, then he smiled that alien smile. 'What's so special about him? This Leroy?' he asked.

This was a strange question, narcissistic, which was characteristic of Leroy. Across the room, Will was now sitting down talking to Sarah, who was rubbing his back to calm him down. Rex was sealing the tub of biscuits and bickering with Barb. The others were talking amongst themselves. Jake "squirrels", gaunt, in his white vest and leather trousers, leaning out the fire door smoking. The young lady with the manic laughter was nibbling on a biscuit, oblivious and alone. They looked like background artists in a film. Nothing seemed real in this mocked-up church in a community centre.

'What's special about Leroy?' I pondered out loud, playing his little game.

'What's he like?'

'A bit of wanker,' I said – Leroy shook his head. 'A real ego problem,' I smirked.

'Now, come on,' he said, like I was being a mischievous school boy.

'He's just an old friend. I used to be in a band with him.'

'Making music, yes. Harmonising. You miss him,' he told me.

'Not really. I mean, I think about him from time to time.'

'Does that sound like somebody else?'

So, that's your tack. Bring it back to God – always be closing. 'I've done this stuff before,' I said.

'Stuff?'

I'd offended him.

'Please, don't take me wrong. I was in AA. I hear you were in-'

'This is really not the same thing.'

'It really is. We have a spiritual program. It's pretty much identical.'

'It's not!' It was loud. Everybody in the room stopped talking.

'It seems pretty similar to me,' I tried to impress.

'Jesus is the way!' he yelled, prodding me in the chest.

Again, the room silenced, a 'pahaha' from across the room – *the bastard*.

'Ok, ok,' I tempered, embarrassed. 'It's not all Jesus in AA. It can be Jehovah, Allah, Buddha. A higher power. The group, a group of drunks even – g, o, d – but you know all this.'

'Exactly. I know all this. This,' he held his hands out like he was doing the sermon on the mount, 'is not AA. This is the Way.'

'Really?' I looked around. 'Lutley Community Centre? Where we used to play hopscotch? Where we pretended to be the Turtles? Where you clothes-lined me wearing your pink Ultimate Warrior T-Shirt on mufti-day?'

He looked at me, disappointed. I could feel the wall of denial, the trait of an addict. 'Ok, Lee,' I conceded.

He was still wearing the same sickly grin, like we didn't know each other, pitying me. I went to walk off and he grabbed my hand, studying my bandaged arm.

'It's nothing,' I said.

'No,' he smiled.

I remembered the knot digging into my flesh. "If ever there was a sign?" I'd asked myself.

Leroy, the fucker, was in my head. Or God, at any rate.

I wasn't just an ordinary alcoholic, addict, however you want to term it. Most of us would think that about ourselves, of course, but I always refused to be somebody who just drank and took drugs. There were people who did that, just drank and used, by any means, occasionally sleeping and eating, with little ambition beyond it. I always had other ambitions, it never went away, just dampened a little.

We walked back to mum's. I hopped over the little brook, felt it in my arm when I landed. I made my way across the field, which was oddly trimmed. In a new land where gardens and parks were left to grow messy and wild, someone had gone to the effort to cut the grass of this huge field. Perhaps it was someone at the church.

Will and Sarah were ahead of me, laughing away about something, as if all was fine and normal with the world. I felt sombre, lost in my thoughts, forced to think about the dank rooms in musty churches where I'd espoused my daily woes to fellow addicts, of all shapes and sizes. Fat and thin, warm and cold, fearful and brave. We'd lived life all sorts of ways, successes and failures, rich and poor, criminals and pillars of society.

There were the functioning addicts. They'd go to work, conform. Some would try to maintain a happy front, some wouldn't bother, wearing misery and anger on their sleeves. But despite their blighted dopamine receptors, despite the void, despite the incessant need to get out of their head any which way and as often as they could, they functioned. Will was a functioning addict. I never managed to function in this way because the intoxication inspired a morose existentialism.

There were also the creatives, and this is where I'd decided to lay my bag. And it was true, I was a writer, and there was our old band, and we used to sit on William Shenstone's grave talking all serious about art until four in the morning. I pasted my kitchen walls with posters of great musicians, great artists and yellowing pages torn from an old Palgrave's Golden Treasury of English Poetry. To be an addict went hand in hand with being an artist and this kept me drinking for years. But above all, that tragic artist was just a persona which facilitated my addiction.

'Pahahaha,' went Will in the distance.

Sarah punched him in the arm. *Who is this girl?* One minute she was an angry fuck-up, the next she was doting over the mad preacher, and then it was all fun and games with Will.

We walked through the back roads, once again the untidy gardens, caged fronts, barely a car in sight. The scratch of gravel beneath my feet, the echo of their chatter in the distance. The sun was big and midday hot, and this was making me irritable.

Leroy was wearing a strange persona. His service consisted of an hour-long testimony about how he'd found Jesus. But I didn't know any of this story. How he'd lived in Alabama, where he'd stumbled into God in a bar, whilst swigging Wild Turkey to within an inch of his liver. Then there was the school where he'd worked, in Nigeria, as a missionary. He'd known hardships, the noises of the Nigerian nights, the violence, the animals – the "unforgiving land", he'd dramatically called it. There was no mention of the drugs, the past women, wild sex, the STIs, or the way he'd treated people to get what he wanted.

He went on about how he could still hit the wine a "little too hard", and how he asked Jesus to forgive him for this on a regular basis. What about the lines of coke we used to snort off his snare drum? Leroy was a weird fucker in the first place. Now he was just gone. But this was what addicts were like. Step into the rooms of AA for long enough and you meet some real strange people, people who've become who they are, or are trying to. People are strange when they let themselves become who they really are.

I was a strange alcoholic too. I knew this about myself. Bits of Morocco, bits of Nepal, the mountains, the books, the music, the sadness of grief and the stubbornness of sobriety. That was who I was, that was what I'd become.

When I looked at Lee, I still saw Leroy, but he was adamant he was Lee. Was this who he actually was? A preacher, a missionary, a drinker begging for forgiveness?

I tried to catch them up down an alleyway. We came onto Long Mynd and then back round to Purbeck.

'Am I the only one?' I asked them.

'What do you mean?' Will said, sounding surprisingly sober and sensible.

'Leroy.'

'Leave it, man,' he said, side-glancing towards Sarah.

'You didn't have to come,' she said.

I looked to Will, he just stared at me.

'I'm glad I did. I'm glad I witnessed for myself the absolute madness of my old friend.'

'You don't know him,' she insisted, sick of this conversation.

'Sarah, I've known him since I was a kid.'

Will smiled at her and then turned to me, 'it's not the same guy, is it.'

'Are you for real?' I put the key in the garage. 'Do you mean that literally?'

'Oh, come on, Tom, the world's changed.'

'Yes, I know. I know it fucking has.'

'You need to get with it,' Sarah said.

I was gobsmacked. I stood there shaking my head thinking about this stupid girl and her ridiculous boyfriend, scuttling around the estate, and her strange church, and my dead mum, and poor Maureen. 'Fuck off, Sarah. Just fuck off.'

I could hear the sound of banging and something being smashed. I jumped out of bed and ran downstairs.

'What the fuck you playing at?'

'Bastard-cunting-bollocks-bombs-it-doesn't-even-work-like-that!'

Will had the kettle in one hand and was using it to smash the radio, on the floor, in the middle of the living room.

'I think you've done it,' I said.

He looked up at me, then down to the little DAB radio that blarted out Elaine Page on Sundays, mum humming along to Phantom of the Opera. It was now just shards of black plastic, a broken speaker and wires. He burst out laughing. It wasn't normal-for-Will laughter, but high-pitched and hysterical. He looked at me again, giggling, dribbling, wiped a bubble of snot from his nose.

'Why?' I asked.

'Because.'

I walked around him into the kitchen. Kettle smashed, I took a saucepan and filled it with a little water, turned on the hob. 'Any sign of him yet?' I called through.

'Fuck him.'

I rang Loz. When he answered, in the background I could hear an argument between Jenny and one of the kids. 'You'll find another boyfriend,' Jenny shouted.

'You will,' I said.

'I hope so,' deadpan.

'Have you seen Marcus?'

'Funny, ain't ya.'

'No, seriously. Bit of a mad un yesterday. We bumped into Leroy.'

'Leroy? No way!'

'Long story short, now Marcus has disappeared.'

'Probably just with Will.'

'Will's here.'

'*Leroy*?'

'I seriously doubt it.'

Will walked into the kitchen carrying the kettle. 'Is that Loz?' He plugged it in. The light didn't come on.

'Yeah.'

Will spotted the water on the hob and he grabbed the coffee. 'Tell him to bring beer.'

'What happened?' Loz asked.

'Will says bring beer.'

'I can't.'

In the background I heard his daughter scream, 'I'm an adult!'

'Sounds like she's staying,' I said.

'She's not! I'll be there in an hour.'

'Come up ya fanny!' Will shouted.

'He's on his way,' I said, putting my phone in my pocket.

Will poured the steaming water into the mugs and handed me one. He looked disturbed. I wondered if it was because I'd sent Sarah home.

'Thanks for that,' I said, pointing at the broken kettle.

'Fucking radio. They were talking a load of shite,' he said. 'China wouldn't bomb London. How is it even possible? Russia?' he asked himself. 'Maybe.'

Here we go.

'Russia dropped the biggest bomb known to man,' he continued, 'and the radius of the blast was half that of the London bomb – "apparently",' he did the inverted commas.

'When was that?'

'Of course, I know, there's bigger bombs, Tom,' he said, like I was calling him out. I wasn't. I didn't have a clue. 'And I know the '61 Tsar Bomba was only released at half capacity, everybody knows that.'

I didn't.

'And now there's warheads with twice the yield, at least 250 megatons, theoretically – thing of fiction if you ask me – but this brings me back to the point.'

I sipped the coffee, enjoyed the scalding, warming my gullet. It made me feel hungry. *Food*. That's what I needed. I started eyeing up the cupboards, whilst still trying to give Will the time of day. 'Go on.'

'80 miles,' they said.

'55.'

'Just as ridiculous, but my point is the first figure they plumped for was 80 miles. Even the mythical 400 megaton China claims to have built wouldn't stretch that far.'

'Yes,' I said, watching him, but edging towards the cupboard.

'And how would they get it here? A sub? Airspace? Wouldn't we pick up on it? An ICBM? And it wouldn't be one bomb. They'd triangulate,' by now animated and cocksure, which was irritating me.

'I've gotta eat something-'

'And why would they nuke London? *Nuke?*'

I was listening, but I didn't really want to hear it. I opened the cupboard and rummaged for something easy. It was all tins. There had to be a biscuit!

'Why didn't we nuke them back?' he asked.

'Because they took out our control centre,' I mumbled, lifting up a tin of mushy peas.

'*The control centre?*' He burst out laughing. 'And that's why I smashed the radio. Why haven't the States bombed them then? Europe? Why haven't we nuked them back?'

'Oh, I don't know. Because they'd blow the rest of us up.' Tinned pineapples. I hated pineapples.

He laughed and slammed the cupboard door shut, which angered me to the point of making fists. 'Why?' he asked. 'We're nothing now, just a bunch of plebs bombed back to the dark ages. Pleb Britain. Don't be so stupid.'

'Don't call me stupid!'

'Oh, don't be a dick.'

'Because you know it all, don't you, Will?' I snapped.

'Yes,' he said, smug.

'I saw it first-hand. The second bomb. *Bomb*, singular. I watched it hit Burnham. I saw the fucking cloud. You would've been stuck in your own little cloud, smoking weed, reading articles written by other people smoking weed. Who's the fucking idiot?'

He just looked at me and sighed. I'd pissed him off, but he knew not to go there. He understood what was going on. We'd had nearly a year of this, a year of this strange reality. A year of loss. And now mum.

Will had a sip of his coffee and looked into the garden. His willingness to not say anything moved me.

'I'm sorry. I… I just want a cracker,' I said, tingling with emotion. 'That's all. Or a measly fucking biscuit.' I stifled a tear, but the room was thick with it, an underwater silence. I could feel my heart beating in my chest. I tried to sip my coffee but my hand was trembling, so I put the cup down, embarrassed.

'This,' Will started, breaking the quiet, 'is a great start to the day. I smash the radio and the kettle, and you break down over a shortage of crackers. All we need now is Marcus to come back and tell us he's gay… Again.'

I tried to laugh. I looked out of the window at mum's grave. I was glad she was gone. This was no world. I missed her already, but not as much as I missed… I still couldn't even say her name.

'Was it because of Sarah?' I asked.

He looked taken aback. 'What?'

'The radio. Because I sent her packing?'

'No, you silly twat. Chinese radicals could be responsible maybe, but not the Chinese government. It doesn't-'

'Alright,' I butted in.

I could see he was itching to continue with his tirade about the situation and the misinformation in the media, looking to the ceiling, nodding, agreeing with himself. But then he looked at me and I watched the subject leave him. His expression changed to a warm smile. 'Is this another Tammy?' he asked.

'I don't see her like… I mean, she's fit, but she's like 20.'

'So was Tammy.'

'Yeah, but so were we.'

He shrugged.

———————

I woke up thinking about Sarah.

Leroy and Sarah, was that a thing? If that was ever a thing, Will and Sarah was a possibility. They seemed to be getting on really well. And, if it was a possibility with Will, even I stood a chance. He was better looking than me, physically stronger, but I was more sane by a long shot. And Sarah was becoming more sane, wasn't she? Isn't that what she was trying to do? *And I bet she'd be great-*

'What are you on about, Tom?' I was shaking my head in disgust, but I was also lying naked on my bed, visibly aroused. 'You're an animal, you're 50 for God's sake.'

I recalled what Rex had said about how humans *are* animals. 'I have no control over this stuff,' I said to my erection.

I listened to the birds outside. Crows, pigeons – *is that a nightingale?* Chirping of small finches and a woodpecker tapping. The trees, the skies, were filling up. Nature restoring itself. It was like the big bushy lime trees cracking the pavement by Picks, destined to be there long after the pub had turned to dust. Soon this whole estate would be abandoned to trees, weeds and wild grasses, with no one left to do anything about it. But did we need to do anything about it? I thought about the big field behind the community centre, neatly trimmed. *We just can't leave things alone, can we?* 'But then we *are* nature,' I reminded myself. 'Animals!' I looked down at my diminishing cock. An animal cut the lawn with an animal-made lawnmower. An animal built these houses and the bombs that caused so many of us to abandon them. Was that just nature restoring a semblance of balance?

Outside, in the distance, I heard the sound of rumbling. I figured it must be the binmen. Mum's house was filling up with empty tins, bottles and food wrappers, not to mention broken gadgets, but I couldn't be bothered to move.

Then on a tannoy, 'three days to the last bus, three days to the last bus. No water, no electricity, no full English on a Sunday morning. Three days to the last bus.'

I got out of bed and went to the window.

'Three days to the last bus. No binmen, no mobile phones, no happy face emojis. Three days to the last bus.'

I couldn't see the truck at first, but eventually it drove past Purbeck Close. It was the binmen, but they were also acting as a government announcement. I didn't hear them stop anywhere to pick up rubbish, but then who was likely to check up on them?

'Three days to the last bus. No television, no sanitation, no Toilet Duck. Three days to the last bus.'

There had never been anything like this before. We'd had captions scrolling government plans across the bottom of the three TV stations we could still tune into, Dave+1, BBC Gold and Channel 32, the Chinese shopping channel which resembled soft core porn at certain times of the day – or maybe that was me. The buses were to take us to half-way houses in Derby, Manchester and Newcastle, but resettlement could happen anywhere between Derby and the Shetlands, Northern Ireland and Skegness – I can't pretend the idea of being shipped off to the Shetland Islands wasn't appealing, but it was obviously highly unlikely too.

'Three days to the last bus. No Friends re-runs, no Celebrity X-Factor, no watching footie down the pub. Three days to the last bus.'

They must've been making it up as they were going along. Whose idea was this?

'Three days to the last bus. No food, no loo roll… Three days…'

As it moved further away, the tannoy faded out to mumbles, which were more than likely echoes in my mind: *three days to the last bus, six toes and three eyes, Halesowen left to fester in the nuclear winds.*

They were compelling arguments and, if I could've been bothered, I'd have tried to follow them to see what else they came up with to persuade all the hangers-on. The elderly, too old and stubborn to leave – perhaps Maureen was in this category. The infirm and the mentally ill, too unwell or depressed to leave. The addicts, a danger to themselves and everybody else – where were they even getting their gear? There was also the community church congregation, but perhaps it was made up of the old and the sick.

What would it take to persuade these people to leave?

I went downstairs. The living room was an assault course of booze cans and bottles, a dusting of ash and nub-ends, a sticky stain on the rug. Mum would've had a fit. I noticed the picture of the dogs playing pool was at funny angle. I straightened it.

Late last night, a bottle of gin sunk, Loz and Will had gone off in search of Marcus. In vino, "persuaded" by Will, Loz had decided he was going to stay in Halesowen. And, if he was going to stay, there was no way he was letting Marcus leave. "Fuck Jenny and the kids," he said, but it was undoubtedly the juniper vapours – and apparently an ongoing argument about leaving his electric train set behind. I offered no opinion.

In the kitchen, the kettle was in bits where Loz had decided he knew how to fix it. I tidied up and made myself a cup of coffee with the saucepan.

'Why do they care?' I asked.

Maureen had been to see her friend on Hambleton Road and on the way back had stopped by to see me. We were stood in the kitchen drinking lemon and ginger tea.

'Unity. They don't want the country even more divided.'

'Really?'

'Don't look at me like that,' she said. 'If you want to talk conspiracies you've let the wrong person into your house.'

She looked old. She seemed old when I was at primary school, but everyone seems old at that age. Her face was gridded with lines above and below her lip, which told of a teacher's snipes, the constant correcting. Her eyes showed signs of laughter, but she was clearly tired.

'You should go,' I said.

She looked a bit taken aback.

'I mean, take the bus,' I laughed.

She smiled. 'So should you.'

I tried to imagine a future in Halesowen. Perhaps we'd find a big detached house somewhere close to town – or two big semi-detacheds with a door knocked out in the middle. I could do the same for Sarah and Maureen. We'd need to find somewhere with solar panels, or else remove them from somewhere else. I'm sure we could figure it out – I made a mental note to Google it whilst we still could. The town would inevitably need somebody to run it. *Maybe that would be me, once I get over...* I stopped myself thinking about her. *One thing's for sure, I'll be sober, and Sarah will be sober too, I'm certain. Maybe even Will. Hell, if it helps, he can have Sarah, if she wants him.*

What are you bloody on about?

'On weekends, when she was little,' Maureen said – I had the sudden fear I'd said that stuff out loud – 'she used to go downstairs and make me Marmite on toast and a cup of tea, and she'd bring me breakfast in bed with the Guardian. The tea was vile, the Marmite was too thick, but I'd finish it when doing the crossword – or sometimes pretending to, because she expected it of me.'

I laughed, inwardly cursing myself for my thoughts. 'Where's her mum?'

'Claire? She didn't tell you?'

I shook my head.

'Sarah found her.'

Maureen's eyes told the story. 'Drugs?'

'No, never,' she said, offended. 'It was ever since my son Robbie died-'

'Your son? The one in the army?' I smiled, sympathetically.

'My only child, yes,' she nodded. 'I know, Tom. I was scared when you came to the house.'

'I remember. Your son died in Afghanistan?'

'Sarah was just a baby. Claire was never right after that. She even had a spell in the mental hospital in Dudley.'

'Busheyfields. I detoxed there a few times.'

'It wasn't drugs,' she insisted. 'Depression. We kept it from Sarah, but one day she came home from primary school and found her mum in the garage.'

'That's so sad. Her mum and her dad. Your son.' I didn't know what to say. 'He was a war hero,' came out of my mouth, trying to be nice.

'Come off it,' she immediately dismissed.

'What?'

'Tom,' she rolled her eyes. 'It's just a way to earn a living. A nurse, a teacher, in the army, whatever. Pick a career and fall in line. Robbie chose just about the daftest, but then he was never going to university.'

I was surprised. 'But he… died fighting for us.'

'No, he died getting paid to do a job. The same as nurses have died, teachers have died – I'm glad I retired when I did, the last decade's been worse than ever. All kept in our place, on the right amount of money, as little as possible without starting a revolution. That's the job of government.'

'I thought you weren't one for conspiracies,' I smiled.

'Tom,' she said, in a way which made me feel like I was back at school. 'People are people.'

I was expecting her to say something else but she stopped and looked out in the garden at mum's patch. Unsure what she meant, I added, trying to be philosophical, 'people are animals.'

She turned to face me, 'Sarah?'

'No-no, I mean, we're animals really.'

'Animals?' she asked, unsure what I meant.

'I mean, all of us are,' I stumbled. 'Like nature.' I felt like I was lying, spouting Rex's philosophy to be clever. I stopped. Took a deep breath. 'What do you mean, people are people?'

'We're all just amateurs trying to do a job, born at the level we're born at. High up, low down or in the middle. I've never stopped feeling like an amateur, no matter how old, especially when I was at school. Some days I knew my experience helped, but things changed all the time and then you're right back where you started. The government are the same, the people telling us to leave.'

'A right bunch of amateurs,' I laughed.

'And so are the people who tell the government what to do, the civil servants or whoever else has a say.'

'The illuminati,' I smiled, thinking of Will.

'Who? We all are. As parents, friends, bosses and employees. And in all those roles, eventually we rotate out. Such is life.'

I wasn't fully sure what she was trying to say, but it sounded wise, or maybe it was just grief, her way of dealing with things. She'd lost her son, her daughter-in-law and, as far as she was concerned, her granddaughter.

She put her cup in the sink and turned the tap on.

'I'll do it,' I said, turning the tap off.

She went into the living room to get her coat, a long purple mac, overkill in this sunny weather. She stopped and pointed at a rug I'd bought mum from Morocco. 'A stain,' she said.

'I tried to get it out. Mum would never forgive me,' I laughed.

'You tried,' she said, her hand on my arm.

She seemed sad. When she left I had the feeling that I was never going to see her again.

I spent the rest of the day pottering around the house. My house. How different it all should've been. In any other time, this house would've been legally left to me. Now it was just going to be left abandoned. Who owned it? Mum wasn't even legally dead. If Halesowen was ever officially deemed safe again, could I stake a claim to my house? Would we have to dig her up to prove she was dead? And if we did dig her up would I be arrested for not going about things properly? We still had a government, there was still a channel and presumably some way of dealing with this stuff, a crematorium perhaps. There just wasn't actually anybody here to enforce anything.

I sat looking out of the window. Aside from the caged fronts and bits of furniture and rubbish on scruffy lawns, it still had the potential to be a place for families to lead good lives, perhaps better lives than before. Down the road I could see old Arthur loading black bags onto his drive. He was the only other person still living on Purbeck. He must've been about mum's age. I'd never spoken to the guy. I didn't even know his name, I just called him Arthur because he looked like an old Arthur type of guy. *Who will look after him when he can't look after himself?*

'Stop it, Tom!'

I knew what I was doing. There was a part of me that saw this as an opportunity, like finally I could be somebody, a town hero. Someone to look out for old Arthur, to protect Maureen and her friend. Was that why I'd wanted to help Sarah? To be a hero? But then, really, Sarah was helping me, and I knew not everyone understood that, least of all Sarah. I never understood it myself when my AA sponsor said it to me. It was something I learnt over time.

But it was one thing one addict helping another, but taking on the town was just a barm-pot idea, an ego-trip.

'You can't even look after yourself, Tom'

I'd spent the day watching re-runs of Big Break on BBC Gold, thinking back on a time when Jim Davidson was not only an acceptable entertainer but a loved one – I guessed he was another celeb who went with the bomb, or had he already gone with the viruses? I'd eaten a freezer-burned lamb curry which I'd had to break free from an ice-shelf. I'd managed to read a few pages from Ian Rankin's Valley of Blues, one of mum's books – the one where Rebus dies. After that, I'd had a hell of a battle retrieving photos from the loft. When I went to climb down I managed to kick the ladder over. I had to hang down and drop, praying I wouldn't break my ankle on the bloody ladder.

And now, in the back of my mind, I had a delusion of grandeur about building a utopia in a nuclear wasteland. I used to think like this when I was drunk. I'd read a page or two of Marx, something about Lenin visiting the miners in Wales, or just about any Orwell book, and then I'd wander around the town telling everyone about it like I knew. Then I'd have Ross North, a vitriolic socialist, his big hand dwarfing his pint of Banks's bitter, telling me to stand for Labour at the next election. "Some day I will," I'd say, and I believed me.

I sat in mum's chair and switched on the TV. I had a choice of Electric Gear, Laura Kuenssberg's car show on Dave+1, or Mrs Brown's Boys on BBC Gold. I searched through mum's saved films and drifted off to Oh Mandy, the Barry Manilow musical, telling myself this was all I needed in life, my house, solar power, a quiet life with books and films.

My peaceful sleep was broken by the sound of the garage door being forced open. People were making their way in. Dark outside, it must've been the early hours. My heart thudding, I panicked and picked up the nearest weapon, a fork from the curry tray.

'Pull it out, pull it out,' Loz was screaming.

'I'm sorry man, I didn't know. You can't just come barging in and expect me to do nothing,' I said.

Loz had both hands on the counter and was looking at the fork hanging out of his upper arm, like it was some animal biting him. 'Pull it out!'

'Calm down,' Will said. 'How are you going to cope in the years to come?'

'Shut the fuck up!'

Will pulled the fork out and Loz yelped, a small bubble of blood seeping through his lumberjack shirt.

'Did it hurt?' I asked.

'No,' deadpan.

'I'm really sorry, the light was off–'

'Why was the goddam light off?' he yelled.

'Because I didn't want them to know I was in.'

Will laughed.

I took a loose plaster from the cutlery drawer – mum had been gone less than a week and already there were plasters in the cutlery drawer.

'You silly twat,' Will said. 'Who did you think we were? We've got the fucking key?'

'It sounded like you were breaking in.'

Loz took his shirt off, but couldn't look at it. 'Is it bad?'

'Nah,' I said, putting the plaster on it.

'He was turning the key the wrong way,' Will said, 'and trying to force it.'

I paused, looked at Will, then to Loz, 'your own bloody fault then.'

'Fuck you man!' He pulled his shirt back on. 'This is why I'm going. I'm not going to stay and put up with all of you taking the piss out of me and sticking fucking forks in me and making me drink and take drugs all the fucking time!'

Will bit his lip, but then we both burst out laughing. 'Who's making you take drugs?' I asked.

'Not you.'

'I haven't made you take drugs,' Will said.

'You tried to get me to go to Jay's and I don't want to take drugs. That's why I'm leaving.'

'So, you are going?' I asked, nodding. 'Makes sense.'

Will was shaking his head, 'that's not why he's going.'

'Oh, cos you know, don't you, Will,' he said. 'You're so fucking clever!'

'Yes,' he responded, opening the fridge. 'You're just scared of her. You don't even want to be with her.'

'I love her.'

'You were trying to fuck Stacey the other day!'

'Six-Kids?' I asked.

'Yeah.' Will opened a can of Carlsberg.

'I was drunk! Everyone's leaving. My mum and dad have already left. What about my kids?'

'They're all grown up.'

'That's not how it works,' Loz said. 'Is it, Tom?'

'Don't,' I said.

'Sorry.'

'They're adults!' Will shouted.

'That doesn't matter,' I said, starting to feel irritated by Will's arrogance.

'Don't you chip in,' he defended. 'You're both scared. Loz, you're scared of the truth, and Tom, you're scared of imaginary burglars. What about when they're for real?' he asked, angry, banging the work surface.

'I'll stab them with a fucking fork!' I yelled, banging it back in response.

'What's that gonna do?'

We heard the garage door start to lift. Will grabbed my arm in abject terror. Loz inexplicably at the top his voice yelled out, 'mum!' but we were too scared to laugh, and I reached for his hand to try to squeeze him straight.

'Knife,' I whisper-shouted, my back against the fridge, blindly grabbing for the cutlery drawer.

Loz pulled out a butter knife, Will reached for the bread knife and I grabbed the fork. There we stood, in silence, listening to somebody make their way through the garage, brandishing three pathetic weapons from the cutlery drawer. Why didn't we grab a carving knife?

'What are we gonna do?' I whispered.

'Fucking stab them?' Will shrugged.

The door opened. 'Tom,' she said.

'Bloody hell,' I sighed.

I heard the sound of the butter knife hit the floor. Loz tugged on his hair, like he was anchoring himself to a riverside, shaking his head to make sure he'd got a solid grip.

'It's Sarah,' I said.

'I can't. I can't,' he mouthed. 'I can't take it anymore.' He was close to tears, his cheeks trembling. He took his glasses off. 'This is madness,' he squeaked. 'The world. It's.' He ran out of the kitchen, the sound of heavy feet running up the stairs.

I looked to Sarah. 'He's struggling-'

'There's no time,' she said. 'I need your help.'

She had a small holdall with her like she was ready to move in. She rifled through it and pulled out a plastic bag, from which she removed a small pistol.

―――――――

It was a warm night, purple, the orange shapes of houses in the light of the street lamps. If I could turn the volume down, I might still remember those gentle evenings stumbling home as a drunken teenager, but the 'yow'm gonna fuckin' av it', as we neared Doran Close, was abrasive and frightening. More so because we had a gun. All my ideas of a paradise in the Squirrels were swiftly disappearing in the reality of life on this doomed estate.

Somebody yelled, 'we'll ram a crucifix up ya arse.'

'He's gonna get it for that,' Sarah said, marching down Portsdown Road.

Will was marching alongside her, determined to prove himself.

'What are we supposed to do?' I pleaded, trying to keep up with them.

'Use the gun,' Will said.

He was acting like he had no fear at all, but he'd dug his nails so hard into my bad arm when Sarah entered the garage, I was bleeding.

'We can't use a gun,' I said. 'Have you ever used a gun?'

'You know I have.'

'Shooting each other in the arse with a gat gun doesn't count!'

'Same principle.'

'Exactly,' Sarah said, wielding a hatchet.

'I feel like I'm in a fucking comic book!'

Then my mind drifted to the TV series idea. I saw Sarah's character with her axe, and Will, the hero, with his gun. *Why did she give him the gun?* I'd been relegated to a side character, carrying a bloody cricket bat, English-Tom. I was sure to go early on in this farce. Maybe I'd make the second season, but sooner or later I'd be done for, knifed by an addict or taken out by the mad preacher because I was the only one who'd seen through him. *And here we are helping the bastard. Perhaps this is where it ends. The first episode. Will and Sarah can expect to go on for much longer. Together, in the Addict Wars. But who's gonna write it?*

'Fucking stop it,' I told myself.

'Tom, we're doing this,' Will said.

'Just wait,' I said.

They stopped. There was the sound of breaking glass in the distance and more shouting.

'Look Tom,' Sarah said, 'this is partly your fault.'

'Don't you go there,' I said.

But she was right, in a roundabout way. Jimmy, his name was. The little rodent I'd chased off the first time I set eyes on her. Our little friendship had caused a rebellion in the rat ranks and now Jimmy wanted everything back he'd stolen for the church. Leroy was holding them off with a gun apparently, but Sarah said he would never shoot anyone. She was probably right, but then desperate times and all that. I certainly doubted God would stand too firmly in his way, but how was I to know?

'How many?' I asked.

'Four, I told you.'

'Ok, so three against four.'

'Bloody Loz,' Will moaned.

'It's his family.'

'I've got family, too,' he whined.

'Do you wanna go find your mum and dad?'

'No.'

'Exactly.'

'But it's not the-'

'Stop it,' Sarah shouted.

'There's only three of us against four,' I reasoned.

'And Lee,' she said.

'It'll be fine,' Will stated.

'Fuck you, Will, now's not the time for bravado. We need to use our heads.'

'Now's exactly the time for bravado,' he said. 'It's how we won the wars.'

'*How we won the*?' incredulous. 'And how we got bombed,' I said.

'You don't know what you're talking about. The UK lost its balls decades ago. It was only a matter of time.'

'Come off it, what's that got to do with-'

'For God's sake, stop it!' Sarah demanded, grabbing our hands. 'Will, hold the gun like you own it. Shoot if you have to. Tom, hold the bat firm.'

'Don't you worry. I'll hit a fucking six if anyone comes near and be sure to bloody run.'

'Good.'

She led the way down to the corner of Doran Close. Will looked over to me and nodded in appreciation. 'Remind you of anyone?' he whispered.

It'd been a long time since I'd really thought about Tammy, but he'd never really got over her. Sarah was a little like her. Tough, boisterous, a leader. Tammy had been a classic ladette and used to front an 80s cover band way before the 80s was cool again. The last I heard she was married with grown up children, living in Perry Barr. She was a taboo subject, unless Will brought her up himself.

We turned the corner. There were the four men. A small one, a fat one, a tall one and one with a small head and a beanie hat with ears which made him look like a rabbit. A rat and a rabbit. They were volleying abuse at Leroy, from the middle of the road, I felt my stomach roll over – was it the lamb curry?

'We've tried to be reasonable,' the little one said – that was Jimmy the rat.

'You broke my windows,' Leroy shouted, aiming a rifle at them from the bedroom of the semi-detached.

'I'll break ya neck,' the chubby one jibed.

I turned helplessly to Will, who was trembling. The gun in his hand looked heavy and he was slowly lifting it, like it weighed ten kilos. The bat in my hand was welded tight, tendons aching.

Sarah raised her axe. I wanted to say something, to stop it, this seemed like madness. 'Boys,' she yelled, waving the weapon.

Fuck.

All four of them looked to us, but then a gun suddenly fired from the house and tarmac went up. Everybody panicked and covered their faces. I turned to Will, but he was legging it around the corner. One of their guys, the rabbit, had the same idea and was hopping off in the opposite direction – which was a dead end.

'Baz!' someone shouted, but he'd disappeared into a bush.

'Sorry about that,' Leroy said, 'but next time it'll be your skull, Jimmy.'

'Lee,' Sarah shouted, 'aim higher.'

'Very fucking Christian!' the rat spat.

I was paralysed with fear, still holding my bat in the air from when I'd tried to cover my face with my arms. I felt like a child pretending to be He-Man. It was a wholly impractical stance and I looked daft, but I was frozen. I couldn't even shout after Will, who'd legged it with the only sensible weapon. I felt like I was going to throw up. I would've run with him if I could move, and fuck Leroy, or Lee – *who is he to us now?*

I looked over at him. He was half naked, the rifle pointed in the general direction of the three remaining men.

'You're gonna fucking av it, now,' Jimmy the rat shouted. 'Remember, yow hurt me and Baz's dad'll av yuh. I just want the stuff. Yow've got one last chance.'

The fat one, a guinea pig, podgy and neckless, threw a rock which smashed another window. I heard a scream from inside.

'Who's in there?' I asked Sarah.

'Put your fucking bat down,' she said.

I moved it down, ready to bat – I was never any good at sports. 'I heard somebody scream.'

'It was just the echo from the glass.'

'I don't want to kill you,' Leroy said.

'Just shoot them, Lee,' Sarah shouted.

'You're a little bitch traitor,' the rat said.

'Rapist!' I yelled – it just came out.

'Yuh fucking what?' the rat demanded.

'Called yow a rapist,' the guinea pig said as if the rat hadn't heard.

We were about 50 feet away from them, but now they started slowly walking towards us down the middle of the road. *You idiot, Tom.*

'That's right,' Sarah said. 'Come closer. I've got an axe.'

'I've… I've…' *be brave,* 'got a bat.' I sounded more English than I'd ever sounded in my life. 'And I know how to use it.'

The rat laughed, the guinea pig grunted and behind them there was a tall one, a meerkat, 'we… er… we getting them or… er the vicar?' he asked.

'All of 'em,' the rat said to the meerkat, and then he pulled out a knife.

I looked behind us. *Where's Will?*

'What's all this about?' I asked, again English, all claim I had to being born and bred in the Black Country had left me.

'Sooo, is this your mate Tommy? What was it he said, "I'm not the feds",' he laughed. 'I don't care if yow'm the bloody police.'

Be like Tony Dale. I took a deep breath and steadied myself. 'You want this off your face, come a little closer.' I lost an octave and sounded surprisingly convincing.

'I… ay scared of… yow,' he shouted back. But he clearly wasn't sure about it.

'Fucking av him, Jim,' the guinea pig said.

They were moving more slowly than before.

'Go for it. I'm just waiting,' Sarah said.

The rat stopped, turned to the guinea pig, the meerkat peered over their heads at us. Jimmy was muttering something, and then he spoke, arms open: 'what is the point in all this?'

He sounded entirely reasonable. I had no doubt he was scared, but so was I. I didn't want to get anywhere near that knife. The meerkat backed off, leaving just the guinea pig and the rat.

'Listen Tom, mate, I've got no problem with you. I doh really know ya. *She's* a bitch, but I can let that shit go. All we want is the stuff we nicked and gave to the church.'

'Ok,' I said. 'That doesn't sound too-'

'No way,' Sarah said. 'You'll have this axe before you take that stuff.'

'Sarah,' I reasoned.

'No, Tom.'

'Give it up Leroy, it's just stuff,' I shouted up.

'Lee,' he yelled from his window – like now was the fucking time.

'Whoever you are, just give it up.'

'Coward,' Sarah cursed.

'It's just things. Material stuff. We can get more.'

'It's your mum's stuff too,' she argued.

'I don't care. If I cared about that I wouldn't be here with you now.'

'These things,' Leroy cocked his rifle, 'are used to help those who really damn well need it.' He was leaning out of the window, his hairless chest on show, a naked chest I'd seen so many times paraded around the flats in drunken summers, or on the Magaluf holidays when we were teenagers, or in the swimming baths when we were just kids, the same bare chest with slightly bigger moobs. 'We have to help the weak links to make the-'

In the terror and confusion of it all, we hadn't noticed but the meerkat was nearing Leroy's front door.

'Now,' a disembodied voice shouted.

The rat and the guinea pig came quickly towards us, my mouth dried up, my heart sped up, and I held the bat ready to knock the rat for six. Sarah started to move towards the guinea pig who also pulled out a knife.

'Sarah,' I panicked.

BANG. The shot echoed throughout the estate and the meerkat yelled out, 'Baz!'

All of us turned to see what had happened.

On the front door step, the rabbit lay still. His friend looked down at him and up at us, fighting with his conscience. He decided against helping him and legged it over gardens, past us, and off down Portsdown Road. Jimmy suddenly turned and came at me with the knife. With blind hope, I swung the bat and smacked him around the face. He fell to his knees, scrambled up quickly, dazed, and ran through us and towards Portsdown Road. He fell over, got back up, fell over again, got back up, and then went off in the same direction as the meerkat. His podgy mate dropped his knife and trundled after them, stopping to pull his jogging bottoms up.

I looked up to the window. 'What did you do?' I shouted.

'It wasn't me,' Leroy yelled down. 'It wasn't. It wasn't.'

Across the road, on an overgrown lawn, Will was standing holding the gun. I could see he was shaking. 'Is he dead?' he asked, lost, vulnerable.

'I don't know.'

Sarah went over to him. 'Baz, Baz,' she was calling. 'Baz.'

She kept shouting his name even when she was sitting holding his head in her lap.

'I just aimed for his arse,' Will said, childlike.

'Baz,' she said, one last time.

I finished digging the hole and pulled the body in. He looked about 16 in the cold blue of early morning. A grey-faced child, mousey hair twitching as the breeze scanned us. The blood from his torso had seeped through the bedsheet and I tried not to think about it, but I could feel it on my hands as I clenched my fists, sticky, barbecue sauce.

Leroy was standing over me in a maroon gown, watching. He'd mumbled a few monk-tone prayers and then bowed his head in silence.

'I couldn't do it,' he finally said.

'I had to bury mum a few days ago.'

'Shoot somebody, I mean.'

I looked up, incredulous. 'We were just trying to protect you, your bloody stuff. The kid died for stuff.'

'Hardly a kid.'

'Compared to us.'

'How old do you think I am?' he asked.

I climbed out of the hole, handed him the spade. 'You can fill it.'

'Wait, er, Will,' he said, pretending he didn't know my name.

I ignored him and walked through the double glass doors into his back room.

Leroy's house was cluttered. Boxes everywhere, used to vaguely categorise all the things they'd presumably stolen from houses on the estate. There was a box of china dolls, one of which had lost the nose on its pale dainty head; a box of metal objets d'art, candle holders, ornate bowls, trays, a giant spoon with a filigree handle; a big plastic box with paintings and photography, a canvas of a lighthouse which looked like a holiday snap that had turned out particularly well – or maybe it was from the Range. A box of toys, military police, nurses, shop-worker figures, from the Hasbro Heroes craze; sun-faded Lego, bagged up in smaller individual zip-bags, ready to hand out. Then there were the big laundry bags of shoes and clothes, fabric skins, left behind in the light of cancer-risk predictions in frightening news articles and closed hospitals. Against the wall, books bricked, crime fiction, Harry Potter, the dystopian fiction from a decade of writers trying to keep up – I was even cheered to notice a copy of my own book amongst, Not Thinking Normal, a recovery memoir.

Most of these things would normally end up in a charity shop. At best, this was what Leroy's house had become. But I noticed a small cardboard box full of jewellery and, on top, I could see quite clearly the stolen silver necklace with an amber cross I'd bought mum in Vilnius. I remembered buying it from an arty shop on Pilies Street. Mum had never been religious, but I was going through one of my spiritual phases and it seemed like a nice thing to get her. I contemplated stealing it back, but she didn't like the thing anyway, and I never saw her wear it. I laughed out loud thinking about it and woke Sarah up.

'What's funny?' she sulked.

'Sorry.'

She was lying on the settee. Will was sitting on an armchair holding a guitar he'd found, eyes glazed, absent. He played the first few notes of "Stairway to Heaven".

'Just thinking about my mum,' I said. 'She was a funny old bird.'

Will stopped, lifted the guitar over his head and, with a hollow clunk, rested it against the back of the chair.

'Baz's mum left years ago,' she said. 'I expect they'll have told his dad by now.'

Will looked up. 'He's got a dad?'

'Of course he's got a dad!' she spat.

Will went to speak, looked down to the gun which lay on the floor by his feet and stopped himself.

'Jackson,' she added.

'Jackson?' I asked.

'His dad.'

'First name or last? It's not Paul Jackson?'

'You know him?'

'I went to school with him. Ninny fucking Jackson.'

'Who?' Will asked.

'Oh, some little scag rat.'

'Is he hard?'

'He never used to be. I dunno. Sarah?' I asked.

'No, he's…' Her jaw jittered, emotion vibrating behind her face. 'No, he's-'

'Are you ok?'

'Baz… I…' The pain hissed. 'I can't take it. I can't fucking take it!' Burst. She pulled the back pillows down, so it looked like the settee was swallowing her. 'I'm listening to you talking about your mum,' she mumbled, muffled, 'and I'm thinking about Baz – he was a cock, but he was my mate – and all I can think is I need hez.'

'Hez?' I looked over at Will confused and worried.

'Heroin, H, gear, scag – as you call it, like you're in fucking Trainspotting.'

'Ok, of course, heroin,' I said, relieved. This felt like a crack in her wall. 'What do you want to do about it?'

'Here we go,' she said, 'he's got his cape on again.'

Will laughed. I looked over at him, hurt. 'Oh, come on,' he said. 'How many times? You're always trying to be the hero. You ran through the goddam brook to save her.'

Sarah laughed from under the pillows.

'She was being raped!'

'He was my boyfriend!' Muffled.

'Your *boyfriend* and his merry band of rodents just tried to fucking knife me!'

She pushed the pillows back. 'Don't be a fucking girl.'

Ego-pricked, 'you're the girl! I'm not a… or a boy… I'm a grown man, adult.' It was pathetic. 'I'm a man, damn it!' The tin echo of my voice bounced off the walls and we all fell silent.

I could see Will wanted to laugh, but he held it in like a schoolboy being told off. Standing in the middle of room, I felt exposed, vulnerable to attack and it was making me angry.

I looked around for something to do, somewhere to sit, something to break, steal or just distract me. Blue walls, brown carpets, a large cross on the wall, wooden, two feet long. I wanted to snap it in half. Surely that wasn't taken from a house. Perhaps they stole it from a church. Perhaps it already belonged to Leroy, a gift from a "saved" Nigerian, *halle-fucking-lujah*. Not knowing what to do with myself, I blurted out the first thing that popped into my head, 'Sarah, you need to fucking man-up and quit the shit then, don't you!'

She sat up, her white top, grotty and figure hugging, 'you don't have a clue,' she said. 'I *neeeed* it!'

'Don't have a clue? Ok, I was never addicted to smack, or *hez* – what the fuck is that, sounds Scottish? But I was addicted to weed-'

'Weed, hah!' she laughed.

Will laughed too.

'You can't get addicted to weed,' she added.

'I got addicted to weed, then booze, pills, prescription drugs, food, fags and many other things over time – too many to list –

which were not quite as detrimental. You're 20. You're just a baby, for God's sake.'

'I'm 25!'

Will glanced over and nodded – this was a more acceptable age.

'25 then. You're young, you've got hardly any life experience. I know you've had a hard life, but you're still in the honeymoon of addiction.'

'Why does it always have to be about addiction?' she argued. 'You should talk to Lee about this. He could teach you moderation.'

'Let me get this right. You're telling me, you just want to take heroin sometimes?' I asked, perplexed.

'I didn't say that.'

I looked to Will, who shook his head: *don't give her a hard time.*

'Chase a small line on weekends, yeah?' I mocked. 'Special occasions?' I was being a bastard. 'Find a vein after a hard day at work?'

'I don't inject! Fuck off, Tom.'

'Well, what then? What do you want to do?'

'I just don't wanna take fucking hez anymore! I don't wanna think about it! I don't want my mind to go to it whenever there's a quiet moment!'

I felt the pain. I had a flashback of the day dad died. They took him away and I sat in that empty moment, the void. Then half a bottle of whiskey sunk, I found I was still alone in my flat, the magnolia walls, a blank TV screen. Alcohol didn't work any more.

'Then stop, Sarah. I know it's not easy, but just don't take it. A day at a time. Or even an hour at a time,' I smiled, or tried to. I felt my cheeks crack a little as if I was working a much under-used muscle.

There was a silence, before Will spoke up, 'it isn't always about addiction, mate.'

Was this in her defence or his own? Either way I was tired of the excuses. 'No, it's not *always* about addiction, Will,' patronising and cold.

'Fuck you.'

I sighed. 'Moderation is all well…' I decided to rephrase it, group therapy empowerment, 'for *me*, moderation didn't work.'

'Yeah, but that's you,' he sniped.

I stared at him, trying to telepathically impress: *she's 25, she's addicted to heroin and sooner or later it will kill her – if not her body, her soul.* But what was the point?

'It's two days to the last bus, Will. We need to go to the Supra shop before it closes, amongst other things.' I didn't want to say cashpoint in front of her. 'We need to find Marcus and say goodbye to Loz.'

I made for the door. 'Where you going?' she asked.

'I'm going to see what else Lee-*roy* has in the house, then I'm going to get my shit together and leave.'

'You can't just wander about,' she said.

'Can't I? It's not even his house. You know who used to live here?'

'Who cares?' she said.

'Steve Harris. You know who he is?'

'Who fucking cares?' Will stressed.

'He was Leroy's best friend. I used to sit upstairs being made to listen to Iron fucking Maiden–'

'So,' Sarah.

'Shit,' Will laughed.

'Exactly – fucking *raaaa*. I suppose it's just a coincidence, Sarah, that Leroy lives in this house.'

I went into the hall, closed the door behind me.

I listened to hear what was said. Will told her to give me some space. 'Mr fucking AA,' she moaned.

The kitchen was surprisingly neat. Wood laminate floor and grey work units. I washed my hands in the sink, scrubbed hard to get the blood out, making them so red raw I couldn't tell if they were bloodstained.

I relived the image of the crumpled boy bleeding on the doorstep. It was one thing burying mum in the garden, but this was violent and harsh. This was gang warfare. This was something from the news, only it would never make the news. *Is this what happens now? Is this what we have to adjust to?*

We had to move away from this estate as soon as possible, move down town, which was ironic when I thought about it. The Squirrels used to be the safe side of town. The town centre was where the drugs were, the knife crimes, where the poor people lived. But now it wasn't about being well-off, poor or slightly less poor, it was about safety in numbers and somehow finding a common ground. Maybe that's what Leroy's church was about. To me it looked like a bunch of half-soaked nutters, but then what were we? It was becoming clearer by the minute that anyone left in Halesowen after that last bus must be barmy.

I remembered my old AA sponsor back home persuading me to stay in Somerset in that first year of sobriety. "Why would you go back to the town where you were an active addict? Maybe you want a drink. I'm not going to stop you," he manipulated – successfully. There was a part of me wishing I hadn't listened to him, because I just couldn't stand seeing her face and his little face and then an inescapable image of the nuclear blast cutting through them like a knife. 'Boom.'

I opened the fridge to close my mind, a cool waft, the light came on and then flickered, as did the kitchen light. Cans of beer, half a stick of chorizo and some orange juice which smelt sour. On the side, there was half a bottle of wine, without a cap, next to two wine glasses. Then I heard something upstairs, a *thunk*.

Two glasses? The scream. I was certain I heard a scream when the guinea pig smashed the window. Someone else was in here.

I took a couple of cans out of the fridge, went into the living room and tossed them one each. A peace-offering, medicine, moderation.

'I don't want it,' Sarah said.

Will cracked it open, necked the best part of a can in one and then, half-gasping, reached for the second: 'I'll have it.'

I went back into the hall, determined. I shut the door behind me. I stood at the bottom of the stairs, nervous, but curious. *Who does he have up there?*

As I climbed the stairs I heard something shudder like a fence panel in the wind. I stopped and thought about it. It was bound to be some woman, a sexual conquest. This was Leroy. It had crossed my mind this could be the whole reason for his performance as the mad preacher. Everything he ever did, there was a woman at the end of it. Perhaps it was the young woman I'd seen at church, manically laughing, tossing her hair back seductively. There was a little bit of me hoping it was her, the thought excited me and a brief image of her naked on the bed popped into my thoughts – *what's wrong with me?*

There was a room on my right. This was Steve Harris' old bedroom. I flung the door back like a pro and sidled in, my back against the wall. I stopped and listened, expecting a response –

whoever was up here, they now knew somebody was looking for them. There was nothing. The room had a big unmade bed, the covers were blood red, a silver cross above it on the wall. It was almost satanic. *Christ only knows what that sick fuck gets up to in here.*

There was a mahogany wardrobe at the side of me. I tapped it, slowly, knock... knock... knock. I felt like the killer in a slasher flick, *here's Tommy*, but I was fully aware I might also be the victim. *Be. Fucking. Brave.* I took my shoe off to use as a weapon.

I tried to swiftly move past the wardrobe, opening the far door on my way, but somebody immediately fell out and pushed me to the ground. It happened so quickly I didn't know what was going on. I had this big weight on me, like a fat fish, gasping for air. It felt like there was a pile of clothes between us and I put my arm around the wriggler's waist. We were now two fat dolphins, squeaking, 'get-d-fuh-o-me-get-d-fuh-o-me,' aimlessly headbutting.

I finally landed one.

'Ow, fuck!' he cursed.

I stopped. 'Marcus?'

'Yeah,' he rolled off me, took deep breaths, rubbing his head.

I sat up and looked at him. 'What the hell are you wearing?'

'A vicar's smock.' He was trembling, still breathless.

'What you doing?' Will shouted up.

I got to my knees and awkwardly stood up. 'Nothing,' I shouted down, before turning back to Marcus. 'I can see that. *Christ*. Why the fuck are you wearing it?'

'Who's here?' he panicked, getting to his feet.

'Will. Did you see what happened?'

'I heard somebody was shot. I've been in here since. Thought I was gonna fucking suffocate. My clothes are in the bathroom.'

I heard the door open downstairs. 'Come back down,' Sarah shouted up.

'Who's here?' he whispered.

'Leroy's burying the kid outside,' I whispered back. 'Will and Sarah are downstairs. I'll be down in a bit!' I shouted. 'I tripped up on the bed, fell over.'

We heard somebody coming up the stairs.

'Please don't tell. I've had too many years of it.'

'What were you doing?'

'Nothing. I wasn't doing anything. I␣was-'

I started ushering him in the wardrobe, 'get in,' slammed it shut.

'What's going on in here, dear boy?' Will asked in an old English accent, already two-cans-tipsy.

'Nothing.' I leant against the wardrobe, holding my foot.

'Where's your shoe?'

'I stubbed my toe.'

'What's in there?'

'Where?'

'The wardrobe.'

'Old dirty clothes. Come check out the other rooms with me. See what else they've nicked.'

Will was looking at the cross. 'Like a Hammer Horror,' he said.

'Tell me about it.'

We crossed the landing to the master bedroom.

'*Fuck*!' Will had found the motherload.

On the back wall, wine racks, dozens of bottles, a sign pinned to it: Communion Wine. The metal graze of a bottle top, Will was already drinking scotch before I'd even noticed the boxes of spirits which lined the side wall.

'This is what they were after,' I said.

'Who?'

'The fucking animals outside.'

He stopped drinking. Trembling, he tried to put the cap back on but dropped it. He handed me the bottle and sat on a box. 'I didn't mean to kill him, Tom. I aimed low.'

'I know, brother. At least you came back. I thought you'd done a runner.'

'I wanted to.'

'Me too.'

He put his head in his hands and started to cry. 'How old was he?' A mumble, hiding his face.

I didn't really know what I needed to say to pull him out of this. He'd killed somebody. And Will had been in some fights in his time. He had a big punch, he'd bloodied noses, broken teeth, left the victims purple, yellow and green. But in our young pub fights, street brawls, you just took it on faith that no one was going to die or get seriously hurt. We were never soldiers, we weren't gang members. We were just drunk, paranoid and angry.

I pictured the body again, crumpled. We'd carried him through the house, his wiry arms and sinewy biceps still wriggling with our movements, but then I looked at his head flopped over his shoulder, his face greyed, lips black in the grainy light.

'Will, you did what you had to do. This is the world now. You're right, we need to move away from here. It's too big and open.'

He looked up at me, his face wet. He wiped the bubbling snot away and sniffed, 'we could get the last bus.'

'We… could,' I said.

I handed him the bottle of whiskey.

———————

Will was anxiously looking around the estate, expecting Ninny Jackson and the rodents to be on the hunt for us. My memory of Ninny was that he was a coward, forever threatening us with his brothers. I'd seen him a couple of times during the summer, wandering around shirtless and skinny, and we ignored each other as if we'd never met. I wasn't scared of him in the least. But now his son was dead. A father had lost his son. I knew what that felt like. I felt my mind falling down a tube, a kaleidoscope of meandering images, the nuclear knife, his blond hair, green eyes smiling, trusting, present and oblivious.

I smacked myself on the head. Will turned at me, puppyish, beaten. 'It'll be alright,' I lied.

'You've never killed anyone, Tom!' he protested. 'How do you know it'll be alright?'

'You're right,' I apologised.

'Maybe… maybe we should kill them all,' he said. 'No, I don't mean it,' he reasoned. '*Could we?*'

'Maybe,' I half-laughed, not really knowing how to respond to such a ridiculous idea. 'Why don't we wipe out all of the addicts? Then the estate would be fine and we could start a little settlement, Squirrelsville.'

'I'm fucking serious, Tom.' He waved the gun in the air.

'Put the thing away! I know you are. What am I supposed to say?'

'Nothing, if you can't think of anything useful.'

I'd got him drunk enough to leave Leroy's, to face the big, bright empty streets, but his nerves were shot. As we left, Leroy tried to stop him pocketing half bottles of whiskey and rum. I grabbed his gown and pulled him towards me, 'consider it a bounty for killing the fucking rabbit, *Lee-roy*.'

'Yes, of course,' he trembled, for the first time not denying his name – and probably wondering why I'd called the boy a rabbit.

When we got back to the house, I started to pack the few meaningful items I had. Mostly bits of writing. The most important piece was the Yellow Pages apology. Perhaps it was the first meaningful thing I ever wrote, and mum had kept it all these years, which was something. She just wasn't like that. She wasn't sentimental. I don't think she'd even read my book. If she hadn't been so neat and pragmatic, I would've assumed it'd just been left in there and forgotten. It was clear she'd made the decision to keep it, to remind her there was still some good in her rotten son – not enough to give me a goddam key, but enough that she wanted me in her life.

I sat down and started to drift off thinking about it, but there was a knock at the door.

I jumped up, expecting it to be Marcus. I grabbed the gun and held it behind my back just in case. Black and heavy in my hand, I wasn't sure I'd be able to fire it, despite the magnetic desire to see what happened. As soon as I saw Maureen's silhouette, I put it on the floor and kicked it under the sofa. It hit the wall and startled Will, who sat up, then fell back down, gargling snores.

'Tom,' she said, sombre and serious. 'Tom,' she repeated.

Before I could say anything, she walked quickly past me and into the kitchen. Without saying another word, she started boiling water on the hob.

'Is this about Sarah?'

'*What?*' she snapped.

'Ok. It's not about Sarah.' I tried to laugh it off. 'How about we sit outside?'

The morning was hot, but there was a cold breeze to keep me from falling asleep. I could see Maureen had something she needed to say. So did I. I needed to make sense of the previous night's tragedy. Would Maureen understand why it had happened? Why we'd done what we'd done? Would she believe there were good intentions, when she heard we'd killed somebody? How much did she even know about Leroy and the church?

'I'm surprised to see you,' I said, 'thought you might be preparing for the last bus,' I smiled, half-joking, half-serious.

She was nodding, absent.

'*Really?*' I asked.

'Last night my friend died,' fell out of her mouth.
'*Died?*'
'Yes.'
'Hambleton Road?'
'Yes.'
'What happened? How?'
'He was only 62-'
'*He?*'
'They wanted what was in his house, so they took it. And then they killed him. They hit him over the head with a mallet and he's dead now.' She was very calm about it. It was disturbing.
'Who did?'
'Oh, they did!' she broke. 'The *animals*!' She said this pointedly, reminding me of our conversation the previous day.
'I wasn't excusing anyone… I mean-'
'Druggies, Tom! The estate's full of them. They've been a problem in Halesowen for decades! Rabid animals trying to get the… to get a fix, or whatever you call it.'
'Maureen, please-'
'Don't, Tom! They bloody caved his…' she stopped, swallowed her emotions.
There was silence. 'The animal thing,' I said, 'I don't really know-'
'I know what you were trying to say and why you were saying it. I've tried my hardest to forgive Sarah but I can't. *Animals*, Tom!' She bit her finger, her cold anger cracked. I thought she was going to cry.
What was happening in Halesowen? First the rabbit, and now Maureen's friend. Once again, I saw the replay, like a YouTube video. The boy dropped immediately on impact, nothing came out of his mouth, the bullet entered his heart and he crumpled, dead before he hit the ground. Emotion sucked at my throat, I saw Sarah with his head in her lap. Baz the rabbit dead.
If Maureen had seen us on Doran Close armed with a gun, an axe and a baseball bat, surely she'd think I was one of those "animals" too. I decided not to say anything. It wasn't the time.
'I think you misunderstood me, Maureen. The animal thing-'
'I don't care, Tom,' she said, tired of it.
'It was just something someone… it was some, I dunno, philosophising. That's all.'

'Sarah's gone and I have to accept that. Now he's gone too. That's why I'm here,' she said, resigned to it. 'I've decided I have to get the last bus.'

My mind was scatty with tired, the sun was giving me a headache and the coffee made me feel worse, teeth fuzzed, arms aching from digging my second grave in as many weeks. I couldn't be bothered to try and explain myself or make sense of the whole thing. I knew Maureen was making the right decision, but I felt sorry for Sarah.

'She is trying,' I said.

'I don't want to hear it, Tom.'

'She's quit drugs-'

'Tom Hanson!' Silenced by the teacher.

I sat still, wearing a sympathetic smile, unsure what to say. 'I'm so sorry, Maureen.' *That's what people say, right?*

But I needed to say so much more. I needed to hear the words coming out of my mouth.

My name's Tom and I'm an alcoholic. Last night my friend killed somebody in a fight, which I was just as much complicit in, to protect charity shop junk and alcohol. After burying the boy in Lee-pretending-to-be-somebody-else's garden, I passed out the beers to active addicts, one of whom refused – there's hope! Then I went upstairs and found my lost friend in a vicar's smock in a wardrobe. I put him back in the wardrobe to hide him from my other friend, who I made drink whiskey, mostly so he would get the idea of getting the last bus out of his head, if I'm honest – and I know I can be honest with you lot. I need sleep.

'I'm glad you're taking the last bus, Maureen.'

'I need your help with a couple of things.'

'Give me a few hours. Why don't you stay here and make sure Will doesn't choke on his own vomit.'

Then he can tell you how we killed a rabbit.

I shoved Leroy out of the way and went upstairs. I could smell the familiar reek of bittersweet bile which seemed to be peculiar to Marcus. I pushed open the bathroom door, his head in the pan.

'Put some clothes on.'

Downstairs the mad preacher tried to impress upon me that Marcus had similarly got him mistaken with this Leroy chap. 'That's why he followed me home,' he said.

'Ok, Lee,' I said, worn down by it. 'I just need his help.'

'I've been trying to help him,' he added. 'I could help you too.'

Sarah was still asleep on the settee, or pretending to be. She trembled a little under a thin bedsheet she'd taken from one of the jumble bags. I wanted to stay and try to keep her clean but we had things to do.

'No thank you,' I said, categorically, and went to wait outside.

We made our way quickly down Portsdown Road, Marcus behind, struggling to keep up. 'I really thought it was Leroy,' he called after me, out of breath.

Patience lost, I swung around and grabbed him by the throat. 'I'm not a fucking idiot!'

Lost in rage for a few seconds longer than I needed to be, first Marcus's cheeks, then his forehead and finally the whites of his eyes turned red. I had my thumb on his windpipe – a trick my dad had inadvertently taught me when he was trying to teach me an altogether different lesson. Grabbing at my hands, Marcus didn't even think to kick or punch me. He looked so helpless and pathetic, I found myself welling up with emotion. Overcome with guilt, I let go. I couldn't look at him. I kept on walking, exhausted, hungry and disappointed at myself.

'Don't say anything,' he begged, chasing after me. 'Please, Tom. I'm not fucking gay. I just-'

I shook him off me, 'Not now! Please!'

I felt close to tears. We cut a corner across the scruffy grass on the verge of Lutley Park, the tall reeds and shrubs buzzing with life, gnats and butterflies. For a brief moment, I let myself be transported to high up in the Spanish mountains, the green and wet Siete Lagunas in the Sierra Nevada, the hot steamy morning dew. The sensory memory vanished as soon we hit the tarmac.

Perhaps Will was right and we needed to kill them all. Ninny too. Maybe they killed Maureen's friend, boyfriend, whoever he was – I'd been assuming it was a little old lady she'd been feeding liquidised stew.

We've got a gun. I knew I couldn't kill anybody with a knife, but perhaps I could stand across the road and blindly fire a bullet into somebody. Like one country firing a missile at another, I might feel removed from the reality.

Or we could just get the last bus with Maureen. I considered asking Marcus for his thoughts on it, but it seemed that right now his answer would most definitely be "yes". Will was verging on it too.

Loz was already leaving. This sudden threat of leaving made me realise I definitely wanted to stay. But why?

Walking up Bassnage Road, everything felt different. The Co-op had been broken into, the thin metal boards cut open with some tool, refrigerator units removed, white organs left to rust. I found myself wandering over, the desire to climb in and explore the dissected creature.

'Come on. Let's just get down town,' Marcus sulked.

'Do you understand what the fuck's happening?' I shouted at him.

'We've… er… got to get shopping and use the cashpoint before it closes,' he said, like I was asking him a literal question.

I wanted to scream at him, to grab him by the shoulders and shake him until his chubby, balding head saw sense. But I quickly realised he was absolutely right. This was exactly what we needed to do and he had exactly the right head for it. My tired mind was slipping and sliding all over the place.

We continued on and I tried to reason with myself: were things actually all that bad? Had I been looking at it all wrong? There were neighbourhoods in Chicago worse this. And what about Johannesburg? And these cities were in supposedly civilised countries. What about the war-torn Middle East? Or Pakistan – although I'd had no trouble from the moment I'd landed in Skardu, traipsing across the Karakoram, to the last three nights in verdant Islamabad. In Mexico City, the kidnapping capital of the world, we were told to avoid certain parts – I still went and bought a nice pair of shoes in Tepito, and then she went mad at me because I lost the way back to the Centro Historico. The world had always been a dangerous place for millions, even billions of people, we were just lucky to have been born in the UK. *How did people deal with living in dangerous places, where horrible things happened all the time? I guess it's not about what happens, it's about how you respond to it.*

And not long before, I'd pressed my thumb into Marcus's windpipe to stop him breathing. I felt sick about it. I slowed to let him walk alongside me.

'I'm so sorry, man,' I said, squeezing my neck.

He brushed his hand across his neck. 'It was pretty scary, mate.'

And he meant it.

'Do you remember that time when we locked you in the Cornbow Hall office?' I said. 'At that Indian wedding we crashed?'

'Yeah, I had to tell the father of the bride that I was a cleaner and that I'd been locked in there most of the day. "You-nut-allow-t'-be-he-uh,"' he laughed, doing a somewhat offensive impression.

'We were proper dicks.'

'Yeah,' he said, in all sincerity, bowing to the pavement.

We continued walking towards Huntingtree Park in silence. En route, I noticed activity in three separate households. People were gutting their homes and leaving everything on the drive in black bags. Old Arthur on mum's road had done the same.

'Everything's fucked,' I said, rubbing my temples. 'My mind feels like it could break.'

Marcus burst out laughing. 'Ark at the drama queen!'

'It's not funny.' I stopped by the corner of Huntingtree Road, the old primary school across the way, hidden behind tall evergreens, a sign hanging off the gate. 'How will we ever be normal again?'

He snorted a laugh.

'I'm serious.'

'I think you just need a good night's sleep, mate,' he said, unwilling or unable to entertain my neuroses.

I pressed the button to the traffic lights as we passed it. A few seconds later, the bleeps echoed throughout the streets. I turned around, walking backwards. Marcus looked up at me. 'I didn't fuck Leroy.'

'I don't wanna know, mate. Not now.'

'Just got pissed.'

'I don't wanna know. It seems like nothing in the middle of all this.'

He looked sad. I didn't want offend him or belittle him, I'd done enough of that, but I just didn't have the brain for it.

'What will you tell them?' he asked.

'I met you on the way to Ally's.'

'Yeah.' He thought about it. 'Yeah, that'll work. We going to Ally's?'

'It's happening everywhere,' she said.

'Oh, great!' – a sardonic understatement.

Marcus was asleep on a bean bag. Next to him was Ally's little girl, Colette, making pyramids out of plastic beakers.

'Jay Bird pissed off Gary Bennett because he broke into the old TV store and stole a booster.'

'What's that got to do with Gary Bennett?'

'God knows, but Jay's been ferreting around for things for a number of people.'

'He has for us.'

'Me too. Which means he's made just as many friends as he has enemies. Gary was found knifed outside the old post office.'

'*Dead*?' There was a sudden bang and the sound of tumbling bricks. 'What the hell was that?'

'Tony and Ross are knocking through the next door neighbours' wall. They left a couple of weeks ago.'

'Ok…?'

'I'm getting an extension,' a twinkle in her eye.

'Ross North?'

'And Tone, from Picks.'

'Why's the landlord from Picks extending your flat?'

'I'm pregnant.'

'*What*?' Ally lay on the settee, sipping from a cup of tea, the bulge of her stomach I'd assumed was her gut. 'You're 50!'

'52,' she smiled. 'What can I say, I've always been very fertile.'

'Besides the fact the hospitals have all gone, isn't it dangerous at your age?'

'I was 49 when I had Lettie.' The little girl looked up. 'She was out in 40 minutes, the quickest of the lot. Tony's building me a bigger nest.' She had a big grin on her face.

I looked around the place. It was still as grimy as ever, red carpets with black cigarette burns; the brown curtains, perpetually drawn, thick with smoke stains; Yankee candles of all colours stifling the place with myriad smells, musky like a brothel.

'So why Tony?' Then it dawned on me. 'You… you fucked Tony Dale?'

'You don't fuck Tone, believe me! He fucks you,' she smiled, proud, excited.

'Alright, alright,' I dismissed.

'He takes control of me like-'

'I really don't want to know.'

'You're so funny. You've always had an issue talking about this stuff.'

'Except when I was pissed.'

'Only when you were completely out of it,' she laughed.

'What can I say? I'm British.'

There was the sound of toppling bricks down the hall, followed by cursing.

'So am I,' she laughed.

'Yeah, but you're proper working class and liberated.'

'What are you?'

'I'm working class, but mum brought me up to think I was middle class.'

'But you always used to rave about being working class.'

'I was aspiring to it.'

'You're so strange, Tom.'

'I know I bloody am,' I laughed. 'Not that class means anything these days.'

Ross North walked into the living room, his belly fat and free. 'I dunno about that, comrade.'

He took a drag on a thin roll-up which smelt strong and appealing for it. It stuck to his lip, reminding me of the times I'd lost a bit of skin when I'd pulled it off too quick.

'Oi, fuck face!' Ally yelled. 'I'm pregnant.'

'Oh, sorry, shit… sorry, Ally,' he grovelled, tapping it out on his thumb nail and sticking it in his shirt pocket.

'Fucking think so, coming in here with your "comrade".'

'Tom knows what I'm on about,' he said, with a waggle of his fat finger. He sat down on the arm of my chair, his arse cheek trapping the flesh of my forearm. 'I remember them days pontificating on the demise of socialism in the George, eh?' he nudged.

'I was telling him about Gary,' she said.

'Bennett? "What is genuine is proved in the fire", eh, comrade? "What is false we shall not miss-"'

'Hang on a minute, Ross. Gary Bennett was knifed,' I said.

'No time for it. Don't belong here.'

I was stunned. 'He's dead! What the fuck are you talking about? Quoting bloody Engels to justify murder. Who did it?'

I yanked my arm free and he stood up. 'Don't you come here telling us how to suck eggs,' he said. 'You was like this at school. You don't even live here. Yow come here,' he said, appropriating a thicker accent, 'talking 'bout classlessness with yuh middle class conk-'

'I'm working class!' I insisted.

'Yow don't even drink, 'bout as working class as Phil the fucking Greek,' he laughed, proud of himself.

'How does that make any sense? I used to live just there,' pointing to the back door, to Block 5 Ankerdine Court. 'Dad lived in the high-rise behind.'

'Your dad was posh.'

'He lived in a two bedroom council flat.'

Marcus was starting to stir in the background, he sat up and *coochie coo'd* Colette, who looked nonplussed.

'All I'm saying is, class will always be around. It's in us,' he said.

'And I'm saying, I don't really give a shit. Marcus,' I summoned.

'What've I missed?'

'Let's go.' I stood up, eyed Ross, provoking the red rage.

He lifted his fat finger and was about to let rip in Marxist angst, when Ally yelled, 'no!'

His face dropped in servile terror, *of course m'lady*.

'We've gotta go anyway, Ally.'

'Ross, piss off back to Tone.'

'But…' She halted him with a glance. 'The door,' he mumbled.

'What about it?' she demanded.

'That's why I came in here. Does there need to be a door to the other flat or can we just stick a curtain up?'

'Of course there needs to be a fucking door.'

'Yes, of course. Yes. I'll see you in a bit, Ally. Tom,' he nodded. 'Marcus.'

'Tood-a-loo,' his impish response.

Ross gave him a funny look, then left.

Ally sat up and pulled a packet of tobacco out of her bra. She started to roll a cigarette. 'This is him with his bastard smokes,' she said. 'I was doing well. Don't tell Tone.'

'We do have to go, Ally.'

'Tom,' she said, serious, 'you need to avoid fucking politics-'

'I was thinking of standing at the next election,' I joked.

'I'm serious. The last thing we need to be doing right now is arguing about things which don't really mean anything. Things are changing fast around here and after they've left on Friday, people will start making rules.'

'*Rules?*'

She was looking at me, shaking her head, 'for all your talk about politics, what do you really know about anything?'

'I don't give a shit about politics.'

'You always talk about politics.'

'I gave it up many moons ago, when I realised there was no getting to the truth, if there even is such a thing.'

'Ever since the papers murdered commie Corbyn,' Marcus laughed.

'Oh God, we've lived lives since then,' she said.

'Yes, we have,' I nodded. 'I have.' *Boom* – I remembered the nook in my shoulder where her head lay, the bowl of his hair.

'Life goes on. You need to move back to town.'

'That's the plan.' I opened the back door. 'Ally, who killed Gary? Was it Jay?'

She burst out laughing. 'You kidding? Jay Bird couldn't kill a fly.'

———————

There was a surprisingly long queue outside the Supra. Even shaded under the big bulbous lime trees we were sweltering. Mel was in front of us, she turned to me. 'I went to school with your mum,' she said. 'How is Pat?'

'Sorry to say this Mel. Mum passed away last week.'

'Yow'm kidding? Does Barb know?'

'No, I haven't told her.'

'She'll be in pieces. She's always going on about how they used to go to Snobs and the Rom to try an' pull a black un.'

Marcus snorted a laugh. Mel laughed with him, 'crackers, ay they? No offence kidda.'

'Mum once told me about how they ended up in a car with Hot Chocolate. Barb went off with Errol Brown, but mum just stayed in the car. She went mad at her after because the guys were all smoking weed.'

'Pah! Barb and Errol. She's never said that to me. Cor be true. Er would've dined on it by now.'

'Who knows?'

'Dark horse, Babs,' Marcus said, a wink in his eye.

A family of four came out of the shop with about six bags each. 'No eggs, no kitchen roll, no pasta left,' the man said.

'You staying, Ant?' someone behind us asked him.

'Nah, last bus for us, mukka.'

'Why so much then?'

'Yuh fat fuck!' someone shouted.

'Yuh fucking what?'

'Leave it, Ant,' the woman said.

'Yow can talk, fatty bum,' one of their kids mocked.

'You fucking what?' the man argued. 'Control yuh sprog!'

I thought I recognised the voice and turned to see it was Ricky, my old school friend, a white half-moon of gut hanging under his orange Wolves top.

'Leave em, Rick,' I called up. 'Bunch of chavs,' I joked.

'Right, ay it? Yow alright Tom?'

'As good as the times,' I laughed.

We watched them waddle up the high street, a skirt of bags. A number of people protested but none were prepared to lose their spot to confront the family.

'A bit mental, ay it?' he said.

A bit mental? I thought about it. Being back in town actually felt a bit less mental than it did on the Squirrels. With so many people around, it was easier to conform to the madness – the boy's lifeless body, a YouTube clip. I imagined Gary Bennett's corpse around the corner, stiff with morning cold, like a poisoned rat. I hadn't seen it for myself, but it was easier to dismiss it – or even to accept it, like it was the way of things.

Down the street, I watched councillor Ray walk into Picks, a book in his hand, probably the history of the Black Country or some similar fare. He was a true regionalist. I was certain he was staying, and for some reason that gave me hope. As much as I might disagree with him, he always wanted the best for his town. Maybe we could work together to rebuild our broken home. I thought about Ally and her talk of rules and politics – *is this what she means*?

The Supra had been extended through to the back and into the adjacent premises, which used to be a pet shop. It was cold and felt like a warehouse, shelves bulging with low quality items for exorbitant prices. We filled our bags with tins, crisps and biscuits mostly. There was one pack of four loo rolls for £17.95, far exceeding the post-Greek recession hike. What would they even do with the money? I heard people arguing with Anis at the counter to which he responded, 'don't buy it,' without feeling. Or, 'government, init,' which seemed like a party line at best.

'£922… let's call it £900,' Anis smiled at the counter.

I handed over part money and part Will's Supra Rations.

'I can't accept these from you, mate,' he said, waving the vouchers.

'Fuck off Anis. You know Will.'

'You robdog!' someone shouted from behind.

He looked at me, then at the vouchers, then at the queue. 'Is he the lanky un?'

He knew full well who he was. He was just trying it on. I nodded.

'For you, Tom,' he fist bumped, like we were 17 again.

'You staying?' I asked him.

'Nah, man, well out of here.'

'Last bus?'

'Nah, got wheels.'

'You got a car, Anis?' someone asked from behind.

'Yeah, Glenn. A sweet Transporter.'

'Fit us in?' Glenn asked.

Anis laughed. I handed over the money.

As I left, I heard Glenn genuinely pleading for a lift, but there was no space.

Outside, Marcus held both his hands out to show me he was trembling. I remembered those violent hangovers only too well. It'd been a heavy couple of weeks for him. We popped into Picks to cure it, the orange sour swill for him, a coffee for me. It was good to get out of the sun.

In the back of the bar, the usual wad of blokes, but this time ghosted in a cloud of pipe smoke, cigarettes and cigars. This was new. It hadn't taken long for the smoking ban to be overturned. The bus hadn't even left. Technically they were breaking the law. I laughed, thinking about it. The police were gone, laws were meaningless. Other than the rare sight of the binmen and the nuke buses, government was reduced to a scrolling caption on TV screens. Everyone was on the rob, at least three people had been murdered. Baz was dead, Maureen's fella and now Gary Bennett. Where would it end?

'Three murders already,' shaking my head.

'Yeah,' Marcus' nonchalant response – *and your point?*

At our usual table, the other side of the bar, Christian and Anita were sat drinking, holding hands – the archetypal love birds. We went to sit at another table but he gestured for us to join them.

'Tom,' he laughed, like I'd just told a joke.

'Yow alright me mon?' I said, putting it on.

'I bay three bad,' he joked back, laughing. 'Always cracks me up this one,' he said to Anita.

'Laugh a minute,' Marcus sneered.

'What's with the face?' he asked Marcus.

I could see he was all set to say something sarky, but I gently stepped on his toe to prevent causing another scene in Picks.

'Just a bit knackered mate,' Marcus said.

'Hungover more like,' I smiled.

Christian laughed. 'Remember… remember the golf hole?' excitable.

I fake laughed. I kinda liked Christian. He was a tit, but we had a bit of a history. A few benders in the school days when it was good, piss ups in Penorchard meadow, a big field near Clent Hills, far enough away from the road to avoid getting into trouble – not that it ever really stopped us. By the time I got to college though, he was already just an old face, a pub chat, a drink to nostalgia, but sometimes that was all you wanted. We'd reconnected over the last year because he'd been drinking too much and I'd become someone to talk to.

'You seem really well,' I said.

'Just the cider for me, now.' He lifted the swamp juice, gave it a little shake. 'You're definitely staying then?'

'The town seems a bit crazy but,' I nodded. 'Not seen this many people out and about since the cancer-winds scare. Makes you realise how many of us are still here.'

'Not for long, my friend,' he said with authority.

'Good riddance,' Anita added.

'A,' like he was teaching her the children's alphabet.

'So, you can say it, but I can't?' she argued.

'And this is how it starts,' he said, resignedly.

I looked at Marcus. He took it as his cue to drink more quickly.

'What do you mean, Christian? Not for long?' I asked.

'The feds-' Anita butted in.

'What did I fucking say to you?' He was angry. 'Don't listen to the stupid bitch.'

'I'm not staying here taking this crap from you.' She stood up and waited for him to say something.

'Go,' he ushered with a camp flick of his hand.

'Ooooh.' Marcus couldn't help himself.

Christian turned to us, then back to her. 'Let the big boys speak.'

Anita walked a few steps, then turned, 'big boy? Yeah, right.'

I put pressure on Marcus's foot.

'You… you… took it… you fucking took it good last night,' he said for our benefit, but she was already gone.

'What's going on?' I whispered.

'She never stops,' he moaned.

'Just words, Chris.'

'Just words?' he yelled, then caught himself and laughed. 'Just words. Not actions, eh?' he gyrated in his chair, chortling to himself.

The back bar was misted over with smoke which choked me a little and made me crave it. Tina was behind the bar. She leant over to give Percy and Jack their drinks and her breast almost popped out of her strappy top, which was not uncommon. I often thought it was a play for a drink. She adjusted her top, 'not that you'd care, eh?' she tittered. She caught me looking and I turned away immediately. I heard her titter some more.

'You like her, eh, Tom?' Christian was still gyrating and I could feel the laughter welling up in Marcus.

'No, I'm… you know. I'm married.'

'Tom,' he shook his head and then looked me straight in the eye. 'Fuck. Tina.'

Did he mean leave her alone or fuck her? 'Anyway, sod that silly bollocks,' I said. 'What were we talking about before Anita-?'

'Interrupted us like the irritating-?'

'Yeah, sure.'

'Lots of people are going to leave on Friday. Most people, I reckon.'

'Why?'

'Because that's what they want us to do.'

'Ok,' Marcus chipped in, 'so what about the federali?'

'Federali?' he laughed, clearly hiding something. 'Who said anything about the federali?'

'She did,' he replied, without thinking.

'No, she mentioned the feds.'

'Ok, feds,' I reasoned. 'Federals? Federalis? Federal bureau…?' I pretended.

He tapped his nose, 'more will be revealed.'

More will be revealed? They used to say that in AA – not that I expected him to know this. It meant peeling back the onion, learning more about ourselves and experiencing more of life. We said it to ourselves to remind us that life will keep getting better if we live an honest life.

'What do you mean?' I asked.

'You'll be alright, Tom,' he affirmed, and I thought it best not to go there.

Something strange was going on – I preferred the onion just as it was, big and round and in one piece.

As we passed the Supra, we saw Stacey and Damien in the queue, Stacey in a skin-tight short black dress, aquamarine veins unsure where to seam up her loose-skinned legs. Damien was in a baggy black t-shirt and slightly flared frayed jeans, his green parka in his arms.

'I hope you like petit pois, pineapples and carrot and coriander soup,' I joked.

'And fucking lentils,' Marcus added.

We were hulking eight bags each, and I could see this offended some people.

'Are you staying too?' I asked, loud enough so people would hear.

'I'm staying,' Stacey flirted, her face sunken and grey.

'Got the... er... the barge,' Damien mumbled.

'Of course. You'll be off sailing the canals. All the best with it,' I said.

'Um ta, but I'll be um... here and there, she... needs... er...'

Stacey shielded her mouth, 'he thinks I need his willy.'

'Um!' Damien's cheeks blossomed. 'No, Stace, er... I'm-'

'I wish you the *sincerest of luck*, my friend, but we've got to make a move.'

'Er, yeah... um, bye... er, Tom, Marcus.'

I looked behind us and watched Stacey squeeze Damien's cheek – *oh, the liddle baby*. I had the feeling this was going to be my last image of Damien, scorned by Stacey to the very last. I hoped it was. She'd been in his life for too many years, a perpetual prick-tease. He'd never seen anything for his love, as far as I knew, and he'd fought with her to save her six kids, all of which had been lost, scattered in foster homes to a life of poor odds, even in the best of times.

We passed the cash point, which was now closed. It was after 1pm. We'd already taken out the maximum of £500 each. We had one day left to get more, the day of the last bus. I wasn't sure what use money would be or how any of that was going to work, but better to have than have not. Sooner or later the financial system was going to change for everyone in the UK. It had to. Like Will said, we'd been bombed back to the dark ages, to "Pleb Britain".

We made our way to Ally's flat. There was a feeling of carnival on the estate. People were drinking on the grass, the enticing smoke of barbecues. Some were celebrating leaving, some were celebrating staying. We said our hellos to familiar faces, but the ache of bags and the sweltering heat made me want to get away from everybody, especially as they were all so happy.

'You ok with us leaving this stuff?' I asked. 'We'll be down for the last bus.'

'I think most of the town are off,' Ally said.

We were standing in her living room.

'Why?'

'Because that's what they've asked us to do.'

'So bloody what? That makes me want to stay more. Also, while we're on it, who the fuck are the federalis?'

'Who told you about that?' the voice came from another room, it was deep and strong.

I held my nerve. 'You did, Tone.'

Tony Dale entered and the room felt smaller. Lettie giggled to herself, Marcus looked down and pulled a daft face. She didn't react.

'You're the federali,' he said.

'Me?'

'And you,' he pointed to Ally. 'And him,' he pointed to the bump.

'It's a boy?' I asked.

'I reckon,' he smiled. 'And even him,' he tapped Marcus on the arm.

Marcus flinched like he'd been given an electric shock. 'What? Me?' he asked, nervous.

'You're all federali.'

'Ok. I think I get it,' I said.

'You don't,' he said, 'and, to be honest, neither do I.'

I laughed. 'What the hell are you on about, Tone?'

'All a bit bloody daft to-'

Ross North entered mid-sentence, like he'd been standing listening in the hall. 'You keep saying this, Tone. It's very simple. Tom'll get it.'

'Will I?' suspicious.

Over the years I'd agreed with Ross on many things. Left-leaning ideas which helped the many, and didn't just enable the money-men to keep widening the divide, gaining more power in the process. But he was militant about it, an anarchist, and I never had that in me, even back in the thick of addiction. He would hurl vitriolic abuse at those on the other side of the fence, the police, neo-liberalists, the right and most of the left. I had to talk him down from punching councillor Ray one drunken night. Maybe he was right about some things, and maybe I was wrong about some things, but I just didn't have the violence in me. That's where I drew the line.

'The federalis are the people,' Ross said.

'Aren't they the police?' Marcus asked.

'Oi,' Tony warned.

'Tone, don't get me wrong,' I said, 'but that's who the feds-'

'That was then,' he menaced. 'This is now.'

'What are they then?'

He went to prod the air in anger, then stopped and looked at Ally, who looked nervous. He laughed and punched Ross in the arm, 'ask this plonker. Whatever it is, they mean well.'

'They?'

'Tom,' Ross said, professional voice. 'It's not the police. It's all of us. The police is a them-against-us organisation. A government can be a bit like that too but perhaps, in the future, who knows… we might need some sort of representatives for the areas of Halesowen.'

'Councillors.'

'Kind of. But who knows? Maybe you have some ideas. The federalis is just something I thought about and people seem to like it. We'd all be federalis. If we wanted to be. Which we oughta.'

'We oughta?' I was sceptical.

'I don't mean… what I mean… it's like a neighbourhood watch.'

'A neighbourhood watch,' Tony nodded.

'A collective consciousness. No laws.'

'So why call them the federalis? Why not the neighbourhood watch?' I asked.

'Ok, mukka. To be blunt. We're about to lose all our systems, some of them we should be glad to get rid of, like law and order, and capitalism. But we need something, we're not animals-'

'We kinda are,' I interrupted.

'Co-op-er-ative fed-er-alism,' he said, ignoring me, breaking down the syllables in case we didn't understand.

'Thought we were doing away with government,' Tony said, objecting.

'It's not about being governed, it's about working together, being on the same page.'

Marcus yelped a laugh. Tony shut him up with a glance.

'We're all federalis,' Ross insisted. 'But it's just something to talk about.'

I'd had enough talking about it. I was sweating and irritable. I didn't trust Ross North. The idea didn't seem terrible, but where was the democracy? Wasn't this just his ego? Or maybe I was being unfair.

'You should move down here,' Ally said. 'Get involved.'

'Yeah, Ally,' I smiled. 'Maybe.'

We went back out into the steamy heat. It was so hot it was hard to move. Tony, Ross and Ally, Christian and Anita too: who else was in on this? Councillor Ray? All the guys hiding in a cloud at the back of Picks? We'd been in the pubs too, we'd watched most of the town leave, the boards and cages go up, nature start to reclaim the town. Why were we only finding out about this stuff by accident? Perhaps they thought we weren't bright enough? Or that we'd disagree? Already we were adapting to the madness, developing a necessary willingness to accept the unthinkable. We were about to head back to a potential war with Ninny Jackson and the other ferals. And we wanted stay in spite of this. Or I did. Loz was leaving. Will was talking about it.

'Do *you* want to leave?' I asked Marcus.

He paused and thought about it. I could tell he was looking for the right answer. 'No?' he half-asked me.

'I want to stay and give it a go.'

'Me too.'

I wasn't convinced.

'Come on, Marcus. Let's get back. It's too bloody hot. We need a storm or something,' I said.

And, as if by divine intervention, then came the storm.

2032

February and cold.

I closed the notebook, stroked the glittery front. It felt romantic, but then this was one of those defining moments in life. I found myself thanking Sarah for enabling me to the say the things I just couldn't say. And I thanked Lucy, who would always be the one soul I felt truly in sync with, but this wasn't like the story I just wrote in my notebook, I couldn't just write a different ending and magic her back into existence. There are some things you can change, and some things you have to accept.

There was a big yellow bedroom in Burnham-on-Sea. One morning I awoke to find a lump digging in my side.

'Lucy,' I said.

She opened her sleepy eyes. 'What?'

'Are you pregnant?'

'What are on you about?' She wasn't impressed.

The lump wriggled.

I started feeling about manically, grabbing his nose, his hair. 'You're pregnant. You've got a big hairy baby.'

She smiled.

The lump giggled and wriggled his way up.

'Dylan!' mock surprised and disappointed. 'I thought mummy was pregnant again.'

'Dad-dy,' he said, like I was being silly.

Every day I opened my eyes and I knew I would see him, and every day we had a new baby, our beautiful boy, Dylan.

I climbed out of the tent and started packing my things away. The sun was bright, but it was bitterly cold. I needed to get moving to warm up. It would've been a great day to climb Tryfan, assuming there wasn't too much snow.

I looked up at the biscuit ruins of Castell Dinas Brân on the top of the hill. That was going to be our first landmark hike on our walk to Wales. It was now protected by a circle of green wind turbines with black blades, the same turbines which lined so many of the hills. I considered trekking up to the medieval castle, but I didn't have the time and there wasn't really any point now.

I made my way out of the field and towards the cottage. Helen was outside, smoking.

'I'm gonna go,' I said.

'The mountain?'

'The aqueduct.'

'You are not going without breakfast,' she nagged, warm and Welsh.

'I haven't got time.'

She held her finger up and ran into the house, then a few moments later came out with two little plastic bags, one containing a bun, an apple and some cheese. The other containing blackberries – of all the fruits. I nearly cried when I saw them. I saw the flat, the brew, Tony Dale's blood on the wall. I saw Loz and Marcus on their settees, Will standing in the doorway to the kitchen telling them to drink. The memories turned inside me, churning energy. It felt like trauma.

'You'll be alright,' she said.

I thanked her for the use of her field, the warm breakfasts and the company and started hiking down the A5.

2031

'Woah, Tom, just… um… I'll make you a hot drink.'

'Where's Sarah, Damien?' I panted.

'She's in the gallery.'

I moved towards the stairs, my consciousness slipping away. *Get it together.* I knelt on the steps, took a deep breath.

'Just um… sit, Tom. Have a tea.'

'Tea?'

'From the Jetboil. She's trying to meditate.'

I stood up but, feeling light-headed, immediately sat down on the stairs. Damien was standing at a big table, the seashore roar of lighted gas, a roll-up in his mouth.

'What's the panic?' he asked.

'I just need a minute. I'm convincing myself I'm having a heart attack.'

He laughed.

'Will said you'd gone back to the barge,' I said.

He poured the water into a tin cup which had been clipped to his rucksack. 'Wanted to see Sarah. Make her… um… see sense.'

He put a spoonful of green powder in the cup.

'What's that?'

'Matcha. Good for um… immunity, they say.'

He handed me the drink. It was warm and milky. Restorative. It made me feel safe, a child eating digestive biscuits in front of the Two Ronnies with dad, or even a grown man sitting on a bench with old Mick watching Morecambe and Wise.

The big entrance space to the baths had been mostly cleared. There used to be photo boards of swimmers and squash players brandishing cups and medals. Now it was just beige rectangle upon rectangle, dystopian Rothkos. The vending machines had long since been emptied and upturned, and were currently being used as beds, topped with interlocking karate mat mattresses. There was a single big round table, Damien's Jetboil, Sarah's Calor gas stove and two chairs.

Damien picked up the chain of old tin cans lying by the entrance. A make-shift alarm system. He carefully hung the string over small hooks on the reception counter and attached it to the big front board, which on the other side read "Renovation Pending". We hoped not, although Sarah didn't expect to be here long. This was one of many temporary hide-outs she'd used in a bid to stay clean. But she was here for a reason. The not so distant past was still simmering inside. I just hoped she'd eventually find a way past it and out of Halesowen.

'Can't persuade her then?' I asked.

'I think if you went.'

'Will maybe,' I smiled.

'*Really*?' she asked.

I leant back, glanced up the stairs. Sarah tossed my headtorch down. 'Forgot this.'

I caught it. 'Thanks. It nearly got us into trouble.'

'Will?'

'Just nagged me for losing it, doesn't suspect anything.'

She made her way down. Beige baggy trousers, a black shirt open, army green vest. She looked like a war correspondent from the noughties.

'Do you really think he's the reason I'm hanging around?' she asked.

'Maybe.'

'That's hardly a good reason for staying in Halesowen. Emotional sobriety,' she squeezed my balding brow and then kissed me on the cheek. 'Hello, you.'

'I wish I hadn't given you that book.'

'I wish you'd read it,' she teased.

'I'm having enough trouble staying free from substances never mind anything else.'

'What do you mean by that?' She sat at the table, opened the lid on the Jetboil and poured the remainder of the warm water in a cup.

'God, Sarah. There's so much to say.'

———

I woke up on the vending machine bed, my back killing, bag of cobs nuts digging into my leg. I went to take them out, but found the blister pack of co-codamols underneath. I took my hand out of my pocket and tried not to think about it. It was dark and felt like the early hours of the morning, but it was just gone 9pm. Damien was hunched over a candle in his green parka, biting the skin on his thumb. He looked thoughtful.

'Tell me about the north,' I said.

He turned away from the candle-light, his expression masked in the brown fabric of the evening. 'I wouldn't say it was better than here.'

'Ok. Is that a healthy point of view?' I asked in all seriousness.

'Um, depends on what your view of... er... healthy is.'

'That's what I thought.' I sat up, the hollow *clomp* of metal.

'I... like... the dark,' he said – morose old Eeyore. 'But the north is better for you.'

'Me?'

'Er, um, yes, but *you* in general. For, um, people. It's like it was.' He stopped and thought about it. 'And it's not... at the same time, if you, er... get me?'

I didn't, but I knew it was going to be hard to learn much more from him. Damien was an artist. He was on a slightly different plane. He painted surreal images, usually thin men in a haze of aura, blues, greens and browns. This was Damien, a short stick in a big green parka with blue jeans and brown hair, often in a haze. I don't think he would say he was painting self-portraits, but that's how it seemed to me. They were very good and he'd made a decent living in the old world.

'Where is she?' I asked.

'I'm here.' I saw a flick of movement the other side of the room. I imagined she was sitting with her back against the wall, her arms wrapped around her knees. 'Can you hear it?' she asked.

I listened. 'The genny at Picks?'

'Ommmm,' she said.

I laughed.

'Don't laugh at me!' she snapped.

'I'm not.'

'It's in everything. You know you told me it was in the sound of the stream?'

'Yes, I stole it from somewhere.' I'd read it, but I'd sat many hours in more peaceful times listening to the "om" of the estuary in Burnham.

'Damien was saying that if you randomly mix paints,' she continued, 'it eventually turns to brown every time. Right now, I can hear the generator at Picks and the din of music, the rumble of voices, the stream outside and the breeze, and they're all just strings which when twanged together give us "ommm".'

'Ark at the budding Buddha,' I joked.

'Don't take the piss, Tom! I'm trying.'

'Really, I'm not. I've been there.'

I understood what was happening. Sarah was in exactly the place she was meant to be in. The key to it was sustaining it. She was receptive and trying to be her better self. This is what happened to me in the best of times, when I was really sober, not just abstaining from drink and drugs.

'You know… er… you don't have to stay up there,' Damien said, bringing it back to the north. 'You can always come back.'

'I know,' she replied. 'But now's not the time. Tony Dale's dead – Tony Bonham too, it seems! Tony Moran is more dangerous than ever. And the rest of the town aren't bad,' she defended.

'They're a bit, er…' Damien interrupted, without qualifying it.

'He's like the putrefied tip of a carrot in a plastic bag,' she added.

'The bag being Halesowen?' I asked.

'Yeah, man,' Damien agreed. 'The bag.'

'Yes,' she confirmed. 'If we can open the bag and let him run out, the rest of the carrots will last a little longer.'

She wasn't mad. No more mad than a few years of this existence made any of us. I recognised the desire to help people, but it was so exhausting. I didn't have it in me. I just needed to survive.

'See, um… what, I er… mean, Tom.'

I wasn't sure whether Damien really believed she was onto something or whether he just had a crush on her. Perhaps he just wanted to see how it all played out. The intrigue and observation of an artist. I totally got that, but I was too tired to even sit and watch.

The room went quiet. I guess we all drifted off into the play in our heads. Mine involved mountains at that moment, the jagged ring of Helvellyn, a cold freshwater lake numbing my naked feet, tufty grasses cushioning my tent. Perhaps Damien was on his barge painting. Or perhaps he was thinking about Sarah.

'How *is* Will?' Sarah asked.

That was clearly her little play. The mountain vanished and my stomach filled with an encroaching sickness. Fear, guilt, jealousy, I don't know. I pulled my headtorch out and shone it on her across the room. She shied away from the light, her pale, serious face. I switched it off again.

'He'll be alright. They'll deal with the body. I'm not hiding from the situation,' I said.

'I didn't say you were,' she said.

'Can't I tell him?'

'No!' She meant it. 'He can't know I'm here. No one can.'

'Why? I'm so sick of it all,' I sulked. 'I don't understand what's going on anymore. Why did Ally send me into town? It all made sense at the time.'

'You ballsed it up.' She was categoric about it.

I laughed out loud at the honesty, but it was anxious laughter, adrenaline-filled and loose. It was followed by a dead silence, like I'd laughed a little too long and made them worry for my sanity. It reminded me of the paranoiac hangovers and comedowns. I hadn't taken anything for years but there was an insecure scattiness inside me, like I couldn't quite keep up with what was going on. Ally's plan made complete sense when she said it, but now it was all feeling like some strange ruse. Anita was drinking wine in Picks too, what did that mean? Had she even stopped? Or was this a way for Ally to find out where Sarah was? But why would she want to?

Because of Will.

But this was madness.

'It's all a bit mental,' Damien said, out of nowhere, just to remind us he was there.

'I guess, I could've told Christian that Stacey had killed Tony Dale. He might've helped me. But then I think we'd all still be implicated somehow.'

'And Stacey would find a way out of it, anyway,' Damien remarked, bitter.

'Someone will pay for this,' Sarah said.

'Unless we drain the bag,' I laughed. I only said it for some sort of literary continuity. I had no real intention of involving myself in any plot against the Sons. I wanted to, but after the confrontation with Tony Moran in Picks, I knew I didn't have it in me anymore. I wasn't sharp enough or fit enough. The time had come for me to leave, I knew it. I just didn't know how.

'At the moment,' Sarah said, 'Tony Dale's just missing.'

This was true but, if Ally's plan had gone ahead, his body had been removed from Dan the dealer's old flat, bumped downstairs and battered across the path to the back of St John's graveyard where it would've been unceremoniously dumped in the Greek Grave. It was just a matter of time before someone spotted him. And we might not be the immediate suspects, for the sheer bravery of it, but sooner or later they would unearth the truth or a version close enough to it.

'I want to go and help them,' I lied, 'but Ally said-'

'Shush!'

'What?'

'Shush,' she repeated.

'You better go,' Damien said, before I even knew what was happening. 'Both of you.'

Then I heard the boards move. At first I thought it might be the wind, then a can rattled.

I shone my torch on Sarah and made for her. 'Which one?' I asked her.

'The men's.'

'Damien, come on,' I whispered.

The cans fell off the hooks with a nerve-piercing clatter.

'Go,' he whispered back.

We ran into the changing rooms, the torch shining our way across the grimy floor tiles. We moved around the corner by the sinks. She grabbed my hand, took the torch, and switched it off.

We listened as someone awkwardly made their way in behind the boards, the flicker of torchlight.

'Who's there?' Damien asked.

'Oof… is, erm, Tom Hanson here?' the jittery man uttered, a Black-Country chirp.

'Councillor Ray,' I whispered. 'You wait here.'

'No,' she said, squeezing my hand. 'Listen.'

Our backs against the wall, we slowly slid down to the cold tiles.

Sarah put her head on my chest and pulled my arm around her. It felt good, but I tried my best not to think about it.

'Just, um, me, Ray,' Damien said.

'Ar sin Tom walk this way earlier. He disappeared and there was a loud clanging noise like the one just now. Come on, yow,' he urged, 'Ar know he must've bin 'round at some point.'

'Not seen him, Ray.'

'Something's going on in this building. I walk Wolfie by the baths every morning. Sometimes I see the flash of a light.'

'I stay here, Ray, when I'm in Halesowen.'

'When yow'm in Halesowen?' he sounded surprised.

Alarm bells were ringing for me too. Damien was about to out himself to a Son. He wasn't allowed to just come and go. I went to get up, but Sarah held me tight to stop me.

'He'll get in trouble,' I whispered.

'No, he won't,' she said.

'When I'm not on the run,' Damien said, with more clarity than I was used to hearing.

'On the run?' confused.

Damien laughed. 'The tobacco run for Tony.'

'Moran?'

'Um. Dale.'

'I don't know anything about this,' he said, slightly irked.

'Neither did I,' I said to Sarah.

She lifted her face to my ear, I felt her breath on my cheek. She spoke slowly, 'you didn't need to know. The guys especially didn't need to know. He does what he has to do to stay safe, like all of us.'

I heard what she said, but I was more distracted by the warm breath in my ear, transported to the pillow. I thought I was past all this. We'd become real friends. Siblings in a war against our natures. But when this lump of woman was against me in the dark, I couldn't fight the animal. When she stopped talking she lingered by my ear. I took it as a sign, it was a moment, and I grabbed it, wasn't this life? Life against all odds? I turned to face her and kissed her. Immediately she recoiled, then I felt a punch in my side.

'Fuck,' I groaned.

She didn't say anything but she was standing above me. I was half-expecting a kicking.

The commotion alerted councillor Ray who was uttering in nasal yam-yam terror, 'who goes there? What's this all about?'

Sarah dragged me up and pushed me out of the changing rooms. Blinded by torchlight, I covered my face. 'Switch it off, Ray. It's me, Tom.'

'Why yow hiding?' he chided. 'Who's behind ya?'

'Me,' she said, strong. 'Shine the torch to the ceiling, Ray.'

He fumbled with the torch, trying to balance it on the table, 'Sarah,' he was nervous. 'We thought yow'd gone up north to find your nan.'

'Sit down, Ray,' she asserted, calm.

Ray sat down immediately. Damien had been standing up the whole time watching the scenario unfold. He went into his rucksack and pulled out some big candles. He lit four of them and placed them on the table. He then switched the torch off.

'What do you want, Ray?' I asked.

'Shut it, Tom,' Sarah commanded.

With a sulky clomp, I sat on a vending machine, ashamed and sick inside. *Pathetic wretch.* Sarah went over to the other side of the space. I could hear her fumbling for something and, as she approached Ray, I saw she had rope in her hand.

'What are you doing, Sarah?' I asked, nervous.

'What else can I do?'

She had a point.

'Think about it,' I said. 'There'll be no going back. Not the way things are. You might have to do something unthinkable.'

'Have the courage to change the things you can,' she said as a matter-of-fact but with an air of criticism. Was she quoting the serenity prayer in reference to my lusty actions, or to justify tying up Ray?

'What yow doing?' he panicked, as she spun the rope around his mid-riff like she'd done it a hundred times.

Why does she even have rope? Again, my mind wandered, this time down some desperate alley to sexual foreplay and I slapped myself on the forehead.

Damien moved to hold Ray back against the chair, but he wasn't fighting it. It was hard to watch, but I was paralysed, lost in my head. *Why did I try to kiss her?*

'Please, Sarah,' Ray said. 'I had nothing to do with it.'

She pulled hard on the rope. 'Ow, please,' he was a little louder. 'I'll bloody yell, I will.'

'I'll gag you,' she said, taking a piece of cloth out her pocket to show him.

'Come on, Sarah,' I said. 'He's just a bird.'

'Stop it,' she snapped.

'A wittering skylark,' I added, with a smile, hoping she'd thaw.

'Quit with the animals!'

'I'm a Christian,' Ray manipulated. 'I wouldn't do anything like that. I don't have any power. I'm just there because I was a councillor. There's hardly anyone living in Hasbury anyway. I'm a Son of nothing.'

'How can you call yourself a Christian?' she said. 'Lee didn't hurt anyone.'

'Leroy lied,' he said.

'Lee!' she slapped him hard around the face which stunned him quiet. 'Who are you to tell someone how they should live their life?'

'I'm… I'm sorry. I'm just a Christian. Forgive me.'

She looked like she was about to slap him again. In the flicker of candle-light, I saw him prepare for it. He looked small and scared, like he might breakdown and cry.

'Sarah, how's this going to change anything?' I asked.

'You've no idea what you're talking about. You're just a dry-drunk lording it over everyone else. You think you're so different. You're a million miles away from the caterpillar.'

'Caterpillar?' Damien asked.

'You're exactly the same as my nan,' she added.

'I'm sorry, Sarah. I shouldn't-'

'I told you from the very first moment I met you, that I wasn't going-'

'To fuck me, yes. I know! I got muddled and mixed up. I'm not pretending I wasn't in the wrong. But now you're "lording it over me" whilst tying up councillor Ray.'

'What… um… happened?' Damien said, slow to catch up.

'It doesn't matter,' she said.

'Why did you come here, Ray?' I asked.

'I-I-I came to see if yow were alright. Look, I'm not saying anything bad against Tony-'

'Dale?' I asked, on purpose.

'Moran, yuh daft prat. He was on yow 'ard earlier.'

'Untie him, Sarah,' I said.

'I can't?'

Sarah was a potential target, no doubt. Since Leroy's demise, Tony Moran had been out of control. Supposed deviants had gone to spend a penny and never came back. Who they determined a deviant and how, we never knew, you just heard someone was no longer around.

'I won't tell anyone,' Ray said. 'I don't even want to be a part of this anymore.'

'I dunno,' Damien said, wary.

'He's a thug,' Ray added. 'Tony Moran's a thug. There, Ar've seddit. Yow have something on me.'

'Hardly. We'd record it on a phone, but…' she said, cynically.

Damien sat on a chair opposite Ray and started to roll a cigarette. Tiny canines of flame flickered on the table, warm, violent and alive, like an ancient ritual. I remembered candlelit AA meetings, fuzzy faces of anonymity telling stories about how their day had gone wrong and they'd shouted at the poor bastard at Costa who'd accidentally made them a latte rather than a flat white, and how they'd now realised the error of their ways and would make amends with an apology and the offer of a slice of cake. What part had I played in Tony Dale's death? Or in hounding Leroy to death? In Jay Bird's death? What about ripping teeth out of a dead man's mouth? What about my lust for Sarah? And my disloyalty to Will? And now, here I was, watching them tie councillor Ray up, a man who's only crime was fear – he'd actually come to see if I was ok. How would I ever make amends for it all?

'He means well, Sarah,' I begged.

'He won't be able to lie to them. I don't want to have do this, Ray, but-'

'*Do…*' he looked over at me, terrified. 'Do what?' His voice was filled with terror. He looked all around him, manic.

'Keep you here,' she replied. 'I can't risk you telling them where I am.'

He let out a deep sigh of relief. For a brief second even I thought she was going to stick a knife in him. Perhaps this was the mark of Halesowen, jumping to the most violent conclusion.

'The kiss, Sarah… it was just a random urge,' I said.

'Ray, look at me,' she ignored, pulling the rope up. 'I'm not going to hurt you.'

'It was dark-' I continued.

'I won't say anything to the Sons,' Ray begged.

'We were up close-' I said.

'It's just until I find a way around this,' she told Ray.

'But I'm claustrophobic.' Ray was wriggling in the chair.

'Just keep still,' she said.

'I was confused,' I pleaded.

'Tom!' she yelled. 'You've stopped doing what you need to do.' She went behind Ray to tighten the knot. 'All the things you told me.'

'Please, Sarah,' Ray panicked.

I found myself nodding. She was absolutely right. I knew now was the time. I reached into my pocket for the letter. 'I need to give you something.'

'What about Wolfie?' Ray shouted.

Sarah took the piece of cloth out of her pocket and muzzled him.

I made my way home via the old Cornbow Hall where we used to gatecrash private functions on weekend nights, where I used to watch the town pantomimes as a kid. Underneath it there used to be a Wilko's, before that it was a Safeway's – both companies had gone under before the bombs. Across the road, there used to be a chip shop run by an old Greek whose Greek father had owned it before him. It flourished in the wake of Covid 19, and easily survived the lockdown formality of the Western Flu which wiped out nearly a fifth of us, only to fall prey to the Greek Riots, coincidentally. Or not – we can be a funny bunch of nationalists.

'Of course, Phil had a hand in all of those things we read about,' Will once told me of the Greek Riots. 'Of course he masterminded Diana's and Dodi's deaths. But that's not what it was about. He was dead for fuck's sake. Like Jimmy Saville.'

'What was it all about then?' I asked him.

'It was when there was a big uptake in Christianity – a natural response in difficult times. It was a moral reaction to obscene greed which was initially directed by the media towards politicians who really had nothing to do with anything. They were just the team leaders, deputies and managers running a big shop. Remember the big image of Boris Johnson merged with a gopher, when he went into hiding?'

'"Go-for Boris the Gopher", of course.'

'He took the brunt of it from the media, and he was just an ambitious, morally bereft buffoon – we all grew up believing in ambition, Eton and comprehensive schools alike. But they didn't realise just how pissed off we all were and so before the workers started to unite they gave us a way to vent it. They sacrificed the Royal Family.'

Will made a lot of sense at times. I didn't know whether these things were true. It rang true, but then lots of things rang true. If only he could just break free from this place and the booze. But did I really want that? Did I want him to be happy and free and able to live a fulfilling life? I had to ask myself. I thought about Tammy, our beautiful punk, the love of his life. The girls always wanted Will, even as a broken-down wretch. Only he'd stopped seeing it. And Sarah was still here, but I couldn't even tell him. Maybe it would've helped him break free from his addictions.

But I knew I couldn't say anything for her sake. I couldn't tell any of them. Maybe I could tell Loz, but it was a risk. I certainly couldn't tell Marcus with his jabber mouth.

I felt so sick thinking about Sarah, everything that she'd been through and everything she was trying to overcome. And there I was, a middle-aged man-child trying the old AA thirteenth step – what would my sponsor have said about it?

'Oi, sad sack!' came from behind me.

A jolt of fear. I looked over my shoulder and walking towards me, a stumble in his step, clearly half-cut, was Tony Moran.

Oh fuck. 'Tone? I mean, T-Tony… Tony Moran?' I fumbled, adrenaline tremble in my voice.

'Call me Tone,' he said, a big stubbly smile on his tough, old face.

He was on his own. I couldn't see anyone else around.

'Erm, ok… Tone,' I nodded.

'You know, Christian tells me you're alright and maybe I was a little rough on you earlier,' he burped. 'Was I?' straight to the point.

'What? No,' I lied – *coward.*

He laughed. 'You're a nervy fucker. Don't you miss it?' He was swaying and looked ugly-drunk, but seemed to be in good spirits.

'Miss… er… what?'

'Drink, a bit of the old dutch,' he grinned. He lifted his arm over my shoulder. I crouched to accommodate him, a piquant waft of boozy apples for my troubles. 'Relax, Tommy. I know I can be a bit of an hard-nut, but I don't really mean any harm. The boys, you know how it is. You should come round more often.' He paused, turned and looked up at me, 'I mean that.'

We continued walking towards the flats, his drunken arm yanking on my neck, my back acutely aware of it. 'Yeah, you're right, Tone. We don't come around enough. Too busy breaking down metal-'

'I remember when you were young. You drank with the best of them. The George on Sundays, you'd sing on the karaoke, Oasis shit and what-not. We'd sell ya a couple of wraps.'

I'd completely forgot that we bought speed from his crowd, sweet, bitter, pasty and grainy. It was cheap and effective – whatever the true ratio of amphetamines to filler. There was a gang of them. Four or five lads in their 40s, five or six girls from 14 to 30, sometimes mother and daughter – wandering hands breaking laws.

'Good times, Tone,' I placated.

'Where's *he* gone?'

'I'm… er… here,' I laughed, nervous.

'You're shy, shaky. You need to act like a man.'

'Just who I am, who I always was. Keeping it real.'

He removed his arm from my shoulder. 'There's nothing fake about having a good time and letting your hair down. Alcohol's a need,' he said. 'You can renounce it, but it's written. Biblical. Ask the preacher,' he winked.

'Look, Tone,' I bit, 'you do what you need to do and I'll do what I need to do.' It was firm, because he'd angered me – I relived Leroy's bloodied head on the Christmas tree, his detached arm on Doran Close.

'Oooooh,' his deep wavering voice. 'I like it, Tom. I like it.' He was nodding. 'We had to do that to the preacher. It was for the good of the town. It's crazy times and crazy things happen. The George… well, *you* know all about that,' he smiled.

'That wasn't me!' I snapped. 'It wasn't my fault. It was Jay Bird!'

'Woh. All I'm saying,' he navigated, 'is maybe we wouldn't do those things now. We were *all* losing the plot back then.'

That was true. We'd all done things we wouldn't normally have done, things we never thought were in us. That was the mark of a civilised nation – those human behaviours which had lain dormant. But then I thought about Dan the dealer, chased out of a window to his death by Tony and his son, Aaron. That was before the bombs. Those animals were wild and free long before the new world.

'To tell you the truth, Tom. I've been shaking off a mean bastard my whole life.'

'What do you mean?'

We crossed over to the flats.

'This. The Sons. Being a Son is my attempt to redeem myself. Maybe I've not been altogether successful, but I'm trying damn it! I'm… I'm…'

I looked at his round, Irish face. He looked away, shy almost, pushed his hair back.

'Go on,' I said.

'I'm not a good man, Tom.'

It was probably just words, but it was good to hear. 'I've done bad things too,' I smiled.

'You what? Come off it, Tom!' He was angered by that. 'What have you really done?'

'I stopped drinking for a reason.'

It looked like I'd offended him. Was it a disparaging remark about his beloved drink? Or did he feel like I was playing him? Only then did it occur to me: did he already know about Tony Dale? What was actually going on here? Where did he come from?

I felt faint. If it'd been daytime, he might've seen my face turn white. I could feel the pulse beating faster in my temples, wild animal drums.

'I'm just… er, saying… What am I saying? Women, you know,' I said. 'I treated women bad. I still can, *believe me*. But I used to be very selfish. I treated my dad bad, my mum–'

He grabbed my wrist hard and looked me in the eye. *What does he know?* 'Family is everything.'

Most of his family had fled north. 'Exactly, Tone, and I was a shit. So I tried to stop being a shit.'

He stared at me and then burst out laughing, squeezing the back of my neck so hard, I had to suppress a squeal. 'Come on yuh shit, let's go to Ally's and treat some women nice. My lad's there, you know Aaron, went to school with him, din't yuh–?'

A sudden, loud eerie howl stopped us dead. In the still of the night, it echoed across the whole town. First it was one lone voice, then another joined in, frightening, until more followed suit and then it sounded like a pack of drunks pretending to be wolves.

Tony Moran looked up alert, he glanced around trying to gauge the direction. 'Come with me,' he said.

My immediate instinct was to argue my way out of it, but I really had little choice. That howl meant something serious had happened and I guessed I knew all about it.

———

Moving beams of torchlight, a frantic laser show across the graveyard.

'What's happening, Tone?' I asked as we speedily made our way alongside the graveyard wall.

'You tell me!'

Was that a threat? I had to stop myself responding.

There were people everywhere, but it was too dark to make anybody out. Just shadows of movement in distant beams, men scanning the area. The howling had been replaced by moans and shouting. A town usually stilled was alive with panic. It had to be the discovery of Tony Dale's body.

'Over here!' somebody shouted, and three or four beams converged. It was towards the middle of the graveyard by the wall.

Tony pulled out his little pen torch. The light was strong and lit up a group of men gawping over whatever they'd found. 'There!' he yelled to me.

I fumbled around between getting my headtorch on and pointing in the direction of the side entrance around the corner.

'The wall!' he said, grabbing my shoulder and trying to lift me over four feet of sandstone.

I lifted my leg up and let out a howl. 'My back!'

'Get over!'

'Ok, Tone, ok!' I swung myself astride the wall and rolled off the other side into grasses, against an all-but-buried gravestone.

I heard Tony scrambling over and looked up to see him making his way towards the men. It felt like my chance. It felt like the moment for me to run. I could fling myself back over and scarper towards the baths. Then we'd just need to find a way to get to Damien's barge without being spotted. But in the brief moment I lay in the sweaty grasses contemplating getting up, Marcus popped into my thoughts. Surely he'd be the one who'd end up being punished. It was always him. He was just so frigging helpless. And then I thought of Leroy, savagely torn apart in the wake of Jay's Law. I knew I had to go along with it. I had to risk it and play the game. *Fucking Ally*! It was her fault.

I got to my feet and stumbled my way through the grasses and gravestones. All I could think was one of them had left something behind after dumping Tony Dale's body. It had to be something to do with that. Maybe Marcus had dropped his buggered headtorch, or one of them had left behind a bottle of berries. Loz? Had Loz even gone with them? I couldn't imagine him dragging Tony Dale's dead body. He would've found something to do back home, like guard the bloody brew. Will would've mocked him but secretly been glad there was somebody at the flat.

But, as I got closer, I could see somebody's naked feet, then legs. I couldn't make much else out because there were people around the body.

'She's dead,' someone said.

'She don't look it,' another.

'Check her fucking pulse… honestly.' Tony turned, shined his torch on me. 'Tom, you do it.'

The men turned in stunned unison.

'Tom, mate.' Ricky broke the silence. 'Come see if Barb's still ticking.'

My heart sank. '*Barb*? Barb and Rex, Barb?'

I moved between them and Barb was lying on the floor, her pink dressing gown splayed open, white nightie exposing her lower half. Immediately I pulled her nightie down. I touched her face and she felt cold. There was a big bruise on her forehead as if she'd fallen and hit her head on the wall, or something much worse. 'Barb! Can you hear me?'

'Ark at the nurse,' someone said, laughing.

'Fucking shut it!' Tony warned.

'Sorry, I didn't… sorry,' the voice grovelled.

'She's alive,' I said.

'Pick her up, pick her up,' Tony nagged, irritably.

I reached under her arms and tried to pull her up, but this sent a bolt of pain down my back. 'Cunting hell!' I blurted.

'His bloody back,' Tony excused. 'Get her up, lads.'

I felt somebody push me aside. I fell on my knees, sick with the pain. I took a deep breath, half-grateful it was nothing obviously incriminating, half-grieved it was poor Barb.

'What's happened?' I heard Tony ask.

'Someone robbed St John's. Terry's dead,' someone answered.

'Who?'

Robbed? Perhaps they hadn't got around to dumping Tony Dale's body yet. God forbid they carried him over now.

'Terry Goddard,' someone said.

'I don't know a Terry,' Tony grumbled.

'Goddard's Fields,' he prompted.

'The milk?' he asked. 'Owns the cows!' epiphany.

I felt a wave of relief at not having to play ignorant, but then we heard someone shouting at the top of their voice, 'the Greek, the Greek!' followed by a howl, then another.

On all fours, I turned my head, felt a pang of pain run from my neck to my tail bone. 'Fuck,' I barked. 'Fuck, fuck!'

I watched the beams begin to converge from various directions across the whole graveyard.

'Come on, Tom,' Tony called.

'My back.'

He reached for my hand and helped me to my feet. 'You got any of them painkillers left?'

'I'm alright,' I said.

'The fuck you are. Give.'

Tony Dale was dead in the Greek. The town was about to make this gruesome discovery. Tony Moran was staring deep into my nervous eyes and it had already been too many seconds. I reached into my pocket and handed them to him. There were eight left of the blister pack of ten. He eyed me suspiciously and then took two out.

'I don't... I don't have a drink. At St John's?' I asked, hopeful.

'Use spit,' he said.

'I can't swallow like that,' I lied.

'Better still.' He took one capsule and turned the top half, pulling it free from the bottom. My headtorch lighted a mound of powder in the half capsule, he carefully held it between grubby finger and thumb. 'Open,' he said.

I held my hand out.

'Mouth,' he tutted.

There was no option. The situation. And my back did hurt. *It did*! I opened my mouth and he poured the powder in. It coated my tongue and teeth, the bitter taste numbing but oh so familiar, two decades on since I last experimented with any mind-altering drugs. He opened another and repeated it.

'Nasty, eh?' he laughed.

'Yeah, huh, yeah,' I tried to laugh.

I licked it into my gums, grainy. There was no going back.

'Now, let's go see if we've found ourselves a robber.'

I limped purposefully slow behind, overwhelmed and in pain. The bitter taste in my mouth was only a temporary distraction from what I was about to encounter. Tony rushed ahead, to see the body being pulled from the grave. I heard him yell, 'someone's gonna pay for this!'

I stood in the big circle, a face amongst many, inside St John's church staring at Tony Dale's dead body. The men, like pallbearers, had carried his coffin-stiff corpse on their shoulders across the graveyard. I'd held back, using my injury as an excuse.

He now lay in a rigor mortis recovery position, on the cold red and black tiles in the middle of the building. His bloodstained face was yellow and grey, already his cheeks were sunken beneath the stubble. His mouth, frozen slightly ajar, made him look like a much older man. I hadn't noticed before, but his hands were swollen and purple. I couldn't smell anything, but it had only been a day since he'd died. It usually took a couple of days before that stench infected the air and everything else around it.

Lying on his back next to him, was Terry the milkman. Terry was fat but much shorter. Tony Dale faced him, whilst Terry, white-faced and wide-eyed, stared up at the ceiling like he was day-dreaming about making cheese. There was no obvious evidence of a murder and his lips looked blue in the white LEDs which hung from the ceiling. There was also no evidence of a robbery either. The church looked organised and mostly tidy.

The circle was made up entirely of men, heads bowed, occasionally mumbling about who could've done it and what had actually gone down. Tony Moran paced up and down where the altar used to be, unofficial president of the unofficial confederation of Halesowen – which, if the rumours were true, was about to make a move on the tiny population of Quinton.

'It's so sad,' fell out of my mouth, staring at the doomed couple.

One of the Price brothers, a Son, looked up at me but didn't say anything.

It'd been well over a year since I'd been in the church, not since the time of Jay's Law. Before that, I recalled the voting of the Sons, when we stood at the back with the Church of 7 congregation – a happier time. Sarah had been newly sober and seemed happy. Leroy was Lee but not the Lee he would've liked to have been. Jake was made a Son. Rex was alive, batty as ever, and Barb was Barb.

Poor Barb. At the front of the church, behind Tony Moran and below the big stained-glass, she lay on a long table like the grotesque expression of a sacrificial virgin, a Bosch painting, her multicoloured face just visible above the white sheet. She'd been somewhat forgotten in the wake of Tony Dale's discovery, but the doctor – who wasn't technically a doctor – had been called. Her mind was already lost to Wernicke-Korsakoff's, it seemed to me, and maybe it would be best for her to fade out like her beloved Rex had, his cancerous goitre a second head. Life must've been so long for her. 80-odd years, the majority spent in the most fruitful period of history in our country. It was only the last decade or so when things had morphed and we'd started to taste something darker, something we'd been protected from for so long.

St John's was now primarily a trade hall, a place for the Sons and the nons to keep track of what we were looting, deeming it's worth – according to their standards on any given day – and valuing it in shillings and guineas. Either side of us, running down the left and right wings of the nave, were the trade stalls, covered with insulating sheets to keep some of the produce from going off, mostly breads, fruits and vegetables. Behind the stalls the hum of tall meat and milk fridge-freezers, like an army of white robots. Against the sandstone brick, on every side, were tall lines of tins in various shapes and sizes, metal walls in a solemn trench. Everything was priced in old money terms and each person/group had an account, audited by the town, us, the federalis – supposedly one and the same thing. The lay-out seemed very neat, the ideas behind the economics, simple and sensible. I found myself thinking this was a really good system and that actually we were very lucky. If only we had better leadership what a wonderful town it might be.

I looked back to the poor slab of Tony Dale, a tragedy next to the round comedy of the milkman, who I didn't really know. Tony Dale was a good guy. I'd never had any trouble with him and he was the father of little Ethan. *Poor Ally.* I started to feel overcome with emotion, said a prayer to myself: *God grant me the serenity to accept the things I cannot change, the courage to change the things I can and the wisdom to know the difference.*

The building was once an actual living and breathing church. St John the Baptist, C of E. I was christened in it. My mum and dad got married in it. I remembered singing Christmas carols from the pews with both my primary and high schools, in the far from bleak midwinters. I remembered the arm ache, which I refused to show, leading the scouts as a flag bearer in Remembrance Sunday parades to the church. I'd studied the building when I was at school, and still recall being told that there was a time when, if you held the big iron door handle outside, they couldn't arrest you. The church was once a sanctuary for criminals. It was once again.

Or perhaps I was looking at it all wrong. Maybe I just needed to take part. I felt a sudden wave of love come over me. Isn't this what Ally had been trying to get me to do? She understood I could make a positive contribution in the difficult task of running a town.

I looked around the circle at the sombre men I'd known for most of my life. It was a dutiful show of grief for their compatriots. I had goose-pimples – a warm feeling of patriotism for my home town.

The back of the church had been converted into a big hardware store. Ladders hanging over the big stained-glass windows. Tins of paints and varnish in tall precise and wonderful circles. Then there were aisles of shelving, which reminded me of my beloved library – *we need to reopen the library again* – but it consisted of big drawers of tools and smaller drawers of nails, hooks and all the sorts of things people needed to maintain a house, I guess. I wouldn't know, I'd never walked around it before. We had all the tools we needed at the cabin in Leasowes Park.

Oh, Leasowes. Will's right, we're so lucky to have our little home away from home. Why would we ever need to leave? And Marcus, bless him, and Loz, emotionally dependable at times – a good sane person to have around. And Ally's fun, even some of the girls. Life's not so bad.

The last images of Leroy, a mosaic across town, intruded my peaceful thoughts, but I stifled it, denied it. Then I thought about Marcus and I could've cried. Were we in as much denial about his sexuality as we assumed he was?

My meandering mind was interrupted by somebody entering the church, the creak of a heavy door. I glanced over to see Christian walk in. *Good old Christian.* My long-time friend, who'd tried to spare me from being ostracised from the town. I vividly remembered that laughing game when, as a desperate child in a silly sketch, I pretended to fuck a golf hole to make everyone laugh. And still it made him laugh.

He's a good friend, you know, Christian.

'Oh, Christian, oh Christian,' slipped out of my mouth with all the glee in the world, and then I realised why I was feeling so happy. I was high – the chalky dose of co-codamol coursing through my veins.

Following behind him was the butcher, mean and serious, and behind him, the doctor. The doctor looked a little like Penfold from that old cartoon, Danger Mouse, short and chubby, a hazelnut head and small specs. None of them were smiling. I immediately followed suit.

'Just terrible, mate,' I said to Christian.

'Yeah,' he said, cold, as he passed me, straight through the middle of the circle, stopping to glance at Tony Dale and the milkman, before heading over to Tony Moran, conspiratorial whispers.

The doctor opened his holdall and began attending to Barb.

In the midst of my opiate reverie, I seemed to have forgotten that I was culpable, that I was present at Tony Dale's death, that I'd tried to hide his body and knew exactly what had happened, why we'd found his body in the Greek. But I wasn't scared when I remembered it. I found myself staring at his purple patchy hands, nails blackening, lost in a daze. I don't know how long Tony Moran had been calling my name, but he was angry when I realised. 'Tom!'

'What? Sorry,' I said.

'What happened to Tony Two?' he asked.

I looked up at him, then to Christian and the butcher, whose piercing stare made me feel certain he knew. They were waiting. Then there were the other men, about 15 of them, expecting me to say something. These were the men who crammed into the back of Picks, the men I always avoided. Where were the women? It was like being at the Conservative Club on a lunchtime in the 80s and 90s. Ricky was nodding in anticipation, half-smiling. What did he expect me to say? Jordan, the "unofficial" non who chaired the federali meetings grinned at me, gangly and meek – I didn't even know the guy. Jake twitched, 'rabbit-rat!' trying his best to suppress the Tourette's, but his tick flared up with stress and now was perhaps the most stressful time we'd had in Halesowen since Leroy died – Jake being the only Son who'd supported him. Sons, nons and federalis, all the main players were in St John's except for Big Ross North – perhaps he was in the back penning wordy obituaries for the Halesowen News pamphlet which occasionally appeared.

'Tom?' Christian prompted, disappointed.

But I wasn't scared, there was no stress in me, just an easy feeling of everything's opiate-ok. 'He's dead,' I said, half-dumb, my mouth open.

'You don't say,' Tony mocked. 'Fuck sake, you're as bad as the rest of them. Thought you was smart. Fit right in.'

'What?' I half-dribbled, wiped my mouth, bewildered by the whole thing.

'How?' he asked.

'Stabbed,' I said, without thinking.

'How do you know?'

'The knife wound in his neck,' dazed but still unafraid.

'Good. Why?'

'I don't know. But whoever did it is trying to send a message by sticking him in the Greek Grave.'

'Yes, they are,' he said. 'That's exactly what I was thinking.'

I was about to elaborate on the foolish bravery of such an act, but thankfully I was interrupted. The big front door creaked once more. We all turned. Ally walked in followed by Honest John. She immediately ran over to Tony Dale's corpse and fell to her knees crying.

'Weren't even together,' somebody muttered.

She stood up, eyed the circle, found where the voice came from and smacked him square in the face, four times, one for each word. 'He's. The. Baby. Daddy.'

The man fell back into one of the stalls, pulled on the sheet to reveal a mound of spuds, several of which toppled onto him as he sat there, confused. It was like watching a cartoon. The *toot-toot* of Popeye in my head.

I found myself sauntering over to Ally, stepping over Tony Dale's and then the milkman's legs. I put my hands on her shoulders. She turned, making a fist and then saw it was me. 'Tom.'

I nodded. 'Tone, let me take her back,' I said, brave, familiar.

Tony paused, thinking about it. 'Yes. Someone should look after her. Go,' he said.

I turned to cross back over the milkman's legs but Ally put her hand on my shoulder to direct me through the circle to the vestibule, Honest John trailing behind us.

'Tone!' the doctor called. 'She's awake!'

This was followed by three perfectly spaced vixen screams.

We turned to see Barb sitting up and pointing down the church. It could've been at anyone or anything, but I looked up at Honest and he looked terrified. He pushed in front of us to get out.

'Barb,' I called, to try to waken her from the madness.

Ally tried to pull me back.

'Barbara Newton!' It echoed through the church.

Again, a vixen scream, in Munchian terror.

'Tom, what are you doing?' Ally whispered.

'Barbara Newton,' I yelled once more, as if recounting her full name might break the spell of lunacy. It was instinctive, doped but instinctive.

The men just looked at me, bewildered. But Barb had been in my life forever. She'd been my mum's friend since before I was born, then when I was drinking she'd been my friend. And once again, in the good times, when the Church of 7 was being built across the town, she was someone I could call a friend. We lost touch in the wake of Jay's Law, when we spent our days hunting for metals or at the cabin in Leasowes. Then Rex died and I guess she was alone. No wonder she lost it.

'Barb!' I shouted.

Christian and the butcher held her down. Then I realised what was about to happen. She was struggling, trying to kick her old legs under the sheet, but she'd stopped screaming or saying anything. Is this how blind Billy, with his deep chortle and very little else, went? Is this how they took them out? We'd come back from the cabin and certain people just weren't around anymore, erased from the Halesowen landscape.

'Come on,' Ally begged.

Tony Moran held her feet down, turning back to us. 'Go, Tom,' he demanded. 'Take Ally home.'

But I watched the doctor take out his needle to euthanise her. Ally squeezed my arm hard in an unconscious bid to displace my pain. We knew they did it, we'd heard about it, but I'd never seen it. This was the end for a prune loon who was more trouble than they were worth.

'Tom, mate,' Ally whispered.

Eventually I let her drag me outside. As soon as the air hit me, I heaved, but there was nothing to throw up.

'Is that it for Barb?' I said.

'Sorry Tom,' John said.

'Sorry? Why are you sorry?'

'I didn't do it,' he said. '*Honest.*'

Perhaps this said it all, and there was a look of terror in his eye when she screamed. And now there was a look in Ally's eye which suggested this was something to do with us.

'T-Tomatoes,' Honest said. 'Gotta... gotta go. The toms.'

'We can plant tomatoes in the morning, John,' she said.

I heaved again, put my hand to my mouth. This time a ball of grainy phlegm. I wiped it on my shirt.

'Tom, she's better off dead.'

Ally's place was like a beacon. There seemed to be lights on in every room. Torchlight, candles, electric lights, red lights, blue lights, orange, green and yellow. Some of the windows were lit in the other blocks on the estate too. A couple of floors in the Bredon Highrise were lit with LEDs, and there were candles and solar torches staked in window gardens. But nowhere shone as brightly and consistently as Ally's rectangular whorehouse, hidden deep in the estate, opposite our lowly little block, currently blacked-out.

The high was starting to wear off and I was feeling exhausted.

She opened her back door and a familiar whiff of musk greeted me, lads holidays and strip joints, white thighs, and penetrating eyes determined to deter you from looking elsewhere.

The first thing I heard was Stacey's hag-laugh, mean and piercing. She was sitting on the arm of a chair, topless, her breasts like tired eyes. She leant against Loz, who was topless and fat, head-bobbing drunk and ready to pass out. Marcus was standing in the door with a bottle of berries, grinning mid-*ooh-ar-but-yes*, Frankie Howerd mode. Two of the girls were lying on the sofa, chubby bare limbs interlocked like a Henry Moore sculpture, swigging red wine from pale blue ceramic mugs – I wasn't sure where one began and the other ended.

'Where's Will?' Ally asked.

'Anita the meter maid,' Marcus laughed.

Ally walked through him and out of the room. Honest John followed her, an imposing shadow.

Two other women were sat on the floor, legs open and naked. I watched Loz close one eye, trying to focus between their legs. Usually I would do all in my power not to look, but I found myself staring at a shaggy vagina in almost scientific curiosity, lost, and wholly devoid of sexuality, the fleshy stigma of some alien flower.

'Like what you see, Tom?' Stacey asked, before firing laughter at me.

Loz laughed like he knew what was going on.

It was all her fault and I couldn't find so much as a "fuck you", dazed by it all.

I looked to Marcus. 'What's up with you?' he asked, chirpy.

I stood open-mouthed, gawping at him. *Is this just the opiates? Surely they can't be this strong?* But it had been so long since I'd had any mind-altering substance that I felt totally worn down by it.

'Codeine,' I said.

Marcus stopped smiling.

'He needs a line,' one of the vaginas said.

'Do I fuck!' I walked past them and into the hall. Marcus followed me.

'Are you… are you,' he was tapping me on the shoulder, 'are you alright? What the fuck, man? Opiates?'

I could hear people in various rooms, so I moved into the kitchen and closed the door.

'Oh God! He made me.'

'Who?'

'*Tony Moran*. I've just been in the middle of it all. Fucking Stacey!'

'We've already put him in the Greek. Will, Honest and me,' he whispered.

'Did you happen to see Barb?' I asked.

'Um, no… Barb? I don't-'

'Did. You. See. Barb?'

'She's nuts. She won't have a clue about any of this. I don't even think she saw what we were doing.'

'She's *dead*.'

He looked genuinely perplexed. There was no way he'd be able to hide this from me.

'What about Terry Goddard?' I asked.

'Who?'

'The milkman!'

'Fat fella?'

'Yeah. He's dead too.'

'*What the…*'

My eyes felt heavy, my head was in another world. I didn't feel like I had a handle on things. Why did I used to take this shit so much? And these were just the filler drugs, the in-between bender drugs, the drugs to deal with the after-effects of drugs, the drugs when nothing else was there drugs. Codeine, methadone, the 'azepams, these were the drugs that meant I was effectively high for months, even years at a time, drugs which stopped me seeing the light of day. Then Sarah popped into my thoughts again.

'I can't believe I tried to kiss…' I nearly did it, I nearly said her name, but I couldn't. None of them knew about Sarah and I really wished they did. Only Ally and she wouldn't want them to know, because she was in love with Will and Will was in love with Sarah. But I needed to vent, to talk, to let it out, *my name's Tom and I'm an alcoholic and…*

I could hear a row upstairs. I knew what was happening.

Marcus was pacing up and down the kitchen. 'We didn't do anything to Barb. Or the milk guy. I swear!'

'They euthanised her.'

He stopped, slammed the counter with his fist. 'Like Lee!' He was so angry he'd forgotten to call him Leroy. Loz, Will and me always called him Leroy, in spite of it all and, because we called him Leroy, Marcus called him Leroy too, but if anyone of us knew him as Lee it was him.

'Not quite the same,' I said. 'She went with the needle.'

'It's the same fucking thing, Tom!' He slammed the counter again, hard, and then immediately subdued a scream from the pain it caused.

I opened the fridge and took out a jug of water. I started to pour it into my mouth, spilling it down my cheeks, cold, numbing, giving me some sense of feeling. I lifted it higher and drenched myself with a big splash. Marcus jumped back.

There was a loud thud upstairs and we heard Will shout, 'fuck off, you mad woman!'

'What's this about Tony Moran?' he asked.

'I bumped into him on the way back.'

'On the way back from where?' he asked.

I wanted to tell him. I wanted one of them to know. I shouldn't have to keep carrying this secret around with me. Secrets make you sick, they used to say in rehab.

I looked Marcus square in the eye. 'Talk to me about it.'

'About what?' he lied.

'Tell me about Lee and I'll tell you where I've been and how the hell we're going to survive this mess.'

Jay's Law

I climbed into the sandstone pulpit, councillor Ray looking up at me.

Ray: Did yow see Nigel's body, Tom?

Me: No.

Ray: Why did yow goo in the George?

It was the first time I'd been in St John's since they'd removed the pews. It made the church look much bigger. The other six Sons were sat amongst the townspeople on chairs of varying shapes and sizes, haphazardly spaced. Jay Bird was sitting restlessly behind me, where the altar used to be. He looked tiny next to John Bosko, the gardener, who'd been told to stop him leaving his seat.

Me: We went in to see if they'd really left.

Ray: Had they?

Leroy was sitting amongst them all, next to Marcus, in a yellow robe. As much as Lee wanted to leave Leroy behind, the guy I'd once known and grown up with was at last looking back at me. He half-smiled, but he looked worried.

Me: I assume so. The van was gone.

Ray: Ok, Tom.

Someone booed, one of the nons. A few people laughed.

Ray: He may be a lot of things, but ar doh think Tom's a killer.

Tony Dale looked troubled, arms crossed, which made me think the worst. He was standing behind Ally, who was cradling little Ethan, his son. Lettie was playing at the back with the other children – whose idea had it been to bring kids into this circus?

Me: I really wasn't there very long.

I looked back to see Jay Bird. He stuck his thumb up, like a bloody idiot. I turned away quickly.

* * *

Loz came running into the flat and through to the bedroom in a state of panic muttering about Jay and the collective judgement. 'And they've left the George!' he insisted.

'What?' I asked, sitting up in bed. 'Where? How?'

It was an old Ford Transit van which they'd converted to serve burgers in the tiny concrete beer garden of the George. It looked like an Um Bongo drink carton, colourful jungle animals painted on the sides. It would've been a sight to behold on the move at any time, but it was 2029 and rare to see a vehicle on the road. Jay Bird had been sitting on the balcony of his maisonette when he heard the rumble of an engine. He then watched the colourful van trundling around the roundabout and disappearing out of view.

He went down to see if there was anybody still at the George. Apparently, there wasn't.

Will and Loz had been up the road at the King Edward. Will had his guitar and they'd played an impromptu set of Christmas songs, which Loz would've loved and Will hated, consoling himself with a drink or two for requests.

'He spotted us and dropped the bomb,' Loz said, plonking himself on the bed and rolling a cigarette, 'and then he swore us to secrecy.'

'Shit.'

'He was like all, "come on manz",' he added. 'You know in that weird-'

'Attempt at a Jamaican accent-'

'Fucking Gollum!' He lit his roll-up, trembling. It looked like a burst zeppelin, zig-zagging in and out of his mouth. 'What are we gonna do?'

'But the George has been closed for weeks,' I said. 'Is it even a business anymore?'

'God knows! Maybe? Jay just told us they had beer, two full barrels-'

'And Will?' I asked, nodding an answer to my own question.

'The Edward was heaving too.' He took a hard drag on the damp wick and coughed.

'Did anybody hear you?'

'I reminded them about the federalis. "We *is* the fedz," Jay kept saying.'

'He knows better than that. Especially now,' I thumbed behind, the continuous crack of sledgehammers and domino-topple of bricks, where they were dismantling dad's old high-rise. 'All for a goat-shagger – Ground Zero, they're calling it.'

'What are we gonna do, Tom?'

'You should've stopped him.'

'You kidding?'

'Or at least stayed as a look-out.'

'He'll be alright... won't he?'

Ross North had defined looting as "the act of pillaging and plundering in a lawless land", and Halesowen had no laws. Instead, according to the recently ratified *Declaration of Freedom*, we had the "collective judgement". Laws were unnecessary, "an imposition on sound-minded adults".

'After the Supra, it's not worth the risk,' I said.

'Exactly!'

Anis Devi and his family abandoned the Supra shop the day after the last bus. One family looted it a couple of days later, which seemed fair game to us, all things considered, but it angered the Price brothers, who then riled the rest of the town into a lynch mob who looted the family back. One was looted to death. The collective judgement in the wake of this was: don't steal from our businesses, don't steal from each other.

It spread around the pubs as if it had been in the Daily Express. When it came to the *Declaration of Freedom*, the Supra shop incident was cited as the perfect example of the collective judgement and, by luck or genius, nothing like it had been repeated since and nobody had died.

'One way or another,' I sighed, 'booze is destined to kill me. We've gotta do something.'

'I've got a family to think about.' He was sincere but his face twitched like he was trying to swallow a lodged painkiller. 'Second Christmas without them.'

There was a huge bang outside and someone shouted, 'timmm-berrr!' We instinctively crouched as if the whole high-rise was going to topple onto our little block. We heard the bricks hit the ground like a pool break, balls quickly coming to a standstill, and then the jeers and laughter of a near miss. This was happening a few times a day.

'You'll see them again,' I said.

'I sure as hell won't be here forever.'

'Don't tell Will that.' I got up, pulled a jumper over my linen shirt. 'I'm gonna have to go down there.'

He looked panicked, 'he'll be alright! Won't he? He's with Jay. There was nobody around.'

'It's too close to St John's,' I said, putting my old down jacket on – memories of cold Himalayan teahouses, a million miles away.

'What if someone sees you there?'

'I'll walk by and, if it looks risky, I'll keep on walking.'

'Should I… come?' he asked – he didn't mean it.

'You want to?'

'Where's Marcus?'

'With Sarah at the post office.'

'I'll… go let him know,' he said, giving himself an excuse.

I grabbed his arm. 'Don't say anything to anybody, especially not bloody Marcus. Just go help them out.'

He followed me out of the flat, the *pock* of sledgehammers intensifying. We looked up to see a small gang of men, fags in mouth, wrapped up warm, banging away. A couple of floors had been lopped off, brick by brick.

Two old guys were sitting on a settee, swigging from a bottle of booze, as if they hadn't realised the walls had fallen down around them. There was also a young girl sitting in an armchair like she was supervising the workmen building her a rooftop terrace, pink bobble hat and scarf. Her legs were crossed and she looked serious, young heir to the Halesowen throne. God knows what she was doing up there. If I'd had my phone, I'd have taken an award winning photograph of a town devolving in the nuclear wastelands. On the floor below them, we heard woodpecker taps where they were knocking out the window frames.

It'd been five months since that summer night when the Sons came into being. The bus station was still coated in glass and debris. The smashing up of the town was a symbolic gesture instigated by comrade Ross. It went on for days. We would tear it down and then build it back up.

At the old post office – or Church-1, as they were calling it – the big windows showed a busy congregation, wide-eyed and smiling, setting up shop with homemade Christmas decorations. Barb was making drinks and Rex was fast asleep in one of the seats on the front row. The double doors were open and Jake, Son of the Squirrels, was leaning against the wall, smoking.

'Squirrels,' he twitched. 'You come to give us a hand?'

'I can help,' Loz said.

'Maybe later,' I smiled.

At the selection of the Sons, Jake uncontrollably fired 'sheep-deer-squirrels!' to all at St John's. Leroy saw this as "an act of God" and urged him to put his hand up. We voted him Son of the Squirrels for fun, but he was already proving to be quite good at it. Leroy seemed the obvious choice, ever willing to take centre stage, but he'd had discussions with councillor Ray and clearly wanted to be the pope in this play.

Sarah spotted me and called me over.

'Where's Will?' she asked.

'Will?' I replied.

'*What?*' She knew there was more to it.

'Edward probably. I dunno. You doing alright?'

She was sat at a table with a Bible in front of her.

'Yeah.' A half-smile. She tore a page out of the Bible.

'Is that the truth?'

'Is he wrecked?' she asked, avoiding the question.

Sarah was coming up to six months free from drink and drugs. I knew how hard it was, especially in Halesowen and with the way those around her, specifically Will and Leroy, got wasted. I'd been in her situation and I'd never managed to stay sober. The only way for me had been to leave Halesowen.

'I think he's pretty gone, yeah.'

'Can't he just go a day?' she pleaded, before swiftly tearing another page out of the Bible.

'I'm gonna go find him. Don't worry. We'll see you later. You keep doing… what are you doing?'

'I'm making origami doves.'

'Isn't that sacrilege?'

'No,' came from behind.

'Hi Lee,' I said, without turning.

'A book is just a book, a church is just a building. The words matter, and then it's all about this,' he said, coming over and jabbing me in the chest. He grabbed a box of her efforts from under the table and held it out with a rustle and a shake. 'Take one.'

'I've really gotta go, Lee,' I said.

'Go on,' he teased.

'Tom,' Sarah insisted.

I took a paper dove.

'Open it,' she added.

I opened it up. The first verse I saw, '"whosoever putteth away his wife, and marrieth another"…' I stopped.

'Oh, Tom,' Sarah squeezed my hand.

I walked away cursing Leroy. *Please Lord, don't let this meaningless building falleth on Leroy's head.*

As I went to leave, Loz whispered, 'I'd say call me but,' he shrugged, 'just be careful.'

'Don't fucking say anything.'

———————

Sitting towards the front of the nave, Ross North leant over and whispered in Ed's ear. Ed had been made the College Son — he was the only one who'd put his hand up. The College Son represented the area formerly known as Hawne, but there was vague talk about using the old college for educational purposes in the future. In his early thirties, Ed was enthusiastic and confident, but education was not his strong point.

He tipped his trilby to Ross and stood up, a youngster finally getting off the subs bench. He pointed at Will.

Ed: Geeze, you's up.

I climbed down from the pulpit, nodded solemnly at Will, as he made his way up. I sat on a chair between Loz and Stacey, adjacent to the pulpit. Ross had called it the "witness queue". Loz had already said his bit, which corroborated my story.

Ed paced back and forth with a swagger. He stopped, clasped his hands together, then looked up at Will.

Ed: Did you kill Nigel?

There was a shocked reaction from the townspeople. Ross was smiling.

Will: What the fuck? I didn't even see him.

Ed: Hey, don't shoot the lawyer.

He faced the crowd, tossed his trilby in the air, before suddenly turning, ready to fire another question.

Ed: Did you steal any loot?

Will: Yes.

What the hell! Will wasn't supposed to say that. We had our story. Leroy immediately glanced at Marcus. He noticed but looked straight ahead, his hand squeezing his bad knee, forever testing to see if the sensation had returned.

Will: We have a right to loot. Is there a law which would suggest otherwise?

Ed looked stunned. Jay Bird jumped up. 'Yeah, manz!' he said. 'We have the rightz!'

Christian gave the nod to John Bosko, who put his arm out and pushed Jay back in his seat.

'Woah, John, manz,' Jay Bird laughed, nervous, straightening the collar of the white shirt he wore as if we were at Birmingham Crown Court.

Ed: But… the collective… judgement.

* * *

I went into the graveyard and alongside the church to get an idea of who was around. As I passed the entrance, I heard people inside, the scraping of chairs on the stone floor. My plan was to convince Will and Jay to give up the George loot to the Sons. They'd surely get something out of it and order would be maintained.

Jay Bird epitomised one of the darkest periods of my addiction. His permanently pin-head pupils rolling around his pale face, his bald pinhead rolling around his string pin body. He was more *addict* than any I'd ever met. He wasn't simply addicted to drugs, because that suggested there was a way to change it. It was who he was. He was fearless with little awareness or thought for consequences. A doomed relationship with Six-Kids-Stacey, many years ago – he was father to one of the six – started him down this road. To him there was only her, so much so he still believed it was happening despite her absence in the pairing. There'd been only one way to move forward and that was to deny reality.

He took a shine to me from very early on in my addiction, and I just took a shine to dark days and they were never more grungy than when I was with Jay. We searched out the dives in Dudley and Birmingham, £1 a pint of Banks's bitter, four bottles of Diamond White for a fiver, happy hour double-doubles. We'd snort crunched up sleepers and tranqs – usually his prescription – off porcelain pub toilets. We'd counteract the down with big Rizla-wrapped balls of doughy amphets, all the time swallowing as much booze as we could afford. The bacchanalia was accompanied, innocently enough, with karaoke singing. He would sing Bob Marley, a terrible offbeat refrain of "Jamming", whilst I sang Radiohead tracks and the odd Lennon song. We sang the same duet almost every time we were together, "Twist and Shout". I took the lead and he chipped in with the backing vocal. Jay was always very proud of this. For my friendship, he let me in on some of the stories of his criminal life, robbing pubs, family, mostly people close to him. If I'd had anything to steal, I probably would've avoided him, but instead I went down many murky rabbit holes with Jay Bird. I felt like I was about to follow him down another.

I only saw Jay once in the good in-between years, when back visiting mum. He was bloated, his legs swollen, face blotchy with heart disease. I tried to talk him off the dope, but he could barely grasp what I was saying. A year later, I heard he'd been diagnosed with early-onset dementia and was in the Brett Young Centre, at the ripe old age of 40. His older brother, Sean, said it was just to get the meds. Naïve, as ever, I didn't believe him and felt sorry for my old hopeless partner in escape. But, post-bombs, when the care home was about to close, many residents dragged north with family, Jay Bird made a miraculous recovery – and apparently cleared them out of meds. He moved back in with his brother across the road from the George, relieved of his swollen sickness.

When I got to the George, I could hear the crash of drunks fumbling about. There was nothing clandestine about this plunder. Out the front, the door to the cellar was wide open. I looked around, saw nobody.

'Will,' I whisper-shouted.

Nothing.

'Jay?'

I took another glance around me before making my way down the steep steps and into the cold stony underworld of the cellar, the sweet familiar reek of yeast, the tinny taste in the air. Stainless steel barrels lay next to each other, droids in a futuristic hospital, freed from their lines, the barley stained tubes which fed the beer pulls in the bar above. I could hear people up there. 'Will?'

'Tom?' he called down. 'Loz is a goddam coward, did a runner.' He made his way down the stairs from the bar.

He had a full black bag in his hands. 'Here,' he handed me an empty one. 'Open it.'

I started to look for the right end. 'We can't do this, Will.'

'Open it.'

'It'll fuck things up.' I opened the bag and he doubled it up. It was heavy and jangling. He took it from me and left it at the bottom of the stone steps.

I heard someone else coming down. Jay Bird appeared, swigging from a bottle of wine.

'Jay, we've gotta tell the Sons.'

He went over to the barrels. 'Nah, manz-'

'Fuck that!' Will added, now carrying a huge white plastic barrel, which looked empty.

'What you gonna do with that?' I asked.

'About 18 gallons I reckon,' he said. 'That's about 150 pints.'

Jay Bird started rolling a steel barrel over, the wine bottle in his mouth. It wasn't as big as the plastic one, but it was full – one person wouldn't be able to carry it very far. 'We can't do this, boys. Think about the Supra.'

'The barrelz is full Tomz-y boy!' Jay said, stopping to swig.

'Just grab it,' Will said.

'I don't wanna be murdered by a lynch mob!'

'Look, I know you don't drink,' he manipulated, 'I get it, you tell me every other fucking hour, but just-'

'It's nothing to do with that.'

'Yes, it is.'

'No, it's not.'

'Tom, this is happening!' Will's overpowering boom bounced off the stone walls.

'Alright, alright, just be fucking quiet.' Helpless, I whispered, 'St John's is only around the corner.'

I ran up the stone steps to see if anyone was in sight. Then I went back down and grabbed the steel barrel, heaving it up backwards, lifting and stopping until I was on the pavement.

I took a moment to get my breath and looked around. The huge Earl's roundabout, stilled, sulking under a wet hairdo, a neglected sprawl of weeds and grass. Up the Stourbridge Road, two shop fronts were boarded, one of which had been graffitied, "Looting for the Living, Leave the Living to their Loot, Federali Rule" – a nervy reminder of the collective judgement. Further up, the condemned Wagon and Horses, where real ale had fought craft beer and lost, before the riots killed craft beer shops – Amazon's EcoBooze-Tubes, the beneficiary. There were the side roads, the council maisonettes with the same peeping windows and concrete balconies where Jay Bird had spotted them leaving the George. No one seemed to be around in any direction, but if anyone spied us, I had no doubt the repercussions would be murderous. But even if nobody saw us, it felt like bad karma.

'Jay, pass the plastic one,' Will said, surprisingly calm and professional, midway up the steps.

'Nah, manz, there's another full one.'

'Stop fucking calling me manz and give me the 18 gallon.'

'Woah,' Jay laughed, trying to save face. 'I got this for yuz. I scored this, Tom.'

'Keep it down, both,' I whispered.

Will looked at me and I knew something more was going on. Surely there had to be, in the face of this risk.

'Just get him the white one,' I called down.

Jay looked at me, pleading.

'Please, Jay.'

'Alright, manz, twist and shouts manz,' he shot me a finger.

We pulled the white one up, not heavy, but awkward.

'The bag,' Will pointed.

Jay sighed, looked to me for support.

'Shake it up, baby,' I half-sang.

'Yeah, baby,' all smiles. He grabbed the bag.

Will snorted a laugh. He took the bag from Jay and passed it to me. It was clearly bottles.

I grabbed Will's hand and pulled him up.

Jay was trembling behind him. I offered my hand, but he waved it away. Pale and completely bald, he scuttled up the steps Gollum-like.

'Now what?' I asked. 'If they see us-'

'Jay, you roll the steel over to yours,' Will said.

'Yeah, what about the other full, rudey?'

Will closed the cellar door with a clatter, I looked to see if anyone was around.

'We'll get it later,' he said.

'It'll be gone manz!'

'Guard it from your balcony.'

'What are *we* gonna do?' I asked.

'You grab the bag, I'll take the plastic. We'll come back later, have a drink at Jay's and then get the other.'

'Woah, manz,' Jay looked annoyed. 'What'm I getting? You gets the bagz man.'

'Fuck's sake, Jay, you've got the full barrel. This is just empty bottles.' He pulled one out to show him. 'Gonna brew. That's why I've got the barrel. You'll see some.'

Jay looked wary – too crooked to trust.

'Share and share alike,' I smiled. 'You can have my share.'

'Yez? For yous, Tom, manz.'

Will hoisted the huge barrel on his shoulders. I lugged the heavy bag. We turned away from Jay up Hales Road, one side the ancient sandstone wall at the far end of the graveyard, the other side, the 1970s council maisonettes – between a rock and hard place. I glanced back to see Jay rolling the barrel a foot at a time, stopping and getting his strength, before fighting on. Needle-jabbing, eyeball-spiriting, try-anything-to-escape Jay Bird – how had he lived so long? Every time I saw him, I thought it might be the last.

'Empties?' I said, trying to lift up the bag.

'Nah, even found you some dandelion and burdock. There's even a sheet of scratchings.'

'This feels dodgy.'

'It's somebody's home and they've left,' he said. 'Not the Supra.'

'I'm not so sure.'

'It's done now,' he said, impatient. 'We can use this gear to brew cider to trade.'

'That's not a terrible idea,' I conceded. 'Why'd they leave it?'

'The old man's in there. Dead. Looks like she snapped.'

'*Fuck*!' I panicked, dropped the bag on my foot – he just looked at me. 'You fuck! I knew it! I just had a feeling about all this!' I was freaking out, pacing up and down, punching the sandstone wall.

He stopped, put the barrel down. 'Just calm down. I didn't know.'

'There's been crazy fights, wild parties, the tearing up of the town,' I rattled off quick-speed, 'and now the tearing down of the high-rise. Everyone seems to be getting crazier by the day, but no one has died since the Supra killing… Until now.'

'People die.'

'It's murder. We can't just accept this. Remember after mum died, Baz the fucking-'

'He's not a goddam rabbit!' His face full of anger. A full stop.

'If it was illness or old age,' I panicked, 'but you reckon she killed him?'

'Maybe he had cancer, I don't know.'

'Was it? Did he look… cancerous?'

'No, he was battered on the head.'

'Fuck! This feels like it means something, like a line's been crossed, and we're involved.'

'Stop writing a bloody novel.' He punched me in the shoulder, the bag jangled in my hands. 'This is what you do, Tom. Today is Tuesday-'

'Wednesday.'

'Who knows anymore? Some shit has gone down. We didn't do it.'

'Thursday-'

'Whatever!' he yelled.

'No, it is Wednesday, because it's the 15th and Christmas Day's a Saturday.'

'It doesn't matter! The point is, it's just another day and I'm trying to find ways for us to survive in the new world. Brewing is a good idea.'

I *was* being a bit Garcia Marquez. The Curse of the Collective Judgement. I had a habit of building things up and getting caught up in my own narrative. 'You're right, I'm just being dramatic.' I took some deep breaths, scanned the area. There was no one in sight. 'This is good, yeah. The barrel. It's good. A way to trade. For food and shit.'

I helped him lift the barrel onto his shoulders, picked the bag up and we continued across the road to the back of the flats, the pock of sledgehammers in the distance, the pool break of bricks.

Will stopped at the allotments and looked through the gate. 'We need fruit. You reckon you can get in?'

'Climb? Probably.' I dropped the bag on the grass, put my foot in the bolt hole to try.

'There's apple trees up the back,' he said.

I pulled myself up, so I was now towering above the top of the gate. 'I could just ask Christian to open it,' I laughed.

'You have to apply for an allotment,' he moaned, 'and it has to be voted on. How long's that gonna take? We could just come at night, pinch a few apples from under the tree – it doesn't matter if they're rotting.'

'He'll give me the key.'

I jumped down, the rattling gate clattered and immediately grew into something much bigger and louder, thunder, a tsunami. The roar of tumbling bricks echoed throughout the flats – was the whole highrise coming down? We saw a cloud of dust and heard people yelling and screaming.

I immediately started running towards it.

'The bag,' Will shouted.

'The flats!' I yelled back.

He stashed the bag in the overgrown brambles, lifted the barrel over his head and followed.

I ran straight into the cloud of dust, heard voices of panic, but saw nobody. 'Down there!' someone yelled.

I covered my mouth with my shirt. I could just about make out the shape of the high-rise, most of it intact, but it looked like a whole floor had come crashing down. I coughed, spat dust.

'Your dad!' a voice called down.

Our block slowly revealed itself. It was mostly in one piece, except for a settee which had smashed through the main entrance, leaving a gaping hole. Just beneath it, I saw a shoe, and then a leg. There was an old man trapped under the settee, not moving. He had to be dead.

Engulfed in dust, 'Will!' I yelled.

'Your dad!' the voice shouted down again.

'Down here!' I called up.

In front of the high-rise the mountain of rubble was becoming apparent behind the veil of dust. It was like the crumbled temples in Patan, reduced to rubble after the Nepal earthquake.

'Will!'

Under the rubble I could just about make out the tips of a pink scarf. Then it dawned on me.

I went to call Will again but nothing came out. Then I felt him grab my shoulder and drag me down the grassy bank.

'The girl,' I yelled. 'Down here. The little girl!'

The curse of the collective judgement.

Will: I grabbed a barrel so we could brew plonk to trade with everyone. I imagine there was lots of other stuff in the building, but we just went in the cellar. We meant to report back, but then the high-rise incident-'

Ed: And yous boys just upped and left, when the town was in crisis?

I could feel the judgement of the whole town weighing on us. A wall of stony faces, familiar faces, the ones I'd known my whole life. My dad's old mate, Mick, was shaking his head, disappointed.

Will: There was an old man dead in the doorway to our block. Tom lost his mum not so long ago. It brought shit back.

I looked down, trying my best to look sad and sincere, without laying it on too thick.

Ed: Where did you go?

Will: The Squirrels. Tom's mum's old house.

Sarah looked at me. I felt sick about it all. This was not the way to do things.

OUT OF THE SIGHS

* * *

Will put another log on the fire, then went inside the cabin and came back out with a quilt. He gave it to Sarah and sat next to her.

'I don't know his name,' she said, 'but it was definitely her dad who did it.'

'Mark? Ricky?' I asked.

'No, stop saying names, I can't remember. One of the old men who died was Ricky's dad.'

The little girl's dad had been hammering the walls on the floor below before they'd started removing the ceiling. This caused the whole front wall of the floor to collapse and a large portion of the top to slide off. Two old boys and the young girl died, and several were injured. In the absence of a doctor, a little man with a St John's Ambulance certificate bandaged the survivors up and was heralded a hero.

Will swigged from one of the bottles he'd pinched from the George. I caught Sarah watching him. She noticed and tutted at me, like I was judging her.

'You really should've been in town,' she nagged. 'The church has been holding services every night.'

The night of the incident, we left for Leasowes. It had been three days, which we'd spent doing what we could on the cabin, but mostly I'd been using tarpaulin to protect it from the rain whilst they were on a bender.

'Don't you think it's a bit weird that everyone's all of a sudden Christian,' I said.

'Tom,' Will warned.

'No, I don't actually,' she said. 'This is a time of need. It's only natural that people should turn to God to make sense of it all.'

I looked at Will. I could see he was biting his lip.

'You of all people should get that,' she said, 'after the things you tell me.'

I sat back and looked up at the trees. There was a bitter breeze but I was warm in my down jacket, remembering cold Chamonix evenings on the clean and overly priced Rue du Docteur Paccard, Lucy on my arm. Will was shivering, near to passing out. He put his arm around Sarah and went to kiss her cheek, but she looked over at me and then pulled away.

'Oh, fuck ya then,' he said, getting up. He grabbed his guitar, *clunk*, 'I'm going to bed.'

'Stroppy fuck,' I laughed. I waited for him to go inside, before saying what people say, 'and then there were two.'

'I'm not gonna fuck you,' she smiled.

I half-laughed. 'Boom,' I mumbled under my breath.

She looked over at me tenderly, 'Tom.'

'It's nights like this when I'd like a drink,' I said. 'It's not about missing Lucy.'

'What about your son?'

'Or this high-rise crisis, or even our situation,' I said, ignoring the question. 'Perhaps it should be about those things, eh? It's sitting in the woods, around a campfire. Or listening to Christmas songs. It's those normal times when normal people drink like normal people.'

'There's no one normal here,' she said. 'Especially *him*.'

'You won't change Will, believe me.'

'He wet the bed the other night,' she whispered.

I laughed. 'Haven't you ever done that?'

'When I was like eight maybe.'

'I used to from time to time. You're lucky to quit so young.'

'It doesn't feel like that.'

'I think it's amazing you have, under the circumstances.'

'It's because of you!' she accused.

'Shut up. It's because of *you*.'

'I wouldn't have done this if I hadn't met you.'

I didn't know whether that was a good thing or a bad thing. I'd had to give it up for me. It was a purely selfish decision, which I was certain had helped me sustain it for so many years. 'What would your nan think if she saw you now?'

'She'd think there was another angle.'

There was a little bit of me that was wondering the same thing. Had she really stayed sober all this time? Was she really into Will? I couldn't help but remember some of the things she'd done. But I knew I had to put my faith in her completely.

'Can I ask you something?' she said, getting up to stoke the fire.

I nodded.

'Why do you keep having a go at the church? For all your talk of "God consciousness,"' – even hearing those words made me cringe – 'you won't accept that people want to find God in a way which means something to them.'

She was prodding the fire and glancing up at me. I didn't know what to say. I didn't know what I really thought any more. I remembered God working for me in those early recovery years and life being easier and more magical, and I didn't want to put a dampener on anything she was going through. 'I don't know, Sarah, maybe it's everything that's happened,' I lied. 'My family, this place.'

'I don't believe you,' she said. 'What about the caterpillar?'

I laughed.

She sat back down. 'Tell me again. Please tell me again.'

I saw the boy, blond hair, green eyes. "Tell me the one with the apples," he'd say. It was a story called *The Giving Tree*, about a relationship between a boy and a tree. The tree provides for the boy throughout his life, food, money, a boat. He believed the tree was magic, because it could give so many things. *I never got round to building him that treehouse.* I could feel the tears behind my eyes. I tried to hold them back, but they burst with a snort. 'God, I'm so sorry.' I wiped my face.

'It's ok,' she smiled. 'Tell me about the caterpillar.'

I laughed at her persistence. It helped me forget myself. 'I thought I was in love with this girl, Dani,' I rolled off. 'I just kept thinking about her all the time.' I'd told Sarah the story three times already.

'It made you really happy,' she said, eager.

'And it made me really sad. We were both new to being sober, but she was much more experienced at life than me, only I couldn't let her in on that. I lied about a lot of things.'

'Why?'

'I don't know. I didn't really think about it. I guess I was just living life as I was, a liar.' I remembered feeling powerless at the time, like I had no control of my actions, good or bad.

'Carry on...'

'Yes, ma'am,' I laughed. 'When I was younger. There was this girl-'

'Tammy,' she said.

I stopped. 'Why do you like this so much?'

'Just tell me.'

'It's embarrassing. I thought I was in love with Tammy,' I cringed. 'But she ended up with-'

'Will-'

'Yes, and when I'd talk to Dani about my past relationships, I'd bring up Tammy as if we'd actually been in some serious relationship. I even had an old picture of the two of us.'

'That's so sad,' she laughed.

'Fuck off.'

'And so you'd go walking in the hills,' she prompted. 'It was when you realised you liked walking up mountains.'

I looked at Sarah, leaning forward on her seat. Her face looked so young in the light of the fire, spitting and cracking, the bitter-sweet of the wood. There was hope for her if she could just stay sober, I knew it. But Will was never going to sober up.

'It wasn't a good relationship, Dani and me,' I said in all seriousness. 'Those early recovery ones rarely are. I was hurting for months after it ended and I wanted to drink. I found out all the other ways I was an addict, the food, the running, the mountains, the romantic fantasies.'

'The little voice,' she said, dismissing the sermon.

'I'm getting there! Yes, when I was out and about walking on my own, I could hear the little voice in my head. God, my better self, whatever you want to call it. It told me Dani was a bad idea. But I would fight it. I'd argue with it.'

'Is that what you're doing now?' she said.

'No, I've never really been a Christian. It's not the same.' It probably was. 'Anyway, I was out walking and I got lost in some woods in the Mendips.' I could remember it so vividly, the cool shade of the trees, the green smell, the chocolate shavings of dusty earth. 'I had to carefully climb down a particularly steep bank, but I was so consumed with the thoughts of this girl that I tripped and fell. I rolled and rolled, certain I was going to do some serious damage. I found myself blindly reaching out for something to grab hold of and I caught a branch, which stopped me falling. I looked up and a green caterpillar was staring at me.'

'The instant!'

'In less time than it took to formulate a sentence, I realised I was a caterpillar and there was nothing wrong with being a caterpillar, it's just where I was in life. I was as experienced as I was, no less or no more, and I had to stop pretending to be something I wasn't. In the same instant, I knew this was God consciousness, a hyper awareness of reality, and that everything happens for a reason because it's all undeniably connected to itself.'

'And then you walked back full of the holy spirit,' she smiled.

'I did, yes,' I admitted.

'And you broke it off with Dani.'

'It was never really on, but I knew I was never going to let it go any further. I just knew this was the right thing to do.'

'Don't you think that's just amazing and wonderful? You were so in tune with it, and you listened. Just like you said to me. It's all about the listening.'

I stared into the dying flames of the fire, ghostly, heavenly, a brief roar in a small gust, hanging onto the branches like it was hanging onto its life. Sarah was smiling, innocent, excited about a life free from drugs. This was the power of one addict talking to another. I'd experienced it many times.

But I wasn't being completely open with her. We still hadn't told her about The George, worried she might let it slip to Leroy which was a risk. And there'd been no mention of it from her so, presumably, the town was too distracted to realise what had happened. I wanted to open up to her about everything, because that was the right thing to do. I wanted to tell her about this curse of the collective judgement which was playing on my mind, as ridiculous as it sounded. I wanted to say it out loud to somebody who believed everything happened for a reason.

'The God stuff really helped me, Sarah,' I said. 'I'm really happy for you.'

'Why wouldn't it help you now?'

'I'm sure it does, I just don't think about it so much,' I smiled. 'I'm not sure it matters now.'

Her face changed, 'don't patronise me! Of course it matters!'

'I'm not-'

'Maybe you're still a caterpillar,' she sulked.

She got up and dragged the quilt towards the cabin. 'You can be really depressing, Tom.'

'I didn't mean anything by it-'

'I don't care.'

But clearly she did.

The next morning, I opened my eyes to the dark of the cabin. It was light outside, I could see a haze of white sky through the tarpaulin covering the roof slats. Outside, they were laughing and chatting, the smell of coffee and the caramel of overly cooked baked beans. My face felt damp with cold, but I was snug in a thick sleeping bag. I heard somebody come into the cabin.

'Wakey wakey, lovey.' Marcus pushed through the curtain.

'We need a door to this room,' I grumped.

'At least, you weren't made to sleep on the fucking floor. When we going back?'

I heard someone else enter. 'What you boys up to, eh? Eh?' Loz said, before laughing too hard at the suggestion.

'Very witty,' Marcus sneered, pulling back the curtain.

'When we going back?' Loz said. 'It's Christmas in six days.'

'And Santa only comes to Halesowen?' Marcus, dry.

'Christmas Eve drinks, like the old days,' he said. 'Besides, I don't think I can stand anymore of them two flirting out there.'

'I think we should go back today,' I said.

'Cos of The George?' Loz asked.

I shushed him with my eyes.

'I know you looted the place,' Marcus said. 'Will told me.'

'We looted the place?' I asked.

Loz was looking at me, gently shaking his head – clearly Marcus didn't know everything.

'Yeah, all the wine we've been drinking, and dandelion and fucking burdock,' Marcus laughed. 'I'm not stupid.'

'Don't say anything to Sarah! Or anyone for that matter.'

Marcus zipped his lips.

I sat up in my sleeping bag. It felt too cold to step out of it. I stood up and edged towards my down jacket but lost my balance and fell over. 'Damn it!'

I wriggled about on the floor.

'Look like a fat caterpillar,' Marcus laughed.

———

Will: When we got back, we offered our support to the whole town.

Ed: And yous still didn't tell anyone you'd seen Nigel lying dead in the George?

Ed bounced in his pink Filas and put his trilby back on, proud of himself.

Will: I'm gonna come down there and smack you in a minute, you little prick. Don't play games with me!

There was laughter from the back of the church. It was Tony Moran. He walked forward and whispered something to Ross, before walking back. Ross called Ed over and said something to him.

Ed: Would Jay Bird come to the pulpit.

Ross stood up and called us over. Loz, Will and I left Stacey sitting in the witness queue alone. We were now sat amongst the rest of the town. Were we absolved? It all depended on Jay keeping it together.

* * *

As we neared the flats, we could hear the sledgehammers. Business as usual. But the closer we came the louder the voices became. It seemed like the whole town had descended on the high-rise. Deckchairs and garden furniture, hats and scarves, some of the women were cooking sausages and burgers on barbecues under a gazebo. Barb waved a spatula, wearing the same sad smile she wore every time she'd seen me since mum had died. Under another gazebo, plastic pints of the orange swill people drank in Picks. Rex was clearly supposed to be manning it, but he was just sat in a plastic chair with a blanket wrapped around him, a straw hat on his head, drinking. If it wasn't for the squelching earth and icy damp, you'd be forgiven for thinking it was a summer fete.

'Where've you been, boy?' Rex asked me.

'Exploring,' I said.

Will immediately reached for a drink. I noticed Sarah watching him lift the cup to his mouth to slurp off an inch.

'What do you think you're doing, boy?' Rex chided.

'Having a drink,' Will said, uncaring.

'You can't just turn up and take a drink. These are for the workers.'

Will ignored him. I shrugged apologetically.

In a long orange robe, reminding me of a Buddhist meditation class I once attended, Leroy was hammering in a poster board. On fluorescent pink paper it read, "in God we trust, Ground Zero we must." Below the words there were old photos of the two men and the little girl.

Sarah ran over and gave Leroy a hug. I caught both Will and Marcus looking irritated by it. Loz was oblivious, watching them dismantle the building, ants on a sugar cube. 'We should help,' he said.

Marcus looked offended by the suggestion.

'We should,' I agreed, feeling a pang of grief. 'They're nearly down to my dad's floor.'

'I'm starving,' Will added. 'If we did a bit, they'd probably feed us too.' He headed over and shouted up, 'who needs a break?'

Loz followed suit and Marcus begrudgingly joined them.

'You boys are unbelievable,' Rex said. 'You do see what's happening?'

'The town's gone mental,' I said.

Rex looked disappointed. He took a sip of cider, put the pint down, picked it up again and took another sip. 'These are your people,' he said.

'I thought we were animals?' I smirked.

'Animals? What?' his philosophy which captured me a distant diatribe. 'These are your people! Your town, boy!' His valleys-boom weaker than it had once been. 'You've been here your whole life-'

'No, I went away-'

'I'm a foreigner. Only been here 30 years and they mean more to me than my own kin back in Merthyr.'

I looked up at the men, hammering bricks, taking apart the walls and windows and tossing small bits of furniture off, eagerly awaiting the smack and echo of their landings. It all seemed so bizarre.

'What's it all about, Rex?'

'Have you asked Him?' He pointed upwards.

'Who?' I half-smiled.

'Tom, boy, when will you listen?'

There'd been a time when Rex would've given me a detailed theory encompassing social behaviours and patterns, or at least an artistic interpretation. It had used to bore me, but I found myself longing for it. Now all that thought was behind him. He'd totally let go and let God. I noticed there was a lump on his neck. He saw me spot it.

'Just a goitre, boy.'

'Are you sure?'

'Quite sure,' he said. 'I'm being looked after,' he smiled, full of faith.

As he glanced away from me, I got a proper look. It was surprisingly big and solid. I wondered how long it had been growing. Perhaps this was why he'd turned so stridently to God.

I went over to Leroy. He was reading something to Sarah from a small bible, followed by the old "spectacles, testicles, wallet and watch" routine.

'*What?*' she asked me, reading my mind.

'*Nothing.* Can I have a word, Lee?'

'Of course,' he smiled, sanctimoniously – *stop judging, Tom*!

Sarah looked suspicious and unsure what to do with herself. She went over to Barb. We headed towards a block which was being converted into Church-2, away from the sad carnival, the chorus of pocks and crashes, laughter and banter of all pitch and volume. 'It seems a bit crazy,' I said.

'The town has come together over a terrible accident. It's quite beautiful really.'

I wanted to hit him. I couldn't help it. 'I don't want to feel like this,' I said.

'I know. AA gives us something but it's not–'

'Please,' I said. 'Let's not talk about specifics. I accept you're Lee the Christian preacher. I'm happy to go along with that.'

I could see he wanted to say something else, but he held back. 'Good. That makes me happy.'

'And mostly I want Sarah to be ok and this church works for her, keeps her straight, so I want to try and make it work for me.'

'Sobriety isn't everything,' he said.

'Please, Lee.'

'Sometimes we have to accept difficult truths.'

'Oh, you're so infuriating! I'm really trying.' I glanced behind to see Will in a tussle with Ricky over a sledgehammer. Sarah shouted and he gave it up.

'I used to be an alcoholic,' he said.

He still reeked like one.

'And so I gave it all up,' he continued. 'It wasn't difficult. But it didn't feel right. Then I realised, moderation is the more difficult and Godly path. I quote: "for God gave us a spirit not of fear but of power and love and self-control."'

'What about the one about not being filled with wine but filled with the spirit?'

'Where?'

'Oh, I don't know, the Bible. I tried moderation, you know I did, but I kept failing at it and ending up in terrible benders with dramas and fights–'

'But that was then–' he tried to interrupt.

'Vomiting all the time, anxiety so bad I couldn't leave the flat. I argued with my family and made everyone get wrecked with me, like Will–'

'His choice.'

'And this Leroy chap you've heard so much about. We had some wild times, some good, but in the end they were mostly twisted and bad.'

'That's you, Tom. Not Will. Not Sarah-'

'You need to stop filling her head with this moderation shit. Please, *Lee*. I'm gonna support you to build the seven churches and be an active member of the congregation-'

'You're going to support-'

'She's just a kid and she was a junkie. *You* know how many young people have died in Halesowen on the brown. We went to school with half of them. If she drinks, all bets are off. Help her out.'

'Or what?'

There he is, my old friend. I looked into his eyes and saw the burnt soul of my coke-snorting, sex pest, ex-bandmate. I saw the bitterness, the anger. He knew I saw him too.

'I'm just saying,' he justified, 'we have lots of support for the Church of 7. It's become such a big part of the town. Perhaps the biggest.'

I didn't want to say it, but I had to try it. 'What if they thought you were gay?'

'Then you'd be giving up Marcus to the wolves.'

We stared each other down, two old friends in some strange stalemate, two animals, stags locking invisible horns. The interesting thing about humanity is not that we're animals, it's that we're forever trying not to be.

I shook my head, broke the lock, glanced behind at the other animals on Ankerdine high-rise. Brick by brick they removed the ceiling to floor three, where dad drank whiskey after giving up his life as husband and chemist; where I lay on the floor, leg reddening in the light of the electric fire, swallowing biscuits and missing mum. I didn't know he was an alcoholic, nor that I'd become one. Our base nature was greed and I never thought I'd need to fight that impulse to stay alive.

'Why would you risk her recovery?' I asked.

'Moderation is the key to it all,' certain, stubborn.

'What? To everything?' I said. 'What about lying? What about crime? What about sexuality? You're in denial, my friend,' smug.

'This is why I left AA!' he sniped, stepping out of the pious façade. 'The sanctimony.'

'Said the preacher,' I laughed. 'Have it your way *Leroy*,' I said, walking off. 'I'm going to go and help them destroy this building… God only knows why.'

He looked annoyed, but I walked away before he could say anything. After a few seconds I heard him call out, slow to quip, 'yes… yes, He does.'

———————

Ed: Jay, tell us how you didn't kill Nigel, and how you didn't even see him in the George.

Jay looked confused. I could see him looking at his brother, Sean, who was sitting in a wheelchair, drunk enough to hold his head up, but mostly oblivious.

Jay: I didn't see nobody, manz. Sad like, but nothing to do with me like.

Ed: Who then?

Jay: I don't know, manz! Nige was a good soul, didn't deserve someone clobbering him on the head.

Two questions – that's all it took.

The town reacted in shocked mutters and whispers. Nobody knew what had happened to Nigel. No one had said anything other than he'd been found dead in the George.

I unconsciously grabbed Will's knee and he immediately pushed me off, aware of how it looked. I looked behind and Tony Dale was glaring at me. I smiled. He didn't. Leroy glanced in my direction, shook his head helplessly.

Ed turned to Ross, who stood up, fat, strong and slow, the executioner.

* * *

You never saw cats any more. There were always cats in Halesowen, like anywhere else in the UK, but within a year of the bombs they were all gone. I could never understand this and rationalised that cat owners were more sensible than dog owners and had left, taking their beloved pets with them. You still saw the odd dog, you still heard dogs. This absence of cats separated the town from almost anywhere I'd been to in the world. Perhaps cats were a mark of civilisation. Whether civilisation was a good thing or not was something else, but keeping cats as pets stretched back to at least ancient Egypt. Was our catless society an historic change for humanity?

A sudden bang on the back door startled me out of my thoughts.

I nudged Will. He didn't budge, a gas mask snore. 'Will,' I whispered, giving him another shove. He rolled over and took the quilt with him.

Bang, bang, bang!

My first thought was they'd finally found out about the George – perhaps Jay Bird had owned up to our involvement in the looting. I pulled the quilt back. 'Will, there's someone-'

'Get off!' he moaned.

Bang, bang, bang, bang, bang!

He sat up. 'What's that?' he panicked.

'I've been trying to-'

'You think it's about…?' He stopped, whisper-shouted through, 'Loz.'

'Yeah.' Loz had been standing just outside our bedroom door.

'You watching us fucking sleep?' Will jibed. 'Who's at the door?'

Loz slipped into the room, dragging his quilt behind him. 'I dunno. They sound angry.' He sat on the bed.

BANG! BANG! This time rattling the bedroom window.

I jumped, Loz yelped, Will punched him in the arm. Three men in their 50s.

'For fuck's sake, come on!' Ally shouted. BANG, BANG!

Loz sighed, rubbing his arm. 'Thank Christ.'

We sat in the living room, the fetid reek of morning and men perfumed by the piquant sweet of rotting apples. After a late night raid on the allotment, we were now cider brewers. Apparently all that was needed was sugar, apples and time. Time would tell.

'What've you heard?' I asked her, sitting on the edge of the settee.

'That they've left and you looted the place,' she said.

'A plastic fucking vat!' Will justified, next to me, two boys on the naughty bench.

Loz was pacing, biting his thumb. 'I didn't… I mean, it wasn't-'

'Sit down,' Will said.

'I wasn't even there, I didn't do-' he worried.

'Sit down, you prat,' Ally said.

He sat next to her, looking at her, pathetic and lost. 'Sorry, Ally.'

'It'll be alright,' she said. 'We'll do a line, everything will get a little lighter.'

He sat back and sighed. Loz had mostly given up drugs, but the unbearableness of the situation since his family had left changed that. He wasn't a wreckhead in the same way Will was but, without his wife and children, he relied more and more on drink and drugs to get through the day.

'Who told you, Ally?' I asked.

'Sarah came over,' she continued. 'She's not happy with you,' she laughed, wagging her finger at Will. 'Naughty boy-'

'*Sarah*-?' I said.

'*She knows*?' Will asked, passing over a Verve CD case. He looked at me. 'I didn't say anything to her, Tom!'

We turned to Loz.

'Don't look at me!'

Ally tapped a little coke out of a baggy onto the CD and started to chop three lines with an old library card, the big feet of Richard Ashcroft, now behind white bars. 'And she's not the only one who knows.'

'How?' I asked.

'I suspect half the town know by now. You need to speak to Jay.'

'Jay?' I panicked.

'He was with you wasn't he?'

'Who told you that?'

She snorted a line. 'Sarah, I already told you. You need to flip this before they start jumping to conclusions.' She passed the CD case to Will.

'Jay Bird!' I thumped the arm of the settee. 'This might land us right in the shit. Where's Marcus?'

Will did a line and passed it to Loz.

'He was with the church lot at Picks,' Loz said, the grains of cocaine shifting on the jittery CD case.

Ally pushed his head forward. He didn't resist, picked up her five euro tube, laminated with Sellotape, and *sniff*.

'And the rest,' she pointed.

He chased the remainder of the powder, before gargling, 'urgh, gone down my throat.'

I got up and went to the back door, looked through the curtains and then closed them again. I didn't know whether I was more bothered about the town knowing or Sarah. 'You're a fucking idiot, Will,' I cursed.

'You what?' He looked shocked.

'We were going about our business-'

He jumped up, cocaine-emboldened. '*I'm* an idiot-?'

'…just looting houses. No one had died-'

'*Who's died*?' Ally asked.

'I didn't kill anyone!' he threatened.

I gave him a look.

'What's that supposed to mean?'

'Whatever happened, you looted the place, and that's why we're in this mess.'

He grabbed me by my pyjama shirt. I went to grab him back but he was topless and hairless and I just grazed his skin. 'Put a fucking shirt on!' I shouted.

'Gay-boy!' angry.

'What the-?' confused.

Ally got up and stood between us. 'Tell me what happened at the George.'

'They left,' I said, my eyes on Will.

'What does that mean?' she asked.

'They've fucking left!' Will yelled, his eyes very much on mine.

'You really need to tell me,' she said, holding two collapsing walls apart. 'You remember what happened after the Supra.'

'I do,' I replied, smug and justified, already certain the high-rise incident was a direct result of the cosmic disturbance of the George – *Sarah would understand.*

'Don't pretend you knew this was going to happen,' Will gnarled, pushing his chest up against Ally's hand. 'You're just pissed off because I got with Sarah.'

'I... what the... I'm pissed off because you wouldn't listen,' my chest pushing against Ally's other hand. '*Sarah?*' I yapped.

'Just like Tammy,' he laughed, vile, arrogant.

He knew how to wind me up and this felt like a punch to the gut. I quickly moved around Ally and, without thinking, smacked him the face. It shocked him, his lip bleeding. Then anger. The moment I'd done it I knew it was a terrible mistake. I'd awoken the beast in him. I backed away and he charged, grabbed me and pushed me up against the wall, his big hand pressing hard against my cheek.

I flinched, preparing myself for a hail of punches and kicks. 'I'm sorry, don't smack me,' I cowered.

'Leave him, Will,' Ally was yelling, trying to pull him off.

He shook her off. I tensed, ready for it, but someone was trying to open the back door. We all turned and Marcus fell in, steaming drunk, his trouser leg dripping with blood.

'Sweeeeet Caroline,' he sang.

Ed sat down. Ross North faced Jay. He rubbed his nose, sure of himself. Jay still hadn't realised what he'd actually said.

Ross: Were you the only one to see Nigel?

Jay: Nah, manz, I didn't see him, manz. We just looted, got the rightz.

He pointed in our direction and winked, a quick shoulder shimmy, sure he was in the clear.

Ross: Do you know how many people have seen his body?

Jay: Who knows manz? Not me.

Ross: I've seen it. Tony Dale has seen it. Tony Moran has seen it and Dave White prepared him for the funeral. Dave, have you told anyone about the state of his body?

Dave was sitting amongst us. He shook his head.

It was hard to watch. Jay still hadn't cottoned on.

Ross: No one other than the four of us know that he was "clobbered". Did you go against the collective judgement to kill Nigel for loot?

It was a huge leap but nobody batted an eyelid. We *certainly daren't*. We knew we had to conform, to look straight ahead and let this play out with the hope he didn't tell the whole town that *Will* had actually seen the body too.

***

'Perhaps we should've told Ally everything,' I said, climbing the stairs.

'What's to tell?' Will banged on the door. '*I didn't see the body*. You *didn't* see the body. Simple. Marcus knows nothing about that either.'

'You think Marcus told Sarah?'

'I hope so. Anyway, as far as Sarah knows, we looted an empty barrel. Deny anything else.'

'She's not stupid. When they find the body she might… think-'

'What, that *I* did it?' He banged the door again, frustrated.

'It wouldn't be the first time.' I was still reeling from the Tammy taunt.

'Fuck you, Tom.'

'I'm not saying,' all innocent.

'Fuck off! You're lucky I didn't clout you before.'

'Ok, forget it. I shouldn't have said that. Sorry.'

Jay answered the door to his maisonette shirtless and shivering, sleep in his eyes. His face was blue and yellow, his cheeks cut, a curtain of dry blood. One arm was holding his chest, as if to keep his innards from spilling out.

'What happened to you?' I asked.

'Stace,' he said.

'Did you tell anyone?' Will demanded, straight to the point.

'Tell? What?' He put his finger on his lip to shush us. 'Come in, manz.'

With a slouch and a limp, a Black Country Iggy Pop tribute, we followed him inside.

The house was littered with letters and newspapers which must've accrued over many years, starting long before the bombs. By the toilet there was a white bucket filled with dark opaque piss, a custard plaque building up around the sides. The place smelt like sweet rotting flesh and soiled cat litter, but there was no cat, it was human shit, piss and bile, liver juices.

In the living room, his brother Sean was sat in low light in an armchair under a coverless quilt stained with all manner of things. Coffee perhaps? Blood? Shit? His eyes were closed, breathing laboured. 'Bloody arse-ache,' he mumbled, shifting slightly.

Jay pulled me to one side, opening the curtains to let the morning in. 'He ay got long left, Tom,' his voice quietening to its natural Black-Country-*spake*, losing the strange mask which drove us all mad.

'Sorry, man,' I whispered back. 'You ok, Sean?' I raised my voice, trying and failing not to talk down to the frail man.

'Is that you mum?' he asked – mum long dead.

'It's Tom.'

'Tom, that's what I said. Oh, Tom,' he suddenly realised, opening his eyes. 'Have you come for my brother? Jay,' he shouted.

'I'm here, Sean.'

'Tom's here to see you.' He noticed Will, 'and some other chap.'

'It's Will.'

'Will. How am ya son?'

Jay looked a little sad below his beaten face, and then he winked at me, cajoling me into play. 'Tom, manz, nice to see you.' He sat on the arm of the chair, next to his brother.

'Hi Jay,' I played along. 'I've just come to see how you're both getting on.'

Will was looking around the room for the barrel.

'Jay's escaped the Brett Young Centre, now, Tom,' Sean laughed. 'Miraculous recovery, eh?' sarcastic.

'It's been years, Sean,' Jay said. 'All better now.'

'Bah!'

'He's a sod,' I said.

'Naaah,' Sean broke into a phlegm filled cough, spat an oyster on the floor. 'Just the same old druggie. Town's crawling with them.'

The last time I saw Sean, he was fit and all-day-drinking-strong. He was over ten years older than Jay Bird and now well into his 70s. He'd been a builder by trade and always had a solid strength. He was a loyal Halesonian, born to die there. Even now, he was wearing his blue Halesowen Town football shirt, phlegm-crusted and filthy, much too big for his dwindling frame.

Sean belonged to a popular tribe, with strong opinions which often seemed to chime with the Sun and the Mail. He'd supported Thatcher and gone against her, only to support her again years later, when he and many of his generation had naturally aged to the right. He'd supported Blair too and gone against him, only to change his mind in the wake of the Greek Riots, when students became such a smug nuisance that the Express told us they deserved to pay for education. He opined with the best of them when they brought down Corbyn, the old Labour leader; likewise, he did his bit in pub-stir to help bring down Boris Johnson, the old Conservative leader, too. Drinking was his drug. Druggies were deviants, the heroin and crack addicts at least – I'd seen him do a line of coke from time to time, and he might smoke a joint, acceptable drugs in the building trade.

I moved a pair of jeans hardened by time and bodily fluids, and sat on the settee.

'Got anything to drink?' Will asked, still standing, barrel detective in this awkward situation.

'All out,' Jay said.

'Don't even have tea,' Sean moaned. 'Barely gives me water. I'd love a beer. Tom, d'yow have a beer?'

'I don't, mate, but I'm sure Jay does,' I prompted.

'I don't, sorry boyz.'

'But surely you have some sort of barrelled beer,' Will urged.

'Nope. We could go to the pub and get my brother a drink, maybe a big one.' He made the shape of a barrel, clearly referring to the one we'd left at the George – he hadn't been to fetch it, that was something.

Will mouthed, *what the fuck*?

'I don't have a beer, but I have some painkillers for your "bad shoulder",' Jay said, a poor performance.

Will shrugged, confused.

'Ooh, I've got a terrible back,' Sean said, 'but it's my arse that really hurts. He keeps promising me a new chair.'

'My shoulder's fine,' Will said. 'Strong as anything.'

'But I thought you wanted some of those *strong* painkillers,' he winked. 'The sort you can get off Tony Three?'

'Three?' I asked.

'I want some, Jay,' Sean said, oblivious to the charades. 'Please give me a painkiller.'

Jay turned away from his brother and pulled blister packs out of his pocket. Diazes, temazes and tramadol. He then disappeared and came back with a brown bottle. He shook it, smiling. Methadone. He'd clearly traded the beer for drugs. *Shit.*

'But I want a beer,' Will urged again.

'Magic beanzes,' Jay said, trying to get him to understand. 'Trades'iz for the mooz.'

But who had he traded it with? Tony Three? Was that Dale or Bonham? Did it matter? Especially as half the town knew. If it was Tony Dale, would Ally be able to help us out.

'Who with Jay?' I asked, trying to be casual.

'Tony Three.'

'Is that Bonham? Which one is Bonham?' I asked Will.

'The chemist.'

'Drugs!' Sean suddenly shouted, startling the shit out of us. 'Bunch of druggies! Druggies, the lot of you!'

'Cool your boots, Sean,' Jay said, prompted into action, pushing two capsules out of a blister pack. 'Here. Trammies.' He inserted them in his mouth like coins in an old cigarette machine.

'Water,' Sean said.

'Bloody chew em!'

'Bloody miserable… doesn't even give me a cup of…' he started to bite into them, the cracking of shells. 'Please, give me water… 'orrible, 'orrible bastard.'

'Get him some water,' Will demanded, by now angry, the coke worn off and clearly in need of a beer himself.

Sean sat chobbling on a wasp. He turned to Jay to let him have it, then his expression suddenly changed. 'What happened to your face?'

'I told you. We've talked about this. I fell off the front step.'

'You told me nothing. Your face, your face,' he panicked. 'This is drugs-'

'Get him some fucking water,' Will shouted, going over to Jay and pulling him into the hallway.

I went to follow them, but Sean reached for my hand, close to tears. 'Tom, what's happened to our Jay's face?' He started to sob. 'I just can't take this anymore, do me in, please somebody do me in. I've had enough!'

This was Halesowen. A man tethered to his seat by illness, with no help from anybody, wanting to die. I looked around the grimy room, the white walls stained with handprint upon handprint where they'd held themselves up on drunken, drug-fuelled nights. A settee with the indent of a body, clearly used as the bed, a scrunched up bedsheet. Clothes in balls, clothes everywhere in fact, more clothes than any man needed. Pill packets, empty cans, dirty mugs, cigarette butts. No carpet anymore, a rug kicked half way up the skirting board, and the flooring tiles, old, cracked, revealing concrete underneath. The nasal-staining reek of bodily fluids throughout. A 70-odd year old man who'd worked all his life on a building site, sobbing and sniffing away, adding to the bodily fluids on his already rank quilt innards.

'Why did you stay, Sean?' I shouldn't have said it, it just came out.

'What do you mean?' he grizzled.

'In Halesowen.'

'Cuz of him,' he said bitterly.

I could hear them muttering in the background. Will was annoyed and Jay was trying to appease him with methadone and benzos.

'But wasn't it the dream? That night in St John's?'

'What dream?' he snapped. 'What night?'

'When we gave up our phones, laptops, TVs, the outside world? When we started again?'

'What yow on about?' He was angry.

The Declaration of Freedom, I wanted to say, but what was the point? Ross North and Tony Moran, Jefferson and Washington – although to point that out would've caused a hell of a stir. And we bought it too, Will, Sarah and me. The idea of reconnecting to a global world didn't seem appealing. Control always seemed so far away, little empowerment, no voice. This seemed like the better option. It didn't feel like ego and ambition and power. Ross North had his twisted socialism and Tony Moran was an imposing thug, but that summer's night, months after the last bus had left and we'd been cut off, it felt like a group of flawed humans trying to make the best of it, animals nesting, apes forming a tribe. We forgot about what we'd lost and shared a hope for a kinder future. I wanted to say all of this to Sean, but he wasn't there anymore. 'I don't know what we're in, what this is,' I muttered.

But as I sat in Sean's fetid living room, wondering what the hell had really happened to Marcus's knee, fearing the future burden of the collective judgement, and the imposition of Leroy's brand of Christianity, I realised this was it. A dying man, one of their own, in a rotting room with a junkie brother, not even a decent chair or a beer, or even a glass of water to take two measly painkillers with. Why didn't he give him a swig of methadone, tell him it was Oramorph to deter any bias? Perhaps the kindest action would be to give him the bottle, one long, last swig. This was Halesowen, a dying man who put his hand up with the rest of us, even if he couldn't remember it. This was it, rats in a sewer town of old Britain, either doing what you want and living in fear or, paper dove and sledgehammer in hand, blindly patriotic.

I heard the gravelly grate of a cap being turned in the hallway. One minute later Will came in, smiling, calm.

'We should go and get a drink for his brother,' he said.

'Where?' I asked, slightly worried.

'Ooh, Stella, ta,' Sean begged, like we lived in a different world.

Jay: I ay killed nobody. Tomz!

Jay was pointing at me, pleading for support. They all looked at me. I shrugged. I didn't know what else I could do. I glanced behind at Leroy and he immediately looked down. Marcus just stared at me, unsure what it all meant.

Ross: Was Tom there when you killed him?

My heart beat hard in my chest, I could feel my face filling up with blood. I hadn't even seen the body, but God knows what was going to come out of his mouth.

Jay: No, he came down after.

Phew.

Ross: After you killed him?

Jay: Nah, manz. This ay right. Sean!

Sean looked up, struggling to focus on his floundering brother, and then waved him away as if he were asking for a couple of quid for a pint. Jay Bird knew what was happening. He was about to take the rap for killing Nigel. We didn't believe he'd done it. He was a crook, he'd always been a crook. He was a fighter too, but he wasn't a killer.

Ross: Perhaps Will killed him then?

Will grabbed my leg. I had to brush him off this time.

Jay: He came down after!

Was this a confused response or was he just purposefully clearing us both from any responsibility in this?

Ross: After you killed him? Nothing's going to happen to you, Jay.

Jay: I saw the body, Ross! Ok! It must've been Sandra. I saw the body. That's all.

Ross: Why wouldn't you tell anyone?

Jay looked over at us, then around the building, clearly trying to find a way to escape. John stood up, big and strong, but unsure of himself. Christian must've given him the nod.

I heard somebody get up. I glanced behind to see Christian going over to the front entrance, he locked the door. He then pulled the inner gates to, the click of the padlock.

* * *

'There is absolutely no way I'm going back into the George,' I said, as we made our way towards it. 'You're both high, you're not thinking straight.'

'Nah, manz, we getz the goodiz,' Jay said.

'Will, listen to me. If they haven't been there already, it won't be long. You heard Ally, half the fucking town knows.'

'Oh, what yuh scared for?' he said, switched off in opiate fearlessness.

'My life! Marcus's knee, for fuck's sake.'

'He fell… on broken… glass,' he spoke slowly, rhythmically, 'dancing… to Sweet… Caroline.'

'He's not telling the truth, is he,' I said. 'We need to go and find Sarah – she's gonna be stewing. That's more important than this.' I wanted to tell him her recovery was on the line, but he wouldn't have cared or understood. 'Sod Jay Bird.' I turned to him, 'no offence, Jay.'

'You owe me, manz.'

'Seriously? You owe us! You've fucked us. What did you do, Jay?'

'What?' he snapped. 'What?' befuddled. 'Nah, Tomzy manz.'

'What did you tell Tony Bonham?'

He looked at me, shrugged, 'nothing. Don't know him manz.'

'But you said… What did he do with the barrel?'
'Have to ask Tony Two.'
'Who?'
'Two.'
'Pahahaha, that rhymed,' Will stamped his foot on the pavement, doubled-up.

'Will, wake up! Jay,' I slowed, 'I thought you said Three? Who's Tony Three and who's Tony Two?… Please, we just need to know who we're dealing with.'

He didn't respond, drifted, eyes pinned and Gollum-dazed. I shoved Will. He looked startled, came-to a little. I gestured to Jay.

'Alright, Tom. Jay Bird. Jay, bird like a jay,' he said from his little cloud, arms open in some messianic pose. 'Who did you go through? Our sober friend, Thomas of the Hanson wants know?' He burst out laughing.

'Shit, manz. Tony Two.'
'I thought you said Tony Three?'
'Tony Two, Tony Two!'
'Tony Two? Tony Dale?' I asked. 'You went through him?'
'Yeah. Look!' He pointed.

We looked ahead of us, saw Tony Dale open up the cellar door to the George. I grabbed Will and pulled him up Hales Road. Jay was standing watching.

'Jay,' I whispered.

He looked over at us, annoyed. 'Your faultz, manz. We lost it.'

'Jay!' I begged, gesturing for him to follow us.

He sulked towards us. 'We could've had that, manz. Paydayz.'

Will had gone quiet, half dazed by the benzos now surely joining forces with the methadone. I started slapping myself on the head to try to make Jay understand. 'There's a dead man in there,' I said. '*A dead man.* There's a dead man. *A dead man.*'

Will grabbed my arm like he was about to say something, but he just stood there, dumb, holding onto me. He wasn't used to methadone. I looked up at him: *how's this helping?* Then I watched him disappear into his mind again and he let go.

'But the barrelz boyz,' Jay said, stamping his feet. 'We lost the beerz manz.'

I wanted to smack the zeds out of his head. 'Get real for a second.'

'I'm going down there,' he said.

I reached for him, pinched flaccid skin through his acrylic cardi.

'Ow! Tomz manz.'

'Did you tell Tony Dale *we* got the barrel from the George? Or *you*?'

'Nah. You had the bagz manz!'

'The barrel was all of ours, man,' Will whined, betrayed. 'The three amigos.'

'*The three…*?' I cast a glance at him, but his lubricated synapses were clogged. He'd stopped working properly – two plus two made methadone cakes, endorphins and dopamine, a goose-pimply peace. 'That's right, Jay,' I impressed, hoping Will understood my tone. '*Fair's fair, the barrel was yours.* Did you… mention us, Jay? Er… Will and… um me?'

'Nah, manz. Just tradez'iz.'

He made to go down there again. I tried to grab him, but missed and he disappeared around the corner, only to immediately return, his face straight. 'Tony One's there, ay he,' zed-free and Black Country.

'Moran? Did he see you?'

'I doh think so.'

I glanced around the corner. Tony Moran was followed by Ross North and Dave White into the cellar.

'Dave White?… *They know*,' I said to myself. 'They already know, Jay. You need to go home and say nothing about seeing the body, yeah?'

'Yeah,' he was nodding.

'Go up the road and back home that way. Will?'

'Wha?' He looked up at me, hopeless. 'We lost the bloody beer?'

'Yeah, yeah, we lost the goddam beer! Listen,' I asked slowly, 'we need to find Sarah. Can you go home and see if she's there or at Ally's? And I'll go down the old post office.'

'I wanna see Sarah,' he said, doped and pathetic. 'I love her.'

'She might be at the high-rise. If she is, take her to the flat and ask her to wait for me. If not, I'll bring her back up with me. Yeah?'

'Promise me?' he said, grabbing my hand.

'Yeah, sure,' I smiled.

'Tom,' Will paused, tried to make eye-contact. 'I didn't mean it, brother.'

Because now was the time to talk about Tammy!

At the top of the road, we heard the sound of sledgehammers and the tin of muffled music at bloody Demolition Fest, "it's Chrissstmas!" Will crossed the road to the back of the flats, Jay turned right and I turned left down Church Croft to make my way to the new church.

Ross: You're telling me, you didn't steal a barrel of beer from the George?
Jay: Beerz?

I looked behind to see Tony Dale now sitting down and holding Ethan, trying not to pay too much attention. Ally shook her head at me: don't get involved.

We watched Jay judge a jump over the pulpit, away from John, who was now standing at the bottom of the steps. He was too old for that shit. It'd be sure to end in broken bones on the hard tiles of St John's. He was trapped.

Ross: And you're telling me that you didn't trade it with Tony Three-
Jay: No!
Ross: ...for a list of drugs you claimed were to help you deal with your addiction and your brother's illness? If we were to get Tony Three...
Jay: It was Tony Two!

There was a gasp. Nobody cared whether it was Tony two or three, four, five or twelve. This was another admission of guilt, a step towards convincing the town he was responsible for Nigel's death. Even I was starting to wonder, but I knew in my heart of hearts it couldn't be possible.

Ross: I rest my case. Sean!

We all turned to see the old man in his wheelchair. He grunted, wiped dribble from his mouth with a tissue, then dropped it. Leroy got up to fetch it, wearing the pious smile of his new persona.

Ross: Sean, did Jay give you medication to help you with your illness?
Sean: Whaaat? He don't even bloody feed me anymore.

There were more gasps and groans amongst the townspeople who now, apparently, cared about this man they'd left to rot. I stood up to contradict him, but Will pulled me back down.

Jay: I gave you trammies!
Sean: What?
Jay: For the arse ache.

People started to laugh and Jay laughed with them.

Sean: That was for mum, she's stuck in her chair all day and gets sores.

Will was tugging on my shirt. He knew I wanted to defend Jay from this absolute madness, but it was a losing battle. It was no good yelling "your mum's dead." It would seem insensitive and probably implicate me. I looked at Leroy and I knew he saw the injustice too. I felt like we were about to witness something truly horrific.

Ross: I put it to you, Jay Brettle, you murdered Nigel Burton at the George – a town business no less – to pilfer a barrel of beer and anything else you could get your hands on. You "clobbered him" on the head, as you put it, in a fever of violent greed. Will and Tom came down to try and stop you taking everything. Will, wrongly, took no more than a plastic vat with the intention of brewing to trade with his fellows, but due to the high-rise tragedy, he didn't get chance to tell us. You left with a full barrel of beer which you traded for drugs, and not out of any decent need to help your brother, like you promised Tony Three-

Jay: Two.

Ross: But nihilistically-

An old woman 'oooed' at hearing a big word – "ark at mister big shot".

Ross: Um… selfishly, with no care for the future of this town or the people in it.

I saw a sad acceptance in his Will's eyes, but I felt sick and guilt-ridden. Why had we been protected from the implication?

Jay: I dint do it man! I dint! I never murdered no one.

Ross: What about Gary Bennett?

'Good bloke,' came from somewhere behind us.

Jay: Nothing to do with me.

Ross: I believe that was after you robbed the old TV shop.

Jay: I nicked a booster for one of the Price brothers.

Ross turned to address us.

Ross: We are not animals in Halesowen. I'm sure you feel, as I do, the murder of Nigel Burton is a clear injustice, but we have to be sure. We can't damn a fella on this alone.

I heard somebody behind me say, 'he's very good,' like they were watching Cradley Heath Amateur Operatics perform Wicked at the town hall.

Ross: It's fair to say, even though we know he's capable of looting from town businesses, we don't know for certain he knifed Gary Bennett or "clobbered" Nigel Burton-

Jay: Gary…? I bloody d'ay!

Ross: We have to be sure the man is capable of such an act. Stacey, dear.

* * *

I moved quickly down Church Croft, one side of the road St John's graveyard, the other side, the flats. Rain gently spat, grey skies and skeleton trees.

The town was deserted. It was usually deserted. People were always somewhere, Church-1, the high-rise, Picks or the Edward. There were no cats on the streets and no people. The only people I ever saw were the prune loons and scag rats, who didn't want to be somewhere or had nowhere to be.

I turned quickly onto the Queensway and walked straight into Mel. '*Shit*! Sorry!' my hand gripping my chest hairs.

She laughed. Then she laughed some more, a little too hard, like the off-button had a loose wire, sparks spitting. 'You ok, Mel?'

'Ar know you,' she said. 'Barb wuz on about your mother.'

'Have you seen Barb?'

'Don't talk to me about that bad-mouthing slut!'

She reeked of stale booze, her grey hair matted to her face with rain and grease.

'Thinks er's all high and mighty now er's gone all God,' she laughed again, too hard – I wanted to bash her on the head like an old detuned TV.

'Ok, then. I… er, better be off,' I smiled.

'Yow know mar boy,' she called after me.

'Erm, I knew him, yes,' I called back. 'Everybody knew him. Places to be, Mel.'

When I got to the old post office, I noticed fluorescent signs in the window. Green, pink and orange, on top of each other, a punk Mohican. "Church-1. Renovation. Christ is the Way."

The front door was open. I walked inside. There was nobody, no sign of Sarah. Presumably they were all up the high-rise. They'd put the Christmas decorations up, a big tree, decorated with the bible paper doves. I pulled one off and opened it up.

"For you know that we dealt with each of you as a father deals with his own children, encouraging, comforting and urging you to live lives worthy of God…"

What is it with these bastard things? I screwed it up and tossed it on the floor.

I was about to leave when I heard: 'ow, ya fucker!'

I froze and listened.

'Yow be more gentle,' the voice mumbled.

I followed the voice to the disabled toilets. *Fuck it*. I turned the handle.

'…Jason?'

He turned, half-gouching, eyes pinned. Leroy got up off his knees.

'T-Tom,' he said – Leroy, not Lee.

Jason put his cock away and held his hand out. Leroy fumbled, panicking, reached into the pockets of his fuchsia robe and handed him something. It looked like a little wrap, a small black paper rectangle. Jason had got what he was there for and he squeezed past me. 'Alright, Tom,' he said, like we were passing on the street.

'Erm… good, mate,' I replied, stunned.

Leroy sat down on the toilet, eyes to the ground, like he was waiting to be punished. He looked up at me, the person I knew and had known for most of our lives. His cheeks quivered and his eyes softened. 'My whole life,' he cried.

'I don't… know what to say.'

'My whole bloody life!'

'What about it?'

'You don't understand, Tom.'

'But all the women?'

He laughed, like I just didn't get it. 'What about it?'

'The sex… the women sex.'

'What do you want me to say?' he asked.

'But the men?'

'Yeah?' He wiped his nose on the sleeve of his robe.

'*Jason*?' incredulous.

'Don't judge me, Tom. You've done your fair share of fucked up things.'

I was nodding. I wasn't going to deny it, and this Jason transaction seemed relatively minor in the light of his preacher façade. 'The *church*?'

'I grew up C of E,' he defended.

'Really?' I disputed. 'Your family were, but we did a lot of crazy shit, took a load of drugs, had a lot of… *you* mostly had a lot of sex, and-'

'What's that got to do with it? For an AAer you're a bit shallow.'

'I don't mean… I mean, God, yeah… sorry. It's a lot to take in. Perhaps I was starting to believe you weren't Leroy… Oh, I don't know. But the church? *This*? It just seems a bit-'

'That's because you're a million miles away from it, from God-'

'*But all the women*. They used to come crying to me.'

He looked like he was about to launch into a tirade, but he stopped, jutted, like the tectonic plates of his breast bone shifted. 'Oh, God,' he cried. 'I did, I did! I hurt a lot of women. I'm so sorry about it. God forgive me!' The emotion intensified. 'When I think of the way I treated women,' he sobbed.

I was standing watching my old friend in meltdown. It was a much bigger reaction than I'd expected. The only time I'd ever seen him emotional was, ironically, when we went to the cinema to see Boys Don't Cry. He always took a lot of cocaine, drank a lot of whiskey and seemed to manage his feelings much better than I ever did.

I found myself picking at a roll of toilet paper. *Where did they even get this from?* We'd long since been using old telephone directories, we'd looted from the library. I wanted to give him some to dry his tears, but I recalled being warned not to in rehab because it was like telling someone to stop feeling.

'There, there.' I inwardly cursed myself. 'We've all done bad shit, mate.'

It was a sad sight, but I was happy to see it.

'Why are you smiling?' he asked.

'I'm sorry, but it's kinda nice. It's good to hear the regret. It's good to be talking to Leroy, my old friend.'

'I'm not Leroy,' he said.

'Oh, for fuck's sake!'

He flinched, as if I was going to smack him. 'Wait, Tom… I was Leroy, yes, but I'm not anymore. I know you might not understand that, but my name's Lee and I want to be called Lee. That's all I can hope for in all of this. *Please!* I mean, what do you want from me? Do you want me to tell everyone I am who you say I am, even though I'm not?'

'Everyone who matters knows, except Sarah.'

'She knows who I used to be,' he said. 'And she knows who I really am.'

Standing in the cramped disabled toilet, the emotion was stifling. 'Let's get out of here,' I said.

The place was still empty. Leroy was vibrating with anxiety. I grabbed a jar of coffee.

'Electric?' I asked.

'Use the Calor.' He shook a metal kettle to check for water, then switched on one of the hobs on a double camping stove.

I looked around the old post office. 'This is some crazy feat. There's really gonna be seven?'

'There is,' morose. 'Just transforming them to fit the brand.'

Brand was such a crude but appropriate word to use. No matter what he told me, it didn't feel congruent, or spiritual, just another corrupt organised live-a-lie religion. We were just building another western civilisation, only with fewer idealists. Ross North had once been an idealist, but now he seemed to be revelling in the power of his position, the desire to be a leader amongst the mostly apathetic.

As Leroy poured water into the cup, I noticed the familiar tremor. That wasn't anxiety. We'd cured our tremors many mornings with double Wild Turkeys at 'Spoons. 'You need a proper drink,' I said.

He reached into a cupboard and uncorked the remainder of a bottle of wine. 'Just for my nerves.' He drank from the bottle.

'When did you know?' I asked.

'What?'

'That you were gay.'

'Gay?' he looked confused. 'You mean, liked men?'

'I guess.' I felt awkward.

'It's not like that...' He looked like he wanted to say something, but was struggling. 'You remember Steve Harris?'

'When we were at primary school?' I was shocked.

'Nothing happened. I just realised I liked him a bit more than a friend. That's when I realised there was something different about me, but it's not black and white.'

'Nothing ever is.'

'No, but...' he started, but then changed tack, 'I was maybe six or seven.'

I suddenly remembered where he'd chosen to live. The very same house where we used to make Transformers fight Thunder Cats. Steve Harris' house. Was it one big unrequited love story?

'Whatever happened to him?'

'Steve? God knows,' he caught himself and laughed, looking up to the ceiling. 'Last I heard he'd moved to London.'

'Shit.'

'Yeah.'

'I can't get over all the women though,' I laughed.

'I like women, I like men. I like people. I'm not...' he stopped, looked up at me, then away.

'What?'

'Please, Tom.' He took a big swig of wine, loose, broken. 'I know you might want me to be someone else, but I'm not him.'

'Ok, ok. I get it.'

He scoffed, tearful, then drank wine. 'I'm sorry.'

'What for?'

He walked over to the Christmas tree, stopping to pick up the dove I'd tossed on the ground. He tried to remake it, but quickly became frustrated and threw it down again.

'Why didn't you just come out?' I asked.

'Oh, for God's sake!' he clenched his fists, suddenly angry. 'It's not as simple as all that.'

'But you were always fairly open… Marcus.'

He stopped, smiled, 'Marcus.' Then his face soured. 'Tom. It was nothing to do with me.'

'What?'

'What happened to Marcus. He's a danger to himself,' he insisted.

I looked into his vein-cracked eyes. He'd turned from a man who'd always looked much younger than me to a man who was tired and old.

'What did happen to him?'

Stacey was escorted by Ross like she was a Southern belle, her flip flops clopping the back of crusted heels, wearing the same black and white plastic tube she wore three days prior.

Jay Bird held his hands in the air as he walked with John back to his lonely seat, facing the town. He sat down briefly, looked over at me, winked, and then jumped up to run off. John instinctively put his arm up, smacking Jay back to the chair. 'Bloody hell, John,' Jay blurted. 'It was a joke.'

'I didn't mean to,' he said, looking over towards Christian. 'Sorry, Jay Bird.'

I glanced behind to see Christian sticking his thumb up. There were jeers and laughter from the townspeople, a simmering excitement.

Ross: Calm down everyone. Let's continue with the proceedings. Now, Stacey, you've known Jay for many years. Jadon's dad, yes?

Stacey: He's little Jay's dad, yeah, but he wore there for him and we lost him to Social Services as you know.

Ross: I don't want to rehash painful memories, Stacey. Tell me what happened in Picks a few days ago.

It was a foregone conclusion. The only thing we didn't know was what they would do about it. This wasn't the Supra incident. We were sitting somewhat civilly in something which resembled a court of law – in a Lord of the Flies manner.

Stacey: I was singing on the karaoke. What was the bloody song?

Leroy was now standing at the back, looking thoughtful. But wasn't he just one of them? Part of the establishment? Not only that, he was the moral compass of the town. Leroy the Lee, straight-gay-bi vicar, functioning alcoholic.

I glanced over at Marcus. He looked sad and in pain with his leg, next to an empty seat. What had really gone on with those two? I didn't want to think about it.

Stacey: *It was by Fairground Attraction.*

Ross: *Was Jay on drugs?*

Jay jumped again to protest, but was knocked back down. 'Fuck off, John! I only had a Jägermeister!'

John looked anxiously over at Christian, standing by the entrance, who put his hands up to try to calm him, mouthed 'it's alright'.

In the old world, Christian had been a businessman. He owned a huge sporting goods store in Quinton, before the Greek Riots killed it. He part-owned a hotel in Newport which drowned in the Burnham-bomb tsunami. And he'd also owned a day centre for adults with learning disabilities in Old Hill. This service had flourished in the post-virus NHS privatisation, but finally went under in the evacuation. Christian was left with nothing. He turned to drink, found himself in an up and down battle with depression. Being made the Outsider Son seemed to fix this.

Standing at one side of St John's we had the church and the other side, business. But behind both of them, sitting at a little round table with a glass of something gold and strong, was Tony Moran. How had this supposedly equal, dutiful rep seamlessly become the unofficial leader of our town?

Stacey: *Perfect! I was singing Perfect.*

Ross: *When he attacked?*

Stacey: *Let me tell it! Please let me tell it!*

The town was transfixed on this court room drama. Jake was sitting near the back, next to Ray, both intently focused on what they must surely have seen as an injustice. In front of them were Tim and Alan Price, brothers who'd been made the Manor Way and the Huntingtree Sons, respectively. Tim had stood and lost as a Conservative for Halesowen at the last general election. They'd owned a Wish warehouse which took a big hit after the government supported the US internet-shopping embargo. The embargo was quickly lifted but they lost a lot of money. All around us, old faces, young faces which had turned old, dumb faces, hanging onto every word as Six-Kids-Stacey made the most of her fifteen minutes of fame.

Ross: *Of course, Stacey, carry on.*

Stacey: *I was just singing the bit, "well, I have been foolish too many times…"*

* * *

I opened the back door to find a party in full swing. The place reeked of sweaty cider and weed. They all looked up. 'Alright, Tom,' Ally said. 'Carry on, Damo.'

'I… er… no, Stace and me were in Picks and um, well, it was funny really… er-'

'You want me to tell it?' Stacey asked, impatient.

They were both sitting on the floor, recounting some drunken tale which was evidently supposed to be hilarious.

Will had clearly been revived from his benzo and opiate dope by cocaine and was rolling a joint on the settee. Loz was next to him, wasted, sitting tight against Ally and staring at her in some strange awe. On the other settee, Marcus had his leg up, laughter in his eyes, swigging from an orange pint of Picks' juice – presumably pinched from under Rex's not so watchful eye. If Jay Bird hadn't told anyone about Will and my involvement, it had to be Marcus. I glared at him, but he was oblivious.

'Where's Sarah?' I asked.

Will shrugged. He'd forgotten her in phase three of his bender.

'Sit down, Tom,' Stacey insisted.

'I'm ok standing.'

'They had Jägermeister,' Damien continued. 'Technically… er… I brought it from up north,' he whispered conspiratorially.

'That's not important, is it?' she laughed. 'Let me finish.'

'Alright,' he smiled. 'She loves to tell stories.'

'One of you just bloody tell it!' Ally laughed. 'Sit down, Tom. She'll turn up-'

'Leroy said she was with you.'

'*Me*? Earlier, when she said about… Now, sit! You're making the place look a mess.' She swigged gin from the bottle.

I sat against the back door, trapped in my own home, tired and dazed by it all. The dead landlord at the George, Sarah's disappointment – perhaps she'd relapsed – and Leroy's revelations. I was carrying it all on my own. They were free of the responsibility, twisted and loose, made mad in the bender.

Will lit his joint, took a big drag and laughed about something. Marcus chortled, high-pitched, a stabbing laugh. I could feel the paranoia rising up in me – maybe it was the green cloud stifling the room.

'I'll tell them,' Stacey insisted. 'It was me he came for.'

Outside, they were banging away at the building, most of them already drunk. Last I'd seen they were removing the floor to dad's old flat where, in the middle of the night, he would come and rail us for being loud and I'd tell him I loved him, the ecstasy lighting up my veins, brain, the world.

'I was singing *Perfect* on the karaoke, you know, "it's got to be-e-e-e-e-e perrrfect".' She sang like she was auditioning for Billie Eilish and The Weeknd in Past Prime-Time – it was grating. 'I'd had like six Jägermeisters. Yeah, we had Jägermeister, mental!' she teased, taking the piss out of poor old Eeyore. 'And two or three of the guys were looking at me, you know, like they were undressing me. I had this on.'

Packed in a plastic tube of zebra skin, red tights, laddered. I found myself staring through the gaps to her bare inner thigh. Loz caught me and smiled knowingly. I looked away embarrassed.

'Then,' she said, 'Jay Bird came over-'

'*Jay?*' I asked.

'Yeah, Jay,' she said.

'*Jay?*' Will parroted.

'Yes, Jay Bird. I'm spaking English, ay I?' eyes rolling in the coffee rings. 'He's still obsessed with me, and he starts looking at these fellas-'

'Who?' Will asked.

'I dunno, a Son, a non-'

'Tinker, tailor,' Marcus chipped in.

'Shut up, you,' hag laugh.

'When was it?' I asked, all serious.

'A couple of nights ago.'

'Get on with it,' Ally heckled.

'Yeah, stop interrupting you lot!' She stood up to perform. 'I'm getting to the good bit. I was like, "well, I have been foolish too many times,"' she sang, 'and then out of nowhere he shoves one of the guys over, threatening to kill him-'

'*Jay?*' I asked again.

'Jay Bird, yes! Yow following me? I think it was Tim… or Dave. No, Alan? I dunno. He'd cracked his head and was bleeding loads. Then Jay grabs me, like he's bloody Tarzan, the scag head, and tries to take off with me.'

'Nooo!' Ally.

'I er… wouldn't mind, but er… he didn't start on *me*,' Damien laughed.

'Why would he?' Stacey asked, deadpan.

'Because… well… er-'

'It's not all about you.'

Damien looked hurt. He'd had years of it. So had Jay Bird. Damien had just been the next Jay Bird, except Jay had been elevated to Tarzan in this little play and Damien was barely credited as Jägermeister provider.

I stood up needing to do something, go somewhere, figure it all out. My palms wet with anxiety, my heart nauseously whooping fast, slow, unsure how to beat to this story – *maybe I need a pacemaker*?

Stop it!

'Jay Bird's been making enemies in Picks,' Will said to me, knowingly, before dragging on his spliff.

'He's not the only one,' I said, glancing at Marcus.

'Very funny,' Marcus said. '*What*?'

It wasn't the time to pursue it.

'Jay's been fighting over me,' Stacey said, proud, 'after all this time. Bloody idiot.'

'I wish someone would fight over me,' Ally said.

'Aw, Tone still cares, bab,' Stacey said.

'Sod him. Just Ethan's dad.'

'You'll find someone else,' Loz said.

She already had. Many. In orgies which sometimes went on for days. It both terrified and intrigued me.

'Someone who really cares about you,' he added.

'Bless.' She rubbed Loz's head.

Loz blushed, unashamedly staring at her tits. He looked up and was about to say something I was sure he'd regret.

'You alright, Loz?' I smiled.

He looked startled, glanced around the room and then started singing, 'Rudolph the Red-Nosed reindeer, had a very shiny nose…' whilst doing a little jig. 'Five days to Crimbo!'

Will stood up. 'Sod this.'

'Sarah?' I asked.

'She'll turn up. I need some food. Let's go hammer the high-rise.'

'Oi!' Ally called after him.

Will took a big drag and then handed her the spliff.

'Ta, big man,' she winked.

'Not what I heard, luvvie,' Marcus tittered.

Stacey stepped down from the pulpit. Alan Price seemed fit and well, despite corroborating her story, blood supposedly spurting out of his head after Jay's "murderous" attack. She faced Jay Bird and shrugged. They made eye-contact and he smiled, hopelessly hopeful. When she turned away from him and came to sit with the rest of the town, he disappeared into himself. He was clearly more heartbroken that she'd been the one to stick the knife in than worried about the reality of what was surely a guilty verdict. It was now just him at the altar on his lonely chair, John Bosko next to him, a lumbering guard, blank faced and dutifully dumb.

Ross North addressed us all.

Ross: Many of us would like things to be different. We'd like to think Jay is just a common thief with a drug problem. Unfortunately, what we see from Stacey's eloquently expressed – and beautifully sung – witness statement, is Jay Brettle has a history of violence, potentially murderous violence. But, perhaps the saddest part of all this, is that an expression of greed has once again brought tragedy to our town after a period of calm and flourish. Greed leads to tragedy. We saw it after the Supra looting and we're seeing it now. Greed, one of the seven sins. Our town must not be founded on it. We have to use these examples to grow, to better ourselves, to change the way we live our lives. We must say no to greed. My friends, we have a difficult decision.

An old 'un jumped up and yelled, 'an eye for an eye, ay it?' I looked over at Mick, who I remember reminiscing with my dad about the 70s "when a nigger was a nigger and a Paki was a Paki and they didn't mind", and he was nodding in agreement. As was Ricky, who'd just lost his dad, and Pete, the fella who'd lost his daughter, both in the high-rise incident. Barb and Rex also agreed, amongst a Guess Who of flapping heads, who all looked similar in that moment, siblings, soldiers uniformed in righteous indignation.

Jay Bird looked up at me with more seriousness and sensitivity than I'd ever seen in him. I felt compelled to say something. I looked over at Leroy. He knew I was about to do something and he looked panicky, shaking his head to warn me. I felt sick, my hands cold and clammy, the blood rushing to my head. Jay Bird sat pathetically in his chair, a puppy about to be put down because he wouldn't stop scratching at the furniture, that's all.

A woman leapt to her feet, 'he cor get away with it!' The mumbles turned to short sentences of anger.

I had to do something. What was there to live for anyway? And maybe I'd make a difference. Sarah had been sat quietly watching the proceedings, annoyed at us for holding back the truth. She was now looking to Jake who blurted back, 'squirrels, mouse, rabbit-hutch!' The whole show had been a drama of twisted truths. Sarah knew Will had seen the body, she knew Jay wouldn't have killed Nigel. What would this do for her recovery? Leroy caught me looking at her and he smiled. He looked sad. Perhaps he knew what I had to do. I took a deep breath, ready to make a stand.

'I'm a woman!' Leroy shouted.

We all looked over and he dropped his robe.

* * *

'Get down!' Sarah called up.

'Me?' I said, wobbling on a tall ladder, removing loose-teeth bricks from the wall

'And him.' She gestured to Will, hammering out a window frame.

A few of the fellas warbled a sarcastic, "oooorr".

'What?' Will asked, playing the game.

'One word,' she said. 'Marcus.'

Shit.

I climbed down to the second floor. Ricky was sat in the corner, his gut in his lap, swigging from a bottle of vodka and mumbling to himself tearfully. Three lads were tightly packed on a two-seater each eating a full English big enough for a family and slurping it down with cans of lager Tony Dale had donated to the cause.

Will grabbed my shoulder. 'The soppy prick has dropped us right in it this time.'

'*You* told him.'

'And I'll regret it til my dying day.'

'A tad dramatic.'

'Do you think she knows about…?'

'Marcus didn't. Ally didn't. Just the looting,' I said.

She was standing under the gazebo, where Rex was emptying a bag of cider into a plastic pint glass. 'I can't even look at you,' she said.

Rex looked up, followed by his goitre, but didn't say anything.

'Me?' Will asked.

'Both of you. Everybody knows what you've been up to,' she said.

I looked around us, ears pricked up. Rex sipped cider. Barb glanced across, uneasy, flipping eggs.

'Walk,' I said. 'Who's everybody?'

We carefully edged down the muddy bank to the back door of the flat. Will stopped, pulled out his tin to quickly roll a cigarette. She watched him briefly, then turned her attentions to me. 'I can't believe you wouldn't tell me. I feel like such an idiot.'

'You haven't…?' I asked.

'What? Relapsed? Course I haven't! Is that what you think-?'

'No, no,' I held my hands up. 'I was just worried. I'm really sorry… Who's everybody?'

'Them,' she gestured behind us. 'The Sons, everybody. Why didn't you tell me?'

'I wanted to,' Will said, catching up. 'But he made me promise not to.' He lit his roll up.

'Fuck you, man! This is *your* fault.'

'Here we go, always my fault. I suppose the bombs were my fault? The Greek Riots? What about Trump's murderous cock?'

'Another fucking conspiracy.'

'A conspiracy? The two school girls who died of syphilis because they thought it was flu? That's a fact! Trump was the only one who had syphilis. Fact! Like Epstein's island-fact, Ted Heath's boat-fact, Westminster kid cabin-fact!'

'*What*?' She clenched her fists.

'Don't ask,' I said.

'He knows nothing,' Will argued, taking a drag.

'Just stop it, both of you!' she screamed.

We looked at each other, nervous, school boys trying not to laugh.

'Who said all this?' I asked. 'Marcus?'

'Eventually, but everyone knows.'

'But,' I lowered my voice, 'knows what?'

'That they've left the George and you've been there looting the place. Jay Bird traded a barrel of beer with Tony Dale-'

'That was all Jay!' Will said. 'We had nothing to do with that. All we did was take a big empty vat and a couple of bottles of wine.'

'It's a town business,' she stressed.

'It's a house and they've gone,' he argued. 'Just like all the other houses we've looted.'

'I tried to stop them,' I said.

Will looked at me and was about to spew vitriol, but he knew I was right. This was always a murky business, no matter how he tried to spin it. Sarah didn't know just how murky, but sooner rather than later they'd all know the dead landlord was in there. I wanted to tell her, I should've told her, but it felt too dangerous.

'They're talking about a trial,' she said.

'A trial?' I nervously laughed.

'To prevent another lynching.'

Will looked at me, put his hands on his head, incredulous. 'For… *looting?*'

'Is there more to it?' She wasn't stupid.

'When did you find this out?' I asked.

'Last night.'

'They're saying it goes against the collective judgement.'

'How can they… can they,' Will twitched, 'say that? Who? What? What collective? You? Me?'

'You need to speak to Jay and get your story straight,' she jabbed him in the chest. 'Whatever that is.'

'We saw him earlier,' I said.

'And find out what Marcus has been saying.'

'I'll break his goddam neck first,' he said.

'Don't blaspheme!' she nagged.

I immediately looked at Will and he laughed. 'I'm sorry,' he half-smiled, grabbing her hand – it was the wrong move.

'Fuck you, Will.' She yanked herself free and crossed the grass towards Ally's.

'You better speak to him, Tom. I'll kill the prick.'

He chased after her.

I opened the back door to the flat. Stacey and Ally were staring at me. Damien picked his nails. They'd clearly heard everything that was said. Marcus looked white, yellow, clammy and cold, legs up, the one wounded, the other a restless tremor. He swiftly necked the dregs of his pint and then chewed the plastic rim, giving him a duck beak. He poked at his knee. Blood had seeped through the bandage and his trousers.

'We, er… I mean, um,' Damien mumbled, getting up. 'Come on Stace.'

'May as well stay now,' she said.

'Stace,' Ally warned.

The three of them got up to leave. I watched them head over to Ally's, where Will and Sarah stood arguing. He would never understand the whole sobriety thing, but our lies – mine especially – were a total betrayal. I felt sick with guilt.

I slammed the door. 'What the hell, Marcus?'

'I don't know, Tom,' he panicked. 'I know I told Sarah. Maybe she-'

'No! This is *you*, pissed-up. It's one thing screwing yourself over…' I slapped his leg.

'I fell… Sweet Caroline… I was dancing,' he looked pathetic – it was so hard to be mad at him.

I sat on the other settee and sighed into my hands.

'I'm sorry, Tom,' he said, *little brother getting us in trouble with mum.*

The toilet door opened. Loz stumbled into the living room, clearly struggling to focus. 'Where is she?'

'Who?' I asked.

'My love.'

'*L*ove?'

'I mean,' he stopped and tried to come up with something. 'The… Ally.'

'My love?' Marcus laughed.

'I don't know what you're laughing about,' I said, 'waving your cock about like you're on goddam Hurst Street.'

'What?' Loz.

'Eh?' Marcus. He looked clueless.

'Loz, leave,' I said. 'She's across the grass.'

'Who?' He reached for the wall to steady himself.

'The love of your life!' I got up and helped him to the back door.

'What's he been doing with his cock?' he laughed, as I pushed him outside. I slammed the door, the windows shook.

'Marcus, man, I know what happened. Leroy told me.'

'I fell over! I was dancing to-'

'Sweet Caroline, so you told us.'

'What did Leroy say?'

'A hell of a lot more than I wanted to know. He said you were in Picks acting all "ooh fucking matron".'

'Alright, alright, I genuinely can't remember. I was wrecked. I remember Jake helping me out of Picks with Neil bloody Diamond in the background. What happened?'

'Tim Price was talking about how he'd had a lovely bit of sausage on the high-rise barbecue-'

He snorted a laugh.

'It's not funny man.'

'What did I do?'

'You pulled your cock out and asked him what he thought of your lovely chipolata.'

'It was Tim Price who did this? The cunt!'

'Leroy didn't say, but it caused a massive scene and three or four of them jumped you. One of them gashed your knee with a broken bottle.'

'It's proper fucked, Tom. I can't feel my kneecap. It's just numb.'

'You can't pull your cock out in Picks! Not in a gay way.'

He laughed, 'ark at madam.'

'*Listen to me.* You couldn't do it before, but now it's worse. Let's face it, they're a bunch of drunken homophobes, and now there's nothing to fear.'

'I was wankered.'

'You can't get wankered then.'

'Fuck off! I'm not joining your AA brigade.'

'I'm not saying you should. But look at your leg. Why do you think Leroy-?'

He sat up, 'there's nothing going on with Leroy!'

'Maybe not anymore.'

'What did Leroy tell you?'

We'd had so many years of bravado and piss-taking, the subject of his sexuality had long been a joke. This was how we went about things. I looked over at my old friend, anxious, on the edge of his seat, it was written all over his face, carved deep in his knee. But I didn't want him to tell me he was gay because I didn't want him to deny it again.

'Just that he was bi, I guess.'

I'm Tom, alcoholic. Sometimes I don't know how to be a friend.

I sat back and put my head in my hands, tuned out. All around us, the irritating cough of pocks and woodpecker tapping; the maddening echoes of the town voices bouncing around the blocks, Black Country yelps, nasal cackles and football jeering. Working cogs in a broken machine or viruses in the matrix? I opened my eyes and Marcus was looking at me.

'I'm sorry, man.'

'Who did you tell? What did you say?'

He looked nervous, old, restless leg quivering. 'I said Jay dragged you down the George, that we were gonna brew booze, I think. I'm sure I didn't mention you nicked the wine, just the plastic barrel. I told Leroy and Sarah… Maybe Jason-'

'Jason?'

'Only in passing.'

I looked him in the eye, but he immediately looked away. A regrettable image passed through my thoughts.

'They're talking about a trial,' I said.

'A *trial*?'

I nodded.

He clenched his fists and banged the wall. 'I'm such a fucking idiot!' He slapped himself in the face, hard, then shook his head, dizzied. 'I need a drink.'

―――――――

Leroy stood naked. The town faced him in shocked disgust.

'You ay a woman!' a woman.

'Where's yuh tits?' a man.

'I'm a woman! *Look*.'

He had small moobs and no hair on his chest, but from the waist up he was a man, he was Leroy, the guy I went to Primary School with, played in a band with, listened to recount the most intimate details about his sexual conquests. But from the waist down he… she was someone altogether different. Pale, bare gangly legs, cock gone, scarring that more resembled the criss-crossy self-harm on my angst-etched arms than a sex change operation – not that I'd ever seen the results of a sex change operation.

I found myself shaking my head in utter disbelief, somehow aware of everything that was going on around me, whilst transfixed on the absence of cock like it was the third eye.

'Fucking fake!' someone.

'Freak!' another.

Leroy just stood there. More nervous than I'd ever seen him. In fact it wasn't him. Obviously it was her… I guess. But I mean, she was different. She nervously smiled and it didn't look like Leroy. Was it humility? If I'd first seen this person perhaps I would've honestly believed Leroy was Lee… or Lee wasn't Leroy.

'Deeve!' College Ed yelled.

Councillor Ray looked terrified and ran to the wall. Tony Dale scooped up Ethan and ushered Lettie to the caged entrance. Ally herded the other kids, some of whom were intrigued, peeping between her legs at the nude vicar. Others were terrified and crying, sensing the change in the air and looking for safety in the guise of their parents who were morphing and twisting into Bruegel beasts in the crowd.

Tony Dale rattled the cage, but it was padlocked. He started kicking it. 'Key! Key!' he yelled. Christian was frozen until Tony grabbed him and screamed 'key!' in his face, 'kids!' prompting him into action.

'Sick fuck!' someone growled at Leroy.

'Yow'm disgusting!' another.

I felt surprisingly calm and slow in the midst of this. God maybe? I don't know. Perhaps this was Lee the preacher? Lee just stood there, naked and white, an orb of light in St John's, whilst the world spun dizzily around her.

But then someone picked up a chair and threw it at him and the orb popped, everything suddenly speeding up. Lee flinched and dodged as shoes, chairs and keys were flung at her. Man or woman, he adjusted naked limbs in a pathetic attempt to protect organs, eyes, liver and genitals. There was mania, jeering, yam-yam anger. Tony Dale had managed to open up the cage and he ushered the kids out, but the front door had been locked too, so now he was caged with a bunch of kids in the entrance, as madness gripped St John's.

'Stop!' Jake screamed, trying to shield Lee. 'Squirrel-sheep! Fuck! Stop! Fuck!' It was the first time I'd heard him swear.

'Move Jake!' Ricky shouted, ready to toss a framed painting of St John the Baptist's head on a plate. 'He's a freak!'

'Pahahaha!' Will laughed. I looked at him in anger. 'I don't know. I don't…' he mouthed.

Sarah had her hands on her head and looked like she was going to implode. I ran over and grabbed her. 'They're gonna kill Lee,' she said. 'They're gonna kill her!'

'Yuh fat mother-fucking prick!' suddenly came from behind us. I turned to see Jay Bird trying to get away from John. 'Just piss off!'

This was followed by some woman screaming, 'Jay Bird's trying to escape!'

Everyone stopped for a full moment, the gap between a breath, and turned to see Jay Bird run up into the pulpit, kicking John down the steps.

'Jay,' I called. 'Stop it!'

'Get him, John,' Christian yelled.

'John, John, John,' someone chanted, then more joined in, 'John, John, John,' until most were chanting his name. I even caught Barb joining in. Rex was too tired and stood nodding his head in contribution.

John looked like he was about to have some sort of a meltdown, trapped, he kept turning to us, then to Jay, then to us, confused.

'Jay, sit down!' I yelled, thinking this was the only way he could save himself.

'John, John, John,' the room throbbed.

'Tomz,' he yelled back, 'shake it up baby!'

He kicked John hard in the face, which made him scream like a child having a tantrum.

'John, John, John,' they boomed, faster, angrier, out of time with themselves.

Jay went to kick him again, but John grabbed his leg and charged up the steps. Jay Bird rose into the air and came crashing down off the pulpit, his head hitting the tiles with a smack which immediately rag-dolled him and silenced St John's. A large pool of blood quickly spread from under his Gollum-bald head, face down, dead.

'I didn't, I didn't,' John spoke, broken.

Everybody stared at him. He was agitated, scratching at the sandstone pulpit. 'No. The toms.'

The crowd had got what they wanted and it had stunned them still, captivating them, an isolated mutter of 'is he dead?' But not even Jay Bird could've survived that. I felt the hot oil of adrenaline fall to my stomach, too sick to cry, but the emotion was there somewhere, put aside for processing.

John didn't seem to realise what he'd done. 'The tomatoes?' he asked, looking for Christian.

'John.' Christian slowly edged towards him.

'The tomatoes will be red by now,' he said.

'John,' he whispered.

'What?' petulant.

'It's fine. Listen to me.'

'Yeah, yeah,' nodding.

'We can go out into the garden, tidy the leaves and plant some potatoes,' Christian continued, with surprising calm and experience.

'The tomatoes?'

'It's the wrong season for tomatoes, John.'

This made John laugh. 'I didn't do it.'

There were a few nervous titters from the townspeople.

'That's right,' Christian said.

'I didn't do it,' he grinned, the smile failing to mask the anxiety. 'They made me do it. *Honest.*'

Slow laughter came from a solitary voice behind. It was like we'd all been party to a ruse, a test and it all was about to become clear. The herd turned back to see Tony Moran laughing and Leroy still standing naked. Why hadn't he made a run for it? Why was he still naked?

There were murmurs of shock where people had forgotten there was another side to the story. 'Deeve, Deeve,' College Ed started to chant, but no one else was on the same page, everyone was too sickened for it, or were they just exhausted? Tony Moran laughed again. *Why is he laughing?* It seemed like bad acting.

'"I didn't do it. Honest,"' he quoted, still laughing.

There were conforming titters and half-laughs amongst us, nerves, confusion. Intermittently, we looked over our shoulders to check Jay was still dead, then back to Leroy and the laughing Son.

Tony Moran put his arm around Leroy's bare shoulders. She half-giggled, girlish, pale, unable to hide. This made everybody laugh, anxious laughter, but relief. I found myself laughing along, like everything was going to be alright. Perhaps Jay's death would break the curse of the collective judgement.

In the entrance, the kids were still caged with Tony Dale, his big gorilla hands, patting little ape heads. Ally was the other side failing to block their view. The future of Halesowen scarred for life – they fuck you up your mum and dad, but this was another level.

I looked for the boys. Marcus was leaning against a pillar, squeezing his numb knee. Loz was behind us in the far corner of the church, a mouse looking for a crack in the wall. Most of us were standing in the nave, a clag of humans, giggling like we were all in on the joke. In the middle of us, Sean, Jay's brother, was sat in the wheelchair. He was awake, but he didn't look like he knew what was going on. I remembered the sad panic when he saw Jay's battered face. How would he feel when he realised Jay was dead?

I caught Leroy's eye. '*Why?*' I mouthed. His face dropped. Was it redemption? Was it because of our conversation? He was done for. If not today, not too far in the distant future. Marcus's knee for getting his cock out was one thing, but *Lee?* All it would take was a bender in Picks turning sour.

Will was looking at me, hands holding his chin up, stunned by what we'd just witnessed. Sarah held onto me, hid her face in my chest, juddering with hysterics. There was no laughter.

She pinched my back in anguish.

'It'll be ok,' I said.

Because that's what people say.

———————

Will locked the back door. He lit two candles and put them against the wall on plates. 'Just us tonight, yeah?'

I nodded. Loz didn't. Marcus looked straight ahead, legs up, morose.

The townspeople had relieved their tension by reducing the high-rise to the ground floor. The sledgehammering had now stopped, the barbecue extinguished, ciders sunk. Everybody had gone their own way. Sarah had gone with Lee to prepare for midnight mass and a hasty funeral. It was just the four of us. I found myself thinking this was how it all began and this was how it would end, but I was probably just writing another story. Outside it was purple and cold, a frosting of stars. In the flat, burnt orange candlelight, big coats and damp.

'Ally's?' Loz suggested, clearly with an agenda.

We could hear music. A party which would inevitably turn into something more bacchanalian, and terrifying for it, especially in the wake of the trial.

'Just us,' Will stressed.

'It is Christmas Eve,' he tried.

'Just the boys,' I said. 'Jay Bird, Leroy, it's all a bit too real.'

'What about Sarah?' he manipulated.

'Fucking hell!' Will stood up and stormed into the kitchen. 'Are we speaking Gaelic?'

'He's come over all queer,' Marcus said, making an effort, but without a smile. 'Calm down you big lank.'

He came back in with a half bottle of vodka. 'Great, Marcus. We've established *I'm* tall,' he grumped, 'and *you're* gay... *again*.'

'Cunt.'

'Where did you get the booze?' Loz asked.

'Ally.'

'Does she know?'

'Are you the fucking federali?' He unscrewed the cap, took a huge swig and then passed it to Marcus, subduing the impulse to heave.

Until I went to rehab, Christmas Eve had always been our night. The days around it spent with family, we'd always come together on that one evening. After midnight, blind drunk, we'd say our merry Christmases and then go our separate ways. We looked forward to it – if the four of us had been a company, it was like our work's-do.

'Remember the last Christmas Eve before I left?' I asked them.

'Stacey-gate,' Marcus said.

'*She was fit*,' I insisted.

'I never saw it,' Will said.

'I know you didn't. You never did like an older woman.'

'You didn't even fuck her,' Marcus laughed.

'No, but we kissed, man. It was something. Look what's happened to her.' I felt sad thinking about it.

'Crack and smack,' Will said. 'I mean, what did you see in that?'

'She had a real spark. There was life in her.'

'Six of them,' Marcus, dry.

'But she'd dance and sing, "find my love, find my love,"' I half-crooned. 'She was round in the right places. I thought she was hot.'

'Eeyore thinks she still is.' Will reached for his guitar. 'Come on then, Loz, one bloody day to Christmas, what do you want me to play?'

He looked surprised and excited and sang, '"come they told me pa rum pum pum…"'

'Bowie and Bing,' I smiled. 'Go on, I'll do Bowie. "Peace on earth…"'

We were sat on the front row of a packed Church-1. A somewhat normal and boring Christmas service – *nothing to see here* – had followed Jay's rushed funeral.

I looked out of the big windows, across the road to St John's. The cold, sunny skies gave everything a shape. The bare yew trees looked like splintered dinosaur bones. The sandstone building, a big tombstone. Both were framed in Jurassic grasses surrounding the church, small graves poking out like chipped teeth in the mouth of an underground monster.

'…And Christ was born…' Lee said, from under his green and red robe.

Sarah sat next to me. She looked depressed and had spoken very little since the trial, when Leroy bared all. But the town had seemed to accept it. On the surface, at least.

'… And He taught us forgiveness, a virtue which we hold dear in our civilisation,' Lee said, 'which we take with us into our new independent land of Halesowen…'

There were mumbles amongst the townspeople. They weren't really listening. Councillor Ray was sitting adjacent to Lee, after giving a reading. I noticed he would glance in her direction but he just couldn't look up at her. As mild-mannered as he was, he was always going to struggle with the truth of Lee. They'd been close friends.

'… All that it remains for me to say is, I wish you a loving and merry Christmas.'

Merry Christmases were muttered, as people started to get up to leave.

'Come on,' I said, grabbing Sarah's arm.

Ross North came to the lectern. 'Wait, if you could just take a seat for a few minutes' – there were grumbles of disapproval – 'then we can go for one on the house at Picks' – which turned to cheers and bums on seats.

'I know there's been a lot of talk in the pubs and the high-rise recently about laws and rules, after what happened. We want you to know we've been listening. We've come up with something which covers all bases. Jay's Law, named in honour of our fellow townsman, who was merely a victim of his own greed. I know what you're thinking, but it's not a law, it's a rule, like Newton's law of gravity. A few clauses about trade,' he mumbled quickly, 'to help us avoid another situation like this one,' he gestured out the back, where they'd awkwardly carried Jay's coffin. 'Essentially it's our collective judgement on paper.'

Our collective judgement, as if we'd all voted on it. I caught his eye and conformed with a solemn nod.

'Now, regarding this murder. Whether Jay killed Nigel is neither here nor there,' Ross stated. 'We will never know. The van has gone. They've left the George. Nigel left this mortal coil, and Sandra left on wheels – whether out of guilt or fear is not for us to say.'

In the wake of Jay's death, of which the town had absolved themselves of responsibility, most believed he hadn't killed Nigel. They knew he wasn't capable of it, just like he wasn't capable of killing Gary Bennett. Jay was a lovestruck dope with a lifelong dope habit. He had it in him to do a lot of things, but wilful murder was not one of them. Sandra Burton had murdered her husband – wasn't this the collective judgement?

'The Sons have suggested, and it's merely a suggestion,' he said, 'that vehicles are given up.'

Councillor Ray didn't seem so sure, refusing to look up where others nodded in agreement.

'It's only the same as we did with our communication devices,' Ross added. 'We know many of you don't have working vehicles, but if we could, as a town, remove the tyres from *any* motorised vehicles, this would be a show of solidarity, a symbol of our commitment to Halesowen.'

Most were nodding. Apparently it was a good idea – or they just wanted to get down Picks.

'Just pile the tyres outside St John's and the Sons will get rid of them. Those of you who are able, please assist one another. We need to look out for each other, my friends.'

Bert stood up, he was a mechanic and now a non-bureaucrat. 'I'd like to offer my services to help remove tyres,' he said.

'Thank you, Bert.'

'I can help too,' Mick said.

'Yeah, me and the lad,' someone else added.

'Thank you all,' Ross said. 'Town spirit,' he smiled, condescendingly.

'I can change a tyre too,' Lee said, stepping forward.

The room silenced. Ross looked to him, to the town, then down at the lectern, 'yes, yes, thank you,' he muttered.

Sarah squeezed my arm. I looked past her to Will. It felt awkward, dangerous even.

'There needs to be some sort of order,' Ross said, changing the tone. 'Times have changed and we need to come together no matter how difficult things might get in the future.'

I remembered smoking outside Picks many moons ago with comrade Ross pontificating on whether or not there could be order without chaos. He would talk about the flaws of communism, about Orwell and the Spanish Civil War, and I would agree with him, lubricated, sure of myself in that eternal moment which had no beginning or end, no consequence, no meaning. Were our brains just too small for utopia?

'We need to listen to each other,' he continued. 'The collective judgement bubbles and difficult courses of action need to be taken. How can I explain it?' he asked his ego. 'Aha! We all thought the Iraq War was a mistake. I marched with the students-'

A conflict Ross was once so indefatigably against was now acceptable. As original a thinker as I used to think he was, from my sodden perch in Picks, Ross soon dutifully fell in line. First it was the working class battle for UK independence. And then Red Ross, his beer gut growing, testosterone levels lowering, turned his back on Corbyn for being too red. Then he turned his back on the students and unions in the horrifying wake of the viruses, as they fought for fair pay for key workers. And, when the unemployed rose up to tear down the buildings of the establishment during the Greek Riots, he stood back and chastised them in line with "is he red, is he blue" Blair, during his revival.

'But I was naïve,' Ross continued. 'Sometimes bad things need to happen so that we can have a semblance of order. Iraq was-'

'Alright, alright,' Tony Moran yelled. 'Get on with it. There's a pint with our names on it.'

A few cheered.

Ross blushed, 'sorry, my friends, I just care so much about my… our town. Now, some of you have already formed groups and chosen looting trades. I'd ask you all to follow suit. This is Jay's… Jay's Law… of tranquillity,' he laughed hard. No one else did. 'Yes, well, look down the list to make sure there's no trade duplication. If some good can come from this sad tragedy,' he said magnanimously and with little self-awareness, 'it is this: we can choose a humble life less of greed. Times are hard and I implore you to focus on an existence which is about need and nothing more. A life in which we are true to ourselves and each other.' He gave a sideways glance to Lee, who smiled.

Then it hit me. The Iraq war? Difficult decisions? Was this bubbling collective judgement about Lee? Most of these people disregarded gender politics even before the bombs. I had trouble myself seeing my old male friend as female. I would forever have to work at it. Will didn't even believe in the idea. How would they handle this? Another trial? What was the crime? Not being "true" to himself, or herself? They could spin it either way.

Marcus rubbed his knee, looking down, forever looking down. He wasn't going to last in Halesowen. Sooner or later we would have to leave to save him.

I looked up at Lee, who was smiling, proud of what he'd built. Couldn't he see what was going on, what they thought of him now that he was a her to them?

His revelation hadn't been overshadowed by Jay's violent death. The image of Lee's naked body, scarred androgynous, was surely a memory they would strive to remove. Unless he removed himself.

We had to leave this goddam town.

'Are you alright?' I asked Sarah, leaning against the front entrance.

Most had made their way down to Picks for their free drink. Inside, Lee was sitting alone, reading his bible.

'She's alright,' Will said, his arms around her.

'I'm fine.'

'In rehab, that meant-'

'Fucked up, insecure, neurotic and emotional! I know! You've told me many times,' a sulky teenager.

'Just stop asking her,' Will griped, roll-up hanging out of his mouth.

'It's only because I care!'

'What's that supposed to mean?' he argued.

'Nothing. I'm gonna go and speak to him,' I said, looking at Lee.

'Her,' she corrected.

'Alright, alright, him, her, give me chance.'

'It's not that difficult,' Will said.

I stopped myself short of calling him out. It wouldn't help the situation. He was a bastard at times.

'You better hurry up if we're getting Sean's chair,' he said.

Lee smiled when she saw me. She looked ridiculous in that Christmas robe. Were her robes part of the whole thing? I knew pretty much nothing about it, but enough to realise I probably shouldn't ask that question.

'You coming to Ally's?'

'I don't think so,' she said.

She closed the book and I saw the familiar tremor. 'When did you last have one?'

'After the funeral I took a swig. I might have another in a bit.'

It didn't feel like the time for a "told you so" about moderation, but I was feeling quietly smug about it. 'Has Sarah said anything about-?'

'I'm not leaving, Tom. They'll get used to it.'

'And if they don't?'

'It's God's will.'

'What will be will be,' I said.

'Exactly.'

'Let go and let God,' I smiled.

'That's a bit AA,' she said, 'but yes, in a way.'

It was still Leroy. Broken down and lost, but Leroy. How can the best part of 50 years be erased just like that? Sarah was young, she'd only just met her.

'When did you have the op?'

'The op,' she laughed.

'What?' I asked.

'Sorry, Tom. It's just tiring spending your whole life telling people who you are. "The op" is just something people used to say on TV. A punchline in old sitcoms. The truth is,' she stopped, clasped her hands together to try to control the tremor, 'this journey, the operations, the therapy, has been my life. I just want to live now.'

She looked tired and ill, beads of sweat in her furrowed brow.

'But there's surely better places to live?'

'No!' she jabbed the air, the tremor extending down her arm – I was immediately transported to detoxes on a psych ward, the memory of trying to scoop up peas with a fork.

'Maybe have a drink?' It was hard to watch and surely there was a risk of a seizure if it was this bad.

Lee got up and fetched a small flask from behind the lectern.

'I had my first three operations in the states. The last one left me… oh, it doesn't matter, Tom.'

'You can talk to me, you know. I'll try to understand. I can't promise I'll say the right things.'

I wanted to ask why she hadn't had a boob job, but that was bound to come out wrong. Wasn't "boob job" a punchline too?

'Some day. Maybe,' she said.

'In the states? Was that when you found-?'

'He was always there. That was when I turned my life over to Him.'

'Were you in AA in the states?'

'Not for God.'

Her face was still his face. She was still my old friend, but bruised by life, like we all were one way or another. Maybe someday we would talk properly and learn to listen to each other.

'Will you come to Ally's later?' I asked. 'It's Christmas.'

'Maybe. I've got a lot to do here.'

When I left Church-1, I had a feeling this was going to be the last time I'd see Leroy. Or Lee, for that matter.

'Where's Sarah gone?' I asked Will.

'Up Ally's with Loz.'

'He really wants her,' I smiled.

'He better fucking not!' he threatened.

'Ally, you prat.'

'He can have her,' he laughed. He held up a bag. 'Two cans of Stella and a turkey sandwich. Do you think he knows?'

'I hope not.'

'He should've been at the funeral.'

'No one wants that kind of reality. Where's the chair?'

'Tony Dale left it outside the George. I'm not being his fucking carer, Tom,' he moaned.

'We'll figure it out.'

'Marcus will have to do it. He does bugger all.'

The chair had been covered by a black bag which had half blown off in the wind. It felt slightly damp. It didn't weigh very much, but it was clean and had to be better than the one Sean was using.

'Maybe we should put our name down as furniture traders,' I said.

'Too much like hard work.'

We wheeled the chair to Jay Bird's flat, awkwardly lugged it up the stairs. The door was open.

'Just Tom, mate,' I yelled. 'Sean, it's just Tom.'

There was nothing.

Even before I entered the living room, I knew it. The stale air, still and cold, the reek of piss and toxic shit, vinegary bile. How was he ever going to survive?

His head back, mouth agape, I curiously inspected the stiff and withered body which once belonged to Sean. Yellow cheeks sucked in, one eye was closed, the other half open, a sliver of eyeball. Was I already desensitised to this horror? His hands in his lap, knuckles twisted and frozen – one looked like he'd been trying to make a duck shadow.

'Makes life easier,' Will said, cracking open a Stella.

'Yes,' I agreed, coldly, gawping at his tongue, dried and shrinking back.

But then I recalled Jay winking, acting for his brother to spare him the embarrassment of his failing brain. There was a warmth to Jay Bird. I'd seen it all those years ago when he'd shared his prescription drugs in old, dirty Black Country pubs, the stale beer sweating from every pore of the upholstery. Somewhere inside he genuinely cared for his brother and his brother reciprocated those feelings. And Jay never pretended to be kind. I never saw him play that trick. Whether he was too kind, too dumb or too honourable, I would never really know, but he wasn't all bad.

I felt his absence in the chill of the room. Then I heard him, almost as if he were there, "yuh jammin', jammin', jammin'…" he sang, spoke really – a truly terrible singer.

'Curse of the collective judgement,' I said.

'Don't start. Just starved,' Will said.

'Like a neglected animal forgotten in his cage.'

'You know,' he said, looking into Sean's mouth.

I noticed the golden glint in his back teeth. I knew exactly what he was thinking and I started to shake my head.

'We need a trade,' he said.

'That's sick.'

'Survival,' he said, putting his hand in Sean's mouth.

'What you doing?' I grabbed his elbow.

He turned to face me, irritated. 'Just accept it.' He said the words slowly so they reverberated in my head.

So much of life was about acceptance. *Accept the things you can't change, have the courage to change the things you can, the wisdom to know the difference.*

'Wouldn't we be breaking a rule?' I pathetically put out there, just to show where I stood if it came back on us.

'The only rule is Jay's Law,' he said, pulling at his teeth. 'If this is our trade, it's game. Valuable metals. There's gold, platinum and palladium in all sorts of gadgets and vehicles.'

Valuable metals. I quite liked the idea of it. Like we were at the forefront of a modern gold rush. Maybe I could write about it, like Jack London of the new age, a sober adventurer into circuit board wildernesses.

'Do you even know anything about gadgets and the workings of things?'

Then I heard the twisting and clicking of gums, followed by a crack.

Will was playing "O Little Town of Bethlehem" on his guitar. Loz had his bass with him but was too drunk to play it. He was singing with an accent to a calypso beat. Marcus kept trying to sing along in a high-pitched opera voice.

'Shut up, man,' Will moaned. 'You can't sing. You can't even keep fucking time.'

Stacey was dancing in the middle of the room on her own, Damien watching her, puffing on a roll-up. They were all smiling, like it was any other Christmas.

Against the wall, a table full of booze. Bottles of spirits. A fancy tequila which looked particularly appealing. I found myself contemplating it. No one here would mind. Perhaps they wouldn't even notice. Maybe I could have one sesh a year. Christmas Day. Or just special days. And birthdays! New Year's Eve and Christmas Eve, like the old days. Or make it a weekend thing?

Christ, I haven't even had a drink and I'm already talking it up.

'She should be here,' I said to Ally.

'She'll be back soon, don't worry about it.'

'I'm not worried,' I defended.

But I was. I was worried for myself and I was worried for her. She'd gone to fetch Lee from Church-1 over an hour ago and it was nearly Boxing Day already.

I stood up. 'I'm gonna go down there.'

Ally stood up too. 'Tom, she'll be fine, just leave her.'

The way she intervened made me more worried. 'What's the big deal, Ally?'

'O, little, towwwn,' Marcus sang, full on Dame Melba.

'I'm not playing it then,' Will sulked.

Ally grabbed my hands.

'Oh, come on, man! It's Christmas!' Loz demanded.

'Let go of me, Ally,' I said. 'I'm just going to check she's alright. You coming Will?'

'Where?'

'To get Sarah.'

'She'll be fine. Just chill out. Have a bloody drink,' he laughed.

They all laughed, except Ally, who was just looking at me, 'I wish you would,' she said. 'I know that's bad of me.'

'What are you hiding?' I said.

Stacey came between us. 'O, little town of Bethlehem,' she sang, sexily, before grabbing my balls.

I jumped back. 'Fuck off, Stace!'

'Not much to play with there,' she cackled.

'Nothing,' Ally said. 'I just think she wants some time alone with him-'

'Her,' I corrected.

'Whatever. Before they come up here. Just trust me, Tom,' she said.

I didn't, and normally I would. I sat down to appease her.

Will started playing Elvis.

'"We're caught in trap,"' Marcus sang.

'Not yet,' he yelled. 'Let Loz do it. Or Tom, you sing.'

'I'm not in the mood.'

'You need a drink,' Loz said, laughing.

'Leave him alone,' Will insisted.

'Alright for you!' he countered.

'"We're caught in a trap, I can't walk out,"' Stacey sang.

Ally sat down, tapping her foot prescriptively, watching me. Damien was playing the drums on his knees. Will joined in singing, '"because I love you too much, baby," that's fucking ace, Stace.'

They'd been drinking all day. The town *I* was living in was no longer the town *they* were living in. They were numb to Jay Bird's passing, Leroy's plight, the energy-expending hoo-ha of the high-rise all because a man shagged a goat in the 1980s.

Loz started to sing along, Marcus was rocking and trying to sing. Stacey danced, rubbing her body, putting on a show. She hadn't used to be like this, she had a kind of class, a power. She held you with her eyes, but now she was relying on you looking anywhere but, which Damien was content to do, transfixed on her body, her old legs and arms, all elbows and knees.

Marcus got up, his balding head dripping with the beer sweats. He tried to dance with Stacey, humped her leg, but it was as dry as his wit, and Stacey shook him off, leaving him to dance alone, hobbling and out of sync. Loz couldn't stand up. He wobbled on the settee, glancing at Ally and singing, '"we can't go on together, in suspicious minds".'

Had Will forgotten that not so long ago we'd pulled gold crowns from Sean's dead leathery mouth? He looked happy, playing well, lost in the music. Everyone was moving. Even Ally, but there was a flat incongruence in her expression. Something was going on and she knew about it.

I stood up. '"We can't go together,"' I sang, dancing, '"in suspicious minds…"'

'That's it man,' Will said.

I danced to the door. I looked over at Ally. She knew what I was doing. I opened it, slammed it shut and ran out into the cold dark of the flats, the hard buildings, the spongy grass. I didn't hear the door open behind me. She'd let me go. I had my headtorch in my pocket. I put it on my head, but left it off for the time being, slipping and sliding on the frost-dewed grass.

I came to the next block, which was now Church-2, but it was blacked out and empty most of the time. I walked alongside it, off the estate and onto Andrew Road.

It was one of those nights where the sky looked brown. Some of the solar powered streetlamps were still working, orange cones of light like lily pads into town. I had a bad feeling, but I always had a bad feeling. Then I heard somebody yelling incomprehensibly in the distance and the feeling intensified.

By the bus station, I saw a figure step into a cone of light and stay there. I realised quite quickly it was Sarah, putting her shape and the voice together.

My stomach felt icy and empty, like I might throw up, watery mouth and dry lips. I found myself looking behind me, but there was nothing. I wanted to turn around and go back to Ally's, pretending I hadn't just run out suspecting she was in on something terrible, but my cold, stiff legs kept moving forward, against me. 'You always have a bad feeling,' I told myself.

As I neared, I could make out the silhouette of a bottle. *Is she drinking wine?* 'Shit.' She looked drunk – was this Lee's moderation?

I crossed the road making cold fists, my fingers weak, like I wouldn't even be able to hold her hand. It looked like she was reading something. *Why I am still walking?* Then she saw me. I must've been the last person she wanted to see. She started spitting words, kicking and punching the streetlamp, which flickered but would not go out.

'Sarah, it's ok,' I said. 'Relapse is all a part of it.'

Laughing, manic and cynical, 'this is a good one,' she said, waving the page, before swigging wine.

I wanted to take the bottle and smash it, but I knew better. 'Where've you been?' I asked softly.

She held her finger up to shush me. '"And they said unto her, there is none of thy kindred that is called by that name."'

There was oil or wine on the crumpled paper and I reached for it.

'Wait, there's more. "And they made signs to his father how he would have him called."'

I took the page from her hand and looked at it under my headtorch. It was one of the doves from the Christmas tree. But it wasn't oil or wine. It was blood.

'*She* was called *Lee*,' she yelled, at the unravelled dove. 'Ah-fucking-men.'

2028

'This is completely insane!' I shouted.

A growl of thunder after leaving Ally's turned to the slow pitter patter of rain as we made our way up Andrew Road in the suffocating heat. To begin with it was a welcome relief, but the wet-heavy droplets quickly turned into a frightening downpour.

Marcus gestured back towards the flats.

I pushed him on. 'We're not gonna get any wetter!'

With two days until the last bus we had to get back. Maureen needed my help and God knew what state Will was in after shooting the rabbit. Would they talk about it? How would she react? What *would* they talk about? Perhaps he'd tell her I was married and then she'd know me for the lying wretch I was.

I grabbed Marcus's shoulder. 'Let's run!'

We began pounding our way up the hill against the storm, Marcus stopping intermittently to catch his breath. Eventually we reached the top, the road flattening out. We sheltered behind a hedge next to the old red-bricked Button Factory pub, where we used to pop pills and sing, falling in love with anyone who took a moment to talk to us. A half-sunken roof, it was now barely standing. Long since closed down, it died a death with Amazon's Booze Tubes, when half the country turned their sheds into bars.

A sudden whirling gust shook the fence behind us down, taking half the hedge with it. I shoved Marcus out of the way. We turned to dodge the slats of wood, and watched the winds tear strips of tiles from the roof of the pub. The only time I'd ever experienced anything like this was when I'd caught the tail end of the monsoon in Pokhara, hiking the Annapurna. One night it rained so hard the streets ran with mud. The next day it was brilliantly clear and we made our way into the Mustang region to find a rain shadow in the mountains.

'Ally's?' Marcus pleaded over the wind.

'No point,' I yelled. 'Get home quick!'

He looked scared, pulling the drenched paisley shirt away from his flab. I dragged him on, fighting through the cage of rain. Pieces of debris broke from houses in slamming winds, bits of wood and strips of plastic. A garden solar light rode a gust towards us, nearly staking us. We jumped out of the way and into the path of a big plant pot, which landed just in front of me with a smash, the red-leaved corpse of a young acer at our feet.

Marcus was crouching behind me to hide from the violent push and pull of it.

'Come on!' I dragged him on.

Covered in leaves, twigs and mud, we moved away from the pavement. We turned off, walking down the middle of Bassnage Road, where black bags of personal items had sailed off gardens, splitting open, soaked in the streams of rainwater. A drenched teddy bear lay plugging a drain, drowned. Plastic nurses and paramedic figures were floating in the gutter. Coat hangers and clothes were tangling up in overgrown shrubs and lawns. Folded chairs and tables were twisted and locked together in muddy garden borders. We'd been out in it for less than half an hour and already the whole landscape had changed, the winds strong enough to move the big white fridges outside the old Co-op into the road.

I gestured to the shop for shelter. Marcus was nodding, desperate to get out of it. Like mime artists, we made our way to the metal boarded windows, to a snipped aperture into darkness. As we climbed in, I caught my shirt on a razor-sharp point. I pulled irritably and managed to catch my bad arm, tearing the bandage and reopening the wound.

Inside the floor was slippy where water had poured in. My hand gripping onto my arm, I slipped and almost fell. 'Goddam it!'

The storm muted to a white noise in the background, the wind folding the sky in paper slaps. A fast alarm was going off somewhere. House or car, it felt strangely unfamiliar, like a town siren warning of an alien attack.

Marcus wiped the water from his brow. 'It's like a bloody hurricane.'

'And it's still so goddam hot!'

My eyes still adjusting to the darkness inside, I needed something to wrap around my arm. Then I remembered how I'd gone about it the last time. I took my shoe off to remove my sock. It was wet, but if I tied it tight enough it would stop the bleeding for now.

'What the fuck's been going on in here?' Marcus said.

I looked up. The shelving had been turned on its sides. On closer inspection, it appeared organised. 'Someone's been living here.'

A matrix of dens, four squares forming a much bigger one, made out of small units of shelving which had been pushed onto their ends and fashioned into four feet high walls. I looked over the nearest unit and the shelves were still attached and formed into triangles of support. There were two mattresses with balled up quilts, bags of clothes, and bottles and cups. The second den, beside it, shared the middle shelving and was similarly cluttered.

'Who?' he asked, walking towards the back of the shop.

'How would I bloody know? Hello,' I called. 'Anyone?' Behind me, the storm rained water through the hole. I stepped away from it and nearly slipped. 'Fuck.'

'Tom! Come here!' Marcus yelled, looking over into one of the back dens. 'Hurry up!'

I started making tentative steps towards him, using the shelving as support.

'*Fuck*. There's a dead guy!' he panicked. 'Tom!'

I moved fast, but immediately slipped and fell to my knees with a crack. 'Bastard! That hurt.'

'Tom!'

'For God's sake, Marcus, I'm coming!' I got back up and hobbled towards him. I leant over the shelving and could see the outline of a man, arched up and bloated. He was clearly dead, but it was hard to make him out.

'Not another. What the hell's going on, Marcus?'

'Dropping like fucking flies,' he said, trying to inspect the body.

'We need a torch.'

'There's one on his head,' he pointed.

'Go on then,' I prompted.

'I'm not doing it.'

'He's dead,' I insisted.

He leant further into the den. 'Shall we just leave it?' he said.

'Help me find a light.'

I edged around the dens trying to find a torch. Each one had a couple of mattresses inside. It was like a refugee camp. So many free houses on the estates and they'd chosen to live like this. Why would anybody choose to live in a grotty little hole like this when they had the pick of the bunch? Who were these people? *Must be smack heads.*

Then I remembered. 'Marcus, forget it! We need to get out of here-'

'I've found a headtorch.' He blinded me with it then lit up the grave. 'Fuuuuck!' he heaved. 'Oh, that's sick.'

I went back over. He shone the light on his face. It was purple and black and partly covered in a pitted foam, a sepia spume ejected when his body had tried to save itself. I knew immediately who it was. 'We need to go,' I said.

'But the storm-'

'Sod the storm. That's Ninny Jackson. This is their fucking lair.'

'*Lair*? Who-?'

'Baz's dad. The fucking scag rats.'

'Who?'

'The Baz, the rabbit-'

'*What*?'

'The one Will killed. I watched one of them run Bassnage Road when I first met Sarah. Now, come on!'

But above the roaring showers outside, I heard a panic of voices. 'We're too late.' I grabbed the light off him and switched it off. 'Get in the den.'

'How?'

'Just do it.'

'With *him*?'

'Marcus, they'll kill us.'

I clambered up with the grace of an old drunk, slid awkwardly across the shelving supports and into the den, crouched by Ninny's corpse. Marcus followed, climbing awkwardly on top of the units so he was standing, wobbling, looking like he was about to jump. But instead, he lost his balance and with a clattery-crash managed to fall in the middle of the shelving supports, trapped standing in a triangular prison. 'They're in!' he shouted to me, panicking, stuck.

He may as well have greeted them.

I stood up, watched the two familiar men cursing the storm as they scuttled through the hole. They were followed by the fat one who was more careful about it, 'fucking soaked, ay I,' he moaned.

They spotted Marcus almost immediately. 'Who's that?' one of them said.

Without thinking, I shouted, 'we've come to make a deal.'

'A *deal*?' Marcus.

'A deal?' the rat. 'Is that… that better not be… is that fucking Tommy?' he asked the Meerkat.

'It's the one who killed Baz,' he said.

'I didn't kill him! Before we go any further, I've got some bad news.'

'I'll give ya some bad news. A deal?' the rat scoffed. 'Shouldn't have come here. When Jackson's back, yow'm dead.'

In a rash panic, Marcus tried to free himself from the shelving, but they seemed to be tied together.

'Keep still,' I said.

'What ya say?' the rat.

'I was talking to him.'

'Me?' the meerkat.

'Me!' Marcus.

'This chubby fuck,' I said, irritated. 'He's got himself stuck in the shelves.'

The guinea pig made his way over, pulling up his joggers, 'like a… like a fat fly,' he laughed. 'Jackson's got yuh in his web.'

'Nice one,' the rat said.

I took a deep breath. 'Ninny's dead.'

'Who?' the fat one menaced.

'Ninny. He's dead.'

I thought I heard the rat whisper, "Sarah's nan's geeze," to the guinea pig.

'*Jackson*. Jackson's-'

'Jackson?' the guinea pig interrupted, laughing, 'not at all, he made the retard do it.'

'What? No, listen to what I'm saying. Jackson. Is. Dead.'

'Fuck off,' the rat dismissed.

'He is.' I looked down to his misshapen corpse, hands curled at his chest like he'd tried to squeeze his heart. 'I've just been trying to resuscitate him.'

I bent down, felt a twinge in my knee, tried to lift him up. He was too heavy and it was a bit disgusting. 'Just come and have a look,' I sighed. 'He was long dead. OD'd by the look of it, like his brothers. That's the three of them. All went the same way.'

'What would you know about it?' the rat asked.

'I went to school with him. Come look. I've got nothing on me.' I held my hands up. 'I've come to make amends.'

'*A-what*?' the rat spat.

'Amends, to work something out.'

Behind them, rain spattered into the ever-spreading puddle at the entrance. Wind crashed waves outside, the distant drag of debris down the road. They edged slowly towards us. Marcus tried to remain calm, but the closer they came the more he started to panic, trying to free himself. The rat and the meerkat moved two feet to the left of him and entered the den through a small gap at the corner – *of course there's a way in*. I shone the light on Ninny.

'*Fuck*,' the meerkat.

'Dead?' the guinea pig.

'Dead,' the rat.

'*Fucking dead?*' the guinea pig repeated.

'I'm sorry,' I said.

'*Sorry?*' The pig moved towards the entrance to the den, took a big swing and punched Marcus in the side. 'For Baz,' he grunted. Marcus let out a scream and immediately took an even harder one in the back of his head, passing out on the shelving. 'For Jackson, you cunt!'

'What the fuck did you do that for?' I shouted. 'Marcus!'

He didn't answer. The guinea pig was pacing back and forth, fists clenched, ready for more.

I went to claw at the rat on instinct, but he quickly slid out of the den, followed by the meerkat. 'I came to make a fucking deal!' I shouted. 'Marcus is harmless! They want to kill you. The one who shot Baz wants to kill you all! So does Sarah!'

'Like they could,' the guinea pig mocked, rocking back and forth.

'*They have guns.*'

The meerkat looked uneasy, turning to the rat, 'what if… I mean, guns?'

I loosened the ties and tried to pull the shelf back to free Marcus, but he was heavy against it. I pinched his arm, '*Marcus.*'

'Wha?' he said. 'Wha… 'appen?'

'He hit you.'

'Who? The sag wats?' he mumbled.

'What's he fucking say?' the guinea pig threatened. 'Want some more?'

'Just calm down,' Jimmy the rat said, pulling him back.

The pig looked at him in disbelief. '*He killed Baz.*'

'I didn't. Neither did he. We don't give a shit about that stuff at the house. I don't particularly give a shit about the mad preacher. You can fucking have him.' I felt Marcus look at me and then look down. 'But I do give a shit about my friends.'

'So what are you saying?' Jimmy asked.

'I presume it was the booze you wanted?'

'The jewellery too,' Jimmy reasoned.

Marcus had started to figure his way out of the shelving, one tie at a time.

'Ok, the jewellery too. What if I find a way to get you the stuff and we don't start a goddam war?'

Marcus moved the shelf back and was finally free.

'I dunno. You killed my mate,' Jimmy spoke, childlike, hurt.

'*I* didn't. It was a truly horrible thing. Nobody wanted that.'

'How's Maureen?' the pig laughed.

Jimmy put his hand up to shush him.

'Was it you?' I asked. 'Her friend?'

'W-we didn't,' the meerkat, defensive.

'Jackson?'

'No,' the pig, smug. 'He made the retard smack him with his mallet.'

'Retard?'

'The spaz who… you know, mows the fields,' the meerkat said.

'Ok,' I stopped. 'Ok. Two people have been killed for no good reason. They're *dead*.'

'What about Jackson?' the pig pointed out.

'It's awful, but he did it to himself.'

'*You what*?' Jimmy protested.

'It's addiction. The town's riddled with it. Believe me, I've been there myself.'

'He just heard his son died,' Jimmy stressed, with more heart and vulnerability than I thought he had in him.

I relived the boy's crumpled body, remembered the sinewy wriggle of his young arms, his pale dead face. 'I don't know what to say to you. I'm sorry.'

I wanted to say: "I know how Ninny felt, I know what it feels like to lose a…" but I was too cowardly to say it, to let the thought flow and the words formulate. Ninny Jackson's loss was as close as I was ready to get to my own loss.

'Why would we trust you?' Jimmy asked.

'I don't want a war.' I tried to smile, cracked lips. 'It's a waste of energy. Of life!'

Jimmy turned to the pig, who looked ready for a ruck. The meerkat, gangly and hunched, seemed nervous. 'If we did trust you, if we could-?' he asked.

'Wha-the-hell!' the pig squealed.

'Just shut the fuck up, Callum!' Jimmy said.

The guinea pig looked like he wanted to argue, turned to the meerkat for support, but he didn't have it. He tutted, pulled his joggers up.

'I'll put the first lot in the park tomorrow,' I said.

'The fuck den?' Jimmy asked.

'If you like,' I nodded.

He pondered on it. 'No. We want all of it tomorrow,' he asserted.

'*All of it*? I can't. I've gotta steal it myself. I need more time-'

'There *is* no more time!'

I looked down at Ninny's bloated corpse, then up at Marcus who looked pathetic and scared. 'What about the storm?' I tried to reason.

'One day,' Jimmy said, non-threatening but adamant. It made me admire him. Maybe some day I'd help him sober up. Maybe Sarah would.

'Tomorrow,' I conceded. 'The booze and jewellery.'

We side-stepped out of Ninny's grave. I held my hand out. The guinea pig looked away, but Jimmy shook it.

We moved slowly across the wet floor to the entrance, my knee throbbing. I looked back to see them watching us. Three animals dealing with addiction, three boys dealing with the loss of their friends. We climbed out of the hole and back into the storm.

Ahead of us a large branch washed down Bassnage Road, shedding twigs and leaves. We moved as fast as we could, against the wind and rain. I stopped at the bottom of the hill by the park, panting, my brain beat and chest aching. My whole body turned to jelly, hands trembling like I had the DTs, my legs like I'd climbed down a steep mountain. The rain turned my sweat to slime and Marcus couldn't tell I was crying.

His face swollen, 'fucking inspired, mate,' he said.

'But how are we going to do it?'

'Eh?' he stopped. 'You weren't serious?'

Up Portsdown Road we heard a rumble. I immediately mistook it for a vehicle, before seeing the big round bin haphazardly bounding down the hill towards us, changing directions with each bump in the road. Without thinking, I shoved Marcus up a side road, then slipped to my knees again, which were still smarting from the Co-op. '*Goddamit*!'

On all fours, I looked up at Marcus.

He was shaking his head, panicking. 'No, no, please.'

I hadn't even realised it was Doran Close, but we needed to get out of this storm.

'Not Leroy's! *Please*,' he begged.

I got up. 'We need to get out of this!'

'NO!'

Across the road, the wind uprooted a small garden fence, wrapping it around a young tree. The tree flung backwards and then forwards. Top heavy, it was wrenched from the ground and then blew across the drive, landing in the gutter. Behind us, there was a crunching clatter. We turned to see the drain pipes torn from a house.

'We haven't got time for your peccadillos!' I yelled. 'The skies are falling in!' I pushed him on. 'I won't say a word.' He begrudgingly skulked onto the drive. 'Now, knock the bloody door!'

He timidly tapped the knocker. Annoyed, I shoved him out of the way and banged the door hard. Marcus freaked out, and quickly tried to get out of the way, in doing so he tripped and landed his whole weight onto my big toe. I screamed in agony and fell to the sodden tarmac, clutching my shoe.

Jake opened the front door in a sweat-drenched vest. 'What are you… squ… squi… doing d-down there?'

'That fat fuck!'

'Come-sheep-deer… come! … out of the storm!'

I got up and limped in like Quasimodo, my left foot killing, right knee sore, holding Marcus' shoulder. Jake shut the door behind us.

I awoke in the dark on the living room floor, a bag of jumble under my head. I was still damp despite changing into some old clothes I'd found. I could hear them nattering away in the kitchen.

Bare feet, the damp sock still wrapped around my arm. I took my phone out of my pocket and switched it on. I had a missed call from Loz and a text message. "You should come with us mate." I used the Nokia glow to light my foot, a blood blister on the side of my swollen big toe – *bloody Marcus*. I tried to wiggle it, but it was too stiff.

"Glad you're going man," I texted, "but I'm needed here-" I stopped.

I remembered my old sponsor. He would've insisted I leave this madness and head north. That's what the government had suggested, that's where the infrastructure was, that's where AA would be.

"You're sick, Tom," he'd say. "Give your head a wobble, you need meetings."

'I could start my own meeting,' I argued out loud. I considered looking for an online one. Presumably they were still going. New York, Sydney or Blackpool, an English-speaking meeting in Pakistan – there was one in the Hague I used to drop in on which seemed to attract a large international crowd and was always inspiring. In truth, I hadn't done regular meetings in years. Long before the bombs I'd stopped going, sometime after Covid-19, when the face to face meetings started back up. I knew they were there and I'd stayed in contact with my sponsor, but I'd drifted from AA, distracted by life and a little bored with it – how many hours had I spent in cold musty rooms in crumbling churches, coffee-steamed community centres or salty group rooms in addiction clinics?

I deleted the text and called Loz. It rang once before the battery died. *Shit*.

Rain tapped the window, fast tiny bullets. *Alexa, play blizzard sounds.* I remembered lying next to my love, trying to get to sleep by imagining I was in a tent on a snowy mountain.

God knows how long I'd slept for. It felt like hours, but I needed more. What was happening? We'd just come out of a storm straight from the Bible. It was hard not to look at it like the end times Leroy preached about, lofty and sure of himself, like he really knew.

'God,' I said out loud, remembering a time when He, It or That was there. *Maybe I should recite the serenity prayer,* but it didn't seem relevant. 'God, take away my difficulties and let me help those who need it…?' *Or something like that.* Was that the step three or the step seven prayer? It'd been such a long time since I'd spouted that stuff, but I was at that point where I might've found myself on my knees in the shower, surrendering, desperate for outside help, begging the cosmos for the strength to get through life. It was usually work or money worries, or a fight. It had never been because my best mate had killed someone, sparking off a chain of events which would drive me to rob Leroy the mad preacher to pay a murdering bunch of rodents. I knew that was what I was going to have to do. Was it some strange karma?

How had I found myself in this karmic cycle? Where did it start? Will killing Baz the rabbit? Or was it to do with Sarah and me? What were my real intentions there? Surely this cycle of retribution was bigger than me, than us? What were we doing in Halesowen, all secrets and lies and *feds* and people being killed – what was this Gary Bennett business?

Ross North's big fat face popped into my mind on a big red flag, an army of "federali" marching, chanting: "what is genuine is proved in the fire, what is false we shall not miss." *We'll be dead in no time!*

I heard Marcus squawk a laugh in the kitchen, and then muffled voices. There was just Jake when we arrived, but now there were definitely more. It sounded like they were having a party, drunks gathered in the kitchen. 'Am I going to have to save them all?'

Oh yes, Tom, I heard my old sponsor say, sarcastically. *Not only are you the hero in your own story, but everyone else's too.* It irritated me, but he was right.

Sarah seemed like the key to it all. If I could just focus on helping her, one addict helping another. *What are you on about? You do realise you're being utterly ridiculous, right?* 'But that's not a bad thing, is it?' I asked my super-ego. The id briefly imagined her naked just to remind me he was there.

I sat up.

'Ow!' *My knee.* 'Damn!' *My arm.* In the darkness the damp sock looked blood soaked, which made me feel queasy. I got onto my good knee and pushed myself up. 'Shit!' *My Toe.* I felt like an old man, remembered dad in those last years, frail, all bones and trembly aches.

I tried to tune in to the conversation in the kitchen.

'We're *all* animals.' It was Rex.

Marcus snorted a laugh.

'You may laugh, boy, but if you can wrap your head around that it all makes much more sense and it's so much more acceptable. We're all animals. To accept that is kindness.'

'F-fox, f-fox-speciesism,' Jake laughed.

'Don't get me started, boy. I was in Oxford when those nuts were at it. Animal-testing is cruel, of course, but we've slipped out of that realm. What about lions?'

I was lost. I hobbled into the kitchen.

'Here he is,' Rex boomed, wine-smiling.

Barb was sitting on a stool with a glass of wine and a blanket wrapped around her. Both had clearly been caught in the storm.

'Terrible out there, eh?' I said.

'Someone's trying to tell us something,' Rex said, glancing up.

'Are you ok, Barb?'

'What?' She looked at me and burst out crying 'Am-am-am *I* ok?' She shed her blanket and ran out of the kitchen. I went to go after her.

'Let her go, boy,' he said. 'She loved your mother. She needs to let it out.'

He poured a glass of wine and offered it to me. Jake took it. 'Tom doesn't drink.'

I smiled, surprised. Sarah must've told him. 'Thanks, mate.'

'Don't drink, do you, boy?' Rex asked.

I'd told him many times. 'Where's Leroy?'

'Who? Oh, Lee, boy. He's gone to help one of yours,' he said.

I glanced at Marcus, he shrugged like Rex was talking nonsense. I looked to Jake and then to Rex, 'but if we accept we're animals,' I said, 'doesn't it just give us carte blanche to do what we want?'

'To do what's right,' he clinked Jake's glass, wine spilled from both. 'To do what's meant. To let go.'

Marcus laughed, drunk.

I limped out of the kitchen to go find Barb. She was sitting on the settee in the dark. I switched the light on, noticed she'd knocked her glass of wine over, a pool of red soaking in. She followed my gaze.

'Oh, no, no, no,' she panicked, jumping up. 'First your mum and now…no, I didn't mean… I'm not-'

'Barb,' I grabbed her hand. 'Calm down. Mum was ill. I'm going to get a cloth. Sit down.'

'Yes, yes, she was ill. I'll sit down, you're right.'

I went back into the kitchen.

'Aristot-tot-turtle-sheep, *damn it*,' Jake clenched his fists, frustrated, 'said we're the only rational animals, distinguish-duck-ing us from-'

I moved in between them looking for a cloth.

'Aristotle, yes, boy,' Rex said. 'But Voltaire and Darwin came along many years later to remind us we're just like every other being.'

I grabbed a sponge and went back out to Barb. She was sitting staring at the blood red stain, crying. I bent down to sponge the carpet, making it worse.

She screamed at me.

'I'm sorry,' I said.

'Salt and white wine,' she shouted, jumping up.

'Please sit, Barb. I can do this.'

Foot, 'ow,' *knee*, 'shit,' back to the kitchen.

'But you assume man can solve all the world's problems, boy-'
'No,' Jake said.
'We're not all powerful,' Rex asserted.
I looked to Marcus who was a million miles from their conversation. 'I need white wine.' He seemed confused. *'For Barb.'*
'Oh.' He opened Leroy's fridge like it was his own – I briefly imagined them playing house, Marcus in a dress or, worse, that green robe I'd found him in.
'We're not even top of the chain, boy. You know why? Because there is no top.'
Marcus handed me an opened bottle of white.
'Salt,' I said.
'Salt?'
'For Barb.'
He didn't question it and started looking in the cupboards.
'Tetrachromacy,' Rex stated.
'What?' I asked.
'Birds, fish, reptiles, all have the ability to distinguish more colours than we do. We always think we're superior, the best. A dog, a goat and many other mammals are dichromats…' He looked at me and could see I was confused. 'Black and white vision, boy.'
'Oh.'
'Whereas humans are trichromats. We distinguish a wider spectrum of colours than, say, a bull, but not as many as some, say, fish.'
'Salt,' Marcus said.
'Thanks.'
I walked out recalling the pulsating strawberry grass on throbbing aurora-green nights, wondering if the visual experience of acid was akin to that of a fish.
'Give it to me,' she insisted.
She poured the wine on first, wiped it with the sponge and an old shirt she'd taken from one of the jumble sacks. She then sprinkled on the salt. 'We just leave it, now,' she said.
'And that'll do it?'
'I hope.' She took a deep breath and smiled sadly. 'I'm so sorry for you, Tom.' She patted the seat.
'Maybe it's for the best,' I said, sitting down, 'what with everything.'

'Don't say that! Your mother went far too young. She lived such a good life. I know your dad left and that probably didn't help her… no, I'm not… I mean, he was a good man was your dad.'

I smiled. Barb seemed older. She was always so vivacious, highly strung but bubbly. Now she was mithering and old. Mum had gone a bit like it too. I guess that's what happens to us all – if we're lucky.

'Dad was a drunk,' I smiled.

'We've all got a bit of that in us. Your mother too… don't look at me like that. In her day, she drank with the best of them. We'd dance down the Rom til gone midnight. The things we got up to.' She zipped her lips. 'That goes with me,' she laughed loud, which almost immediately turned to tears.

I put my arm around her shoulder. 'She was a funny old wench in the end,' I said.

Barb laughed again. 'I know we didn't see eye to eye on everything, but she was my best friend.'

She hadn't seen her for years. They lived less than two miles apart and they never spoke, they never even bumped into each other because mum never went into the pubs. She rarely went anywhere. Occasionally she took the bus into town when she had to, but she'd long had Amazon deliver her shopping.

'Ooh, we did laugh – some of the blokes she used to pull…'

I half-laughed out of politeness.

She pulled away from me and held my hand. 'You need to be strong, Tom,' her face serious but smiling.

'I'm ok.'

'It's ok,' she said.

I didn't know whether it was her smile or because she was holding my hand and seemed to care, but I could feel the tears. I swallowed them and tuned in to the voices in the kitchen.

'Perhaps we *are* all animals,' I said.

'Oh, him and his bloody theories,' she shook her head.

'The last bus hasn't even gone and already the town feels wild.'

'The druggies?' she asked.

I laughed. 'Yobbos, mum used to say, but that ended up being us.'

'We all know what happened last night,' she said. 'To protect the church belongings. It's important. That's why we're here. The tall one-'

'Will?'

'It wasn't his fault. Lee will help him.'

'What do you mean?'

'That's why he left. To exorcise his sins,' she said, in all seriousness.

'Oh, Christ,' I laughed. 'He'll love that.' I wondered whether Maureen was still there. What would she make of it all? 'Has Sarah gone with him too?'

She nodded. I got up and went to the window. The storm was still strong, the drag of debris, the crack of things breaking, fences, houses, civilisation.

'It's just stuff,' I said. 'That poor kid died for stuff.'

'*Poor kid*? It's much more than that, Tom,' she defended, and she believed it.

It made me think of the people in pubs who'd steadfastly defended the wars in the Middle East and who were happy to hear about sinking dinghies full of refugees. "I don't want 'em to die," they'd say, "but we haven't got the space." Now, we were having to cram refugees from the south into a country halved. It was like some twisted poetic justice. And I was all for listening to each other, however extreme the opinion seemed, but I had my opinion too. The rabbit flopped once again before my eyes, dead before he hit the ground. He died for stuff – that was my opinion.

'Your friend's a hero,' she added.

I wanted to laugh. *A hero*? It made me feel certain of what I had to do, what my role was in this. I had to steal back the booze and jewellery – including some of mum's things, which was my sacrifice, my peace-offering – and give it to the scag rats. This was justice. It felt more right than anything else.

'There's a toilet upstairs, yeah?' I asked her, knowing full well.

'Yes, of course.'

I hobbled out of the room.

'Squirrels!' came out of the kitchen as I passed.

'The loo!' I squeaked, turning, startled. 'The loo,' I smiled. 'Need a pee.'

At the top of the stairs was the room where Marcus had fallen out of the wardrobe, begging me to keep his sordid little secret; the room where years before Snarf and Battle Cat fought against Optimus Prime and Bumble Bee, where in little clothes as little boys we listened to Iron Maiden. God only knew what went on in there now, blood red sheets below that huge silver cross.

Opposite that room was the booze store where Will fell apart at the seams after killing Baz. 'This is justice,' I whispered. I opened the door.

Fuck.

I stood inside, looking at the walls. It was empty.

Behind me: 'squirrel-sheep!'

I turned quickly. 'Jake, where is it all?'

'I thought you didn't drink.'

———————

I lay my damp linen trousers over a case of beer. In the pocket, a wad of plastic cash, drenched and stuck to each other. I was separating the colourful slips of money, wondering whether they'd ever be used. Why were we still using these tokens? According to Will's forecasts we should've been chipped years ago with little silicon slave tags, bank details, payroll number and Top Trumps credit scores.

'But what if they still want revenge-rabbit after?' Jake asked.

He was sitting on a box of wine, smoking a roll-up in the garage. Leroy had moved all the alcohol in here after we'd found it. Once I'd explained our "near-death" run-in with the scag rats, Jake took us to it.

'They've already taken their revenge,' I said, wondering how the hell I was going to tell Maureen about it.

'We should tell Lee,' he said.

'There's no time, is there?' I prompted Marcus to corroborate.

He shrugged and pulled out a bottle of rum from one of the boxes.

'Look,' I said. 'I can understand you not wanting to part with this stuff. You're here to look after it. But don't you think it's weird. I know it might just all be a coincidence-'

'No such thing as coincidence,' Jake said.

'I'm beginning to think the same thing,' I said, by now certain this was all meant to be.

'Oh, God,' Marcus laughed, swaying-drunk, swigging from the bottle.

'Go back to sleep,' I said.

'Mate, I feel like I'm in an AA meeting. Is this what you all twitter on about?'

'Witter-'

'You said it,' he burped. 'Ooh, how rude,' he chortled to himself, sipped on the rum and then half-heaved.

'There's a price to pay for my sobriety,' I said to Jake. 'I'm sure it sounds nuts to Marcus, but there's certain things I've had to accept.'

'What do you m-mean?'

The lights flickered out, then back on, putting me on edge, like they were warning me. I walked to the kitchen door, for some reason nervous, embarrassed to be saying these things out loud.

'Rex and Barb have goph-gone,' he said, 'to squirrel-sheep-rabbit-hutch bed.'

I felt Marcus look at me, he wanted to laugh, totally oblivious to what was actually going on in the conversation, never mind the town, the country, the world.

'I feel like I've got to help Sarah.'

Marcus groaned. 'Fuck, you mean.'

'*Really?*' I insisted. He looked down only too aware of what I wasn't saying. 'Sarah came into my life at the very moment I was about to relapse,' I said to Jake. 'I had the pills in my hand. Was that a coincidence? And then everything that's happened around it. Bumping into Maureen. The church. Even Rex and Barb. I'm not saying I can make sense of it. The tragedy of that poor kid, bastard or not.'

Marcus looked at me like I'd gone mad.

'And then,' I said directly to Marcus, 'there's a massive storm, in *September*. By chance we find ourselves looking for cover in the worst place possible, but he was dead. Ninny was dead. The boy's dad was dead.' I turned to Jake. 'Then the others come back while we're there. I was sure we were goners, certainly this fuck-'

'Fuck you!' Marcus said and burped.

'But words just started coming out of my mouth. I don't feel like I had a say in any of it. And now here we are, Leroy isn't home, off helping Will-'

Marcus cast a glance at me. I ignored it.

'I'm sure Lee would see G-God the goph-ferret in this,' he smiled.

I wasn't. If it was the Leroy I knew, that alcohol meant way too much to him. 'You're probably right. This just seems like the right thing to do for everyone. I don't know… am I going mad?' I asked him.

'Yes,' Marcus said.

'In AA,' I added, 'they talk about first and foremost helping other addicts. I've not always stuck to that, but I keep coming back to it. I'm not trying to be a hero,' I said to my super ego, my dead sponsor and anybody else who happened to be listening.

'I don't know about AA,' Jake said, 'but I used to have a crack habit which made me totally selfish. I figured the antidote to the crack habit must be the f-fox-opposite.'

With half the words and far more humility than I could muster, Jake had explained it beautifully. 'Wisdom, my-'

'Mate,' Marcus interrupted, addressing Jake, 'why the fucking animals?'

'Fox-fox-fox-squirrel,' Jake blurted fast, in a panic.

'Marcus!' I cursed.

'My f-fox family, m-mum.'

'You don't have to answer him,' I said, embarrassed.

'No, it's Tourette's, n-no, she trained me early on-the-rabbit-sheep, the hutch-bad words, f-fox-rabbit-dad would f-fox at mum and she would sh-sheep-hutch dad,' he stopped, took a deep breath. 'I grew up thinking animals were words I wasn't supposed-to-sheep-deer say. My mum.'

'Shit, that's fucking incredible,' Marcus said, laughing.

'Because it was more acceptable,' I said. 'That's so clever.'

'I ended up on crack,' he said, with a sardonic clarity which made us laugh. 'Ok, Tom, let's f-fox do it.'

'Do what?' Marcus asked.

'Get rid of the booze,' I said.

'All of it?' Marcus asked.

'Where've you been?' I said. 'What about the jewellery, Jake?'

'Sounds like it's meant to squirrel-bee-be. It's just material possums,' he laughed. 'Possess-possums.'

Shoulder barging the wind and rain, the lights went out with a fat clap, as the two of us wheeled a bin-full of booze down Portsdown Road.

'*Shit*,' I cursed.

Jake was nodding in mild-mannered agreement, one hand pulling his hood down to stop the wind taking it. He mouthed something. Animals, I guess. I couldn't hear him.

We were already struggling to see more than a few feet ahead of us, but now we'd been plunged into third-world darkness, the streetlights just empty metal tubes rattling in the fierce storm. I saw no lights in any of the houses here or anywhere in the distance. Perhaps the whole town was out. Was this the beginning of a life without electricity? A barb of lightning lit the sky as if to prove me wrong. I counted. 1, 2, 3, 4, 5, 6, 7. The sky cleared its throat, then cracked like a giant pterodactyl flapping its wings.

This had to happen sooner or later. With one day left until the last bus, to government services and systems, was this power cut signalling the beginning of our new existence? From here on would we be reliant on battery and solar power alone? Maybe electricity was just one of man's problems anyway, polluting the atmosphere and keeping us from a decent night's sleep. I certainly remembered feeling peace those nights we'd camped in the mountains, the fuzzy purple ether all around, above us the molecular structure of stars, atoms in a much bigger body.

Lightning shocked the sky once more. There was no moon, just the brief wiry veins of light. I moved quickly.

'Wait!' Jake grabbed my shoulder, his face close to mine. 'Fox-squirrel!'

I stood waiting, water streaming down the hill, the wind dropping debris all around us. It was hard to judge where the sounds were coming from. We found ourselves flinching with every crash and clatter. 'What?' I asked.

'Six miles,' he said, thunder grumbling above, the voice of a bigger being. God? The devil? It all seemed possible.

We carried on towards the park and I found myself splitting, thinking this would make a great episode of my TV show idea. *The whole thing could have a spiritual element, like a Paulo Coehlo novel. People like that stuff.* But this wasn't a TV show, every crack snapping me back to reality. Gary Bennett knifed. Maureen's friend bludgeoned. Baz shot, Ninny OD'd, father and son no more.

Still, Jake would make a great character. Can I have a character with Tourette's? Is that crossing a line?

'How do we get to the f-fox-den?' he yelled.

'Round the back of the park!'

Lightning struck again, the count began.

We'd left Marcus in the garage, guarding the rest of the booze, but he'd probably passed out by now. He wouldn't have got very far in his state. How many seasons would Marcus be likely to last?

'Five!' Jake yelled.

Not likely.

We were wearing raincoats and fishing salopettes we'd found amongst the jumble, but they'd already proved useless in this storm. We were drenched through. Jake flicked on his pen torch. It lit the shrubs and trees at the back of the park briefly, but then it went out. He kept smacking it, but it was no good. It was the only light we had.

'There's another way, but-' I stopped. It was no good trying to explain it. 'Follow me!'

It was impossible to find the back way in the dark, through the shrubs and bushes where I cut my arm. I knew the brook was the only way. Even at it's deepest point it couldn't rise much above our waists and we were already soaked.

Wheels spinning, catching knots, we pulled the bin through the sodden grass to the far side of Lutley park. Lightning struck once again and showed us the gap by the brook. I couldn't help but think we were being guided.

'Eleven,' Jake yelled, the grumbling voice in the sky advising us the lightning was getting further away.

'We have to go in the water,' I shouted.

'B-*brook*?'

'It'll be fine!'

The moment I stepped in, I felt the cold on my injured toe. I looked down to my arm, squeezed it, the sock still in place. My body battered and bruised, the elements unleashed, the dangerous task in hand. 'Faith,' I mumbled in prayer and I felt it in the veins in my wrists.

I reached up and grabbed the handle to the bin and wheeled it towards me and in. Jake climbed in behind it.

With each step I felt the pain in my knee, followed by toe. *Knee, toe, heave, ho. Knee, toe, fuck, no!*

'It's not too far, Jake!' I yelled at the top of my voice, but before I'd even said his name the storm suddenly stopped.

'What you sheep-deer-horn shouting for?'

His stuttering Tourette's somewhat spoiled the timing, but we were laughing.

We stopped still in the water, the pitter patter of droplets trickling off the leaves. This sudden absence of the ever-present downpour was like a small wow of ecstasy, an LSD revelation or that first beer in those early benders which cured my crippling shyness.

'Peace,' Jake said, his purple shape dotted with twinkling green and red atoms – my trichromatic vision was clearly trying to make out more than it physically could.

We left the bin in the den after the third and final load. The sky had lightened so I could now make out the gaunt figure of my partner. He smiled.

'I have to go home,' I said. 'Will you tell Marcus I'll see him later.'

He nodded. 'Are you ok?'

'Me? Honestly, I'm overjoyed,' I said.

'You look p-pig-pen wrecked,' he laughed. 'Sorry. Sheep-baaad rough. *God.* Sorry. Will you tell them about this?' he asked.

'I'll take full responsibility,' I said.

'No,' he shook his head. 'I played my part.'

The sky rumbled. 'We better make a move.' The slow pitter-patter quickly turned into the same wet-heavy droplets of earlier. I laughed at the timing.

'Meant to squirrel-sheep-be,' he said.

When we shook hands on the corner of Doran Close, I noticed the sock was no longer on my arm and the wound was bleeding. I'd forgotten all about it. In fact, my knee, my foot and any other aches and pains had all been anaesthetised by the adrenaline of our mission. But as I made my way up Portsdown Road, my toe started to hurt, my knee ached – I was sure gangrene was setting in, somewhere.

The morning sky, wet and moody, I staggered onto Purbeck Close in the rain, right knee sore, left foot swollen, arm tense and curled up. Bruised and battered, but I felt smug. The storm had stopped just long enough for us to deliver all of the jewellery and most of the alcohol to the den for the scag rats. It was meant to be. God, fate, coincidence, call it what you will.

Leroy would be angry, but he'd struggle to deny the hand of God when I told them of our mission. I'd stopped the war escalating and hopefully anybody else getting hurt. This was the sort of decisive action expected of a leader. *Maybe that's what fate has in store for me and this is the first of many such actions.*

Up the road, old Arthur's bags had been upturned, a spread of clothes and papers in the road and on gardens. I was half-tempted to go over and see if he was alright, but I knew my first task was letting everyone know what I'd done to save them.

Sarah opened the door, sleep in her eyes.

'*Your arm*,' she whispered. 'Come out of the rain.'

'It needs attending to but I'll be-' I tripped in the doorway, reached for the handle, pulled it towards me and headbutted the door. 'Fuck!'

'What you playing at?'

'Sorry. I tripped.' I rubbed my head, hunched and hobbled in. Right knee, 'oo,' left foot, 'oo-a,' cradling my weeping arm, 'oo-a, oo-oo-a,' like an ape on hot coals.

'Are you ok?' she asked. 'You look really unwell.'

I was starting to feel it.

Will was on the settee, asleep. Leroy was sitting in mum's chair, beginning to stir. 'It's been a challenge,' I said. 'Is your nan still here?'

'She couldn't leave in the storm. She's upstairs.'

I looked up to the ceiling, 'are you getting on?' and lost my balance. I fell to my knees, dizzy, 'oo-uh-oo,' a sudden wave of nausea.

Sarah tried to help me up, 'you look grey.'

'I'm fine.' I pushed her hand away and got up off my knees into a crouching position, took a couple of deep breaths. I looked up at her. 'Are you speaking to her?'

'Not really. The same as ever. That arm looks disgusting.' She gave it a little poke with her foot.

'Oo-oo-oo, stop it!' I said, still crouched, waving her off.

'Guess what?' she said, patting me on the head. 'I haven't used. I haven't even had a drink.'

Leroy caught my eye, nodded solemnly.

'That's amazing, Sarah.' I pushed myself up using my good arm, felt the blood rush to my head. 'I have some news… ooh, hold on,' the room spinning, I reached for the wall. 'That's better. Everybody up!' I yelled.

'*What are you doing?*' she whisper-shouted.

'I have something I need to say.'

She looked at me like I was crazy. I moved to the arm of the settee and sat down, a little woozy.

'Are you drunk?' she asked.

'Of course I'm not. Wake up, Will!' I shook his leg. 'It's a bit dark in here, Sarah. Put the lights on.'

'They're not working because of the storm,' she said.

'But they're solar powered.'

Will sat up. 'That's not how it works. What's the matter with you?'

I looked at Will and his face clouded over. I rubbed my eyes. 'What's the matter with *you*?' I asked.

'You've just fucking woke me up. You better have a good reason for it. Where's Marcus? Where's Loz? Have you seen them?'

'Maureen,' I yelled.

'Don't wake her,' Sarah snapped.

Leroy was glaring at me. He didn't look very happy. He was about to feel much worse but they would surely understand when I explained everything. 'Maureen, I know what happened to your fella!' I called up.

'Tom,' Will shouted. 'What the hell are you doing?'

'You'll see,' I said, jabbing the air, before losing my balance and falling on the settee into Will's arms.

'He's ill,' Sarah said.

'I'm not ill!' I said, pushing myself up off him, so I was sitting on the arm again. 'I have things I need to say,' I asserted. 'I'm Tom and I'm an alcoholic, and I need to speak my mind.' I heard Maureen coming down the stairs. 'She'll understand. Maureen!' I stood up, but feeling dizzy, sat back down on the arm.

'Tom, what's going on?' Maureen panicked. 'Are you drunk?'

'Of course I'm not. I know what happened to him! What was his name?'

She stopped dead. Sarah moved towards her. 'Don't,' she warned, things clearly much the same. 'Jan,' she said to me.

'What?'

'His name was Jan.'

'Jan?'

'He was Polish,' she said.

I turned to Will, I wanted to laugh. I've no idea why. I felt hysterical, but I managed to stop myself. There was an awkward silence. I felt like I was playing a cruel joke on everybody, but I wasn't. I'd just come back to lay down the hard truth.

'What happened to him?' Leroy asked.

'They did it,' I said.

'Who?' he asked.

'The scag rats. The rat, the guinea pig, Ninny.'

'What the fuck, Tom?' Sarah said, annoyed. 'What do you mean?'

'Jimmy, Jackson and the fat one, although Jackson's dead now. OD'd. He was in a right state when we found him in the lair, frothing at the…' They were all staring at me like it was my fault. 'Say something then.'

I'd nearly died, braved treacherous storms to save them. I was exhausted, felt sick, a migraine coming on, and all I had in return was a mute, dumb, incredulity. Sarah moved to sit on the settee next to Will. He put his arm around her – *why was he putting his arm around her?* Maureen was frozen in the middle of the room. Leroy looked annoyed and somehow sanctimonious – I hadn't even told them about the booze and jewellery and already he was looking sanctimonious.

'Who killed him?' Maureen asked, her voice full of revenge.

'Jackson. Well, actually, it was the retard.'

'The retard!' she screeched.

'Ninny Jackson made him do it with a mallet. They said it was the retard who mows the lawns?'

'The retard!' she screeched again and fell to her knees. 'No, no,' she cried, taking deep, fast breaths.

'Nan!' Sarah jumped up, crouched beside her cradling her. 'Nan, nan, I'm so sorry,' she said.

'Get off me! Get off me! Tom get her off me!'

I got up and Sarah jumped up immediately. 'What *you* gonna do, you fucking deeve?'

'I don't understand,' I said, anxiously. 'Does Maureen know about the rabbit?'

'What's fucking wrong with you?' Sarah screamed.

'I don't know.' I was starting to feel very strange. 'My head.' I moved across the room, right knee, left foot, arm throb, 'oo-oo-a-a,' hunched, rubbing my brow. I walked back. Knee, foot, arm, hunched, scratching my head, 'oo-a-oo-a.'

'What's happened to you, mate?' Will asked. 'It's like you're on fucking acid.'

I stopped and leant in the doorway, all of them watching me, expecting something of me, something I didn't have. Leroy frowning, Maureen fraught, Sarah like she wanted to break my neck. Will was the only one who didn't look offended.

He pulled out his tobacco and started to roll a cigarette. 'We had some wild times on acid,' he smiled, inappropriately nostalgic.

I had the urge to run out. I felt like I *was* on acid, in the middle of a bad trip.

'Remember the panda,' Will said, laughing.

'Panda?' I panicked, confused, like I'd missed a beat.

'The cop car.' Everyone turned their attentions to Will. 'What you all looking at me for!? Tom remembers,' he said. 'We thought it was a police car, but it might've been a taxi or it could've just been sounds in the distance creating visions out of nothing.'

'Will,' I said. 'Please.'

'The more I think about it,' he laughed, 'it was just a visual. We ran a bloody mile.'

'Will,' I repeated.

'What you nagging me about? You got yourself into this.'

'Will!'

And then I threw up. I don't know what I'd eaten or drank to have thrown up, but a red and orange streak came out of my mouth, a whip of Pollock's brush on mum's Moroccan rug.

'Shit. Are you alright mate?' he asked.

'I don't know,' I said.

'To be fair, you look dreadful.'

Maureen was trembling on the floor, confused. Leroy hadn't moved, just sat there with a sanctimonious smirk. Sarah couldn't even look at me. I heaved again but nothing came up. I crouched down, breathing, 'oo-a, oo-a, oo-a.' This seemed to offer some relief and made me realise just how weak I was feeling. I banged my fist on the floor to try to gee myself up, but the thud just reverberated throughout my body and left me feeling worse. I slapped my chest as if to kickstart my heart. *Is this how it ends?*

Without looking at them I told them what had happened and what I'd done. The Co-op, the deal, all in this violent storm, and with Jake's help to stop a war. 'It's just things,' I stressed.

Leroy got up without looking at me and walked into the kitchen. Sarah followed him. Will was shaking his head. Was he gutted about the booze or killing the boy, which was now rendered even more senseless? Surely they'd all come to understand why I'd done what I'd done.

Maureen was on all fours, she looked up at me. 'How could you?' she barked.

The room was spinning. Was I dreaming? 'Will, am I dreaming?'
He stretched his head and leant forward, sniffed the air, a big giraffe. 'Nuh,' he said.
Maureen was yelping words, anger, a high-pitched yap. I heaved again, stood up, felt woozy. My other foot had gone to sleep. The room whirling as I made my way to the kitchen, foot, knee, arm, hunched, 'oo-oo-a-a, oo-oo-a-a,' scratching my head. The giraffe sneezed behind me, the dog yapped at my ankles. In the kitchen Leroy wrapped his tentacles around Sarah. I counted them, 'seven tentacles,' I said. 'One for each sin.' The squid squirted ink at me, everything went black and the ape hit the kitchen floor.

2031

Lucy's hair was blowing wild in the concrete beer garden at the George.

'What do you want?' she shouted, above the gale.

'Apple juice.'

'Cider?'

I laughed. 'No! Apple juice!'

Tina was serving from the Um Bongo van. She kept trying to hold her top down in the wind.

Lucy was standing waiting to be served. 'Two ciders please!' she shouted.

I could feel the garden table being pulled from the ground as the gale ramped up to hurricane winds. Raindrops started to splat the concrete around me, until there was a prison of rainfall between Lucy and me. I looked over at Tina and her top blew up over her face as she juggled with two pints of cider. I found myself transfixed on her breasts, before noticing Lucy had spotted me.

'What?' I shrugged, now drenched.

'I'm not getting you cider again!' she nagged, dry under the van awning.

'Eh?' I heard her, but pretended I didn't so I could drink the cider, under the pretence it was apple juice.

Tina took her top off and handed the pints to Lucy. 'I just need to put the brake on!'

She moved into the front of the van and, as soon as she wrenched the handbrake on, the table took off, taking me with it, high into the stormy sky.

'Lucy!' I called down.

'What about your cider?' she yelled.

I held tight to the table, but it felt like it was coming apart at the joins. Lucy was getting smaller and smaller. From the back door of the George, Will and Marcus walked out holding pints of beer. They looked up.

'Will!' I tried to shout. 'Will!'

Above me and through a gap in the clouds, the skies were blue, the sun shining. What was going to happen when I left the cloud, with nothing to pull or push me? I pulled myself up so I was lying on the table, my hands gripping tight to the wood slats. I closed my eyes as I came into the blue. When I opened them again I couldn't see anything below the grey storm. Silence. Lucy was gone. Will and Marcus had disappeared. But I wasn't falling, the table had steadied and I found myself afloat in the skies. I rolled onto my back and lay in the warmth of the sun. It felt wonderful. 'Is it because I'm going to heaven?' I asked myself. 'Or leaving hell?' I noticed a smell, like burning wax. I glanced to the side of me and saw the joins of the table had started to melt and trickle. 'Shit!'

'Wax!' I woke up with a jolt on Ally's settee.

Loz was staring at me, head in his hands. 'Yeah,' he said, morose. 'Wax.'

'I can smell it!' I panicked.

'Calm down, my head's banging,' he sat back. 'I just blew the candles out.'

'What!'

'What?' he half-laughed, sitting back on the armchair. 'You alright?'

'Christ!' I sat up. 'I just had a nightmare.'

I put my hand down on the cushion and felt something wet. 'Urgh.' I rubbed it on my knee. *Booze? Cum?* Then I remembered pouring cold water over myself in the kitchen. Then I remembered being force-fed codeine.

'You want coffee?' he asked.

I nodded, distant.

I followed his sight to the jug on the side table, murky and cold, like a pint of Guinness beheaded. 'I think we'll leave that to them,' he said.

'It's just cold.'

'Trust me, Tom, I'm not going near that. I'll make some fresh.' He left the room with a groan.

As soon as I heard the kettle come on, I started fumbling in my pocket. They were still there. I fingered the blister pack, six pills left. I recalled the high in the church, a temporary bliss. For a good hour everything had been acceptable. *That must be what the dream's about.*

As I leant forward to take them out of my pocket, I felt the sudden throb of pain, like an invisible being reaching into my body and squeezing my coccyx. I sat back, my hand tight in my pocket, cupping the pack. I knew I ought to throw them away, but I also knew I couldn't.

Loz came back in and, guiltily, I tried to pull my hand out of my pocket quickly, nerve pains shooting.

'You want sugar…?' he stopped. 'What you got?'

'Got? Nothing.' I felt my face burning up.

'Tom?'

'*What?*' Then I remembered. I dug a little deeper. 'Here!' I threw the bag of Honest's cob nuts on the floor. 'What do you think I've got? A bag of fucking brown?'

He gave me a funny look. 'What's up with you?'

'Just… just a bad back that's all. Sugar, yeah. That'll help.'

He left the room.

It was like hiding half bottles of vodka down the side of the settee all over again. Two codeines and I was right back in it.

It was early blue and throughout the building I could hear noises, the groans of hangovers, the sex bumps and moans where some were still at it. Little Ethan was crying somewhere – too young to truly understand his dad was no longer around – and Lettie was confidently demanding something from somebody, somewhere in the block – just like her mother. There was a lingering whiff of Christmas from the recently extinguished Yankee candle. I was reminded of Leroy, Christmas forever tarnished with that macabre image of the tree, his eyes open, glancing in opposing directions, doves smeared in thick blood.

'Marcus!'

Shit. I'd told Marcus about Sarah and he'd told me about Lee – as he called him, her, whatever. He finally admitted his feelings.

I pushed myself up, pains pranging, lightheaded and angry at myself.

Loz entered with two cups of coffee. 'You're up then.'

'Why did I fucking tell him, Loz?'

'What you bloody on about now?'

I don't know if it was the way he said it or his pained face, pale with hangover. 'Why the fuck are you still here, Loz?'

He looked taken aback.

'Seriously. You've got a wife and kids. Isn't that what you always wanted?'

'Where's this come from?'

Thoughts from the previous day started hitting me, like nerve zingers. Tony Moran. The butcher's smirk. Barb euth'd. The milkman dead. Councillor Ray gagged! *Codeine*! Not to mention they'd found Tony Dale. The hunt was on. It was only a matter of time before they turned to us. And now Marcus was on the loose, armed with dangerous information. Sarah was in trouble. We all were.

I wanted to shout all this, to let it out, but I looked at hopeless Loz, concerned and confused, two cups of coffee trembling in his hands.

Somehow I've got to get us all out of Halesowen. But is it even be possible to get us all out? How can I wrangle them all together?

Loz was here and I knew where Sarah was. Perhaps it was too late for Will, wild and determined to stay. And Marcus, with his loose tongue, had he passed the point of no return? *What are you saying?* But it entered my mind. Were they ever likely to escape the chemical cycle of self-harm and the socially acceptable – or not – suicide? What hope was there for them?

Loz, on the other hand, didn't even know how to drug himself. Not properly. He could barely drink. He'd never been very good at it. It just wasn't who he really was. He wanted family and work and Christmases. He never should have stayed. 'Loz, what do you really want from life?'

He laughed. 'A good woman, a strong drink and a fag,' he bragged. But it wasn't real, it didn't even sound like him. It was this bravado, this costume we'd always wore.

'They euthanised Barb, for Christ's sake!' I said, frustrated. 'Do you get it? We-we have to… Yes, we-we can't… No, we won't… Do you even understand?'

'Tom?' He looked worried. 'What's going on? Your brain's spitting.'

'It is. It is,' I was nodding furiously, which made me think of my dad, his Parkinson's tremor. 'I haven't got Parkinson's!' I yelled at myself.

'Parkinson's-?'

'I know I didn't speak to Barb much,' I rolled off.

'Ok,' the cups of coffee jittering, 'and?'

'She was part of Halesowen,' I stressed, certain he would intrinsically understand. 'I remember mum telling me why she stopped speaking to her. "She was just a ruddy drunk," she told me. "You were a baby, I was too old to be out drinking. It looked ridiculous."'

'Sit down, Tom.'

'Barb was just doing what people did. She had low self-esteem, she'd only ever worked in retail,' I insisted.

'You sound a bit like a mad person.'

'Barb's dead, Loz.'

'I know,' he said.

I sat down, felt the invisible squeeze at the base of my spine. 'After my mum had done her nurse training, Barb told me she didn't want anything to do with her.'

'That's harsh,' he said.

'Hold on… How do *you* know she's dead?'

'Marcus.'

'Goddam!' I shot up again, as if someone had jabbed me with a hot fork. 'Ow! Blabber mouth! Back! My goddam… Where is he? What did he tell you? He's lost, he's lost, he's lost-'

'Tom, just stop! Here, have this,' he said, handing me the coffee. He glanced around conspiratorially. He shut the living room door and then sat on the settee. 'Marcus said you'd been at St John's and that they'd found Tony Dale and Barb was dead too.'

'And the milkman.'

He nodded. I waited for a bigger reaction, fear, anger, something. At the very least, incredulity. Why wasn't he scared?

'Loz,' I said, still standing, the coffee spilling onto my hand. 'None of this adds up. What's *really* going on?'

He was looking at me like I'd gone barmy. 'This is how it is,' he shrugged.

'Why did Ally send me to town, Loz? Why did she tell me Anita's not drinking?'

'She was well on it last night.'

'Exactly. How did Tony Moran just "bump into me" after I'd left-?' I stopped myself. Loz had mentioned nothing about Sarah. Perhaps Marcus hadn't told him.

'Sit down, you're freaking me out. It's not the first time people have died here, you know.'

'How can you of all people be ok with this?' There was nothing, no reaction, cold – is this what had happened to us? I sat down next to him on the settee. 'Why did they have to kill Lee?'

'*Lee?*' That stumped him. 'What's Leroy got to do with anything?' Marcus had even used the "L" word. *Marcus.*

'Leroy was just an old perve,' he added.

'She wasn't.'

'*She*? What you on about?'

'She was just a person.'

'*She*?'

'He, she, whatever!'

He looked at me and he knew I was being serious, he knew there'd been some kind of shift in my thinking. 'You know what I mean,' he smiled. 'Lee/Leroy was always a perve, wasn't… she/he?'

'Why did they did kill Jay Bird?' I added.

'*Jay*?'

'Why did they kill him?'

'*They*? It was Honest John-'

'Come on, Loz. Just like he killed his dad?'

'Where's this coming from?'

Then I remembered Barb, her nightie open, half-dead. I remembered the way she screamed when she saw him.

'Tom,' serious. 'Leroy? Jay Bird? Honest John? What do they have to do with last night?'

'I don't know.'

'You sound like sodding Will, putting two and two together and coming up with chemtrails and Jewish paedos.'

'They're just in my head.'

'Tom. Drink your coffee.'

I looked down at the cup, a bitter mist twirled. I took a big sip. It was warm and wonderful, of another time. It was cafes and conversations, cinnamon sticks and a biscotti. Loz was looking at me like he cared, like he was worried, but he didn't understand anything. If he had, he'd be terrified. 'Is that all Marcus told you?'

'Why?'

'He didn't tell you anything about any… special place… or any people we might know.'

'People we might…? No, he said you were high as a kite and drenched yourself like a madman,' he laughed.

'I wasn't high. I was tired and annoyed at having to take codeine.'

'They're just painkillers,' he said.

'*To you*. Where's Marcus now?'

'In the Ganesh.'

'We need to talk. Go and fetch him.'

He left the room and went out into the echoey corridor and up the stairs. My mind drifted, eyes fixed on mum's old Moroccan rug, marked with the debauched stains of time, ash, cum and booze. If

Ally's walls could talk they'd tell of dopamine desires twisted in the meandering synapses of the habitually doped, switched-off, fucking for fucking's sake. There was no romance, no love, nothing for the likes of me – or Loz. It was the old world, like that drunken night many years before, the walls bare, the carpet grimy, when Ally and me entered that realm ourselves. I came out of a blackout mid-fuck, on top of her, and was shocked into silence for fear of offending her. I asked myself, "how did I get here?" Which became a much bigger question, existential and cock-shrivelling. I rolled off her apologetically. She understood. Ally was always very understanding.

I heard Loz coming back downstairs. Did he know about that night? Was our drunken fumble a big secret? I never told anybody. Did she? Did we all have these secrets? Like Marcus and Lee? What did any of them really get up to?

He entered the living room. 'Marcus isn't there. Will is.'
'Ok. Is he coming down?'
'I asked him to.'
'What did he say?'
'"Be gone my child".'
'Is he totally-?'
'Gone, yeah.'
'Is he with Anita?'
He nodded.
I considered going up there myself.
'They were sitting naked,' he said, 'staring into a flame.'
There was no point.

———————

Loz went straight into the kitchen to check on the berries, his role, his hiding place. I'd told him Sarah was still here and it frightened him.

Marcus was nowhere. He wasn't on his settee, throwing up in the bathroom or sleeping in big bear's bed. I found myself thinking something terrible had happened to him, but couldn't help wondering if things were meant to be this way.

I heard Loz pop a cork. 'Nope,' he half-heaved.

It sounded appealing to me. At that moment, those depressing drunken nights of a previous lifetime in this sinking flat, seemed like the perfect escape. I imagined swigging the tart wine. *Has the codeine weakened my resolve*?

Loz came back into the living-room and sank on the settee.

'You understand now that I've told you-' I said.

'You'll have to kill me,' he tried to laugh.

'No,' serious. 'It means we have to leave.' He was looking at me like I'd lost my mind. 'Why would you want to stay, Loz? Why didn't you bloody leave when you had the chance?'

'You know why! It just panned out that way. Booze,' he lied. 'And… and… she wouldn't let me take the electric train set,' he lied again.

I just stared at him.

'And Stacey… you know how it is,' he lied once more. 'She used to be fit!' he justified.

'I remember only too well. I nearly fucked her myself a couple of days ago. Instead, she fucked me. All of us.'

'What the hell's going on with you, Tom?'

'I've got a horrible feeling we're not gonna get out of this town alive-'

'What's new?'

'No. This is different. The way that round-faced little panda was looking at me at Picks.'

'Panda-?'

'The butcher.'

He shrugged, didn't know what I was on about.

'And then at the church… They're on to us, I'm certain of it.'

'What for?'

'For fuck's sake, Loz! *Tony Dale*.'

'How could they know?'

'Even if they don't, do you seriously think it's not all gonna come out?'

'They don't know about the cabin, the store, lots of things.'

'Tony Dale is *dead*. Will could let it slip to Anita in chemical-induced honesty. She'd be sure to tell Christian when they get back together again – and they're bound to. Marcus could tell anyone, wandering hands, a flirt too far. I mean, where is he? He's not here, he's not over at Ally's.'

I watched the colour drain from his face. He'd clearly not considered any of this, his brain switched off to the situation.

'For all we know, he's already dead,' I said. 'And then there's frigging Stacey. She'd hold it over us for a rock or a line.'

'What do we do?' he panicked. 'Tom?'

In my dream Will and Marcus stood below the grey clouds, a pint of beer in their hands. 'We have to get out of the storm–'

'Storm?'

'This town–'

'Get the other two and go?' he asked again.

'Yeah, Loz,' I lied, my stomach whirling with adrenalin and guilt. *Have I really seen them both for the last time?* 'Put some clean clothes on. We can't take anything with us.'

I went into the bedroom and got changed. In a drawer there was a little baggy filled with ash. I put it in my pocket. As I went to leave, I noticed the brown stain from where we'd tried to wash out Tony Dale's blood.

'Why did Stacey have a knife?' I asked Loz. 'What did she steal off him?'

'Drugs. Makes sense, if Tony Dale really is Tony Bonham.'

'*What?* Who told you that?'

'You did.'

But I definitely hadn't.

———————

The skies were white between us and the sun. Already my skin was slimy with the mugginess, my back hurting, soul sick, head fizzing like it needed a good smack – or an ice cold shot of vodka.

I glanced at Loz in his obliviousness – *what is he thinking?* I hadn't told him about Tony Bonham. I found myself plunged into mistrust and couldn't help but wonder if he was in on it – *on what, though?*

Maybe codeine would help. Maybe a drink would. Alcohol had a way of focusing the mind, drowning out the overlays of anxieties, all that incessant noise in my head: "what's he thinking, she thinking? Have I said the wrong thing? Do I look like an idiot, fat, bald and ugly? Does she want to fuck me? Do I want to fuck her? Is the government trying to fuck us? Is it cancer? Early onset dementia? Why are we here? How do we move forward? Should I be in charge? Should I just kill myself?" There was a time when alcohol kept me alive by purely shutting me down.

The town was quiet, no doubt sleeping off the howling madness of the previous night. I glanced around cautiously and casually, stretching my neck – if the federali were watching I didn't want to look suspicious.

'Even if I *could* find them,' Loz said out of nowhere. 'Jenny would never forgive me.'

'Shush–'

'What is it?' he whispered.

I listened. It was just an old lamp post rattling in the breeze. We walked under the Cornbow Hall and towards the swimming baths.

'Sorry, Loz. If you could find them, yes?' I recounted. 'Three years is a long time, mate. She might have found someone else.'

'Fuck you!'

'Why wouldn't she?'

'That's my wife!' There was no crack in his indignation.

'Stacey?' I held my hands up. 'You said it, not me.'

'It was a shag,' he said. 'Ok. Two shags–'

'You said you'd scour the academies to look for her kids,' I laughed.

'Two shags and a drunken promise. That's not why I stayed,' he insisted.

'I know,' I smiled.

'I was gonna leave, Tom!' He stopped, took his glasses off and wiped his eyes. 'That's not why I stayed.'

I couldn't look at him. I knew it wasn't why he stayed. I looked up at the car park where we used to drink and hang out, vagrants, yobbos, as mum called us… *kids, really.*

'Do you remember,' I said, 'when we found a bunch of out of date peppers in the bins outside Safeways?'

He scoffed a laugh, wiped his nose. 'We went up on top and threw them off and they made a huge popping sound, like bombs.'

'Why did we do that?' I asked, laughing.

'Something to do,' he smiled.

'Being kids, I guess,' I said, walking on.

'We were in our twenties!'

Where were the kids now? Where were the youths? Occasionally you saw them in the pub, but where were they the rest of the time? We'd have been exploring derelict buildings, climbing things and breaking stuff, desperate to get our hands on booze. What was Ed teaching them at the college? What *could* he teach them? Fashion? Drama perhaps? PE? Perhaps I was being unfair. Fashion requires creativity, PE is about technique, and drama is art, teaching us to think for ourselves. How would Ed's "curriculum" compare to what they'd taught Stacey's kids at the academies? Perhaps her kids were at war. *The madness of it all.* Was Ed turning the youth into little federalis, gestapo policing the town, whilst the UK government turned our ex-compatriots into soldiers?

We crossed over to the baths. *Note to self: write a love story between an indoctrinated federali and a young person of the north – possible name, The Federali and the Northern Child (or the other way around).* It'd been a long time since I'd thought about writing. Perhaps the idea of leaving was opening me up to it.

'Loz,' I said, in front of the baths. 'You need to be mentally prepared for what you're about to see.'

'Has something happened to her?'

'No, but you have to remain… open-minded.' I hadn't told him about councillor Ray. 'There's no way we're gonna survive in this town now Tony Dale's dead. This is the beginning of our way out.'

He eyed me suspiciously. 'What about Marcus and Will?'

'Yeah… I'll figure it out.'

All around us, the boarded-up buildings in our boarded-up town, "awaiting renovation". The Olde Queen's Head long gone, with its collapsed wall and a smashed fruit machine leaning against the remains of the bar. New brick offices with smashed windows, perhaps no less stale than in its previous guise as a law firm. Across the road, the old Zion church where we stored our metals through a tight gap in a dilapidated corridor.

I gently tapped twice and then started to move the big board. I heard the chain of cans hit the ground and we squeezed through.

It was dark, empty and quiet, but there was the oily singe of a recently blown out candle.

'Sarah?' I whispered. 'Damien?'

We heard footsteps in the changing rooms. Damien came out, his green parka in his arms. 'Tom, I thought… Oh, um… Loz,' wary.

'Where is everyone?' I asked.

'*Everyone?*' Loz.

'*Everyone?*' Damien.

'Loz knows Sarah is here.'

'He knows *Sarah* is here?'

'You and Sarah, yeah,' I said – Loz seemed oblivious. 'It's kicked off. They found Tony Dale.'

'We… er… heard the howling.'

'We have to leave. Where is she?'

'Have a cup of tea,' he said.

'Tea?' Loz.
'Where is she?' me.
'Matcha,' Damien.
'Matcha?' Loz.
'It's good for you,' I said. 'Where is she?'
'You know, um… Tom,' hesitant, protective.
'I know. I was an idiot. It's all getting a bit on top.'
'But… er… still-'
I looked around. 'Is she in the changing rooms?'
'Have a cup of tea,' he said.
'I'll tell you what, you make one for Loz and I'll go looking.' I started to make my way to the changing rooms.
'Wait… I suppose… um.' He pointed upwards.

My back pinching with each step, I hobbled up the stairs and into the dark, musty corridor. A glass door led up a few steps and into the light of the long gallery, stretching almost the length of the building, rows of benches overlooking the empty pool, a layer of black slime in gold rectangles of light. Sarah was sitting, eyes focused on the glittery dust in the beams. She looked peaceful and strong.

'I knew it was you,' she said.
'Where's Ray?'
'The squash courts. It had to be you.'
'Sarah, I'm-' sorry felt too weak. 'The town's gone mad. Ever since Stacey did Tony in, we've had the curse all over again, like when Lee-'
'I heard the howling.' She wouldn't look at me.
'I couldn't leave it like this.' *That's what people say, right?*
'Two gentle knocks on the big board like a timid gentlemen,' she laughed, ironic.
'I feel awful.'
'It's not the end of the world,' she said. 'It's just a shame.'

My heart broke hearing her say that. The consequence of my lust. Without thinking, I put my hand in my pocket and fingered the blister pack. *Can of Tennent's Super would be nice about now.*

She turned to face me, pointedly. 'Do you even like me like that?'
'What?' I wasn't prepared for that question.
'Do you like me like that?'
'No, what? Yes. I don't know. I mean… I miss Lucy.' I stopped, took a breath, remembered her head on my neck. 'I like you more than anyone else-'

'*Thanks.*' She turned away.

'I'm not… That sounds… No… it just happened. I'm just an animal,' I reasoned, pathetic.

'Rex has got a lot to answer for,' she laughed.

Ok, she's laughing. 'I can't blame old Rex. My first addiction wasn't drinking, it was bloody thinking. Always fantasising.'

'I was just a drink? Except the drink bit back.'

'It always does.'

'I was like Dani?' She looked over, I looked away.

I sat down on a bench about 20 feet from her, the squeeze in my spine. *Codeine.* 'My sponsor said getting into bed with Dani was like getting into bed with a bottle of scotch.'

'But you didn't.'

'No.'

'So, if we fucked?'

'Please, Sarah, can we stop this conversation?'

'Why?'

'*Please.*'

'That's what you were thinking about. So let's have it out.'

'Stop it!'

'It's honest?'

'*I'm begging you.*'

'Why, Tom?'

'Because even talking about it makes me think about fucking you!' A silence hung in the air. It just came out. 'Shit. I can't help it. I'm a man.'

'Are all men like that?'

'Animals? I don't know… Addicts maybe. I don't know.'

She went quiet. What was she thinking? What did I sound like?

'What about your son?' she asked.

'What?' confused.

'Do you think he'd have been like that?' There was another silence, glitter twirled all the way down to the edge of the pool and then vanished into the shadowy murk. 'Is that how you'd have brought him up?' she asked. 'The boy?' I could feel her words picking at a scab. 'Your *son?*'

Was this some kind of punishment for trying to kiss her? 'What about him?'

'Will you say his name?'

Why was she asking this now? *Maybe she has feelings for me and I've rejected her and she wants to hurt me – shut up Tom!*

'Tom, why did you drink?'

'I haven't!' defensive.

'What?' she laughed. 'Never?'

'You mean back then? Why…?' I asked the ether, casual, innocent.

'Just tell me.'

On top of everything that was going on, the secrets and lies, Marcus blabbering, the bubbling Loz conspiracy, and already riddled with guilt coming to see her, now she was bringing all this stuff up. *This is bloody recovery. This is what it does to you! It's a life of fucking therapy. Exposure, pain, blush-burn, one of those dreams where you find yourself naked on a stage inexplicably aroused by a horse or a relative.*

'I guess it was social anxiety,' I said, trying to keep my cool. 'And grief around family stuff. Maybe childhood trauma. And my dad drank, that's just what we did. And the boys, you know.'

'What was his name, Tom?'

He was just the lad, the boy. The little man with the blond bowl and the green eyes. 'What's this about, Sarah?'

'I'm trying to understand things from your side.'

'It's just this, everything, last night was-'

'I used to feel like your daughter. On the Squirrels. And then you were like my big brother, my mate, looking out for me. Will said you had a thing for me but-'

'Oh, fuck Will!'

She gave me a look.

'It's not… I'm not jealous.'

'I didn't say you were.'

'You're attractive, Sarah. I've always found you attractive. I don't know. These things pop into my head.'

'And then you escape in them?'

'No, it's not like… yes, probably. Oh, I don't know. I'm just a guy. It's just who I am. I don't usually over-step the line, but my thoughts wander… I don't drink. I don't do-' I stopped myself, codeine tight against my thigh, melting into my leg. 'I don't have too many ways to quieten myself down.'

'There's no mountains in Halesowen,' she smiled.

'Exactly!'

'What about God?'

'Please, Sarah.'

'How long can you go without saying his name?'

'God?' I knew what she meant and she knew I knew what she meant.

She waited for an answer. 'I know his name,' she smiled.

'Yeah, I know. The boys would've said.'

'Lee told me.'

'*Lee?*'

'Whatever you think about her, however messed up she was, she cared.'

'We're all messed up. Was it L-e-e or L-e-i-g-h?'

'Tom,' she said, stern.

I got up and stepped down to the front of the gallery, leaning on the railing. I closed my eyes and remembered when this abandoned space was full of life. The echoes of kids playing. I learned to swim here. Lee too. The bright yellow lights flickering on the blue glassy ripples in evening classes. The little strip of fabric sewn into our Speedos, red, green and blue, 25 metres, 50 and 100. The chlorine which got in your hair, towels and clothes, which filled the air in and around us. The burst of warmth in pee, the cold as it dispersed. The diving down to fetch plastic block weights. 20p coin in the locker which, when returned, bought a vending machine Kit Kat.

'Do you remember?' she asked. 'The day before the last bus?'

I nodded.

'You forgave me, after all I'd done,' she smiled.

'You came back.'

'What's his name, Tom?'

Was that what was wrong with me? I had a sudden flashback of rehab, sitting in group therapy, bursting out crying. I didn't stop for 30 minutes or so. I missed lunch. My addiction worker said to me, "we've been waiting for this," like we were in a film, Good Tom Hanson. But it didn't feel like that, like I'd let go, surrendered, or done whatever it was he'd been waiting for. Nothing changed after it. I just continued on this up and down path of sobriety.

'I need to tell you about Barb,' I said.

'Tom,' she responded, this time annoyed.

I could hear it in my head, bouncing back and forth, each time followed by a typewriter ping. I remembered when we chose it. We were in Mister Beans, a café on Burnham high street. I'd been reading Dylan Thomas and started quoting a poem, Out of the Sighs.

"Before the agony; the spirit grows, forgets and cries; a little comes is tasted and found good". I never truly understood his writing, just odd snippets hit home and that was enough. He was cryptic – like the Bible. The words sounded good when they came out of your mouth, *rage, rage against the dying of the light.* His writing was deeply spiritual and seemed to encapsulate that life is hard and inexplicable but can also be simply beautiful. Lucy suggested the name and I was chuffed about it.

'Dylan,' I cleared my throat. 'Dylan.' I looked up at her. 'Dylan.'

She came over, sat down behind me and tugged on my hand. I tried not to cry.

'I need to leave,' I said, hot with emotion.

'Thank you,' she smiled. 'For saying his name.'

Hi, my name's Tom and after three years I've managed to say my son's name. Dylan. His name's Dylan. Like the poet. Thomas, not Bob.

I looked into the black grime of the pool, remembered Paramedic Peyton and Care Worker Wade, the characters on Dylan's armbands from his favourite animation. 'Sarah, we have to leave. It's time.' I paused, took a breath. 'Loz is downstairs too.'

'*Loz?*' she panicked. 'Is Will here!?'

'No.'

'Marcus?'

'Just Loz. Last night it went off.'

She waited. 'What aren't you telling me, Tom?'

So many things. People had died, Marcus had blabbed, and we probably wouldn't see Will again. Not to mention, I'd accidentally relapsed. But I was too ashamed to tell her, as if somehow I'd willed Tony Moran to pour that bitter opiate powder down my throat. Or was I just scared she'd take them off me?

'I don't think Loz is in on anything,' I said. 'But there is something I need to put out there.'

———————

'But why?' Loz asked, working himself up.

'*Shush,*' Sarah said.

It was a long, dark corridor overlooking three squash courts. All the windows had been smashed and boarded up, the rustle of leaves outside. Damien was shining a torch down on Court 1. Ray was tied to a chair in the middle, gagged, shying away from the light. He looked sweaty and ill, his greying-black hair flat with grease.

'Because Ray won't be able to lie,' I whispered, 'to the Sons, nons, feds, whoever.'

'But if they find him, they'll-they'll,' he panicked, 'chop us up and spread us around town like they did with-' he suddenly stopped, looked at Sarah.

'With Lee,' she said. 'You can at least say her name.'

'Lee!' he screeched, 'like Lee!'

'Calm down, Loz,' I said. 'We're gonna get out of here, aren't we, Damien?'

'Oh, um, yeah. North. Might have to do a couple of trips.'

Sarah looked annoyed with me. She gave me the nod. I didn't fully understand the plan and I wasn't sure it was the right way to go about things, but so many things just didn't make sense. Loz's assertion I'd told him about Tony Dale being Tony Bonham was just one of them. Sarah said we needed to make sure.

I nodded back, hesitant.

'You've got to trust us, Loz,' Sarah said, her change in tone disarming.

'Trust?' he looked at me.

I smiled sympathetically.

'I need your help,' she added. 'Come with me.' She made her way down the corridor.

'It's dark,' he said, nervously pushing his glasses up his face.

'Oh, just go,' I said, playing it down.

He followed her to the stairs, looking back to me, confused. I stayed up top with Damien. 'Is she doing the right thing?' I whispered.

'Oh, um, yeah. He'll be alright. She... er knows what she's... er... yeah.'

Below us, we heard them drag the cabinet away from the door and then watched Loz and Sarah enter the court.

Sarah removed the gag from councillor Ray's mouth. She gave him some water. Loz was pacing. He didn't have a clue what was happening. I felt so bad about it. He looked up at me and I put my hands up to try to calm him.

'What do you know about Tony Bonham, Ray?' she asked.

'He's the chemist,' he said, morose, looking down. 'That's what they call the chemist.' He looked up at Sarah. 'I'm worried about my Wolfie, please, Sarah.'

'Finish the questions first,' she said.

'What've you done to his dog?' Loz panicked.

'Nothing-' she snapped, irritated.

'He'll starve,' Ray said.

'What does the chemist sell, Ray?' she asked.

'He doesn't sell. He trades. We don't sell in Halesowen. We only trade.'

'Without er… the um… party line,' Damien called down.

Loz glanced up, anguished. Was it because he knew something or because he knew nothing? I felt like I was betraying him.

'Look, I know what yow'm getting at,' Ray said. 'He trades drugs which aren't essential, but for recreational use. I'm not saying it's right. But Tony Bonham won't trade with addicts.'

'What's your definition of an addict?' I scoffed.

'Well, Tom,' he said, awkward. 'Yow and Sarah know.' He looked up at her. She seemed oddly offended.

'What about Jason Higgins?' I sniped. 'Scavenging on the streets like a rat?'

'He doesn't trade with Jason.'

'Only because if Jason trades anything he'll be accused of breaking Jay's Law,' I said. 'He's just left to die.'

'He stole a pack of double A's! We have to have rules.' He turned to Loz, 'there has to be rules.'

Loz looked up at me completely bewildered. It seemed like he knew nothing about anything, but why would he say I told him about Tony Dale being Tony Bonham?

'Jason's besides the point,' Sarah said. 'Surely that means Tony Bonham is breaking Jay's Law?'

'That may be,' he said, 'but he cor be arrested,' he chirped.

'Why?' Sarah asked.

He paused, sighed irritably, 'because he doesn't exist.'

'But he does,' I said. 'Tony Dale is Tony Bonham.'

'Tony Dale's dead,' Loz said.

'Eh?' Ray.

'*Loz*,' Sarah.

'What?' Loz.

Sarah looked up to us, prompting Damien.

'I better… er, go,' Damien said to me, heading to the stairs.

I shook my head at Sarah, and she knew what I meant. This wasn't necessary. Loz had heard about Tony Bonham from someone else and was obviously confused. A weird smile grew on her face, she completely disregarded me and turned to throw the gag to the far end of the court. 'Fetch it, Loz,' she shouted.

'What?' Loz, confused, manic.

'The gag,' Sarah, urgent, insistent.

He looked up and down the court fast, up and down again, then chased after the gag, loyal and hopeless. Sarah immediately ran out and slammed the door. Loz turned and charged towards it, yelping, banging it.

'Loz! Stop it! Shu-shush.' I put my finger to my lips. 'Calm down. I promise it'll be alright. Sarah,' I called down.

I heard them drag the cabinet to secure the door, then the patter of footsteps up the stairs.

'T-Tom, what's going on?' he called up, banging the door, close to tears.

'Loz,' I said, 'there's nothing to worry about. You have to stop banging.'

'Doh trust em,' Ray spat. 'Help! Help!' echoed around the court.

'Loz,' I called down. 'Look at me. Gag him before we have the Sons on us.'

He was panicking, pacing, he ran back to fetch the gag.

'They're in here, in here!' Ray was shouting. He tried to howl, but a cooing *oo-oo-oo* came out, followed by a coughing fit.

Sarah and Damien came over to me. 'Hit him,' she shouted down.

'Hit him?' he called up, surprised.

'Slap him to prove yourself!' she yelled.

'What?' me.

'Er-' Damien.

I was looking at her in shock, Damien seemed unsure and Loz was freaking out. He ran to the wall and then back to the chair.

'Hit him or die!' she shouted.

'*Sarah*,' I warned.

She shrugged.

Trembling with fear, Loz slapped Ray harder than I'd thought he was capable of. Ray went quiet, terrified.

'I'm sorry Ray, I'm so sorry,' Loz was mumbling.

I pulled Sarah to one side. 'What the hell?' I whispered. 'What's the plan here?'

'Find out what he knows,' she said.

'Clearly he knows nothing.'

'The plan worked then,' she smiled.

Damien was watching us, listening intently, looking a little uncomfortable about things. He had absolute faith in Sarah and I had more faith in her than I had in myself, but looking down on the squash court, councillor Ray tied to a chair and Loz pacing like a hamster on a wheel, I realised we'd all gone mad.

'I had to do something,' she defended, doubting herself.

'Yes,' I said to assuage her guilt.

'Wh…what have you done to Tony Dale?' Ray asked Loz, almost in tears.

'He died… Erm… They found him dead.' He looked up to me and nodded – *just to give the game away.*

'Oh, no,' Ray wailed. 'Not Tony.'

'Forget Tony Dale,' Sarah said. 'The point is, there was a Tony Bonham and that was him.'

'He wasn't! He wasn't!' Ray pleaded. 'Tony Bonham is nobody. Nobody and everybody. He's the worst of us. But he ay one person, because if he wuz somebody he'd have to be held accountable.'

'What the hell do you mean?' I asked.

'If yow went to the federali meetings yow'd understand. *Yow all want drugs,*' he said. 'Not Tom. Or Sarah. But most of yow. Loz, Damien-'

'Well, er… I like,' Damien muttered, 'a bit of gange.'

'But Ally said Tony-' I looked to Sarah.

'I never liked her,' she said. 'She never liked me.'

'No, but Ally said Tony Two *was* Tony Three-'

'Ally? Pah,' Ray said. 'Where'd yow fink they keep the drugs?'

'*Why, Tom?*' Loz called up, close to tears, oblivious to anything Ray had just said. 'Am I in prison? What's gonna happen to me?'

'Of course not,' I said. 'Sarah.'

'He's definitely not in on anything,' she added.

'*What?* What do you think I… Tom, it's me,' he said, sadly. 'Me. Loz. I stayed for you, Tom.'

I felt emotion bubbling in my gut, remembered waking up that day to see his pitiful face at the foot of my bed. *What have I done?* 'Loz, I'm so sorry.'

'Who told you Tony Dale was Tony Bonham?' Sarah asked.

'He's not!' Ray yelled.

'Shut up,' she shouted, 'or I'll kill the animal.'

He went quiet.

Loz looked confused, picking at his lip. 'Tom did.'

'I didn't. I only found out yesterday. Ally told me, and I went straight down to Picks-'

'You wanted to see Tony Bonham-' Ray said, thoughtfully.

'Then I came here to see Sarah,' I added. 'When I left, I ended up at St John's, where they found Tony Dale-'

'Marcus then? Or Will? Or Ally? I don't know,' Loz said. 'I didn't... I haven't done anything.'

'You killed Tony Dale,' Ray said to me. 'You came down to Picks asking for Bonham, thinking he was Dale, but you knew he was dead, didn't you? It was some sort of an alibi.'

'Let me out, please,' Loz begged.

Sarah and Damien went downstairs.

'Ray, I didn't kill him,' I said. 'We didn't kill him. Some of us knew about it. But he's not the only one. Barb and the Milkman are dead too.'

'The milk-' Ray drifted. 'The butcher. It's happening.'

'What's happening?'

'It'll be the gasman next,' he said.

'What?'

'Aaron Moran. Then maybe me-'

In the distance we heard the yelp of a howl, as if right on cue. This was followed by another, then more. That terrifying wolf howl in stereo across town. Only it wasn't a pack of wolves. It was people. And nothing was capable of hurting people more than people.

'There you have it,' Ray said, smiling.

In an instant an image of Marcus flashed up in my mind. Just a glimpse. He looked calm and at peace. I took a sharp intake of breath. He was dead. I knew it. I didn't know how I knew it, but this image was a goodbye.

Loz had his glasses in his hand and was wiping his eyes. 'What's going on, Tom?'

I heard Sarah and Damien move the cabinet. Loz ran out. Ray glanced at me, a man resigned to his fate. 'The changing of the guard.'

My hand moved to my pocket. I stroked the blister pack. *Shot of brandy.*

Sarah came back upstairs.

'There's something I should've told you,' I said. 'I told Marcus you were here.'

The howling had stopped, nobody had come to the baths and not one of us had anything wise, sensible or funny to contribute. I felt like we'd come as far as we could. Three years in a town hell-bent on destroying itself was probably not a bad innings. We'd lasted more than some, but not as long as others. We all have a lifespan wherever we are. This ending would just be the mark of our survival skills. Perhaps they'd find me here, a heap of bones on an upturned, empty vending machine.

'Fag,' Damien said, like he'd had an idea, then proceeded to roll.

Marcus's calm face flashed before my eyes again, as I tried to process my vision. Was it my fault? Had Marcus told somebody we were planning on leaving Halesowen? Did they confront him and ask him how? Maybe he refused to tell them to protect us. Maybe that's why they killed him. I felt sick with guilt. How could I have thought about leaving him?

'We should move Ray up here with us,' I said.

'Yeah,' Loz agreed, jittery, elbows on the big table, biting his thumb nails.

Damien sat next to him rolling his cigarette. I had to do my all not to ask him for one, forever fingering the blister pack in my pocket. In fact, right then, the pills, the booze, the fags, Sarah, everything seemed appealing, my mind moving back and forth between them, cursing myself for it, irritable. If Lucy was here she'd tell me to go to a meeting. I'd take it as an insult, start an argument. Then I'd go away and think about it. Eventually I'd slip out to a meeting, tell them all about my problems and they'd nod and laugh because they understood. On my return, I'd apologise to Lucy.

'We need to find out what's happening out there,' Sarah said, next to me, the clomp of the vending machine as she sat up.

'It's too risky in daylight,' I said, thin sunbeams through small gaps – voodoo pins to kill vampires.

'It might be... um, er... nothing to do with us, the howling,' Damien said.

'It's for Ray,' she countered, adamant. 'He's missing. All that went on last night and there's still no sign of Ray. They've lost one of their pack. That's why they're howling.'

'Er... yeah, I bet that's right that is,' Damien said, the click and hiss of the lighter, suck.

I wasn't so sure. 'Ray will know more about it than us.'

'What about er… the wolf… the um, dog? Would Ray help?'

'Sooner or later one of us is going to have to go out there,' Sarah said. 'Then we can feed the stupid thing.'

'Don't look at me,' Loz said.

'We weren't,' she mocked.

He looked wounded, but there was no way he was going to be able to hack it out there. Assuming he wasn't stopped en route, he'd head straight home, close the door and have a drink to steady his nerves, asserting his position as brew-guard. 'Let's fetch him back up here then.'

'Definitely!' Loz said.

'Go on then, Loz,' Sarah told him.

'*Me?*'

'Why not?' she said. 'Pretty soon we're gonna have to leave here. It's gonna take balls. If you can't go downstairs and get Ray what hope do you have?'

There was silence.

'Loz,' I prompted. 'She's got a point.'

He didn't respond.

'Oh *God*,' Damien said, irked. 'I'll um, help you move the bloody cabinet.' He got up and paced towards the stairs. Loz looked at me and Sarah, who was shaking her head, before begrudgingly following him.

'He has to leave,' she said.

'We all do,' I added.

She looked upset and had every reason to be. By talking to Marcus, I'd forced her hand.

'Why are you still here, Sarah?'

She sighed. 'Why are *you*?'

'What's here for you?' I asked. 'Your nan's gone. You've seen so much tragedy in your short life. Your dad, your mum-'

'My mum?' she looked completely thrown. 'Why are you talking about my mum? Is this because I got you to talk about Dylan?'

'No, not at all.' *Was it?* '…I don't think so. It just popped into my head. We don't have to talk about it.'

Downstairs, we heard the filing cabinet being shifted, the mumble of voices, *to-me-to-you*.

'I don't really think about her anymore. I was young. I just grew up with it. I certainly didn't carry it around…' she caught herself and glanced at me, 'I'm not saying-'

'Aren't you?'

'No! Why are we even on this?'

I half-laughed. 'I asked you why you were still here and you didn't answer me.'

'Neither did you.'

'My sponsor always used to say you'd have to be mad or depressed to go back home,' I laughed.

'Is that an answer?'

'I want to bloody leave! I want you and Loz to leave too.'

'What about Will-?'

'Ohhhh-'

'Let me speak-!'

'That's why you're still here-' I don't know why it hurt.

'I was going to say "what about Will and Marcus", if you'd let me finish.'

I shrugged.

'What does that mean?'

'I wish they'd leave them, but…'

'But what?'

'Last night I had this dream outside the George and-'

'A fucking dream!'

'Sarah! The last we saw of Will he was high on hallucinogens at Ally's. He wasn't alone-'

'So!'

'He wouldn't come! Marcus has vanished completely. There's not much hope and there's no time left. You heard the fucking howling.'

She was shaking her head, disgusted at me.

'What are we supposed to do? They'll kill us! You haven't been out there. You don't know what it's like.'

There was a silence. I looked at Sarah, but she wouldn't look at me.

'We can't all go on the barge, anyway,' she sulked.

'There you go. There's not enough space for everyone.'

'No,' she said. '*We* all can't. Damien only allows three at a time. Any more is a risk.'

'We'll fit,' I said.

She shook her head, smiling, like a little child who was getting her own way no matter what. 'He won't do it.'

I laughed out loud, like the universe was playing a trick on me. *Am I tethered to this town until the bitter end?* 'Fine, Sarah. Have it your way,' I decided. 'You and Loz go. He needs to find his family.'

I was doing the right thing and that was what it was all about. She could start again and have a happy sober life.

'No!' she slapped the vending machine. 'Absolutely not. You go!'

'Hold on-'

'Don't you come all this hero bullshit with me, Tom.'

'It's my fault Loz is here!'

'Then *you* take him! Who do you think you are?'

'Wait a minute. Is this about bloody Will?'

She was about to have a go at me but she stopped. 'Honestly, Tom,' she shrugged, 'I don't know.'

I shook my head. '*Yeah, right,*' smug.

'I don't know! If I say I don't know, I mean it. What's wrong with you?'

'Nothing's wrong with me. I just care!'

'*Yeah, right,*' she mimicked. 'I'm not gonna fuck you or kiss you or suck you off!'

'I said I'm sorry!' I yelled. 'What do I have to do!?'

There was a long, bitter silence, tight fists and grimaces. I was beaten. Downstairs we could hear mumbles, where they were figuring out how to bring Ray up. I put my hand in my pocket and started poking at the co-codamols, nails scoring the foil, secretly trying to pop them out, but the room was too quiet and the packet too noisy. I couldn't risk it.

Had I ruined our friendship? Would it always come back to this?

'Sarah, I don't want to argue with you.'

'My dad was a bully.'

'What? I'm not a-'

'Tom. It's not all about you,' she interrupted. She turned to me and smiled, sadly.

'Where's this come from then?'

'I think more about my dad than I do mum.'

'You said you didn't know him-'

'Just the stuff nan told me.'

I smiled remembering Maureen, wondered what she was doing now. Was she alive? Perhaps she was sitting in a big hall somewhere listening to an orchestra play a symphony wrong.

'Did you read the letter?' I asked.

'She picked at her cuticles, nails rigid and dirty, before reaching into her pocket and pulling it out, her hands trembling. 'I'm not sure I can.'

I put my hand on hers and gently squeezed, partly wondering whether I'd been too hasty in giving it to her. 'There's no rush.'

She moved her hand away and put the letter back in her pocket. 'I'm not,' she looked at me, 'ready. Just time, Tom.'

I wasn't sure whether she was talking about the letter or us. Perhaps both.

I thought about what she'd said upstairs in the gallery, that I was like her dad. It made me feel guilty and protective, like I had a responsibility. Maybe that's what I needed to deal with myself and my wandering mind. 'Your dad?'

'He made me, I s'pose,' she smiled.

'For right or wrong that's generally the way.'

'Mum loved him, but he was a bully. No, he was more than that. He was violent – I guess he was trained to be. He wasn't faithful-'

'I'm sorry-'

'He'd get drunk and sleep around. She knew about it, but he told her she was imagining things. The army really screwed him up… and her.'

'It took his life.'

'Nan said he was already dead.'

'It must be hard not knowing him. I had my dad until I was 30 and I still feel like there's so much I don't know, but you were just a baby. I was lucky.'

'You said he used to beat you.'

'People are like diamonds. We have lots of sides but if you look close enough you can see through it.'

'That's pretty good,' she smiled.

'Probably stole it from an old meme,' I laughed. 'Dad was a good man, a bad man, strong and weak. He was very useful in some ways and utterly useless in others. Your dad was probably the same. Lots of sides. Me too.'

'*Don't I know it*,' she said, looking at me and laughing.

'I'm ok some of the time, and then I'm a… what did you call it?'

'Deeve,' she laughed. 'Maybe in your head. The kiss was a shock because I spent so much time telling Will he was wrong.'

'He was.'

'Was he?'

I'll never forget the night Will told me about Tammy and him. He was quite sweet and gentlemanly about it, because he knew I was obsessed with her. We drank a lot, it hurt like hell and the hurt lingered until the hangover the next morning and far beyond it.

'Just my head, Sarah.'

'We can't leave them behind,' she said. 'What would you do without them?'

We heard them coming upstairs. I went to help. Ray was still strapped tight to the chair, wriggling and pained, several rows of rope digging into his gut.

'We didn't know what to do,' Loz said.

'After every incident there's a federali meeting. Jordan chairs them,' Ray said.

'Jordan,' Damien said. 'He's alright he is… er… um, made me an easel.'

'I thought he made musical instruments-?'

'If yow cared about your town, yow'd know all this,' Ray added. 'Now, please let me feed my Wolfie.'

'Ray,' Sarah said, loosening the rope, 'we want to let you go, but the first sign of pressure and you'll tell them where we are.'

He sighed in relief, 'I can breathe again. Ar doh wanna see them. Yow doh understand, I'm more likely to be done in than anyone.'

Damien was shining a torch on Ray's face. Beads of sweat had smudged the muck of his ordeal making it look like he was wearing make-up.

'What might they want with me, Ray?' I asked.

'Yow?' He seemed confused.

They were all looking at me. I felt myself blushing, like somehow I was making it the Tom show. 'Tony Moran just *happens* to bump into me,' I said, 'and then I'm dragged into his crazy world.'

'You're a nobody-'

'He was grooming me-'

'A periph.'

'A periph?'

'Like Jason.'

'We trade!' I said, offended.

'Yow've got friends. Christian talks you up. Jake seems to like you, but your trade is challenging and time consuming-'

'Not really.'

'And not especially useful, unless we joined Blackheath or Quinton. Batteries are very useful. If the butcher's taken the milkman-'

'The butcher was at St John's,' I insisted, 'when they were trying to figure it all out. He came in with Christian. They didn't have a clue about any of it, Tony Dale, Barb or the milkman. Or the robbery-'

'Robbery? That's more like it.'

'Honest John had something to do with it.'

'*The gardener? A robbery?*'

He stared at me like I'd gone mad. Sarah too. Loz was paying attention for once and looked like he wanted to say something, get a little dig in, pay me back for what I'd done to him. Damien couldn't even look in my direction. He looked down to his feet, scuffed irritably.

'Barb was found half-naked. It was like John had been, you know… The milkman was dead next to Tony Dale and John looked guilty. He practically ran out when Barb pointed at him.'

'She was alive?' he asked.

'They injected her.'

'Oh,' he looked sad. 'All I know is, I have a good stock of batteries and someone has to feed Wolfie. He's getting on. He'll die and then I don't know what I'll do with myself. Please,' he begged.

'It's too dangerous, Ray,' I said.

'He's all I've got left.'

'No way,' Sarah said.

'I love my Wolfie more than I love myself,' he cried.

'I'll go,' Damien said. We all glanced over at him. 'I'll um… go,' he asserted.

'You can't,' Sarah said. 'You have to get *him* out.' She was pointing at Loz.

'That's his dog! You lot er… have um… obviously never had a bloody pet.'

'Of course we have,' she said, 'but there's more important things than a bloody pet right now!'

'It's his frigging mate!' Damien shouted.

Everyone went quiet. It had all come a little out of the blue. We weren't used to hearing him raise his voice like this.

'You alright, mate?' I asked.

'Um… er… No.'

We sat in silence, Loz rolling his thumbs – he clearly wanted another roll-up but was too scared to ask Damien. Sarah was sat on the floor against the vending machine in tomboy boredom. We seemed to be stuck in an ethereal mud, a morphine sag which got heavier with every passing minute. Marcus flitted into my mind and I heard him say, "matcha tea anyone?" in high-pitched humour, to break the tension. *Maybe he's not dead and these fleeting images are a telepathic cry for help.*

Damien was shaking his head like he was fed up with us all. He wasn't much older than me but in that moment he seemed like a grown up amongst a bunch of kids. For all his umming and erring, which made him appear dithery and unsure of himself, he was regularly back and forth from the old world to the new world, whilst we were just mucking about in this wild playground. He was living life and had apparently been trading with Tony Dale – what the hell was that about? Now he'd decided he was going to feed the dog, Sarah was telling him no and I found myself judging him for raising his voice, when really he made me feel like a coward.

There was nothing else for it. I was going to have to go out there. 'I've got it,' I said. 'Jordan.'

'What?' Sarah looked confused.

'That way they won't think we're leaving,' I said to myself more than anyone. 'Sarah, I have a plan. Can you stay here with Loz and Ray?'

'Yeah?'

'Ray where do you live?'

'Blackberry Lane, not far from the old police station, on the right. No number. The one with the blue door.'

'When's the meeting gonna be held, Ray?'

'It's probably done and dusted now but Jordan will still be at the Fed-House.'

'Ok. Damien you go to Ray's and I'm going to find Jordan.'

I knew it was a risk. It seemed like so many things could go wrong. What were they howling about? I was going to have to go to Ally's – who knew where she really stood in all this? And I was going to have to bare-face lie to her. She probably already knew I was planning on leaving.

'What's going on, Tom?' Sarah asked.

'It's my fault. All of this. I told Marcus. I'm gonna go and find them and then we can leave, yeah?'

Sarah looked unsure.

'Sarah?' I prompted.

'I don't know.' She was glaring at Ray, who wouldn't look back at her.

'It wasn't my fault, Sarah,' Ray said, looking down. 'He was my friend, too.'

'*She*.'

'Yeah, sorry, 'er was my mate. What they did, I knew nothing about it.'

'I know it was Tony Moran, but the whole idea of the Sons was yours.'

'No bloody fear! Ar put forth an idea for a council, something proper. The Sons is a bad American TV show. It was yow're commie mate, Tom.'

'None of it matters anymore,' I said. 'Sarah?'

'Be careful Tom.'

Back in the mad fire of New Halesowen. The sun was all but down, leaving a beige sky, a blank page with which to write the ending to our time in Halesowen, the town we were born in and might yet die in. Every sudden sound a danger, a leaf dragging on the tarmac, a bird chirping up high, the rattle of a lamp-post. It was like the old days, when I was scared to face the world sober, I just had to get to the offy. Now there was no offy, nowhere to hide.

There's codeine. No!

In the distance, I could hear the familiar din of music, the whirr of the generator. Picks was open. That was probably a good sign. Business as usual.

I just had to stick to the plan and stay calm. If I did bump into somebody, it was alright to be a bit jittery. *Last night was enough to make anyone nervous.* Whatever had happened since, I knew nothing about it and was free to plead ignorance.

But as I walked under the old Cornbow Hall, I saw something I couldn't ignore.

'God, not again.' My heart sped up, temples throbbed.

The trainer was still on the foot, the leg was wedged into the door handle of the old Greek chippy. It was the same place they'd left one of Leroy's arms. The thigh was naked and pink, flesh frayed, jagged bone visible as I crossed the road.

It wasn't Marcus because he didn't wear trainers. I stood looking at a man's amputated leg, at first desensitised, a thought which reduced me to tears, until I was eventually biting the skin on my palm to stop myself screaming.

In the pool of blood and gristle there was an old penny. An old, old one, like a medallion. In the knee cap, a small rectangular, black wrap. I had a flashback to the toilet in the old post office. Then I realised who it was. 'Oh, why? He never hurt anybody. He was like Jay Bird, harmless and hopeless. Poor Jason.'

'Yeah?'

'Fuck!' I jumped about three feet, turning to see him, 'you fuck, you fuck, you fuck!' I punched him in the arm. 'I thought it was you?'

'Me?'

'The wrap?'

'The wrap?'

I pointed to it and he removed it from the knee without a second thought. He opened it up. There was nothing inside.

'Goddam,' he screeched, 'the same!'

'The same?'

'As the other. I just need something. Tom, have you got anything? Come on man, don't let me down!'

'Here, for God's sake!' I pulled out the packet of co-codamols and threw them at him. 'Go wild!'

He looked at the packet on the floor, then at me, then the packet again. 'Tom, you came through for me,' he smiled. 'Always knew you were a good un.'

He started popping the pills out one at a time. He put three in his mouth and cracked them open with his teeth. He licked the grainy powder into his gums, just like I'd done myself the previous night.

I stood there watching him, shaking my head at my own stupidity. How could I do it to myself? Pain or no pain, why had I been carrying them around in my pocket all this time? I lifted my arm to lean on the door and, without thinking, put my hand on the bloodied flesh. I screamed, wiped my hand on my shirt. Jason found it hilarious.

'One last laugh for Aaron Moran,' he said.

'Tony's son?' *Ray was right.*

'His head's on a stick by the Fed-House. Ed put his trilby on him.'

'Aaron? But what about Tony? What about the Sons? The federalis?'

Jason shrugged, smiling.

'Have you seen Will or Marcus? I need to find them.'

'Not for days.'

'What's the town looking like? Is it safe?'

'Is it safe?' He seemed confused. 'It'll be safer without that cunt around. Be Tony's head on a stick soon.'

'You hope.'

'Too right! I can trade again.'

Jason walked with me to the flats, thanking me every two minutes for off-loading the pills. I felt relieved of temptation, and I was grateful I didn't have to walk alone. The town was empty. As we came up to the Fed-House it looked like it was closed. Perhaps they were all in Picks celebrating – or just forgetting.

'There it is,' Jason said. 'Another empty wrap.'

Aaron Moran's head. Yellow and purple, looking to the old penny on the ground. It didn't look real. It was like a Halloween decoration. He wore Ed's trilby at a jaunty angle. My first thought was heads are heavy – I'm not sure it would've been my first thought had I stumbled on it by chance, alone. Lee's head had rested back against the wall, the Christmas tree slightly arched.

Was this what we were reduced to without the UK government? Even if *all* of Will's conspiracy theories were right, what was worse? But then, was this not the actions of Halesowen's "government"? Perhaps the answer is no government. *Christ, Tom, now's not the time for social-politics.*

'Where is everyone?' I asked.

'It's been a mad un. You hear what happened last night?'

'Tony Dale,' I said.

'Tony Dale, Tony Bonham…'

'Tony Bonham?'

'Didn't you hear, Tony Dale was Tony Bonham?'

'What!? Who told you that?'

'The Halesowen News.'

'The what?'

'Came out earlier. That's why they reckon he was done in.'

'The News?'

'Barb went too,' he said. 'Er was alright. Often got me a drink before she lost it. Probably for the best.'

'And the milkman,' I said, absent, trying to take it all in.

'Honest John, I heard. The paper put out a request for information.'

I stopped and looked at him. 'Honest John? Who? The milkman?'

'And clobbered Barb too, I reckon.'

'Why though?'

'Er was always pulling up those weeds in St John's,' he laughed. 'Him and his bloody gardening. Fucked up, man.'

Nothing made any sense. Conflicting stories, half-truths. The Halesowen News chiming in. Councillor Ray was saying one thing, Jason another, and now there was some sort of press release.

I went over to the entrance of the Fed-House.

'What yow doing?' Jason said.

I had to speak to Jordan. I turned my back on the decapitated head and knocked. There was no answer. I pulled on the handle and it opened.

'Hello,' I called in.

'Hello,' came back at me. 'Just a minute.'

'I've gotta go,' Jason said, nervous. 'Thanks for the pills, Tom.'

He scuttled up Andrew Road, probably off to inject the rest of them.

Jordan came to the door. 'Tom Hanson,' he said. 'I've never seen you here before.'

'I've never been here.'

'That would be why,' he smiled. 'Come in,' he said, warm and friendly, like there wasn't a bloodied head behind me.

'I can't right now. Another time.'

Checked shirt tucked into his denim shorts, he looked like a good Christian – the sort that Lee would never have been.

'How can I help?' he asked.

I felt crazy asking this, having seen what I'd just seen, but I didn't know what else to do. 'You… er, make guitars, don't you?'

'That's right.'

'I don't suppose we could do a trade.'

'You know, Tom, that would make me really happy. Ally said you're a lovely guy and I've been looking for a way for us to meet properly.'

There was something in his eyes. I couldn't tell whether it was sinister or just that God thing – a kind of blind faith that everything was how it was supposed to be.

'What do you want for it?' I asked. 'We break down precious metals, but we also brew. Or I could trade to get you something else.'

'Electric or acoustic?'

'Electric?'

'I can do both. I have battery amps.'

'That would be frigging amazing.'

'Electric?'

'Electric, yeah.'

I was momentarily lost in a genuinely exciting prospect – we were used to playing an old bellied-up Tanglewood. It seemed a shame we'd never play the handmade guitar, but whatever the hell was going on, we had to leave Halesowen and, to leave, it needed to look like we wanted to stay.

'I've got a good stock of lime wood leftover. I don't have a pressing need for anything, so it would be wrong for me to ask. How about you attend the federali meetings?'

'How many?' It just came out, like I was bartering with the rehab about how many AA meetings I had to attend every month. It didn't matter whether it was one or a hundred, we wouldn't be here.

'Just come,' he smiled.

Standing in front of this friendly man, I almost forgot what Halesowen had turned into. Was this why Ally had wanted me to trade with him? Maybe we just had a few bad eggs. I remembered what Ray had said, but Ally wouldn't lie to me, would she? And clearly Tony Dale was Tony Bonham. It said it in the Halesowen News. That made sense, even if it made no sense at all.

I shook Jordan's hand then, as I turned to leave, I once again came face to face with the reality of Halesowen. Aaron's staked head forlornly looking down as if he was trying to find his body. A sad head on a stick? A smiling gentleman inviting me in? A cold dead head? The warm leader of the "neighbourhood watch"?

But then it *was* Aaron Moran, the bully who used to terrify us at school, who chased Dan in the upstairs flat out of the window to his death. Perhaps this was karma catching up with him.

I turned back and Jordan was still smiling like customer service in a fast food restaurant. It made me feel uneasy. 'Where is everyone, Jordan?'

He shrugged, 'Quinton?'

'Quinton? What's happening in–'

'Tom!' came in a panic from up the road. 'Tom! Help!'

Before I could even turn to see Jason, I heard a gunshot echo through the streets, followed by another. I watched Jason falling, his arms seeming to give up life before he hit the tarmac, the sound of flesh scraping on the road. I saw no one else in the street, no one chasing him. I quickly moved towards the Fed-House but the door locked with a click. 'Jordan,' I yelled, banging on the door.

I turned expecting to see the gunman, but there was nothing, no sound, stillness, and Jason lying in the road.

'Jase,' I whispered.

Nothing.

'Jason.'

I edged to the corner of the block. Ally's place was the other side of the grass. I ran, hunched half-expecting a bullet to hit me.

'Open, open up,' I yelled. I turned the handle but it was locked. It was never locked. I banged the back window. 'Ally!'

'What? What? What d'ya want?' angry. She opened the door topless, pulling her leggings up. 'Bloody hell, Tom!'

As I entered, I heard the door to the stairs close. I pointed out into the hall, taut, enquiring.

She looked at me as if to say, *what do you think I was bloody doing*?

'A gun! Did you not hear it?'

I ran to the side table, poured a cup of cold coffee.

'I wouldn't,' she said.

'They just shot Jason!'

It looked like the same coffee Loz had vehemently refused earlier, but I needed a drink. I swigged it down like it was booze. I poured another and sat down with it, agitated.

'They? Who shot Jason?' She flopped to the settee, her breasts like bean bags resting on a sack of flour. 'It'll be Tony.' She sat up and reached for her purple tie-dye top and pulled it over her head.

'Moran?' I asked.

'Of course bloody Moran, who else is there, *thanks to you*?'

'*Me?*'

'Oh, Stacey, you know what I mean!'

'No, I don't. I didn't kill Tony Dale! Will didn't. Loz didn't. Marcus didn't. Stacey, one of your fucking whores, came over to fuck me – and I didn't fucking ask for it – and she stabbed him in the fucking neck!'

She waited. 'Better?'

'What's going on, Ally?'

She gave me a curious look, before answering, 'Tony's on the rampage. They've killed Aaron.'

'I bloody know they have! I saw! Both of him!'

'Both? He's everywhere. Did you see his cock?'

'What? No. I just saw his head by the federali block and a leg at the old Greek chippy.'

'His cock's on the clock outside Picks.'

'Christ.' I swigged the coffee off, put my head in my hands. 'Where's Marcus?'

'Gone.'

'Gone?' I panicked. 'I knew it!'

'I don't mean bloody dead, do I?' she laughed. 'What's wrong with you?'

'Gone where?'

'Off with one of the Prices. Or both of them.'

'Both of them? The Prices? That's who did him in last time.'

'There's been a lot of water under the bridge since then,' she smiled. 'They're as bent as old Percy and Jack.'

'The Prices?'

'Old Tory queers,' she laughed.

'Why are you laughing? Jason is lying in the road, dead presumably. Aaron Moran's head's on a stick. Not to mention what happened yesterday! Tony! *Ethan's dad.*'

'What am I supposed to do, eh?' she snapped. 'Cry? Beat my head against a wall, "oh why did it happen?"' she wailed, mocking.

'That would be a bit more human.'

She looked at me, shaking her head. I couldn't help but feel I'd done something terribly wrong.

'Where are you?' she asked.

'What do you mean?'

'What planet-?'

'Earth. Halesowen. Land of the anything-but-free.'

'And what are you doing about that?'

I started rubbing my legs irritated by the question, by the suggestion. I stood up. I sat down. 'I need another coffee.'

I went to the side table.

'I wouldn't, Tom,' she said.

'I don't care.'

I poured a cup and took a sip. It was room temperature, bitter and vile, but good for it, like a shot of grappa. I topped it up and sat down.

My head a stew of thoughts and conspiracies, as I sat there with Ally, it seemed the easiest thing to do was to trust her. But that didn't mean it was the right thing to do. Could I trust her?

'Do you remember,' I said, 'when, you know, we–'

'What? *Fucked*?' she said.

'How did you know that's what I was thinking?'

She laughed.

'What's so funny?' I asked, irritated.

'Why are you going on about that?'

'Did you ever tell anyone?'

'You mean Will? The "boys"?' she laughed. 'No, I never mentioned it. It was between us.'

'I wouldn't have cared,' I qualified.

'Did *you*?'

'Well, no.'

She laughed again. 'You'm a bloody odd-bod Tom. You rush in here to tell me Jason's been shot dead, have a go at me for not reacting in the way you think I should, and now you're asking me if I told anyone we'd had sex over 20 years ago?'

Why was she laughing? I wasn't laughing. I was deadly serious. How could she be so calm in the midst of this madness? Medication? Alcohol? 'Did you hear it? The gun?'

'I was in the middle of something,' she smirked.

'It's not funny. Poor Jase.'

She got up and poured herself a small glass of fruit wine on the side table. She drank it in one and then tossed me the lighter. She poured herself another and sipped it staring at the wall.

The scent of candles had faded, instead there was the piquant whiff of cider wine and the sweet, sweaty smell of fresh cum. Who knew who she'd just been with. Maybe Will popped down for a quickie – probably another secret. She looked old and grainy in this light, her brow furrowed, body huge, Shane Meadows real, This is Halesowen.

I moved around the room lighting the candles, small globes of orange light. I felt like I was setting up shop, an Elizabethan bordello, and soon the girls would turn up for work and the customers would trickle in and disappear into the various themed rooms to make their own little secrets.

'You know what *is* funny?' she said, still staring at the wall, 'I'm pregnant.'

'Fuck off!'

'Will's,' she answered.

'*Fuck right off.*'

She glanced over her shoulder and nodded, smiling.

Shit. What did this mean?

'Will's? How do you know? Does he know?'

'No. Only one I don't use a johnny with. I didn't tell you,' she warned, swigging off the wine.

'Should you be drinking?'

She cast a glance, *give me a break*, and flopped back down, covering most of the settee, like it was a throne. I got up to pour another coffee.

'I really wouldn't,' she said.

I poured and swigged. 'Where's Will?'

'With *her.*'

'Anita?'

'So much for sobriety,' she said. 'Drinking me out of house and home.'

'So, she was sober?'

'I told you.'

'I know-'

'But you thought I was lying?'

I don't know if it was the way she said it or the situation but I had the sudden urge to laugh. I squeaked a chortle.

'I did warn you,' she said.

I laughed.

'The coffee,' she tutted.

'What?' I laughed again, this time bent over with it like a school kid, high-pitched and nervy.

'You should probably get Will. You're gonna need his help.'

'What do you mean?' I laughed. 'Why can't I stop… laughing?'

I laughed for what felt like ten minutes until I started to feel panicked, until I started to feel like I couldn't breathe. Ally got up and walked out into the hall. 'Will,' she called up.

I pushed her out of the way and ran up the stairs. I swung open the door to the Ganesh. Will was smoking a joint with Anita.

'What does she want now?' he asked.

'Hello Tom,' Anita said.

'I drank the coffee! What's in the coffee!' I laughed. 'Hello,' I giggled. 'Hello, Anita.'

'Oh, the coffee!' he said, suddenly excited. 'Oh… the coffee,' he suddenly realised.

I was laughing but it wasn't funny. Nothing was funny. The situation, the world, the Sgt Pepper coloured room, my inability to control myself. 'Is it-is it acid?' I panicked.

'No, just some mushrooms. Tea.'

'Mushrooms! But it was coffee, I drank coffee. It wasn't tea.'

'Yeah, I put it in the coffee so Marcus would drink it.'

'Marcus!' I screeched, the blue-gold paisley vibrating on the wallpaper as if to forewarn me of what was to come.

'Yeah, he drank it,' he laughed.

'You cunt!'

'Tom, calm down, you're gonna have a bad trip.'

'A bad fucking trip! Marcus has gone off with…' I shouted, but then realised there were people everywhere, I could hear them twitching on their beds, clanging keys and chattering through the walls in a rollercoaster of pitch, buh-de-buh-de-buh-de-buh-de. 'With the Prices,' I whispered. 'He's with the Prices.'

'That's not good. It was very strong.'

'Very strong! I drank like four cups.'

'You shit! Is there any left?'

He got up, said a prayerful goodbye to the elephant in the room – the pink statue of Ganesh. He kissed Anita on the forehead, like he was off to work, and made for the stairs whilst pulling his top on.

'Where you going?' Anita shouted, annoyed. 'You coming back?'

She was sitting topless and I was stood there staring at her. 'What do I do? Coca-Cola? Orange juice? They never stopped it. Can I throw it up?'

'A bit late for that,' she said, swigging from a bottle of wine.

'Breasts,' I said. 'Shit, sorry, that just came out.'

'Bye Tom,' she said, flat.

'I haven't gone anywhere.'

She got up, covering her breasts and pushed me out of the door. The door closed and I was standing alone in the corridor, listening to the buh-de-buhs. The red tiles were the same red tiles of these blocks all those years ago, prettied with various rugs. There was a niggle that I hadn't actually gone anywhere since 2010, merely imagined it in an eternal hallucinatory second. But I knew it was a niggle, another promise of what was to come – it hadn't quite got that bad, yet. I went back downstairs and watched Will devouring the coffee.

He was necking a cup. 'Four,' he said. 'If you're having four I'm having–'

'Will,' I said, like a frightened child, 'I haven't had it in years.'

'Good point.' He poured the last of it into his cup and drank it. 'Nearly five. Come on. We better go home.'

We were standing in front of the living room wall, transfixed on a squashed mosquito which had dried to it. Every so often, Will would laugh briefly and gleefully which would start me off. I'd forgotten the euphoria. In truth, I had no recollection of it at all. This felt different, cleaner, as if somehow my decades-long battle with spirituality had all been for this moment.

'Bill Wilson took hallucinogens, you know,' I said.

'Did he?' Will asked, intrigued.

'To fight depression.'

'Yes, it's supposed to be good for that.'

He moved to touch the mosquito.

'Don't!'

'No, you're right,' he said.

We continued to look at it, its wings multiplying in rounds with my breathing. *I am breathing, aren't I?*

'I'm not breathing,' I panicked.

'You are,' he said. 'Also, remember: your heart hasn't stopped, you can't fly and you've not shit yourself.'

'Thank you,' I smiled. 'I forgot about that.'

He opened the back door.

'Where we going?'

'The Greek.'

'Why?'

'For answers.'

'Answers?'

'Answers.'

'What about the mosquito?' I asked with a tinge of sadness.

'He's moved on.'

I glanced up at Will and he looked so sincere I knew what he said meant more than I could conceive or needed to. I turned back and the mosquito flew off. I went to tell him, but I assumed he already knew and dutifully followed him outside.

'Who's Bill Wilson?' he asked.

'The founder of AA.'

'Oh, so you can take mushrooms? It's like part of the program?'

'I guess so.'

The flats swelled in tandem with the ether, a jelly, but we were part of the jelly. It was yellow and it was green but it was still night time and they were the same brown bricked blocks with deformed expressions, Pompei petrified. When we were looking at the mosquito it felt like our minds were the start point of a billowing hallucination and every so often a slip in our focus caused the hallucination to start again. Outside, I realised it was impossible for our minds to be the start point, because that would mean we were independent of it. If we were independent of it, we could be suffocated in the visual throb of the jellied ether or we could trample through it breaking its form, like a blunt knife parting a blancmange, but we were part of the jelly. It was us and we were it.

I glanced back and a wide beam of light shot out of Ground Zero and high into the sky. Inside the beam, ash twirled. 'Dad,' I said.

'Yes, son,' Will spoke, deep.

I gasped. He laughed.

'Bastard, I was connecting.'

We looked across to the graveyard. A light shone. It was moving fast and then it went out.

'Did you-?' I asked.

'That was real,' Will said.

We heard the sound of smacking, then the light turned on again and moved further up the graveyard. 'That's definitely not the 'shrooms,' I said.

'I just said that!'

'You just said that.'

'Stop it!' he nagged.

'Sorry.'

We moved more quickly towards the graveyard. Then the light went out again and we heard the same smacking sound.

'It's definitely real?' I asked.

We climbed over the sandstone wall with the energy of much younger men. I felt what should've been pain in my back but instead it was a sensation like somebody lifting me up by my shirt.

'It's definitely real, Tom. Do you have light?'

I fumbled in my pocket for the headtorch. Up ahead the light came on again, more towards the middle, near the Greek. 'There it is again,' I said. 'Are you thinking what I'm thinking?'

'Marcus.'

Shit. My stomach throbbed with the surroundings, face-burning, sweat glands expanding. I went to shout out "Marcus" but something stopped me and I didn't argue with it.

The light went out again, followed by another series of smacks. I got hold of my headtorch and tried to switch it on. 'You sure we're not tripping, Will? It wouldn't be the first time we've shared an hallucination.'

'It's real, Tom. I'm not as gone as you.' He was serious, clambering over headstones towards the light. 'This isn't the same as the fucking cop car.'

I shone my headtorch, looking around. 'Panda,' I yelled.

'Tomate-o, tomarto,' he said.

'No! *Panda.*'

The butcher looked up, 'the periphs.'

'What are you doing?' I asked.

He was astride Mel, his hand over her mouth, his fingers melting through her face. 'Mah, mah, mah,' she said, which seemed to translate to "I know your mother."

'I know, Mel,' I said.

'You what?' he menaced.

He got up and brushed the grass off burying Mel. I wanted so much to run but I was frozen to the spot. 'Will,' I called.

'Hurry up,' he said. 'I need the torch.'

'I can't.'

'The light,' he said. 'Marcus!'

I turned to see the light come on once more. It moved along, before sliding quickly downwards and disappearing into the earth.

'The Greek,' Will said.

'The panda!' I called back.

I turned back to the butcher but there was no one there.

'Where's Marcus?' I shouted.

From under the grass, Mel sat up, brushed herself off. 'He's gone to spend a penny.'

2028

A nerve pain needling, the left side of my head, I opened my eyes to the bright of an empty room. *What happened? Where is everyone?*

'Hel-' I coughed, a sore throat, caramel vinegar. 'Hel-loo?'

My face was cold outside the warmth of the quilt. I was lying on the settee in just my pants. When I moved it felt like I was wearing an iron coat, my whole body aching. I looked to mum's Moroccan rug and noticed a big damp patch where someone had clearly tried to clean up my sick. On the wall, the dogs playing snooker were at an angle, but elsewhere it was clean. There were no cans or bottles.

I remembered arrogantly telling them all about my quest to surrender the booze. I cringed, covering my face to hide from it.

'Anyone in the house?' I called.

Nothing. Outside, the storm had stopped, not even a breeze. There was an eerie stillness which removed me from everything and everyone. I had the feeling that everybody had left Halesowen and I was now fated to spend the rest of my life alone in some kind of purgatory.

My nose was clogged and I could smell smoke as if someone was smoking at the far end of the settee, but there was no one. Clearly I was having olfactory hallucinations. It wouldn't be the first time. I used to think it was the sign of a stroke but, after many Google searches, it seemed it was probably a sinus infection. Right now, it felt like spiritual punishment, condemned to fires of hell. I envisaged some half-man/half-beast, car-sized feet traipsing around town looking for me in an eternal game of hide and seek.

'Anybody?' I called.

I relived the pained expression on poor Maureen's face as I recounted the story of the "retard" killing Jan a mallet. What had I done? I was clearly high on ego, certain I was the hero in our little drama, the writer, director and actor in my self-conceived show. How would I ever keep my wild ego in check in Halesowen? No sponsor, no AA, my love long gone – she was always quick to point it out, with a look or a laugh, when I was ranting and raving about my undiscovered talents as a writer, or unrecognised leadership skills in the workplace. *Maybe I should get the last bus. What day is it? Maybe I've missed it?*

I sat up looking for my phone but the smell of burning distracted me. *It's not actual burning, is it?* All but naked, I walked into the kitchen. In the sink, there'd been some kind of fire – I wasn't hallucinating. I moved closer and there on top of the burning pile was a damp edge of the Yellow Pages note. I could just about make out the "t" off the end of my vanished words, "I'm really sorry, mum, I can't help it."

I leant against the counter, sick and swimmy.

'Sarah.' She was the only one wild enough to burn my things. Underneath it were the soggy ashes of burnt pages and photographs from a fire someone had clearly tried to put out. I picked up the pages of my old writing, things I'd written as a child, all gone; the blackened photos were mostly old family ones, they broke up when I looked through them. That little note my mum had kept meant more than any of it. I went to the window and looked into the garden. Leaves and branches, the clothes line wrapped around a tree, and a cylinder of bird seed stuck in the mud of her final resting place. The storm had proffered a vision of mum's grave as if it had been left unattended for years. I immediately put some flip flops on and went into the garden with a broom.

The sun was shining but it felt like autumn. The grass squelching, I was still in my pants but somehow the cold was refreshing and the effort of sweeping the leaves and moving the debris seemed to stretch out the pains in my body, my arm sore and red with infection. *Mum. She had such a simple life and didn't ask for much.*

'Mum,' I said out loud, and the word felt funny, somehow distant and incomprehensible, a sound, a mum-ble.

So much had gone on since she'd died, I hadn't thought much about her. *Died. Mum.*

'Mum's dead.' As I said the words it felt alien and new, like it was supposed to feel, how it felt when my grandparents died when I was young, when grief and the idea of never seeing a person again was a new concept to me. When dad had died, I was drunk, trying not to be, but mostly consumed in the battle of addiction. How do these things ever resolve themselves? I could feel my son – *my son* – and my wife – *my wife* – knocking at my self-built wall, but I just couldn't let them in.

I started to cry, at first gently, but quickly losing control until I was struggling to breathe. I threw the broom down. 'Why did she have to burn the note?'

I pictured my mum holding open her empty purse, that last tenner burning a hole in my pocket. 'What couldn't you help, Tom, you twat? Stealing? Drinking? Lying?'

I couldn't help hurting you, mum. 'I wanted to drink, I wanted to steal,' I cried, 'and lying was just part of that. I never wanted to hurt you.'

I heard the back door open. I turned immediately, shocked and embarrassed. It was Maureen rushing towards me with a dressing gown. 'What are you doing half naked, you silly man? No wonder you keep having these funny turns. You're not a youngster anymore.' She lifted the dressing gown over my shoulders.

This made me even more emotional. 'Maureen… you're here… Where is everyone?'

'I had to go and fill the black bags.'

'But you came back,' I cried.

'It's a good job. You'll make yourself ill.'

'Maureen. It was *years*.'

She grabbed both of my hands, the cold, bony fingers of my old teacher, weakened by a long life lived.

'A whole decade of it,' I continued, 'after I wrote the note which promised, I don't know, some kind of redemption.'

'This is redemption,' she said, squeezing my hands. 'You. The person you are now. The one who wants to help people.'

'Only to help myself.'

'What difference does that make?'

'When I lived with dad, I'd only visit her once a week or when I thought she might lend me money. Every Thursday at 11 and already I'd be stinking of cider.'

She tutted and let go of my hands. 'You can spend a lifetime thinking like that, dwelling in misery, but where will it get you?'

She picked up the broom. 'Do it up-'

'What? Oh,' I wrapped the dressing gown around me.

'Finish what you were doing,' she insisted. 'Grief has a way of dictating how we deal with it. This seems like a good start.'

She handed me the broom and went to walk inside.

'I'm sorry, Maureen, about-'

'You… weren't well,' she said. 'Sweep.'

———————

'Why did she do it?' I asked, my hands warming around a hot cup of coffee.

We were standing in the kitchen, unsure what to do about the stinking mess in the sink.

'Anger, bitterness. That's what she's like, Tom. She kept saying it's just stuff. Your friend, the one obsessed with Prince Phillip-'

I nodded apologetically, 'Will.'

She raised her eyebrows. 'He was trying his best to stop her and in the end he managed to drag her out of the house.'

'Where did they go?'

She shrugged.

There was a niggle inside telling me they were all just on a bender and it irritated me. Here I was, dealing with my grief and they'd probably gone to save the booze. *After all I've done to help… Stop it!*

'It is just stuff,' I made myself say.

'*Tom*. That's not just "stuff". It was your family photographs.'

'But what does it matter now?'

'She's drinking again, of course – didn't last long. God knows what else she's on.'

'I'm not bothered about the photographs, maybe I should be, but the note… I can't explain it.'

I could. I just wasn't sure it made much sense. It was my first honest piece of writing and mum had kept it. It was like a kid's first picture magneted to the fridge, and mum just wasn't the sort for that.

'You don't have to explain it. It meant something to you, that's enough.'

'When I found that note in her purse, I could feel my mum's presence. I could see her.'

She smiled.

'Her face full of anguish.' I stopped, felt it. 'I can remember feeling there was no way out of it. I'd stolen her last tenner, there was no denying it, no pretending she might be mistaken.'

'I can't lie,' Maureen said. 'I probably would've felt the same. But you had a choice.'

'I could've run away with the tenner and got drunk.'

'But you didn't, you gave it back.'

I found myself shaking my head, because it wasn't about that. Encompassed in those few words, "I'm really sorry, mum, I can't help it", was the battle I spent the next decade fighting. Did mum see that too? I doubted it, but it didn't matter. She kept it. She might not have been great at showing it, but she loved me and I always knew that. Perhaps that's why I was one of the lucky ones who managed to stay sober. Whatever I thought about myself, I was still loveable to somebody. Sarah had that too.

'I don't believe Sarah wanted to do it,' I said. 'She couldn't help it.'

Maureen shook her head, clearly disappointed.

'I know what you're thinking, Maureen.'

'Do you?' she scoffed.

I assumed she was thinking here's a silly man infatuated by a young woman. I hoped not, but it made sense. Or maybe she just thought I was too nice for my own good. But I just couldn't believe Sarah, deep down, would want to burn those pictures and the note. Sure, she'd had a difficult childhood, but she'd also been brought up with the love of a grandmother – in that, there was hope.

There was an awkward silence. Maureen went to pick up the burnt mess in the sink, but stopped herself. 'It was his son.'

'What was?' I asked.

'If those animals are telling the truth, it was Jan's son.' It was matter-of-fact.

'His *son*?'

'He has a learning disability.'

'Who *killed* him?' I covered my face, emotionally spent and unable to react like a normal human being.

'And you… rewarded them, Tom-'

'It wasn't a-'

'Let me finish. That's why I was angry at you.'

'Giving booze to an addict isn't a reward,' I defended.

She just looked at me. We both knew I'd said the wrong thing.

I sipped my coffee to hide my face.

'We'll probably never know what really happened,' she said. 'John won't be able to tell us, not fully and certainly not in any detail.'

'Is he severely disabled?'

'He's quite capable, but his emotional intelligence is lower than say yours and mine.'

'Would he be able to… with a mallet… do it?'

Maureen looked away, reached into the sink and picked up the black mass of my writing and photos. 'Shall I throw this away?'

I nodded, absent. I wanted to ask her if she was alright, but I could see she wasn't. She started scooping the soggy remnants of my life into a plastic bag, getting on with it, forgetting perhaps. I felt somewhat detached from the reality of it from her point of view. I didn't know Jan, I didn't know his son. I kept thinking about Jackson and how sick he must've been to do such a thing. I was sure his overdose wasn't accidental. It was too much of a coincidence. I relived the gunshot, the rabbit dropped, Jackson's lad dead. One moment of madness, and Will was broken by it, Sarah was already broken and this just made things worse. We were all broken and I just wanted to fix us. But there was no fix. There was just living with yourself and taking it a day at a time. I learnt that in rehab and Sarah was going to have to learn it too, if she really wanted to get clean.

Maureen scrubbed at the carbon stains on the sink. She didn't have a clue about addiction. She understood the damage and pain an addict can cause, but not the pain that was being masked.

'When I was in rehab they chucked a guy out once after they caught him kissing one of the girls.'

She stopped cleaning. 'Is this about Sarah?'

'It was on New Year's Eve of all days. They sent him off in a taxi. But they didn't chuck her out. Just him.'

She looked confused.

'We didn't want either of them to leave. It's was just a kiss, that's all.'

'I expect they had their reasons.'

'They just told us it was against the rules and that they were doing it for the greater good. We couldn't understand it. It seemed so cruel, especially on New Year.'

She continued scrubbing, 'what's the moral of this?'

'The last time I saw him, not so many years ago, was in an AA meeting in Weston-Super-Mare. He was trying to get sober again and seemed pretty well.'

'Look, Tom, you're a good man-' she said.

'But I never saw her again,' I continued. 'Jess her name was. She finished treatment, was given the obligatory keyring and Big Book,' I laughed. 'We were Facebook friends. I saw the relationships, the bad boys, which always looked like dubious choices. One day I realised she hadn't posted in a while, so I went to her profile. Turned out she'd died of an overdose.'

She put the scourer down and looked at me. 'That's truly sad, Tom. But what's this really all about-?'

'I suppose they thought they were protecting the one who had the best chance of making it, but you can just never tell. People change. People die.'

'She's already got your friend wrapped around her little finger. I see the way you look at her, Tom-'

'It doesn't matter.'

'Doesn't it?'

'I'm not perfect, Maureen,' I insisted. 'But I'll always try to do the right thing.'

'I'm sure you will. But sometimes even our best intentions are not enough-'

'I'll look after her.'

She laughed. 'I'm not worried about *her*.' She squeezed my hand. 'Go and get dressed. I need your help.'

———————

I heard the front door open and made my way downstairs, hoping it was Sarah.

'Tom, you're ok,' Barb said, sounding relieved. 'They said you were at death's door.'

Maureen let them in, introduced herself and went into the kitchen to make drinks.

'I'm absolutely fine, Barb. Nervous exhaustion, I think. The storm, maybe.' I glanced down at my arm, bandaged tight by Maureen.

'You shouldn't have done that, boy,' Rex said.

Barb came through and sat on the edge of the settee, her hands in her lap. Rex sank deep into it, crossing his bony legs.

'Maybe you're right, Rex. I thought I was doing the right thing.'

'You've made us look a right pair,' Barb said. 'Lee wasn't happy at all.'

'What are they doing about it?' I asked.

'None of ours or your business,' Rex said, adamant and drunk.

'I suppose not,' I smiled. I couldn't help but think this was going to end badly. Perhaps Jake would steer them in the right direction.

'I see the old place hasn't changed much, has it?' Barb said, looking around the room. 'I can remember you crawling across this floor as a little baby. Bless, still got the picture of the dogs too – I do like… I've always liked the dogs.' She sounded emotional.

'Where is the dog?' I asked.

'Ben?' a sad smile.

I nodded, enquiring.

The smile fell from Barb's face. I glanced at Rex who was shaking his head.

'I didn't want to say,' she said. 'With your mum-'

'The animal is dead, boy,' Rex confirmed.

'*Rex*!' Barb cursed. 'Yes, Tom, I'm afraid it's true. It's been a really difficult time. I did love that dog, and your mum-'

'*Ben*,' Rex said.

'*Pat*,' Barb corrected. 'Oh, no, silly me… no, Pat and Ben,' she turned to Rex and squeezed his hand. 'You see, it does bother him.'

'What happened to Ben?'

'Old age,' she said.

'It happens to us all,' Rex added.

'He just didn't wake up. Hopefully we all pass away as peacefully as he did.'

I sat down, aware I was in the armchair mum fell asleep in for the last time. Barb was nervously smiling, hands in lap. Rex put his hands behind his head and looked like he owned the place. I felt an encroaching loneliness, a cloud, an invisible knot in my gut, digging in.

'You know what dog is backwards, boy?' Rex suddenly spouted, pulling me out of it.

'What? Oh,' I nodded. 'Yes, Rex' – I couldn't disguise my irritation with it.

'Leave him alone,' Barb said.

'Ha,' he scoffed, restlessly bouncing his leg. '"God is missing at the altar where I'm the victim",' he almost sang, reciting a poem or lyric.

Maureen walked in. 'That sounds familiar.' She handed them coffee. 'Is it Nerval?'

Rex immediately uncrossed his legs and sat forward, 'why yes, it is. Or Tom-' he laughed to himself.

'I saw an opera about his life-' Maureen smiled.

'*Or Tom*?' I asked, defensive. 'What does that even mean, Rex?'

'What does it mean?' he asked himself. 'Does it mean the übermensch are coming?' he asked Maureen, laughing.

She shrugged.

'"What is ape to the man, no?"' he pressed, clearly off on his own thought-track.

Maureen looked over at me without giving anything away – I was sure she thought he was barmy.

'Don't listen to him,' Barb said. 'You sound like a bloody mental patient.' She slapped his thigh, giggling out of embarrassment, before catching herself, 'oops, no offence, Tom.'

I laughed – it had only been 20 years, although I was fully aware I still had all the hallmarks.

'You know what I mean,' she waved off, like I was teasing her. 'Your electric works then.'

'Came back on this morning,' Maureen said, hands clasped, standing awkward.

'No one then? Ape to the man?' Rex asked, like we were all still listening to him. '"It's just what man is to the superman!" The ape? Yes? Now, how did it go?' he asked Maureen, but she didn't know what he was on about. None of us did.

'Stop it, Rex,' Barb said out of the corner of her mouth.

This seemed to inspire defiance and he stood up and boomed in Welsh grandiosity, '"he turned to those waiting for him downstairs, dreaming of being kings, but",' there was a pause for dramatic effect and, with a waft of wine, directed towards me, he continued: '"they were lost in the sleep of beasts… boy… shouting God does not exist."' Rex stopped and waited – for applause perhaps. 'Yes?' he asked Maureen.

I had no idea what he was referring to. The superman? Nietzsche maybe? Bowie perhaps? I'd never heard of this Nerval fella. Even so, Rex had somehow managed to make me feel like I was the devil incarnate.

'That was Nerval, right?' he prompted Maureen.

'I don't… I really don't remember,' she said. 'The opera was called Missing at the Altar – the Madness of Gerard de Nerval. It was written by a student at the Royal Conservatoire,' she smiled, awkwardly.

'Leave her alone,' Barb said.

'Interesting synchronicity, nevertheless, don't you think.' He fell back into the settee. 'There's nothing more to us than God, boy.'

'I prefer the animal stuff,' I said, deadpan.

'What?' he shot. 'What, boy?'

I reached for my phone, which was charging at the wall. 'Excuse me a sec, I've gotta make a call.'

I went into the kitchen and turned my phone on. I had a message from Loz. "Where are you? Need to figure out goodbye drinks (coffee!!!)."

I went out into the garden and rang him.

'Where've you been?' he asked. 'I've been trying to-'

'Hurry up,' I heard Jen shout. 'we've gotta go round mum's.'

'I'm talking to Tom… no… yes… of course. Christ, give me two minutes for the love of God! You there, Tom?'

'Yeah, I'm here.' I was pacing up and down the garden. 'I'm thinking of coming with you,' I said.

'Shut up!' He didn't believe me.

'I don't know. I don't know what's gonna happen here. You've missed it all. The town's gone crazy.'

'I heard about Gary Bennett.'

'That's just one! You went home at just the right time.'

'I had to. It was hard enough listening to Will harp on, but then you stabbed me in the frigging arm with a fork. It still hurts.'

'I didn't mean to-'

'And the brook bird had a gun! What's that about? Come with us, Tom. What would you be staying for?'

I knew the answer to that and I knew he wouldn't really understand it. I didn't really understand it. It was an instinct, a calling.

'But then, what would I be leaving for?'

'Let me think,' sardonic, 'your health, your sanity, a better life. A new life, Tom,' he tutted and sighed. 'She wouldn't want-'

'I can't even say her name.' I felt a gulp of emotion rolling in my throat, found myself manically stamping the edges of mum's grave, where the rain had turned the mud a little swampy.

'Lucy,' he said. 'Her name's Lucy.'

I heard her name out loud for the first time in months and it made me feel physically sick. If only I'd headed straight to Burnham I could've died with them. 'Do you believe in God?'

'*What*?' He sounded a bit taken aback. 'I don't know, Tom… Why?' he asked cautiously.

'Do you think things happen for a reason? People come into our lives-?' I looked over at the house and Sarah was staring at me from the kitchen window.

'Yeah, I guess.'

I laughed and looked up to the skies.

'What?'

'Maybe I'm supposed to be here.'

There was silence on the other end of the phone.

'Hurry up!' Jen shouted.

'Just fuck off, woman!'

I heard her yelling something at him.

'I'm sorry, Jen, I shouldn't have said… I'm sorry, but Tom needs a friend-'

'I'm alright, Loz. I'm just thinking out loud.'

'You don't sound alright.'

I looked back to the kitchen. Sarah wasn't there.

'Go sort your shit and we'll chat in a bit.'

'Promise?'

'Of course.'

I ran into the house, through the kitchen and into the living room.

'"God is not! God is no more! But they were still asleep!"' Rex performed from the edge of the settee.

'I honestly don't remember all the words,' Maureen said. 'I remember a violinist dropped their bow-'

'So?' I asked, manic. 'Where is she?'

'Who?' Maureen said.

'Sarah.'

'She went off with the tall one, I told you.'

'But-' My head felt instantly swimmy. *Don't you dare, Tom.* I leant in the kitchen doorway.

'Are you alright?' Barb asked.

A vision?

'Yes, I'm fine… I… um… just need to find her,' I said.

Could I have imagined it? Sarah had been standing in the window, clear as day, her hair a mess from a rough day drinking. *A brain tumour? No, don't be daft!* Earlier, I'd thought I was having olfactory hallucinations but the smell had been real. I was certain it was a vision. *Has she died? Perhaps she came to me at the moment of her passing.*

'Tom?' Maureen said.

'Yeah?'

'Are you ok? You zoned out a bit.'

'Just thinking. I have to find her-them, all of them.'

'You need some rest,' Barb said.

I went into the kitchen and put my shoes on. 'Maureen, you need my help?'

'At Jan's,' she said.

'Let's make a move. Not a lot of time left.'

Maureen fetched the cups and brought them into the kitchen. She grabbed my arm. 'Why don't you come?'

'The bus? Maybe. I need to find everyone first.'

When I made my way back into the living room, Barb was standing awkwardly, clearly she wanted to ask something. 'Tom,' tears in her eyes.

'My mum?'

'We did used to be very good friends. I want to pay my last respects.'

'In the garden.'

'"The earth is intoxicated by this precious blood."' Rex said, standing up.

'Oh, stay here!' Barb yelled, losing her temper.

'Um, yes, um,' he bumbled. 'Of course, love.' He looked at me and held his hand out. 'I'm sorry, boy. She loved your mum.'

I watched her go into the garden and stand by mum's grave, suddenly she was a little old lady in grief. She knelt down on the wet grass, juddering with emotion. Was it mum? Or Ben the dog? Or even the reality of our situation? Perhaps it was all the same.

'"What is this new God that is imposed on the earth?"' Rex asked, over my shoulder.

'God only knows,' I said.

'That's Nerval,' he said. 'Le Christ aux Oliviers'

She'd asked for my help in such a casual way, I'd assumed I was moving bags and furniture, instead I finished digging my third grave in two weeks and headed back inside to fetch Jan's body.

'I wish you'd told me sooner, Maureen. I feel so bad he was left like this.'

'You had your own problems, Tom. Besides, he wasn't going anywhere. I'll grab his feet.'

He'd been covered but his head had been so badly caved in the sheet couldn't hide it. As I went to lift his shoulders, I felt something damp and gritty on the floor which I assumed was part of his head that had come away. That, combined with the sweet smell of rot, had me doing all in my power not to gag.

We put the body on the grass by the grave. I wondered how many other people had endured these problems in the last few weeks. If not in Halesowen, in all the other towns where people were refusing to leave their homes. Was there a mass epidemic in the UK of violence inspired by, or at least aided by, drink and drugs consumed to deal with this crisis? Halesowen was certainly not the only town in the UK where drink and drugs were such a prominent means of escape.

'He's been here,' she said.

'Who?'

'His son.'

'How do you know?'

She walked over to the greenhouse. The windows were smashed, plants on the floor – I assumed it was due to the storm. She pulled the door back. 'All the tomatoes have gone.'

I followed her. 'He's taken them?'

'They did them together. John comes over a couple of times a week.'

'Why's he taken them?'

'They were red. It's the right time for it.'

I had so many questions, but it didn't feel like my place to ask. I went back over to the grave, climbed in and started pulling the body towards me.

'I'm going to fill the black bags,' Maureen said, sounding sad.

'Why's everyone filling black bags?'

'That's what they've told us to do.'

'Who?'

'The government, on the TV.'

'But so many of these bags got washed away in the storms?'

'I don't suppose it matters.'

'So why do it?'

'What else am I supposed to do?' she said, slightly irritated.

I smiled, 'no, of course. Is that why you're leaving?'

'Why?'

'Because that's what they've told us to do?'

'What are you trying to say, Tom?' she argued.

'I'm not… nothing. I was just wondering.'

'You sound like your nutty friend.' She went to walk inside, and then turned around and marched over to me. 'What are you doing, Tom?'

'What do you mean?' I climbed out of the grave and grabbed the spade.

'Who are these people? Stoners and drunks? Who was that old man? Raving on about God like he was religious, clearly pissed out of his mind?'

I nearly laughed. It was strange hearing my old teacher swear. I felt about 12.

'Just Halesowen people.'

'What does that mean? I'm from Halesowen. You're from Halesowen. They're nutcases. That preacher chap, Lee, is it? He's not right in the head. Came out of the toilet with a smear of powder on his nose. They must think I'm stupid. They're just druggies, the lot of them.'

I was kicking soil into the grave. 'They're messed up, I know. But there's a lot of it about.'

'If you stay here, what hope do you have? You'll be back on the booze and whatever else it was you were on.'

'I didn't take crack or smack,' I pathetically responded. 'I mean, I tried it, but it wasn't really my-'

'Tom, grow up!' She shook her head and stormed off inside.

I looked to Jan's body, thought about my mum, Gary Bennett, Baz and Jackson. All dead. Were more about to die in a battle for booze and jewellery? Jimmy and the other two, they were just boys, children, caught up in addiction, the town sickness. They were much younger than I was before I gave it all up. There was another world out there for them if they could get free from drugs. I wasn't just there to help Sarah. I needed to help them too. Perhaps Jake would help.

I shovelled mud onto the poor man's body. What a way to die, killed by your own son. I thought about my dad. I remembered that day when he collapsed. I was drinking but I wasn't drunk. A few hours before he died he'd told me he didn't feel right. He was in a grave mood but I ignored it because I'd heard it so many times.

Maureen came back outside holding letters. 'Are you definitely staying?'

'I need to find them all to see if they're alright.'

She laughed, bitterly. 'They'll be fine. They'll be drunk. You know that, I don't need to tell you.'

She handed over two letters. One was addressed to Sarah and the other to me.

'Don't open it yet,' she said. 'Not until after we've said goodbye.'

'What about Sarah? Wouldn't it be good for her to read it before you leave?'

'Not until she's completely off whatever she's on. Read the letter.'

'Maureen-'

'This is it Tom, after you're done. I won't see her now. Or you. I really don't want to.'

'Obviously we'll say goodbye at the bus.'

She sighed and smiled, before walking back inside.

———————

The house was dark and quiet. I clicked a light switch.

'Ooh,' Maureen jumped, nothing came on. 'Scared me half to death. There's no electric, Tom. It's probably just tripped, but I don't know where they are.'

'I can look,' I said.

'No sense. I'm leaving shortly.'

I pointed to a picture on the wall. 'Is this him?'

Maureen came over. 'That's Jan and that's his first wife, Alina. Over here, this is Margaret. That's John's mum.'

'Is that John?'

'Yes, planting tomatoes with his dad.'

'I've definitely seen him about.'

'He gets the bus on his own. Or he used to. He liked riding buses. They all knew him.'

'Will he get the last bus, do you think?'

'I don't know. It's not my problem.'

'Which bus are you getting, Maureen?'

'Tom,' she squeezed my hand. 'It's so strange to bump into you after all these years.' She led me to the front door. 'Please take care of yourself.'

I knew there was nothing I could say. I stood at the front door wanting to say something, 'I didn't steal that lollipop,' came out.

'I beg your pardon,' she said.

'You once accused me of stealing a lollipop off Zoe Hackett.'

She laughed. 'It was an orange, wasn't it?'

It came flooding back to me. 'It was! It wasn't a lollipop, it was an orange. God, you remember?'

She nodded.

'I didn't steal it! Why would I steal an orange?'

'But you would've stolen a lollipop?'

'Oh, yeah, totally.'

She laughed.

'But then I'd have given it back.'

'You probably would, Tom Hanson.'

We said our goodbyes. I walked up Hambleton Road and back onto the hill of Portsdown. I didn't realise just how many people were still here, but there were a number of black bags lining the street, like flags conforming, informing each other of who was leaving.

The sun dropped off the horizon and a red glow shone over Halesowen. It would be a sunny day tomorrow, but the future was perhaps less promising. I sat on a wall and opened the letter.

Dear Tom,

Firstly, I have to say – and I know I don't always show it – Sarah is a special girl and I love her more than I could possibly tell her or she could hear. She will always be my granddaughter. I know you think you know her, but your tales of stealing money off your mum are child's play in comparison to the things she's done. I forgive her for everything, but I won't do it to myself anymore. I thought perhaps the despicable act of burning your photos and writings might've been enough to show you what she's like but you seem hell bent on discovering the extent of it for yourself.

I am not without hope. Alas, my hope in her redemption through the church was dashed upon meeting the strange man at the helm – the blind leading the blind. But perhaps, and I mean no pressure here, you will be the person to help her out of this pattern of self-destruction, by whatever means necessary.

I'm not a total fool, Tom. You might be thinking that old teach doesn't know what she's talking about. When I first met you after all these years, I was certain you were on drugs. How wrong I was. I can only apologise. Of course, you didn't let me in on everything, did you? I know what it's like to lose a child and spouse…

I stopped reading, my heart thudding against my chest wall. It wasn't only that she'd found me out, it was seeing those words on the page, "lose a child and spouse." I had a lost a child and a spouse. Lost them. I got off the wall and sat on the pavement, my head in my hands. The sound of scraping gravel made me look up.

'Tom?' Sarah said.

'What are you doing here?' I rubbed tears from my eyes, half-wondering if this was another vision, the night darkening around us.

'I was coming to find you.' She sat down next to me and put her head on my shoulder – I could smell lager, wine, the sweet stench of metabolised booze. 'What you reading?'

I quickly folded the letter up and put it in my pocket. 'It doesn't matter.'

'Is it from her?'

'Who?' I asked, suspiciously.

'Your wife.'

'My wife?'

There was silence.

'I'm sorry, Tom,' she said. 'Will told me. Why don't you talk about her?'

I didn't respond. I didn't know how to. I felt hot with emotion, thankful the sky was getting darker to hide my face. Eventually, 'why don't you talk about your mum?' came out, sharp, and it felt mean, a low blow, a distraction. I cursed myself for it.

'Mum?' she asked, lifting her head from my shoulder. 'I don't know.' She knew why I'd said it, she knew I was hitting back at her because she'd dared to mention my wife. 'I don't think about her so much.'

'I'm sorry,' I said.

'I know. Me too.' She reached into a pocket and pulled out a small article of some kind and handed it to me.

It was a drug baggy with black stuff inside. I opened it up and smelt it. 'Ash?'

'No one could stop me, Tom,' she said, squeezing my arm. 'I was so angry you'd given the stuff away. Baz was killed and it all felt like it was over nothing.'

'It's ok.'

'It's not ok. Those pictures were like decades old, before-computers-old.'

'Not quite.'

'I know it doesn't bring it back and it's not even from the actual stuff, but I didn't know what else I could do. I'm such a fucking waste of life!'

There was a real stillness in the air. The sky was cool, her body warm against me. 'No, Sarah, it's nice.' I felt protective of her. 'In fact, it's better than that stuff. None of it matters, Sarah. Not really.'

'I was so angry. I just couldn't help it.'

'You know-' I stopped myself. I was going to talk about the Yellow Pages apology which seemed to map out my life.

'Yeah?' she asked.

'Doesn't matter.'
'What was her name, Tom?'
It's just a word. Her name is just a word. 'Lucy.'

2032

I kept my head down in Llangollen. After my time in Halesowen, the UK still felt a little alien to me. It wasn't too busy, but everyday life buzzed about me, or behind walls and glass, people walking dogs, the odd cyclist whizzing by. It was hard to face it, to trust it. On the ground, the same black circles we'd seen in Shrewsbury, sensors, cameras, solar panels, who really knew? The slow and menacing blades of small red turbines poking above and behind most of the shops and houses.

'Oi, careful!' someone called out.

I looked up and saw the pole just in time, a Wales Welcomes You flag, narrowly missing it. It was the same image that was in the corner of every window.

'See where you're going, mate,' he said, smiling.

'Yeah,' I said, out of sync with him, with it all.

It was quieter the other side of Llangollen and I felt better about things. Once I'd passed the You Are Leaving a Car Free Town sign there was no one, just old roads, dead roads I'd driven down many times en route to Snowdonia for a mountain trek. It was a relief crossing onto the fields at Froncysyllte. The roads made me feel lonely, reminding me of everything that had been in my relatively minute timeline. But, crossing into the sun-creamed fields, I felt a part of everything again, a cog in the machine, atoms vibrating in the big tapestry. It made me think of everything that is and ever was.

I crossed the aqueduct, the sloppy canal in a bracing breeze, alone and warm in my down jacket. I thought about the night I spent in the cottage with Helen. It wasn't meaningless, but we made love, awkward and sober, and I woke up snug in her bed, awkward and sober. I went back to my tent the following night and it wasn't awkward, but I was sober. I started to write it all down, everything that had happened, but I didn't know how I could end it. Had I slept with Helen as an ending? It seemed to be a sort of ending for the protagonist, me. A change had taken place. It was as if somehow I'd finally come to terms with Lucy no longer being in my life. But it wasn't just about grief and death, was it?

I wrote a different ending in my tent.

I pulled out my glittery notebook, sat down on a wall and read it.

I made my way up the A5 to Betws y Coed. It was early, sun cresting over the mountains behind. The small village was unchanged. There was still a Cotswold Outdoor, a Hawkshead, the little Spar and the Stables Bar where I ate gammon with Will the night before we scrambled over Crib Goch all those years ago. It was the only place I'd been to which hadn't changed at all, which didn't seem to be affected by the bombs or time. I walked past the village and by the side of the road there was a drunk, swaying and muttering incomprehensibly, perhaps he was speaking in Welsh.

'You ok?' I asked.

'Fucking brill,' he said, sarcastic.

'I know the feeling,' I smiled. His head swirling, one eye closed as he tried to focus. I sympathetically patted him on the shoulder. 'I've been there,' I added.

'Yeah?' he asked.

I was fully aware that I might be misreading this situation. He might've just been out for his birthday or on a stag do and not found his way back to his mates, but I just had a feeling he was one of us, one of me.

'I'm going up Tryfan,' I said.

'Yeah?' he asked, uninterested.

'Yeah.'

'Yeah?' he asked, just saying words.

'You should come.'

'Tryfan? … Ok.'

That was easy.

He followed me, tripping up and falling into the road. Tryfan wasn't just a hike in the hills. We would have to climb up over rocks. It was a little dangerous, but then swaying into the roads without anyone to help you was even more risky. I could help him up the mountain one step at a time.

'Why… the mountain?' he asked.

'Sometimes it helps to get perspective. I used to climb mountains all the time. It helped me sober up.'

'Egg,' he said.

'What?'

'Raw egg. My grandad used to crack two eggs and stir in some Worcester sauce.'

'I don't mean it quite so literally.'

'Urgh,' he heaved. 'Just the thought of it.'

He clearly wasn't hearing me, but it didn't really matter, as long as I was hearing me. If he heard it was a bonus.

After an hour or so of walking we made it to the gate at the north face of Tryfan. It was cold and sunny, a mist of dew an inch off the ground.

'I don't wanna go up,' he said.

'I know, but I don't want to go up on my own.'

'I don't even know you. Besides,' he stumbled sideways a few steps, steadied himself on the wall, 'I'm not gonna make it up there, look at the state of me.'

His shirt was mostly open, he'd lost a button half way down. His hair was long and sticking up to the left, like a tree on a hill, petrified by the wind.

'I'll help you.'

'I don't want your help,' he said, defensive.

Here we go again. I looked to the winding path which mostly disguised the rock face I was going to have to climb.

'Are you going to be alright?' I asked.

'I'll be fine. Don't you worry about me!'

I looked into his angry eyes and sensed the sadness underneath, but maybe that was just me. 'Ok, I get it. I've been there. You take care.' I shook his trembling hand and went through the gate.

The first part was just a steep muddy path, some grassy sections, stepping up over the rocks. When I came to the top of it, I looked to my right and saw the north face of Tryfan, a huge cracked egg of rock. It looked insurmountable. But I carried on towards it and came to a plateau of rocks. I looked ahead of me and, lying on the ground, like a siren washed up on a rock, was a woman. I moved quickly towards her, drawn to it, but also fearing the worst.

'Are you ok?'

'I'm fine.'

She wasn't.

'Really?'

'Yeah, Fucked up, Insecure, Neurotic and Emotional.'

I was stunned. Who was this random woman, attractive, but clearly struggling at the foot of the north face. 'Rehab?'

'They tried to make me go,' she sang, then burst out laughing.

'What are you doing here?'

'What do you think I'm bloody doing here?' I caught a wave of whisky which enticed and disappointed me at the same time.

'Tryfan?' I asked in disbelief.

'Of course,' she said. 'But I can't do it.'

'I feel the same, but I'm gonna.'

'Why?'

It was a good question. Why didn't I just mill about at the bottom with the normal folk? 'I want to get a better perspective on things in the wake of the bombs.'

She held her hand out. I yanked her up and she fell into my arms. She looked into my eyes and I knew what she was thinking. 'This isn't about that,' I said.

'About what?' Then she realised what I meant. 'Why do men always think I want to-'

'No, I mean,' I was embarrassed. 'I'm sorry.'

'It's ok,' she said confidently. 'Just help me get up this mountain.'

We clambered on in silence. I felt like a fool. Even after everything I'd been through, my mind had jumped to the wrong conclusion. I tried to forget about it. Besides, she needed my help.

Behind us and below, the path was misting over with a low fog. Ahead of us, the craggy limestone of the rockface, seemingly impenetrable from here. But I'd read all about it. It was best to ascend the mountain from the left side. The right side was more risky. As we came up close, I could see a rock we could climb up which kept us firmly on the centre-left.

'There seems be a route here.' I put my hands on the rock ready to pull myself up.

'I don't know,' she ummed. 'This rock looks easier.'

'Ok, I can see your point,' I reasoned, 'but we need to think ahead. I've read up on it. That path could veer to the right which is more dangerous.'

'No, your way looks much harder,' she said.

'Have you been up it before?'

'No, but I've climbed many mountains in my life,' she said. 'If you know what I mean.'

'I'm... er... not meaning to blow my own trumpet,' I excused, 'but I've been up actual mountains all over the world, and the advice on this one is to stay to the left.'

'You go left then,' she dared.

'What?' I worried.

'You go left and we can meet at the top.'

'You might fall.'

'Yes, that's true.'

'I don't want you to get hurt.'

'Are you scared?' she teased.

Am I scared? I was scared she might fall, but then that was her choice. Was I scared to go alone? Reluctantly I found myself following her.

She climbed up over the first rock, which was a stretch, but fairly simple, but the following rock was long and looked like a hard one to get back down from.

That was the main rule when scrambling in unknown territory. You had to be sure you could climb back down safely. We were breaking it from the off. I tried to tell her.

'The worst we'd do is twist an ankle from here,' she said.

'But then how do we get back down to safety?'

She ignored me and continued, confidently. I felt envious. I'd been sober for years and still I had so little confidence. I steadied my nerve. It's do or die. Come on, Tom! I felt a sudden burst of adrenaline and followed her, but as I grabbed the rock my hand got stuck in a crevice, my foot slipped and I twisted around, so I was facing outwards.

'Help!' I yelled, panicking.

Immediately she turned around, 'don't panic, mate, you're alright.'

My feet flailing, I could just about reach a ledge with my left foot.

Breathing fast and hard, it shook me up. I was thinking about what could happen rather than what I should be doing. That's another rule broken. Be present, one step at a time.

'Just pull yourself back around,' she said, hanging from one hand and looking back at me.

I untwisted and reached over to another handhold at the side of me. I yanked my other hand out of the crevice, grazing my knuckles. 'Thank you,' I called up, steadying my breathing.

We pulled ourselves up over a few easier rocks, getting a good grip on the limestone and building my confidence a little. But all the time we were veering to the far right.

I looked down and the mist was rising. I could no longer see the plateau where we'd met. Ahead of us, we reached the first challenging move. This is what I'd warned her about. Because of my height, it actually wasn't so hard for me, but she was much shorter.

'You'll have to go first,' she insisted, for the first time sounding nervous.

'You sure? We could-'

'Just go,' she snapped, angry at herself.

'Ok, ok.' I climbed up. Ahead of us, I couldn't see a simple route. Just to the right there was a big drop into the mist.

'Help me then,' she yelled, irritable.

'Of course, sorry.'

I leant over the rock and pulled her up.

'Where next?' she asked, as if the route had been my idea.

'Just there, behind us is a gorge, careful where you step. The only way I can see is up there,' I pointed, assessing the situation. 'Then we'll have to see where we stand. Yeah?'

She didn't answer.

I put my hand on the rock but, before I could pull myself up, I heard a loud clap echo throughout the whole terrible face. I turned and she was gone.

'Where are you?' I shouted, panicking. 'Girl?' I called, sick to my stomach, blood-sugary weak. 'Woman, where are you? Where are you?' I muttered, circling on the spot, as if she might be hiding behind my back.

I knew, of course. I knew before I'd even turned around. I looked down into the mist covered gorge. 'Are you ok?' I yelled, hopeful.

'Are you ok?' came back at me, my own words, echoing.

'No,' I shouted.

'No,' came back at me.

'No!'

'No!'

'Stop it!' I yelled at my echo.

'Stop it!' its hollow response.

I waited for another voice, but there was nothing. Why didn't she listen to me?

The mist was still rising like a fast tide. Soon, I would be engulfed in it and then I'd be lost climbing up an unknowable rock face. I started to panic, breathing fast. I felt like I was going to pass out. I didn't want to go on.

I looked down into the misty gorge once more. I didn't want to leave her, but there was nothing I could do.

Sometimes there isn't. No matter how much you might want to help, sometimes you can't. She was lost.

I looked to the rocks and started to climb, racing the mist. I got over one rock and then onto a small ridge which at the end overlooked a drop. I climbed down, touching the mist and then climbed back up. It was easier now, I could see at least a couple of moves ahead at a time.

I didn't even know her name, I thought, my instincts taking over, carrying me up the face. She was just another anonymous soldier in an endless war. But she got me this far. It might not be the easiest route, but she got me further up the mountain. I wondered how the drunk at the bottom of the mountain was doing. Was he still there? Perhaps he'd stumbled into the road and been killed by an oncoming tractor.

It wasn't long before I could see the two big rectangle Adam and Eve stones poking out at the top. Now it was just a clamber over rocks, the mist all around me like I was on a small island in the middle of a swamp. My plan was to stand on the highest rock. I wasn't going to jump from one to the other like tradition dictates. I just wanted to stand on the highest point. But as I neared them I started to see I wouldn't be able to. I was too old to lug myself up. I'd come as far as my body would take me. I patted the rocks.

'Ello.'

For a brief second I thought the rock was talking to me. 'Hello?'

'Oh, ello mate,' the voice said, a thick Somerset accent.

Behind the rock, a man was standing looking out over the sea of mist.

'We're right in it here,' I said.

'Oi like it, Oi do. Not a thing in sight. The perfeck escape.'

'Why are we always trying to run away from things?' I asked.

'We're not, are we?'

'I think I was.'

'Oi know nothing about thaat.'

I couldn't tell whether he was joking. 'What are you… er… "perfectly escaping" then?'

'Same thing you're 'scaping I 'spect.' I assumed he meant life, work, bills, responsibilities. Those were the things most people were escaping in the hills or on holiday. 'The bomb,' he said.

'The bombs?'

'No, just the one. The one that 'it Burnham. Oi was driving back that day, somewhere near Worcester when it 'it.'

'On the M5?'

'Aye.'

I was dumbstruck. I couldn't speak. No words. I remembered lying on the road after it happened, and then it was like I was on rewind, I jumped back into the car. The cars on the other side reversed and straightened up. The cloud sucked back in and the earth was restored. I found myself driving backwards, then I noticed another car also driving backwards towards me. It caught up with me and passed me. I looked into the car and saw the face of a man — could it be him? I tried to ask him but I just couldn't say the words.

'Need a leg up?' he asked.

'What?'

'You wanna get on Adam?'

'Oh, yes, I do actually. How did you know?'

'Highest point, ain't he.'

As the man awkwardly helped shove me up on the rock, I caught a whiff of cider on his breath, a whiff of Burnham-on-Sea, a whiff of home. I took a few breaths on my knees before tentatively standing up. I watched the mist rise half way up Adam, until the man disappeared. I was standing on my own, on the top of the mountain.

I closed the notebook. It seemed like a nice way to end the story. But that wasn't the story and it wasn't life. It was in a way, but it didn't actually end on a mountain. It hasn't ended on a mountain.

My phone buzzed. I pulled it out. "Here. L x" it read. I looked around but couldn't see him.

A story never ends on the top of a mountain. Not even a mountain climb ends on the top of a mountain. That's the midway point. And even when you get to the bottom, that's not it. Maybe you get in a car and you go home. Then you have a shower, eat, sleep, wake up, go to work. At some point there's another mountain. You go up, you come back down, you go up another. I didn't just hike up one mountain, I kept doing it. The keeping doing it was the bit that made sense.

'Tom!'

I looked up and Loz was walking towards me. He looked so normal and solid, stronger than when I last saw him. I stood up, it felt like my limbs were loose in their joints, my bones loose in my skin. It had been eight months since I'd last seen him, but it felt like years.

Maybe the story ends here? When they've turned up. Survivors reunited. But I knew this whole experience wasn't just about getting out of Halesowen, it wasn't about Halesowen.

He put his arms around me and embraced me. He seemed so in control and strong. He looked so… British.

'How are they?' I asked.

'Jen's happy with her new fella.'

'You ok with that?'

'God, yeah! I'm a world away from that.'

'The kids?'

'It's gonna take a bit of time.'

'Of course.'

'It's so good to see you, Tom!' He looked well, but he also looked older, his grey beard spread wide, digging the air with an excited nod, the laughter creases, fault lines which had slowly driven down the mantle of his face.

'She's not with you then?' he asked, a mischievous smile.

'Who?'

'Who?' he bounced back. 'The Welsh bird.'

'Helen?' I asked, shaking my head. 'That was one night. She was lonely, I was lonely.'

'Yeah, right. It's a bit more than that,' he smirked.

'Maybe,' I said, full of melancholy.

He looked over my shoulder. 'They're coming.'

We watched the old green barge slowly float up the lanky Pontcysyllte aqueduct – ancient and grand, it looked like a harsh winter wind could topple the stone giant, spilling the murky green drink on the fields below.

We saw a little head pop out and thumbs up. We waved back.

'Reckon you'd ever go back?' he asked, laughing.

I looked at my friend, saw my reflection in his glasses. 'It's really good to see you, man.'

'What does that mean?'

The canal widened, but the barge juddered against the side as Damien tried to keep it in. He threw the rope out.

'Take it back! Take it back!' a voice shouted from behind.

An old man had come out of the visitor centre. Big trousers held up with braces, he looked like he'd been there since the 1800s.

'Take it back! He needs to carry on further up.'

'Um… er… I, yeah,' he started pulling the rope back onto the barge.

'You on your own?' I called.

'Um, no… but… er.'

'Are they there?' I asked.

Marcus limped up from below, waved his stick.

'Where is she?' I asked.

A ginger cat jumped up from behind Marcus and onto the deck. It hopped off the boat and tottered towards us.

'Aw, the little puttycat,' Loz said.

2031

'It's just a trip, it's just a trip,' my mantra as I moved towards Will, feeling for the headstones in the grasses.

I glanced behind and the light turned with me as if it was coming out of my eyes. I felt for the headtorch, the rectangular reality in all of this, and in the billowing beam there was nothing. No butcher, no Mel telling me Marcus was dead, just the empty graveyard throbbing in this escapable new world given to me by the mushrooms.

'What've you done?' Will shouted into the Greek.

At that moment no human existed other than Will and me. We were consciousness expressed, combined. There was no one in any of the blocks across the road, on the streets, down the town or even in the Greek grave. No humans, but everything was alive, especially the buildings, the gravestones, St John's. All of them had sharp edges which I could seemingly touch from here, because all of them were in this seamless web, a net which contained everything and ebbed and flowed with the breath of time. When I thought about it, I wasn't breathing. And I wasn't. All those times we used to remind ourselves we *were* breathing and our heart *hadn't* stopped under the influence of hallucinogens, we'd missed the point. We were never breathing. *It* was breathing, the animal which held this little bit of God.

'Over here,' Will called. 'I need your help.'

A beam of light shone out of the earth up at him. It joined forces with my light and we held Will's head in place, one quick move from either of us and I was sure we'd decapitate him. I briefly closed my eyes to banish the horrific notion, but his head fell off his body deep inside my mind and rolled down my throat. When it settled in my shoes the thought vanished and there was just as much warping the silence of my vision, a churning kaleidoscope of mauve, orange and green. 'It's impossible to imagine nothing and that's why something has always existed,' rolled out of my mouth.

I opened my eyes to the sound of mutters coming out of the ground. *Marcus.*

'What've you done to Marcus?' Will yelled.

'Leave me alone,' the voice nagged.

It's not Marcus!

The light went out again, followed by the sound of smacking.

'Fuck off,' the voice said.

I recognised it, but I couldn't place it. The tone was universal, God, Jesus, the Holy Ghost. It was telling us to leave.

'Marcus has moved on,' I said to myself. His face passed through my mind again, calm and at peace. *Marcus has moved on*. The drugs knew, the ether knew, I just had to have the faith to tune in and listen. I looked over towards the flats and a huge black skyscraper grew out of Ground Zero, inking a shape, cutting through the purple throb of the night sky. Above it, I saw translucent faces like Jedi spectres, mum, dad and Marcus. 'Not Lucy and Dylan,' I said. *They're in a skin pocket on the side of my face.*

'Tom, snap out of it!' Will said.

'I drank way too much coffee, Will.'

'Tom, listen to me, help me get this fucker out,' he said.

'Tom? Is that Tom?' the voice enquired.

'Yes,' I answered.

'Pull me out,' he called up.

Will reached in and was dragging the Holy Trinity out of the grave. 'I'm not sure we should,' I said.

'Tom, you're fucked. Whatever you think is happening right now is not what is actually happening. Now come and help me. We need to find Marcus.'

As I moved towards him, I knew before I even saw his face. It wasn't the Holy Trinity. It wasn't even Jesus. It was Tony Dale.

'How?' I asked. 'How are you still alive?'

'For fuck's sake, Tom!' Will raged.

'Help me, Tom,' Tony Bonham said.

Tony Bonham? 'You're Tony Bonham,' I said.

'So what,' he barked. 'That's no crime!'

'Isn't it?' I grabbed an arm and heaved him out, all pain in my back gone. Then I saw the voice for who it really was. 'Tony?' I asked. '*Tony Moran?*'

'Yes, for Christ's sake. You fucking tripping-?'

'Yes-' I said.

'They killed him, Tom! Oh, Christ. They've killed my lad.'

In the torchlight, I noticed one side of him was covered in blood. *Is that real?*

'Yes-' he said.

I didn't say anything. 'I didn't say anything-' I said.

'Look,' he pointed. I looked into the grave and above the headless and limbless torso of a man was Aaron's barely recognisable head. 'My boy, Aaron,' he cried. 'They goddam killed him!'

'What does he mean?' Will was saying.

'Why've you got Marcus's headtorch?' I asked.

Will angrily tore it from his hand. 'It is, it is,' he said. 'Is that Marcus?'

'My boy!' Tony knelt down at the Greek. 'My little lad!' He took a small flask from his pocket and tried to take a swig, but it was empty. He tossed it into the darkness – it landed with a splash of orange. 'My lad, my only lad.' He sat down, his legs in the Greek, muttering to himself inconsolably.

He no longer looked like the terrifying leader of the corrupt Sons, nor the violent thug who'd terrorised the town for years prior to the role. He looked like an old man in grief. He looked like my dad. I glanced to the side of us, the black skyscraper was now swirling with the purple sky which surrounded it. The stars above looked like diamonds and made up my dad's face, if I closed one eye. When I opened it, it was Sarah's dad. I didn't even know what he looked like, but it was him. When I closed both eyes, it was me.

'Tom!' Will demanded, pointing into the Greek, 'is that Marcus?'

Dazed, I stared at him without responding, wondering if I was ever going to find my way back from this state.

He turned to Tony for answers, bravely tugging at his hair. 'Where did you get the fucking torch?'

His head thrown back and with no will to fight, 'I found it,' he cried.

'Liar!' Will spat.

'I ay no liar! In Bredon high-rise… My boy, my lad… Tom, you know… The girls all went north. It was just me and the boy left.'

I was doing my best to focus on what was happening, but as I moved my head towards him it was suddenly daytime. I could hear cars and voices, mums nattering, babies crying, people going to work, addicts sitting on benches drinking Kestrel Super, silently screaming about getting their next fix, an inner howl, a primal scream, a pitch too high for anybody to hear other than addicts. Was it 2001 in Halesowen and had I dreamt the last 30 years? The bombs, Lucy and Dylan, Burnham-on-Sea, rehab? I could feel my heart racing, the wrinkles dropped off my face, my hair grew, I looked at Will and he was just a boy, no more than 20 years old. Was dad still alive? I immediately turned to look at Ankerdine high-rise and Honest John's face came at me. I screamed.

'What the fuck?' Tony blurted.

In one terrible second I aged 30 years and saw Barb dead, the milkman, Tony Dale, Stacey grabbing at my cock. I'd been tricked by the beam of my headtorch. It was night time. *It's just the fucking 'shrooms, Tom. It's 2031.*

I took a moment and then asked him, 'what were you doing at Bredon?'

'What's fucking wrong with you?' Tony replied.

'That fuck put mushrooms in my coffee. I don't know if I've ever been this fucked.'

'You have,' Will said, making patterns with his hands.

There was silence, a thick moment of processing, Tony's features kaleidoscoping on his face. 'They killed my boy, Tom.' His pain-filled sincerity focused my mind.

'What the hell is going on?' Will asked, lost – he'd been standing still for long enough to have let the mushrooms back in.

'Lots of stuff that you don't know,' I said, 'and lots of stuff that I don't know. Tony Moran is with us –' I felt him looking at me – 'and his son has been murdered.' I pointed to the Greek.

'The son of a Son?' he asked in all seriousness, but we both caught it and felt the inappropriate need to laugh.

I nodded, stifling it. 'They killed Jason too.'

'The scag rat?' he asked.

'You got that right,' Tony said, getting onto his knees.

'*You*?' I asked.

'I wouldn't waste the fucking bullets.'

———————

I awoke on the floor in the back bar at the George. The red paisley carpet was still gently billowing bloated shapes but my mind felt surprisingly sharp. Tony Moran was sitting on a bench staring at me. I remembered pulling him out of the Greek, but the rest was hazy, a mosaic of images, day, night, people made out of grass, buildings made out of sky, the dismembered body of Aaron Moran at the centre of it, keeping it real.

'How did I get here?' I asked.

'Through space and fucking time, apparently. Went to sleep in the "hammock of atoms" or some such shit.'

'Oh.'

'Surprised the whole town wasn't on us.'

'Where's Will?'

'Front bar.'

Loz and Sarah would be worried. Why was I here with Tony Moran? Why had this man of all people come into my life? Whatever the divine reason, I needed to get away from him and back to the swimming baths.

'Where's Marcus?' I asked.

'He the queer one?'

'You've got his torch.'

'*What you fucking saying*?'

I sat up, resting back on my hands. 'I'm not-'

'That's alright then. Told ya, I found it at Bredon. Torch was on the stairs next to a sandal.'

Oh, God. 'Just one?'

He nodded.

'Marcus wears brown leather ones.'

'Unless he's Cinderella…'

'Dead?'

'Looks like it.'

My stomach churned with the twirling carpet at the thought of it. *I knew it.* Helpless and hopeless and ultimately harmless Marcus. I remembered playing a gig in this pub. Will playing the guitar like a wannabe Jimmy Page. Loz plucking the bass with a smile, like a big cheesy Paul McCartney. And me louching over the mic like I thought I was Mick Jagger, looking more like Meat Loaf. Just behind me, sitting perfectly still on a chair, like we'd told him to, was Marcus. I never realised it until that moment, but he was the heart of our four-headed beast. We thought we were being cool, but we just wanted him with us, because he was part of us, a quarter. And, now, was he the first of us actually dead?

'They're cleaning up the town, Tom. Changing the… what's the word?' He made a rectangle with his fingers. 'Landscape.' He lit a small cigar, took it back, coughed to dislodge phlegm and then swallowed it. He was still wearing the same clothes as the previous night, smeared with the brown stains of Aaron's blood.

'Who?'

'Whoever's a part of it, I guess. The fat one in his ivory – no, *shit-stained* – tower.'

'Ross?' He lived on the top floor of Bredon.

'Him and the Sons.'

'But you're a-'

'People have different reasons for being a Son,' he interrupted. 'Jake and Ray are made for it. They care about shit. But Christian? Ha! I know he's your bud… And I en't no saint either, but people will always want a good time, Tom – or to forget a bad un.'

He took another deep drag of the cigar. I imagined the smooth, warm smoke streaming down my throat, lighting up my lungs. 'You mean, drugs?'

'I always thought the government should've legalised them, you know? Woulda done me out of business, but it just made sense. Stop people from killing each other, sure, but stop people from killing *themselves*? What fucking right we got?'

The pub was looted and littered, tables upturned, a coating of plaster dust from sledgehammer searches. Windows cracked and boarded up, the door to the kitchen off its hinges. It was the scene of a crime and it felt like it.

I got up and stretched. My back felt surprisingly ok. I leant against the bar, found myself looking at the gap on the wall where the optics used to be, where we'd order happy hour doubles, Glen's vodka, Queen Margot scotch, before necking them like shots. We'd follow them with a beer chaser, because I'd seen Marlon Brando do it in On the Waterfront.

'Marcus is *actually* dead?' I asked the universe.

'How would I fucking know?' Tony spat back, irritated. 'All I am is a small time dealer peddling a bit of whatever makes your fucking dick tick.'

'Viagra?'

He scoffed, 'whatever makes your heart smile, you know. Whatever fills the hole in your floating boat. *You know,*' he insisted.

Do I know? I guess my boat had a big hole in it and I was forever trying to fill it. In the front bar, Will roared a snore from the bench, so much bigger in sleep than he would be that moment when he woke up, trembling at a comma in the self-sentence of his perpetual bender. His hole was even bigger and it took a lot more to fill it.

'Drugs, drink,' he added, 'it's a way of life for us mere mortals.'

It felt like a dig, but it just made him look like a child. 'I guess so. It is what it is.'

'Your "boy"-'

'My *boy*?'

'The *girl*… whatever he was… had no problem with the trade,' he said, 'and he was the real law, no? If you believe in such things.' His finger was pointing upwards like a neon sign to a cut-price heaven.

'You mean *Lee*?'

'That's the one.'

I circled my head and my body creaked, old bones inside an ever loosening skin. But I felt no pain. I reached behind to rub my back and it just felt strange, like it didn't belong to me. There was hardly any sensation at all. It was like I was wearing a coat, an animal skin. Then it came back to me. The revelations of the previous night, the animal and God, like there was a kernel of twirling light at our core, a hologram, the flux capacitor in our bestial engines. It wasn't the first time I'd thought it, of course, but I sensed a renewal of spirituality which made Tony and his talk seem much smaller. I had the feeling that He, the Big Eye, the Everything had come back to me, in all truth or madness, and I felt emboldened by it. I guess I must've believed in such things. It made me want to talk to Sarah.

'What's Lee got to do with anything, Tony?'

He snorted a laugh. 'Everything. He, she – whatever the fuck it was – was good with it, with the trade. Probably a little too good,' he smirked. 'And why not?

'Ok?' I asked, confused.

'It's funny we find ourselves together here, of all places, don't you think?'

'You brought me here,' I said, wondering what he was getting at. 'But I do think it's odd the fates have conspired-'

'"The fates have conspired", that's good that is. That's why they want you-'

'What?'

'You remember what happened here?'

'You mean-?' I knew exactly what he meant.

'Yeah.' He pointed. 'By the window, skull-cracked. Off… The smell, I mean. Like, well, you know what the smell of death's like, don't ya. Followed you around a bit, en't it?'

'What's that supposed to mean?'

'Don't get me wrong, I'm sure you didn't kill the old landlord-'

'You what-?'

'Nor Jay Bird,' he laughed. 'Soft as wool. I couldn't believe he had it in him to hit Alan Price in Picks! But he saw Nigel's body. You too, didn't you? Come on?' he cajoled.

'No, I didn't! Only went in the cellar, like I said. That's my truth.'

He laughed, shaking his head.

'I'd tell you, Tone. What can you really do about it now?' I hit back.

There was a dead silence and Tony glared at me with all his menace, but for some reason it didn't frighten me. Whether it was God or Tony's big fall from grace, I felt no fear at all.

He smirked, suppressing his rage. 'Whether you did or didn't see Nigel dead is neither here nor there. You were saved, Tom.'

'Saved?'

'First by Christian and then by the preacher. Without them…' he took one last drag on his cigar and flicked it at me. It missed.

My head was telling me to argue, but something stopped me. He was absolutely right.

'That day, you were about to defend a dead man,' he continued.

'Jay Bird?'

'He was dead before the whole thing even began. Jay's Law was already written by fat Stalin. Now, I'm not blaming you,' he said.

'Blaming me? Blaming me for what?'

'Aaron's death.'

'What the fuck?'

There was a cold silence. The pub creaked, old boards. I rubbed the bar and the wood grain felt strange, familiar and distant at the same time. It suddenly occurred to me I'd been dreaming about relapsing in the George and now here I was again, but the last thing I wanted was a drink. *Am I dreaming?* Will snored and it irritated me. *Of course I'm not dreaming*! It was quite the opposite. I was having a moment of hyper-reality, when you find yourself in a particular place, at a particular time and wonder what the hell brought you to it, to my dilapidated home-town, post-nuclear event, in a crumbling pub with a crumbling man passively accusing me of having a hand in the death of his son.

'I'm trying not to be angry,' Tony said.

'Me too,' I replied. 'What's this got to do with me?'

He suddenly slammed his fist hard on his knee. '*Fuck, Tom.* That's why he's dead.'

'*Lee?*'

'No, Aaron,' he snapped, 'my boy!'

'Because of *me*? Because of *Lee*?'

'They don't want the drugs no more, Tom! The lines, the little uns, needles and bud – even though they really do,' he prattled off. 'Lee was a great supporter. He accepted our need to escape, us, the mere mortals, the simple working folk, going about our lives. But after his flasher distraction – there was kids there! – to stop *you* from intervening in the trial, they wanted him dead.'

'Who?'

'The town. The fucking Prices! Where've you been, Tom? Even Christian. The business-'

'The *Prices*?'

'I know!' he yelled, 'a couple of old Tory queers! Be easier if they could just accept it like old Percy and Jack – them pair won't be here much longer, be on the slabs like your gay pal.' He took a bottle of something off the table, unscrewed the cap and swallowed a painful slug – it looked good.

'Christian wanted Lee dead too?' I asked.

A sly smile, 'you don't have a bloody clue, do ya? Thought yuh was smart – that's what they reckoned. They wanted you-'

'What? Who wanted me? What do you mean?'

'The business – a bit too square for my liking, like Ray-'

'Fuck off!'

'No offence,' he scoffed. 'They didn't mind-'

'Who didn't? Christian? I barely know the Prices-'

'Christian, yeah. Jake always rated ya.'

'What about The Prices?'

'What about them?'

'Marcus was last seen going off with the Prices.'

He shrugged, lips-tight, eyes-wide. 'There's a cull, Tom. You've seen it yourself. Tony Two, Terry er-what's-his-'

'The milkman?'

He nodded. 'Your mate, Ray,' he winked.

'Is *he* dead too?' I asked, feigning ignorance.

'Looks like it. And my fucking boy-'

'And Barb and Jason,' I said, cold.

He stared at me, severe and irritated – *who was this "square" teetotaller questioning him*? Then his face mellowed. Perhaps it was the reality of his situation. 'There was no way back for Barb, Tom. I can see ya liked her. Difficult… difficult decision,' he was nodding in agreement with himself.

'It was made pretty quick.'

'The doctor-'

'He's not a doctor! He's just got a scout badge!'

'St John's ambulance-'

'Whatever!'

'She was already long gone, you know that. What could we do? Stick her in a hospital?'

'How many, Tony?'

'How many? You've lost me.'

I shook my head, sadly.

'Don't fucking judge me! Four, maybe five. Terminal cases, the quick needle. Her fella would've been better off with it. You know it's true.'

Rex watched the swift death of his beloved church and this was not long followed by his own painful death, cancer we presumed. With Rex gone, and no church around, Barb was all alone, left to go mad on the booze. *Where was I?* We're pack animals. We need each other.

'Tone, why have you come into my life?'

He laughed, 'you pulled me out of the fucking Greek-'

'But the night when they found Barb, round the back of town-'

'After Picks?'

'I wasn't at Picks.'

'No, you weren't, were you?' he asked, sinisterly.

'Hold on-'

'Where the fuck had *you* come from?'

'That's not-'

'No, come on, Tommy-'

Is he playing me? What the hell's really going on here? Why were we here in the George? Why was he in the Greek? Was Aaron Moran really dead? Was it really a Halloween dummy, and was this just a ploy to get to me? *Your goddam ego, Tom!*

'I'm allowed to walk around Halesowen, Tone,' I said, confident.

He laughed.

'I'd been to the metal store, actually,' I lied. What did it matter if I gave that away? We were out of here as soon as possible, and I couldn't compromise Sarah, Damien and Loz.

'Metal store?'

'We've got a place where we store our trading metal.'
'You mean the Zion?'
'How do you know about that?' I asked, shocked.
'I didn't know it was a secret,' he smirked.
'A secret? No, it's not a secret. We just don't tell anyone.' *Bloody Marcus.*

He was laughing. This was a game and he'd just scored a point.

I heard Will stir, a yawn turned into: 'what the fuck-?'

Glad for the time-out, I got up without looking at Tony and went into the front bar. Will was sitting up on a bench, his face yellowed and old, a bruise on his cheek from somewhere. He was trembling plucking beer towels from his lap. I figured he must have used them to keep himself warm, but then I noticed a damp patch on his trousers. He'd pee'd himself in the night. He looked shocked and confused.

'We're in the George,' I said.

'Why are we in the… *what have we done?*'

The windows had long been boarded up, but an inch of light came through above the wood. Dust danced making ribbons in the beams and I couldn't tell whether I was tripping or if it was just my breath stirring the air – I guessed both. I thought about my dad, felt his presence.

'You wanted to look for "answers" in the Greek,' I said, pointedly.

'The Greek?' He hangover-groaned.

'We found some.'

'In the Greek grave?'

'Marcus?' I prompted.

'What about him?' He started to panic. 'Why are we in the fucking George?' He swung his legs around and planted them on the floor, sitting up straight. There was a notable tremor in his hands, which was normal. He clasped them together to try to control it, but it just made it more evident. His hair was stuck to his face, cheeks creased and red. 'Where's er… Anita? Wasn't I with-?'

'Mushrooms? Remember?' I said.

'Yessss, the coffee,' he hunched, relieved, smiling to himself as if all our problems had disappeared – *it was just a bender!* 'Oh, Tom,' he remembered. 'You took 'shrooms! Shit. I'm really sorry, man.'

'Forget it. In a way, I think it's helped me.'

'That's good,' he brushed off, relinquishing all responsibility. 'I dreamt about Tammy, she was wearing those pink leggings. Remember? Fucking camel toe,' he laughed. 'I need a drink.'

Tony got up in the back bar. Will instantly stretched out of his hunch. *Danger.*

'*Wha*?' he mouthed. He'd clearly forgotten, pointing his trembly finger in the direction of the sound.

I nodded, used my hands to calm him.

Tony came in to us. 'Here, big un.' He tossed a half bottle of something at Will.

It bounced off his left hand and he caught it in his right. 'T-Tony, mate, what? I don't-'

'You pulled me out of the Greek.'

'The son.' It hit him. 'Your son,' he nervily recalled. 'The son of a Son!'

Tony leant against the front bar, his orange peel nose turned up, defiant. He was stronger for Will's fear, revelling in it. He knew it and understood what to do with it. But still I wasn't scared of him. He was just a man. My equal. With the death of his lad, in more ways than one.

'We have to find Marcus,' I said.

'He's dead,' Tony threw out there.

'*Dead*!?' Will panicked, fumbling with the bottle, determined to get into it.

As he took a swig, I looked into his vein-cracked eyes and tried to smile to ease him, unsure of the truth. Hysteria was not too far below the surface. I could feel his terror and confusion almost as if it were my own. He looked to the ground, beaten.

After a few seconds, 'I'm still tripping,' he said, oblivious. 'Look at the carpet.'

'Look at the beam of light,' I competed.

He looked up. 'No way. It kinda twirls, like some sort of vortex.'

'It made me think of my dad.'

'The dust?'

'I guess so.'

'Mad shit.'

Tony moved, the floorboards creaked and Will looked up with the sudden reminder. 'What do we have to do, Tom?' he asked, like we were talking funeral arrangements.

'It's obvious,' Tony said. 'Leave.'

'Leave?' I responded, incredulous, acting on autopilot. 'But I've er… just traded for a new guitar.'

'Guitar?' Will.

'I saw,' Tony.

'*You saw?*'

'Are we really gonna play this, Tom?' he asked. 'I saw you talking to that federali fuck.'

I relived Jason running towards me and then hitting the road with a flaccid smack. *He must've killed him.*

'I didn't kill Jason,' he said.

'I didn't… say-' I stuttered.

'I just went for my boy.' He looked away, tamping down emotions. 'I went for Aaron, that's all.' He bit the skin on his finger.

For all Tony's toughness, when he talked about Aaron he looked broken. Weak. His ego cracked like his round Irish face, the unruly spider veins sprouting from his bulbous nose, whiskers etched by years of booze. *Perhaps this is what he needed. Perhaps this is why we're in each other's lives?*

'I'm sorry, Tony,' I said.

He half-laughed, but his inability to look me in the eye said it all.

I imagined him removing Aaron's heavy head from the stick, like removing a dagger from his heart. It made me think of Dylan, blonde bowl, green eyes. And then, once again, the nuclear blast cutting through them. They were in the kitchen. They were always in the kitchen, normally on the floor sticking bits of things to things, PVA fingers and "look at this daddy." Half the time I wasn't even there. I mean, I was in the room, but I was elsewhere. Some call it trauma, some call it being a man. In my old circle they called it untreated alcoholism. *I've gotta help Sarah. I've gotta help Sarah to help me.* I looked at Will, trembling, the bottle in his hand.

'I saw Jason go down,' Tony said.

'He was calling me-'

'Probably just after a fag,' he smiled. 'Your mate, the funny one. He en't gonna be alive. They're cleaning up.'

Will unscrewed the cap on autopilot, forcefully oblivious. He swigged the medicine and suppressed the urge to heave as the strong liquid bit at his throat. He squeezed his gut and I remembered the warmth of it, and the pain. He burped acidic, grimacing. Then he drank some more before leaning forward to hand it back to Tony.

'We've gotta know for sure,' I said.

Tony's face soured. 'That world out there is not the same as yesterday, and yesterday was bad enough. It has to get worse.'

'I don't care,' I insisted.

'Where's this come from?' he asked, eyeing me up.

'What?'

'The balls?'

He had a point. I could only think it was the mushrooms. 'I just need to know my friends are ok… or… I just need to know.'

Will stood up to get ready to leave. He patted his pockets looking for baccy.

'*He's* staying here,' he said.

'M-m-me?' Will asked, nervously tapping his chest, an involuntary SOS. 'No, Tony, I've gotta check the brew.'

'Nah, you haven't, mate. I en't taking no chances. Tom's gonna go chat to Christian to find out what's happened to your bum chum. He's not gonna say anything about me, nor listen to any of the horse shit Christian says about me. Then when he finds out they've done your mate in, he's gonna sneak back here and we're all leaving. Tom knows how.'

'I do?' I lied.

He just looked at me.

'What you talking about?' Will said, still trembling.

'It's ok, Will,' I conceded, making eye-contact with Tony. 'That's the way it has to be.'

'No, no way, Tom!' Will sulked. 'This is one of your fucking ploys to get me to leave!'

'Listen, you lanky prick, he's the only one looking out for ya!'

Will looked stunned.

'The town's on fire,' he continued. 'You're a wreckhead, you don't stand a chance.'

Will was clearly annoyed with me, but my unlikely ally stopped him from reacting in a bigger way. He was too sober. 'Ok,' he started to argue. 'But what about Loz? Where's he stand on all this?'

'He knows,' I said.

'Knows fucking what?'

I carefully lifted the cellar door, the warm sun thawing the cold underground world of the pub. My eyes level with the pavement, I saw nothing. Upstairs I could hear the mumbling voices of Tony and

Will, who were now drinking themselves out of their respective hells. I was glad to leave it.

I edged open the heavy metal door and climbed out. It had to be late May, the sun blinding, the tropic of the Earl's roundabout with its overgrown grasses and wild flowers, spilling onto the road, Play-Doh squeezed through a strainer. Free from the George, I felt an undeniable wave of euphoria. Why did I feel so good? I looked around and everything seemed so alive and wonderful for it. It wasn't billowing and blending into itself like it had last night but, if I stopped still for long enough, the visuals would start, reminding me I was just one part of the whole, a small cell in an ever-expanding organism. Feeling strangely fearless, I asked myself: *am I going into Halesowen with a blinkered fight or flight mechanism? Have the mushrooms broken me?* But I didn't care. Every outcome seemed acceptable.

It is what it is.

I walked towards St John's, the scene of last night's visions and, as I passed the old C of E primary school, I heard the eerie sound of the playground. This was followed by somebody pretending to do the trombone. I knew I wasn't hallucinating. I had more clarity of mind than I'd had in a long time. *Footsteps. The spike of laughter. Someone's coming out the graveyard.* I found myself drawn towards it, curious, and then out walked college Ed, a stick in his hand like he was leading a parade. Behind him, little ducklings, eight infants marching two by two. I couldn't remember the last time I'd seen so many children together.

'Tom,' he said, seemingly happy to see me. 'What are you doing?'

'What are *you* doing?'

'Taking the kids to school. Today we're going to learn about Remembrance Day.'

'Ok,' I was nodding.

'Yeah, you "remember", hahaha,' he pointed gun fingers, smiling.

The kids were looking up at me, interested in the strange middle aged man wandering around town so early. 'Right,' I said, acting daft. 'Cadets! Hup, two, three, four. Companyyyy, march.'

'That's the spirit,' Ed said. 'Sometimes bad things happen, but as long as we remember it happened for a good reason, like killing Hitler, it's ok,' he smiled. 'That's right, hup, two, three, four, come on kids.'

I felt like I'd walked onto the set of Sesame Street. Was he teaching me or them? I watched the small people, with their little legs, march onto the road and around the roundabout towards the college. Children led by a man who yesterday put his trilby on Aaron's Moran's decapitated head.

It is what it is.

In the graveyard I passed William Shenstone's tombstone, now buried under grasses. Those nights when we'd sat on his sandstone tablet talking about Radiohead, Herman Hesse, Coleridge and the romantics, drinking and smoking, were innocent and beautiful times, a host of golden daffodils chirping like nightingales. They called this idyllic recollection *euphoric recall* in the rooms of AA, but I didn't find myself missing alcohol and drugs. My euphoria was the recollection of the camaraderie, the conversation and curiosity. There was a quest for truth and gut-wrenching honesty. But it was easy to be honest back then because we were mostly on the same page. Now we were writing different books. What would my honesty be to Will? On Tammy, Sarah, Halesowen or alcoholism? Where was I on these subjects? *God, the Ether, the Eye, I guess I'm asking you.*

As I came out of the graveyard I recalled chatting to Mick. "He was an old sod," he called my dad. Everyone was an old sod in his day, rabble-rousers, drink-drivers and arse-pinching "deeves" alike. It sounded so innocent. Dad *was* an old sod and I loved him, but it wasn't all dipping biscuits in tea and watching the Two Ronnies.

It is what it is.

Why did I feel so good? From the moment I woke up I'd felt stronger, physically, mentally and spiritually. It was like someone had pushed the reset button. Things were slotting into place and my brain felt more capable than ever on this beautiful May day.

I made my way across Church Croft into the flats, the town atoms alive around me. The crumbling buildings were not just the sad remnants of our pillaged town, but mountains eroded by time. I marched straight to the highest peak, Bredon high-rise, without a thought for who might see me. None of it seemed to matter. I had a simple mission and I wasn't scared about it. The main front door was open.

Inside, the same cigarette-scuffed red lino floor from my youth was transformed into the Martian-red sand of Mount Teide. The lift shaft was open, or I could take the stairs. I knew I was going to climb up the rickety ladders all the way to the seventh floor. For the sake of adventure, and because I felt able to. I might never make Everest, perhaps this was my mountain.

About half way up, aluminium creaking and out of breath, I looked down the shaft, light interrupting the dark from the floor below. It made me think of the old recovery allegory about choosing a new life, *you don't have to get off the lift at the bottom floor.*

I continued to climb until I reached Christian's floor, where the red lino had been disguised by wood laminate. There was a door directly in front of me. After getting my breath, I knocked.

The door opened, Christian looked past me and then ushered me in. 'Just you?'

'Yeah,' I said. 'So, what's going on, Christian?'

He looked stressed, stroking an imaginary beard. 'Oh, Tom. It's all gone crazy. Changing-'

'Of the guard?' I interrupted, nodding.

'What?' He looked confused. 'No. Changing-'

'Landscape?'

'No,' he snapped. '*Changing times*, Tom. What's up with you? You seem different.'

'It's been a mad few days.'

He stopped and stared at me like he was trying to figure something out. 'Yes, it has. People have died. T-Tony's on the war path-'

'Who's died?'

Four flats had been knocked into one big apartment. A short corridor opened up into a huge living room which used to be three rooms, sunlit and pale blue walls. Aside from the faint whiff of beer and cigar smoke, it was very clean. It felt like a private club. In the middle, there was a glass table with a few books, an old Times Atlas and a dictionary on top. It was surrounded by three plush leather chairs, and four leather dining chairs were against the wall.

'You were there, Tom,' he said, flat.

'I was at St John's, but since?'

'You mean Aaron Moran?' He seemed cagey.

'And Jason, too.'

'That's… right…' he half-enquired.

'Christian, I want to know where Marcus is?'

'… Marcus?' He scratched his cheek. I was certain he knew something.

He was wearing a thin dressing gown over shorts and a vest, casual, but he'd combed his hair. I wondered whether he'd seen me walking up to Bredon – he inhabited the whole floor, one of the bedrooms looking out onto Church Croft and the canopy of yew trees.

'Why can't you lot just contribute a bit?' he asked, overly-irritable, taking me by surprise.

'By us lot, you mean, Loz, Will, *Marcus* and myself?'

'Of course!' His tone seemed defensive and tired.

'We trade.'

'You trade metals so far we haven't really used. Essentially you're on welfare.'

'Here comes the bloody Tory in you,' I tried to laugh it off.

'You don't know what you're talking about, Tom,' he argued. 'Things need to move on in Halesowen. Quinton are ahead of us in many ways.'

'Is this why you're stressed?'

'I'm not stressed!' he defended.

'Ok, you're not,' I held my hands up. 'What's all this about Quinton?'

He tutted and walked over to a small fridge, 'you should know all of this.' He took out a beer.

'Bit early, isn't it?' I asked, knowing he was not the world's best drinker.

'I've got no issues with you not drinking, Tom.'

'I know,' I said, confused – it wasn't so long ago I was helping him off the spirits.

'For God's sake, Tom!' he riled. 'It's all out there, isn't it? They've got to go! Tony Two-'

'Dale?'

'Yes, Dale, bloody Bonham – like an albatross – and Tony One, sooner or later.'

'The Holy Trinity.'

He laughed. 'The Trinity! Exactly,' he pointed. 'You get it, you understand-'

I didn't.

'The three of them entwined,' he continued, 'keeping the town sozzled and useless. Ross didn't think it was such a bad idea numbing us all either.'

'And now?'

'He's not as smart as he thought, but he was useful. He wrote the Declaration of Freedom.'

'And the Halesowen News.'

He laughed. 'Don't believe everything you read in the papers.'

'What does that mean? Where is Ross, anyway? I haven't seen him in quite a while.'

Christian took a swig and then put it on the table. He sat down on one of the big chairs and put his head in his hands. 'Remember the golf hole,' he mumbled.

I laughed out of politeness.

'We were kids,' he said. 'Why did you pretend to fuck a golf hole?'

'To make you all laugh.'

'But why would you even think that? That's what we need. *Entertainment*.'

'TV?'

'Maybe.' He sounded depressed. 'Or a play. You did that stuff, didn't you?'

'You could get old Ross to write an adaptation of Animal Farm,' I tested, resting my hands on the back of one of the big chairs.

'Tom,' he patronised.

In St John's, the bodies laid out before us, Barb euthanised, I felt like I'd been in the belly of the beast. But standing here with Christian, I felt much closer to the dark heart of the Sons. I'd never really thought about it, but many of the figures central to the town occupied floors in Bredon. Perhaps this was where the real decisions were made, not in the "democratic" meetings in St John's or in the Fed-House.

Tony had said there was a cull. He was right on that front. But he put Ross at the top of the tower. It made me realise how little Tony Moran knew and where he really stood in the town. They'd put him at the top, but he was just a looming figurehead to scare us into order.

'What's happened to Ross, Chris?' He didn't respond. 'Christian?'

'The Prices,' he sulked, like I was nagging him. 'They mean well.'

'Christian?'

He looked up at me. 'I don't know!' he yelled, anguished. 'He's just not here anymore. The Prices saw to it.'

'All I seem to be hearing about is the Prices-'

'Hearing about? From who-?'

'Tell me where Marcus is!'

He leant forward and took a sip from the beer, before sinking back into the chair. 'They want you to stay.'

'The Prices?' confused.

'You can write.'

'What the fuck are you talking about?'

'They think we need someone who can write.'

'What does that mean?… Forget it,' I waved the notion away, I wasn't being pulled into anything. 'Where's Marcus?'

'I want you to stay,' he pleaded.

'Christian,' I asserted, standing back from the chair, my arms wide open. 'I'm not going anywhere-'

'Marcus, he told them-'

'The Prices?'

'They do some weird shit together with robes. Marcus is an odd bird-'

'Robes?' A flashback. 'What did he tell them?'

'That you were all leaving on a canal barge-'

'A barge?' My heart was beating just a few beats faster, fear knocking on the wall of peace and acceptance. *It is what it is*! I found myself gripping the back of the chair again. 'What barge?'

'*Tom*.' He looked me straight in the eye.

'*Christian*,' I unconsciously mimicked. 'I've just ordered a guitar off Jordan.' It felt like a pathetic attempt. 'I'm trying,' I lied as honestly as I could.

He half-smiled, stood up and went to the fridge. He grabbed a beer, before breaking the tension with laughter. 'Golf. It just tickles me. It's perverse but in a gentle way. Like an X-rated Mr Bean.'

'Mr fucking Bean?' I was mock-offended.

He spat beer, laughing, but the smile soon left his face. He poured beer down his throat.

'You haven't even finished the first one,' I said, trying to show I cared. 'What's going on, mate? You alright?'

'Yeah, great. Yeah. I'm… yeah.'

His dressing gown had shifted off his shoulder. He looked loose, stroking the parting of his hair as if that might be the answer to his troubles. There was something he wasn't saying. Or maybe he thought he was saying too much.

'Why did they kill Jason?' I asked.

'*They*? Who? *Us*? No… No. It was that madman.'

'Who?'

'Tony!' He slammed the second bottle down next to the first, then fell into his chair.

I moved and sat down opposite him. I found myself staring at the dregs of his beers, the first two notes of an instrument I once played every night – actually it played me. It was Coors Light. A terrible beer even in the most desperate of times, but right now I could almost feel the cold liquid and the bubbles. Perhaps a Perrier would sate it.

'Just tell me,' I said. 'I'm prepared for it. Have the Prices killed Marcus?'

He looked up at me. 'I don't know.'

'Ok,' I nodded.

'They were angry.'

'Are they in the block?'

'No.'

'Where are they?'

He stood up. 'I don't know, Tom,' he whined, going over to the fridge. 'I'm not their keeper. Marcus is a strange man. He's... you know...' He seemed to struggle for the word.

'Gay?'

'Well, yes, but, er... what does that have to do with anything?' he asked the fridge.

'It's not exactly... Halesowen.'

'Isn't it? He's just strange, he's strange... just strange, strange,' he mumbled into the fridge.

I got up and wandered over to the window. Outside, I could see Honest John sharping the blades on his lawnmower. *What's his part in all this?* 'Did John really kill his father?' I asked him.

'What did you say?' He sounded annoyed.

'Honest John.'

His big hands holding a hand-propelled lawnmower upside down. The ones that were heavy and hard to push.

'Why are you talking about John?' He was clearly offended.

'Just a question.' I watched him pulling grass from inside the blade chamber. 'There's something frightening about him.'

'There's nothing frightening about John!' he shouted.

I immediately turned around to face Christian and he was pointing a gun at me. 'What the fuck?' I flinched. 'What are you doing!? Put it down, man!' My flailing arms unsure what to protect. 'Chris? Is this because of John? I was just asking?'

'John?' he laughed. 'What's he got to do with anything?'

'That's what I was wondering. Just put the fucking thing down. Christ!'

He aimed lower. I had no idea where this had come from, but he seemed sketchy and broken, rubbing his head. *Is this how it ends*? I took a deep breath. *It is what it is.*

Fuck that!

'John killed Jan, yeah,' Christian said. 'Hit him with his mallet.'

'How do you know?'

'It came out in a roundabout way. I've known John since he was a little boy. A sweet thing. The day service had an allotment and he tended it for years, still goes there most days.'

'To the day service-?'

'The allotment,' he laughed, like we were having a normal conversation and I'd said something daft, but there was a gun between us. 'He came back the day Jan died with a bunch of tomatoes. That was odd.' He stroked his parting down.

'He didn't do it on purpose,' I said, trying not to focus on the gun. 'Jake told me.'

'Did you… perhaps you knew Ninny… er… P-Paul Jackson?'

'A little. I didn't know the other guys at all.'

'They took the last bus. Two of them did.'

'If you say so,' he smirked.

'What does that mean?'

He raised the gun again, a flat expression on his face.

I felt like this was it. No explanation. 'But why, Christian? What about the golf hole?'

'Don't,' he warned. 'This is hard enough.' He looked sad, but seemed to gee himself up closing one eye, preparing to shoot, but then he suddenly dropped his aim, 'why were you friends with that freak?' he shouted, anguished.

I sighed a breath of relief. 'What freak? Who?' *Think quick.* 'Do you mean Lee?'

'Lee?' he laughed. 'Tony never liked that sort of thing.'

'Tony? What about the Prices? A pair of old-'

'Queers, yes,' he mused, rubbing his cheek with the gun barrel – I half-hoped it would go off, stunning him so I could run. 'But Marcus? He's strange, strange… urgh. He was the instigator in all this deevery.'

'What? But the Prices? They beat him.'

'They beat him regularly, from what I've heard, but it has to change!' he stressed. 'It just has to. I'm sorry. I am. It just has to. Pervert!' He hit himself in the head, stifling tears.

There was a heavy silence. What could I say? All my senses had been overrun. I could feel the pain emanating, he seemed tortured. 'Are you alright, Christian?'

He looked at me, his eyes watered up. He raised his gun, but I just knew he didn't want to do it.

My body felt strong, my mind tired and drained, but my fears had evaporated with the tears in his eyes. 'Ok. I understand, Christian. You have to do what you have to do.' Perhaps this was the way it had to be, one event in the fabric of time and life goes on, the twirling hologram of light can't go out. It will just move on and find another animal.

I'd expected my earthly life to pass before my eyes, like they say, but even Lucy and Dylan were mute, in my neck, on my shoulders, out of my head. I found myself walking towards the table.

'Stop, Tom.'

'If this is it, I'm going to have a drink.'

He laughed, unsure what to do with the information, 'you don't drink.'

'Christian, I've recently been force-fed opiates and I'm still coming out of a magic mushroom high. A drink feels like the logical progression. I'm ready for it.'

He laughed nervously, unsure whether I was making a joke. I sat down on the chair and grabbed one of the bottles. 'Coors Light? Not really my idea of a last drink.'

'I still don't touch the strong stuff,' he said with an odd smile of gratitude. 'Cider's all right, but that's pretty much all they have lager-wise.'

'Who?'

'The UK. It's all American beers these days.' His hand had started to tremble and the gun dropped. He seemed a little lighter in mood, distracted, but one wrong turn in the conversation and I was certain the gun would go off.

'How do you know what the UK has?' I asked.

'It's my job to know.' He used his other hand to support his arm, but still the gun wavered with the lightness of his mood.

'Where do you get them from-?'

'Look, Tom, of course I don't want to kill you... You helped me during a difficult time.'

'The drink probably wasn't helping things.'

'Thank you,' he said in all sincerity.

'You're very welcome,' sarcastic – he didn't pick up on it.

I sniffed the beer. It smelt like wet beard. *Would I be able to throw it at him and then run out of the door? What if I missed?*

He itched his cheek with the gun, and then supported his arm again. 'I'm not mad,' he said.

But he looked mad. The parting in his hair, slick and tight like the seal of an ego. His dishevelled dressing gown, the looseness of his mind. His legs were bald, I wondered if he shaved them. I started to think maybe he was the real deeve in all this, repressed by his own expectations, unnecessary expectations in the existential possibilities of the new world.

'Do you ever wonder what we've created?' I asked.

'You haven't created anything,' he scoffed.

Out of the corner of my eye, the walls throbbed, reminding me the psilocybin was still in me. I was still open to another world, one where we were all connected and we were all responsible. And it was true, wasn't it? I couldn't deny my part in the creation of this Halesowen.

'It was supposed to be exciting and new,' I said. 'An independent Halesowen. I'm sick of it.'

'Me too,' he conceded, the gun lowering and now aiming at my liver – a poetic place to be shot at least. 'I want my old life back, Tom. The businesses, like when I was looking after John, when he was little. I was… good with him,' he pleaded for brownie points. '*I was*,' he insisted, his tone darkening.

'I don't doubt it. I saw you with Honest, that day in St John's.'

'What day? Jay's Law?'

I nodded.

'I was good, wasn't I? I was good, Tom,' he begged, looking tearful again. 'I want my houses back too,' he said angrily. 'And her, I want…' he stopped, his face went blank.

'Anita?' I asked.

'Don't,' he said, rubbing his eyes.

'Is that what this is about?' It was sad to see it. He looked like he was losing his grip on reality. I wanted to help him out of it. 'What a shit life, eh?' I laughed to lighten the mood, sniffing the beer. 'Maybe I *should* just drink the fucking thing. What do you reckon?'

'No, Tom,' he smiled, shaking his head. 'You know it won't help things. Look at me,' he laughed sadly, then he laughed some more, a little too hard, and mumbled, 'the golf hole.'

'Easier times,' I smiled.

'Will and Anita?' he asked, his face tightening.

I shrugged.

He just glared at me.

'I don't know, Christian.'

'Just tell me, Tom. I know you'll be honest with me.'

'I came here to see if you'd seen Marcus and now you're pointing a fucking gun at me. You really want me to be honest?'

He looked at the gun, removed his support arm and let it drop. He started to cry. 'You really care about your friends, don't you? Even that, that…' he turned angry again, 'twisted fuck with the twisted knee. He's sick, Tom. Really sick. Who knows what he gets up to behind closed doors?' He stopped still and took a deep breath.

'Please, Chris. Where is he?'

'They took him to the store.'

'Store?'

'Your store.'

'To Zion?' *Blabber mouth* – I smiled to myself, it felt like grief.

'I'm an alchy, Tom,' he cried.

'We're all alchys,' I smiled.

'Pah!'

'You're threatening to put a bullet in me and rather than thinking about Lucy and Dylan I'm thinking about drinking Coors frigging Light.'

He tried to laugh, but the engine faltered. 'Always tickled me, you did,' he wiped his eyes, smiling. He looked down at his gun, then at me and all the warmth and humour fell from his face. 'Everybody's fucking fucking!' He turned the gun up, leaving no time to do or say anything, and fired a bullet into his jaw.

I jumped up and immediately fell to my knees, ears ringing, dizzy with it. His body stumbled forward, his balance wavering. Maroon ribboned out of his throat and spat out of his eye. He dropped to the floor with a thud, then a crack, his head on the laminate. Briefly, he trembled in seizure before stopping dead.

I crawled towards him. 'You fuck, you fuck, you fuck! Christ, Chris! Christian!' I grabbed his hand, it was clammy. There was no movement. He was dead. 'You fuck!' I wanted to punch him, but I didn't want to get covered in blood, so instead I punched my hand. 'You bloody idiot, Chris! What did you do that for?'

I stood up, panting stress breaths, then sat down on the floor looking through the rough bloodied hole in his chin to the back of his splintered teeth, a tide of blood gently growing towards me. For a few seconds I found my head circling, hypnotised by it. I stood up again and went to open the window, but I saw Honest John talking to the Prices. *Shit.* They would've heard the gun.

There was an urgency about them. It was hot and they were wearing big suits and ties like they were on the campaign trail in 1979. Honest pointed and they glanced up. I jumped back. 'I've gotta get out of here. How the fuck am I gonna get out of here?'

Shit, Christian. Why did you have to do that?

When I opened the front door, I heard the echo of feet. I couldn't tell if it was coming from above or below. I went to the stairs. It sounded like there was someone above and below. I went to the lift shaft. There was no way I was going to leave quietly, but I had little option. It sounded like someone was coming down the stairs from above, so I decided to go up the shaft a floor, hoping to bypass them. I climbed onto the ladder, my legs trembling, every step feeling like I was going to miss a rung and fall to my death.

I got to the eighth floor and climbed out.

'Of all the people,' a voice said.

I held my hands up. 'I'm not a periph. I bought a guitar.'

'Shush, sounds like they're at his floor.' He was standing listening at the front door.

'That's what happened, I promise.'

'I believe you, calm down,' the butcher said. 'Sit.'

I sat on the arm of a big pink chair, probably as old as me, ready to move if I had to. He came and sat opposite me on a brown, beat-up old sofa. He picked up a half-drunk bottle of Coors Light and supped on it. It looked small in his hands – a panda chewing on a piece of bamboo. The room was dim and dirty. Quite the opposite to Christian's, two floors below. There'd been no modern decorating done to the place. One wall had been knocked through to make it bigger, a Roman plaster column in the middle of it, as if he'd had an idea about decorating but hadn't followed it through. The fluffy red carpets looked old and filthy. I wondered if he'd lived here before the bombs. After finishing the bottle he dropped it into a small bin by the side of him.

He didn't seem in the least bit frightening. I'd just seen Christian kill himself, but somehow the man put me at ease. He was certainly not the same guy astride Mel in my vision, nor the man who seemed fixated on me in Picks.

'He's never been right,' he said. 'Stick one drink too many in him and he becomes arrogant, angry, macabre even. Why do you think she left? She chose a life at Ally's over a life getting smacked around. Besides, they hadn't fucked for years.'

'I just came looking for my mate, Marcus.'

'At Christian's? He never liked poofs. Not like them down there,' he laughed.

'The Prices?'

'Shush!'

We both froze, listening. We could hear mumbling. It sounded angry.

'Have they killed him?'

'The poof? Doubt it.'

'Why? Look at what happened to Lee–'

'Who? The preacher? That was *him*,' he gestured downstairs. 'Christian wasn't right in the head. Get him together with Tony… the pair of them were twisted. Christmas Day for Christ's sake!'

'Tony? Moran?'

'Yeah, he's sick… did you hear the story about the cat?'

'Cat?'

'He hates em. When he was a kid he used to tie a piece of string around their heads and their tails. Then he'd tie the other ends on door handles on houses opposite each other and play knock door run.'

'Shit. And the cat…?'

'It didn't end well for them. That's what I heard anyway.'

'Christian and Tony Moran did Lee in?'

'On Christmas Day. That poor wench found him-'

'Sarah?'

'The one who wor drinking – Tony didn't like that either, but then it's hard to trust someone who don't drink. No offence.'

I was shaking my head, thinking about Sarah. She followed it with a six month bender which almost killed her. Then one night she nearly killed Tony Moran with a broken glass. She went "north" the following day. I looked up and the butcher was glaring at me. 'What?'

He half-smiled like a good soul and it irritated me.

'"I'm Tony Bonham",' I reminded him. 'That's what you said in Picks-'

'I know what I bloody said. What can I say? Sorry, fella. Tony just brings out the worst in all of us.' He took the bottle out of the bin and sipped on it, making sure he hadn't missed a bit. 'In a way, though,' he added, 'I am Tony Bonham. I've got a pig stomach in the fridge with a bag of pills in it.'

'A pig stom-'

'I expect most of us are hiding Bonham supplies. We're all responsible for him.'

There was a sudden popping sound below. 'What the-?'

'They're just opening the window. Probably need a bit of air,' he laughed. 'Sorry. Not funny.'

His round face looked glum and stupid. Had it been Tony's influence? He certainly didn't seem like a bad man. He reminded me of Mick or my dad, one of the old boys in the pub, who just went about life working, a drink or five every night. An old sod.

'But Tony Dale was Tony Bonham, wasn't he?'

'If you like.'

'It said in the Halesowen News-'

He laughed. 'Tony was a keyholder to the stock rooms at Ally's place, that's all.'

'That day in Picks-'

'Your alibi-' he laughed.

'How did you know?'

'You hid it pretty well,' he nodded.

'Stacey did him in,' I pleaded.

'Stacey didn't kill him,' he brushed off. 'She put the knife in him, but she wasn't behind it.'

'Who was? Tony Moran?'

He laughed. 'No. The business.'

There was a loud bang below like somebody had punched the work surface or a wall. I got up and went to the front door. There was some shouting. I went to open it. How would I get out of the building? The walls and floors were cheap. I'd lived in the other high-rise with my dad, heard the noises all day and night, TV, arguments, dogs barking and fucking. They'd hear me.

'They're not happy,' the butcher smiled, sitting comfortably on the settee.

I went over to the window. Honest John was still down there, trimming the lawn outside Ally's.

'You can't take the window,' he laughed.

'Can't take the window?' I asked, distant.

'It belongs to me,' he laughed harder. 'Besides, it'll hurt.'

His laughter was abrasive, grating. What was he telling me? I couldn't judge whether he was making silly jokes or saying something more sinister. *Is this the mushrooms? Is it right to trust this man? He seems like an ok guy. An old sod, yeah.*

'You'll have to hide here,' he added. 'From the Prices.'

'No, I really must find Marcus. The other two will be looking for me too.'

He laughed like he didn't believe me. Only then I remembered what Ray had said and my heart skipped a beat, before glooping speedily back into action, *the butcher killed the milkman.*

'What happened to the milkman?' slipped out of my mouth quick-speed, against my better judgement.

'You know nothing about that!' It was angry. 'That man, he was a bastard to them cows. You think Robert Parsons was bad to that goat-'

'The milkman shagged the cows?'

'No, not quite, but he didn't keep them properly. Hardly any food and water, locked up in small sheds. I've never seen such poor quality meat and I used to sell American mega-farm beef.'

I shook my head, confused.

'I didn't kill him! But I'm glad he's dead!'

The yelling below us intensified. They were arguing about something. We heard a door swing open and slam shut. Then the patter of fat feet on the stairs.

The butcher glared at me. 'Get in there. *Now.*'

'What? Where?' I panicked.

'Trust me, writer or no writer, they'll do you in if they think you killed Christian.'

I couldn't move, unsure what to do. He gave me a shove towards one of the rooms. I opened the door, it was the bathroom, a tiny piss-smelling closet with a plaque bottomed bath.

When he closed the door, I found myself in what should've been the dark, but the absence of light seemed to wake up the psilocybin. *How much did Will stick in that frigging coffee pot?*

Every little sound, the drip from a tap, the bath creak, the scuff on the floor was accompanied by a small light show, streaks and sparks. Every sensation, heat, sweat, the clothes on my skin, gave a smudge of colour. Every breath a brown cloud which, deep inside me, was accompanied by a fog horn, like I was in the Liverpool docks at the turn of the 20th Century. All fear disappeared once again. It was as if my nerve impulses were outside of me. I accidently kicked the bath and a thin spine of electricity cut through the dark and it made me wonder if the sparks were a projection of my synapses. *Am I broken? Will I ever return to the frantic, nervous, neurotic man I'd come to know so well? AM I FIXED?*

No knock, I heard the front door swing open like we were in a saloon bar. 'What's going on?' the butcher asked.

'You tell us,' a Price insisted.

'I heard a gunshot,' the butcher said, calm, perhaps too calm. 'Has Tony done someone in?'

'Come off it,' one Price.

'He smells like beer,' the other. 'You been drinking?'

'What of it?'

'There's a dead man down there, a bullet in his head.'

'Made it look like a suicide,' the other.

'Listen boys,' the butcher said. 'I don't know what you're trying to say-'

'But there were two unfinished bottles of beer down there. He wasn't alone.'

'Always been tight with Tony One, haven't you?' the other said.

'Self-preservation. I was tight with Christian too.'

'Who said anything about Christian?'

'What you doing?' the butcher panicked. 'What about the plan?'

'Tell us how you didn't kill him,' one menaced.

'I didn't. I was drinking here, alone-'

'Not enough-'

'Wait!' It was loud and desperate and I knew what he needed to say. I understood. *It is what it is.* It was just an event in the fabric of time.

It's time to die, Tom.

Immediately, Dylan's voice came to me in the bathroom: 'daddy,' loud, causing a small firework to explode in the air. 'I love you,' Lucy whispered, a mauve cardiogram. *I love you, too.* It all made sense. I was having a God moment. Everything was happening at the same time, overlapping itself. All of this came to me at once. The mushrooms, my absence of fear. *I've become a man. I've completed the game, now's the time to move into the next realm.* I was looking around for a butterfly, no longer was I the caterpillar. There were little sparks here and there, I was sure the tetrachromacy of my improved vision would come up with a butterfly. *Not even a moth?*

'Fuck it,' one of the Prices said.

There was a loud bang and the sound of a body hitting the floor. *Fuck, they've shot the butcher! Tony was right they're cleaning up the town!*

Without any further thought I stepped out of the bathroom and into action. 'Thank God,' I lied.

'Who the-?'

'What?'

They said.

'Thank Christ you shot him. He was about to toss me out of the window, until we heard people downstairs.'

I stood facing them, the poor dead panda between us, a bullet in his head.

'Tom Hanson,' Alan Price said.

'At your service.'

Alan was tall and thin, Tim was shorter and round. Both were all but bald. Alan just had the sides and Tim had combed a dry wave, but it was sticking up and he was sweating from the jog up the stairs. They were both probably in their late 40s but they looked older. The grey suits reminded me of the sort my dad wore before he gave it all up to drink in the early 90s.

'What we gonna do with him?' Tim asked Alan.

'He didn't like the alliance,' I pretended. 'The butcher never liked me. Fat panda.'

Tim snorted a laugh, eyeing the one-eyed corpse, a dark patch of blood soaking into the carpet. 'He does look like a panda.'

'Christian was recruiting me,' I continued. 'I can't believe he's dead. Said you needed a writer and I'm ready for it.'

'We've got Ross for that,' Alan said.

'Ross?' I stumbled, surprised. 'Like I said, you need a writer,' I smiled.

Alan laughed. '*You'll* have to let him know.'

Is that a threat? A promise? There was an uneasy tension. What was really being said here? Was Ross alive or dead? *How can anybody know anything in this goddam town?*

'Whatever you need me to do. I need a challenge. I've gotta get away from the fuckheads and do something positive or I'm gonna go fucking crazy.'

'Fuckheads? Fucking crazy?' Tim asked. 'You like a fuck.'

Is he asking me?

'What do you think, Tim?' Alan said. 'Christian had a lot of faith in him.'

'Yes, but so does Jake,' he said.

'But so does Ray,' Alan countered.

'Look, boys, I don't know what other people think about me. I don't honestly care too much,' I said, full of confidence. 'I was on the fence, I've gotta be honest. I've been on the fence for a while. But Christian was just killed for trying to bring me in and I just narrowly avoided being killed thanks to you.'

Alan walked over to the window and looked outside. I had the horrible feeling he was judging where I'd land. Tim was half-smiling at me, a drop of sweat on his forehead glistening brighter than a drop of sweat normally does. I started to wonder whether the answer was in his sweat. A troubling thought.

'That's all very well,' Alan said. 'But you just *barge* in here-'

'Yes,' Tim said. 'He did just *barge* in here.'

'I get it,' I said. 'I see what you're getting at. I spoke about leaving. Marcus told you, the stupid fuck-'

'You what?' Tim yelped, offended.

'Tim, calm,' Alan said.

'I'm calm, I'm totally calm.' He clearly wasn't. 'But what is it with these guys and their "fucks"?'

Is it the swearing? 'I apologise, Tim.'

'Mr Price, it's Mr Price to you,' the younger man said.

'Tim, stop it,' Alan interrupted.

'I'm not denying it,' I said. 'We discussed trying to find a way out of here and back into the UK-'

'With the importer-' Tim said.

'The importer?'

'Damien,' Alan said, turning around.

'Ok. With… Eeyore, we call him, yes,' I laughed – they didn't. 'But I went off and thought about it and decided to listen to Ally's advice. Then I went for a chat with my old pal downstairs – God rest his…' I looked down at the butcher and spat on him. 'Sorry, but-'

'So, the guitar?' Alan said.

'The guitar, how do you know..?' I played the game. 'I need something to help me relax. I was thinking of learning Cavatina-' slipped out. If they knew anything about music, they'd know an electric guitar was not the best choice for a classical piece.

'Of course we know!' Tim sniped. 'A man was shot dead just after you'd ordered it.'

'Jason? That was nothing to do with me!'

'Calm down, Tom, we know,' Alan said. 'So, he didn't tell you?'

'Christian?' I asked. 'That Tony was on the warpath?'

Alan laughed. 'He didn't even tell *you*. That's interesting – I wonder why. It seems poor old Chris caught wind of Jason doing the deed with Anita-'

'You're kidding?' Only then did I realise Anita actually must be a bonafide alcoholic – somebody trying not to drink, regularly slipping up, and then making all sorts of disturbing life choices.

I stepped over the butcher and sat down on the settee. 'I can't believe Christian killed Jason.' *Did he kill Marcus? The butcher said he didn't like poofs? Is that why he killed himself?*

'He's – he was – a funny sort,' Alan said, coming over to me.

'There's too much killing going on,' I said, my head in my hands.

Alan sat next to me. I thought he was going to put his arm around me but he didn't. 'Yes, yes,' he coddled. 'I think you'll be a good fit.'

'Yeah,' I mumbled, distant, mostly wondering whether I should ask them about Marcus.

'Now, come on!' Alan perked up. 'You listen to me, Tom Hanson. There'll be none of this moroseness. It's just the way it is. But it won't always be like this. I like to think this is our dark age, but it won't be long before we get to the enlightenment.'

'You sure about this?' Tim said, from behind me.

'You ignore him, Tom,' Alan said to a baby – I was about 10 years older than him. 'I need you to go to Ally and say "operation typewriter".'

'Operation typewriter.'

'Just say those words to her.'

'Now? "Operation typewriter"?'

He nodded.

I stood up and he smacked my arse, making me jump, 'go, go!' – one for each "go."

I walked past Tim who was clearly unhappy.

'Operation typewriter,' I muttered to myself, playing the game.

I stepped over the poor butcher and left the flat. Tim closed the door behind me. For a second I listened but heard nothing.

What a performance! I couldn't help but feel amazed by my ability to step up to the mark in a crisis. *That's what you need to survive in Halesowen. Sarah has it. Will had it on a good day. Loz doesn't, and Marcus…?* I felt certain he was dead. I realised I had to accept I'd probably never know what happened to him. The only lead I had was the metal store, but as everybody knew about it, it didn't feel like a safe place to go.

It just is what it is.

———————

I walked across the estate. I could feel the brothers looking down on me from Bredon high-rise. I refused to look back and walked straight to Ally's, just as I'd been told. When I came to her block, I noticed Honest John was using shears to cut away the grasses which disguised our kitchen window and the brew. He looked over at me. I smiled. He didn't react and returned to shearing the grasses. *They're keeping an eye on us.*

Ally answered the door in her dressing gown. 'Operation typewriter,' I said, with a cocky smile.

'Really?' she asked, testing.

'For sure,' I nodded.

I didn't know where Ally was on any of this. I just knew I needed to play it out like I was staying, before going to find the others.

I followed her inside.

'That's great, Tom. It really is. The Prices?' she asked.

Ricky was lying asleep on the settee, the full moon of his gut above the little star of his cock, twinkling in a black night of pubes. The room smelt of Christmas, paper doves sprang to mind.

'Yes. Alan seems alright, but that Tim's a bit off.'

'Ok,' she said, thinking. 'Probably the other way around for me.'

She was standing in the middle of the room, looking unsure what do with herself.

'You ok, Ally?'

'Me?' she said. 'Yeah, good.'

'You sure? Is it the baby?'

'Everything's absolutely fine.' She sat down on the settee. 'You didn't tell Will?' she whispered.

'No, course not. That's for you to do, unless you want me to.'

She shook her head.

'Operation typewriter,' I smiled. 'I've finally cracked it, eh? I'm in! Sounds interesting,' I laughed.

'That's great, Tom.'

She didn't sound especially pleased. It felt like she'd been trying to integrate me for years, but now she'd got her way she wasn't bothered. Perhaps she'd had a rough night between the sheets, Ricky beached beside us, a faint odour of beer and sweat emanating off him.

I gestured to him, mouthed, '*really?*'

'Eh?' She looked over at him. 'Oh,' she laughed. 'Why, jealous?' she tried to joke, but she really wasn't on form.

'I'm bigger than that!' I played, wiggling my little finger.

'Only just,' she laughed. 'Yuh prat.' She edged forward to reach for her glass of swamp juice. A tit popped out of her dressing gown, which she casually tucked back in.

'Ally, what's up?'

'No, nothing. I'm chuffed, Tom. Don't you worry about the boys. They'll come round.'

'I'm not worried, Ally. They'll pull their weight too, no doubt,' I lied.

'Did you find Marcus in the end?'

'No, have you seen him?'

'No,' she replied, expressionless. 'He'll turn up.'

I had a feeling she knew what had happened to him and that was why she was in this strange mood.

'We went looking for him,' I said, 'but got a little Lucy-in-the-sky distracted. I'm only just coming out of it.'

I daren't tell her about my bathroom light show, Dylan and Lucy coming to me to call me into the next world. I wanted to tell her about Christian and the butcher, but something wasn't right. I just needed to get out of there without arousing suspicion.

'Do you want a coffee?' she asked.

'Very funny.'

She looked confused, absent. 'What? Do you want a coffee or not?... Oh, of course, the mushrooms. No,' she scoffed a laugh. 'A hot one? From the kitchen?'

'Not now,' I said. 'Are you sure you're alright?'

'Me? Just baby-brain,' she smiled.

'Ok. If you're sure. I better go find the boys, fill them in.'

'You can't,' she sat forward.

'I can't?'

'No, I've gotta show you operation typewriter first.' She said it earnestly enough, but she sounded disturbed. *Will and Anita, maybe?*

'Show me? What? A typewriter perhaps?' I laughed, putting on a front.

Alarm bells were starting to ring, but maybe I was writing a novel again. Out the corner of my eye, I noticed Ricky stir. I glanced over.

He flinched, cupping his cock and balls, 'what you fucking looking at, Tom?'

'Sorry, Rick, mate. Just came to see Ally.'

He rolled onto his knees and stood up. 'Why d'ay ya cover me, wench?' he moaned.

'I en't your keeper!'

'Alright, alright, calm down,' he said, leaving the room.

She took a big gulp of her drink and heaved herself up off the sofa. 'Come on then, Tom.' She sounded a little bit more friendly. 'Come and see where it all happens.'

'Happens?' I asked, trying to mask an encroaching sense of panic. 'I really have to find Marcus. I can come back later, but first-'

'*Tom.*'

She meant it. I knew I was going to have to go and see what it was all about. This was why the Prices wanted me to see Ally, so she could show me what my role was in all this.

'Of course,' I conceded. 'Show me operation typewriter then.'

I followed her out of the living room, the echoing trickle of Ricky's piss down the hall. We went out of the main flat and into the cold stairwell, made warmer for a patchwork of rugs but still maintaining its essence d'urban on the floor beneath. She gestured up the red tiled stairs. I climbed up, two steps at a time, passing the Ganesh room. I wondered if Anita was still in there, how would she react to the news of Christian's death? Had he really been abusing her? Maybe she'd be glad.

'Next floor, Tom.'

'The top?'

'The penthouse,' she smiled, breathless.

I carried on up and as I neared the top, I saw the room ahead of me had a big grey metal door. It looked like a panic room – not that I'd ever seen one for real.

'This,' she panted, coming up behind, 'is the safest place in here.'

'Looks it. What is it?'

'Everything. The meds, weapons. The truth.'

'The truth?'

'Everything, Tom.'

'What's that got to do with me?'

'You need to know,' she puffed, 'what Halesowen's really all about.'

'Meds and weapons,' I laughed.

She took a big breath. 'Too old and pregnant for this malarkey.'

She opened a big padlock, slid a bolt and pulled the door back to reveal a second door made of wood. She opened this one with her key and stood out of the way. The lights were very low, but I could make out somebody sitting at a table. 'Go on,' she insisted.

The fetid odour hit me immediately. It was not quite death, but near-death. It reminded me of my dad in his last year. For a split second, I thought that's what I was walking into, a mummified icon of him. To me, that smell would forever be the truth of mortality and aging, the rot from within, piss, fish and faecal impaction. 'Ally,' I asked, disturbed and confused by it, but still compelled to investigate, 'what is this place?'

She gently nudged me inside. I recognised the figure at the typewriter.

'Ross?'

Fat in his chair at a desk, he was wearing a t-shirt, but no bottoms, his big red cock on show. On a grimy bed, out of it, Stacey lay naked but for a sock on her hand. *Fuck knows.*

'They got yow too then?' he asked.

'What do you mean-?' It was like a nightmare. Instantly, I recognised the vile truth. I turned around and Ally slammed the first door shut. I went to open it but she turned the key. 'Ally, what the fuck are you playing at?'

'I'm sorry, Tom. I tried.'

'Tried? What do you mean?'

'I really wish you could've joined in.'

'Joined in? What the fuck do you think I'm doing? I bought a guitar!'

'Yuh don't buy anything in Halesowen, comrade,' came from behind.

'Fuck off, Ross!'

'Come off it, Tom,' Ally said. 'That was a trick, a blatant lie. Marcus told everyone about the plan to go to Netherton and head off on a barge.'

'It was just a plan, an idea!' I banged the door. 'I changed my mind.' *Marcus. I hope he is fucking dead!*

'They obviously don't think so,' she said. 'I really wish it didn't have to be like this. This is operation-'

'Typewriter,' Ross joined in, before laughing. 'That's what this is. Our little news room. It's alright though, we've got Stacey for a bit of fun.'

I turned to look at her. The room was dim, but she looked bruised and filthy, her head rolling in opiate-contentedness. 'Ally,' I shouted.

I heard the second door closing. I banged on the wood, shoulder barged and kicked it, but all I managed to do was hurt myself. 'Ally,' I screamed, but I could hear nothing outside the room.

'Tom, calm down,' Ross said, clearly doped up himself.

'How can I calm down? They've got me cooped up like a prisoner.'

'Not like,' he laughed. 'You won't get out of here, believe me. I've been here for a couple of weeks, ay I.'

Stacey started to laugh, coming-to. 'Yow as well, eh?'

'Stace, what the fuck's going on? I've gotta get out of here. The boys-'

'Yow can say goodbye to them,' she cackled.

'What the hell is this? Why are *you* here?'

She sat up on the bed, pulled a sheet over her legs, breasts like a spaniel's ears. 'It was them,' she said. 'Wor it? I d'ay wanna kill Tony Two. I d'ay nick nothing.'

What the hell was going on? All the fear, which had been banished in the wake of my spiritual experience, came back to me. *Old Tom.*

'Why did you kill him then?' I asked.

There was a silence, before Ross burst out laughing, followed by Stacey, their laughter hitting the walls hard, bouncing a short, sharp echo which made dim blue lines, the mushrooms all but out of my system. 'Is there a fucking light in here?' I begged.

'Just this lamp in the corner.'

'How can you see?'

'Would you want to?' Ross said, pointing at Stacey, laughing.

'Fuck you, fatman!'

'You didn't mind my fat cock-'

'I don't want to know,' I said. 'For fuck's sake, why did you kill Tony Dale?'

'For this,' she gestured the room.

'What are you talking about?'

'A beautiful prison,' she cackled.

'Ross, maybe I can get some sense out of you.'

'We never should've elected the Prices,' he said. 'You chose them.'

'And you did. I just went along with Ray.'

He let out a small piercing fart and laughed. 'Councillor Ray. He's behind it all, you know. His vision.'

'He just wanted a council, representatives, civilised order.'

'Order?' Ross yelled, standing up, his cock flopping onto the desk. He turned away from us, taking the huge thing with him and started pissing. 'I spoke of order-'

'What are you doing, Ross?' I shouted. 'Stop it!'

'It's the piss corner,' he said. 'Instead we have chaos.'

'What am I in?' I yanked on the few hairs I had left, and sat down on the bed.

Stacey sidled over to me and put her head on my shoulder. 'It'll be alright, Tom.'

'Here,' Ross said, handing me a sheet of paper. 'We've got work to do.'

I read it. It said Halesowen News No.9. Headline: Bonham Gone.

I started to laugh. Will was with Tony. Loz and Sarah were at the baths with Ray and Damien. And Marcus was probably dead at the metal store.

'I'm never gonna leave, Halesowen,' I muttered.

Ross chuckled. 'That's the spirit.'

2032

'You... er... don't have to. I mean... um... you have a choice, Tom,' Damien said, securing the rope to a bollard.

'It's not a choice,' I said. 'You guys will do what you'll do, and I'll do what I'll do. And the world will keep on turning. Until it stops.'

'What are you rambling on about?' Marcus said, still on the boat, leaning on his stick.

'You wouldn't understand. Sarah would,' I said. I looked at Loz. He was shaking his head in disgust. 'What?' I snapped.

'I can't believe you! We were so close to all getting out,' he said.

'Not all of us!'

Loz held his hands up. 'I'm sorry, Tom. I'm sorry we weren't there. It must've been horrible, but-'

'I'm talking about Sarah.'

'Fucking hell, mate,' Marcus said, disappointed.

'Obviously I wish Will had made it too,' I backtracked.

There was a heavy silence, my face and hands numb with the cold. In the distance, the old man in the braces watched us, making sure we were mooring correctly – Damien knew what he was doing but dithered. Neither Marcus nor Loz could look at me, smarting at the fact I put Sarah over our lost quarter. But they hadn't been there, they hadn't seen what I'd seen. I'd spent months in a damp tent in a field trying to make sense of everything and, no matter how I rationalised it and bent it into a recognisable shape, it was just meant to be. Those who died, died. Those who lived, lived. What we did, how we lived and where we ended up was all ok. We just had to roll with it. Of course, it wasn't what I wanted. 'Why didn't she come with you, Damien?' I asked, frustrated.

He glanced up, could see I was conflicted. He pulled hard on the rope, before moving to the next bollard. 'She's staying... er... because of you, Tom,' he said.

'What do you mean?' defensive.

'Not... no. Because you... um... stayed for her,' he added. 'She wants to stay for *them*.'

For them? 'Oh.'

He nodded.

I was worried she'd stayed because she was sick of me, but she was just trying to do the right thing, supporting our lost town, something I'd not had the strength to do. Was I too lazy? Apathetic? Or just wrapped up in my own problems? I could've been a voice in Halesowen, a pair of hands. I was no politician, but my heart was in the right place.

Comrade Ross came back to me. Whatever I'd thought about him, at least he'd being doing something all that time. The last day in our prison, in the piss and shit, the reek of death, I gave up on the news, certain my job was done, just grateful I'd managed to stay sober. 'How did I stay sober?' I asked myself.

I caught Loz glancing at Marcus, shaking his head.

'Rehab,' Marcus moaned – he'd heard it all before.

'But first I had three spells on a psych ward at Bushey Fields,' I said. 'Four years later, I went to rehab and, yes, I finally quit.'

'What are you on about?' Loz asked.

'Why am I here now, if I'm going to go back? I was imprisoned to write for Halesowen and now-'

'What?' Loz, annoyed.

'I must go back to write. Things just happen,' I said. 'In whatever order they're supposed to. Like dots.'

Marcus made the crazy gesture, smirking at Loz.

I pretended I didn't see it, *I'm Tom and I need to say this stuff.* 'In 2008, three years before I quit, I was in 'Spoons and this random fella started espousing the virtues of recovery to me. I thought he was a nutter and I argued the toss with him. I knew nothing about it, just what you see on TV, but I thought I knew everything.'

'I remember,' Marcus quipped.

'Not as bad as Will,' Loz laughed, caught my eye.

Goose-pimply sad, I laughed with him.

'I tuned out,' Marcus said.

'He drove me fucking mad!' Damien said, getting up off his knees. 'Arrogant-' he stopped, the three of us were glaring at him. '*What?*'

It just wasn't his place to say anything bad about Will, especially now. He looked at me, awkward and nervous. He knew it. I laughed to break the tension.

Loz followed suit. 'Remember how he used to go on about there being nothing inside the sun-'

'Oh, God, barmy fuck,' Marcus chuckled. 'A hollow egg. No fucking fusions or fissions, no light years.'

'I don't remember that one,' I said.

'You escaped to Burnham for half a lifetime!' Loz laughed.

'I just got 12 foot lizards, satanic rituals and paedo-rings.' I thought about it. 'He wasn't all wrong, you know.'

Marcus squeaked a giggle, Loz burst out laughing.

'You can laugh, but if we close ourselves off to possibilities we'll never get the full picture.'

Marcus groaned. 'Here we fucking go…'

'An open mind saved my life. And Sarah's, whether she knows it or not. And now she's trying to *help* others,' I said, proud. 'That guy in 'Spoons talked to me about spirituality and the 12 steps and, at the time, I thought it was a goddam cult-'

'But now, halle-fucking-lujah,' Marcus mocked, 'here I am to save your souls.'

'Too late for you,' I smiled.

'What… er… happened to the… um… 'Spoons fella?' Damien asked.

'Never saw him again. He was drunk at the time. I guess he'd relapsed. He came into my life and left, like an angel-'

'Hah!' Marcus laughed. 'A fucking angel!'

Damien climbed back onto the boat and fetched the gang plank. I grabbed the other end. Once it was in place, Marcus hobbled down. He looked the worst of all of us. Gaunt and all but bald, his eyes beiged and red. He nearly lost his footing and I grabbed his arm. 'Steady. You alright?'

He laughed. 'Yes, luvvie.'

'Serious, man?'

Our eyes met and for a brief moment I thought he'd actually heard me, but then he turned to Loz, awkward, 'nothing a drinkie-poo won't fix,' and I knew he'd never change. If being left for dead at the Zion wasn't enough of a rock bottom to make him stop and see, perhaps nothing would be.

'What's your plans, Damien?' I asked.

'Head back. Food, fags and… um… booze drop. There's not a lot of space but… er…' he smiled. 'Or… um… Why don't you stay? I can catch you next time round.'

But there was no reason to stay. Loz and Marcus, my brothers since the baby-faced days of college, had made it out. They didn't need me. Wherever we were, we'd always be brothers, but just as I'd walked away from them 20 years ago, it was time to do it again. 'Fuck,' came out.

'We've only just caught up,' Loz said, crouching down to ruffle the ginger-crown of the cat. 'You're really going back already?'

'That ok, Damien?'

'Um, er… yes… er… space… yes, I guess.'

'You'll be back,' Marcus said.

But somehow I knew I wouldn't. This was the last time I would see them both. I held my hand out. Loz stood up, solemn. A handshake turned into a hug. 'Love you brother,' he said.

'Always, brother.'

I hugged Marcus. He'd lost a lot of weight. 'Just be you,' I whispered.

He laughed. 'Ark at Oprah.'

It was sad. I didn't expect anything else, but then we all had things we weren't saying, one way or another. For whatever reason we'd all been living a life of secrets and lies. 'Did *you* know, Marcus?'

'Know? Know what?' he half-panicked – what was I going to say?

'That night in Picks, before the last bus.'

He looked to Loz.

'Did *you*?' I asked Loz. 'It's alright, I'm not bothered about it now, am I.'

'Yeah.'

'I was there when it happened,' Marcus said.

'*How did you not tell me?*'

'I didn't care.'

I tutted, but it was honest. 'What about Will?'

'He knew,' Marcus said, 'but he was with Sarah.'

'Of course.'

'She didn't know,' Loz added. 'We thought we were protecting you.'

'Don't get me wrong,' Marcus said, 'it was fucking horrible, mate. The one begged-'

'Jimmy?'

'I don't know. The one Jake shot in the brook-'

'The guinea pig,' I nodded. 'Callum.'

'Probably. The other two tried to run away, but.'

'What happened to the bodies?'

'We buried them.'

'*You*?' Loz laughed.

'Yes, me!' he defended. 'I'm capable of digging a fucking hole! When I want to. Then Lee said a few, you know, a-fucking-mens and shit.'

Damien was watching us. 'Bloody… um… scag-heads, eh,' he said, just to say something.

'Rats,' Marcus corrected, looking to me, which made me feel complicit. I'd only ever meant it in the scavenging sense of the word, but they'd been exterminated like vermin.

There was a moment of awkwardness between us, the big lie, one of many, finally broken.

We looked to Damien to move us on. Unsure what to do with himself, 'Christopher,' he called, taking something from his pocket.

'*Christopher*?' I asked.

'The puss. Christopher,' he called again.

'As in Christopher Robin?' I laughed, side-smiling at Loz and Marcus.

'Just… um… Christopher.'

The cat tottered over to him on the barge, baited by some sweet-smelling flesh. I followed behind.

'Fuck,' came out again. '*Fuck*,' and again. It felt real, like my life was ending and starting all over again. Back in Halesowen, to write.

Notes for the News

Halesowen News – No.12

FEATURE – Life in the UK
Sadness in Shrewsbury,
The walk to Wales,
Camping in Llangollen,
Saying goodbye to the boys,
Car free zones and renewable energy.

SCULPTURE ARGUMENT –
Buttons and Nails,
Aynuk's argument against (Art has no function),
Ayli's argument for (Art doesn't need a function).

WHO KILLED GARY BENNETT –
An incomplete play. A call to start a theatre company.

PUZZLES PAGE –
Sudoku,
Crossword,
Join the dots!!!

OBITUARIES –
Remembering the euth'd.
Abstract – the death of the regime (a bit dramatic?)

2028

At the top of Andrew Road we heard the thump of music coming from different directions, saw the flash of disco lights like creatures jumping between the buildings. The flats had all been adorned with small flags like it was a VE Day celebration, the people linking arms singing "so, Sally can wait…" in wellies like they were at a festival. The roads were littered with debris from the storm, the grass churned up, but none of this mattered, the whole town was in a festival mood for the eve of the last bus. It was hard to believe the Squirrels was only a mile up the road, a tense and sparsely populated dystopia.

'And Jimmy was happy with that?' I asked sceptically.

'*Jimmy*?' Will asked, irritated.

'The scag rat.'

'I should fucking think so!'

Half of the alcohol had been retrieved from the scag rats in exchange for all of the money I'd taken from the cashpoint. 'I thought you weren't bothered about money?' I said.

'I'm not!'

'Marcus?' I asked. 'Are you pissed off too?'

'I'm not pissed off!' Will snapped.

Marcus laughed.

'Fuck you, fag!'

'I'm not a fag!' he defended.

Marcus glanced at me, I shook my head. I hadn't said anything, the green robe still burning a disturbing and perplexing image on my retinas.

Will noticed the silent exchange, 'what's going on?'

Marcus shrugged, innocent, '*what's going on?*'

Ahead of us, in the orange light of the streetlamps, a half-naked woman wandered across the road singing. '"One night, oooh, one night in heaven…" Classic! Turn it up, ay it!'

'Tits!' Will laughed, distracted. 'Can we *please* just forget the scag rats and try to have a good time?'

'I agree,' Marcus said. 'Just fucking forget them. Where's Loz?'

'In Picks,' I said.

'Jen there too?' Will asked.

'Yeah.'

'*Great*,' Marcus sneered.

Will laughed.

Gazebos had been set up on the grass, disco lights twirling beneath. There was a DJ, people cooking burgers and hotdogs, serving drinks and cake. I wondered who was paying for it? Was this a legitimate community effort? All it took was a couple of nuclear bombs.

'And Sarah's definitely coming?' I asked Will.

'Tom,' he sighed, irritated. 'I'm not her fucking keeper, am I?'

'I was just-'

'But you keep asking-' he said, frustrated.

'What? Once… twice, ok-'

'You've seen her since me-' he said.

Marcus gave me a sideways glance, but wouldn't make eye-contact.

'Yes, and she went off in search of God knows what-'

'She'll be fucked, no doubt,' he said. 'She's a wreckhead, like me, like you used to be.'

'Exactly! That's what I'm worried about.'

'Why? Why are you worried, Tom?'

'She's using. Anything could happen.'

'So what! She's some girl you've just met. Are you in love with her or something?'

'What? No!'

'Good.'

'Good? What does that mean?'

'Can we just have a nice time for one night?' he pleaded. 'No Sarah, no fucking recovery, and no goddam scag rats? I just need a break from it.'

He clearly did. His face was tired, his eyes black. I wondered where he was on the Baz stuff. We hadn't spoken about it since the morning after he'd killed him.

'Ay, ay, Tom lad,' someone called, from behind us.

I turned to see Ricky, a can of Strongbow in his hand, his orange Wolves top damp with cider dribble.

'How do, Rick?'

'Cor complain.'

'You've got… er… shit on your top,' I said, pretending to be a man.

'Yow still Baggies then, thought yuh'd gone all lah-di-dah.'

'What? No, can't be bothered with it,' I winked. 'I mean, you've dribbled.'

'Piss off,' he laughed.

'You heading down Picks?'

'Later on. Me old man's down there. Just gonna grab me some grub first, then said I'd meet the old sod. In a bit boys.'

He crossed onto the grass and headed towards the waft of burger fat, dad's old high-rise the back drop. Ricky reminded me of the days I'd go down the pub to meet dad, when he was vital and clear-headed, opinionated and funny. When I looked up at floor three, that image disappeared and I saw his blue lips on that last day. It was always there, the day he collapsed, somewhere, even if I didn't word it to myself. It happened on a Sunday, I'd been drinking but trying to control it. I hadn't drunk enough to deal with it. Once I realised it was more than a fall, I jumped up, panicking and called 999. They talked me through CPR. When the paramedics arrived, he still had a pulse.

'Tom!' Will called. I was stopped still, transfixed, looking up at the looming brown-bricked high-rise. They were at the bottom of the road. 'Hurry up, man.'

'Yeah,' I said, absently, walking towards them. 'Should knock the bastard thing down.'

In the bus station, Damien was sitting on a wall smoking a roll-up. He handed the baccy to Will, who proceeded to roll.

'Still here then?' I asked. 'Where is she?'

'Who... um?' he lied.

I just stared at him.

'Stace? Oh... er... she's in Picks. Doing me head to be... um... honest.'

'You let her treat you like shit,' Will said, sparking up.

'What you... er... on... er... about?' he defended, irked, grabbing his baccy. 'She's... um... just my mate.'

Will was shaking his head. 'You've gotta treat 'em a bit rough. Have a bit of respect for yourself.'

He looked bullied and downtrodden, unable to argue his point.

'What would you know?' I laughed. 'When was the last time you fucked anyone, let alone had a relationship? Not since the days of Limp Bizkit,' I laughed.

He knew I was alluding to the time of Tammy, but a smug smile grew on his face. 'This morning actually.'

'*Fuck off.*' I glanced at Marcus, who immediately looked down.

I could feel my face turning red. *This shouldn't bother me.* But it did. Of course I knew it was Sarah he was referring to, but so what? She was nothing to do with me, just a friend, someone I wanted to help. For myself as much as anyone. I didn't want anything more from her. Yet somehow I felt humiliated.

Loz was sat at our table next to Stacey. We squeezed through the fat of the drinkers which filled Picks, in a cloud of smoke. In the back, a throng of football voices sang "The Drugs Don't Work". It felt like the late 90s, transported back to easier times when we just drank and tried to get off with someone.

'Where's Jen?' I asked.

'Fuck her,' Loz said. He was clearly drunk.

'Er's a right selfish cow,' Stacey said.

'You'd know all about that,' Will muttered under his breath.

'Yow what?' She stood up, defensive.

Loz grabbed her arm. 'It's alright, Stace. Watch it, Will!'

Will immediately turned to me with a childish smile. Ordinarily I might have laughed with him, but I was still smarting from the revelation.

'Pahahaha! What you gonna do, Loz?' he prodded.

'Just… just… leave it,' he backed down.

Will sat at the table, laughing. 'You're staying then?'

'Piss off,' Loz sulked.

I sat down, mostly removed from it all. I looked behind for Marcus, but he'd disappeared. Then I watched him squeeze between Jake and Leroy at the back bar, muttering something discretely in his ear. Leroy noticed me and immediately turned away.

I felt a hand on my shoulder. 'Hello there, boy.'

Rex and Barb had come in through the back door. Barb looked shy, hiding behind him. I smiled to greet them. 'You ok?'

Barb shook her head, burst into tears and immediately scuttled back outside.

'Let her go, boy. For God's sake *let her go!*' he stressed, trying to make a joke of it. 'Out with the boys, eh?'

'Boys? We're men,' I nodded, smiling.

'What, boy?'

'They're not boys, they're men,' I half-laughed. Will was looking at me like I'd gone mad and clearly Rex didn't remember the conversation.

'Men, boys, what's the odds, boy?'

'Good point. Take a seat, Rex,' I said, getting up.

'No… no… Well, I suppose I could rest the old appendages.' He handed me his stick and pushed in front of me. 'So, boys, will you be taking the much publicised bus?'

'I ay a boy!' Stacey sniped.

'You most certainly are not,' Loz declared, embarrassingly transparent.

Will looked to me again. 'Pahahaha!'

He wanted me to laugh with him, but I just couldn't. 'I'm gonna go see,' I rested Rex's stick against the table, 'if Barb's, you know…' I went outside.

I found her sitting under the big clock, a balled up tissue in her hand. She'd always been an emotional woman, but she looked lonely with it.

'Please, Tom,' she sobbed. 'Leave me. I'm ok.'

'Is it mum?' I asked.

'No… Oh, Tom,' she cried.

'The dog. Is it Ben?'

'No. In a way, yes. But I don't know-'

'Is it this whole situation? Because it's enough to reduce us all to tears, but we get caught up in it and-'

'Yes,' she said. 'That's it. Caught up.'

The night was mild, but she was trembling. I put my arm around her, aware of the bones in her shoulders. She reminded me of Maureen. They were both so frail but so strong. Barb didn't think she was strong but she was. It took strength just to age and it was hard enough in the old world, let alone this new existence. She rested her head against my shoulder.

'Are we doing the right thing?' I asked her.

'What *do* you mean, Tom Hanson?' she said, suddenly flirting and pulling away with a smile.

I burst out laughing. 'Bloody hussy! That's the Barb I remember.'

'I don't think I've ever known what the right thing is,' she added, more sombrely. 'Your mum would tell you that.'

'Why would we even consider staying? No healthcare, electricity, what about food? What about water?'

'They'll find a way,' she said.

'Who's "they"? That's us, isn't it? How have we got to a point where so many people think it's ok to split up from the rest of country? Because that's what's happening-'

'I think many are leaving-'

'Were we brow beaten by the bombs? Or was it the Greek Riots? The viruses? Or the years of austerity before it?'

'Ooh, you think too much,' she dismissed. 'As bad as bloody *him*,' she gestured to the pub, where Rex was no doubt regaling them with something nobody understood but himself. 'It's just-' she stopped.

'Yeah?'

'The… the young. That boy and-' she started to cry again.

'Baz?'

'Yes, and-' she sobbed.

'What?'

'So young. Please, leave me, Tom. I need to be on my own for a little while.'

'What's the matter, Barb?'

'Go inside, Tom,' she pleaded.

I glanced around, confused. She was hiding something, I was sure of it. I stood up, 'of course, Barb. Sorry.'

When I opened the door to Picks, I was greeted by a line of women, arms around each other singing with the jukebox, '"he left no time to regret, kept his dick wet…"' the pub thumping with the mournful drums – above it the not-so-soulful wails of embittered women many ciders past the point.

The whole place reeked of smoke, sickly sweet apples and a garlic of sweat as I squeezed through the chubby punters, between breasts and limbs, dodging fag ends and slopping pints. The voices rumbling, mumbling, stabbing Black Country chortles from different directions – it was now another language, sounds, words I didn't recognise.

'Tom!' I heard Will call from down the end of the pub.

Just hearing his voice, his dumb beery voice, I was irritated. *Why do I bother*? I looked behind me and saw Tony Moran, an old dealer. He squeezed his missus, Big Val's, nipple, – she used to work behind the bar at the Edward. Aaron Moran was sitting on a stool, some girl much younger than him, probably legal, sitting on his lap. There were other faces, some I recognised, some I didn't. Christian was in the back, his arm around Anita, laughing away like a school boy. I could hear the chatty Black Country natter of councillor Ray somewhere. The Price brothers, short and tall business men, like a comedy duo but for the dour faces. Ricky's dad, small and old, sitting neatly against the wall, quietly supping on his pint. Some younger chap in a trilby, bouncing around like Scrappy Do.

Will looked over and he knew something was going on with me. I turned away, shaking my head, and made my way back up the pub, an arse in my groin, elbow in my ear. Will called me again. I gestured I was going for a pee, but I had no intention of returning.

At the back bar, Marcus was *ark-at-madam* about something, Leroy was laughing. Marcus looked *happy*, and Leroy looked like a real person, his round red face had a shape and life, elasticity. For the first time there was a person there – *in vino veritas*.

I could leave now. I could just walk out of this pub and keep on walking and no one would notice until I was miles away. I could walk north and start again, find my alcoholics and recover. I've done it before. There will always be people, there will always be friends to help each other muddle through life. Perhaps there's a novel in this last year since the bombs. I could find a quiet corner to write it, get a little job to pay my way. They'd be alright. Loz will start his new life with Jen and the kids. Marcus can mix with the church lot and Will can have Sarah.

The other side of Marcus, Jake looked sad, smoking and sipping at his drink. Was it my fault? The scag rats, the booze and jewellery? Had he been vilified by the congregation for our crimes against the church?

'Stop it, Tom,' I muttered under my breath. 'You meant well.'

'Eh?' some fella asked.

'Pardon?'

'You say something to me?' He was angry.

'No, no,' hands-in-the-air-surrender, 'just trying to get through.'

'Should fucking think so!'

'Sorry, mate.'

I pushed through, foot stamped on, cider splashed. I was standing at the door. *Could I really go*? It felt huge. I was scared, scared about leaving my friends, about starting again and having to address the things I was avoiding. To be totally honest, I was scared of walking through the night on my own. But I knew it was the right thing to do.

Then I thought about Barb and what she said, or didn't say. It was a loose end, a page to turn. And Jake was depressed at the bar. We made eye-contact. I smiled. He tried to smile back, tight-lipped and glum. I called him over. He shook his head.

Forget it, Tom, whatever it is. Take the hint. Listen. See it as a sign.

I looked down the bar to our table. Loz with his drunken crush. Stacey cackling – how I'd once longed for her with every bit of my boyish lust. Will swigging off his pint, finally given the apocalypse he'd always dreamed of – *perhaps he'll go on to lead the town to brighter days*. Old Rex opining on something, God, animals, fucking Nietzsche, who knew?

I scanned the pub for posterity, the old faces. Percy and Jack reminiscing over some spirit. Little old Doreen, who used to be the cook at the George. Tina leaning over the bar, offering an eyeful for a drink. Big Tony Dale, sitting at the end of the bar chatting to Dave White and some other fella. And all the nameless faces I'd drank with many a night in years gone by, all blurring into each other, the Steves and Pauls, the Katies and Gemmas. The mutter and grumble of voices, the high-pitched squeak and squawk of laughter and flirts, a background track for the background artists in this strange film, moving picture, series of photos which, as I walked outside into the dark of night, morphed immediately into a Picasso swollen Pollock painting on the beige background of a Francis Bacon triptych. And that would be the memory, as it so often is for me, colours, light and shapes.

Barb was a blur under the clock. She looked up. I waved and quickly walked away, *goodbye Barb*, off under the canopy of bulbous lime trees which someday would seed children to eat up the whole of Halesowen.

2031

I heard the slow creak of the outer door. Ally opened the inner door a crack.

'Come on, Tom,' she whispered.

She smelt like musk, it made her seem attractive.

Stacey was spooning me on the bed. Ross was lying on the floor against the back wall, naked, snoring, his bare feet slopping in the piss corner. In his hand he had a pen, where he'd fallen asleep mid-article. I couldn't help but smile – I'd miss him and I'd miss the newspaper. I gently peeled away from Stacey, but I felt her tense-up.

She grabbed my cock and squeezed. 'Where yow going?'

'Nowhere,' I lied.

Ally pulled the door to.

'Yow wuz trying to get away from me.' She steered my cock, until I was lying on my back. She started to pull the foreskin back. 'Ooh, still works then. After all these years.'

'Yes,' I said, a little surprised.

She knelt over me. 'You'll like this, Tom. Close your eyes.'

I looked to the door, it was closed. I saw a shadow move over the keyhole. *She's bloody watching us.* I shut my eyes.

'Now, imagine yow'm on a beach. It's 1999. I'm walking over in a skimpy tiger-striped bikini with a piña colada.' She pulled my foreskin back and forth.

'M-m-mojito,' I muttered.

In the background I could hear the sea lapping on the shore. I could feel the sun beating down on my naked body, the young, shapely Stacey coming over with a cocktail.

'Mojito,' I repeated.

'Yuh wha?' she asked, her grip tight.

'Mojito. I never liked piña colada.'

The sound of the water seemed to get louder, as she turned up the meditation track.

Meditation track? We don't have a player. 'Where's the sound-?'

'Shush, Tom. Soon be done.'

I opened my eyes and Tina was on top of me, one mottled breast flopped out of her basque. 'Stacey? Where's-'

'*Who?* Want a pint, love?'

The sound of the sea intensified. I looked to my right and saw the bed was afloat and Ross was swimming towards me in a murky lake of faeces and piss. I pushed Tina, Stacey, whoever the fuck it was off me, and she fell into the sea of shit.

'Tom,' she called, 'save me.'

I looked into the murk and for a brief second it looked like Lucy, her face vanishing below the liquid. Thinking quickly, I yelled, 'Ally, open the door!'

The door opened, the liquid quickly rushed out, washing a pregnant Ally down the stairs. 'Tom, you've killed us. You've killed us all,' she screamed.

'Serves you fucking right!' I shouted, jumping off the bed. 'Lucy!'

All that remained on the slimy, sodden floor was a fish.

'Tom,' Ross said, standing naked beside me, dripping shit. 'We'll have to…'

'Yes,' I nodded, fully accepting. 'Eat her.'

'Or fuck it.'

I woke up to the low light of our prison, sandwiched between fat Ross and the ever-dwindling Stacey. We were all naked. One side of me was hot, the other cold. I peeled Stacey's breast off my arm.

I looked to Ross, blue in the light, his mouth agape and dry. 'Oi, Aynuk,' I whispered – that was his pen name.

Nothing.

I poked his upper arm, the width of my thigh, despite a diet of little more than crack, smack, cider and an occasional tin of mushy peas. 'Ross? We've got work to do.'

His hand was on his chest, clutching pages. I guessed it was the article he was writing on why we shouldn't have a town sculpture – I was writing one about why we should.

'Oi, comrade.' I slapped his arm. It felt cold.

There was no breath coming out of him, no snoring, he was blue and cold. I knew, of course I knew, but still, 'Aynuk, move. I need to write.'

Weak and trembly, I climbed over the icy slab of body and fell to the floor with a slap. I got up and sat at the old Olivetti typewriter, inky letters on the same thin paper we used for the toilet – a beige bucket I'd fought for with an article about, amongst other things, sanitation: *Two Bombs and a Bad Education*. I was commenting on how, through the centralisation of power, we'd lost what the Romans gave us. I was proud of it.

In the typewriter was Ross's sculpture article for the debate section in Halesowen News No.12, our third collaboration. I looked to my stiff opponent, the crumpled pages on his chest. 'What's in your hand, Aynuk?'

'Nothing,' he didn't say.

I removed the sheet from the typewriter, put a blank one in and started to write.

Day 41. I'm not Him. 40 days have passed and I've decided I'm not Jesus – no more than we all are. I'm not Buddha, I haven't reached my age of Nirvana. I'm ok with that. I choose a different path. I'm ok with coming back in whatever form You, It, the Life-Cycle will have me.

Ross doesn't look well. Last night he couldn't even muster the strength to fuck Stacey. She seemed relieved. He went through the motions with me, trying to get me chase the dragon, puff his pipe or "just have a thimbleful of cider" as he calls it, which is what a mug's reduced to in his big hands. Once again I resisted. Today, day 41, who knows?

Stacey seems stronger than both of us, despite the bones protruding through her skin, collarbone like scaffolding around her neck. I've come to the conclusion women are just generally tougher than men.

'What do you think about that, Aynuk?' I asked him. 'Women tougher than men?'

'Ha,' he didn't snort. 'Some men, Ayli' – that was my alter-ego – 'some men, sure.'

I knew what he was trying to say, but now more than ever I was content to admit my weaknesses. I'd spent three years grieving, not contributing to our town, telling myself I was strong just because I'd managed to avoid drinking. And here I was in this fetid little prison with my cold comrade and withered boyhood crush. It was my own fault. I created this existence for myself.

Lucy wouldn't have grieved for this long. I remember splitting up in the early days, riddled with guilt and mixed emotions, unsure what it all meant, what my feelings were. She just got on with it. She told herself that was that and accepted it. Women are hard-wired to survive. Men are much more ready to click the switch to self-destruct. Women are more like men than men. Look at Ally, Sarah, my mum, Anita and Barb. Women keep on going until they stop. Men dig their heels in and judder to a halt.

'You write some shit, Ayli,' Ross didn't mock.

I looked to his body, bloated and hard, like a poisoned cat. 'What about you, Aynuk?' I reached for his sculpture article. '"A sculpture serves no purpose. *Art has no function*," you quoted. I think Gertrude Stein meant a little bit more than that. And what about these pages?' I asked, tearing the sheets from his hands.

'Oi,' he didn't argue.

The first pages appeared to be a transcript of Jay Bird's trial. Underneath, there was a title page. *What is Genuine is Proved in the Fire – The Gary Bennett Story.*

'What's this, Ross?' I asked intrigued.

'My masterpiece,' he didn't say, smug.

'Another one,' I scoffed.

The bed moved, Stacey sat up, 'who you talking to?'

I looked over at her, she scratched her hairy armpit.

'Ross has written a play,' I said.

'You kept telling me to,' he didn't say.

'I said you wouldn't know where to start,' I laughed.

'What yow on about?' she asked.

'I was talking to *him*.'

She gave Ross a shove. 'Tom, he's dead.'

'I know.'

I was pacing up and down the steamy cell, reading the play. 'We all knew it wasn't Jay who killed him,' I told Ross.

'But who did?' he didn't ask.

'I bet *they* did.'

'What yow on about now?' Stacey moaned, irritated.

'Who killed Gary Bennett.'

'Yow've frigging lost it.'

'It's Ross saying it!'

She sat up, her breasts flapping under her arms. 'Ross is dead!'

I knew he was dead, but even dead he was a better conversationalist than Stacey. I'd spent hundreds of hours talking to Ross during the course of our friendship, relationship, whatever you want to call it. He'd lost his senses a little in the last few weeks, doped on sex and drugs, determined to get me to join him, but had improved somewhat in the hours since his passing. '*In his play*, Stace.'

I climbed over the icy body and sat next to her. 'Do you remember Gary Bennett? He was stabbed outside the old post office.'

'Ar doh care.'

'We thought it was over a TV booster–'

'There ay no TVs,' she said, perplexed.

'Nothing to do with it,' Ross didn't say.

'I can see that now, Ross.'

'*Ross*?' she yelled. 'Tom, please, just shove him off! He's sending yow loopy, and he's making the frigging bed cold–'

Three in the bed, the little one trying to get me to roll the big one, who was saying very little, over.

'Just let me finish reading this first.'

(standing at the bar in Picks)

ALAN PRICE
For you (hands Jay a shot of Jägermeister).

JAY BIRD
Nice one, Al, manz. Yow alright?

ALAN PRICE
Gary Bennett was a good man.

JAY BIRD
(looks confused) Gary? (necks shot) He wuz yuh mate, wor he?

ALAN PRICE
He didn't deserve it, did he?

JAY BIRD
What yow on about?

ALAN PRICE
Sad, what happened to him.

JAY BIRD
Well, ar d'ay touch him!

ALAN PRICE
Neither did I.

JAY BIRD
What yow saying?

                        ALAN PRICE
        Oh, nothing. (whispers) I mean, you pinched a TV aerial-

                         JAY BIRD
                         For you, ar.

                        ALAN PRICE
    Looting troubled Gary. And then he was knifed. Who would do such a thing?

                         JAY BIRD
                         It wor me!

                        ALAN PRICE
                      I didn't say it was.

                         JAY BIRD
                     Must've bin yow then!

                        ALAN PRICE
                  (laughs) Don't be silly. I'm a Son.

                         JAY BIRD
                            So.

                        ALAN PRICE
    But you're not (laughs, turns and overtly ogles Stacey as she sings on the
                    karaoke). What a tramp, eh?

                          STACEY
          (singing) "Well, I have been foolish, too many times…"

                         JAY BIRD
    (shoves Alan, who falls into the karaoke speaker, cutting his head open) Ya
                             prick!
              (Tim Price rushes over to help his brother)

                        ALAN PRICE
           (rubs his head, smiling, to Tim Price) The trial.
    (they look over in the direction of Ross, sitting drinking cider with the workers.
                        Ross nods, smiling).

I punched Ross in his fat thigh, all buoyancy gone, the flesh hardening. 'You fuck! Tony was right! He was done for before the trial. It was all contrived.'

'Contrived?' Stacey asked.

'Jay's Law. Jay Bird didn't even hit him.'

'Jay Bird-?' she said, like she'd never heard of him.

'Just gave him a shove.'

'Dunno what yow'm on about.'

'It must've been the Prices! I have to write this story in No.12, Aynuk.'

We heard the outer door open – it must've been that time of the day, "pea-time" we called it. Stacey grabbed my cock, '*tell them.*'

'Let go!' I pushed her hand off.

There was a gentle knock on the inner door. 'Tom,' Ally called.

Naked, I climbed onto Ross's hard corpse, the cold of his clay gut transferring into my hands. I stopped and looked into his matte face, remembered a trip to Moscow, begging Lucy to go in with me to see Lenin's preserved corpse – she thought it was morbid. '"The most important thing when ill is never to lose heart,"' I said. 'Eh, comrade?' I kissed his cold forehead and laughed.

Stacey looked disgusted. I climbed off him and stood at the door. 'Yes, Ally?'

'You have a visitor,' she said.

'Tell her!' Stacey nagged.

'Shut up! A *visito*r?'

'Tell me what?' Ally asked.

'Stacey's being dramatic. She thinks I've lost the plot, but really I've just discovered it,' I laughed, proud of my words.

'Yuh what?'

'Ross is dead. He doesn't smell. But if you could remove him before he does.' There was a silence. 'Ally?' She didn't respond. 'Ally?'

'…Still here… dead, is he?' she said, as if she was stifling emotions.

'He's fucking rotting!' Stacey yelled.

There was another silence, the scuff of feet.

'Ally?'

'Ok, Tom. Stand back from the door. We're coming in.'

I stepped back towards the desk. The door slowly opened and Honest John was staring at me. They usually came up together, but normally he would stand somewhere in the background. This was odd and I wondered whether I was supposed to feel afraid.

'Oof, Christ!' Ally stepped back, covering her mouth and nose.

'It's not Ross,' I insisted. 'It's just the bucket. Close to needing an empty.'

'Oh, *Tom*,' she mumbled, from under her hand. I knew she wasn't really happy about the situation but she sounded a little sad, which was unusual.

Then it dawned on me. 'Is this it?' I asked. I looked to Ross's cold body, his lips blackened. 'Is it time?'

'Just,' she stuttered, 'cover yourself up, Tom.' She said it in a tone which made me feel like I was being dramatic, but I didn't feel capable of hamming it up.

'Of course, sorry.' I grabbed Ross's article off the desk and held it at my waist.

'Tom-'

Why does she keep saying my name? 'Yeah?'

'John found out what happened to Christian.'

'What does that mean?'

'You were the last person to see him alive.'

'I was the last…? But I didn't do it,' I said, matter-of-factly. *It all made sense*. 'This *is* it. Is this it, Ally?' I took a breath and smiled. 'Whatever you have to do, I want *you* to know – I don't care about the rest – Christian did himself in.'

I instinctively looked to the old typewriter. Even if I'd wanted to fight my way out, I barely had the strength to pick it up, let alone use it as a weapon against the big man. And even if I could make it past him, I'd have to get through Ally. In ordinary times I might've laughed.

John came towards me, emotionless and slow. I can't have been that much shorter than him, but I'd lost a lot of weight and felt tiny in his muscular shadow. There was nothing I could do. I closed my eyes, absolutely certain this was it. Then I heard the rustle of paper and Stacey's cackle. I opened my eyes and John was holding out a brown paper bag. 'For me?' I asked.

He nodded.

I took the bag off him and looked inside. It was tomatoes. I looked over his shoulder at Ally, who was stroking her ever-growing bump.

'Why? What's this all about?' I asked. But I knew why. The tomatoes clearly represented my death. It had been the strange motif in all of John's murderous actions. Something he'd grown with his dad, before killing him. Something he mentioned after killing Jay Bird and after we left St John's, Barb still warm at the altar. I didn't quite understand the poetry of it, but it was there. And now it was here.

And was there a poetry in it for me too? There was a father/son theme. *Is John the universal son, and am I the universal-*

'Tomatoes,' he blurted.

But I hadn't killed Christian, in fact I might've been his only friend in the end. 'I was there when he picked up the gun, but I didn't-'

'Tomatoes,' he suddenly pointed to the bag.

I flinched. 'Yes, thank you, John. But… They look very… red.'

'Red,' he repeated, staring at me.

I kept looking to Ally. She was shaking her head and stroking her tummy. '*Don't,*' she said, cryptically.

'Don't what?'

'Just don't.'

I could only think she thought I was going to say something sarcastic, but my wit had left me.

I looked up at John. He looked frightened, like he'd been placed here against his will, like he looked the day of Jay's trial. I felt sad looking up at him. I knew I was implicating myself but I couldn't stop myself saying, 'sorry.'

'Picked,' he said, pointing at the bag.

I guess I have been. I looked over his shoulder. 'Before it ends, tell me, have you seen… you know… the baby-daddy?' I asked Ally, patting my stomach.

She shook her head, but I couldn't tell if she was lying.

'Any of them?'

'No, Tom. *Enjoy the tomatoes.*' She glanced at the cold elephant in the room. 'There's been some… changes.'

'Yes,' I said, looking to Ross. 'I didn't do that either.'

'He needs to fucking go,' Stacey said, scrunched up in the corner under the bedsheet.

I stared at Ross's stilled face and felt a pin-prick of emotion. I was suddenly overpowered with the realisation that I had to finish No.12, I had to tell the town the story of Gary Bennett, for Ross. I looked up at Ally, panicked, 'but we can still finish this edition, yeah? I mean, it's nearly done. I mean, we have to-'

'*We?*' Ally asked.

'Tell them, Aynuk,' I said to Ross. 'We can, can't we?'

'*You* can, Ayli,' he didn't say.

'Same difference.'

There was a silence. Ally looked genuinely upset. 'Tom...' she tried to speak. 'Not. Long. Now. Not long...' She stopped, tearful, and turned away from me.

'Not long? Ok,' I nodded. 'But just give me two days... a day... Ally. I can write it.'

'No, Tom, you don't have to,' she said, without looking at me. 'John, grab Ross.'

'Don't you dare,' Ross didn't say.

'Aynuk doesn't want you to,' I insisted. 'Ally, listen to me. Just let us finish No.12.'

'What yow fucking on about?' Stacey yelled, from her corner. 'He's lost it! He keeps talking to it, Ally.'

Ally rustled in her pocket and pulled out a little black wrap. She turned and skimmed it towards Stacey, before turning back. It landed on the bed and Stacey dropped the bedsheet and scrabbled to get it. Honest John was transfixed on her gaunt naked body.

'Yow ain't having me, ya perve,' Stacey sniped. 'Now get that fat dead fuck out of here!'

He moved towards my comrade and reached under his arms, but his body was too heavy.

'Please leave him,' I stressed. 'If we...I... don't finish it by the time he smells, then do what you need to.'

John grabbed Ross's feet and dragged him down the bed.

'Stop him, Ayli,' Ross didn't say.

I shrugged helplessly. 'What can I do, comrade? My fate is your fate.'

'Just until No.12-' he didn't beg.

'Just No.12,' I pleaded. 'Please!'

'Tom!' Ally screeched, her hands on her ears.

John pulled Ross off the bed with two smacks which sounded like a broken pelvis and skull. Not that it mattered. Ross didn't even not say anything, and John dragged him out of the room.

'I'll still keep the News going, Ally,' I placated. 'I promise. I can do it. I can-'

'Tom, listen to me,' she stressed. '*Eat the tomatoes*. You don't need to do the news. *Not now.*'

'I can write it-'

'The tomatoes!' she shouted and pulled the door to, turning the key quickly. 'He's not got long,' I heard her mumble to John.

'I can do it,' I banged on the door. 'Ayli can still write! I can write Aynuk, too, if you need me to! Ally! We can still argue about the sculpture!'

The outer door closed. I fell to the floor, my back against it.

'You'm really not well,' Stacey said.

I would've cried if I'd had the liquid inside to tear. Instead, a waft of toilet hit the back of my throat and I dry heaved. *Be brave, old soldier. Soon be over.*

Stacey was looking at me pityingly. She proffered the spoon.

I shook my head.

'Hold it for me.'

I wanted to laugh, but who could blame her? I got up. 'Maybe I *should* fuck you. Day 41, Tom fucks Stacey.'

'Think y'could,' she cackled.

I held the spoon whilst she burnt the brown powder and sucked it into the syringe, then watched as the drug hit and she melted, needle in arm. She flung the sheet back to offer herself to me. 'If you want.'

I picked up Ross's play and continued to read it.

———————

'You'll be left all on your own,' I said, inspecting a tomato.

'I don't mind,' she murmured, still half-gone.

The first week had been the hardest. Ross had gone on endlessly about how he was Solzhenitsyn in a Siberian prison. It reminded me of all those years I spent drunk, thinking I was Jack Kerouac, a tragic aberration waiting to be discovered. Stacey just lay open, waiting to be filled by crack, smack and Ross. Mostly I stood and watched in the corner, the thwack of flesh and the reek of bodily fluids making me wretch. We didn't have the bucket back then and slowly the piss and shit crept out of the corner towards the bed. I soon accepted sharing a bed with them for this reason. By the third week, the sun warming up the walls, we were all sleeping naked, my clothes used to mop up the shit and piss, Ross's fat cock against my thigh, Stacey's flaccid breasts on my arm, neck or face.

I bit into the tomato, the juices slightly salty. *Poison?* 'A-ha! Is this how they want to kill me?' *Perhaps this is Ally's mercy. I'm not stupid.* I remembered Jay Bird's head cracking open on the cold hard floor of St John's. I threw the tomato in the direction of the bucket.

We won the bucket on week four. We'd just finished No.11, our second joint effort on the Halesowen News. Ross was the named editor, but we wrote under the pen names Aynuk and Ayli. Ross was writing what he knew, communism and the workers, need over want, espousing the virtues of his Halesowen ideal. I was writing about Hollywood musicals and the traditions of British comedy, my silent tribute to Christian, his last request for entertainment.

I pictured Christian's young face all those years ago, as I'd pretended to fuck a golf hole. One 15 year-old pissing himself laughing at another 15 year-old desperate to entertain, desperate to be liked. Almost four decades later and the fates had conspired to have me accused of his murder. I couldn't kill anyone if my life depended on it.

'I don't want to die,' I muttered.

Stacey put her hand in mine and squeezed. It was comforting and transported me back to better times, to a time when she was really there and every man knew about it. 'Remember the millennium?'

She squeezed my hand again. It was the best response I could hope for.

'Do you remember it?' I tried again, but nothing.

Auld Lang Syne sung, we'd left the George and made our way back to my dad's. Four of us were on my bed. Will was sitting legs folded, skinning up, Marcus was telling us he had to go home whilst falling asleep against the wall. Stacey had her leopard patterned tight-fitting dress and skin-toned tights. Her face was angular and strong, dark freckles, red lips, deep and meaningful brown eyes. She was sharp and spoke smart, maybe 26 or 27. We were all about 20, and I tried to kiss her. "You don't want this, Tom," she said, grabbing my hand.

But that had just made me want her more. I tried again, but she turned her cheek. I tried once more but she pulled away and jumped up. "Da da da da," she sang, ""cats are crying, gates are slammin'…""

I'd never heard of Fairground Attraction before that night. It was her CD. I watched her dance. It dawned on me she didn't want to kiss me, she was letting me down gently, which depressed me but I just kept on drinking and forgetting, my normal.

Many years and many kids later, we kissed on my last Christmas Eve in Halesowen. I knew I wasn't her type, just a drunken pest. But I was an alcoholic and pathetic and I let myself believe it meant something.

I looked at her now, sitting against the wall. She was pushing 60 and grotesque, a Hogarth mother, only rather than gin she had a needle in her arm. Her skin was tight on that angular skull, the brown of her corneas bleeding into the yellow of her eyes. She spoke slowly and without the street smarts of those days, and that cackle, hollow and jagged. Smack and crack had not been kind to her. She had that forever young thing that scag rats have, like a teenager with a terminal illness. And that smell, like chip paper. But we'd had a past, and I was about to die. I rubbed the fur of her pubis and for a moment I forgot everything, but she didn't respond. It was like stroking a dead cat.

'Did we ever stand a chance, Stace?' I asked.

She turned so slowly I heard a creak in her neck. 'Yeah, man.'

'*Really*? Do you remember, then?'

She half-nodded.

'Millennium? You wouldn't let me kiss you. Then Christmas Eve?'

She moved her head towards me and went to kiss me. I let her peck my lips but it was cold and terrifying, I could feel her teeth behind those withered lips. She rested her head on my shoulder, the stench of grease in her hair.

'You played "Find My Love" by Fairground Attraction. I'd never heard of them but pretended I did.'

'Oh,' she whispered, '"on nights like this feel like falling…"'

'Do you remember?'

At least we had this, this memory together. At least we weren't alone in our dying days. However we'd ended up, we had this youthful moment when we were vital and excitable.

'You had a leopard skin thing on.'

'Leop-ard skin?' she spoke slowly, then cackled. 'Nah, man. Never had one.'

'You did. It was tight. You looked so good. Those hips-'

'Yeah?'

'You remember?'

'Nah, man.'

'What?'

'Not me.' She was shaking her head.

'What! It was!' It hurt. For some reason it hurt. 'And then Christmas Eve? The kiss?' I panicked.

She was shaking her head.

'What do you mean!?'

'Yow never kissed me,' she said.

'I did! I'd been dreaming about it for a decade!'

'We en't that,' she said.

'I know, but-'

'You want it now?' she asked, eyes half-closed, naked and open.

It was like realising Lucy had gone all over again. I don't know why, but that's what it felt like. I looked to the bag of tomatoes. *No!* Soon my executioner would be here. My world was ebbing away and all I had was Stacey and the few memories we could've, should've shared. *Have I imagined it?* 'No!' But I started to doubt myself. Doubt something which wasn't even that special or beautiful, in fact it was sleazy and warped, but it was real. I thought. Maybe she never had a leopard skin dress, maybe it was a zebra, a tiger, a catsuit? Maybe it wasn't even her, maybe I dreamt the whole thing, made it up, like a story in a book. I had a sudden vision of Lucy asleep lying across me on our brown settee, the baby asleep at her breast. A blessed memory. But then it hit me… it was just a photo I put on Facebook. *That's not memory! It's a photograph!*

'You got up and danced, Stace,' I pleaded. '"cats are crying, gates are slammin…"'

'"Wind is howling,"' she sang.

'Yeah, you remember?'

'I love Fairground.'

'I know!'

She lifted her head and moved back, 'do a spoon, man-'

'What? No!'

'Chase a line, then.'

I got up and walked to the door. *John, kill me. Come and kill me now.* Jay Bird popped into my thoughts and I saw it again, the impact as he hit the floor, like an exploding pepper. Dead. *Because of her, let's face it!* Then I thought about Damien. *Poor old Eeyore.* Where was he now? Did he get them all out?

I lay on the cold floor, naked, curled up in a spiky womb, regretting everything, coming back to Halesowen, staying in Halesowen, stopping outside dad's flat until it was too late for me to die with them. I tried to cry, I wanted to cry, but I was too weak and ill to cry. I could see a half eaten tin of peas. I tried to reach it, to eat and cry. It was too far. I closed my eyes, my head hurting. Eventually I fell asleep.

'Dad!' I woke up shivering.

'Who yow spaking to now?' Stacey asked.

'I'm sorry I left you lying on the floor naked.'

'What?'

I'd been drinking in 'Spoons when dad called to tell me he'd had a fall. I told him I'd be up in a bit. I had another drink, then another. A few hours passed. 'I didn't know you were naked, dad. You just said you'd had one of your falls – but the way you'd treated me!'

'What yow saying? What's up with ya?'

I sat up. The cold was sinking into my stiff bones. *Is this what it felt like?* I felt delirious. I could see his face in front of me, calling me. I remembered those old bones in his pale thin skin, curled up in the foetal position, trembling.

'I made it up to mum, but you…' I could see his white face, the Parkinson's tremor in his jaw… 'you were dead before I-'

'Stop it!' Stacey interrupted, annoyed.

'Before I-'

'Stop being mental!'

'Before I came back to life, before-'

'Please!' she screamed.

I stopped. She was on her knees on the bed, begging me, her face pale and dripping with sweat.

We heard the sound of the bolt, the big door was opening.

I looked up to the ceiling. 'Before I started to do things right-'

'For fuck's sake, Tom. *The door.*'

'*I know*, Stace.'

I got onto my knees. 'Forgive me, dad'

'Bloody hell, yow'm right off.'

I smiled. *It's not her fault she doesn't understand. There's so much of life and people we just don't get. Like this.*

I would never understand why it had come to this, I would never find out what happened to my brothers. I would just transcend into the next phase of existence, whether that be to fertilise new life or something else which I'd never figured out. I smiled, resigned, and used the bed to pull myself up. There was nothing I could do now but leave this life with dignity.

'Woh,' she smirked, pointing.

'What?' I looked down. It was an erection. 'How did that happen?' I inspected it and it looked bigger than normal, like an old Italian statuette.

Stacey was cackling, reaching for it.

I stepped back, feeling a little off balance. It was as if all the blood in my body had pooled to one place in a last affirmation of life. I looked to Stacey and considered making her a last request, but there was no sowing my seed there. No legacy to be had.

The key turned. The inner door opened. I faced my executioners, hands in the air. 'I'm ready. Take me.'

'What you doing?' Ally asked, looking away.

'I'm ready to face my fate.'

'Have you been… with…? Never mind. Put this on.'

She handed me a jacket and some baggy shorts.

'What's this for?'

'Did you *eat* the tomatoes?'

'No,' I smiled, smug – *you'll have to face me and do it.*

Behind her, John was looking nervous, his white t-shirt speckled with blood. 'Tomatoes. Toms,' he said.

'You really should've,' Ally said.

'What's going on?'

'Toms-the toms-' he was pointing at the mostly full paper bag.

'I tried,' I said.

'Did you see?' Ally asked. 'The tomatoes? You're free. Did you see? You're free,' she insisted. 'Did you see?'

'See? Free? What do you mean? *Dead?* What was in them? Acid?'

'No, yuh prat. You're free to go.'

'Free?' It hit me like a pang of conscience. 'No! No, you're wrong.'

'The tomatoes,' she repeated. She was nodding, half-smiling. 'Do you understand?'

'Do I…?'

John came towards me, I ran to the bucket. He grabbed the bag of tomatoes and left the cell.

'What's happening, Ally? Why are you doing this to me? Just shoot me! Where's my comrade?' A strange noise was coming out of me, a whimper, like I was crying, but even I didn't believe it. 'Dad!' I shouted. 'Dad, I'm sorry!'

'*Dad?*' Ally asked. 'John, give me the bag.'

John started taking out the tomatoes and putting them in his pocket.

'They were nice, John,' I said, kicking the tomato I'd thrown across the room behind the bucket. 'I would've eaten them eventually.'

'Forget the bloody tomatoes,' she snapped.

John handed her the paper bag. She turned it inside out and held it out for me. I edged towards her, grabbed the bag and ran back into the cell.

'Read it, Tom.'

The next time I come, you will be freed. You need to mentally prepare yourself for this. Alan and Tim Price will no longer be here. The Sons will not exist. TVs and radios are in use.

'TV?' I asked.

'Yes, Tom,' she smiled. 'It was you.'

'What do you mean? What was me?'

'Fork handles,' she said.

'Fork handles?… "Handles for forks?"'

'Exactly,' she clasped her hands together.

'"Hoes,"' John spoke, before laughing, slow and deep – I don't think I'd ever heard him laugh. '"I thought you meant hoes",' he chortled.

'Hoes? Yow all sound fucking barmy to me,' Stacey moaned.

'The article, Tom. You reminded people about the Two Ronnies.'

All I'd done was write about Saturday evenings watching an old convex box of flickering lights. 'So, I don't need to write anymore?' I asked. 'Is that why I don't-?'

'You don't need to write because you're free,' Ally said.

'I did it in No.11,' I smiled, as if somehow that had been my intention all along. Ally seemed truly happy, any lingering feelings of betrayal evaporated. *I did it.* 'But Gary-'

'Gary?'

'It doesn't matter. It wasn't me, the article. It was Christian really-'

'Don't,' she warned, nodding behind.

Honest John looked up after wiping blood off his hand on his trousers. '"Tins of peas",' he laughed.

'What about Stacey?' I asked.

'What about me?' she defended, back to the wall, scowling, her long thin hair pooled in the grooves of her collarbone.

'Stace,' Ally whispered, edging inside.

She shook her head like a stubborn child. 'Nah! Tony Dale, ay it.'

'That doesn't matter now,' Ally said.

'Tony Dale! That was the deal.'

'*Stace*,' I pleaded.

She pulled the sheet over her naked body, still shaking her head. She reached for her spoon. 'Tony Dale!'

I looked to Ally. 'Is this all for real?'

'Yes, Tom. You're free.'

I climbed onto the bed and grabbed Stacey's cold, bony hands. 'Please come. You can have a better life than this spoon.'

'No!' She pulled her hands away.

It was the wall. I knew it. I recognised it. There was nothing I could say. She wasn't ready for change. I looked into her cold eyes and remembered Sarah. I'd looked into Sarah's eyes and I'd seen me. In the corner of the room, were my balled up piss soaked clothes. I rummaged through the pockets and found the little baggy of ash. I handed it to Stacey. 'Remember?'

'Weed?' her eyes lit up.

'Ash. I told you about Sarah.'

'*Fucking ash*!' She opened it up and poured the contents onto the bed, as if somewhere inside there might be a little nugget of something worthwhile.

Ally pulled out another black wrap and tossed it to Stacey. She grabbed it, blew the ash off the bed and then immediately started unwrapping it.

I put the jacket and shorts on and grabbed Ross's play. I appealed to Stacey one last time but she just held out the spoon. I shook my head. 'Bye Stace.'

'Fuck ya then!'

Ally ushered me to the stairs. As I made my way down, I heard Stacey close the door to our cell.

On the floor below, Honest John went into the Ganesh. I glanced inside and I saw the naked leg of a man. Ally noticed and silenced me with a shake of the head.

She stopped at the bottom of the stairs and, stroking her tummy, 'you know he's dead, right?'

I had a sudden panic, 'Will?'

'No, yuh prat! Ross!'
'Aynuk?'
She nodded.
'Was that…?' I asked, pointing upstairs.
'No!' she said, like I was being ridiculous.
Scratching my wiry beard, I looked into her dark eyes. *Who knows what's real anymore?*
'You *do* know Ross is dead, right?'
'Yeah. But he's alive, too,' I said, thoughtfully. 'We're all alive and dead, Ally.'
'Tom,' she stressed. 'You sound like a nutter. Up there, you were talking to a corpse-'
'Ross-'
'Stop it!… Look,' she struggled, '*I'm…*'
She was trying to apologise. I nodded, smiling. 'I know. And yes, my comrade is dead.'
She looked unsure. 'Let's leave it at that then.'
We entered the main flat, the sickly sweet reek of a vanilla Yankee candle, and I could hear a rumble of voices in the living room. The sound of so many people made me panic. 'What's going on?' I mouthed.
'They want to see Ayli,' she said, rolling her eyes.
'You what?' I whispered, confused.
'Tom.' She seemed conflicted. 'Oh, Tom, I thought it was for the best. For Halesowen. Operation typewriter-'
'It is what it is. There's no point looking at it any other way. I'm alright.'
'You're not alright! Look at you. Your face, all bones, talking to dead people. You're messed up.'
'*Thanks*,' I snorted a laugh. 'Don't worry about me. I just need to try and find the boys-'
'They're gone, Tom!'
'Dead?' I gasped.
'Who knows? I don't. I just know they're not here and nobody has seen them since you… disappeared. Now, everybody wants to see you,' she shrugged, incredulous. 'Not you so much as Ayli.'
'That is me. Why-?'
She held her hand up to shush me, listening at the living room door. 'Just go with it.'

'That's all we can ever do, Ally,' I found myself saying. 'Cells transformed amongst other transformed cells, which will ultimately transform again.'

'What you on about now?'

'That's what we are.'

She looked confused.

'People. We build complex things out of other transformed cells and then we destroy them.'

'Tom, please.'

'If ever there was a trait of this animal, it's build and destroy.'

She was circling her bump faster.

'Who killed the Prices?'

'It doesn't matter, Tom. Let's just say the Prices, and Christian, weren't such wonderful people. They did some bad things.'

'What did Christian do?'

'What's the worst thing you can think of?'

'After living here for 4 years? Well, it's certainly not shagging a goat,' I laughed.

'No, but,' she stopped. 'You're John's hero.'

Without saying anything else, she swung open the living-room door.

The room of townspeople immediately silenced when they saw us. Ally entered and I followed behind, my grey jacket wide open to my baggy-skinned torso, the beige shorts above the knee of my bone thin legs.

'Oh my God, Tom,' Anita cried.

'We d'ay know,' Ricky said.

'Yow'm Ayli?' Mick asked. I nodded. 'Yuh dad'd be proud, kid.'

'What's going on?' I said.

Mick started to clap, the others joined in. There must've been 30 people crammed into the room, clapping. Why were they clapping? Was it because they could watch TV? Was it because I'd been freed? Or they'd been freed? It didn't make any sense. I didn't know whether to laugh out of hysteria or cry with relief.

'Well done, son,' someone said.

'Blinder,' another.

'Was alright, that was, mukka,' came from behind, with a pat on the back which sent a nerve-pain judder through my bones.

'Yow can write,' an old woman said.

I smiled a thank you, but I felt like a fraud taking credit for something I hadn't done. All I did was recount a memory. I was desperate to run outside to get some air, but it felt rude.

'Come on folks,' Jordan said, standing up, his checked-shirt neatly tucked in. 'He needs room to breathe.' Slowly, they stopped clapping. 'Tom,' Jordan continued, with an air of authority. 'I can see this is difficult, but it's really good to see you.' He reached down and picked up an electric guitar. 'For you,' he smiled.

'Is this from the federalis?'

He laughed. 'It's from me. For what you've done. Mick,' he prompted.

'Ar.' Mick opened his little DVD player, the disc whirred, the light came on.

'Morecambe and Wise?' I asked him.

The BBC screen came on. It was the Two Ronnies. He skipped ahead to the sketch, Four Candles.

'But where from?' I asked, astonished and bewildered by it all.

'Quinton,' Jordan said.

Within seconds, the town were laughing, stretching and bending to get a glimpse of the screen, of a savvy little man irritated by a dumb bigger man buying things in a hardware store. "You're having me on," the little one said, which made me laugh too. I remembered lying on the floor, leg-reddening by the old electric fire. In front of me, a ceramic mug of sweet milky tea, bits of biscuit floating in it. Dad was sitting on his chair, glass of whisky on the arm, flicking cigarette ash into his hand. He took one last drag, leant forward and poured it into the heavy glass ashtray. "Watch the film after this," he smiled. "Your mother wouldn't let you stay up this late."

'I just need some time, please,' I said, stepping outside, fanning away mixed emotions with the pages of Ross's play.

'Where do we go from here?' someone asked.

The whole room was looking out at me. 'I don't know,' I shrugged. 'Quinton?'

'But this is our home!' Ricky shouted.

This was followed by grumbles in agreement, one or two shaking their heads at my apparent disloyal response.

'I don't mean move,' I said, 'I mean, Quinton is probably a good place to ask… oh, I don't know.'

What was I supposed to say? Not an hour before I was stewing in a cell on the top floor, waiting to die, after spending 41 days stone cold sober, living a senseless existence I couldn't even have dreamt up – and I was a writer, supposedly. Now I was being asked advice on how we move forward, my head needing to process not only a new reality for myself but for the town.

'Come on Ayli,' Mick winked.

'Yeah, come on, Tom,' another voice.

'Ooh, don't forget the guitar,' Jordan said.

'Just everybody calm down,' Ally yelled, barging through the bulging crowd. 'You're all bleeding barmy. Let him have some time. Go Tom,' she said. 'Go!'

I walked quickly backwards away from her block, tripped and nearly fell over. She slammed the door shut and the muffled voices rose, arguments about what they would do next.

The back door to the flat was wide open. Weak, trembly and baffled by it all, I stepped inside and was immediately hit by the reek of the brew, stale booze steaming out of the pores of the furniture. *Is this what it always smelt like*? The settees looked as they usually did, old and worn with balled-up quilts. Had Marcus and Loz returned at any point? Had Will? Nobody had seen them. Everybody assumed we'd all left together. The town didn't know I was rotting away in a soundproofed hole, writing under the nom de plume of Ayli.

In the kitchen, the floor was wet where a barrel had been tipped over, bottles had been taken, someone had clearly been here. I went into the bathroom. My gaunt face, barely any hair on my head, oily rings around my eyes. My beard was grey, wild and greased to the right. 'Tom,' I whispered into the mirror, 'what has happened to you?'

Jacket open, my skin looked scaly and flaccid. I'd even lost hair on my chest, just a few grey whisps. My legs were thin and bald, my bare feet filthy.

I went into the bedroom, saw the brown stain of Tony Dale's remains on the carpet, relived the spitting blood as his life left him, when the whole drama began. *If I do write about this, this could be where I start. Maybe I could write a kind of whodunnit.*

I grabbed one of my old Moroccan shirts. It was huge on me. The shorts would do for now. I stepped into an old pair of trainers.

'That's better,' I muttered.

'Who'm yow?' came from behind.

'What the fuck!' I turned and lying down the side of the bed, surrounded by bottles of the brew, was Mel. 'What are you doing here?'

'I know yow,' she said.

'I know, I know, Mel.'

'My Leyton,' she said, tearful.

'Leyton?'

'My boy, my boy, you're back.'

'It's Tom. You know my mum,' I reminded her.

'Don't yow play games, my boy. Yow've come to nick my money! Couldn't even say hello to your old mum,' she nagged, trying to stand up.

'Mel, it's me, Tom. You know, Pat's son.'

'Pat?' She got up and walked towards me. 'Pat! I went to Walton Girls with Pat!' She sat on the bed. 'I thought you was my Leyton. Thought he was back.'

'Back? Leyton's…' I couldn't bring myself to say it.

'They want to blow him up,' she spouted, bitter.

'Who?' I asked.

'Them lot in Picks! He didn't nick any money off him!' She was trembling. 'That Warren was a piece of-'

'Of course, Mel.' I reached for a bottle which had the dregs in it. 'Here, maybe you should-'

She snatched the bottle from my hand and swigged it off. Did she know? She must've known at one time what they'd done. It was the only Greek in the whole of Halesowen. Was this a Wernicke-Korsakoff rewrite?

It made me realise what I had to do.

I went into the kitchen and fetched the fruit trowel. It was the only thing we had at the flat. It would have to do. I went back into the bedroom.

'Will you be alright, Mel?' I smiled.

'I know your mum,' she said.

What was the point?

I left the flat through the front door, up the stairs and out the hole which had been smashed through in the high-rise tragedy, the sulphurous whiff of Ground Zero sticking in the back of my throat. There was no hanging around reminiscing. I said goodbye to dad for the last time and headed towards the back of St John's. There were no people, the only sounds were the screech of the seagulls scavenging on Ground Zero and the scant tweet of small birds in the yews of the graveyard.

God consciousness, madness, or for some sort of literary continuity, I knew I had to fill the Greek grave. As I neared it, my stomach churned at the thought of what or who I might find in it. I smelt it before I saw anything, the summer only speeding up decomposition. I pulled my shirt over my mouth and nose, edging towards it, terrified I was going to see the limbs or faces of my lost brothers.

'God!' *Why are they naked?*

The entwined limbs of Alan and Tim, their faces side by side, like a two-headed beast from a circus freakshow. They were newly dead by the looks of it. Alan's eyes were closed, his mouth glum, resting on what looked like Aaron Moran's rotten tattooed torso. Tim's eyes were open and staring at me, opaque and glassy, his mouth wide and smiling, his nose bloodied. *What on earth had happened and why?*

I started counting the limbs. My heart was pounding, there were at least seven legs. Was I going to have to climb in to discover what belonged to who? One foot was coming from under Alan's arm, another under Tim's. It was like some terrible scene from a concentration camp. Then I noticed somebody's bloodied brow below Alan's balls. I started panting, hyperventilating beneath my shirt. I was going to have get into the Greek to learn the terrible truth.

'God,' I started muttering, 'grant me the serenity, courage and if all else fails the wisdom…'

I sat on the edge of the grave and dipped my foot in to try and kick Alan's leg up. It barely moved, but enough for me to see the butcher's face. I wondered if they'd put him there after they'd shot him and now in some poetic justice, Alan had found himself in the dead jaws of his victim – *perhaps they liked that sort of thing.* In the bottom corner was the top of another head but, despite the rot, I could see it was Aaron Moran's. I felt satisfied there was no evidence of the boys. It was just a stew of Sons and nons, which seemed appropriate.

I began digging around me and filling the grave. It felt ritualistic. Two Ronnies or no Two Ronnies, I was certain this was my goodbye to Halesowen and this strange chapter in my life. I recalled that very first hole I'd dug after the bombs. The day I met Sarah. My mum's. It was quickly followed by more holes, more casualties, young and old.

After filling the grave, I flattened out the soil and stood atop the Greek. I felt a sense of freedom as if all our troubles had stemmed from this crazy act, which occurred before the bombs. If only Halesowen could've found a way to ignore the stirring tabloids, the provocative memes and television opinions. I mean, who really cared about the Greek and what he did or didn't do? But they told us we should and so most of us did and the mob sunk to new depths.

If I do write that book, I could end it here. I could start it at Tony's death, jump back and forth, and then end it here, the portal closed. Maybe everything would zip back in time, Ross would bounce back to life and stop writing the news. The Prices would survive. The butcher, Christian and Aaron Moran would breathe once more. Barb would be resurrected at the altar, perhaps the milkman could tell us who killed him. Poor Ray would be free to go about his business and feed Wolfie. Tony Dale would have the knife pulled from his throat, Stacey would let go of my cock. And all the other terrible things, the pennies spent, Rex's shrinking tumour, Lee's head lifted from the tree and reattached, the re-rooting of Sean's gold teeth, Jay Bird jumping back into the pulpit, the two old men and the little girl would fly back to floor eight and the high-rise would rise again. We'd zip right back to those early days of the church and the scag rats and mum, and beyond, down the motorway the bomb sucked out of the earth, Lucy and Dylan...

I stopped myself. I felt a sense of dumb bliss in rewriting history. 'It happened, Tom.'

I was stood solemn on the Greek, my mind racing. Where would it end if I really had such a power? Would I take us back beyond the Greek Riots, the royal scandal, the viruses? Or would I go further to austerity, the banking crisis, the wars in the Middle East? Or beyond me, to the three day week in the 70s, the swinging 60s, the Suez Canal, the World Wars? Could I even go back that far? What would happen if I erased me in this flight of fancy? *Of course, you could just erase you now and all of this would be true.*

I felt hot with self-pity. *You can't rewrite history. It is what it is.*

I looked over to where dad's high-rise used to be and remembered how I hadn't looked after him in his final years. He would forgive me, but deep below the surface where I might now readily accept that forgiveness, lay the real guilt, something I'd never attempted to work through. *I should've gone home to Lucy and Dylan.*

I left the graveyard, not a soul in sight. Even before I got to the George I knew they wouldn't be there. It'd been six weeks since that night of the mushrooms, when Mother Nature, Allah whatever you want to call it suddenly reawoke in me. And it hadn't left, but it'd lost its importance. I'd stopped feeling special about it. It just was and I couldn't explain it and I had to live with that.

I listened at the pub windows, there was nothing. I lifted the cellar door. 'Hello?' My voice hit the walls and bounced back. I gee'd myself up and stepped down into the cold cellar and then quickly up into the bar. 'Hello?'

Nothing.

'Will? Tony?'

There was no sign of life. The same coating of plaster dust and upturned tables and chairs; sharp beams of light through cracks in the window boards; broken glasses, bottles, and ashtrays full of cigarettes long dead. It was still easy to remember it as it once was, throbbing with life, wet with drunkenness, when going to the pub had been the best thing in the world. Four awkward college kids taking the piss, nervous around girls, egging each other on and drinking and laughing in the face of failure. Those years were few and they went fast, before our minds, hearts and bodies began to show the cracks, but that war we fought on ourselves was a war we shared. We came out the other side of it brothers.

Now I'd lost them. Loz was perhaps the only one who'd been in safe hands, but where were they now? They'd been waiting for me to come back to them six weeks ago. Did they think I was dead?

I left the pub and headed towards St John's. As I neared the graveyard, I thought I heard the sound of the playground again, but it was just the wind carrying the ghosts of my memory – *or is it the vision of a new town?*

Through the graveyard, I passed old William Shenstone, his sandstone box buried under three feet of weeds. I stopped briefly and sat on the bench where I'd seen old Mick with his DVD player.

I carried on into town, the cobbled path leading to Picks, which was closed. Despite the sun, it felt cold, like I was at altitude, my bones aching, head throbbing. Was everything dead here, where the lime trees once canopied the High Street, where shops once bustled with yam-yam natter? I felt like I was the only person in Halesowen, but of course that wasn't the case. There was a roomful of old Halesonians, dreaming up a new future, perhaps a much brighter one. And there would be other people, prune loons, scag rats, and people keeping themselves to themselves, like anywhere. But at that moment, I was alone in a strange purgatorial peace, stuck at a comma.

I sat to rest under the town clock but immediately stood up when the sentence picked up, the stillness broken by the sound of glass smashing somewhere in the distance. It didn't startle me, but intrigued me. I looked around, curious. *Perhaps it's a scag rat or prune loon looting, freed from Jay's Law.*

I continued on, curious, and noticed something move by the old Greek chippie. It looked like a man dashing under the old Cornbow Hall.

SMASH. More glass. I headed towards it. *SMASH.* Once again, but this time I saw something, a spray of debris. Then somebody shouted, 'quick, another riffer!' from up high, and I heard the scuttle of feet echoing above on the multistorey car park. It was a young voice. *Kids tossing off bottles? Is this a return to normal?* But on the ground below, amongst a smattering of broken bottles, an old prune loon was curled up against the wall. 'The little fuckers,' I said. 'Mate, are you alright?'

He was groaning. I edged towards him, caught a whiff of piss and fish, that familiar smell of internal rot. I put my hand on his shoulder. 'You alright?'

He rolled onto his back. 'W-w-weasel-rabbit. Where? Where!?'

'Jake!?'

'T-Tom...' His face was grey and bloodied, a black eye. Gaunt and aged, he had wisps of hair on his chin which looked glued on, rather than a real beard. He was trying to speak. 'W-w-where?'

'It's ok,' I said. 'They're gone. I've scared them off.'

'No!' he yelled, annoyed.

'No? What?'

'I-I turtle-duck killed them!'

'Killed? What?'

'I-I-I don't turtle-quack-sheep-steer know! Don't look at me! Don't squirrel-sheep-'

From behind me, I heard the gravel. I turned, ready to smack the little bastards. *'Tom?'*

'Shit!' His hair was matted and long, his body thin, face bloated and yellow. 'Will, what's happened to you?'

'I could ask the same of you. Look like a prisoner of war! Pahahaha!' His laugh turned into a cough, his face reddening with it. He took out his tin, lit up a roll-up and coughed again to clear his throat, spitting a greeny-brown mass on the tarmac. 'We waited for you for days. It's been mental, shacked up with this fuck. Where've you been? Thought you were dead. Thought they had you.'

I looked back to Jake on the pavement. He was now sitting up and lighting a pipe, the icing-sugar sweet reek of crack. 'They did. The Prices put me in a cell and made me write a newspaper-'

'Eh?' Will asked.

'Have you not seen a newspaper?'

He looked confused.

'Pamphlet really… Don't worry about it. What's going on?'

'God knows. But the Sons are done.'

'D-dun-turtle. Gone. We're gone,' Jake laughed, brightening with the pipe. 'N-nuff-rabbit-sheep-nothing left to do.'

The sound of more smashing glass came from the other side of the car park.

'Fucking-cunting kids,' a familiar voice yelled. 'Where's that fuck gone?'

'Tony!' Will called.

'You're still with *Tony*?'

'Will!' Tony cried, desperate and old. 'Where's Jake? I'll kill the bastard!'

Will followed the voice under the old Cornbow Hall.

'He w-w-won't,' Jake said. 'The Sons are no sheep-squirrel more. And n-now the town's overrun with sheep-squirrel-baa yobs.' He laughed, 'f-f-pheasant karma.'

2028

I just couldn't stop crying.

After leaving Picks, I'd made it as far as St John's and decided I needed to say goodbye to William Shenstone, where many a night we'd talked about art which leeched into love and the obsessions of our youth. I'd pulled back the weeds and was sitting against his sandstone back, reading the rest of Maureen's letter by the light of my phone.

'Damn you,' I sobbed.

I read the lines again.

Sarah is too young to understand love, Tom. I can't wait and watch as she kills herself. It's not helping me and it's not helping her. It would make me very happy to see her again in the future, in better circumstances but, if I don't see her, then so be it. I'm too old, I've seen too much. We come into each other's lives and we leave, family or friend. That's what it is to be a human.

You're not to give the letter to Sarah until she's clean and sober and has grown into a proper adult. It's down to your discretion and I have faith you will know the right time, if the time ever arises.

'How am I supposed to do that if I'm not here? Eh, Maureen?'

Something always pulls me back to Halesowen.

'Hold on a second, Tom,' I said to myself. 'What's really going on here? You know Maureen would sooner you get out of here, letter or no letter.'

'But she doesn't understand addiction.'

'Do you?'

'Don't you fucking start!' I yelled. It was loud. I looked around, listened. Heard nothing but the distant tin of Britpop at Picks and, up the flats, some RnB beat.

'What *are* you doing?' a third voice asked. 'Sitting on Shenstone's grave, talking to yourself like a madman.'

I laughed, two of us did.

She doesn't get it though, the more serious voice thought. *And maybe I do have feelings for Sarah*, it reasoned, *but isn't that just something I have to accept and deal with?*

'You could still help her,' one said.

'And it would help you, too,' two added.

'What's up north anyway?' three asked. 'There could be a real book in this experience.' *The last year has been more a novella, let's face it. Or the beginning.* 'You need a middle.' *And an end. What about the TV drama?*

'Hang on a minute,' a fourth voice joined in.

'Shut up!' one.

'Let him speak,' two.

'What about the book?' three.

'*Tom!*' a disembodied voice, as loud as if he were merely a couple of feet away.

I jumped up off the grave not wanting to appear disrespectful. 'Hello?' I switched the phone to torch, but I couldn't see anyone. 'Hello?'

The voice was familiar, gruff. Deep down I'd suspected there was nobody there even before I got off Shenstone. It was just pretend, a game I was playing for myself – the small fear a real person was there. I knew it was my dad's voice. Concocted in my own brain, by the spirits or God, none of that really mattered. I remembered being on a psych ward for the first time, 30 years ago, barely an adult, emotionally far from it. I was lying on the bed when all of a sudden, as loud as if he was sitting next to me, I heard my grandfather shout my name. It startled me – I wondered whether I'd caught schizophrenia off one of the patients. But as time went by I came to accept it was meaningful. Whatever it was, it meant there was always something there to stop me veering too far off path.

I sat back down on Shenstone.

'I don't know, Tom,' I answered myself before the question even entered my brain: *why do you have to stay?* 'You'll never really know.'

'I guess.'

'You're nuts, you know,' the third voice said.

The fourth voice stayed quiet. He was the little voice inside that made more sense than any of the others. The voice that once told me I was a caterpillar after tumbling down a hill because I was too busy thinking about Dani.

'Dani,' wistful.

I drifted into fantasy but she was probably long gone with the bombs. Tina popped into my thoughts, leaning over the bar, her breasts slipping out-

'T-Tom!' a loud voice, not me, my dad or the Gods.

He was clearly very drunk, stumbling into the graveyard, his white vest hanging off his slight body.

'How did you know I was here?' I asked.

'Mick squirrel-slaw-saw you,' Jake said.

'Old builder Mick?'

'Yeah, said you was p-p-pig-pissed.'

I laughed, shaking my head.

'Don't j-judge me!' he yelled. 'I can dray-rabbit-hutch-drink! I'm allowed!'

'I'm not judging.' I gestured for him to sit next to me on the grave. 'I was laughing because I probably looked pissed, crying and talking to myself.'

'Crying? I d-didn't...' he tried to say. 'I'm t-t-t...' he took a deep breath... 'truly sorry, Tom.'

'*You're* sorry? I really thought I was doing the right thing.'

'You were.'

'What was the point? I hoped it would stop-'

'T-Tom,' he interrupted, his head circling with the drink.

'If I'd known all it would take was money,' I said, 'they could've had it there and then in the Co-op-'

'Tom,' he grabbed my arm to get my attention, steadying himself, 'l-lamb-listen.'

'What?'

No words were coming out of his mouth, as he tried to focus on me. I didn't know whether he was stuck in a silent-stutter or fumbling for the right animal to precede whatever it was he needed to say. Eventually, 'Picks' came out.

'Oh, no.' I waved him off. 'I'm done with that place. Jake, I've made a decision to stay in Halesowen, but I don't have to spend any more time in that hell-hole.'

'P-p-'

'I'm too old-'

'Pigeon-'

'Too sober.'

'P-pig-Picks.'

It was a little bit like having a cat trying to communicate his needs. 'Are you alright?'

He shook his head, using my thigh to push himself up. 'Tom.' He was serious.

'I've just said goodbye to the place,' I sighed. I knew I was going to have to go back there. 'Ok. But I'm not staying long.'

Jake was making three steps forward, falling back a step and then stopping to steady himself. I had all the time in the world to change my mind, but William Shenstone, Maureen's letter, Mick finding me "drunk" and Jake's sudden inebriated appearance seemed strangely serendipitous. Halesowen had me, and all that entailed, the drunken, debauched theatrics – which is what it always had been to me. The little voice inside was trying to tell me something about my feelings around Sarah, but without a hill to fall down, a caterpillar or frankly a sledgehammer around the face, I was probably not going to listen to it. One thing was certain, going back to Picks certainly didn't feel like a conscious choice, so somehow it felt right.

The door to Picks opened with a clatter and Jason fell out. He glanced up and saw me. 'Alright, Tom?'

'Yeah, Jase. How you doing mate?'

He was itchy and fidgety. 'Yeah,' he said. 'Gotta… yeah.' He continued on.

Clearly has other "priorities".

Behind me, there was the sound of a splat. I turned to see Jake on the floor. 'Shit!' I helped him up. 'Maybe we should get you home.' He pointed to Picks. 'What's going on, Jake? Can't you just tell me?'

He opened his mouth to try to speak but gave up, jabbing his finger at the entrance to the pub.

I opened the door, the sweaty heat, the waft of smoke and booze, the Picasso punters once again coming back to life, shapes and colours reanimating, bodies mock-cockney chanting "park life" to the music.

'Tom,' Leroy called, smiling that distant smile, a sideways glance at Jake. 'Come and have a Coca Cola,' annoyingly magnanimous.

Jake held onto my arm. 'Turtle-tell him,' he demanded.

Leroy looked surprised, loosening a third button on his red robe, exposing his hairless chest.

The boys in the back all turned to have a nose. At the side of me, Tony Moran looked intimidating – if this were a western, he'd just unclipped his gun holster.

I shrugged, awkward and apologetic, to all around. 'Tell me what?'

'Jake,' Leroy condescended. 'Have a drink.'

Marcus was standing next to him, his face serious, not knowing where to look. I squeezed through to stand next to Leroy at the bar, my elbow wet in cider spillage. 'What's going on?'

I could see there was something he wasn't saying. He wouldn't make eye-contact. I looked around us, people immediately turned away, like we were playing a game. All except Tony Moran who was clearly irritated, glaring at me for some reason – what had I done?

Tina put a coke down in front of me. '£5.90, luvvie.'

'Cider, Jake?' Leroy asked, placating him with that pious smile.

Jake twitched.

'Cider for Jake. And for that one,' he gestured Marcus. 'And do you happen to have Wild Turkey?'

'Wild Turkey,' I laughed. 'The strong stuff, eh?'

Leroy immediately looked at me and I knew he remembered those mornings in 'Spoons, curing tremors with swift doubles of the throat-biting spirit. 'It was… er…' he fumbled, speaking to Tina but for my benefit, 'when I was in the states, they, it, we… it was common.'

I couldn't help but smile.

'Nah. We got Grey Goose,' she winked.

'That's vodka,' he patronised.

'Yow doh say.' She rolled her eyes.

Jake, seeming even more drunk, grabbed onto Leroy's arm, partly to get his attention and partly for balance.

'Ok, Jake. Just give me whiskey, Tina. Two ciders and a whiskey.'

'Is this anything to do with Barb?' I asked.

'Barb?' Leroy asked. 'What do you mean?'

I looked through to the other side of the bar. Loz was out of it, his head on Stacey's shoulder. Rex and Will looked like they were arguing. Barb was laughing at them. The bar was full of the same sounds and noises, the other language – I used to speak it.

'She was very… I don't know, emotional-'

'She looks happy enough,' Marcus chipped in.

We made eye-contact. What was going on? I could see it in him. He picked up his pint glass and drank from it, but it was empty.

'L-L-lemur-Lee!'

'Alright, Jake,' he snapped. 'Tom, I'm not saying you were right.'

'About what? Is this about the booze?'

'I d-didn't mean to-' Jake mumbled, leaning against the bar.

'Jake,' Leroy insisted. 'You did what you had to do. You saved my life. And,' he paused, looked up to the ceiling, '"and the dead in Christ will rise-"'

'"*The dead in*…?" What the hell did you-?' I glanced over my shoulder, Tony Moran was still staring in our direction. I lowered my voice, 'what did you do?'

Leroy hesitated. 'We were in the park exchanging the booze for money – you shouldn't have stolen from the church,' he whisper-shouted.

'Lee-baa-sheep!' Jake demanded.

'I'm telling him. The one was mouthing off, the big one-'

'C-Callum, squirrel-sheep-stack!'

'Callum,' Leroy confirmed.

'And you *killed* him?' I asked.

'He went for me,' he added, pathetically.

'What about the others? Jimmy and… the meerkat?'

Jake couldn't look at me. Marcus either. Tina came over with two pints of cider. 'I'll just get the scotch,' she said.

'Do you have bourbon?' Leroy asked but caught himself, 'no, yes, scotch. Whatever, Tina-'

'You'd think there'd never been a bomb,' she moaned, clicking the e-optic.

'There was little else we could do.'

'They were just kids,' I said. 'You *killed* them?'

'It's not quite like that-' Leroy said.

Jake picked up his pint and proceeded to neck it. It looked like an act of self-harm. I tried to stop him, 'that's not gonna help.'

He pulled away and stumbled back. Trying to regain his balance, he dropped his glass before falling onto a table, knocking several drinks over and rolling onto the floor amongst the smattering of shards and the swill of cider. People jumped up and out of the way.

'Dickhead!' Sean, an old boy shouted, wiping cider off his blue Halesowen Town FC shirt.

'Goddam lightweight!' another.

'Druggies more like!' Sean was muttering. 'Town's full of the fuckers.'

'Alright, move!' Tony Dale pushed people out of the way. He pulled Jake up and sat him against the wall on a bench. 'Oi,' he yelled. 'You'm bleeding on my furniture!'

Jake was out of it, writhing in drunkenness. Tony slapped him and he stirred, but he was clearly too far gone. Tony turned to Leroy. 'This is *you*!'

'Me? It's not my fault he can't take his drink.' Leroy looked awkward and weak.

Jake was broken, swaying and muttering "sheep-squirrels" to himself. Across the other side of the bar, Will and Loz were oblivious to the scene, Stacey joining the chorus of booze-sodden girls singing, "I kissed a girl and I liked it, the taste of her cherry Chapstick."

What had they done? 'All for stuff!' I yelled, disgusted.

'Ah, shut up!' someone shouted. I turned to see it was Tony Moran. 'Virtue-signalling cunt.'

'You can pay for all this, Lee!' Tony Dale was demanding.

I felt light-headed, the whole sorry situation sinking in. I made for the door to get some fresh air but somebody put their foot out. I tripped and hit the floor. I got up to see who'd done it, but they were all shrugging, stifling giggles, Tony and Aaron Moran outright laughing. At the bar, Marcus looked away, too cowardly to look at me. Behind him Christian and Anita were blatantly staring at the wall, pretending they hadn't noticed.

I watched Leroy pluck money from a wad of cash, handing it to an angry Tony Dale. There was nothing I could do or say. I pushed my way out of the pub.

I ran up towards the Queensway. I wanted to scream into the night, helpless and hopeless, at the situation past, present and future. *Is it all my fault?*

The primary purpose of this alcoholic was to help other alcoholics stay sober. That was the key to it all. That was how I'd stayed sober all these years. I was by no means the best at it, but I tried. In my attempt to make things better I'd made things so much worse. Jimmy was a good rat deep down, I knew it.

I passed the Wetherspoons. *How could they do it?* Then I remembered Will's suggestion to kill them all. Was he in on it? I felt nauseous, stabbing groans in my hollow gut, blood sugary weak. Will was my brother. Marcus was my brother too. What were they playing at? I fell against the old post office, clammy cold, panting. *Maybe I need a shot of insulin?* I wasn't a diabetic as far as I knew. I glanced inside the building. Tables had been moved. There was a collection of chairs and boxes of books. I pushed myself off, trembling.

As I came to the bus station, the sound of music and voices overwhelmed me. The party had leeched out of the flats and reached the town centre. There were people in the road, dancing and singing. "'I'm in love with the shape of you…'" umming and ooing, bumping and grinding. I could smell the sweet stench of fruity alcohol and the hairy-burp of wheat beers. A woman grabbed my arm and tried to dance with me. I shook her off, trying my best to give people a wide-berth. Someone called my name. I knew who it was and I ignored him.

'Tomz,' he called again.

I continued onto the hill of Andrew Road and "Shape of You" faded into a chorus of "'sooo… before you go,'" a group of lairy lads singing at the top of their voices. By the side of the road, a girl, probably no older than 16, was throwing up.

I made my way into the flats, the flashing disco lights bringing on some kind of twirling sickness, like I was in a Hitchcock thriller. A sudden red flash illuminated a couple fucking up against the wall of one of the blocks, like a warning, but then the jangling piano of "Let Me Entertain You" started up and I found myself uncontrollably moving to it, transported from 2028 back to 1998, in the persistent euphoric recall of Halesowen. "'I'm a burning effigy of everything I used to be,'" meant something, as the words fell out of my mouth. I wasn't sure what, but it felt poignant. I was heading for the throng of people surrounding Ally's flat and as I came into the circle, I felt arms clamp around either shoulder, "'let me entertain you,'" they all sang. "'Let me entertain you…'" I sang with them. I remembered Loz singing it on the karaoke at the George, taking speed-bombs and snorting poppers, swilling double-doubles, sweaty dancing. I stepped away from the arms and into the centre of the circle of singers, "'come on, come on, come on, come on…'" I sang at the top of my voice, the screeching saxophones, throbbing bass, people clapping and cheering. And I kept singing, on and on, I didn't realise the song had morphed into the electronica of "Poker Face".

'Tom!' they were shouting.

'Come on, come on, come on…' I continued.

'Tom!' I felt somebody wrench me from behind.

Digging my heels in, I tripped over somebody and landed into the strange reality of "my, my, poker face," on the muddy ground.

But there was no poker face. No stiff upper lip. No pretence. There were tears and screaming and pulling the grass from the churned up earth. I felt arms tugging on me from all sides, muscles tugging on me from within. Synapses spitting sparks, the town was alive with fun and festival, but people had died, my people had been murdered. 'I tried to stop it!' I screamed. People were on me and I couldn't understand why. I started lashing out.

'I can't leave now, can I? Not like this,' I heard somebody say, a man.
'What about her?' a woman. 'The kids?'
I wasn't totally sure if I was dreaming. I was definitely on a bed. My head was throbbing and all down my side felt sore.
'She'll be alright,' he replied. 'And they're grown up. Tom's completely lost it, hasn't he? I thought I was bad.'
I groaned and opened my eyes on a tar-stained magnolia ceiling. Outside, the music had stopped, there was just the patter of rain, punctuated by the erratic yelps and jeers of a festival dying down. I recognised the bedroom, I'd been here once before and only once. I glanced to the side of me expecting to see Ally.
'*Sarah*? What happened?'
'You're back with us then?' She was sitting at my bedside like she was visiting a sick relative. 'You hit Ricky.'
'Ricky? I hit…? *Why*?'
'Er… um… you said he was a fat… um… Wolves fan,' Damien said, laughing.
I turned to the other side of me, 'Damien? What are-?'
'We carried you in,' Sarah said. 'After you'd passed out.'
'Passed out?'
'Ricky um… hit you back,' he laughed.
'That's why I feel sore.'
'You completely lost the plot, man,' came from the foot of the bed.
I lifted my head. Loz was sitting on the floor against the door.
'What plot?' I asked, nauseous and dizzy, my heavy head falling back to the pillow. If I'd drank anything, I'd be convinced I'd been spiked. *Concussed*? 'Must be.'
'Must be what?' Loz asked. 'Ally said you were singing Robbie Williams and-'
'*You* were,' I accused, and I believed it.
'I wasn't even there. I was at Picks.'

'The George,' I said, smiling to myself. 'In… 98.' I closed my eyes. '"Hell is gone and heaven's here there's nothing left for me to…"' I sang, before drifting back to sleep.

I awoke to a faint snore, but I didn't open my eyes. Then the jagged knife of a loud snore, which startled me. I was on my side. I opened my eyes expecting to see Will, but it was Sarah fast asleep.

The low light of the morning backlit the red curtains, thunder rumbling above the rain. I stretched my legs and kicked someone the other side of me. *Oh, of course.* Sandwiched between Sarah and Will. I laughed to myself like it was a sick joke, but my feelings about it paled when I remembered the fate of the scag rats. *Does Sarah know? Did Will have anything to do with it?*

I shuffled down the bed, half expecting to see Damien, Loz and Marcus on the floor. But we were the only three here. I quietly turned the handle to the bedroom door and made my way down the cold corridor to the living room. Ally was awake under a dirty quilt, smoking a cigarette.

'The baby,' I said.

'Don't you start. Especially after last night.'

'I'm sorry. I had some bad news.'

'The junkie?'

I pulled the curtains back and looked outside, the remnants of the festival, cups, plates and bottles awash in the rain – would we ever clean it up? 'Three kids. That's all they were.'

'Yuh what?'

'Rats,' I said, 'exterminated.'

'*What?*'

I turned to face her, the burning paper of her cigarette every bit as appealing as it had ever been. 'I know you don't get it, nobody does. But when you've been an addict-'

She laughed.

'Ok, when you've been an addict who has to give it all up, you feel an affinity for those like you. Jimmy, his name was, and there was a way out for him.'

'Jimmy?'

'Jimmy, Callum and… the meerkat.'

'Meerkats and rats? You'm off your tree, Tom,' she laughed. 'And Jimmy en't dead.'

'What you talking about?'

She reached beside her for a glass of something cloudy, took a sip. 'They shot the fat un because he went at the vicar with a knife. The skinny one did it.'

'Jake?'

'Probably. He's dead in the brook, they said. The other two "rats" went off with the money and jewellery.'

'Who told you that?'

'Will.' She took a last drag and dropped it in a can, a short fizz.

'They're really not dead?'

'The fat un is.'

I looked out of the window at my old flat, sinking in the mud, dad's old block standing tall behind it. It rained hard. A gust blew a table across the grass. 'Another storm. I wonder if this will affect the buses.'

'By hell or high water, they'll go-'

'Poor Jake.'

Will appeared at the door, wearing just his pants. '*Jake*?' he tutted. He sat on the settee next to Ally. He reached over her for her tobacco and started to roll a cigarette.

'Help yourself,' she said, rolling her eyes.

'I thought they were all dead,' I said. 'I didn't even know if you knew or-'

'If I'd killed them?'

'I didn't say that.'

He went to reach for Ally's glass, stopped himself, 'can I?' She nodded. He took a swig of the stuff. It looked like bile. 'Where's your fucking head at, Tom?'

'What do you mean?' I asked, innocent. Ally laughed. 'You mean last night? I told you. I thought they were dead.'

'Who gives a fuck about those dirty little addicts?' he shouted.

'I do. They're still people.'

'That's funny-'

'What's funny?'

'Now they're people. You've been calling them rats and rabbits and all sorts of shit for the last week. You've been having panic-attacks and fighting people-'

'Fighting?'

'Yeah, fighting! Last night!' he yelled, the echo pinging on cold council walls.

There was silence. I stood in judgement facing Ally and Will on the settee. I wanted to cry. I wanted to shout at them: "I'm only staying to help you, to help my friends!"

But it was lie, of course. I was staying because I was scared.

Sarah came into the room, sleep in her eyes. 'What's all the yelling about?' I caught her glancing at the flat juice Ally and Will were sharing.

'Did you know?' I asked her.

'About Callum?'

I nodded.

'I found out last night. I never really liked him.'

'*You never liked him?*' I stared at her in disbelief. 'He's dead, Sarah. Friend or not, he's dead.'

'So what?' Will piped up. 'He tried to kill Leroy-'

'Lee,' Sarah corrected.

Will laughed and she cast an angry glance. '*What?*'

'I'm not saying it could be helped,' I said. 'I wasn't there. I just need people to understand. Where's Loz?' I asked – *surely he'll see the madness in this.*

'Gone, I guess,' Will said. 'The bus. Fuck him.'

'You what?' I panicked. 'I didn't even say goodbye. Where's Marcus?'

'Around,' Will said.

'Around? What does that mean?' I started fumbling in my pocket for my phone.

'It means around! What's wrong with you?'

No battery. I started tapping the buttons in patterns, as if somehow I might unlock a secret stash of power. My chest was tightening, I was struggling to get a full breath. *Not this! It's just a panic-attack, breathe, don't let them see you like this. Not now, of all times.*

'Are you alright?' Sarah asked.

That made me feel worse. 'Me? Yeah, I'm fine… absolutely, one hundred…' I panted. 'Yeah.'

'This is what I'm talking about!' Will yelled, getting up and walking out of the room.

I put my hand in my pocket and felt the paper of Maureen's letters. Somehow it comforted me. I realised this little scene right here was what I was signing up for and I would have to learn to live with it. I looked to Sarah, she kept glancing at Ally's glass. She cared, I could see it, but she was still in the thick of addiction.

Someday I will give you this letter, Sarah. In the meantime, I just have to survive amongst the deluded. I was nodding to myself. 'At least the other scag rats are alive.' I realised I'd just said that out loud. They were both looking at me for something more. I could feel the creep of paranoia.

'That's right,' Ally said, 'two of them are alive and they will get the bus to a new life,' she smiled.

I felt like a patient in Bushey Fields again, the nurses assuaging my neuroses.

I turned away from them, embarrassed, and opened the back door. Rain and wind came through, fresh, pricking the nerves in my face. Paper cups and plastic bags twirled, the slap of a table rolling upside down, the crack of a chair hitting a wall. It was loud and powerful and beautiful, like the waves crashing against the sea wall in Burnham. I saw Lucy's face on that last call on the beach, her hair alive in the nuclear winds. 'Lucy,' I said, still learning to say it out loud.

I felt somebody's hand on my shoulder. 'Come on, Tom,' Sarah said. 'Close the door,' a tender smile.

I pulled it to, cold-faced and wet. 'I need to eat something and then I need to go to the buses. Where's the food?'

'What food?' Ally asked.

'I need to eat something. The shopping?'

'What shopping?'

'That Marcus and me left.'

'I mean,' she said, shrugging, 'everybody contributed. The last night and all.'

'Last night? Our food?'

She nodded.

No food. No money. Nowhere safe to live. The buses were coming to take the sensible ones to a new life, but still I knew I wouldn't leave Halesowen. You'd have to be mad or depressed.

───────────

The town was dotted with drenched people poorly wrapped in macs, dragging bags poorly wrapped in plastic. In the bus station, an old man was leaning against a bus shelter, trying to catch his breath. His wife looked on, irritated.

'I said we didn't need all this,' she moaned, showing me the suitcases. 'They provide clothes and shelter. Only the essentials, Facebook said.'

'Is he ok?' I asked.

'It's his lungs.'

'Can he walk?'

'I'm,' the old man panted, 'fine… just… need a… sec…'

'I can carry the bags-'

'Don't need… help… son,' he said, breathless.

'Really,' I picked up a suitcase, 'it's no trouble.'

As I went to pick up another one, I felt somebody tug it out of my hand. 'Don't go!' Will said, long hair flat-drenched, in just a vest and shorts.

'You'll make yourself ill,' I said.

'Please don't,' he begged.

'*Don't leave*,' I mocked, melodramatic, 'not like this.'

'It's not funny.'

'I'm not going, you div.' He glanced down at the bags. 'These aren't mine. A bloody carpet bag?' I laughed. 'I was just helping this couple.'

'Don't… need-'

'Oh, shut up Brian!' the old lady said. 'Get your breath back!'

At the roundabout a bus turned back on itself, heading towards the last stop in town which was outside the old swimming baths. I could see people sitting on it and wondered if Maureen and the scag rats were amongst them.

The old man moved to pick up a suitcase. Will stepped in. 'Let us do it. We're not going, at least let us help.'

'Not going? *At all*?' the old woman nagged. 'What's the matter with you?'

'Oh… leave it… Joy,' the old man said. 'If you… would,' he conceded.

'They've told us we have to leave,' she continued.

'Stop it, Joy!'

We each grabbed a suitcase and walked slowly alongside them. Ahead of us, wide Botero characters and stick thin Lowry folk were walking fast, hobbling and lugging as much as they could carry, hoping to make the bus. There wouldn't be enough space for all of them, but there would be more buses during the course of the day.

'I'm really sorry, mate,' Will said.

'Why?'

'You know.'

'Don't worry about it. Thanks for saying it, but I'm just trying to come to terms with everything. That must be why I keep having these funny turns.'

'I'm not on about that.'

I knew he wasn't. I knew exactly what he was talking about. 'What you on about then?'

'Sarah,' he said.

'Sarah?'

The old lady was looking at us, curious, the man was oblivious, concentrating on each step and each breath.

'*Tammy*,' he prompted.

'Tammy? What you on about Tammy for?'

'You know.'

There had been many times in my life, many conversations like this, with many people, where I understood exactly what wasn't being said because it was so obviously being said. Sometimes words just aren't the correct units of communication for the subject.

I laughed. It wasn't cynical or hysterical, perhaps it was coy, but it demonstrated we were both on the same page.

'I'd be the same about it,' he said. 'You know I would.'

'I don't even feel that way about her,' I shrugged, shaking my head in disbelief.

'I know,' he smiled.

It was just a deep-seated insecurity. Something inside me wanted to be adored by everybody. I knew I wasn't going to get that, of course. But I guess I felt like I was going to great pains to help Sarah and so somehow that meant she should love me, even though I would never love her back. Certainly not in that way. And then it was Will, and there was Tammy, and that was our thing, a competitiveness between brothers, and some buried resentment which mostly wasn't there but also would always be there.

'She's not your type,' he said.

'She's attractive and she's really nice underneath the bite. But I know.'

'Neither was Tammy.'

'I know!' I laughed. But she was and he knew she was, we were just being polite about it. 'She was a frigging punk and I was a new age hippy!' I laughed again, cementing the lie. 'But she was so bloody fit.'

'Oi!' he jabbed – still, after all these years.

'Sorry,' I smiled – which was the right response, laughing at that particular "oi" was inappropriate, even now, decades down the line.

'I shouldn't have told you about Sarah like that,' he said. 'But you were ragging on me for my loveless existence-'

'*Loveless existence*,' I laughed.

'It bothers me, man,' the mask cracked.

Why was it so hard for us to say these things? It took something big to admit this stuff.

Up ahead, an official in a hazmat suit was loading suitcases into the undercarriage of the bus. Another was seating passengers. People were everywhere, desperate to leave Halesowen and to get out of the bad weather.

'I doubt you'll make this one,' I said to the old lady.

She thanked us for the help and they stood adjacent to the queue, hoping a couple of passengers would take pity on them and swap places. We walked around the bus, looking to see who was on. There was no sign of the scag rats.

'Perhaps they got an earlier one,' Will said.

Sitting at the front, there was Maureen. I went to knock on the window, but she saw me and purposefully turned away. Will didn't notice and I made a point of not mentioning it until the bus turned the corner.

'Why didn't Sarah come with you?' I asked him.

He didn't need to answer, just a slow shrug.

'I think she really likes me,' he said. '*Why?*'

I smiled. 'You have similar hobbies.'

'Yeah, must just be that,' he nodded.

'Shut up, yuh prat.'

2031

I dodged a bottle. 'Who the fuck are they?'

We quickly moved alongside the multistorey car park towards the swimming baths.

'They live in the stairwell,' Will said. 'Bunch of scag rats.'

'*Scag rats*?' I jumped at the sound of another shattering missile.

'Fuck off, sofa-sliders!' one of them shouted down.

I looked up, I couldn't see anybody, just voices and a hail of bottles.

'You boys am dead!' Tony Moran shouted up.

'They don't seem like scag rats,' I said, half-jogging on. 'Too much energy.'

'They live on the piss-stinking stairs,' Will said, 'where we used to drink white cider and suck on gas! Rats!'

Now's probably not the time to quibble over definitions.

We heard the sound of a bottle striking something other than the floor, before smashing. We turned to see Jake fall to the ground.

'Leave him alone!' I shouted.

'Nah!' a faceless voice defied. 'He dopes it!'

Dazed and spitting animals to himself like a broken toy, Jake rolled on his back and stretched his arms out. 'C-c-come on then, c-c-cat-kids!'

'Stop being a prick, Jake!' Will said.

I turned to Will, annoyed. Clearly Jake wasn't well, burnt out by crack and dizzied by the barrage of bottles.

'This is all his fault,' Will moaned.

I quickly moved back through no man's land towards Jake. A bottle landed just in front of me, another barely missed my head, shattering on the wall behind, showering me in glass. 'Bastards!'

Will screamed, 'right, you cunt-scum!' charging towards the entrance of the stairwell. I heard him jogging up the stairs, muttering expletives.

What the hell was happening? Back in the flats life was good, there was the sense of a new beginning, of learning from past mistakes. This side of town, I was with three clearly sick addicts dodging bottles thrown by kids I didn't even know existed.

I grabbed Jake's hand, but he wasn't budging. 'Come on–'

'F-f-f-farm… animals-chicken-no! I deserve-duck-chick-goose.'

I dragged him by his arm until he knew I wasn't giving up. He started to help himself, rolling onto his knees and getting up. I put my arm around his shoulders, quickly directing him away.

'I'm sheep-sorry, Tom-'

'What are you on about?'

'Y-y-you know! I was doing alright-sheep-squirrels-m-m-manure.'

In the car park, I could hear an argument. Will was threatening to beat their brains out. 'Bring it on yuh tramp!' a girl shouted.

'Come on, Will,' I called up. 'They're just kids!'

Jake was rambling sheep, dragging his feet. Tony was up ahead hobbling across the road to the swimming baths. He looked much older than when I'd last seen him, his hair white and thin. *Perhaps he's been humbled by the death of his son and the loss of his place in Halesowen.*

Will was now roaring in anger, panting and garbling like a poked bear, ready to tear something apart. I stopped and looked behind to see him holding one of the kids half over the side, three floors up. 'Please, please,' the child was begging – he looked about 10, this lanky middle-aged man, his face crinkled and yellow like an old newspaper, panting and grizzling in his young, white face.

'Throw a fucking bottle at my mate again,' he said, 'and-'

'Leave him alone-' a girl shouted.

'I'll break all of your necks-!'

'He's only little,' she whined.

'Will,' I yelled up, like he was making a nuisance of himself.

I felt Jake wilting from under my arm until he was once again lying on the tarmac. 'C-c-come scag rats, yuh promised! F-f-pig-pen-have me! I k-killed you all!'

'For Christ's sake, what are you doing?' I said, standing over him.

'This is what he does,' Tony yelled from across the road. 'He's suicidal. He'll be the death of all of us. Leave him to rot!'

I heard the sound of smashing glass and looked up to see Will still in the car park, rubbing the back of his head and throwing fists aimlessly.

'Come on man,' I shouted, 'they're just kids.' I tried once again to lift Jake and had him under my wing. 'What's happened to you? You were more sane than any of us.'

'Come on Jake,' Tony yelled. 'I'll do ya myself, if it bastard pleases yuh!'

'You w-w-won't!' Jake sulked.

'Oh, no you fucking don't,' Will fumed. 'You little bastard-fucking-shitting-!' a trapped tiger, a growl which echoed throughout the car park.

'For Christ's sake!' I yelled to the Gods. '*Will*, just bloody leave-'

My sentence was interrupted by a heavy smack on the tarmac, I immediately turned, panicking, expecting to see the body of a child. But it wasn't a kid. It was Will. He'd been ejected from one of the floors of the multistorey. Sick with it, I laughed. It just came out. Only briefly, a squeak like something had broke inside, a snapped tendon holding my heart in place. I dropped Jake in the road and ran towards him.

From the car park, I heard the echo of retreating feet and worried chattering, as they argued amongst themselves. 'He'll go ape,' a girl nagged.

'Not my fault,' another.

'What the fuck have you done!?' I shouted up, my heart slamming itself against my sternum.

Will was lying on the floor. He coughed and a bubble of blood came out of his mouth. '*Fuck*. Will, what've they done to you?'

His eyes half-opened. 'I didn't deserve…' he mumbled.

'Don't talk. I'm gonna get help.' It was a pointless thing to say.

He reached for my hand, but his grip was weak and trembly, his fingers cold. I squeezed his hand, tears blurring my sight, sickened at the inevitability of it, his body hopelessly twisted on its side.

One eye closed, the other rolled back into his head. Then he suddenly focused on me again. 'Didn't deserve Sarah or Tammy-'

'Don't talk stupid. You always deserved them. You were the better man! That's why they wanted you. Now stay awake, you prick.'

'No,' he tried to smile, gently squeezing my fingers, 'better man.'

'Don't be soppy.'

He let out a little laugh, a *pa-ha*, before closing his eyes, muttering under his breath, speaking tongues.

'What you saying?'

He didn't respond, writhing slowly, unfolding, warping, like a fortune teller fish.

'Listen to me, Will. You've got a kid! You need to stay awake! Ally, she's having a… Will.' I squeezed his cheeks.

One eye opened, he pointed up to sky with his forefinger. 'China.'

I glanced up, half expecting a bomb, a plane, something. When I turned back, his eyes closed, finger came to rest. 'Will!' There was a moment of quiet and then, in a sudden shock of movement, his chest lunged upwards in one last gasp. I gripped his hand tight. 'Will! Come on, brother!' His body fell back, exhaled and then stilled. His yellowed face went ashen, mouth ajar, cheeks sucked in. I froze, unsure what to do. *'No, no you fucking haven't.'* I slapped him gently. Nothing. Then again, this time harder, and his head rolled to the side, his silhouette the shape of a reptile, a dinosaur, empty and inhuman. I rolled his head back to look at him, tears streaming down my face, sucking in sobs. As soon as I let go it fell back to the side, leaving him long, twisted, lizard-like.

'Tom…' Tony called, now dragging a limp Jake. 'Tom! They'll come back!'

'Just go, Tony!' I shouted, strengthening, certain I needed to go and find the culprits.

A gun shot changed my mind.

I quickly got up off my knees and, hunching, as if somehow tautening the muscles created bulletproof flesh, followed them around the corner and out of sight of the car park.

'Who are they?' I panted, back to the wall.

'The kids,' Tony said.

'The *kids*?'

'Of H-H-hen-house-Halesowen.' Jake slumped to floor and started to cry.

Holding his knees he rocked, back-headbutting the wall until, seemingly unbeknownst to him, his light blue jeans slowly darkened around the crotch, but I felt no pity. Just disgust.

'Get up,' I shouted, angry.

He looked up shocked, pathetic, misfiring twitches, swallowing animals.

'Get the fuck up,' I grabbed him by his shirt and held him up.

'W-w-w-'

'W-w-w fucking what?' I taunted.

'W-w-Will!'

'He's dead, Jake!' clenching my fists, ready to punch him.

Tony was watching, nodding. I looked down to my fist, then into Jake's pathetic unfocused eyes, his bruised, scaly pathetic face, nose sores, lip sores, his pathetic cheek bones hanging out over his pathetic mouth. If I hadn't seen it happen so many times, it would be hard to reconcile this was the same man who once jumped in front of Leroy as the townspeople bayed for his blood, the same man who once told me the antidote to his crack habit was selflessness. I imagined my fist making a hole in his head and it felt good, it sated something inside me.

'Go on,' Tony said. 'It's his fault.'

And then I saw what I was doing, what was in front of me. *What good will it do?* I loosened my fists, took a breath and dragged Jake on. 'Come on, you fuck.'

'T-Tom, I'm sheep-skin-sorry-'

'What do we do now?' I said to Tony.

'Hide,' he said, hobbling on, disappointed. 'The Zion.'

———————

Jake was sleeping it off on a pile of plasterboard which had fallen from the ceiling; Tony was sitting on an upturned filing cabinet which used to hold our scrap metal – the store had been looted. I sat against the wall, a bottle of rum in my hands. I wasn't planning on drinking it, instead using it as some kind of punishment, the eternal temptation. I couldn't drink it even if I'd wanted to, and in a way I did, but I'd made a pact with myself all those years ago, a pact that had turned out to be much stronger than I could possibly have imagined back then. Why was I still sober when so many others had relapsed or died from, or with, this illness? Perhaps Sarah had relapsed too. *Why wouldn't she? People do. All the time. For some reason the majority do.* But *I* hadn't. It would've been foolish to think I'd never drink again, but it was hard to see how I would, given all that had happened.

Will was still out on the road, broken and dead, beneath the car park. There was no prospect of burial without risking our lives. he'd just lie there, like those people who die high up in the mountains or those safari animal carcasses that lie out on the plains. *Will's dead.* I don't know why I'd expected things to end differently, but somewhere inside me I'd always believed the four of us would get out of Halesowen. *But he never wanted to leave.*

Now he never would.

'What happened to Marcus?' I asked.

'The funny one?' Tony pointed in the corner of the metal store at a sandal.

I snorted a laugh, it just came out, helpless and hopeless. 'Loz?'

'Who?'

'Our other mate.'

'Dunno.'

'You've not seen or heard anything around town?'

He shook his head, reaching for the rum. I passed it over, the familiar metal graze of the cap, like the sound of a tin of Whiskas to a cat. 'Not been around town, have I. The only reason we were out wuz cos of that fuck!' He tossed the cap at Jake. It hit him on the head but he didn't rouse.

'What do you mean?'

'Been in hiding, en't we. They've long wanted me dead, now all the Sons are gone. Just me and him, I reckon,' he gestured to Jake, took a gulp and grimaced satisfied. 'And look at him. Nothing without the power.'

'Who did it?' I asked.

'Jake reckons it's the feds-'

'Feds? We're all supposed to be feds aren't we?'

'That Jordan's a bit of a freak, too. I thought it mighta been the nons.'

'But why? What for?'

'The taking over of the town.'

He said it so matter-of-fact it made me laugh.

'That's the game,' he defended, certain.

'What if it's not some big conspiracy, Tony?' I said. 'What if it's just a bunch of people with different ideas, trying to make things work?'

He laughed, patronisingly. 'Stopped being that when your fat commie mate wrote everything down. Good riddance.'

'*Good riddance*? What happened to him?'

'Had to be the Prices,' he nodded.

'You think so?' I asked, smug.

'We all agree on that.' He slugged back a satisfying swig, wiped his mouth, confidently.

'What? Will too?'

He nodded.

I could've told him what really happened, but what was the point? It was just an unnecessary expenditure of energy. Besides, I was just as blind as they were, only in different ways. And what did the truth about these things matter? What did any of it matter now? All that mattered was the others. I found myself pacing, wondering where to go from here. I glanced down the corridor, walls crumbling, the light fixtures hanging. A big board rested against the wall, leaving a sliver of crawl space, a triangle, a small gap to squeeze through, which we used to block when we weren't here.

'She's not here,' Tony said.

'Who's not here?'

'No sign of her anywhere. We went to the baths, like you told him – shoulda told me, we'd have gone straight there, instead he made us wait for you for three days, like you wuz gonna rise from the frigging dead!'

'I need to go there,' I said.

'Nothing there. That's why we'm in the Zion. That and your stash of booze-'

'What stash?'

He laughed. 'Another thing they never told you.'

That was a dig, or it felt like it. That was a dig and Will had just died – my brother had just been killed. Tony's red face smiling, cocky, the spider veins cupping his cheeks, bloated with booze. He looked ill, but if he'd survived this long, he was probably gonna outlive us all. I stood over him, 'you know what, Tony, you're a fucking cockroach.'

'What you say?' he threatened, preparing to stand up.

'I'm not scared of you, Tony.' I didn't know why I was saying it, but it was true. 'You're a real shit, you know. You've always been a bully and I've been scared of you, but now I see there's nothing to be scared of, because we all die. That's the way of it. Being scared of you is just the fear of the inevitable.'

'Yuh don't say,' sarcastic, laughing. He sat back, playing it cool. 'Now, how we gonna get out of this mess?'

'It's taken this to bring me to that realisation. I used to go hiking high in the mountains across ridges in icy conditions, my limbs trembling in fear, and it was a buzz, but even that didn't drive out the fear. No, not fear. It didn't give me acceptance of the inevitable. Before that, I did it with drink and drugs, pushed myself to the extreme, purely out of fear.'

'You think too much.' He looked to the wall like a sulky child.

'It's not that I want to die. I don't. But I will, sooner or later and I'm ok with that now. Do you get me?'

He faced me square on like he was trying to suss me out. Should he fear me? What was this fella who'd just lost his mate really saying? I could see it in his eyes. We were having some kind of stand-off, only I had nothing to lose because, to me, there was no loser in a situation like this.

'Tom, you wanna do them kids in?' he placated. 'We can do those—'

'No! I don't want to do anyone in!'

He laughed, weak and old. 'That's good to know. Was wondering what I was gonna have to do and to be honest, I en't got the strength anymore.'

'You should be dead.'

'But I en't. Now how do we get out of here? Or are you happy to stay here drinking, like Will was?'

Will's dead. I glanced around the metal store. Our little shop where we gathered little bits of metal and then traded it for food and tools, or benefits, according to Christian – but then work was always just a trade-off of time and skill for benefits, wasn't it?

I picked up Marcus's old sandal. What had happened here? Who looted the place? And what did they do to him? I had an image of Marcus at peace, but it didn't stop me imagining a bullet entering his head or Alan Price throttling him with his bony hands.

Will's dead. My chest fluttered, stomach creaked. What had happened here since I'd last seen them? Were Will and Tony friends? Perhaps it had been fun. How and why did Jake get here too? Against all reason, I started to imagine it had all been one big party in a debauched bachelor pad – an episode of Friends penned by Samuel Beckett. I had so many questions, but I was too tired to let them out and I knew none of it really mattered, it was just fluff, incidental details, maya, the Hindus called it.

Tony was staring at me, his face making me angry. I tutted. I imagined slamming a big pillow over his grotesque face and squeezing the life out of him, but just below the gratifying violence, the thought of my dead brother was digging at my innards, twisting my sinews, curdling my gut. The last thing I did was nag him for trying to protect me. *Don't go there, Tom. You know better than that. Oh…*

'Grief,' came out of my mouth, like I was greeting an old enemy.

'What about it?' Tony said.

I'm too familiar with it. Familiar, but it was always different. It amounted to the same, a gaping hole, like a missing tooth, but each time I'd lost someone big in my life, it seemed alien and I found myself toying with it, pinching myself with it – just how much could it hurt me?

'I miss the lad,' Tony said, looking for some kind of sympathy. 'The way he went.'

'Aaron?' I didn't care.

He nodded.

'Have we got any food, Tony?'

'Tins.'

Anything but peas.

Tony was on his back, snoring heavily. I grabbed Will's headtorch and shone the light on Jake, he was shivering. Perhaps he was awake, but he looked out of it. I'd never seen him use drugs before. He was generally sober and hard-working, a voice of reason, but a few times the bottle had got the better of him. He was an addict through and through and, like all of us, his habit had lain in wait, ready to go to war on him. Now all bets were off, every day out of the trenches and into no man's land. Maybe I could help him. Maybe he didn't want help. I'd personally seen more people die of this than cancer.

'Just popping out for a piss,' I whispered, in case he was awake. 'Be back in two.'

I crept out of the metal store, squeezed through the triangular gap, the unavoidable crunching of glass beneath me, dodging hanging wires and plaster board tiles.

Outside, the town was black and quiet. Immediately across the road, the old swimming baths. Up the overgrown steps, I trod gently and quietly, feeling my way. There was no light coming from inside, no sounds, but I held hope that maybe they'd heard me wandering over and had gone into hiding. The boards were in place. I carefully moved them, reaching behind for the clanging cans but they weren't attached.

Inside, I clicked on the torch, it echoed like a dripping tap. The big table, the vending machine beds. No Calor gas cookers, just a cold ashtray full of Damien's thin roll-up nubs.

'Sarah,' I whispered. 'It's Tom. Loz? Damo?'

I went to the top of squash courts, where we'd first imprisoned Ray. It was cold and empty. I went into the ladies changing rooms and then the men's, where I'd foolishly lunged for a kiss. I hadn't seen her in weeks and my feelings were so clear now. It was not about sex or any of that, what had I been thinking? It was just about friendship, but more, it was about fellowship, one addict talking to another – our warped souls were connected whether we liked it or not.

I went upstairs into the long gallery, terrifying for its openness. I looked down over the railing and into the grimy pool. I had the sudden urge to dive in head first. I shuddered imagining my skull cracking on the slimy bottom, paralysed in a heap. Then Will came to me again, lying outside – a smack of reality. Perhaps the foxes would have him or the dogs or seagulls. It wasn't such a horrifying thought. Burned, buried or devoured, what's the difference? And he'd feel the same about it.

Besides, nothing is wasted, matter can't be destroyed. We live on. Really we're each of us everything, one ever-growing organism. It's the idea of ourselves which is the illusion, a projection. How had I always known this and why did I forget it so often? I once heard somebody describe the "ism" of alcoholism as Incredibly Short Memory. Every day was a new day and I was forever having to learn it all over again.

I sat on a bench and remembered one of my last conversations with Sarah, how she'd managed to pull it out of me: Dylan. *Is that why we kissed her?* I asked the cosmos. *As a catalyst?*

'Lucy, was it always meant to be this way?'

She didn't answer me. She wasn't into all this spiritual malarkey. She wasn't against it, but she liked science and the BBC and progress and gadgets.

'Christ, where do I go from here?' *One thing's for sure, I'm not going back to the Zion. I'm done with them.*

I left the gallery and went downstairs. At the bottom, I noticed a book on the table. I could've sworn it wasn't there before – I found myself inwardly smiling at the Big Eye, the Organism, the Great We Are. I picked it up. Emotional Sobriety. It was the book I'd given Sarah. My heart beat fast as I held it, as if she were in the room. I opened it up. There was a little note scribbled on it. "Should read this, deeve!!! We got cabin fever and left."

I understood it instantly. 'The cabin!' I laughed, put my hand to my mouth, excited. *How did Will not see this*? 'Emotional sobriety, of course.'

I took a second, held my breath and listened. Silence. Peace. I slid back outside and immediately headed away from the car park towards Leasowes. As I reached an underpass, I flicked my torch on and a moth flew straight into my eye. I flinched, 'sod off!' But it stopped me dead, beyond words. I found myself frozen to the spot, wondering why on earth a moth should hit me in the face right now, of all times? This sort of thinking used to make Lucy laugh, but something inside was telling me I had to go and see Will again. I really didn't feel the need, it was a senseless risk, but something told me I'd understand why when I got there.

'Shit.' I cursed the heavens.

Headtorch off, I made my way back up. When I got to the swimming baths I tip-toed around the building, every contact with the pavement much louder in my brain. *Perhaps I've just got to say a prayer and then I can head off to the cabin.* I could make out the smudge of him, the velociraptor silhouette in the road, and no amount of spiritual thought was stopping the emotions firing off inside me. *The stupid fuck.* I was angry above all else. We'd found each other. We could've left, walked to Wales and started again. *But he was never gonna quit drinking, Tom. He'd gone yellow with it, how long would he have had left?*

As I faced the car park, poised to cross the road, a light suddenly shone on me from up high. 'We can see you,' the young voice spoke.

I panicked. It was confident and steady, which unnerved me. I fumbled for my headtorch and accidentally flipped it off my brow and into the road. Not sure which way to run, I was essentially jogging on the spot, like an avatar stuck in a virtual blip.

'Nowhere to hide, sofa-slider,' a less professional voice spat.

'Stop it,' another bickered.

I was trying to see beyond the beam, 'who the bloody hell are you?'

'You know me,' the calm voice.

'And me,' a young boy said.

'What are you talking about?' I asked, frustrated.

'I never saw you til today,' a girl said.

'You know him!' someone countered.

'I don't know any of you!' I yelled.

'What about me?' the voice seemed to come from behind and I turned quickly, but couldn't see anything for torch-blind.

I fumbled in the road for my headtorch. Found it, clicked it on. There was nothing behind me. I turned back to the car park and the light had gone off.

'I don't know who you are or what you want from me, but I just need to say goodbye to my friend before leaving Halesowen.'

'Why would we believe that?' someone asked. 'We killed your friend.'

I took a deep breath. 'My brother, yes, but I have other-'

'He's not your brother,' a child snapped.

'Look, just tell me who the hell you are!' There was silence, not even the scuff of a foot. They were thinking, I knew it, a multi-headed beast thinking. 'Of course I wish you hadn't killed Will, but in a way he was already dead,' I said, trying to find a way out.

'We're the children,' a girl said.

'What the hell does that mean? We in the middle of an episode of Dr Who?'

Someone laughed. 'That's sweet and seedy, geeze! I remember that classic!'

'…Ed?' I asked.

There was a pause. It was clearly College Ed. 'They didn't mean it, Tom,' he said.

I was searching the levels of the car park with my torch. 'Show yourself. I don't want any trouble. I just want to leave.'

'We can't let you, can we?' Ed said.

I started to back away slowly. 'What's to stop me just walking off and leaving?' I heard the sound of footsteps too late, someone grabbed me, using one hand to hold my arm behind my back, another arm clamped around my neck.

'Let go, you bastard!'

'Don't you want to say goodbye to your "brother"?' the boy said. His voice broken, he sounded about 18.

Christ, why did I walk this way? Lucy, you'd be right to laugh.

'Say goodbye to your friend,' a little girl said, sweetly but undoubtedly menacing.

'How… old are you?' I asked, trying to wriggle free. 'Where's your parents?'

'Picks,' a lad shouted.

Laughter echoed all around. It made me feel like I was surrounded.

'They haven't got parents, geeze,' Ed said. 'Some lost them, others have never really had them, even if they're still around.'

'I lost my dad,' the boy holding me said.

'I'm sorry to hear it, but that's not my fault.'

'That's Jadon,' Ed said, 'Stacey's kid.'

'*Jadon?* I thought you were up north,' I said. 'I was good mates with your dad.'

He pulled my arm up hard, causing me to squeal in pain. *Perhaps this is it, perhaps I was never supposed to leave Halesowen. It was the moth of death!*

'Tom, say goodbye to Will,' Ed said.

Jadon started shoving me forward. 'I know your mum well, too,' I said, trying to placate him.

'You and every other sofa-slider in Halesowen.'

'She's in a cell at the top of Ally's,' I added, edging closer to Will's twisted body. 'Please let go! Please!' I started to cry. I couldn't help it, it burst out of me. I felt like that 12 year old being bullied by dad, blamed for the separation in those moments of drunkenness when he regretted his decision.

He pulled on my arm again. It hurt, but the pain was pleasurable, a justification for my state, each judder of emotion making it worse and better, making a man of me. I heard the patter of feet on the stairs of the car park. They started pouring out into the road. Very quickly I found myself looking down on Will, surrounded by 20 or so children. Some were very young probably not even 10 years old, most were in their teens. As I looked at their smooth faces in the beam of my torch, sans the scars of age, the bags and the wrinkles, my crying became louder, freer, unstoppable, until it was a full sob of exasperation. It wasn't fear, I couldn't have cared what happened to me. It was the warped reality of our situation. It was love.

Ed instructed Jadon to let go and I fell to my knees at Will's feet. His cold corpse just another shell, like the so many others I'd encountered over the years. Sure, it was symbolic of my brother, shared features with him, but it wasn't him. That's not why I was crying. I was crying because of them, because of me, because of Sarah and Loz, because of Jake and Tony, Ally and the hopeless dopes who'd heralded me for writing an article about the Two Ronnies. I was crying for the living. 'Why Ed?' I said through the tears.

'It's simple. We need you to bring us Tony. Dead or alive.'

———————

What had once been the caterpillar of life, was now a moth and transcendence to a moth was the beginning of death. It all made sense. Perhaps there was nothing more to learn.

'Tony,' I whispered, shining the headtorch. 'Get up.'

'Wha-ya-want!?' he grizzled, eyes squinting, curled on his side on the filing cabinet.

'Be quiet. Listen to me. We have to get out of here now.'

I moved over to Jake and gave him a shake.

'Spearmint-r-r-rhino-trunk. What?' he panicked, twitching, looking around.

'Shush. We have to leave.'

He sat up disturbing a smoke of plaster dust. 'L-leave, w-where?'

'What you mean?' Tony pressed an LED lamp, spraying the room with light. He pushed himself up with a clunk and reached for the rum.

'I found this book,' I said, holding up Emotional Sobriety. 'There was a message in it. I know where Sarah is.'

Jake was shaking his head trying to speak, but there was nothing. Not even a quack. Tony was nodding, whilst swigging. 'Sounds good to me,' he said. 'You won't get him to leave.'

'We've all got to get out here,' I said. 'They've killed Will already, next-'

'N-n-no!' Jake said, looking around for something.

Tony reached for his rucksack and started filling it with tins of food and a couple of bottles of rum, revived by the prospect of finally getting out of Halesowen. I felt sick about it, but what would he do in this situation?

'Jake, come on mate,' I said. 'You made a new life once before. You can do it again.'

'I k-k-killed them.'

'Whatever. Just forget it.'

'You d-d-duck understand!'

He clicked on his headtorch, searching manically, slightly panicked. He finally found what he was looking for. In the tin, there was a pipe and a small rock of crack. 'L-l-llama-last one.'

'I've got no more,' Tony said. 'Better let him toot it, then after a duck, a pig and m-m-mongoose maybe he'll change his mind, but I doubt it.'

'F-fuck off!'

Tony laughed.

I've killed ants, I've swatted flies. I'm not a Buddhist for fuck's sake.

As part of the deal, the children promised to bury Will's shell. It didn't seem important, but the suggestion made me trust them a little bit more. I started to hastily pack Will's old rucksack.

'Did you see them?' Tony asked.

'Who?'

'The children.'

'The children? Oh… no, but it's getting lighter. Best get out of here whilst it's still dark.'

Jake lit his pipe, took back a milky-sweet drag, held it in for as long as he could and then let it out with a 'rabbit-rat.'

Tony stopped what he was doing and sat down on the filing cabinet to get his breath and roll a cigarette. 'Tom.'

'Yeah?' The tins had no labels. I packed the big ones, which were less likely to be peas. Pineapple, maybe?

'I've been thinking,' he said. 'I mean, what you said and… you know, I'm sorry.'

'*Sorry*?' I stopped what I was doing. 'What you talking about?'

'I thought about what you said. I am a cockroach.' His face vein-cracked and broken – *this was really not the time for humility*!

'Just forget all that,' I said, refusing to look at him, lifting the rucksack to judge the weight. 'I was just angry.'

'No, I need to say this. You and me, we're not the same-'

'Bat-rat-sheep-rat-a-c-cat!' We both turned to look at Jake. 'W-w-what?'

'Tony, it doesn't matter. Nothing matters anymore. And maybe we're not so different.'

He laughed.

This was the last thing I needed to be hearing right now.

'Come off it! We'm cider and apple juice,' he barked. 'Whiskey and water!'

'We doing a goddam musical number?'

'Yuh what?'

'Just forget it, Tone.'

'I've thought a lot about this. It's my fault Aaron's dead.'

'N-n-no, Tony,' Jake said.

'Just stop it, Jake,' he insisted. 'It is my fault.' He looked genuine.

I had one task. One thing was in the way of getting out of Halesowen. If Ed was to be trusted, I just had to get Tony out of that door first to be in with a chance of escaping. And I had no reason not to trust him. They could've killed me there and then, left me for dead in the road, next to my brother.

'All those people. Gary Bennett, Jay Bird, his bloody brother-' Tony listed.

'*Sean?*'

'We couldn't let him rot. We'd look like right bastards. He was the first one we euth'd. You went in with a chair and that gave us the opportunity to make it look like natural causes.'

'Fucking hell, Tone.'

'The mon-oman, too – your mate, the preacher,' he continued.

'So, it *was* you?'

'As much as anyone. Gerry, Bob, Kate, all euth'd. What about Barb? I'm a piece of scum, Tom, make no mistake. My son paid the price for it.'

He was hardly an angel himself. 'Why are you telling me this now? What's done is done.'

Jake tried to light his pipe again.

'Nothing in it, kid,' Tony said. 'Here.' He offered the rum. Jake looked at it, then at me.

'If it helps us get out of here, you should have it, Jake,' I smiled.

He shook his head and sucked on his pipe, sparking residue.

Tony packed the rum in his bag.

Outside, I heard something, a click. I guessed what it was, but didn't word it to myself. Jake looked in the direction of it and then I sensed him looking at me, but I pulled on the drawstring to close the bag, oblivious.

Tony lifted his rucksack on his shoulders. 'Come on Jakey boy,' he said. 'What've we got to stay here for? Lost one of us already.'

Jake glanced at Tony, then at me, his eyes doped but piercing. He started to gather his things.

'That's a man,' Tony smiled. 'You did your best with this place, but let's leave it to the next lot. Big world out there. Tom's gonna lead us to it.' He patted me on the back.

Why's he being like this? Does he know? Do they both know? Jake kept glancing over at me, but I just looked ahead, thinking about the task at hand.

'We ready then?' I asked.

'I'm ready,' Tony said.

Jake begrudgingly pulled on his rucksack.

'After you,' Tony said.

'No, no, you lead the way,' my heart thudding hard, whooping skipped beats.

Headtorch on, Tony hobbled down the corridor over broken glass, plaster and debris.

I felt sick inside. Was this the right thing to do? *He's just an old man. God, Life, give me a sign?* I imagined a firing squad outside, children wearing saucepans on their heads, poised to throw bottles, Ed at their side, ready to shout: "aim, fire". Only it wasn't bottles. They were going to shoot Tony dead. *Perhaps they'll take us all out? Perhaps that's what I deserve?* I wiped my sweaty hands on my trousers, glanced behind and Jake was watching me, suspiciously. 'What?'

'T-Tony-' he called.

'*What-?*' I asked again.

Tony was just squeezing through the triangle of space in the corridor 'What?' he whisper-shouted.

'R-rabbit-rum.'

'Let's do that outside,' I said.

'Rat-rum!' he demanded.

Tony tutted, 'I just offered you that!' He stopped and took his rucksack off, passed it to me. 'Here, give him that. Pass it back when I get through.' He continued on.

'T-tom,' Jake said.

'What?' I asked, passing him the bag.

'Tom,' he repeated, like the voice of my goddam conscience.

He rummaged through the bag, pulling things out, but didn't take his eyes off me. *Does he know? Is this the frigging sign I asked for?* 'Tony, wait,' I whispered through.

'What now?'

'Come back into the store.'

He sighed, 'for fuck's sake,' squeezing back through the space. When I turned around, Jake had half-emptied Tony's rucksack to get at the bottle, a jacket, tins of beans, an old pair of slippers. Tony saw this and groaned, 'there's a half bottle in the side!'

'Tony,' I said. 'I can't do this. We need to leave the building the back way.'

'What? Why?'

'Because you're right,' I said. 'We're whiskey and water. I've gotta be honest. College Ed's out there.'

'*Ed?* Why…?' He sat down on the filing cabinet. 'Oh… I see,' he nodded. '*College Ed?*' he half-laughed.

'He's leading the kids-'

'Of course. The take-over of the town.'

'I'm not sure it's some big conspiracy. You've just made a lot of enemies.'

He ignored me. '*Ed*? *Really*? Good for bloody him. Ha! So, you were gonna…? Shit. Tom the monk,' he laughed. 'But you couldn't do it.'

Jake swallowed a mouthful of rum and grimaced. 'Woof,' he said, throat clearly burning. 'That's better. I feel human again.' He started to put a jacket on.

'Oi!' Tony barked. 'That's mine.'

Jake ignored him, smiling warmly at me. He moved into the corridor and I didn't even think to stop him. He was already squeezing through the space before it occurred to me. 'Jake! Wait!' I turned to Tony. 'It's dark. They'll think it's you.'

'That's what he wants.'

We heard three loud shots and the children yelped with glee.

We made our way through a collapsed corridor at the back of the Zion, reclaimed by nature, the shrubs and weeds growing into and through the bricks and cement. Out the back, we scuttled alongside a fence which ran adjacent to an old car park obscured by tall grasses. The only way out was the other side of the Zion and back onto the road where College Ed and the children were. We could hear the yaps and nattering amongst them. 'Do you think they've realised who it is?' I whispered.

'Probably.' The sound of glass suggested they were making their way into the building. 'Now's our chance,' he said, grabbing my hand and pulling me on towards the edge of the building.

We looked around the corner. A dim torchlight was moving around, but out of view. It seemed like they were all disappearing inside. We stepped out into the open and carefully made our way down, away from the town, hunched and tense. Then up onto the road by the old McDonald's which at one time had been renamed Church-4. Without thinking, I pressed the button to the traffic lights. Tony grabbed my arm, but it was too late. The lights were blacked out, but a little orange flicker indicated there was something working inside. We froze, waiting for the beep-beep-beep, but nothing happened. Walking backwards across the road, I stared at the dead lights, no stop, no go, no sign of life.

With an hour or more of darkness left, it was unlikely they'd find us as we moved further away and closer to the cabin.

'You really are a bloody cockroach,' I whispered.

He spun around as if he was about to have words with me, but he stopped, processed my intonation and smiled. 'I guess I am.'

We walked to Leasowes mostly without speaking, my old head determined to pore over the whys and hows of it all, but above everything, I knew it was meant to be this way. I was meant to be doing this part of my journey with Tony Moran, not Will or Jake. They were gone. Their part in my journey was over and I just had to accept that.

'Don't feel bad about Jake,' Tony said, as we started up Mucklow Hill. 'He wasn't a bad sort, but once the Sons was done, so was he.'

He was right, but it wasn't about power or status. Being a Son was Jake's antidote to his dark side. With that removed, he was just left faced with himself.

Tony followed me onto the brow of Leasowes park and down into the dark woods, the creak of trees, the cracking of twigs underfoot. I flicked my headtorch on but didn't see the trip wire which let loose a string of clanging cans from a branch. A dog started barking in the distance.

'I can see yow,' a voice said, either from behind or at the side of us, it was hard to tell.

'*Ray*? Is that you?' I asked. 'It's me, Tom.'

'I can see yow,' he repeated. 'Who'm yow with?'

'*Ray*?' Tony stated. 'Thought you was long gone. It's me.'

'I've got a gun aimed at Tony's head,' another voice said. It was Sarah. 'Don't move, Tom, or I might hit you.'

Tony froze to the spot, scared to look about us. He wasn't expecting that. I didn't think for one second Sarah had a gun pointed at him, but I was glad to see him scared.

'I'm… I'm just a cockroach,' he said.

'What?' Sarah asked.

'Sarah, I'm a cockroach.' It was hard know whether it was a threat or a reflection. 'Everything you think you know about me is right,' he continued. 'All the bad things I've done. Not just as a Son, but before it. My whole life. I've never really done anything good. I've always bullied and cheated – I never killed nobody before the bombs though.'

I remembered Dan, chased out of his flat window to death. Did that not count? What about the overdoses? In a town riddled with drug deaths, overdoses and suicides, it was hard to imagine a bag of brown supplied by Tony had not led to someone's last breath. Perhaps he sold the bag that saw off Ninny or one of his brothers.

'But as a Son, one of seven,' he stressed, 'I've done some truly terrible things.' He coughed, to show us he was a defenceless old man.

'What about Lee?' Sarah shouted.

'It wasn't just me,' he said, buying time.

'Wor nothing to do with me,' Ray said.

'That's true. It wasn't Ray. But there were others, Ray, and you know it! We all wanted Gary Bennett gone. He tried to stop the looting before it all began. We all thought it was fair game under the circumstances, so he went too. And what about Sean, Gerry, Kate and Barb, all euth'd. And that's why,' he stopped, paused and had a coughing fit for effect.

It dawned on me that this was Tony's patter. It was clearly calculated. This was the cockroach. *Perhaps if I write this, this can be where my character stands up to be counted. "Tom Hanson suddenly put his arms around Tony Moran's frail neck and drained the life from him." I could call it The Cockroach and the Caterpillar.*

'That's why,' he continued, 'the Gods took my lad, Aaron. If you want to put a bullet in my head right now, there's none more deserving of it than me.'

But Tom Hanson wouldn't kill him, would he? Sarah might though.

'Ray,' Sarah said. 'Put him in one of the tents. Tom, come to the cabin.'

———

'I can't believe he's still alive,' I said, feeling a slight sense of disappointment. It wasn't that I wanted Marcus dead, of course, but somehow I'd made my peace with it. It made sense, it aligned with my dream and powers of intuition. 'I thought it was meant to be,' I said.

'I can't believe Will's gone,' she said, looking out of the window at the two tents. 'I can't believe I won't see him again-'

'But how, Sarah? What happened?'

'What are you talking about?'

'I found his sandals-'

'He was barefoot when Damien found him. Somebody'd spiked his coffee.'

'But the Prices captured him-'

'The Prices?' she turned to face me. 'You do know-?'

'Yes, a pair of old Tory-'

'They'd never hurt Marcus – without his permission.'

'But he told them we were leaving.'

'Ok.'

'And about the store.'

'Apparently.'

'God knows what else!'

'Can we please stop talking about Marcus!? Will's dead, Tom! He's dead!'

'I know.' I held my arms out. 'Hug?'

'*Don't.*' She turned back and looked out of the window. 'I thought I'd see him again. Not for anything other than just to see him.' She started to cry.

It wasn't rational, it wasn't compassionate and it certainly wasn't the time, but still the overriding feeling I had was little more than jealousy. I couldn't, I wouldn't, lie to myself about it. Not now. It made me want to drink to be more like Will. *People like a rogue, Sarah likes rogues, everyone likes a lovable rogue. I used to be a rogue*!

For fuck's sake, Tom! 'I'm sorry, Sarah. I appreciate you're hurting. I am too. But what else did Marcus say? Who looted the store?'

'I don't know, Tom. It's something to do with Quinton and communication devices.'

'Eh?'

'I don't know!' she snapped. 'You'll have to ask him.'

'When will he be back?'

'Damien's dropping Loz off in Shropshire. A few days, I guess.' She rested her head against the window. 'Oh, God. I know he was a bit of a dick, but…' she sighed, her back to me, young and strong.

Was it love? Devotion? Weakness? Or just pure addiction? Whatever it was, I once again found myself lusting after her, admiring her shape, the sinews trembling with emotion below her loose shirt. This vulnerability made her more attractive and I just wanted to put my arms around her, to hold her, to protect her.

Who are you kidding, Tom? You just want to put your arms around her. I could feel the emotions conflicting and setting each other off inside me. Jealousy, rejection, grief, fatigue and sheer hunger. It made me want to run and hide in something. In her.

'*Children?*' she asked again, turning to face me.

I nodded. 'They've been ruined by Halesowen – they're not the first.'

'He was protecting you from *children?*'

'He thought he was. He was trying to be all noble and shit, like the very first day we met when he carried my crate of beer.'

'Why would *children* do this?'

'If you ask Tony,' I said, laughing, 'he'll say they're trying to take control of the town.'

'What's funny about this, Tom?' she spat, angry, her eyes red with tears. 'Why would you bring him here? What's wrong with you?'

'It just happened that way. I told you.'

'He killed *Lee*.'

'You think I don't know that.'

'And Will's dead,' she cried.

I felt for her, I really did, but I couldn't help feeling irritated. They'd had some silly little relationship for a few months, whilst she'd tried to get sober. It was an early recovery relationship, a house built on sand. Will had been my friend for over 30 years and, however much our house had taken a bashing, it'd been built firmly on rock.

I haven't even had chance to grieve for him myself and she's already started venting, and I'm supposed to, what, listen? Be understanding? Be the stronger person?

I reached into my rucksack and pulled out the Emotional Sobriety book. I put it on the table hoping she'd see it and realise she was being ridiculous.

'I need sleep,' I said.

'What about Tony?'

'I'll be in the bedroom – if you need me.' My mind immediately drifted. *Stop it, Tom.*

I didn't sleep. I lay awake feeling irked and jealous. I'd spent six weeks in a cell, an alternative reality, in piss and shit. Somehow I'd inadvertently broken the spell of the Sons regime. I'd found my friend and then almost immediately watched him die. I'd spared Tony Moran out of the goodness of my heart, only to lose Jake. Loz had escaped, Marcus was alive and Sarah was still sober – *thanks to me!* And now, here I was, in the cold, unwelcoming atmosphere of the cabin.

I contemplated masturbating as an act of revenge, imagining the shape of Sarah's naked back. *Revenge for what?*

'I don't know.'

There was a knock at door. 'Tom,' Sarah spoke. 'You awake?'

'Yeah,' sulky.

When she entered, I couldn't deny my feelings, the monkey on my back. Many times I'd hoped and looked forward to seeing her again as a friend, an equal, a sister in the fellowship of our illness, but actually it was proving to be some kind of hell.

'I'm sorry,' she said.

'Me too.'

'What for?'

'I dunno.' I did. For nearly masturbating, for thinking about her in that way, for drinking without touching a drop, for my pathetic inability to deal with my feelings.

She sat on the bed. 'It's always been like this. I have people in my life for a while and then they disappear, like mum and dad. Like Baz, Jimmy and Lee. And nan too. I'm not moaning about it. I'm ok with it. I'm ok with people coming and going. I think I've grown to like it that way.'

I wanted to say, *I'm still here,* but somehow I knew I shouldn't. 'Have you read the letter?'

She clasped her hands together, nervous, 'no.'

She'd definitely aged. At 28 years old, she looked more like she was in her mid-30s. Lines had grown from her eyes and mouth and the smooth skin of her youth had textured, a soft fur in certain lights. But she was all woman and there was something very honest and clean about her face, more so than before, her eyes wide and sharp. She'd been surrounded with balding men, saggy skinned or booze bloated. We'd been shaped by age and eroded by substances. She was slender with a solid posture. She'd escaped addiction early enough to preserve her beauty.

Resentment. That's what I'm feeling. Self-pity.

'You should read it,' I said. 'You're ready. You don't have to trust me. You just have to trust your nan.'

She went back into the living-room. I could hear her opening it. She came back in holding it. She bit her nail, anguished. I nodded. She read:

'Dear Sarah,

I hope Tom hasn't given you this letter too soon. If he has, you'll probably be sighing now, rolling your eyes, thinking old nan doesn't know what she's on about.'

She didn't sigh, she laughed.

'The day you were born, I drove your mum to the hospital. We couldn't find dad. Maybe mum told you, but he was off with "her". He always used to say they were merely "best buds". They'd known each other since school. At the time, this woman was going through a divorce and he was "supporting" her. I didn't want to leave mum in the hospital, but she insisted I find him. Off I went, only to find him with this woman. When we arrived back at the hospital, you were already in the world, pale-faced and sweet. An innocent born amidst chaos. I promised myself that day I would always be there for you, because I knew life was going to be difficult. Now, here I am, breaking that promise.'

Sarah put her hand on her mouth, sensing her grandmother's pain. She stopped reading the letter out loud and walked back into the living room. I followed her to the door, watched her settle on the settee to finish reading it.

Ten minutes later she called through.
I entered the living room. 'Are you ok?'
'Thank you, Tom.'
'What for?'
She handed me the letter and pointed to a section.

My staying wasn't going to help you and it wasn't going to help me. Maybe I'll regret this decision in the future, but there's really no point in thinking like that. Someday you will have to make a difficult decision yourself and then you will understand why I did what I did. Perhaps you already do. Someday perhaps I'll understand why you did the things you did. Tom tried to help with that, but he's a bit soft on you.

He's a good man. Better than he thinks and better than you deserve.

People will come into your life and people will leave, Sarah. You know this better than most. You had a very difficult childhood and I only did what I thought was right. But all I am is human. The same as you. The same as mum and dad. The same as all of us.

I handed her the letter back.

'You a bit soft on me?' she teased.

I felt my face burning up, nervously laughing, but mostly I was distracted thinking about the people who come into our lives and leave it and what the meaning of it all was. My dad died and I went to rehab. Lucy and Dylan left me and I returned to Halesowen. Then mum died and Maureen and Sarah came into my life.

Now Will had gone too, but perhaps there wasn't anything left to say to each other. Loz had gone to find his family. Marcus wasn't here. They were all gone. Sarah was here, but Tony Moran was in my life too, for some reason.

I knew what I had to do. 'I'll take him away from here, Sarah.'

She nodded. 'We'll see each other again.'

But it felt like a lie, not mean or malicious, but just something people say.

She went into the bedroom. 'Where will you go?' she called.

'North, I guess.'

She came back and handed me a Nokia 3310.

'Does it work?'

'It will up north. Just calls. Loz and Damien have phones and the numbers are stored on it.'

'No, I don't want it,' I said, trying to hand it back. 'If it's meant to be-'

'Don't be silly. Marcus and me can come up on the next run.'

I could see she wanted to believe it. 'You really think you'll ever leave Halesowen?'

She nodded hesitantly. 'Yes, I just have to… I don't know. When I'm ready, yes. You get it,' she said.

I could've cried. 'What about Ray?'

'Ray,' she laughed. 'Ray and Wolfie will never leave Halesowen. This place means too much. When the opportunity arises, he'll want to help people get back on their feet in whatever way he can.'

I opened my rucksack and handed her Ross's play. 'Give him this.'

'What is Genuine is Proved in the Fire,' she read.

'It's the story of where it all went wrong.'

'He knows,' she said.

'Everyone thinks they know. Our story's always an iceberg and most people won't dip their head in the ocean.'

She laughed, 'that gonna be your first tweet in the new world?'

She was smiling and happy. I couldn't help but think it was because she was glad to see me go. It was a bitter pill, but really I had a lot to thank her for. I just couldn't say it.

'Try and help people, Sarah.'

She scratched her head, half-smiling.

I was being too serious, sanctimonious perhaps. 'Other addicts, I mean.'

'Like Tony?' she asked, unconvinced.

I put my rucksack on my back. 'A few will make it, but most won't. Whether they do or don't doesn't really matter to you in the end, but it matters that you help.'

'Like Jake.'

'He gave up in the end.'

'Lee made him-'

'Kill them?'

'No!' She was offended. 'Become a Son. *Help*.' She looked me dead in the eye: 'no one ever told me, you know.'

I nodded, 'but you knew.'

'You watched the buses all day and didn't see them.'

I smiled.

'How did you know *I'd* make it?' she asked.

'You haven't yet, and neither have I.'

'You know what I mean.'

'That first day-'

'In the brook-'

'You were asking for help.'

She smiled, but the smile soon vanished. 'Jimmy wasn't a bad person.'

'I know,' I said. I could feel myself welling up.

'Why do you care, Tom?'

It was a big question, one I'd thought about many times over the years. 'I had a family who loved me.'

'So, did I!' she replied, defensive.

'Yes, you did.'

She looked to the letter, folded it up and put it back in the envelope. She sensed I was watching her and she was smiling, shy. I wanted to hug her, to squeeze her hand, just to say thank you, but I couldn't bring myself to say goodbye. *If I was writing this in a story, this would be the last time we'd see each other.* It felt like the end. I opened my mouth to speak. She didn't look up, but heard the intake of air and waited. I shook my head, smiled and left the cabin.

Outside, I kicked the tent. 'Get up.'

'Yuh what?' Tony said.

'Time to leave. We're heading north.'

2028

'I gotta make a move,' the nuke driver said. The storm had stopped, the sun was shining and he was sweating irritable under the hazmat. 'The Rehabitation Halls close at 5.'

Jenny held her hand up, phone to ear, irritated. She shook her head. 'Straight to answer phone, he's a f-'

'You're making enemies,' the driver interrupted, the other passengers glaring at us out of the windows. 'You'll already be at the back of the queue and there's a limited number of beds. Buses coming from all over the south today.'

Jenny was small in frame only. Red-faced and spitting fury, she was certain we were to blame, yet the main reason I was there was to wish Loz and her luck.

'Just let me try once more,' I said, calling him. 'No… Still off.'

'Don't blame me if you're out on the streets,' the driver pressed.

'He's a waste of space,' she said, pacing back and forth. 'Always was. You all are!'

'Fuck off!' Will fought. 'We only came to-'

'You came to give him an alibi-'

'You what? Crazy bitch!' Will laughed. 'No wonder-'

'Stop it, Will,' I said. 'What's the sense in arguing? Maybe something bad's happened to him.' Will glanced at me, we both knew he'd been trying it on with Stacey. 'Jen, I'll call you as soon as we hear anything.'

'Don't bother.' She stepped onto the bus.

Carrie and Alex were already seated and they didn't seem too troubled their dad wasn't there, both engrossed in their phones.

'It's over,' she called down. 'I don't care if he calls next week, tomorrow or in the next half hour.'

The door closed with a clatter and the bus rose with a hiss. The old engine rumbled to a start. We'd watched several buses go, electric and hydro, but this was an old bus – the sort I used to take to Birmingham on Saturday nights out on the piss. We'd watched mini dramas where "so and so was supposed to be here", and "you were supposed to bring that bag", and "we have to say goodbye to nan and grandpa", and now Halesowen was hundreds of largely sensible people lighter.

'She's a mad cow,' Will said out of the side of his mouth.

'*She's his wife*,' I responded, waving.

Initially, she refused to look at us, but as the bus moved off she stuck her finger up.

'Pahahaha!' Will returned the gesture.

We watched the last bus turn the corner, the warble of the engine slowly disappearing leaving us alone in Halesowen in the bright sun, the storm deadened, not a sound, not even a gust of wind in the trees.

'What have we done?' I said.

'The right thing. We're finally off the grid.'

As we made our way back to the flats the reality of our situation dawned on me. All of us had only ever been part of a governed society, and soon we would see just how much we relied on it. I knew this wasn't the right decision. Enough had happened in the last couple of weeks to prove this. But I'd stopped caring.

Will didn't look overly happy himself. 'Are you alright?' I asked.

'*Me*?' he stressed, just to remind me I was the crazy one. 'I'm sound.'

'I mean, you know, the… rabbit.'

'Rabbit!' he bit. 'Fucking stop it, Tom!'

'Stop what?'

'He was a kid, a man, a person, not a fucking character in a cartoon or one of your stupid stories!'

'Ok. I understand. I'm sorry.' Clearly it was bothering him.

'Don't keep dragging it up!' But then he stopped, caught himself. 'You're never gonna fucking stop, are you?'

I shrugged, half-smiling.

'Ok, let's have it out. And then that's it. No more talk, yeah?'

'Yeah,' I conceded, but it was a lie.

'I feel shit about it. I didn't want to kill anybody, of course I didn't, why would I?'

'I know. We're not killers, Will. We're not built that way. None of us.'

'But then,' he pondered, 'in an ideal world, I wouldn't eat meat either-'

'You what?'

'But that's just not the way of things, is it?' he pondered. 'We need meat. If our species hadn't eaten meat we never would've become the superior animals we are-'

'What the hell are you on about?'

'Let me finish-'

'No!' I demanded. 'Forget thinking and rationalising for a minute – *fucking eating meat*? How do you feel?'

'For fuck's sake, I'm trying to say. I feel shit, but it is what it is! Sometimes you have to do things you don't want to do and this is the life we've chosen. What do you want me to say? I just have to accept it.'

'That's recovery talk,' I smiled.

'Whatever floats your boat.' He took out his tobacco tin and quickly rolled a small joint to prove a point.

We walked back in silence, both clearly troubled by our thoughts, of which Sarah was proving to be the least of them. Mostly, I was wondering why I'd really stayed in Halesowen and whether some day I'd end up relapsing. But I looked at Will, puffing on his joint, and I knew it wasn't really about drinking or drugs. Addiction was really just a symptom of the illness. The illness was deeper and more ingrained and it was a real killer. In fact it was the number one killer when I thought about it.

'It's because of you, you know,' Will said, at Ally's back door.

'What is?'

'That Loz is staying.'

'Don't put that on me! He just wants the freedom to fuck.'

'After your little-madam fit last night, he was laid at the foot of your bed like a puppy-'

'Before he went scratching at-'

'Stacey's dirty little door.' We finished the sentence together and burst out laughing.

'Why would we be both say "dirty little"?' he giggled.

'I've no idea,' I said, laughing.

Ally let us in. Marcus, Loz and Stacey were sitting on the settee facing us, clearly well on their way. Damien was sitting cross-legged on the floor, rolling a cigarette.

'Tom!' Loz cheered. 'We've been waiting for you!'

'*We've* been waiting for *you*,' I said. 'Jenny was fuming.'

'Didn't Will tell you?'

Will looked at me. '*What*?'

'Why didn't you tell me?'

'I did. Just,' he smiled.

I wanted to be angry, I felt like I ought to be, but a smile crept across my face. I was glad we'd watched the last bus go together, and happy Loz was here. Lucy popped into my thoughts and I swallowed the rising sadness. At least I had my friends.

Damien stood up. 'I better get going.'

'The canal?' I asked.

'Yeah, well, I've… um… gotta see Tony and then head off.'

'Lightweight, ay he?' Stacey said.

Damien turned quickly and jabbed the air, 'piss off, Stace!'

It shocked the room and we all went quiet.

I could feel Will about to burst, Marcus squeaked, and he succumbed: 'pahahaha.' Stacey cackled, cruel and cutting. Ally tried to suppress it, but let out a giggle. I glanced at Eeyore and he looked truly hurt. I shook my head to apologise for everyone, but he left, glum, slamming the door behind him.

'Ooooh,' Marcus camped.

Loz was laughing.

'Be you next, mate,' Will smirked, eyeing Stacey. 'Pahahaha!' He grabbed a bottle of vodka off Marcus and took a big swig.

'Where's Sarah?' I asked.

Ally gestured down the hall. 'But it's probably not the best time…'

As I entered the bedroom, Sarah immediately grabbed a pillow to hide the paraphernalia. She was clearly doped on something. 'Did you… er… see nan?' she asked.

'She was on one of the early buses. We didn't speak.'

She carefully rested her hand on the pillow. 'Ok. Did you see Jimmy?'

I shook my head.

'Must've got the early bus,' Ally said from behind me.

Sarah stared at me, for a moment roused.

'*What*?' I asked her.

'An earlier bus, yeah,' she conceded.

I remembered the wad of cash Leroy pulled out to pay Tony Dale. 'An earlier one, yeah.'

There was an awkward silence.

'Come on, Tom,' Ally put her hand on my shoulder.

Sarah nodded, 'I need to get some sleep.' She tried to smile but couldn't muster it and wouldn't look me in the eye.

Sometimes it's easier to be lied to than to lie to yourself.

2031

Tony was shaking terribly when we arrived in Shrewsbury, head twitching, itching his stubbly beard as if it was riddled with insects. He hadn't been well for days and he'd barely slept. His face was jaundiced, wrinkles stretched out by the bloat of failing organs. He'd run out of rum even before we got to the ghost town of Bridgnorth a few days earlier, which added to the misery of it all. I told him he needed a drink or he'd have a seizure, but this had made him stubborn and he'd decided I didn't know what I was talking about. I couldn't help but feel I was being punished for something.

He glanced at me out of the corner of his eye. '*I'm fine.*'

'I know,' I said.

'Stop looking then.'

Welcomed by a tall stone column, Lord Hill's apparently, this was the first town we'd entered in the new UK. There were almost no shops, big windows blacked out with signs displaying websites. Amazon, Google, Facebook, Apple and Alibaba amongst. Perhaps they were offices or warehouses, or perhaps it was just a way to advertise – we saw little sign of life in the buildings themselves. These big names reminded me of easier times, but I certainly hadn't missed them. Facebook, which had once been blue, was now green. I wondered if that signified something the company now stood for – the environment… the dollar – or if people had just got bored of the colour. I didn't miss Facebook, Google or Amazon but they excited me in the same way a can of Coke used to make me think of Christmas.

'We've made it, Tony.'

'What d'yuh mean?' he grumped.

'I guess this is it. The end of the road.'

His mood changed from irritability to fear. 'You've gotta help me find big Val.'

'That's not really my job,' I said, somewhat smug with it.

'You want me to beg?' he asked, angry. '*You want me to beg,*' he confirmed, 'like a pervert. Please, Tom,' he mocked, 'help an old – what was it? – cockroach, that's right, find his wife. Oh, pretty fucking please.'

There were no cars on the roads, but the streets were alive with people staring at us from under solar awnings, outside the cafes and bars. Clean people. I felt embarrassed.

'You finished?' I whispered. 'How'm I supposed to find her? She could be anywhere.'

'*You* made me come! I would've-would've stayed in the-in the woods,' he coughed himself into a panic-attack, struggling to get his breath. He leant against a wall. 'Why yuh fucking bring me?' he panted. 'Now, you're leaving me for dead.'

I couldn't tell if it was an act, but he seemed genuinely terrified at the prospect of being left on his own. 'It's not like that. You wanted out. Here you go, you're out.'

'I wanted to survive!' he insisted. 'You know, like a-like a-'

'A cockroach-'

'Yeah!'

'You've played that card enough.'

We must've looked like two bickering homeless men. Did they guess we'd come from a different future, from the "pink zone", the boob? What did the British-leavers think of those of us who'd refused to listen to the government? Were we just the idiots, the nutters, conspiracy theorists? Did they even know about our kind or had we been cut off and cut out? Perhaps some journalist had written an article about the remain-tribes in the National Geographic. Were we even allowed to be here?

'What you looking at?' Tony barked at a group of kids sucking alco-sim gas. 'Can't even fucking drink properly!'

'*Tony!*' I reprimanded. 'You can't – I'm sorry guys – do that here. You're not in goddam Halesowen.'

'This is my country,' he stated, oddly patriotic.

I dragged him up the road. 'Maybe they have a library somewhere. We can find some info on the resettlers.'

'*A library?*'

'I don't know! They might. But that's it. I'm done after that.'

Music, most of which I'd never heard, was emanating from awning speakers as we passed. There was some folk song, which may have been traditional Shropshire fare, for all I knew. Coming from a bar with white painted windows, there was some kind of stripped down drum and bass, punctuated by the jangle of a triangle and the whistle of a flute – it took me back to the ketamine years. One café was playing something which sounded like K-pop or J-pop, squeaky and fast. With so few shops around, it started to feel like a theme park, the crooked black beamed buildings of old, the statue of Darwin, and the winding streets and little churches all part of an exhibition. In a grungy pub called the Old Bell, a three-piece band was playing some kind of folk-rock, violins and guitars, three hipsters in translucent exo-suits, wearing beige bodysocks which made you look twice. Seeing the three of them reminded me that's all that was left of my own band of brothers, wherever the other two were. I felt for the phone in my pocket. *Perhaps I should call Loz.*

I knew what I'd said to Tony was playing on his mind. Could I really leave him? *He'll need a carer sooner or later.* I recalled Sean in his grotty room. Was there some sort of poetic justice in all this? *Tony would sooner euth someone than care for them.*

We passed a place called Tanners Wine Merchants. It had a kind of table urinal for spitting out wine. I noticed Tony staring at the system and I knew he was contemplating drinking the spittle which ran down several pipes into one large glass bottle under the table, a quick smash and grab. He looked like a vulnerable old drunk, trembly and hot. *He looks like my dad. Perhaps I'm destined to care for him, perhaps that's our twisted fate.*

'*What?*' he snapped.

'Nothing,' I immediately looked down to the pavement, guilty for the sudden awareness of our spiritual quandary. 'What do you think they are?' I asked, pointing to rows of black discs built into the paving.

'Looks like glass,' he said.

'I mean, what do they do?'

'How the fuck should I know?'

They were everywhere, like big casino chips. Place your bets on the future. Right now, I was betting on a life with a most unlikely companion.

'Solar panels maybe,' I suggested.

There was an environmentally-friendly feel about the new world, but it also felt industrious – *perhaps the bombs were a necessary evil, in the same way I needed a rock bottom to get sober.* There was a sweet-smelling goodness in the air, a freshness to the town. Some of the buildings had wind turbines, painted red, either behind or in front. A big café called the Darwin Cake Centre was fronted by two small turbines. I soon realised the goodness in the air was being wafted out of the bakery. It was the sweet smell of butter and fruit. Either side there were big vending machines which offered Shrewsbury Cakes, a fiver a piece. They looked incredible.

'Can I… I don't mean,' a lady stuttered.

Tony locked in on her immediately, irritated. 'What-d'yuh-want?'

'No, it wasn't, I mean,' she apologised.

'Bloody foreigners,' he whined.

'*Tony*! Please, ignore my friend,' I said. 'He's old and we've come from another world.'

'I could buy you one each?' she asked, guilty at the suggestion.

'Don't need ya grubby help!' he snapped. 'Don't need-!' he stopped, took a fast breath in, which was odd. 'Don't need,' he stopped again, his face went grey and clammy. He looked weak and small.

'Tony?' I put my hands on his shoulders to steady him. 'Are you ok?' He seemed distant.

'Yes… I'm…'

Behind, I heard a chime. I glanced back and the lady was holding a cake – it looked more like a big biscuit. 'Please,' she smiled. 'He needs food.'

I nodded.

'Don't need…' he said, eyes glazed. 'Tom,' he focused. 'Will said you wuz brothers.'

'Ok,' I laughed, nervously.

'I never had one. But Aaron.' A tear-streamed down his cheek.

'I'll be your brother,' I said.

Behind, I heard another chime. I turned and the lady was now holding two biscuits which she put into a paper bag. I took them off her and put them in my rucksack.

'He's going,' she said, and I realised she was probably right.

'Yes. But I can be there for him in-'

'No,' she pointed. 'He's off.'

I looked and Tony was shuffling away, taking swift, little steps up onto the bridge over the Severn. 'Thank you so much,' I said.

I walked fast to catch up with him. 'Tony, you need to stop and rest. We need to find somewhere to stay.'

'Wha?' he said.

'Together. We'll find big Val, together,' I smiled.

'Pah!' he grunted – I knew this was what I was signing up for, but that was ok. 'Must get to the water. Steps,' he pointed, urgent. His face was matte, like clay, sweat glistening, greasy, separating from the tears on his face. His whole body now trembled.

'Tony, stop.' I held his arm.

'The water,' he insisted.

'You're not making sense,' but then I caught a strong whiff of it. 'Have you-?'

'Must get to the river.'

Behind us there was a trail of watery shit, where it had trickled down his leg. *Poor bastard.* I thought of Sean, tethered to his chair under a piss-stained quilt. There was another way for Tony, a caring way. A few more months, years of company and cheer. *Maybe he'll learn he was wrong all his life. Perhaps he'll change.*

At the top of some steep stone steps, I offered my arm, but he waved me on, too proud. I made my way down, slow and steady, in case he stumbled and I needed to stop him falling. I was nearly at the bottom when I felt a sudden heavy thump in my back. There was no sound, no warning or shriek, just a big weight. I swung around, blindly grabbing at the wall, trying to stop myself, but I fell back and tumbled down the steps, taking a painful winding as Tony landed on top of me, head-butting my chin so hard he broke the ether into millions of flashing particles. The first thought that entered my head was the dribbling diarrhoea which would be soaking through his trousers and onto me, my second thought – I had no control of it – was the fate of the Shrewsbury cakes. The next thought was my dad.

Dad was on his way to the toilet when he collapsed. He said nothing, just fell to the floor. On the ground, his lips turned blue, his face went grey.

Tony had made no sound, was making no sound. I moved his head back to see his lips had turned dark blue, like he'd been sucking liquorice. I let go and his head fell back to my chest. I put my hand on his lips and held it there. There was nothing, no warmth, no breath. If could just move him off me to the bottom of the steps, I could try CPR. But I couldn't, I was too tired, so I just lay there.

I heard somebody coming and I closed my eyes. A brief panic surrounded me and someone called for help. When they lifted him off, I opened my eyes as if I'd just come-to, pretending to be dazed and confused.

In the clean, bright light of a small hospital, the nurses buzzed about the patients and the patients lay bored looking at their phones, the persistent beep of life from medical robots. It was easy to imagine the last few years hadn't happened, like I'd just woken up out of a coma.

I removed my 3310 from the charging desk and looked at myself in the reflection on the screen. With my huge beard and bald brow, wrinkly and weather worn, I looked like Darwin.

I called Loz. 'Hello?'

'It's me,' I said.

'Man! It's so good to hear your voice! Marcus said you were… well, they didn't know what had happened to you. Are you back in the UK?'

'Shrewsbury. Is Marcus still with you?'

'He went back with Eeyore. Are you ok?'

'He's dead.'

'Who's dead?'

I wanted to say my dad. 'Will.'

There was silence.

'When?'

'Last week.'

'How?'

'Halesowen.'

'Can you get to Stafford?'

'I have to walk to Wales.'

'What for?'

The true loneliness of grief was the dreams I'd shared with dead people, but that was also what kept them alive in me. Dad always talked about winning the lottery, "just to have enough money to not care". Lucy couldn't have any more children and wanted to adopt a little girl, "so I can teach her to be a superhero". Dylan wanted to stay up all night, but he just kept falling asleep. I'd poke him and prod him, but he'd be fast asleep.

Epilogue

Damien put down a big box and handed me a bag of notebooks.

'Where is he?'

'He was... um... coming back, but changed his mind, something er... about not being mad or-'

'Depressed?'

He shrugged. 'Isn't that... um... what you wanted, Sarah.'

'You didn't tell him that?'

'Er... course not. He got off in... um... Market Drayton. Said he was going north.'

'On his own?'

He nodded.

I looked through the bag and flipped open the top book.

"Out of the sighs a little comes, but not of grief, for we have knocked down that." Dylan Thomas

2031. I'd managed to lose them all. Right or wrong, I'd needed to. They wouldn't be far, but I felt uneasy...

I flicked through the first couple of pages.

'He er... called it his story, no... share.' Damien picked up the box and patted it. Something moved inside. 'And this.'

He opened it up and a scrawny looking black and white cat was cowering in the corner. I went to stroke it and it scratched me. '*The little...* Why?'

'There was a bunch of strays... um... by the canal. This one was on her own. Angry, but she's alright when you... um... feed her.'

'But why?'

He shrugged again. 'Halesowen... er... needs more cats?' he laughed.

I didn't see what was so funny about it. I left the flat, crossed the grass. Ally was sitting on the sofa smoking away, while little Will was across the room in a cot, crying. I was too emotional to have a go at her about it.

'What's the matter with you?' she said.

'He's gone.'

'*Really?*'
'Yes!'
'Was that not what you wanted?'
'Damien gave me these.' I handed her the bag, and then picked up baby Will. 'There, there, little one-'
'Looks like his diaries-'
'No need to cry. Everything's going to be alright.'
I could feel the tears coming and I tried my best to stop them.
'And he gave me a stray cat.'
'Tom did?' she laughed.
'What's so funny?'
'Maybe he's saying you're like a stray,' she smiled, looking through the bag.
Anita came into the living room, book in hand. I tried to hide my face.
'What's the matter, Sarah?'
'Tom's not coming back,' Ally said.
'Oh.' She sat on the settee. 'I've finished reading it.'
I laughed and then burst into tears.
'What's the matter?' Anita asked.
'Tom gave me that book. I don't think he ever read it. He always tried his best, but he was a bit of a deeve.'
'They'm all the bloody same,' Ally laughed.
'No, they're not,' I said, wiping my eyes.
'Oh, quit your blubbering. I thought you wanted him to go.'
'I did.'
'So why are you are crying?'
'Because he listened.'

Acknowledgments

The creative process of Out of the Sighs has at times felt like a lonely one, spending hours on my own in the shed at the bottom of the garden. But the truth is, I've shared this journey with many people. For that, I'm especially grateful. At the risk of missing someone out, I shan't name names, but you know who you are. You've passed comments throughout, some which have spurred me on and some which have, I'm happy to admit, altered the shape of the book. So, if there's anything wrong with it, it's probably your fault.

In all seriousness, I want to say a massive thank you to those who've taken the time to read each part, especially in such difficult times, when bingeing a boxset on Netflix might prove a more satisfying way to escape. You will never truly know the ways in which the odd comment on social media and those occasional chats influenced me. You are a part of this. Consider it a collaboration.

It would be wrong for me not to thank one person by name, my wife, Beck. She's endured innumerable proof reads and has single-handedly dealt with the tech side of things, sparing me an enormous amount of stress and probably a laptop or two. Without her, I may have written a book but perhaps no one would have had the chance to read it.

I wish you all well in these dystopian times.

Lewis Coleman 2021

www.lewisccoleman.com

Independent publishing depends upon word of mouth and reviews. If you have enjoyed this book, please tell a friend and leave a review on Amazon.

Thank you.

Printed in Great Britain
by Amazon